"Coke?" she asked in a high voice.

He stopped. "Yes, Jessie?"

"You are taking care, aren't you?"

"What?"

She stepped off the boardwalk and came toward him. "This . . . this killing on the Blankenship ranch," she stammered. "Well, it reminded me of the attack on your land only a little over a week ago. You . . . and the others out on your ranch are taking care, aren't you?"

His eyes warmed. "Yes, Jessie, we're takin' care." Then, putting his arm around her shoulders, he kissed her lightly on the cheek. "An' it's sweet o' you to ask."

She put her hand over the place where he'd kissed her as he climbed on to ole Belcher. "You're not playing fair," she repeated.

Smiling down at her, he turned his horse around.

"I know," she murmured to herself. "Not if you can help it."

SOUTH TEXAS

Ann Gabriel

BALLANTINE BOOKS • NEW YORK

Library of Congress Catalog Card Number: 89-91794

ISBN 0-345-35086-3

Manufactured in the United States of America

First Edition: January 1990

To my husband, Rudy, for his love and support, and to my uncles, John and Willie, for their marvelous down-home, country humor.

SOUTH
TEXAS

🌺 Chapter 1

COKE SANDERS LIFTED his hand from the saddle horn and swept the sweat from his brow, casting the droplets into the hot, dry wind. As he did so, his eyes caught onto a half dozen buzzards above a distant ridge lazily spiraling against the glaring metallic sky. One by one, they were dropping to the ground. Another beef had fallen.

On the prairie floor below him, the bonfire convulsed and lapped in the wind, spitting out starbursts of free-falling cinders. Its roar poured over the nagging, hollow-bellied bawling of the starving cattle that milled about it.

The vaqueros pitched more dried brush onto the fire. Popping and sputtering, it tilted and slowly sank into the flames. Amid the waves of heat and smoke radiating from the blaze, the vaqueros looked as insubstantial as wraiths, their hands gloved, hats down-turned, bandannas pulled up over the bridges of their noses. The sweat-slick slivers of skin left exposed on the backs of their necks and wrists blinked fitfully through the haze.

An ox-pulled wagon crept through the herd and stopped near the fire, sending more powdery dust into the air. The two men slumped at the back of the wagon, got heavily to their feet and began slinging chopped cactus over the side.

The vaqueros on the ground spiked the pieces of cactus with pointed sticks and pitchforks and, turning toward the fire, rotated them over the flames, charring the needles sprinkled over them to brittleness. They then hurled the gelded cactus pear into the herd. Sides heaving, the famished cattle jostled against each other to get at the juicy pear, to force it past their missing upper front teeth with sharp forward jerks of their downthrust heads.

A half mile away, another ox-pulled wagon crawled across the prairie. Men moved through the brush alongside, humpbacked and machetes swinging, chopping up the prickly pear and tossing it inside.

1

Chamuscar! the Mexicans called it. Pear burning. When the grazable grass was either cropped to the root or sun-cauterized to straw and the dried-out land looked as contracted and hard as overbaked bread, only the cactus was left to sustain the cattle. Only the cactus remained to maintain the life force in shriveling bovine flesh for perhaps another day or so.

Last month, August 1886, they'd recorded their seventeenth full month of drought. Oh, over the passing months there'd been a few puny showers. Teasers, and nothing more. Not in almost a year and a half had Coke's land taken a drencher, a rip-roaring pounding rain that filled the dried-out creek beds and water tanks and fused the cracks in the callused earth, saturating them to sponginess, spawning new light green grass shoots to proliferate across the land.

The sulfurous South Texas sun kept bearing down, squeezing the juice out of bodies like breakfast oranges, juice that sizzled on exposed skin and soaked anew through already sweat-syrupy clothes. One o'clock in the afternoon, a hundred degrees and just heating up. Coke could tell by the muddleheaded, leaden movements of the men that they were worn out, hanging on by will alone. More often now, they straggled off to the water wagon parked in the weak shadow of the rise and, flinging their hats and pitchforks aside, collapsed to the ground beneath the barrel spouts. Groping blindly up, they pulled out the spigots and, rolling their heads, let the water trickle down over their steamy scalps and necks. Then, lifting their faces, they received the stream in their cottony mouths. Replugging the spouts, they fell back onto their elbows and gulped the air until their sight cleared and sounds sharpened once more. Then, retrieving their hats and pitchforks, they stumbled back into the furnace.

An updraft carried a swirl of smoke and dust over the rise to Coke. Glancing again at the circling buzzards, he nudged his mount, Sin Cerebro, and rode down the slope toward the hide-gathering wagon sitting below. The driver, Homero, lay back on the seat. Feet propped up on the wagon rim, sombrero over his face, he seemed oblivious to the stench of the hides of the dead animals heaped in the wagon directly behind him.

"*Sí, Jefe, los veo,*" he said in a voice that came through the top of his hat when Coke had ridden to within a few feet of him. Yes, Boss, I see them. I see the buzzards.

Shoving his hat back, he sat up, his face furrowing with anger.

Like an exclamation point, he spat on the ground. "That Kansas granger you told to help me! He no damn good! This the fifth, sixth canteen he fill today. No work! No! We do no work. Just back and forth to here. Fillin' up with the *agua* an' pissin' it out."

Coke looked over at the object of Homero's wrath. The granger, Obie Given, stood leaning against the water wagon, one hand on his hip, canteen lapping loosely from it against his thigh, while with his other hand he accentuated his words with the water dipper as he jabbered away. His oration was directed at a vaquero slumped numbly on the ground beneath a barrel spout, the water dribbling onto his head. Words kept clacking forth from the gangly, flaxen-haired youth, regardless of their failure to arouse any response from the poor man at his feet. The dog-tired vaquero could barely comprehend the boy's prattling English to begin with.

"Todo lo que hace es hablar! Me está volviendo loco!" Homero exploded. All he does is talk. It's driving me crazy. Gesturing wildly, he hurried on, now in his own fluent English. "That jaw of his. Flap, flap, flap. My head aches. My ears ring." He stopped, a malicious gleam coming into his eyes. "He keep it up, Boss, could be he find a boot growin' outa that blabbery hole o' his."

Coke wiped his eyes with the back of his sleeve, but the gesture seemed more an irritation than a remedy. "Now, Homero," he said. "Try t'be patient. No need for you t'go throwin' no purple hissies. This bein' his first day an' all, he just don't know how things is done round here."

"Many good vaqueros outa work," Homero held out stubbornly. "We no need a stupid Kansas granger. Kid's not careful, Boss. He rips the hide all crooked. A coyote do it better."

" 'Bout had t'take the boy on," Coke said mildly. "Seein' as how I leased his family that bottomland for farmin' an' their irrigatin' stream turned t'dust soon as this dry-up here started takin' a turn for the worse. The family needs the money. Give the kid a chance. He'll learn."

In midsentence Obie espied Coke. He hurriedly put the lid back on the water barrel, dropped the dipper on top of it, and plodded toward them, summing up his recitation along the way to no one in particular.

Pulling his hat down over his brow, Coke squinted up at the sky. The smattering of clouds he sighted were no more than high, thin streamers.

"Hopin' t'spot a raindrop?" Obie asked sociably, settling back against the hide-gathering wagon in much the same pose he'd held moments before at the water wagon.

"Son, if I was t'gather all them wispy whiskers up there into these two hands o' mine, I still wouldn't be able t'squeeze out enough moisture t'equal the teardrop in a buzzard's eyeball."

"Bound t'rain soon," the boy said confidently.

"That a fact."

"Yup. Less'n a hour ago I heard a coyote a-howlin'. Everybody knows that when coyotes take t'howlin' in the daytime, it's 'cause they scent a drencher comin' on."

"More likely the bastard stumbled onto one o' my beeves too weak an' tuckered out t'stand up no more." Coke nodded toward the spiraling buzzards. "Mebbe that'n over there."

Obie shot a glance in the direction his boss had shown him, and straightened to attention.

"Better go lift that hide," Coke went on. "Afore it gets so pecked an' chewed on, the tanners won't pay me a tinker's damn for it."

"I'll get right at it," the boy declared in a businesslike tone. He hurried around the wagon and bounded up beside Homero. "Let's get goin'!" he ordered.

"Qué?" Homero asked lazily. What?

"Let's go!" Obie repeated, thrusting his arms forward to imitate the motion of the wagon.

Homero gazed dully at the boy, then, rolling his eyes, shrugged in exaggerated ignorance.

Obie sighed. "Really, Mr. Sanders. It's durn hard workin' with a feller who cain't understand nary a word o' English."

"Pendejo!" Homero growled, drawing the word out. Stupid ass.

"Pen *day* ho! Pen *day* ho!" Obie parroted angrily. "That's all he's said all day long." He glowered at Homero. "Now, what kinda conversation is that? It don't make no sense a-tall!"

"Uh . . . Obie," Coke said slowly. "I got a idee. See that fella over there . . . the one with the red bandanna?"

Obie craned his neck. "Yessir, I see him."

"Name's Manuel. Go tell Manuel I want him t'take over your job for you."

"You're durn tootin'," Obie cried, leaping off the wagon. "What you want me t'do, huh? Singe the cactus?"

"Just calm down whilst I tell you, awright? What I want you t'do, Obie, is go to the remuda over there, borrow a fresh horse—"

"Oh," the boy blurted, "you want me t'bring the cattle in t'eat the cactus."

"I reckon they can figger that out for theirselves," Coke said patiently. "What I want, Obie, is for you t'ride out 'bout a mile east o' here, an' goin' real slow-like, check out the cactus."

"Gotcha!" Obie exclaimed, and bounced off. When he'd covered about twenty feet, he skidded to a stop, thought a second, then spun around and came bounding back again. "What'll I be checkin' 'em for?" he cried.

"Burrs," Coke said impassively.

"Burrs?" the boy frowned.

"Yup. See iffen they got more'n the usual number o' burrs on 'em or not. Thataway, we'll know how much singein' we gotta do tomorrow."

"Ah!" his freckled, radish-red face lit up. "I'll get right at it! You can depend on me!" And he bounded off again.

Coke glanced aside at Homero, who was eyeing him devilishly.

"Wayull," he drawled. "It'll keep him outa everybody's hair whilst I figger somethin' better t'do with him."

He climbed off Sin Cerebro. Alejandro, his foreman, was walking toward him. Alejandro Cortez was almost six feet tall, and his high cheekbones and strong features bespoke a strain of Indian ancestry. Though over fifty years old, his black hair turned a powdery gray, he carried himself in the upright manner of a man half his age.

"Better call it a day," Coke said. "Else y'all will wind up coyote bait before my beeves do."

"Sí, pienzo hacerlo," Alejandro replied. Yes, I plan to.

Like many other vaqueros who'd been working with Coke for years, Alejandro had the habit of sliding in and out of Spanish and English while talking with him, the habit being so ingrained that they'd long ago ceased being conscious of it.

"Alejandro," Coke went on. "This mornin' I come upon a line o' fence that was pulled down in our north section. Far as I can tell, 'bout a hundred beeves was run off."

"De veras?" That so? "Lo acabo de revisar hace dos días." I had it checked two days ago.

"Musta happened that same night. Tracks look twenty-four to thirty-six hours old."

"*Cuantos hombres eran?*" How many men were there?

"Three," Coke replied.

Alejandro shook his head. "The second time this month."

"It's probably too late t'track 'em, but have ole Jorge and Francisco give it a try. I think we'd better start doublin' the fence riders along that section."

"*Sí, Güero,* I'll see to it."

Glancing up, Coke saw a cowpuncher galloping hard out of the brush after a calf. "Now, who the hell is that?" He frowned.

Alejandro squinted in the direction. When he brought his eyes back, they had an I-told-you-so gleam. "*Es el* granger," he said flatly. He shared Homero's prejudice against Kansas grangers. During the cattle drives up north he'd gotten his bellyful of the Yankee farmers, armed and guarding their newly fenced little plots of homestead land and blocking the trails to the railheads. For weeks he'd refused to hire young Given. It hadn't been until yesterday, when Coke had returned from a selling trip to Colorado, that the boy had finally been taken on. Smiling to himself, Alejandro turned back to his work. Obie was Coke's baby. He'd leave it at that.

Grumbling, Coke got back on his horse and ambled toward the boy, who sat atop his mount tossing his quirt cockily.

"I thought I told you t'check out the burrs," he said quietly.

"Yessir. I was on my way t'doin' just that when I happened onto that there stray that needed roundin' up."

"Didn't need roundin' up."

"Coulda wandered off an' gotten lost."

" 'Tain't likely. It'd o' no doubt wandered on back again soon as it felt the need t'suck its ma." He nodded toward an ancient, hornless steer. "See that ole muley steer over there, Obie? He's the herd baby-sitter. If the little critter had a-wandered too far off, like as not, *he'd* o' gone for him."

The air seemed to go out of the boy. "Didn't know that. Seemed like the right thing t'do at the time."

"Even if it was the right thing t'do . . . which it warn't, you don't go runnin' a beef like that. You don't hurry nothin' 'round here iffen you can help it. You tire out your horse an' run the weight offa my beeves. An' my beeves just ain't got the weight on 'em no more t'be run off by some fool kid."

"I didn't think—"

"You gotta *start* thinkin', boy. You don't do nothin' t'make my stock any thirstier'n it already is. Look aroun' here. Where the hell you expect 'em t'get a drink? This ain't the middle of a Loosiana swamp, you know."

Obie swallowed. "Yes, sir."

"Now, Obie." Coke softened. "A while back I spotted a little heifer. Seemed t'be holdin' its own in this here die-up. That's the only thing a die-up like this is good for . . . separatin' the fighters from the losers. You think you could take that heifer over to my breedin' herd?"

The boy bounced up. "I'll get right at it!" he cried.

Coke caught hold of Obie's reins, just below the muzzle of his horse, to keep the boy from galloping off. "Take a deep breath," he said calmly. "An' let your feathers settle. I don't recollect pointin' that heifer out t'you."

"Oh . . . that's right." Obie sank down in his saddle.

"See that brown heifer over there . . . the one with the white spot on her flank?"

"Sure do!" the boy exclaimed, bouncing up again. But seeing that Coke still hadn't let go of his reins, he eased back down.

"Obie."

"Yessir."

"Do you, by any chance, know where my breedin' herd is?"

"Uh . . . no, sir."

"It's in my north section."

"I'm on my way!" Obie cried, rising up in the saddle. But Coke still held his reins.

"Obie."

"Yessir."

"You do know where my north section is, don't you?"

"Over yonder?" He nodded in a generally northerly direction.

"That's right. Over yonder. But, son, that 'yonder' over there takes up a helluvalotta space . . . an' that particular section o' my ranch takes up close t'fifty thousand acres of it. Now, the part o' that yonder over there that I want you t'take that heifer to has two windmills on it, 'bout three miles apart. You recollect those two windmills?"

Obie nodded. "Had my lunch at the campsite near one of 'em today."

"That's the well I want you t'take that there heifer to. It's the only one over there still pumpin' worth a damn."

"Yessir. I'm off."

"Now, remember." Coke let go of his reins. "Slow an' steady. Easy does it. Just set back an' let your horse do the herdin'. O' the two o' you, he's the one who knows how t'do it."

Obie nodded solemnly, and ambled off. He held his mount in so assiduously that it moved fitfully in sideways little lurches, as if it were spavined.

Coke shook his head. The pure innocence and pell-mell eagerness of youth could sure get to be one throbbing big pain in the backside.

He rode on, threading his way through the chaparral and prickly pear strewn across his land. Dried cow chips polka-dotted the ground. No steer was around. All the beeves in the area were still crowded around the dying bonfire, clamoring at the remaining vaqueros for their last shot at food and liquid for the day.

Coke was headed in the direction of his north section windmill, the same destination to which he'd sent Obie Given. The boy was nowhere in sight. Coke wondered vaguely if young Given and his charge might end up in the next county or perhaps even Mexico, some twenty-odd miles to the south. He hoped that Obie would recognize the Rio Grande if he came up against it, though he wouldn't bank on it.

Twice in the last thirty days cattle had been taken from his land, the first time fifty head, this last time a hundred. The rustlers were getting bolder.

Up ahead on the grainy surface of a caliche deposit, he spotted a six-foot rattler sunning itself. He skirted by it and rode on. He shot the heads off rattlers only when he was in a good mood. Since four that morning, he'd been riding over his land finding nothing but water holes fried to rock and his tottering, weakening cattle nuzzling uselessly at the balding ground.

Yesterday he'd returned from a three-week trip to Colorado to sell a herd he'd sent there the year before to graze on leased land. He'd hoped that during his absence, the plight of his land would have reversed. A single drencher would have done it. Yes, he'd hoped . . . but he hadn't expected. Hope was like a sneeze, somewhat satisfying in itself, though doing nothing in the way of curing the hay fever.

A year ago, Coke had scented trouble in the wind, that this dry-up had taken a firm hold and wouldn't let go for a long time coming. At about the time he'd sent a herd to Colorado, he'd unloaded another couple thousand head, selling them to a huge new ranching corporation backed by English investors too gullible to know what they were getting themselves into.

Of the ten thousand cattle that had remained on his ranch, a thousand had fallen to the drought. The water, if it held out, could support sixty-five hundred, seven thousand head, at most. That left another two thousand likely to fall in the coming months if no rains came.

But even if Coke and his men could keep the meat on those bovine bones and those bones upright this year, it wouldn't make much difference. The bottom had dropped out of the Kansas City and Chicago meat markets, and any rancher who managed to get a herd to the northern railheads had to sell out at giveaway prices.

A week ago, Coke had marked his fortieth birthday. Thirty-two of those years he'd spent on this godforsaken land. And he could count out that string of time as one year of boom to two of bitchin'.

His pa, Camden, had been a coal miner, born in the green mountains of Virginia, and by the time of Coke's birth, he'd fought and bullied his way up to the rank of foreman. When Coke was eight, Camden was told that he had lung fever. According to the company doctor, the elder Sanders wouldn't last another year if he didn't resettle in a hot, dry climate. So in the spring of fifty-four Coke's ma and pa sold off everything but the bare essentials and, together with their son and their infant daughter, Sarie, climbed aboard a rickety fourth-hand prairie schooner and rambled away into the vast no-man's-land to the south and west. That year spelled the end not only of Coke's Virginia life, but of his childhood as well. From that time onward he was expected to pull his weight like a man.

It was a long and tedious journey, fraught with obstacles and danger, and an uncertain destination lay ahead of them. After five months of meandering, the family rolled into South Texas.

The South Texas land of the 1850s was wide open to them. A century or more before, it had been awarded to the original Spanish and Mexican settlers in vast land grants by the governments of Spain and Mexico. But the Texas war for independence in the late 1830s had left that ownership in doubt. Not even the heirs to those original land grant tracks, many of them living in Mexico, knew if the land was still theirs or not.

Coke remembered his pa climbing down from the wagon and surveying the land, the hot, dry wind twisting at his hat brim and beating through his clothes.

"Well, Bessie," he finally declared to Coke's ma. "It's hot, all right. Hotter'n hades. An' dry . . . damn! It's gotta be drier here than an ole maid's poontang. I reckon this is the place ole doc had in mind."

Since no one was around to object, the family settled at a nearby creek, their home a dugout in the creek bank roofed with leather-tied sticks packed with dirt. Checking the land over, Camden decided that the only thing on it that might be worth anything was the maverick longhorn. Rawboned, with meat tough as boot leather, the Texas longhorn looked like the ragtag outcast cousin of the bovine family. It had been running wild through the brush for over two hundred years. And it looked like it, too. Haggard, with a loose-jointed stance, it had a spooky, mean-tempered cast to its eye. And no wonder. The critter often had to balance on its weedy frame a pair of outlandishly long horns, sometimes, measuring nine feet from tip to tip.

Rounding up the loony longhorns, Camden soon discovered, was akin to trying to herd a roomful of flies into a matchbox. After spending days galloping willy-nilly all over the prairie after them and catching nothing but brush thorns and saddle blisters for his trouble, Camden decided he had some serious learning to do.

He rode off to a settlement twenty miles away. In the saloon he came across two young Mexican drifters who worked maverick cattle whenever their hell-raising money started running low. One of the young drifters was Alejandro. Camden carted the two men home and, when he could see the whites of their eyes, proposed in gestures that they throw in together. The vaqueros counted the change in their pockets, shrugged, and agreed to go along.

With a stray word here and there and a great deal of pantomime, the two Mexican steers taught Camden and his son the art of brush-popping steers and collecting them into makeshift corrals. When they'd collected about enough, the three men and the nine-year-old boy gathered up the unruly slick-ears and chased them east. Barely without letup they chased them. Around towns and farms and over rain-swollen rivers they chased them. Across vast, empty spaces and Indian territory they chased them. Through sticky, crocodile-infested, mosquito-ridden Louisiana swamps they chased them. Until finally, by sheer luck, they all ended up at about the same time in Shreveport, Louisiana. Camden made his first sale, coming home with more money in his pockets than he'd ever laid hands on in his entire life. He'd caught the bug.

Again he rode off. Six weeks later he turned up at their creek bank home announcing that he'd been to Mexico, ferreted out the one man who might hold claim to the land, and had bought three thousand acres outright and another thirty thousand on credit. While Coke's cash-on-the-barrelhead ma went bug-eyed and seemed on the verge of dropping over in a dead faint into the creek, his pa roared, "What the hell we got t'lose? We ain't got nothin' anyway!"

Every year after that the Sanderses headed out with their brush-popped steers, pushing them north, west, or east, to wherever they heard that the price was good, and often not knowing at the onset of a drive what their final destination would be. It depended on the latest rumor along the way. And every year they converted profits to land. Vaqueros drifted in and out. Some stayed on. Alejandro disappeared, then one afternoon two years later, showed up with his young bride and stayed.

Tussling with Comanche, rustlers, droughts, and floods, the Sanderses and their vaqueros pushed herds to New Orleans, Shreveport, and up the Old Beef Trail to Neosho, Missouri. Occasionally they sold out to professional trailers heading for the California gold camps. And if, in a season, Camden couldn't find enough steers on his own land, he and his vaqueros would slip across the Rio Grande and borrow a few out of Mexico. When the Mexicans returned the favor, Camden cussed until he was blue in the face and sent for the Texas Rangers.

Coke remembered his pa as a swarthy, heavy-muscled, hard-drinking, full-bearded man with fiercely glowing black eyes. A man without a trace of religion or sentiment to his character that Coke could make out, over the course of a year, Camden might fight other men over land boundary or water rights, chase bandits, get chased by them, chase Comanche, get chased by them, chase rustlers and get chased by the Mexicans whose cattle he'd rustled, all without betraying any emotion other than outrage. Irascible, abrasive, crude, Camden Sanders was still a man whose favor it was wise to gain, the kind of man to have on your side when sides were drawn. Nothing set his juices flowing more than hitting op-posing forces head on and wrestling them to the ground.

Coke's ma was a spry, wiry woman who could be tender if she found the time, which wasn't very often. She could stretch two bits to last a month, coax a garden to grow in a briar patch, and back every opinion she held with a Bible passage, quoting chapter and verse. Still could. And if, at a given moment, she couldn't come up with the Bible passage to suit her, she made one up, quoting chapter and verse. A tiny, birdlike creature, nevertheless she had held her own with a blustery, bullheaded husband, had shown herself capable of reducing his most potent rages to mere sputters with a hellfire-and-damnation tirade of her own. A dyed-in-the-wool Southern Baptist, Ma grounded her faith on the con-viction that all of humanity—with the exception of the Southern Baptist—was doomed to hell and good riddance to them all. Coke could never quite see where she countenanced his pa in that scheme of things. He guessed that she figured she had enough pull upstairs for the two of them.

Camden and Bessie Sanders, inflexible, tough-minded, opin-ionated. The only force that baffled them, the only being that operated in their vicinity but pretty much beyond their control, was their son, Coke. Soft-spoken and easygoing, he pulled his share of the work and gave them a measure of respect. But he kept his own counsel, gazing stoically off into the distance when the noise level in the house reached thunderous proportions. Al-ways amenable on the surface, he agreed to everything they said . . . then went out and did what he damn well pleased. It took Camden and Bessie Sanders a long time to concede that trying to manage their son as they did everyone and everything else was about as worthwhile a use of their energy as trying to slap sand into shape.

By the eve of the Civil War, the Sanders holdings had grown to sixty thousand acres owned outright and another twenty thou-sand held on credit. The operation had evolved from a brushpop-ping outfit to one in which greater effort and money were invested in improving the quality of the herds through crossbreeding with blooded stock. The least successful results either died off in the harsh climate or were culled out for market.

The Sanders brand became familiar throughout the cattle busi-ness. The lower point of a C connected to the upper curve of a long, sloping S that wound down the hip of the steer; it looked a lot like a sidewinder rattlesnake, and the Sanders ranch became known as the Sidewinder.

During the first two years of the war, Sidewinder profits boomed from supplying the Confederacy. But as more and more able-bodied men were pulled off the land and into the conflict, the region was laid bare to Mexican raiders, Comanche, and marauding gangs of army deserters. By 1863, Coke, as well as half of the Sidewinder ranch hands, had taken off to join the Rebels.

Left with but a few old geezers and wet-behind-the-ears young boys to man a seventy-thousand-acre spread, Camden, despite all his stubbornness and rage, could not fend off the raiders that struck everywhere by night. When the war finally ended and Coke returned home, only a few calves remained on Sanders land.

The following summer, raiders struck into the ranch compound itself, hauling off horses and equipment. Coke, his pa, and a few of the men who'd trickled back home from the war by then rode out after them. Galloping down a hill in the moonless night, Camden's horse twisted its leg in a hole, bringing the man and horse plummeting downward, the horse slamming Camden's body into the hillside again and again. Coke could still picture his father sprawled on the ground, dying at the foot of a hill that he'd ridden over dozens of times before and knew like the back of his hand.

His teeth gritted in pain and outrage, his fist knotting the front of Coke's shirt, Camden Sanders rasped out his final words.

"Steal 'em back!"

At the age of twenty, Coke found himself master of seventy thousand acres of land stocked with but a few scattered calves. But where the father's character was built on rage, the son's was one of unruffled cunning. Where every situation was make or break for the father, and the road ahead fraught with obstacles to be crushed, the son coolly searched out the detours and glided on by. True, he might have to shift and skew to get where he was going, but he always contrived to get there.

That first year, Coke took out a mortgage on his land. With the money, he hired on a crew of battle-toughened men. He bought up every silver-studded spur, bridle, and saddle that he could lay his hands on. Then he met with his old antagonists, the Comanche, who thirsted after silver-plated articles to exhibit as symbols of prestige among their people. The Comanche also knew where to swipe cattle. Trading off silver spurs for fifty head, bridles for a hundred head, and saddles for two hundred, Coke rapidly restocked his land. So long as their source of supply wasn't within shooting distance, Coke didn't care where the Comanche raided their cattle. He figured that anyone who wound up with large herds at the end of the war had probably pinched them off somebody else, anyway.

By the time the first railhead opened in Abilene, in the spring of sixty-seven, the Sidewinder was ready with two thousand head of cattle to push up the Chisholm. It was a seller's market. When Coke got back home, he paid off his mortgage and bought more cattle, and another five thousand acres on credit.

For the next fifteen years, Sidewinder cattle were trailed to Kansas following the westerly push of the railroad through the state from Abilene to Newton to Wichita to Dodge City. If buyers proved scarce at the Kansas railheads, Sidewinder cattle were moved up the Loving-Goodnight Trail to Sumner, New Mexico, or were sent straight through Kansas and Nebraska to the Dakota silver mines. Wherever there was a market for their beef, Sidewinder cattle went.

Homesteaders began swarming into the prairie states, and soon started complaining that Texas cattle infected and killed their livestock when they trailed by. In those states crossed by cattle trails, laws were passed mandating the quarantining of all Texas cattle for a full winter up north to check the outbreak of what was called the Texas Cattle Fever. A sworn, notorized document attesting to that winter's quarantining had to be provided by the trail boss before his cattle were allowed to cross into a prairie state.

Coke complied with that law—if he was in a law-abiding mood that particular year, which usually meant that the market was down. But if the market was up, he was just as likely to buy up the swear papers and the notaries to go with them, sending his cattle straight into the northern states without any winter stop-off in between. The cattlemen had first rights there, to his way of thinking, since they usually were the first through a new territory. And it wasn't until the land was cleared of most of its dangers that the Johnny-come-lately sodbusters crowded in to throw fences around their piddling postage stamp pieces of ground and commenced to bellyaching. It was typical of the Yankee to insult good Texas cattle, the hardiest in the world. If a Yankee cow keeled over and died when a Texas steer strolled by, that was because it was a weak, slab-sided, no-account critter.

When rainfall was good and the market high, windfall profits came Coke's way. When drought struck and the market dropped a mile below purgatory, land came his way when less solvent ranches went under. Good years brought him cash, bad years brought him land. In the twenty years since his father's death, he'd tripled his original inheritance of seventy thousand acres to 216,862 (and a quarter) acres.

Quite an empire, some folks would say. Riding over this barren, sun-shriveled land, Coke could take issue with that. A two-hundred-thousand-acre reject from hell did not exactly make an empire. He just wouldn't know how to live an easier life. He'd get bored, he guessed.

He halted Sin Cerebro and took a long, deep swallow of water from his canteen. Recapping the flask, he surveyed the sky, the squint lines at the outer corners of his eyes runneling deep into his temples. His eyes, dark as his pa's, had the permanently veiled look of a man who'd spent his life gazing into the distance for rain clouds, circling buzzards, smoke, or dust clouds kicked up by cattle or horses. His face looked about as rugged and sun-toughened as his land, and seemed as ageless. Yet there wasn't a hardened twist to those lines, as there was on the faces of other men of Coke's breed. Instead, they sketched out the character of a man comfortable with himself, comfortable to be with. They masked well the iron determination inside. And with his malleable, unpressured manner and eyes that could connect with crinkly good humor, as though they'd peeked inside a person and liked what they saw, Coke could glean more useful information in a half hour of easy conversation over a beer than a well-rehearsed city attorney could in two days before the witness stand. He was stockier in build than the outsider's concept of the long, lanky Texas cowboy, but his weight was solid, concentrated in his shoulders, chest, and upper arms. He had an upright bearing that made him appear taller. He held himself like the master of a cattle empire.

The blazing sun had boiled all the clouds away. Cheerlessly Coke nudged Sin Cerebro on, the smoldering air forming pools of water mirages here and there and jellifying and magnifying the margin of foothills almost twenty miles away to a semblance of close proximity.

Up ahead buzzards were dropping from the sky into the brush. A half dozen of the ugly critters were crowded over the carcass of a steer. As he neared them, they retreated, flopping gawkily into the brush. As soon as he passed by, they lumbered back out again and enveloped the remains.

Off to the side, near a rust-colored boulder that sat like a blister on the scorched earth, Coke saw a coyote gnawing a shredded piece of steer leg. As he drew even with it, the coyote rose to a crouch, eyeing him warily, its pointed snout close to the ground. Coke eased his Winchester out of its boot on his saddle. Sin Cerebro automatically stopped. At the change in motion, the coyote, eyes still riveted on Coke, slunk back into the chaparral. Coke raised his rifle. The coyote broke into a run, skittering in and out among the brush. He fired. The report startled the buzzards, flapping heavily into the air. He missed. The coyote shot into the open, its legs reaching out in long, loping strides, shadow skimming the ground. Coke's rifle barrel followed it. He fired twice more in rapid succession. The coyote flip-flopped and lay on the ground, sides pumping hard up and down, gradually subsiding to a quivery stillness. Coke rebooted his rifle and rode on. Before he'd covered fifty feet, a lone buzzard was already hovering over the carcass.

✑ Chapter 2

SIN CEREBRO PLODDED along the ruts of a narrow, winding wagon trail, carrying Coke within sight of the flat roof and upper-story veranda of the home he shared with his ma and widowed sister, Sarie, and her two young children. Over the years it had grown to be a pretty good-sized house.

Whenever Coke sensed his gingery mother getting on her high horse and about to hit another cycle of lambasting him and everyone else in the household on the hazardous states of their immortal souls, he'd say to her, "Ma, seems like you could use a sittin' room for yourself." Or, "Maybe the kitchen needs enlargin'. What say I bring the carpenters in t'look it over?" And Ma's excess dithers would be siphoned off, with the ranch carpenters getting hit with the brunt of them instead of Coke.

Except for a few juts here and there, the Sanders house had turned out L-shaped. The baseline of the L was the older wing. Long, low, and one story, it now contained the dining room, parlor, and kitchen. Ma had added her sitting room and bedroom off to the side of the parlor. The longer line of the L was two stories tall and joined to the older section at the dining room. Its smooth, sand-colored brick contrasted sharply with the weathered, rough-laid rock of the one-story older section. His sister's quarters were on its top floor, and on the ground floor were Coke's bedroom and his office, the Sidewinder headquarters.

Coke rode through the south gate of the compound. Flanking one side of the roadway was a row of small adobe cottages that housed the vaqueros and their families. Each cottage sported a kitchen garden out back, where corn, tomatoes, frijoles, and chili peppers grew.

As Sin Cerebro ambled along, chickens flopped out of his path. Clothes fluttered from rope lines, simultaneously drying and collecting dust. Small, barefoot children played in the shade, their movements and voices mellowed in the sleepy afternoon heat. Passing by an open doorway, Coke heard a baby coo, and farther down the soft, murmuring edges of women's voices. Few men were about. The vaqueros camped out on the range most of the time, drifting in to be with their families every few days or so. Almost half of Coke's vaqueros were married, and more than half of the unmarried drovers were their brothers, sons, nephews, or grandsons. Coke estimated that the Sidewinder, and those cattle struggling out there to survive, supported over a hundred people.

At the corral by the barn he unsaddled Sin Cerebro and set him free in the nearby pasture. He stopped at the gate and looked up at the windmill. It wheeled above and behind his rambling home, as it had been doing faithfully since the time when nothing had been here but an open field. Today that windmill was the hub of a sprawling operation that included not only the Sanderses' and the vaqueros' homes, but barns, corrals, bunkhouses, tack houses, chicken coops, a granary, a smokehouse, a carpenter shop, and tool, storage, and milk-separating sheds. A newer, abbreviated version of the setup was in Coke's south section, where Alejandro and his family lived.

His three weeks away had opened Coke's eyes anew to what he and his pa had built through their will and endurance, and through his own instinct for when to take a risk and when to let one go. Coke was pleased with his handiwork. Well pleased.

He walked into the house, dropping his Stetson on the longhorn hat rack in the foyer. His eyes adjusting to the muted light admitted by the deeply recessed windows, he heard around the corner in the parlor the steady creak of Ma's rocker, the same rocker that they'd carted here from Virginia a lifetime ago. Ma would be crocheting doilies in her usual spot by the fireplace, which she swore gave off not only heat during cold snaps but "cool" during hot spells. "Idle hands make for the devil's handiwork," Ma often quoted. And with that saying in mind, she spent up to ten hours a day over her doilies.

Boots clomping on the clay tile floors, Coke strode into the parlor. Ma was spinning out a huge rose-colored number, her tiny, liver-spotted hands fluttering as she worked the yarn in triple-time rhythm to the slow creak-creak of her rocker. Her thin, silver hair was pulled up into a nut-sized knot on the top of her head, and on her nose perched a pair of store-bought metal-rimmed spectacles. The spectacles were too big for her tiny features. Each time her face changed expression, they came dislodged, skidding down the roof of her nose to a stop at the upturned end of it.

Abruptly Ma's hands stopped fluttering. Her rocker halted in midcreak. Jaw set, she sent her son a sharp look over the rims of her fallen specs.

"Go back outside an' scrape off your boots," her wiry voice crackled. "You know I cain't tolerate cattle droppin's on my parlor floor."

Coke stopped, did an about-face, and marched back out the foyer door, scooping up his hat as he passed by and planting it on his head. Rounding the corner of the house, he stalked by the clothesline. Over the wires was flung the massive multicolored parlor rug, its weight bearing them down to almost a U shape. Through the open kitchen window, he heard Gustina, the family servant, grumbling direly. As he stepped onto the back porch, he was halted by the sight of the kitchen door cautiously opening before him. Giving herself a space of barely twelve inches, Gustina sucked in her large belly and sidled out through the opening, gently closing the door behind her, her face dark and scowling. She discovered Coke and her eyes fired. She shook the rug beater in her hand.

"Esa madre tuya!" she rasped. That mother of yours.

Blustering on in clipped Spanish, she stomped by him, down the porch steps, and around the corner to the clothesline, where she commenced to punctuating her hot words with blistering whacks of rug beater against rug.

Coke stepped across the porch and flung the kitchen door open. A gust of wind swept into the room ahead of him, bowling over the fort that his four-year-old nephew, Joshua, had been painstakingly building of wood kindling on the kitchen floor.

Taking in the wind-scattered wreckage of his fine creation, the redheaded little fellow opened his pint-sized mouth and let out a shriek that could have knocked a crow out of a tree three miles off. He leaped to his feet, a move that sent more kindling hurtling about the room. "Dammit! *Chinga!* Shit!"

Coke walked over to him, calmly took him by the shoulders, and turned him toward Sarie, who was seated at the kitchen table, stoically snapping green beans.

"Now, apologize to your mama for usin' words like that."

The child rolled his eyes up at his uncle. Coke was the only person whom the feisty four-year-old obeyed with any consistency. Joshua regarded his uncle—the only other male in the household, and at that, absent most of the time—with a measure of the awe he'd seen in the other children on the compound. Coke had never spanked the boy, but he had a way of making him catch his breath and take a hard look at himself. That could be painful. Joshua looked at Sarie, eyes welling with accusation, for as his mother, she was clearly to blame for all misfortunes that came his way.

"Sorry," he said tightly.

"That's all right," Sarie replied, snapping steadily at the beans. "Pick up all them wood chips you flung round here, then go outside an' run that nastiness off. I've had 'bout all I can take for the day."

Coke went to the sink and picked up the cup of water for priming the water pump.

"If you're thirsty," Sarie said, "I made some lemonade fresh. It's over there in the corner o' the counter."

Coke set the primer cup down, then, collecting the lemonade pitcher and a glass from the cupboard, carried them to the table and set them across from his sister.

Joshua gathered the last of the kindling, and in an explosion of energy threw the pieces at the bucket and shot outside, slamming the kitchen door so hard behind that it bounced back open and stayed open. Since the child was already hitting full stride across the yard, raising a hullabaloo among the chickens, Coke calmly went over and shut the door.

"We'd better clean up ole Joshie's language afore we send him off to Miss Muriel's Day School," he said, sitting down at the table across from his sister.

"Will that day ever come?" Sarie sighed.

"Sooner'n we think. An' you know how cussin' riles ole Miss Muriel. At the rate Joshie's goin', we'll be gettin' him tossed back in our laps afore his first hour with her is half-up."

"It'll be damn hard gettin' him t'clean it up. *Hijole*, bein' around you an' the drovers day in an' day out, a body can get t'cussin' like hell in two languages without even realizin' he's about it."

"We never had that kinda trouble with Amy," Coke pointed out. His eight-year-old niece was now a two-year veteran of Miss Muriel's.

"Hell, Amy's prissy. Thinks she's Queen Victoria, Cinderella, Snow White, an' each o' the seven dwarfs all rolled into one. An' she ain't never heard o' any o' them cussin'."

Coke poured some lemonade from the pitcher into his glass. He warily took a sip, and winced. "Sarie, Sarie," he said, shaking his head. "This could 'bout stick a hombre's tongue permanent to the roof o' his mouth. Why cain't you ever remember t'put in some sweetenin'?"

"I take mine straight," Sarie replied, reaching back and pulling open a cabinet drawer. Taking out a spoon, she dropped it into the sugar bowl on the table and pushed it toward her brother. "The rest o' you can season it t'taste."

Coke took the spoon out and shook the sugar straight from the bowl into his lemonade.

"How'd you find things out on the range?" Sarie asked dispassionately as she returned to her pile of beans.

Coke sank down, his chin in his hand. "If trees could sprout outa sun-bleached steer bones, we'd be livin' in Sherwood forest right now."

They fell silent, beans snap-snapping, Coke gazing absently into space. Sarie cast a glance at her brother. It was a waste of breath carping about the drought.

Sarie was a large-boned, full-figured woman of thirty-two. Her hair, once a deep coppery color, had turned white by the end of her second pregnancy. Her appearance was arresting, old hair framing a round, youthful face. The white hair was more becoming to her than the coppery color she'd been born with. It played up her roses and cream complexion and the lively darkness of her eyes, as coal black as her brother's. She'd been widowed three years before, when her rancher husband, twenty years her senior, had been struck down by a heart attack during a midsummer roundup. Sarie's face reflected not the blank-faced, innocent prettiness of youth, but a steadier deeper beauty borne out of having been dealt one of life's major blows and having discovered she could handle it.

From the other side of the wall issued a muffled creak-creak of Ma's rocker picking up speed, a sign that she was closing in on the completion of her latest doily. Outside, Gustina was still walloping the parlor rug, though her cussing was tapering off.

"Everybody's throwin' purple hissies round here," Coke broke the silence. "What put the burrs under Ma's an' Gustina's tails this time?"

"Ma's on another of her nose tangents. You know how she gets thinkin' she can sniff out milk goin' sour in the next room an' a caterpillar burpin' up a piece o' leaf up in the tree out back. Well, all mornin' long she's been traipsin' 'bout, sniffin' here an' sniffin' there an' claimin' the place stinks. Gustina took that as a direct insult to her cleanin'. The thing that finally shot the steam outa Gussie's nozzle, though, was when Ma got down on her hands and knees on the parlor rug, took a giant whiff, an' declared that the thing smelled like it just come offa the henhouse floor."

"Gustina threatenin' t'leave? It's that time o' the year again."

"Yup."

"Well, it's your turn this time round t'make excuses for Ma an' t'tell Gustina how we-all cain't live without her."

Sarie nodded solemnly. "You gonna stay in this afternoon an' get to your paperwork?"

Coke shook his head. He didn't want to be reminded of the letters, bills, and lists of needed supplies that would have piled up in his office during his absence. "I'll get to it tomorrow. Reckon I'll go into town today."

"T'order supplies?"

"Nope, so don't start makin' me out a list o' things t'buy an arm an' a leg long. All I plan t'do is drop by the Easy Come Easy Go for a cold beer an' t'catch up on the news.''

Sarie regarded her brother obliquely. The Easy Come Easy Go wasn't just the only saloon in the area. It was the only bordello, too. "Just a beer?" she asked.

Coke shot a look at his sister. She was the only person he knew who felt she had the right to pry into all the corners of his life. And the only person he occasionally felt an urge to pop on the top of the head.

"A beer is all I'm hankerin' for today," he said evenly.

"Brother mine," she singsonged. "You should stop wasting your time on women of easy virtue."

"Aw, Sarie," he said, deciding to tease her. "The women I waste my time on, why, their virtue's naught but half-easy."

"You should get married," she rejoined flatly.

He regarded his sister. She and Ma and even Gustina had been tootling that tune for fifteen years. "Give up. I ain't interested."

"You need someone t'come home to."

"Did you ever take a gander round here? Hell, I figger at any given time I got close t'twenty-five, thirty-odd folks t'come home to."

"That ain't the same, an' you know it. You need someone special t'love you who you can love special. You need the comfort of a wife an' children o' your own."

"When the time comes, I'll have 'em."

"How much time d'you need?"

"My own time, Sarie. My own time. You ain't the one t'be dolin' it out for me."

"There're lotsa purty girls who'd be right pleased t'marry you. *Nice* girls. Why, just t'other day, Clara Foster was tellin' me that her daughter, Peggy, is right sweet on you."

"Aw, hell, Sarie. Peggy's naught but eighteen."

"She seems purty growed up t'me."

"Yup, but far as I can tell, it's only from the neck down. An' she ain't seen enough summers for life to've kicked some sense into 'er. Last thing I ever wanta be is a pa to my wife. Already got me enough responsibilities."

"I married an older man."

"An' you did most o' your growin' the year he died."

"Oh, so a widow lady would suit you more," Sarie mused.

"Sarie, Sarie," he said wearily. "I know all the gals you could mention. Known most of 'em since the time they first screeched in their cradles . . . the gals whose daddies are always misman-agin' an' who'd be right content t'latch onto some Sanders money—Peggy's pa, t'name but one; the gals with passels o'brothers wild as hell, in an' outa trouble all the time, who'd appreciate me bailin' 'em out. So stop soundin' like a travelin' man sellin' miracle root medicine. I know all the gals you could parade out here, the purty an' the plain, the good-uns an' the bad-uns. The bad-uns are just a sight more interestin'. . . ."

"An' the good-uns?"

"Are like Ma." He gulped down the last of the lemonade and got up. He'd almost reached the door and made good his escape when Sarie stopped him.

"Would you stop by Meg's Emporium when you get t'town?"

He turned and regarded his sister tiredly. "What for?"

"Brown yarn. Ma's clean outa it."

"Seemed t'me she had a good supply o' yarn in her crochet basket."

"Not the brown yarn. An' Ma's set on crocheting a brown doily for the bureau in the back bedroom tomorrow."

"Hell, Sarie, it's already got three doilies on it."

"Ma's tired of 'em."

"All right," he said. "I'll get Ma her yarn. Seein' as how I'm gonna be cooped up in here with her most o' tomorrow doin' my paperwork, I sure as hell don't want her gettin' squirrelly on me." He shook his head. "Sure wish you gals'd do all your stockin' up on your Saturday trips t'town."

The lure of a chilled beer pulling him onward and the hours of accursed sitting work waiting at home prodding him from behind, Coke traversed the fifteen miles to the ranch town of Dispenseme, Texas, at a faster clip than he'd been moving all day. He felt restless, but then, an outdoor man, he always felt restless when-ever the prospect of being penned up in a room glued to a chair loomed before him.

He slept on a bedroll out on the range as often as he slept in his twenty-year-old bed at home, and liked it that way. Liked things plain and simple. His only ambition in life was to own a half million acres before he cashed in, which he didn't deem an unreasonable goal since he was willing to sweat for it.

He hadn't been entirely truthful with Sarie a while ago, for though he did plan to stop by the Easy Come Easy Go Saloon for a cold beer and to catch up on the news, he expected to spend the night afterward with Carol Louise. Carol Louise Carpenter and her husband had divorced several years ago, a first for Dispenseme that had scandalized the town. The ladies' gossip had gone that Carol Louise's husband had been a skirt chaser. And a few of the local males in the know thought it prudent not to dispute that view, for Carol Louise had seldom been indisposed to the occasional pants wearer, either, a couple of them married.

Over the years of her marriage, she'd often sent Coke a special brand of come-hither signals. But he knew her husband too well, which tended to put the lid on temptation. And it wasn't until after his friend, her husband, had walked out that front door that Coke had strolled through the back.

Coke had been seeing Carol Louise off and on for years, and he was pretty sure that since he'd come on the scene, she'd kept from taking other lovers and was willing to go on that way. So long, that is, as she saw an off chance of snaring him. She was a handsome woman in a midthirties sort of way, and their affair had been convenient for him. But it had probably gone on too long, for he was tiring of it. Though shrewd in character, Carol Louise was a fairly humorless and blunt woman, and seldom aroused his curiosity. He did feel affection for her and some gratitude, but little tenderness. Her ripe flesh was invitingly soft and hotly responsive, but he could find little in her soul that was.

Now, if Coke had been sixteen, very likely he'd have been taken by a hot-blooded woman like Carol Louise and would have wanted her for his wife. But he was seasoned enough now to know better. And since he had his druthers, he'd druther be the one snuck than the one stuck.

Coke's gaze came to rest on the magnificent hacienda and compound of El Rancho San Sebastian, set in a valley less than a quarter of a mile away. Dating from well over a century before, when the Spanish Crown awarded a million acres in a land grant to Fernando Sebastian Castillo, the San Sebastian was a harmonious arrangement of buildings, orchards, terraces, and gardens reaching out in dignity and graceful symmetry from the huge, balconied hacienda. It had clearly been planned and built to endure for centuries, and looked very different from the layout of the Sanders compound where Coke had to admit that many of the buildings looked like they'd been thrown up as an afterthought, and with just about as much sentiment could as readily be knocked down. And each time he passed by the San Sebastian compound on his way into town, he felt a twinge of sorrow. The place stood for a way of life that was no longer there. It ended ten months ago, when T. C. Barrett moved in and took it over.

T. C. Barrett's and Coke's paths had crossed once before. Twenty-seven years ago, at the peaceful spot now occupied by Coke's north section windmill, Camden Sanders and the men of the Sidewinder had fought a bloody gun battle with a northern interloper by the name of Saul Barrett, his then twenty-year-old son, T.C., and the men of the Rolling B Ranch.

Camden had been the first to occupy that land. About a year after that, Saul Barrett formed his Rolling B Ranch and began moving his cattle onto it, too. A creek flowed through the land once, and over that innocent-looking creek an intense rivalry developed between the two ranches, for water was South Texas's most treasured resource. It was vital. He who held the water held the survival of his herds in his hands.

For over a year the two ranches moved their cattle in, trying to elbow each other out. The tension built steadily. Then, as he'd done many times before, Coke's pa decided to settle the matter by going into Mexico, finding the land grant heirs, and buying the deeds to the land.

Saul Barrett scoffed at Camden's Mexican papers, calling them "more worthless than the dry leaves my men wipe their asses on." And his men took to stampeding Sidewinder cattle that had been brought into the area. Then one night a Sidewinder vaquero was shot and the herd he was guarding scattered.

The confrontation came to a head two days later, after Camden's men had rounded up their scattered cattle and, combining them with other Sidewinder herds, moved them all onto the fields within grazing distance of the creek. Saul Barrett, his son, T.C., and about eight of his men were waiting by the stand of trees.

Coke was then no more than a thirteen-year-old stripling, all arms and legs. He recalled the men of the two sides facing one another across the field, less than thirty feet apart. He held still fresh in his mind the studied economy of their movements, the steady, unblinking eyes, the scattered bawling of calves to their mothers in the far fields, and the tension in the air so thick that it rippled and crawled at the back of his neck.

Then, out of the corner of his eye, he saw T.C. go for his gun. He saw little after that, for Alejandro knocked him hard into a ditch. Before he hit the ground, the guns started roaring, the blasts coming so close together that he couldn't make out any separation in the sounds. It seemed the gunfire went on for twenty minutes before it slowed to three widely spaced pops and fell quiet. It took Coke awhile to realize that less than a minute had passed.

Saul Barrett sat propped against a tree at a strange angle, a bullet hole through his forehead. Three other of his men lay dead or dying, and two were wounded. T.C. had taken a bullet in the leg. Three Sidewinder vaqueros were also wounded, but only slightly.

Camden Sanders walked over to Saul Barrett, and looked at him thoughtfully. Then he turned to T.C., who was grasping his leg, his face twisted in pain.

"I got the deeds to this land," he said quietly. "But your pa disputed those deeds. I got men who're better shots . . . so there's no disputation anymore."

He had the Rolling B wounded piled in a ranch wagon and taken to the doctor at Warner, the county seat, and his vaqueros moved the Barrett cattle off the Sidewinder range. The land was peaceful for a month, but for about the next six months after, rustlers struck in the area repeatedly. Then the Civil War broke out. It was at that time that the Barrett family, who, as northerners, were presumed to be Yankee sympathizers, sold out and left the region. And good riddance to 'em, most folks around here thought.

But Barrett had returned to South Texas seven and a half years ago with his two sons and settled at the county seat at Warner. He'd come back a wealthy man. Word was that while prospecting for gold in Colorado, he'd stumbled upon a silver vein northwest of Denver, and from this he'd built his fortune. He quickly established himself in Warner, buying control of the Warner Savings and Loan Association. It was from this base that he set out to build his empire.

The owners of small ranches north of Warner soon found that the Warner Savings and Loan under T. C. Barrett was a mighty easy place to borrow money from to help them build new herds, expand their holdings, or carry them through a hard year. They did have to put up as collateral their only assets, their land and livestock; and the interest that the association charged was pretty steep. But as T. C. Barrett told them, money that easily available had to cost more. And cost them it did. For soon enough those ranchers discovered that T. C. Barrett's Warner Savings and Loan had a tendency to call in their loans at the first sign of trouble or when their payments were but a couple of months in default. Foreclosure followed swiftly. Within two years after T. C. Barrett had taken over the Savings and Loan, seven ranches had gone under to it. All were quickly taken over by a ranching company no one had ever heard of before, the Silver Mountain Land Company.

The last Castillo owner of El Rancho San Sebastian had never had serious cash problems. Though most of the million acres of the original land grant to Fernando Sebastian Castillo had slipped out of the fingers of the heirs of succeeding generations, Juan Fernando's branch of the family had always managed to keep a firm grip on its share. Until six years ago, when Juan Fernando Castillo left his ranch to attend to some sort of business in Mexico. He never made it to the border. Less than two miles short of it, he'd been cut down by a single shot fired from a ridge. People speculated that Castillo had become too involved in Mexican politics, which could be murderous. Others weren't so sure. It was known that two days before his death, Castillo had gone to Warner. When the Warner Savings and Loan had been under its former owners, Juan Fernando had deposited money with them. It was rumored that he was growing impatient with the new owner's predatory policies and was considering withdrawing his savings. T. C. Barrett himself soon came forth to substantiate that rumor, but only to the extent that Castillo had withdrawn his money to take it into Mexico. That had probably been the reason for his death . . . robbery.

Up until that shot was fired, El Rancho San Sebastian had been on solid footing. Men would never cheat or go directly up against Don Juan Fernando Castillo, because they feared him. They had no such fears with Juan Fernando's widow.

At the time of her husband's murder, Doña Celestina Castillo was twenty-six years old. She was pregnant, and had been left with four other children under the age of eight. Brought up to gentility, she'd been educated to create a gracious home and to please and placate men, not to order them around, confront them, or fire them from their jobs. Her life had not conditioned her to be tough. And she was taken advantage of everywhere she turned, by outsiders as well as by a few of her own trusted employees.

The resources of the San Sebastian began bleeding out of it, from a trickle at first to a full-scale hemorrhage. And two years ago, Doña Celestina found that she needed a loan to see the ranch through the winter, and the only institution willing to take the risk on so large a loan was the Warner Savings and Loan Association.

Coke wondered how well T. C. Barrett slept in his bed at night in the San Sebastian hacienda, with the small cemetery containing several generations of Castillos, and now Juan Fernando himself, in easy view from the rear balconies. Already the beauty of the compound was starting to fade. The orchard from which Juan Fernando Castillo had distilled sweet peach brandy was drying out. The grape arbors that yielded his table wines looked neglected. No longer did the buildings reflect the thoughtful, gentle touch of people who felt its history and tradition and lovingly strove to preserve them in every stone.

This place was fifteen miles from the borders of the Sidewinder, but Coke didn't like T.C. crowding him so close. And maybe fixing on crowding him even closer. He'd heard rumblings from his contacts in Warner that Barrett was starting to nose through old Spanish land documents. It was possible that he might be planning to use his acquisition of San Sebastian as a basis for going after some of Coke's land—seeing as how two sections of it had once been part of the old Castillo land grant. Coke's pa had bought the land from Juan Fernando's cousins in Mexico, and Castillo himself had never pressed such a claim. Still, Coke was uneasy.

The political power in Warner was becoming divided. The county sheriff, a known gunfighter who'd probably walked the wrong side of the law as often as the right, was firmly a Barrett man. A couple county commissioners were also. And Barrett's older son, Ray, the attorney for the railroad in Warner, was out to get the county attorney's job. The county judge was on Coke's side, and two commissioners as well. One district judge was a Barrett man; the other, Edwin T. Bierbaum, stood in the middle, like a few other county officials, waiting to see which side would prevail before deciding which way to jump. The only people clearly left out of the growing rivalry were the poor Mexicans, who, as always, stood about as much of a chance of coming out on top in any power struggle around here as a junebug crawling up a robin's toe.

Like bees out of a hive, some forty children came swarming out of the sand-colored stone Catholic school next to the road. Ten years ago, Juan Fernando had brought a brown-cassocked *hermano* from Mexico City to teach the good Catholic children of the area reading, writing, arithmetic, and out-and-out terror of the Lord.

On a knoll a little ways back from the school sat the Catholic church. Built over a century ago by a Castillo ancestor, it was close to the San Sebastian compound without quite being in it. At the head of that Catholic church loomed a new, disproportionately tall bell tower. The bell housed in the crown of that tower was so mighty and so loud that its deep, sonorous bonging, summoning parishoners to mass, echoed far out across the Texas prairie. And whenever Coke looked at it, he suppressed a smile.

For three years, the parish priest, Father Dominic, had vainly tried to raise enough money to build his bell tower and buy his bell. Nine months ago the money had fallen into his hands. Coke had made a hefty anonymous contribution through Alejandro, his one condition for giving the money being that when Father Dominic set out to buy his bell, he should be sure to make it one big bugger.

When Alejandro had questioned him about it, Coke had said, "Alejandro, there are some satisfactions in life. An' the notion of a Catholic bell letting loose an' thunderin' through the walls of the Rancho San Sebastian, rollin' T. C. Barrett outa his bed an' shakin' that black soul o' his loose every mornin' at seven, has gotta be one of 'em."

And once he got it, Father Dominic, who'd been close to the Castillos, never went light on that bell, either. Coke had noticed that since it had gone into action, T. C. Barrett had taken to spending most of his weekdays in his house in Warner.

Coke heard the high, chirping voices of children around a curve in the road up ahead. Soon Amy, Coke's eight-year-old niece, rode into view, accompanied by Obie Given's little brother and sister and a few other children from out their way. An ancient Sidewinder ranch hand was performing his sole duty of the day, escorting the children home from Miss Muriel McKenzie's Day School. There, for a dollar fifty a month, they learned reading, writing, arithmetic, guilt, and out-and-out terror of Miss Muriel. The schoolmarm must have been hitting on an etiquette tack lately,

Coke mused, for last night over supper, his niece had taken to blasting the family's table manners.

"Why, good afternoon to you, Unca Coke," Amy called regally from her bouncing pony, chestnut pigtails flopping. She was in her Queen Victoria mood, he noted.

"Hiya, Ame," he called back. "Didn't stir up ole Miss Muriel's hackles too much today, I hope."

"Course not." She frowned indignantly. "What're you doin' goin' into town, Unca Coke? You got a big passel o' ledgerwork t'do. Why, your desk at home's a woeful mess of it." Woeful was Amy's word of the month.

"Listen, my little Miss Prissy," he said, drawing alongside her. "For such a mite of a nose you got there, it sure does hanker t'grow woeful long." He reached out to tweak it, but she ducked away, giggling.

Recovering her poise, she twisted around in the saddle and regarded him tauntingly. "I bet you're on your way to the saloon and that house o' ill repute." The last words had that clipped-out spurt ladies made while gossiping scandalously behind their hands. Coke waited for the hunched-down giggling of Amy's companions to die down. "All right, Miss Smarty, tell your pore ole innocent Unca Coke, what is a house o' ill repute?"

She pulled herself up. "Why, it's a place where improper ladies trounce around in nothin' but their underdrawers."

"Close enough, close enough. But for your information, little Prissy, I'm headed into town t'buy brown yarn for your granny's doilies."

As the little band turned down the lane to the Catholic school to collect the last batch of Sidewinder children, Amy sent her uncle one last squinty-eyed, pucker-lipped look of skepticism.

The child was turning into another Sarie, Coke reflected. Two Saries under the same roof could turn out to be downright disruptive to a hombre's constitution.

Chapter 3

DISPENSEME, TEXAS, LAY sprawled across a sag in the landscape that folks referred to as a valley but that looked more like a warp in the bottom of a tin pan. Two rows of business buildings fronted each other across the dusty main street. It was the only straight street in town, the rest of the roads being nothing more than a convolution of wagon trails and footpaths leading to a hodgepodge of frame and stucco houses, stables, barns, sheds, pigpens, and privies, all strewn out indiscriminately from the business district.

It was believed that over fifty years ago Santa Ana's army passed through here on its way to the Alamo. About twenty years later, a Mexican drifter showed up in the local saloon. As the night wore on and his judgment started eroding under the inflow of tequila, he commenced to bragging about how he'd once been a member of Santa Ana's army. The other patrons in the bar started getting up and inching toward him. And in one last blast of defiance, the Mexican proclaimed that it was his outfit, in fact, that had named this very settlement. Dispenseme en el Valle de Caca Verde had been so christened by his platoon when it had been left to languish behind here after its men had sampled too much tainted South Texas beef. He then charged out the door and was last seen sprinting into the night ducking under a hail of bullets. Somehow, that Mexican's story stuck in the minds of the local residents and in time became a part of Dispenseme's folklore.

Once over beer at a local political rally, Coke had related this piece of local folklore to Judge Edwin T. Bierbaum. Now, the judge was a bigot who, despite over thirty years of residing in South Texas, had learned no Spanish outside of food words. He was a politician through and through, however. And ever mindful of the good faith of his unenfranchised Mexican constituency and enthusiastic at this opportunity to demonstrate to them his deep and abiding affection, he seized upon Coke's story. Leaping upon the nearest stoop, he declared to one and all that he'd see to it that a marble statue depicting that great historical event be erected in the center of town. Coke sometimes wondered if that was the reason why Ed Bierbaum still held back from moving over to his side in Coke's developing tug-of-war with T. C. Barrett.

Plodding down the main street, on Ole Belcher, his second regular mount, Coke passed the big limestone barn that was Ramiro's Stables and Ironworks, the Wilson-Siden Ranch Supply Store and Post Office, Clem's Granary, Meg's Emporium, El Restaurante de Mañana Luis. And in front of the Easy Come Easy Go Saloon and Bordello, he pulled up at the water pump, placed on a wooden platform in the middle of the street like an iron icon. Dismounting, he took the bucket chained to the pump neck, pumped out some water, and poured it into the horse trough close by. He sat down on a corner of the platform waiting for Ole Belcher to drink his full.

"Howdy, Coke, heard you wath back," a familiar voice grunted from the doorway of the saloon. Coke recognized it as belonging to Seth Shaftesbury, the lisping town marshal. "You make a good thell up in Colorado?"

"Coulda done better," Coke taciturnly replied.

Seth had been the Dispenseme marshal for almost the entire fifteen years since his ranch had failed. Greatly respected for his evenhanded judgment, he was over fifty years in age, short and barrel-chested with bandy legs. Now, lugging the top half of a man's body, he emerged from the saloon, backing humpbacked through the swinging doors with the barkeep, Smitty, following behind toting the fellow's legs. As they rotated around for Smitty to take the lead, Coke saw that the man they were transporting was Clyde Stonewall, the town drunk. Whenever he was on one of his binges, Clyde neglected to eat, and Seth, deeming bourbon to be not the best of nutrition, would eventually clamp him in jail to reintroduce him to food.

"Don't thee why you keep on pourin' pore ole Clyde your poithon," Seth grumped as he and Smitty stepped gingerly off the boardwalk.

"We sell top-quality likker," Smitty shot back. "Helluvalot better'n that rotgut he'd be gettin' at the Caudle still."

They slogged across the road in front of Coke, their burden swinging in between, head rocking to and fro, long, prickly jaw lolloping open, and unaware of the change of scenery.

"Had around a hundred steers rustled last night," Coke said.

Seth stopped suddenly, and Smitty stretched Clyde out a bit before he came to a halt. "Track 'em?" Seth asked.

"Sent a coupla men out."

"Probably follow 'em t'Caballo Blanco Canyon, where the trackth'll dithappear on that rocky floor. All the cattle been thwiped around here in the lath coupla monthth wound up there."

"Find where they was moved out?" Coke asked.

Seth shook his head. "Canyon'th way too big. Me an' Hector Navarro, who wath robbed purty bad 'bout ten dayth ago, rode all over it. Flat-out too many rocky drawth an' gapth an' gorgeth t'move 'em out through." He and Smitty started up again. "Tell your men t'be careful," he said over his shoulder. "The vermintth weren't too thy 'bout poppin' off their carbineth when they thwiped Hector'th herd."

They'd almost reached the opposite side of the road when a tumbleweed, nudged by the breeze, came moseying along. Veering gently to the right, it bumped into the back of Seth's legs, snagged on the rowel of the spur connected to his right stovepipe boot, and commenced to dragging in the dust behind.

"Hold it," Seth grunted, and still grasping the snoring deadweight of the drunk under the armpits, he tried to shake the tumbleweed off, kicking high to the side and the back. But the tumbleweed stayed hooked on his spur, bouncing back and forth like a Christmas tree ornament.

"Thit!" Seth barked. Bandy knees poking out at the sides so he looked like a frog on a lily pad, he squatted down and lowered Clyde to the ground. Then he jerked the tumbleweed off his spur and angrily threw it into the wind, where it bounced twice, hesitated, reversed direction, and began following him back down the street.

Coke tied Ole Belcher to the hitching rail in front of Meg's Emporium. Bypassing three boys shouting and tossing a stone on the boardwalk out front, playing keep-away, he stepped into the store.

No one was about the shadowy room, but he could make out women's voices at the back of the store, emanating from behind the curtained doorway that led to the storage and fitting room. Settling back on the counter next to the candy jars, he ran his gaze around the room. He frowned. There was something different about the place.

The potbelly stove stood at the center of the store, gleaming like polished agate. It was flanked on either side by two rocking chairs, the week-old San Antonio newspaper folded neatly in the seat of one. Hanging in orderly alignment according to size from nearby racks were the ready-made shirts, dresses, and trousers. Other cloth merchandise was stacked in neat, well-marked piles on countertops. Cracker, sugar, fruit, and pickle barrels lined one wall; bean, flour, rice, and potato sacks, the wall opposite. There was no spillage anywhere on the floor around them. The Arbuckle Coffee boxes were stacked next to a coffee grinder that fairly shone. There wasn't so much as a speckle of loose coffee grounds around it. Aisles had been cleared so that customers could reach merchandise without having to straddle anything to get to it.

That was it! Everything in the store was neat and in its proper place. Meg was a lovable, big-hearted barrel of fun, but she'd never been neat a day in her life, and her store had always looked like the aftermath of a bobcat fight. Coke was still wondering what had brought on the change in Meg when the boys playing outside carried their commotion down the road, leaving exposed the voices in the backroom.

"There now," Meg's rough voice was saying. "All we have t'do is take up that hem a mite an' you'll have yourself the purtiest weddin' dress this side o' the Rio Grande."

"Well . . . I don't know . . ." a dubious voice replied. Coke placed it to Cindy Blankenship, the twenty-three-year-old daughter of a local rancher.

"What don't you like?" Meg.

"The bodice."

"Seems t'me t'fit just fine."

"Yes . . . but." Coke heard a soft rustling. That'd be Cindy preening from side to side in front of the fitting room mirror. "Don't you think I look a tad flat on top? Now, if you was t'add a little somethin' up here. Ruffle, maybe? Just this once, it bein' my weddin' an' all, I'd like t'look like I got more'n a pair o' chigger bites up front."

"You recollect the last time the circuit preacher hit town?"

"Yup . . . I remember."

"Recollect his sermon 'bout that part outa Luke in the Good Book . . . the part 'bout the widder's penny?"

"Yes . . . sorta. The rich men gave a lotta money to the Lord 'cause they had a lotta money t'give an' this pore ole widow woman gave Him nothin' but a single penny an' the good Lord appreciated that single penny most of all 'cause it was all that that pore ole widow woman had t'give. I stopped payin' the preacher man much mind after that. I figgered he'd latched on to that piece o' Scripture t'jaw away at just so's we-all'd feel obliged to cough up a bigger offerin' for him. 'Sides, Meg,'' she went on impatiently. ''What does that story 'bout the widow's penny got t'do with my undersized bosoms?''

''Why, don't you see? 'Tain't important how big a thing is . . . so long as it serves its purpose.''

Giggling rippled from behind the curtain. Coke's hearing perked up. He detected a third voice mingling in with the others, and couldn't place it.

''Shame on you, Meg,'' the voice said in mock reproach. ''Perverting the Scriptures to suit your purpose.'' Coke's curiosity sharpened, for it was a musical alto voice with a shade of huskiness in it. Made him think of soft fur, running his hands over soft fur.

''Hell, everybody does it,'' Meg was saying. ''They-all go pickin' an' choosin' through the Good Book like it was a crate o' oranges, choosin' out for theirselves only those parts that're sweet to the taste an' payin' no heed to the rest.''

Coke crept back to the open doorway, turned around, and stepped heavily on the threshold. ''Hello. Anybody here?''

The back room immediately fell silent. Meg poked her head out between the curtains. As she saw Coke, her plump face crinkled into a wide grin, exposing the gap in her lower jaw made by the absence of two front teeth.

''Why, howdy, Coke, ole podner. Been here long?''

''Just now stepped in.''

She bustled across the room and enveloped him in a bear hug. ''Sure am glad t'see you, fella. How'd it go in ole Colorado?''

''Fair t'middlin','' he replied. He liked Meg, always had. She gave off the kind of warmth that made folks feel accepted and appreciated right off, warts, buckteeth, bald heads, and all. Plump and closing in on her sixth decade, she had a full, youthful face. Her thick, graying hair was pulled up in a pointy bun on the top of her head. That helped the rest of her—wide shoulders, wider breasts, and still wider hips, with skirts flaring out to the floor— achieve the overall look of a slightly lumpy triangle.

''Drought's bound t'let up soon,'' she said. ''Just t'other day,

Herman, that ole houn' o' mine, took t'movin' real stiff-like. His arthuritis always kicks up before a drencher.''

"Could be his joints is dryin' up same as everything else round here," he replied. He glanced around the room. "What's gotten into you, Meg? Place ain't as sloppy as you usually keep it."

"Got me a helper. Came right in here an' straightened me out. Fine gal, Jessica, though she ain't near as purty as me. Right fine seamstress, too. Made Cindy Blankenship her weddin' dress. You hear 'bout Cindy gettin' hitched?''

"Nope. Who you marryin', Cindy?" he called to the curtained doorway.

"Fella who wrangles for my pa, Coke," Cindy hollered back. "Name's Freddy Winsnap. You ever meet him?''

"Once or twice. Nice fellow. When y'all fixin' t'tie the knot?''

"Week from Saturday when the circuit preacher comes t'town.''

"Hope y'all will be right happy.''

"Thank you kindly.''

"What can I get you?" Meg said. "Now that everything's in its proper place, shouldn't take me long t'find it.'' Glancing up, she caught Coke's gaze lingering on the fitting room doorway, and her eyes danced knowingly. "On second thought," she said, looking the room over and scratching the back of her head, "havin' everythin' in its place confuses the daylights outa me an' I cain't recollect where things are any better'n I could before. Why don't I get Jessica out here t'help you?''

"Fine with me," he replied, trying to sound matter-of-fact.

"Jessica," Meg called. "Come out here an' help Coke. I'll finish pinnin' Cindy's hem.''

There was a pause, the curtains parted, and the loveliest creature Coke had ever laid eyes on stepped unhurriedly into the room.

"Jessica," Meg said. "Meet my ole compadre, Coke Sanders. Coke, this is my new helper, Jessica West.''

"Good afternoon, Mr. Sanders," came that husky voice. "You're from the Sidewinder Ranch, are you not?''

He was so engrossed in drinking in the sight of her, his eyes roving down her slender body to the floor and up again, that her words barely tickled at the outer edge of his mind.

Meg guffawed and headed for the fitting room. "You gotta start fixin' yourself up, gal. Why, you're so homely, soon as folks take a look at you, they stop payin' any mind t'what you got t'say.''

At the curtained doorway, Meg paused and looked back at Jessica a bit uneasily. "Now, be nice to that pore boy, hear?"

Coke's eyes finally settled back upon the delicate features of her small, round face. "Beg pardon, ma'am. Did you say somethin'?"

A tight smile on her face that didn't touch her eyes, she glided by him, trailing the fragrance of lavender. "I only inquired if you were from the Sidewinder."

Like a hound dog that'd picked up the scent, he followed close behind. "That's my ranch. You've heard o' me, I take it."

"I've heard of the Sidewinder," she replied, going behind the counter. She picked up a ledger book that had been sitting on the countertop and patted the pages even. "Can I help you?"

"Uh . . . yup. Like some yarn . . . brown yarn."

"Do you knit?"

"Hell no! It's for my ma!" He caught himself, and frowned. "You're funnin' me, ain't you?"

"One never knows," she answered expressionlessly. "Appearances can be deceiving. Just the other day one of the grubbiest men I've ever seen came in here and bought two boxes of Dainty Daisy Talcum Powder."

"You don't say. . . . Who?"

"He didn't introduce himself. He paid in cash."

"Well, you can take it from me, that yarn I want is for my ma."

"If you say so," she said, strolling around the counter toward the sewing section.

Again he followed close behind, eyes riveted on a fawn-colored curl that had strayed down out of the hairnet-covered chignon at the nape of her neck.

She riffled through the yarn contained in a box on a table. "How many skeins of brown yarn do you want?"

"Six," he said to the strayed curl.

She must have felt his gaze there, for a slender hand appeared and tucked the curl back under the hairnet. As soon as she removed her hand, though, it tumbled free again.

Gathering up the yarn, she turned. A startled look flitted across her face at finding him crowding her closer than she'd expected. She held her ground, giving him a clear-eyed, businesslike look. "Anything else you wish to purchase?"

Her eyes dominated her face. Very full, deep-set, slightly

slanted over high cheekbones, they were luminous light greenish blue.

"Uh . . . uh . . . hooks," he said.

"Fishing hooks? Hooks and eyes?"

"Uh . . . crochet hooks. For my ma, o' course."

"If you say so." She swept around him to a narrow upright cabinet that stood against the wall and pulled out a drawer. "How many crochet hooks do you want?"

"Six," he said, moving next to her into that aura of lavender. He wished he'd cleaned up before coming here. He needed a shave. Smoke, dirt, and sweat saturated his skin and clothing.

"Just six?" she asked, looking down at the drawer.

"Make that eight," he said to her profile. She had a full, rounded forehead, small, slightly upturned nose, neat line of chin curving in to a slender neck, enclosed in a high-collared blouse that looked whiter than white. An earring, a thin circlet of gold, ran through the lobe of her delicate pierced ear, downy, fawn-colored hair brushing over the top of it. "You from these parts?" he asked.

"No. Anything else you wish to purchase?"

"Reckon that's it."

She pushed the drawer shut and walked past him toward the front counter. He followed. The high-button blouse accentuated the narrowness of her shoulders and the slant of her upper torso to a petite waist. A man could get his hands around it, thumbs and fingers touching front and back, tip to tip. She had a small-boned, feline kind of body and the smooth, graceful, feline kind of movements that went with it.

"You kin o' Meg's?" he asked.

"No."

"You kin o' some friends o' Meg's?"

"No." She went behind the counter, and, bending down, took out a cloth sack, dropping Coke's purchases into it. As she pulled the string on top to close it, her attention was caught by the rumble and creak of the stagecoach making its biweekly arrival into town. Absently holding the cloth sack, she drifted to the window and watched as the stage pulled to a stop in front of Lou Wilson's Ranch Supply and Post Office.

"Expectin' someone?" he asked, coming up beside her.

"Merchandise," she distantly replied, eyes intent on the stagecoach. Strands of her soft-spun hair caught the window light and seemed to turn to gold. Her fair skin also captured the light.

She watched the stage empty of its passengers and, with an almost imperceptible sigh that seemed one of relief, turned and walked back behind the counter. "That'll be eighty-four cents."

"Put it on my account."

Turning aside, she lifted the lid off a long, rectangular file box. "What did you say your name was?"

"Sanders . . . Coke."

She leafed through the file cards, pulled one out, and plucking a pen out of the countertop inkwell, jotted the amount down, adding it to the previous total. Giving the card a few wags in the air to dry the ink, she slipped it back into the file box. With a quick, insincere smile of dismissal, she handed him his purchases.

But he remained there, watching her. Shooting him an annoyed look, she pulled a notebook out from under the counter, flipped through the pages, and busily scribbled something in it.

He turned aside as though to get a better look at what she was writing, while instead his eyes were fixed upon the gentle, diminutive movement of her eyelashes fringing out from her downturned face. "What you doin?" he asked softly.

"Making a note to order more crochet hooks. We just sold out."

"You keep good records, eh?"

"Good record keeping is the key to a successful business."

"Reckon Meg could use some help in that department."

"Meg's gracious and kind. People come here because she's such a pleasure to be around," she said, for the first time betraying any warmth. It was only a brief lapse, however. ". . . but she hadn't kept quite the best track of her inventory. When I arrived here, I counted eight chamber pots out on the floor and a dozen more in the back room. Meg had no idea how slowly they were moving, and each month she ordered more. The market was glutted with chamber pots." Pen seesawing back and forth between her fingers, she paused, waiting for him to take his turn and say something. But he said nothing. He just stood there, arms folded, watching her through his squinty outdoor eyes.

She shut the notebook and jabbed her pen back into the inkwell. Grabbing up the feather duster, she began swiping at the already sparkling candy jars. He still failed to move or speak, and her swatting of the jars slowed. She took a deep breath, lowered the feather duster, and tilting her head, regarded him contemplatively. An oily calmness seemed to settle over her. A dimple he hadn't noticed before started playing at the corner of her mouth.

"Uh . . . Mr. Sanders," she began.

"Ma! Ma!" A freckle-faced boy of about seven burst into the room, an unhooked suspender flapping at his knees. "Ma! Come on out and see the turtle Mort and me rounded up."

With a sinking, disgusted-with-himself feeling, Coke realized that the child was addressing Jessica West. He glanced at her left hand. No wedding band was there, but married women sometimes removed their rings when they had work to do, or else due to poverty, had never been given wedding rings when the preacher married them.

A look of amusement crossed her face at his chagrin in discovering that the woman that he'd been entertaining unseemly notions about was A Mother.

"Why, Willie," she said, the timbre of her voice softening to velvet as she came around the counter. "So you caught yourself a turtle?" Bending down, she retrieved his loose suspender, pulled it over his shoulder, and rehooked it. "Is it a big one, precious?"

"Yup! This big." He spread his hands wide to show the size, then impatiently tugged at her sleeve. "C'mon out and look at it."

"First, my love, we must remember our manners. Mr. Sanders, this is my son, William."

"Hiya, Will."

"How do you do, sir," the child replied, manfully pulling himself up and offering Coke his tiny hand. Then he grabbed his mother's arm. "C'mon, Ma."

She allowed her son to pull her outside. He bounded off the boardwalk and picked up a stick. "See? This is how we get the critter t'move," he exclaimed, swatting the tail of a foot-long turtle. Reptilian head poking this way and that, it lumbered forward a few steps and stopped.

Then another child, whom Coke recognized as Cindy's little brother, Mort, gave the turtle another swat on the behind. It lumbered forward a couple more steps.

"Mr. Sanders." Jessica glanced aside at Coke, who was now leaning in the doorway behind her. "That turtle won't bite, will it?"

"Well," he drawled. "If the young-uns ain't careful, I reckon that bas—uh, box turtle could take a fair-sized hunk outa one o' their fingers if he took a mind to."

"Willie," she cautioned him. "Do be careful. Don't get too close to that animal. Stay away from his head."

"Ah, Ma," he protested. "I'm not a baby."

"Ma," she breathed, turning back into the store. "Only a few weeks ago I was still Mommy."

Coke stepped into the street, next to Ole Belcher, and put his purchases into his saddlebags. He could really use that beer now. His letdown feeling was still very much with him. In a twenty-minute spread of time, a pretty little fantasy had been born and had died.

"You waitin' for Cindy t'finish with her weddin' dress?" he offhandedly asked over his horse to Mort.

"Naw, I'm just a-herdin' this here ole turtle," the child said, giving it another whack on the fanny to illustrate his point.

"Oh? An' where are you boys fixin' on a-herdin' it to?"

"Haven't decided yet. Maybe we'll sneak him into Miss Muriel's privy. Naw." He shook his head. "It'd gag t'death before the afternoon's half-up. Happened to that big bullfrog we snuck in there a coupla weeks ago. Died on its back, a deeper shade o' green an' mouth wide open."

Mort was still deep in contemplation over where to secrete the turtle when Willie, who'd been staring wide-eyed up at Coke, found the courage to speak up.

"Sir," he asked shyly. "Are you the Coke that's Amy's uncle?"

"Sure am."

"Coupla years back," Mort put in, "my sister, Cindy, was right sweet on Coke."

"Didn't know that," Coke lied.

"Well, you sure were smart stayin' outa Cindy's clutches," Mort went on. "That flat-chested sister o' mine can be meaner'n a wet hornet."

"Just now heard she was gettin' hitched," Coke replied. "Didn't know she was bein' courted."

"Courted, spooned. And deflowered," Mort declared.

Coke turned away to collect his reins and hide the amusement in his eyes. Deflowered? If all the gossip that he'd heard about her was true, in the years since she'd reached her womanhood, the modest, churchgoing Cindy Blankenship had collected more seeds than a Kansas wheat farmer.

"Well, I sure am glad t'hear she's gettin' hitched," he said to end that line of conversation.

"So're my ma an' my pa," Mort averred. "Seein' as how in six months or so I'm gonna have me a cousin. Or is it I'll be a uncle?"

"Mortimer!" a voice rasped from the doorway of the emporium. And Cindy Blankenship marched rigidly past Coke and grabbed her brother by the ear.

"Youch!" Mort screeched. "Lemme go! Lemme go, Cindy! I got me a turtle t'herd."

"I'm the one doin' the herdin'," Cindy snarled. "And, boy, I'm a-herdin' you home."

Holding her brother by the ear, she jerked him to the buggy and half kicked, kneed, and flung him up into the seat. Then, seizing the reins from the hitching rail, she leaped up beside him.

"Cynthia," Mort tsk-tsked. "A woman in your condition—"

But Cindy had already pulled the horse around, and with a sharp snap on its rump with the buggy switch, they plunged down the road, capsizing Mort to the buggy floor.

"Why's Cindy so mad?" Willie asked. "Mort told us kids at school all about her expecting a baby when he first heard about it a couple weeks ago."

"You got me," Coke said, pulling Ole Belcher around and leading him toward the saloon.

Willie fell into step beside him. "You sure do have a nice rifle," he said, eyeing the Winchester on Coke's saddle. "Do you shoot many rustlers and bad people with it?"

"Mostly coyotes, son. It's agin my nature t'hurt folks if I can help it. Reckon your daddy's a peaceable man, too."

The child shrugged.

"He work around here?"

"No, sir."

"Then I guess you're lookin' forward to his comin' here."

"No. My mother would faint flat on her face if he did."

"Why's that?"

"He's supposed to be up fluttering with the angels."

Coke stopped and looked down at the child with the mother's face in miniature. "That so?"

"Yes, sir. You see, my daddy was the captain of a merchant ship outa San Francisco. One October, just this side of the Sand-

wich Islands, a typhoon hit. The ship went down.'' Willie
shrugged. ''And as far as we know, my daddy went up.''

''That happen a long time ago?''

''Think so. Happened before I started my schooling, anyway.''

''Look, Will.'' Coke nodded toward the turtle, which was waddling down the road in the opposite direction as fast as its wide
bowlegs could carry it. ''Your quarry's gettin' away.''

''Hey!'' Willie cried, and scampered after it.

Coke turned around, led Ole Belcher back to the emporium,
and tied him to the hitching rail. Sighting Meg off down the street
gossiping with a lady friend, he walked back into the store.

🌹 Chapter 4

SHE WAS SEATED on a long-legged stool at the front
counter, bent over a ledger book. At the sound of his step at the
door, her face tightened into a mask of deep concentration. He
walked over, stopped directly in front of her, leaned his elbows
on the counter, and settled his chin against the knuckles of his
upraised hands.

She didn't look up and, frowning even more deeply, kept on
adding the numbers, her pen skimming down a long column of
figures. She jotted a number at the bottom, carried up to the top
of the next column to the left, skimmed rapidly down that, jotted
a number, carried up to the left again, skimmed down that row
of figures, and jotted the total.

''Whoooeeee!'' he broke the silence. ''You are one fast adder.
Sure you got that answer right?''

''I seldom make mathematical errors,'' she replied, flipping to
the next page and writing the total from the preceding page at the
top of another long series of numbers.

''I ain't never seen anyone tally figgers that fast.''

''I use my fingers,'' she said, skimming down the right-hand
column on the new page.

He stared down at the fingers of her free hand, resting on the countertop above the ledger book. "I don't see 'em movin'."

"I move them in my mind." She jotted down a sum and carried to the top of the next column.

He continued watching her. "Was right sorry t'hear o' your husband's passin'," he said somberly.

Her pen slowed. "So was I. . . . 148 . . . 158 . . . 163 . . . Who told you? Willie?"

"Yup."

She'd gone more than halfway down that row of figures when she faltered, backtracked up three digits, shook her head, and started the column all over again. "That son of mine could be the town crier."

"Willie may be a talker, but he shed nary a tear whilst I was with him."

Again, in midcolumn, she halted. And this time she looked up, giving him the full force of those luminous aqua eyes. "A town crier doesn't weep, Mr. Sanders. A town crier was a man employed by townships years ago, before newspapers. It was his duty to walk the streets of the town at intervals, crying out the news."

"That a fact? Sure musta saved folks a lotta fuss an' bother from goin' round tryin' t'nose up information on their own."

She didn't answer.

". . . Like what brought you an' your young-un to these parts."

"The climate."

He backed off a bit. "You got lung fever?"

Faltering again amid her figures, she put her fingers to her temples and shook her head. "I'd like to say I had lung fever. For your benefit . . . I'd like to say it." She took a deep breath. Cool civility settled over her once more and she returned to column one of her work. ". . . But that would be untrue," she went on indifferently. "I don't have tuberculosis, Mr. Sanders. I simply adore warm, sunshiny weather. Who doesn't?"

"I don't," he replied, settling back down on the counter.

She drew a line through the sum she'd written earlier at the bottom of the first column of figures, scribbled another number above it, and carried up to the left again. "I suppose a shower would be welcome," she said. "To settle the dust in the air."

"Lotta our good Texas dust gettin' carried away these days," he mused, his chin resting in his hand. "Downright dreary

knowin' that our best topsoil from these parts is probably shel-
lacking the east side o'some Loosiana gorge right now.''

She didn't respond, skimming down that middle column of
figures for the fifth time.

''Yup,'' he drawled on, looking her slowly up and down. ''Out
at my ranch, so much o' my good ground is weatherin' out from
under me, I've 'bout decided the good Lord ain't fixin' t'wait till
my time comes t'plunk me into hell. . . .'' His eyes settled on
the tempting pliant fullness of her breasts. ''. . . He's already
commenced my descent . . . a degree at a time.''

The sound of the ledger book flipping shut jolted his gaze to
her face. It was transformed by a dazzling smile.

''Mr. Sanders,'' she said through that smile. ''I've an item here
that I think a prosperous man like you would take pride in pos-
sessing.''

''No doubt you have.''

''I show it only to our preferred customers,'' she smoothly
went on, reaching up and taking a key off a hook on the wall. She
unlocked the money drawer. ''It's unique for this part of the country . . . or anywhere else, for that matter.''

She pulled open the drawer, took out a small white box, set it
on the counter before him, and untied the bow on top. As he
watched expectantly, she reverently opened the box. Carefully
smoothing the tissue paper aside, she lifted out in slow, unwinding motion a wrinkled, mottled, sand-colored length of leather
with a buckle at the end of it.

''A belt,'' he said, a trifle letdown.

''That's what it is, all right,'' she stated proudly.

''It's a tad on the ugly side.''

''Why, Mr. Sanders,'' she said, hurt clouding her lovely eyes.
''How can you say that? This belt is genuine Louisiana alligator
skin.''

''I've seen alligator skin belts before. But that-un there sure has
a different kinda color to it.''

''How perceptive you are! For it's the color that makes this
belt so extraordinary. You see, Mr. Sanders,'' she went on, her
voice lowered confidentially, ''the skin on this belt is from an
albino alligator.''

''You don't say?'' He stared at it.

''As I'm sure you can well imagine, there are very few albino
alligators in existence. But did you know that the albino alligator

is one of the most vicious animals in the world today? And what's more, Mr. Sanders, because of its extreme rarity, it is a crime punishable by death to get caught slaughtering any one of them. So in order to get the skin for a belt like this, it has to be peeled off in narrow strips . . . while the animal is still alive.''

''How they do that . . . them critters bein' so mean an' all?'' he asked, eyes fixed on a dimple that was playing like a will-o'-the-wisp at the corner of her mouth.

''The poacher has to wait for the precise moment when the alligator is most vulnerable.''

''When's that?''

''When he collapses on the swamp bank, numb and insensible, from a ferocious bout of lovemaking.''

Frowning, he met her eyes. She didn't so much as blink. He stared at the belt again. ''Looks like they peeled this piece offa the wrong side o' the stripe.''

She laughed. ''Oh, Mr. Sanders, Mr. Sanders,'' she chided him playfully. ''You're quite the tease, aren't you. Now, tell me honestly, have you ever seen anything quite like this before?''

''Nope, reckon not.''

''And just look at this buckle.'' She turned it toward him. ''Hand-tooled by a beautiful Cajun princess.''

He lifted a doubtful brow. ''Cajun princess?''

''Well,'' she said, her smile broadening, ''maybe her bald-headed daddy or toothless uncle.''

''How much you askin' for it?''

''Twenty dollars.''

''Whooeee! I could buy close to thirty acres o' land with that kinda money.''

''With this drought, thirty dusty acres couldn't be worth that much to you anyway.'' She shrugged. ''So you certainly wouldn't be losing out, investing your money in this one-of-a-kind albino alligator skin belt.''

He rubbed his chin in thought. ''I can see your persuasion, but there's a gap somewhere in your reasonin'.''

''Oh, well,'' she sighed, wrapping the belt around her hand to return it to its box. ''I suppose it was presumptuous of me to think that you'd be interested.''

''Hold it . . . hold it,'' he stopped her. ''Let me have another look-see.'' Gazing into her eyes, he took her hand and slowly unwound the belt from it.

"Has a most unusual finish, doesn't it?" she said.

"It's unusual, all right."

"Because we value your patronage, Mr. Sanders, I'm going to make you and only you a special offer. Please don't tell anyone, but I'll let you have that belt for fifteen dollars."

He shook his head. "That's still a helluvalotta money."

"Do you have any idea what a bargain I'm offering you?" she asked, taking the belt back and gesturing with it. "In cosmopolitan areas like New York and San Francisco, *plain* alligator belts retail for upwards of ten dollars."

"That much? Just t'hold your pants up?

The will-o'-the-wisp dimple flitted. "Think of the inconvenience if there were no belts. And you must admit, a useful item that is of such superior quality is worth the added expense." She glanced down at his waist. "And if I may be so bold as to make an observation, you could do with a new belt, Mr. Sanders."

He hooked his thumbs in it. "This is a durn good belt. O' good ole reliable Texas cowhide. Lasted me sixteen, seventeen years, all told."

"And it looks almost twenty years old, too. The leather is scratched and worn. It's shiny in places, dull in others." Her eyes narrowed at it. "Why, it's so old, I can barely, just barely, make out that goat head you have tooled in the buckle."

"This ain't no goat!" he objected, looking down at his buckle. "This is a longhorn steer."

"You don't say?" She squinted at it again. "Well, you could have fooled me. But then, that's because the metal's so worn."

"Well, whatever I have on this here buckle, worn as it is, is a sight better'n that bloated-lookin' water moccasin that you got on that there Cajun belt."

"Oh, but it isn't a water moccasin, Mr. Sanders. Here, look closely."

She leaned forward. So did he. The aroma of lavender surrounded him. Wisps of her hair tickled his cheek. He could almost feel the warmth of her skin, the sweet in-and-out of her breathing, the delicious tightening and slackening of the film of fabric across her breasts.

A slender, tapered finger was pointing to the design on the buckle. "See the swelling," the voice sounded in his ear, huskily intimate, "about the neck. It's a cobra, Mr. Sanders."

"Cobra."

"A king cobra." The voice softened away to a whisper. "Agressive . . . potent. Deadly."

There was a pause, a tantalizing, tingling moment, then she abruptly straightened and the counter was between them again. "But since you're not interested . . ." She whisked the belt out from under his nose and began rolling it back up.

"Twelve dollars," he mumbled.

She stopped. "I beg your pardon. What did you say?"

He cleared his throat. "Twelve dollars. I'll give you twelve dollars for it."

She hesitated, thinking, then regretfully shook her head. "I'm sorry, but we have to make some profit."

"Thirteen fifty."

"Thirteen fifty," she repeated, weighing the amount in her mind. Then her face relaxed into an easy grin. "All right. I surrender. Thirteen fifty it is. But do you always drive such hard bargains, Mr. Sanders?"

"Oh, ever once in a while," he answered modestly. "Just put it on my account."

"Uh . . . about that," she said, seeming embarrassed. "I hate to bring this up, but when you were in here a little while ago buying your yarn and crochet hooks, I noticed that your account was over a month past due."

He reached into his shirt pocket. "How much do I owe?"

"With the cost of the belt . . . nineteen dollars and thirty-two cents," she stated flatly, without checking her files.

He took out a twenty-dollar gold piece and placed it in her hand, his fingers lingering on her soft palm until she snapped her fingers over the coin and hastily deposited it into the money drawer. She counted out his change, placing the coins on the countertop. Then she fitted the belt back into its box and briskly retied the bow on top.

"You know, Mr. Sanders"—she smiled, handing him the box—"from the first moment you came in here, I sensed you were that rare individual with an eye for quality."

"Thank you, ma'am," he said. "I expect I'll be seein' you again soon."

"Perhaps. Good afternoon."

He glanced around, but there was nothing more that he could think of to say or to do to prolong his stay. "Afternoon." He tipped his hat, then reluctantly started toward the door.

"Uh . . . Mr. Sanders," that husky, dulcet voice sounded behind him.

He turned expectantly. "Ma'am?"

"Doesn't look like rain, does it?"

" 'Fraid not."

"Have a nice day."

"Thank you kindly."

🌹 Chapter 5

COKE STOOD BEFORE the swinging doors of the Easy Come Easy Go Saloon and Bordello. He couldn't believe he'd done that. Just couldn't believe he'd let that much money go without feeling anything. He shook his head. He must be getting old. Or daft.

Somehow, that chilled beer didn't seem nearly as tempting as it had an hour ago. Not as tempting, anyway, as going back into the emporium and getting another eyeful of that heavenly face and figure, another earful of that musical alto voice, another noseful of that lavender sachet. But he was scared he might end up buying something else he didn't need. For true, that Jessica West was an angel . . . but what in the hell could an hombre like him wear a highfalutin albino alligator skin belt to around here without feeling like a toe-dancin' dandy?

Sawdust and stale cigar smoke filled his nostrils as he stepped into the saloon. It was that hour in the day when there was a lull in business, the afternoon patrons having taken off for home and dinner, and the evening ones having not yet started to drift in. Only a few diehards, too liquor-wilted to move, remained scattered at a couple of the scuffed wooden tables.

The middle door of the three lining the overhanging balcony crept open. A cowpuncher slipped furtively out and, buckling his belt, came skittering soundlessly down the stairs, the serious expression on his face attesting to the seriousness of the business just consummated.

Over the bar hung the usual painting of a fat nude, this one reclining on her belly on a bearskin rug, pudgy legs folded up, triple chin resting on a plump fist, and mouth half-open as if sighing to heaven at mankind's foibles. When the shine of the light was right, a Circle T brand could be discerned on one pillowy hind cheek, scratched there years ago by some lovelorn cowboy.

Below the painting, Ruby Lamour, the saloon's proprietor and madam, was leaning on the bar chatting in a low voice to Jack Siden, a partner in the Wilson-Siden Ranch Supply Store. Siden had joined up with Lou Wilson, the original owner of the business, about a half dozen years ago. As a sideline he was a broker for some tanneries up north. With his small fleet of wagons he went around to the ranches, collecting their hides and, for a commission, transporting them to a place outside Warner where they were cured before being shipped to the tanneries by rail.

About four or five years younger than Coke, Jack had curly light brown hair, a neatly trimmed mustache, full, even, white teeth, and a complexion that tended to turn a fresh golden apricot color in the sun rather than red or brown. Folks called him "Handsome Jack." Other men might've been embarrassed by such a moniker, but Jack probably just agreed with it. As soon as a young woman—or a not so young woman—felt the full force of his dark green eyes upon her, her breath started catching in her throat. Jack tended to focus those smoldering green eyes quite a lot.

As seen from the rear, Ruby was a fetching sight standing there next to Handsome Jack, red beaded dress clinging to an hourglass figure, tight ringlets of red hair bobbing down to her shoulders. Coke strolled over and blew in her ear, and she swung around, ready to spew out a tongue-lashing. When she saw it was Coke, a broad grin broke her face, exposing tobacco-stained teeth as it animated a tough, painted, seen-it-all face that had more striations on it than a relief map of the Mississippi River Delta. Her right eyelid held a permanent droop from decades of squinting at the world through cigar smoke, her own and the barroom's. And now that Ruby was past sixty, that shapely figure was mainly the product of an old-fashioned lace-up corset that pinched in and hitched up.

"Hiya, hon!" she brayed, slamming Coke hard enough on the back to loosen a bubble up his gullet. "Make a good sale up north?'' Ruby was only being polite in asking. From her station here in the saloon, she had an inside track into everybody's business.

"Didn't come out too far less'n even," Coke replied, then looked at Jack Siden. "Got quite a few hides ready t'be sent out."

"It'll be a couple days before we can make it out to your place," Jack said easily. "Got three other ranches ahead of you."

"You're no doubt gettin' more business than you can handle these days," Coke commented.

"That I am. That I am," Handsome Jack blandly replied. Siden had a soothing way about him that Coke found made him easy to be around but not that easy to know.

"This drought's bound t'let up soon," Ruby put in, delicately picking a red-beaded streamer from her dress bodice out of her puckered cleavage. "This mornin' that ole sow I keep out back was just a-runtin' an' a-pawin' through that sty o' hers like she was expectin' fresh mud any day now."

"Most likely she'd given up hope o' the moisture comin' down from above an' was checkin' out the possibility o' diggin' it up," Coke said.

"Coulda been . . . coulda been. What can we get you?"

"Two beers t'start."

Stifling a yawn, Smitty, the barkeep, stepped over to the beer kegs at the end of the bar. The beer foamed into the glass mugs. Smitty slid them one by one down the bar to Coke, making two slick trails that quickly dulled and evaporated away.

Clasping a beer in each fist, Coke made his way across the room to a table occupied by two old drinking buddies, Cactus Caleb Prolix and Soot Fisher. By the redness of Soot's nose and the rheumy dullness in his eye, Coke judged that his fellow rancher had a good half dozen beers on him.

Without the three men exchanging a word or a glance, their long-standing acquaintanceship nullifying any obligation to be polite, Coke pulled out a chair and sat down. He chugalugged all of the first beer and a half of the second. Then, thirst quenched and leaving the rest for lazy savoring, he sank down in his chair, stretched out his legs, and crossed them at the boot. Head propped against the chairback, hat low on his brow, he gazed up meditatively at the blackened oil lamp on the wall.

Cactus Caleb lowered the stereoscope he'd been peering into. Ruby provided it for her customers, along with a collection of slides showing women posed in various stages of undress. Cactus thoughtfully slid the picture out of the prongs at the end of the stereoscope, dropped it into the box at his elbow, selected another slide, and slipped it into place. Frowning through the lenses, he felt around the table until he latched onto his half-empty beer. He picked it up and, angling the stereoscope up to make room, tilted the beer only halfway into position, pouched his lips out, and sucked the beer up the side . . . *slooooooosh*.

Cactus Caleb was the town mortician, barber, dentist, and bathhouse proprietor. A grizzled, rawboned man who among the locals always looked most in need of a bath and a shave, he had the long, woebegone face of a hound. Clothed in a threadbare, baggy black woolen suit, long in the pants and short in the sleeve, he sported a tan slouch hat with a bullet hole through the brim. Years ago he'd borrowed the hat off one of his newly cooled clients. He called it his conversation starter. But the subject had quickly exhausted itself—except for the occasional outsider, for whose benefit Cactus embroidered outlandish yarns about how he'd come to take the bullet and had lived to tell the tale.

His business building was located farther down the street, the dental and barber part of it in front with a single barber chair by the window to serve both functions. The mortuary was at the rear, and the bathhouse stood separate next door.

Since few people died in a year, since the bathhouse was closed now to conserve water, since folks usually shaved themselves and trimmed their own or one another's hair, and since Cactus's most devoted dental patients were now gumming their way through their vittles, Cactus had a great deal of time on his hands. He frittered it away either here in the saloon or across the street in Meg's Emporium. There at Meg's, from the rocking chair to the left of the potbelly stove, he held forth authoritatively on the events of the day to any passing soul who chanced to cock an ear in his direction. When he was in the mood, Cactus could speechify at great length and even greater detail on any subject that rolled his way, whether he knew anything about it or not.

Wearying of the slides, he set the stereoscope aside, dug into his coat pocket, and pulled out his corncob pipe and a match. He struck the match off the table bottom and, drawing and puffing, got the tobacco started. Slumping forward, he gazed grimly into his beer mug, pipe stem whistling with each draw, lips clicking off the stem as he puffed out the smoke. Whistle . . . click . . . click . . . click.

Soot Fisher, too, was off in a world of his own. Chair tilted back against the wall, he sat wordless, hands folded on a ponderous beer belly that seemed to defy gravity as it hung between his widespread, skinny cowboy legs. His eyes were half-closed in glazed contentment as his jaws swung ceaselessly from side to side over a plug of chewing tobacco. There were more dewlaps down his neck than a well-fed Brahma bull's, and they rippled as his jaws rolled back and forth . . . *schlip* . . . *schlip* . . . *schlip*. Every so often he turned his big head to the side and, with a little bounce, let go a syrupy wad, hitting the spittoon in the corner with dead aim—*ptooey*-ping!

The three men sat in heavy, contemplative silence, Soot chewing . . . *schlip* . . . *schlip* . . . *schlip* . . . *ptooey*-ping! Cactus drawing on his pipe and puffing out the smoke . . . whistle . . . click . . . click . . . click. The minutes crawled along like a peg-legged centipede.

Then suddenly the men were jarred by a discordant *ptooey*-splat! Soot had missed his shot, and hit the already juice-blackened wall behind the spittoon.

Soot's chair legs clunked to the floor. Coke pushed up in his chair. Cactus heaved himself back off the table.

Frowning, Soot took a long, deep swallow of his time-warmed beer, wiped his mouth with the back of his sleeve, and looked soberly from one table companion to the other.

"My lead steer just died," he intoned in an East Texas twang that bent vowels like horseshoes, hit consonants like shotgun blasts, and bore down on *r*'s till they curdled.

"And what precipitationed your beloved bovine's demise?" inquired Cactus.

Soot gazed blankly at the mortician. "*Schlip* . . . *schlip* . . . What?"

"What caused the critter t'die?" Cactus demanded in a loud voice, as though deafness were the rancher's problem.

He thought that over. "*Schlip* . . . *schlip* . . . Loss o' life."

A funereal silence followed. Then Soot turned to Coke. "Heard you got twenty-three fifty a head for that herd you sent up t'Colorado last year."

"Ruby tell you?"

"*Schlip* . . . *schlip*. . . yup."

"Sure wish I had her sources."

"How'd you pull it off . . . that twenty-three fifty?" Soot asked.
"Seein' as how they're fightin' their own drought in Kansas an'
Nebraska an' everybody's dumpin' on the market."

"Didn't dump mine on the market. Cattle I had up there was
prime stock. Sold 'em to a coupla ranchers from Wyomin' just
startin' up operations an' out t'build their herds."

Soot shook his head. "Luck o' the devil."

"Devil's the one that had the luck," Coke said. "At normal
times those cattle woulda brought twice as much."

"Least you got somethin' for 'em, which is more'n the rest of
us can claim," Soot responded.

"Intercoursin' on lucky devils," Cactus put in. "You hear tell,
Coke, o' the high returns that grabby-clawed new neighbor of
ours outside o' town is derivatin' from this here absence o' moisture?"

"Bound t'be sizable," Coke said dourly. "This can be a good
year only for buzzards an' T. C. Barrett."

"That Savings an' Loan o' his holds mortgages all over this
county an' most o' the one next door," Cactus went on. "Ranches
is goin' bust right an' left. Hear tell as of last month that association o' Barrett's has gobbled up close to a hundred fifty thousand
acres."

"Seventy-five thousand acres," Coke said, halving Cactus's
customary exaggeration. "Seems the buzzard business is doin'
purty good."

"Hear the Navarro spread is the next in line t'go under to the
Savings an' Loan," Cactus added.

Coke frowned. "Hector Navarro? He's always managed purty
well. Has a choice piece o' land an' has held on to it for a mighty
long time."

"He was hit by rustlers less'n a coupla weeks ago," Soot said.

"Heard that." Coke.

"Yup," Cactus added. "Hear tell he was just a hair away from
climbin' out from under his debt. Had found hisself a coupla
buyers for his stock in the interior o' Mexico. Wouldna gotten
that much cash for 'em, but from what I heard, it was enough
t'get T.C.'s claws outa his back. Then them rustlers struck. Left
him naught but the milk cows next to his house."

"Won't be able t'make no mortgage payments now," Soot observed.

"Mighty convenient timin' them rustlers had," Coke mused.

"Well, that Savings an' Loan o' Barrett's won't be cleanin' up for much longer," Cactus stated cryptically.

"How come?" Coke asked.

"Drought's definitely gonna secede soon."

"Oh," Coke replied, his interest dying. "Seems I've heard that-un before."

"This time it's based on scientific fact," Cactus assured him. "Last week the stage brung me my latest issue o' the *Terpsichorean Quarterly*. Whilst perusin' through it, I come upon a article that stated unequivocately that the aurora borealis is a-luminatin' all over the far northern reaches o' Alaska."

"So what's that got t'do with the drought we got down here?" Soot twanged.

"Outside o' promptin' the native Eskimos t'swing into some mighty fancy dances 'bout their igloo fires, them lights progmasturbates precipitation throughout the entire northern hemorrhoid."

Coke took some time out to digest this. "Did that there magazine o' yours say that?" he asked.

"Well, not in exact wordage. I deluded it."

Coke shook his head. "Sometimes, Cactus, listenin' to you is like pullin' up to a fancy New Orleans restaurant, orderin' beef soup, and findin' nothin' more nourishin' in my servin' bowl than hot brown water an' a noodle."

"Somethin' scientific like that could spell rain," Soot put in hopefully.

"Soot," Coke said. "When I was sweet sixteen I believed it was rock-hard scientific fact that iffen a gal lowered her eyes an' blushed when a hombre came near, it surefire meant she was a virgin."

"That how you tell?" Soot's interest quickened. "I ain't never knowed any certificable virgins before."

"What's this 'bout virgins?" Ruby asked, nudging the last unoccupied chair at the table into position with her hip as she plunked onto the table her bourbon bottle, shot glass, and Bull Durham Tobacco pouch. Jack Siden, pulling a chair from a nearby table, joined them, too.

Ruby sat down. "I was a professional virgin all my life," she declared, lifting up the undersides of her sizeable breasts and settling them more comfortably over her corset stays. "Till I found there was more money t'be made at poker."

"Mebbe you was just better at it," Cactus said.

"Jawin' 'bout women," Soot put in cagily, "what y'all think 'bout that new gal workin' over at Meg's . . . the Widder West?"

"She's a puzzle," Handsome Jack said, frowning as he reached inside his vest for one of the expensive thin Cuban cigars he always smoked. "A real puzzle."

"Well, I like her fine," Ruby said. "Treats me right nice. Don't ever pick up the feelin' of her lookin' down her nose at me, like a lotta so-called respectable ladies in town do."

"Miss Jessica treats you nice 'cause you're another member o' the female gendarme," Cactus put in sagely.

"What say?" said Soot.

"Miss Jessica's always polite to the members of her own sex."

"So? She was right nice t'me, an' I sure as hell ain't no heifer."

"Yes, she is polite t'everybody," Cactus conceded. "However," he counseled, lifting a yellow-nailed finger, "there's a subtle, but infinitive difference in the way she treats certain o' her clients an' the way she treats certain others."

"What you mean?" Coke asked. "Who she treat different?"

Cactus paused dramatically to shake just the right amount of tobacco into his pipe bowl, tamp it down to perfection, and relight it. "As you-all are well aware, I devote a considerable portion o' my leisure hours implanted, as it were, in Meg's business establishment. Such a vantage point provides me with a singler opportunity t'observe the species homosexian up close. For example, I observe their personal tastes, their mannerisms, their amplitudes, their—"

"We-all know you're a-headed somewhere," Coke broke in. "But we'd be obliged if you spared us the trip in betwixt."

Cactus looked wearily at Coke, then sighed. "Miss Jessica gets her back up at all these gents who drop into the emporium for the sole an' entire purpose o' perversin' her face an' figger."

"What?" Soot again put in crankily.

"Miss Jessica downright detests bein' eyeballed. Trouble is, she's always gettin' eyeballed. All these drovers comin' in offa the range, ain't been near a woman for nigh onto a month, hear tell o' the purty new gal in town, drop on by for a look-see . . . an' keep right on lookin'."

"How's she treat 'em different?" Coke asked.

"In a way that's been profitin' the emporium quite tidily, if I do say so m'self, an' I do. Yup, you hafta give ole Meg credit. She showed some real business acuwoman in bringin' a looker like Miss Jessica into her establishment durin' a slump. Meg's—"

"Ah, hell," Soot cut in. "Cactus, if I wanted t'be treated to a lotta useless clackin' an' blowin', I'd go back out to my ranch an' stand next to a mesquite bush in a dust storm."

"How she act different t'hombres who cotton to the way she looks?" Coke pressed.

"She just turns on the charm, whenever a hombre's got her riled. An' by the time she's through with him, he's strollin' out the door, grinnin' like a schoolboy an' totin' some gewgaw he'd a-never bought in his right mind. Why, Miss Jessica's leg-pulled so many o' the fellas round here, it's a wonder that half of 'em ain't walkin' round lopsided."

"Bet she's unloaded a lotta Meg's old junk thataway," Ruby said.

"Yup. Surplus chamber pots was her specialty last week."

"She sold chamber pots? To drovers?" Ruby asked. "What in the sam hill would a drover need a chamber pot for, livin' out on the open range most o' the time?"

"Tells 'em a chamber pot can serve a wide variety of alternative purposes. Kept in a pure state o' bein', it can make a excellent little servin' bowl. An' seein' as how the thing is bigger than the average tin plate, the drovers'll naturally get bigger helpin's when they line up for chow. While at the same time the elevatored sides'll keep the dust from contaminatin' their vittles an' keep 'em from spillin' out. She tells 'em that a well-made chamber pot can be a fine little head protector durin' hailstorms, avalanches, Indian attacks, an' such. She says—"

"Ah, c'mon, Cactus," Coke said. "I cain't believe any grown man could be took in that easy."

"Sold off all o' Meg's surplus chamber pots," Cactus replied.

Ruby chuckled. "Ain't nothin' like a purty face t'make a nincompoop outa any man."

Coke shook his head. "Durn hard to believe."

"You gotta understand," Cactus went on. "The pore honchos just cain't bring theirselves t'refuse a charmin' little darlin' like her twice in a row."

"What d'you mean?" Ruby asked. "She try t'sell 'em somethin' else first?"

"Yup. An' she woulda sold it, too, 'ceptin' she has this bet goin' with Meg that she can get five dollars for it. An' five dollars is mighty hard for a hombre t'cough up these days. But by trottin' this here belt out first, she softens the pore suckers up for somethin' cheaper."

Coke's eyes narrowed. "Belt?"

"Yup. An' it's *ugly*. Durn ugly. Wouldn't be surprised iffen it was made outa swine hide . . . an' old, sun-bleached swine hide at that.

"I recollect the mornin' Miss Jessica come upon it whilst rummagin' through the rubble in Meg's back room. She immersed outa there holdin' it up kinda doubtful. 'Might as well put this thing on sale,' she said. 'Naw,' Meg said. 'Tried a year ago, couldn't even get two bits for it.' Miss Jessica looked it over a tad. 'You know,' she said, 'oftentimes the packagin' an' the persuasion can be more important in a sale than the item itself. I bet if I do it up right, I could get five dollars for it.'

"Meg really hooted at that-un. Told Miss Jessica if she ever got five dollars for that sorry thing, she, that's Meg now, would do all the cookin' for a week.

"Seein' as how Miss Jessica an' her little sprout is bunked at Meg's house these days, an' I take it Miss Jessica don't cotton much to the culletary art o' cookin', she's right motorvated t'win her bet. She stuck on that belt a buckle one o' Ramiro's younguns made a spell back. I recollect Meg givin' him a nickel for it 'cause she didn't wanta hurt the little fella's' feelin's. Tried t'tool a coiled rattler into the metal, but his little hand shook an' it came out with a bump on the neck. Looks more like a constipated worm."

Cactus rolled his baggy, bloodshot eyes up. "Hell, I'd be tempted t'buy the lalapalooza myself, if I didn't' already know it warn't worth a woodpecker's kiss."

"I almost bought it," Soot twanged. "But six dollars sounded a mite steep even though she told me it was gen-you-wine imported Dutch aardvark hide. Bought me some bath powder instead." He beamed forth his pride in not having been hoodwinked.

"An' what the hell are you gonna do with bath powder?" Ruby demanded.

"Damned if I know. Only take a bath when the crick is up, an' the crick ain't been up for nigh onto two year now. Leastways, the bath powder was naught but three bits, an' I can swing three bits.''

Ruby surveyed the table. ''More beer?'' she asked. And without waiting for an answer, she bellowed at one of the girls who'd just descended the stairs and was leaning on the bar in a dingy dressing gown, yawning and scratching her scalp. ''Felicia! Bring the gents over here another round o' beer!''

''How did Mrs. Jessica West,'' Coke said, stretching the name out, ''come t'be workin' at Meg's?''

''You recollect a few weeks before you took off for Colorado, Meg left town?'' Cactus asked.

''Yup. Said she was goin' to New Mexico t'help her son's wife over her birthin'.''

''Well, it was on the trip comin' back that she met up with Miss Jessica an' her young-un. Struck up quite a friendship along the way, them two. An' when Meg switched stages in San Antone t'come on here, Miss Jessica an' Willie come along with her. By the time they got t' town Miss Jessica had cataracted a touch o' the influenza. An' you know Meg. Magnanimous, munificent, noble o' heart, an' a general all-around giver, she took the two of 'em in whilst Miss Jessica coalesced from her discomforter. Next I know, Miss Jessica was assistin' at the store. Hell, assistin' ain't the word for it. She come right in an' turned the place upside down. That gal is some worker. Regular organizer. An' she's already bringin' in extra money from her dressmakin'.''

''When she met up with Meg,'' Coke said, ''where was she headed for?''

''Don't know. Never did say.''

''Heard she was from San Fran-cisco,'' Handsome Jack put in. ''Ever say why she left there?''

''Well, not exactly. Whenever I bring the subject up, she just a-vassalates an' a-vassalates. Told me once that she'd developed this here terrible itchin' out there an' had t'pull up stakes.''

''What itchin'?'' Soot and Ruby chorused.

''Said livin' all them years so close to the coast, she developed a acute sensitivity t'some o' the wildlife that inhibits the beaches. T'be specific, she grew itchy around seagull dung. Doc out there told her that if she ever wanted t'live a normal life, she'd hafta back away from that coast.'' He paused, scratching his noggin. ''Sure musta been one hell of an itch, her backin' all the way t'here.''

Handsome Jack chuckled. "How're your legs these days, Cactus? Sure one ain't any longer than the other?"

"An' what about you?" Ruby turned on him. "I know she ain't escaped your notice. I see you headin' over t'Meg's 'bout every day t'sniff up her tree."

For a man of Jack Siden's cool self-possession, he looked quite uncomfortable. "Well," he said slowly, drawing in the smoke from his Cuban cigar. "She ain't very reachable."

"You mean grabbable," Cactus amended.

"Her reactions ain't what you'd expect from a normal gal." Jack frowned.

"Ah, Handsome Jack," Ruby breathed. "You just expect that any time you turn on that hot look o' yours, any normal gal'd just naturally break out in a glow an' her drawers come slidin' automatic to the floor."

"She's not agreeable," he said ill-humoredly, blowing out his smoke. "One right pretty night last week I went by Meg's and invited her for a stroll. She told me she doesn't walk if she can help it. So next night I rented a surrey at Ramiro's for a ride in the country. And she told me that the country's too ugly to ride in."

"Cain't argue with that these days," Cactus said.

"What'd you do with the surrey?" Soot asked.

Jack's affable humor seemed to return. "Took another gal for a ride who appreciated it more." He thought awhile, then frowned in bafflement again. "Why, I even bought that Jessica West a book of poems at Warner 'cause she seems like an educated sort. She looked it over, said she knew those poems well, then she handed the book back to me an' told me to read it an' try to understand it myself."

"Did you?" Cactus asked.

Jack flashed his easy smile. "No. I gave it to another gal who appreciated it a whole lot more."

"An' I've had the fur flyin' between two o' my best whores ever since," Ruby groused. "Jack, when're you gonna get it straight that my gals are here for commerce, not for free romancin'?"

" 'Tain't much of a cut Ruby can get outa a buggy ride," Cactus observed.

As if on cue, Felicia appeared with a tray of beers. Poking out her long underlip and blowing a limp, drab straggle of hair off her nose, she slowly rotated a hip against Handsome Jack's shoulder as she set out the beers. Eyeing her as she shuffled away, Soot dug into his pants pocket, pulled out another plug of chewing tobacco, and bit it in two.

"Ruby," he twanged, jaws laboring furiously over the new tobacco. "That new gal o' your-un, uh, what's-'er-name, Fellatia, she may have a all right body, but ye gawd, with that long face o' her-un an' them big buck teeth, when we finishes our business, it's all I can do t'keep from given' her a bag o' oats instead o' the usual three fifty."

"I know, I know," Ruby sympathized, reaching over to give the grubby cattleman a pat on the paunch. "Sure must be hard . . . you bein' such a charmin', temptin' morsel an' all."

"I been thinkin'," Soot went on. "Been almost a year since that last wife o' mine packed up an' took off. I should find me another woman. Place could sure use some cleanin' up. An' it'd be right nice t'have a heifer o' my own that'd cook for me, an' provide me with some good decent home-style lovin' for free."

Ruby loosened the strings on her tobacco pouch, took out a cigarette paper, and tapped some tobacco in a line down the center of it. "Last I heard, Soot, you had you twelve thousand three hunnert acres o' land."

"Twelve thousand three hunnert an' twelve," he corrected her. "Free an' clear. 'Nuff t'make me a good catch for any woman."

"That wasn't exactly what I was a-shootin' at," Ruby said, licking along the edge of the cigarette paper and pressing it to the opposite side around the tobacco. "Seems t'me with that much land, you could afford t'buy yourself some new duds. Just look at yourself, man. The front o' your shirt is held together with nothin' more'n safety pins an' brush thorns. Sometimes, when that there thorn holdin' your pants t'gether up front pops out . . . well, if it warn't for that big *panza* o' your-un droopin' down over everythin', Sheriff Seth could 'bout arrest you for showin' yourself."

"That's indecent explosion," Cactus volunteered.

"Whatever." Ruby shrugged. "You gotta start cleanin' yourself up, man, iffen you want a woman. Start takin' a bath more'n every other year. You give off a aroma that'd 'bout turn a skunk livid." Firing her match with a flip of the thumb, she lit her cigarette. "Why, the way folks strike up their smokes when you walk into a room, it's a wonder you ain't come down with permanent croup."

Scowling, Soot chomped heavily on his tobacco, then spat with a decisive ping into the spittoon. "Ruby, when you die, somebody should take that mouth o' yours to a taxidermist. Iffen they can find a wall big enough t'hold it, it could be put t'durn good use scarin' off mountain lions, grizzly bears, an' wild-assed Injuns."

"Naw," she retorted, words billowing out in smoke, "all they'd hafta do is bottle up some o' that body odor o' yours. Then unscrew the cap when the varmints started creepin' near. Knock 'em offa their feet."

He ruminated darkly on that. "Sure makes a body wonder," he finally muttered.

"Wonder what?"

"How a smartass like you, Ruby, can keep customers comin' back."

"Easy. Own the only saloon an' sagebrush house in thirty-six hunnert square miles."

"An' the pity of it, too," Cactus sighed.

"What you mean it's a pity?" Ruby turned on him.

"Do you realize, Ruby, that in the eighteen years since that straight flush, king high, won you this place, you ain't changed the decorum once?"

"Oh yes I have. Every five years like clockwork I have the walls painted."

"But the same borin' hues. An' look at this here collection o' slides you got for your stereoscope. In more'n ten-odd years, all we got, day after day, year in an' year out, is the same ole half-nekkid wimmin t'look at."

"Well, mebbe iffen you hadna come in here five times a day t'eyeball 'em," Ruby blustered, "they wouldna gotten old on you so fast!"

"But do you know what I dislike the most round here?" Cactus asked.

"Since you're gonna tell me anyway," Ruby muttered, "you might as well go ahead an' spit it out."

"I simply abhor that paintin'."

"What paintin'?"

"The one o' your disrobed lady suspendered over the bar. Reclinin' as she is on her frontispiece, bosoms droopin' like two half-empty flour sacks into that there bear rug, nothin' o' interest is revealed."

Ruby elbowed Coke. "You sure been quiet, fella. You like my paintin', don't you?"

"Hmmmm," Coke said, lost in thought.

She jabbed him again. "My paintin'. What you think of it?"

He turned around and looked at it. "Yup, it's there, all right. Ain't paid it much mind in years."

"See?" Cactus said, smugly folding his arms.

"See what? You bloated-up jackass!" Ruby squawked. "This here is my business establishment. An' anybody comin' in here expectin' more'n what he can get . . . can just get the hell on out!"

"This is depressin'," Coke drawled. "This is durn depressin'. When I left my ranch a spell back, everybody was just a-snarlin' an' a-spittin' an' a-clawin' into each other like a cageful o' half-starved bobcats with but one puny mouse between 'em. I thought that, of all the places in this angry an' confused world o' our-un, I'd find here, in the good ole reliable Easy Come Easy Go, my little island o' peace. Seems I was wrong."

"It's this drought gettin' folks down," Handsome Jack said in his soothing way.

"Yup," Cactus added. "This ceaseless secession o' hot, dry days gets t'be downright monogamous."

"Things is bad," Soot intoned from the sidelines. "Things is just real damn bad, all over."

"Felicia!" Ruby bellowed. "More beer for the gents!"

✿ Chapter 6

A SILVERY CRESCENT moon glowed out of a sky so clear and black, it seemed shiny. In the breeze, velvety shadows stroked the ground, touching and parting and touching again. On a faraway ridge, a coyote let loose a long, lonesome howl. It was answered straightaway by a sharp yelping burst in the brush to Coke's right.

A shiver riffled through Ole Belcher. A raggedy chorus rang out on the distant ridge, and again the howl from the nearby brush split the night. Ears rotating cockeyed, Ole Belcher skittishly lifted his hooves high, setting them down on the rock-hard ground with mincing, irresolute clicks.

Squinting into the blending shadows, Coke quietly drew out his Winchester. With a head-tossing, shuddery snort, Ole Belcher stopped his forward movement and began dancing nervously in place. Coke waited. The ululating chorus on the distant hill rang out. Again, a howl burst from the nearby brush in reply and, in a crackle of rifle fire, veered into shrill staccato squeals. The line of brush swirled and crashed, and fell still, giving way to a thin, shallow whine that drained away to silence. The living earth seemed to hold its breath for a brief interlude, then, minus one coyote, resumed its natural night rhythms.

Coke dropped his Winchester back into its boot and gave his horse a pat on the neck. "Them bastards is gettin' pushier'n pushier, ain't they, ole fella?"

Nudging the gelding, he rode on. He was well inside his ranch now. It had been before nightfall when Coke had left Cactus Caleb at the saloon. He always made it a point to seek out the mortician whenever he returned from a trip of any duration, because of Cactus's habit of anchoring himself smack-dab in the middle of wherever the gossip was flowing. Out of an afternoon of his declarations, distortions, and exaggerations, Coke could glean more useful news of local doings than his ma and Sarie could in a month of church socials.

The news about Hector Navarro had taken him by surprise. After he left the saloon, Coke had mounted Ole Belcher and ridden out to the Navarro spread. The family had just sat down to dinner when Coke arrived, and Hector invited him to join them for their evening meal. Coke had been disturbed by the change in Navarro. The man looked ten years older than the last time Coke had seen him, and appeared not to have slept in an equal amount of time. The atmosphere in the house was uneasy, gloomy, as though they were awaiting news of an imminent death in the family. Hector's wife and children picked at their food, and the way they forced it down their throats, it might have been sand. All kept their eyes lowered and watchful of Navarro. Cactus's information had obviously been true.

After dinner Coke had asked Navarro to take a walk outside. Standing by the corral, he asked the man straight out how much he owed the Warner Savings and Loan.

Navarro shrugged his heavy shoulders. "Six thousand dollars."

The ranch was worth four times that much.

"I'll give you a choice," Coke said. "I'll buy you out, the land

and everything on it for fifteen thousand . . . or I'll loan you the six thousand t'pay off T. C. Barrett plus an extra thousand t'start up operations again. You can have ten years t'pay me back at two percent interest.''

At first Navarro looked shocked. ''I would prefer the loan,'' he finally said.

''You have it,'' Coke replied, untying Ole Belcher's reins. ''When do you need the money?''

''By Thursday, next week.''

''I'll be by with the cash an' the papers for you t'sign Tuesday mornin'.'' He climbed onto Ole Belcher.

''Por qué?'' Navarro asked. Why?

Coke scratched his chin. ''I ain't inclined t'do this sorta thing, you know. I've always held that ranchin' in these parts is akin t'havin' t'follow the rules o' nature, an' it's wise not t'interfere with 'em too much. But maybe with this rustlin' hittin' you when it did, you had a rough shove down that you shouldna had. Mebbe I'm losin' patience with the way T. C. Barrett's been doin' business aroun' here an' am in the mood t'start drawin' the line. An' mebbe, I'm purty doggone sure that the seven thousand I'll be loanin' you ain't money throwed away an' I'll be seein' it comin' back with interest before the ten years is up.'' He turned Ole Belcher. ''I'd appreciate it if you kept our deal under your hat. Let folks think you got a rich cousin or somethin', 'cause I sure don't want 'em thinkin' that I'm goin' soft.''

If he kept on doing the sort of thing that he'd done for Navarro, Coke reflected as he ambled across his dark marbled land, he might start backing into the banking business himself. And he could've gotten the man's land for a song.

He shook his head, and for the second time that day wondered if he was getting old or daft. Could it be that a man could start losing his greed along with his youth and his teeth? What a blasphemous notion to strike the son of Camden Sanders—that anything could ever be enough, especially land and money.

But a man can grow accustomed to other things, too. Like having certain folks around, knowing that they're moving through their lives pretty much the way you are, and fighting similar battles, so you feel a loss when they're gone, feel their ghosts in the places they'd once occupied. That's how he felt about the San Sebastian. The disappearance of the Castillos from their ranch had affected him. It had come suddenly, before he'd known the

straits that Doña Celestina had been in. She would've been suspicious of any offers of help from him, anyhow. He and her husband, Juan Fernando, had never gotten along. They'd been too
much alike, too often rivals vying for the same pieces of land that
had come up for auction. Yet his death had stunned Coke, and so
had the eviction of his family from the San Sebastian. Juan Fernando, his family, and El Rancho San Sebastian were all one in
Coke's mind, fixtures that, without actually thinking about it, he'd
assumed would always be there.

And now that the Castillos were gone, he was the only man in
the region with the money and the clout to go up against T. C.
Barrett. He stopped Ole Belcher, gazing over his land where underneath its dreamy twilight mantle, life teemed and leaped and
skittered, fought and won or died. But then, perhaps, this was
enough. This land.

He was feeling too at peace right now to want to battle anything. He was home. After three long weeks away, he was home.
And here, at night, alone, this piece of earth that was his em-
bracing him all around, he'd begun to gain that sense of comfort
and completeness that he could feel at no other time of the day
and in no other place in the world. A delicate shifting had been
set in motion inside him, connecting him to some deep central
force. This land was home, the hearthstone of his life. Every
single scraggly inch of it belonged to him as he belonged to it,
defining and giving him purpose as he defined and gave it purpose. That had grown to be so out of countless moments of intimate communion with the land, out of many years of protracted
struggles over it, desperate battles, a hundred victories and a hundred defeats. And, the land would outlast him. It would prevail.
Reaching forward and backward through time immemorial, this
land was his linkup to eternity.

And yet, he thought as he nudged Ole Belcher forward again,
he couldn't pull back inside his land now, leaving T. C. Barrett
to have a free hand outside its boundaries. For as sure as the sun
rises each day, sooner or later T.C. would be trying to shove into
his own backyard.

They came to a wide ravine. Ole Belcher picked his way down
the rocky slope to its floor. Coke turned into it and followed along
its meandering course for almost a mile. At the outer perimeter
of a wide bend, the outer slope almost totally eroded away, he
stopped his mount and climbed down out of the saddle.

By looks alone, there was nothing unusual about this particular lopsided spot in the gorge, but Coke had discovered years ago that the wind had a way of coursing by here like being caught in a flue, and it made for pleasant sleeping on warm summer nights. Over the years he'd camped here countless times, and it felt as comfortable and familiar to him as his second-story bedroom at home with the windows thrown open.

He unstrapped his bedroll, dropped it on the ground, unsaddled Ole Belcher, and hobbled him.

"All right, ole fella, you're free for a spell," he said, slipping off the gelding's bridle.

The animal took a few shuffling steps away before he stopped and, curving his head around, eyed Coke past his slow-swishing tail.

"Don't wanta be free, eh? Just flat-out too many varmints out an' prowlin' 'bout t'suit you."

Coke kicked some gravel and dirt clumps aside. Then, kneeling, he slowly unrolled his bedroll, brushing the ground beneath smooth as he went. He got up and, with Ole Belcher tagging along a few feet behind, stepped over the low side of the ravine and wandered about gathering dried cow chips and twigs.

"Gonna het me up some coffee," he said, walking back past the horse and stepping down into the ravine.

Squatting by his bedroll, he swept the cow chips and twigs into a heap and circled them with stones. He struck a match off a stone and lit the chips here and there. He poured water from his canteen into his tin coffeepot, shook some grounds out of his coffee pouch into it, swirled the pot around, and set it on the stones over the flickering flames.

Lying back on his saddle, he looked up at Ole Belcher, who was watching him expectantly.

"Too bad you cain't pull up that crusty ole tail o' your-un an' set a spell."

The gelding took two plodding steps out of the shadows of the ravine and snorted a cloud of dust off the ground.

" 'Bout could make a normal person wonder, couldn't it, Belcher?" Coke drawled. "Got me 216,862 an' a quarter acres. Got more'n a hundred folks dependin' on me an' the decisions I make t'see 'em through. An' how do I spend my evenin's? Jawin' away at a damn dumb horse, that's how. Don't start thinkin' you're anythin' special though, hear? I'd jaw away at any damn dumb

horse that happened t'pass the night with me." He raised his hand
and pointed at the gelding. "Word o' warnin', ole fellow. This is
t'stay strictly a one-sided conversation. No talkin' back, 'cause if I
ever, ever catch you a-sassin' me back, why, I'll a-sassin-ate you."

He settled back, pulling his hat over his face. This had been a
night of decision making, and he'd found that he'd slid into those
decisions with surprising ease. After leaving the Navarros, he'd
gone to see Carol Louise. She'd been expecting him, standing in
her doorway, the glow of the oil lamp in her hand washing up
over her face from below, knitted shawl flung over the warm
cotton skin of her nightgown, thick mane of coppery hair tousled
about her shoulders, and that little expectant smile playing on her
lips. And he had known at that moment that he could not go
inside.

She didn't take well the news that their affair was over. Over
the years he'd been careful to avoid making any promises that
would give her any reason to hope for more. Still, he had gone
back to her many a time, and that *had* given her reason to hope
for more. She called him a few choice names, and he appreciated
that because he deserved them. It would've bothered him if she'd
shed any tears. And by the hot look in her eye, he surmised that
before the month was out, she'd have found another man and worn
the poor fellow down to a staggering daze. He couldn't help feeling a little regretful, and guilty somehow for letting her down,
but he'd been feeling that way about her for a long, long time.

The coffeepot stirred to life, rocking against the stones, steam
bending out of its spout and dissolving in the breeze. He took the
handle in his gloved hand, swirled the pot around, waited for the
grounds to settle, then poured the inky liquid into his tin cup.
He sipped the coffee, the steam rising warm into his eyes.

Opening his food wallet, he took out a biscuit and bit off a
hunk. Munching, he unbuckled the other of his saddlebags and
reached into it. Pushing aside the cloth sack containing Ma's yarn
and crochet hooks, he found the small box. Slipping the fancy
ribbon off, he removed the lid.

Jessica West, late of San Francisco, California, had leg-pulled
him so skillfully, she'd managed to relieve him of eight dollars
more than she'd needed to win that bet she had with Meg. Yup,
he'd gotten snookered worse by that angel-faced lady than a wide-
eyed backcountry farm boy on his first visit to a traveling carnival
sideshow.

As he fingered the belt, he smiled. He'd always gotten a bang himself out of putting over a fast one, but this was the first time in years that he'd found himself on the receiving end.

Earlier that evening, while he'd ridden back through town from the Navarro spread on his way to Carol Louise's, his eyes had been drawn to Meg's house. There at the window, a slender shadow moved back and forth before the wavery lamplight, teasing him some more. Being around a woman like Jessie West could make a man feel a vague privation, like he was missing out on something natural, like a coyote with laryngitis on a night of the full moon.

"Yup, Jessie West," he said, pulling the belt out full length. "There's a helluvalot more to you than meets the eye. You're quick, you're clever, an' best of all, you're ornery. An' I always did take a shine t'folks a shade on the ornery side."

He put the belt back in the saddlebag, gulped down the last of the coffee, and rinsed out the pot. Stretching out on his back, he looked up at the stars sparkling across a glass black, fathomless sky.

"Not a single damn puny cloud up there," he muttered.

The campfire was smoldering now more than glowing, only a few fading embers clinging to life. Crickets kept up their pleasingly monotonous cadence, and the howl of the coyote was far away. The silver-tipped leaves lining the higher side of the ravine trembled in the breeze up above him, and the soft wind wending along the arroyo brushed soothingly over him.

Coke savored his solitude, drew spiritual nourishment from it. Too often, it seemed, he was surrounded by jangling voices that expected something out of him. His own inner voice could become dimmed in the hubbub. The only people whose company Coke could abide for long were those who were not intimidated by silence, but instead could snuggle under it like a feather quilt in winter.

Suddenly a terrific commotion broke out over the top of the higher side of the ravine, filled with clattering, scraping hooves, crackling brush, grunts, clipped snorts, and pressured breathing. Ole Belcher's head shot up, nostrils flaring, eyes rolling.

"Pay it no mind, Belcher," Coke said placidly. "That's just a coupla jabalina screwin'."

Tilting his head, he ran his eyes up the wall of the ravine to its crest, jutting out almost directly over his outstretched body. He settled his hand on the Winchester at his side.

"Just hope them boars don't get so het up that they roll theirselves off."

Chapter 7

GIVING HER SON a look that said she suspected his brains had dried up along with everything else on the place, Ma Sanders took the eight crochet hooks out of the cloth sack he'd handed her. Then, with slow perplexity, she drew out the six skeins of brown yarn and one by one placed them in her crochet basket next to four other skeins of brown yarn.

"Where's Sarie?" Coke asked.

"Upstairs in her room," she replied, still eyeing him dubiously. The house was uncommonly quiet. "Where's Joshie?"

"Sarie felt a mite done in, so she made the little monkeyshine take a siesta."

Leaving his still-puzzling ma behind, he trudged up the stairs to Sarie's room. She was sitting in an overstuffed chair near the billowing curtains of her open window, darning socks.

"You've met Jessie West, I take it," he said, sitting down on the edge of her bed.

"On my last two Saturday trips t'town," she replied, tugging the thread straight from a stitch.

"You know, Sarie, you didn't hafta cook up no errand t'buy yarn t'get me t'meet the lady. All you had to o' done was to o' told me straight out that she was there at Meg's, an' sooner or later, I'd o' moseyed on by for a look-see."

"Didn't wanta give her the kiss o' death," Sarie said, taking another tight little stitch. "All I got to do is point out t'you some gal I think might make you a likely match an' right off that brands her forever as one gal you'd never be able t'tolerate come hell or high water."

"Your past record ain't nothin' t'crow 'bout, Sarie." He shook his head. "It ain't till you start pointin' out who you think'd make me the perfect match that I start into lookin' in the mirror wonderin' what the sam hill is wrong with me."

"This-un is different, though, ain't she?"

70

"Yup. She's that, all right."

"What'd you think of her?"

He considered. "Passable."

"You ain't usually this enthusiastic. Knew you'd be taken by her."

"In more ways than one," he answered slowly, "I was."

"Sure hope you ain't so daggone poky with this-un that she's snapped up before you even get around t'makin your first move."

"Don't think she'll be snapped up that fast. Don't seem like the kinda gal that a hombre would likely get close to that easy."

"Glad t'hear it, seein' as how you don't cotton t'anythin' bein' too easy." She sent him a coy look. "Think you might ask her t'Cindy's weddin'?"

"Might give it some thought."

"Well, you'd better get a move on, 'fore somebody beats you to it—if they haven't already."

"Most likely somebody has. Now, whether she's accepted or not is another thing entirely." He paused, thinking. "You get t'know her purty well, Sarie?"

"Not really," she replied. "Not her, herself, anyways. We talked mostly 'bout our young-uns."

"She ever tell you why she came to these parts?"

"Sorta. Said she thought a small town like Dispenseme was the best kinda place t'rear a young-un. Said that here she felt free for the first time t'let her little boy run loose outside. In the city she was scared all the time t'let him out the door 'cause o' the likelihood he might meet up with a nut or a crook." Sarie's dark eyes danced playfully. "Seein' as how they're city folk, don't you think the lady an' her boy might enjoy spendin' a weekend out here on the ranch one of these days?"

"Might give it some thought. Little shaver might get a bang outa it."

"Little shaver . . . pooh!" Sarie scoffed. "It's the mama you're interested in."

On Tuesday of the following week, his sit-down work accomplished, Coke made it back to town. Delaying to last, like dessert after dinner, the main reason for his being here, he took care of business first, stopping by the Wilson-Siden Ranch Supply Store and Post Office.

On his way into the store he nodded to Handsome Jack, who was out in the road deep in conversation with one of the crew he'd hired to freight hides. Coke had seen the fellow about town before, though he'd never gotten his name. A rough-looking, unshaven man, he had a wary look to his eye and a tendency to keep his head held low so that his face was cast in shadow. He wasn't the most charming-looking of fellows. But considering as how freighting hides wasn't the most pleasingly aromatic of professions and thereby not the most sought after, Siden couldn't be too choosy about the men he took on.

In the store, Coke collected his mail, then ordered from Lou Wilson a resupply of pickaxes, hammers, ten thousand nails, and a few miles of Glidden wire. If the drought and the rustlers didn't get him, he reflected glumly, fencing in 216,862 and a quarter acres of land surely would.

Lou Wilson, the Dispenseme postmaster and co-owner of the store, was a local boy, born and bred. Handicapped with a sweet, apple-cheeked baby face, he'd sought to camouflage the defect behind a thick growth of muttonchop whiskers modeled after a picture he'd seen on a hair oil bottle. But that disguise didn't deter little old ladies from reaching up to tweak his apple cheeks when he handed them their mail, or allow him to get by with a tough, authoritarian act without looking a trifle silly.

Lou was an astute businessman, however. Coke hadn't appreciated that fact until recently, following the revelation that the thirty-year-old bachelor merchant was flat-footed in love with Sarie and had been since they'd both been schoolchildren. It hadn't been until a year ago that Lou had gotten up the nerve to court Coke's sister. Unfortunately for Lou, the slick charm of his partner, Jack, hadn't been contagious. He was so moony over Sarie, in fact, that he'd gained quite a reputation in the Sanders household as a blunderhead, tripping over his own feet, walking into walls, dropping steamy mashed potatoes in his lap at Sunday dinner.

Coke hoped that Lou would get over his awe of Sarie and ask her to be his wife. He was an honest man who would make her and her children a decent husband and father. And best of all, they'd settle in Dispenseme, close to home. Coke sensed that his sister was too hot-blooded a woman to stay a widow all her life; and if she married, he didn't want her and little Amy and Joshua to be taken out of his easy reach. Life was too short for that.

But at the rate Lou was going, it seemed he might never get up the nerve to propose. Sooner or later, Coke reckoned, Sarie would run out of patience and pop the question herself.

Leaving the store, Coke headed for Meg's Emporium to see Jessica West. He stopped, for the stage had just pulled up in front of Lou's store, leaving in its wake down the road a sprinkling of chickens still slowing down to flustered, sharp-stepping struts and what sounded like a dozen mouthy dogs. People on the street were changing direction to come over and ogle at the arrival and Lou and his young clerk were coming out of the store behind Coke to collect the packages and mail.

"Got four big packages for Meg," the driver said from the stage's roof, passing them down to Lou and his clerk.

Standing among the crowd that had gathered, Coke glanced toward the emporium. He saw Jessica at the window, her eyes on the stage, listening absently to the elderly Widow Henry who was chattering behind her. A pair of cowpunchers had wandered out of the Emporium to stand at the door and gander at the goings-on.

Trying to get a word alone with Jessica, Coke thought, would be too much like waiting in line for a haircut at a Dodge City barbershop after three herds and their trail-scruffy drovers had just rolled in.

Pulling his hat down against the sunlight, he spotted Meg coming up the boardwalk. It usually took her a good half hour to make the five-minute walk from her home to her store, interrupting her own progress as she did along the way to exchange greetings, news, and jokes with each and every soul she chanced to meet.

Coke started down the street toward her. Seeing him, she waved and picked up speed.

"Coke," she said, pulling him aside. "That belt Jessica sold you t'other day, it ain't worth the thirteen fifty that you paid for it."

"I know."

"You do? Well, I sure am sorry 'bout this happenin'. I wouldn't blame you iffen you was mad at us."

"I ain't mad, Meg."

"Daggone, I'd a-never o' thought that Jessica woulda tried that trick on you."

"Or that I woulda fallen for it?"

She nodded sheepishly. "That, too. Tell you what, next thirteen dollars an' fifty cents worth o' merchandise you buy at the store is on the house."

"No, Meg. You don't need t'do that. Jessie cheated me fair an' square."

"But I do wanta make this up to you somehow."

He paused, considering. "Well, there is one little bitty thing that you might could do for me."

"Name it."

"Tell me, Meg, is there any particular time durin' the day this week when Jessie won't be workin' at the store?"

"She don't keep regular hours." Meg frowned, then her plump face lit up. "But then again, it could be, Coke, ole buddy, that come this Friday afternoon from 'bout three o'clock on, Jessica just might find she's got some chores t'do at home. That all right?"

"Just fine, Meg. Thanks."

"There's somethin' you oughta know 'bout our Jessica," she stopped him. "She's her own person . . . very much her own person."

"Kinda figgered that."

"An' Handsome Jack still has his sights set on her."

"Is her color startin' t'change when he comes around?"

"No, but I do believe that his color's risin'. An' you should know, too, that besides him, she's turned down close to a half dozen invites t'Cindy's weddin'. An' a good half dozen more fellas come close t'askin' her before they turned snow white from bashfulness an' the words froze in their throats."

"Bet they didn't go away empty-handed, though."

"Darn if that ain't the truth. Why, I do believe my profits is 'bout keepin' pace with ole Ruby's across the street this week." She grew stern. "But that don't mean that Jessica ain't decent. She is a decent woman, Coke. You do have honorable intentions, don't you?"

"Depends."

"Depends on what."

"Depends on what she wants."

"You sneaky ole polecat, you," she mock scolded. "It's a puzzlement t'me tryin' t'figger out which o' the two o' you t'warn t'other to watch out for."

Chapter 8

ABOUT FOUR O'CLOCK that Friday afternoon, Coke pulled up in front of Meg's squat limestone brick house. It was a typical blustery South Texas day. The hot, dry wind flagellated the dirt off the ground, staining the air dusty tan. Somewhere, a dangling milk bucket clanked, an unlatched shutter kept up a fidgety banging.

Coke tied Sin Cerebro to Meg's picket fence, its skin of white paint peeling away from the gray-weathered wood. The wind-splintered whoops and laughter of children, coming from behind the house, reached his ears. He headed toward the sound, rounding the corner of the house. The force of the wind was broken here, and a gnarled rose vine crawled along a trellis on the wall. It had strained out a single pale blossom, petals curling down under the glare of the sun.

In the stable yard to Coke's right, Cuspidora, Meg's old milk cow, stood with her head hanging over the fence, her limpid brown eyes bringing him into passing focus before glassing away again to the hypnotic tempo of her cud chewing. Herman was behind the fence with her, snoozing in the shade of the stable wall. The lanky old hound opened one whiskey-red, doleful eye at Coke, then groaned and nuzzled back into the dirt against the wall.

Coke leaned against the fence. On the far side of the yard Willie was trotting along, prodding with a stick the rusty wagon wheel rim rolling by his side. With a quick stop and a nimble twist of his body, he sent the wheel spinning on ahead of him, bouncing off the dried-out grass hummocks. Just as it was losing momentum, tottering in the wind, another little boy bounded up with his stick and sent the rim wheeling toward his brother. Coke recognized Willie's playmates; they were two of the eight sons of Ramiro, owner of the stable and ironworks.

His attention on the three boys was only fleeting, for the object of his trip here was less than twenty feet away. She was at the

75

clothesline, her back to him, hanging out her wash. The big iron washpot stood by the house, scrub board and wooden stirring stick propped inside. The fire over which the pot was suspended had gone out. Two metal rinse tubs sat on a wooden bench nearby, and attached to the side of one of the tubs was a hand-cranked roller apparatus for squeezing the water out of the wash.

He thought he heard her humming to herself. Her face was hidden under a man's large straw work hat, strapped to her head by a brown scarf that looped over the crown of the hat, dipped through two holes on either side and, hugging her face, was secured under her chin in a knot. Her hair, tied back by a simple black bow, cascaded in a long, honey-colored tail to her waist. She had apparently just washed it, for heavier, darker streamers lined the hair that fluttered and flicked over the apron bow at the back of her waist.

She wore a loose-fitting work dress of a faded brown, lightweight material. Her undergarments must have been in the wash. He could detect no imprint of them from waist to bodice beneath the fabric of her dress, nor did he see any petticoat as she bent over her wash, the wind snapping her skirt above her knees. Her legs, at least the part of them he glimpsed above her high-button shoes, were slender and firm. Even when she thought no one was around to watch her, her movements were lively and full of purpose. And though she was slenderer than his taste in women usually went, every ounce of her body seemed placed exactly where it should be. Her breasts were not too big, nor *chiquitas* either, just right; and her form curved naturally to a petite waist that other women with their corsets and stays gave themselves heartburn to create. The graceful swell of her hips and thighs was smooth and non-jiggly, and completed the perfect picture of a woman in full bloom.

Taking in the sight of her, dipping and straightening as she worked her way down the clothesline, Coke thought how delicate and lovely a woman could be. Delicate and lovely were words uncommon to his vocabulary, but she was about the most feminine being he'd ever laid eyes on. And he would have liked to go up behind her, put his arms around her, and hold her close, blend into that sun-warmed softness. Oh, yes, he would love to do that . . . except he'd probably get walloped from here to Dubuque.

"Oh, hi, Coke," Willie called, bounding up to him, ignoring the wheel rim rolling his way. It boinged, vibrating, to the ground behind him. Jessica spun around. The wind jogged her hat back and she grabbed it to hold it in place. She said nothing to Coke, making no effort to hide her annoyance that she couldn't be left alone even in her own backyard.

"Willie," she reproached her son. "You don't address grown-ups by their given names."

"That's all right," Coke said. "Most of the young-uns round here call grown folks by their first names."

"I don't care what is commonly done around here," she replied. "I want my son to learn proper social etiquette."

He winked at Willie. "Go ahead an' call me Coke. You can practice your proper social eddyket on proper social folk. D'you like livin' here?"

"Sure do. Got me lotsa friends t'play with any time I like. Not like in San Francisco, where most of your friends live far away an' when you wanta visit them you hafta watch out all the time for fast carriages and drunken bums."

"Now, Willie," Jessica said in a low, reproving voice.

"Well, it's the truth," he turned on her. "Why can't I say t'Coke what you used t'say to me all the time?"

She didn't respond and, leaving them to each other, retrieved her rag and wiped the rust and dust off the next length of clothesline. Pulling her laundry basket over, she resumed hanging out her wash, making certain to face Coke this time and to mind the effect of the wind on the skirt of her dress.

"Havin' fun with that ole wheel rim, I see," Coke was saying to Willie.

"Sure am," he smartly replied, pulling a suspender back up onto his shoulder with a pop. "Why, t'other day, I rolled it an entire twenty miles before it toppled over."

"How far?"

"From one end of town to the other."

"Whoooeeee! That shore-nuff is a long ways."

"Willie!" Chacho Ramiro called impatiently. "Are you gonna play or aren't you?"

"Well, I gotta go," Willie said importantly. "Nice talking with you, sir . . . uh . . . Coke."

He scampered off with the wheel rim. And now that he had an audience, he sent his big toy rolling away with extra gusto. He whooped, and turned a flop-legged somersault. Coke strolled over to Meg's back porch and sat down on the top step a few feet from the end of the clothesline.

Jessica's head popped up above a line. She sent him a sharp look. "If you're looking for Meg, she's at the store."

"I know," he replied, folding his arms and settling back against the porch door.

Shaking out a bath towel and fastening it to the line, she contemplated him through the fringes of her eyelashes. His face, what she could make of it in the shadow of his hat, seemed absorbed in watching the children at play.

With a shrug, she dipped back down and pulled one of Meg's blouses out of the laundry basket. He chose to come here. It was up to him to tell her why . . . and she wasn't about to make it easy for him. He was probably just another one wanting to ask her to Cindy's wedding, she mused. She'd never met so many female-starved males as she had in this place. Hand over hand, she pulled out a bed sheet, gathering it against her. Must come from spending so much time out in the hot sun, sitting on bales of hay, chomping tufts of straw, and watching their livestock breed.

As studiously as if she were at her bookkeeping, she drew the wet sheet out along the line, which brought her to the end of it and the point closest to Coke. She paused, looking down at him out of the corner of her eye. His face at this angle was hidden under the brim of his hat. The brim slowly lifted. She whirled around and, plunging her hand into her clothespin bag, marched away, popping the clothespins one right after the other onto the sheet until it looked like the prickled back of a scared cat.

Carefully avoiding looking his way, she wiped the next line, and started her clothes hanging again. What was he trying to do? Make her feel ashamed for what she'd done to him the other day? Well, never would he get her to apologize. She emphatically snapped Willie's socks one, two, three, four on the line. Examining her all over that afternoon with his eyes as if she were a heifer on the auction block . . . it was only fitting that she should make a jackass out of him. Drat Cactus and his loose jaw. Bless Ruby for telling on the old goat. She understood. This was war and women had to stick together.

Nudging her laundry basket along, she set out her own blouse and a washcloth. He was causing her to mix up her wash on the lines, doggone him.

She shook out a pair of Meg's underdrawers. Clasping them to the line, she paused, watching him. Through lazy, half-closed eyes, he was still gazing at the children. C'mon, say something, she willed. Sitting there motionless on the stoop, basking in the sun like an underheated lizard, open your mouth. Say your piece and be done with it. She lowered her head, then looked up quickly. His eyes quickly veered from her to the children.

Aha! Caught you! She dived behind the clothes. She remained bent over the clothes basket, her hand clasped over her mouth. Oh, my goodness, she might start giggling, and then wouldn't she feel like a ninny. She pulled her hat way down until it hugged her brows.

Hanging out Meg's stockings, she glanced at him again. Strange, though he had a perfect right to be angry at her, she felt no hostility coming from him. None at all. Just a relaxed, easy kind of patience. Yes, there was something faintly likable about the man.

Oh, stop it. She straightened her shoulders. All men are devils in disguise.

She'd finish out the line, she resolved as she neared Coke again, and reached for one of Willie's suspenders. She jerked at it. The suspender snapped out of her hand and slapped back into the basket, the fastener on the opposite end probably hooked on the matting at the bottom of the basket. She bent farther down, concentrating on the basket yet keenly alive to his nearness, his scuffed boot on the ground, his quiet awareness of her so palpable that it was like a current of heat between them. She grasped at the suspender again. He moved; she jumped. The suspender abruptly came unhooked, slingshotting out of the basket and popping her on the hat. Putting a hand to the spot it had hit, she gave him a startled look. Their eyes met. Then it happened. A smile passed between then and her smile crumpled into laughter.

Flipping the suspender over a shoulder, she grabbed up the basket and turned her back on him, face tucked down and shoulders rounded and shaking as she went to the last line.

As she clipped on the suspender, she looked down in the laundry basket. Her laughter died. Only her own underclothes remained. She couldn't just leave them in the basket; he'd see them there and know she'd been too embarrassed to put them out.

She sighed. Might as well start with the worst first. Nestled in the corner of the basket like a mauled rabbit was her old frazzled bustle. The only reason she'd never thrown it out over the years was that it was constantly going in and out of style. And as luck would have it, this was the first time she'd washed the pathetic thing all year. Maybe he'd think it was Meg's, she thought, plucking it quickly out of the basket and attaching it to the line. Next worse, her underdrawers. From their size, there could be no mistaking who they belonged to. She gathered them up and, shoving her hat back and giving him a chin-up look, proudly pinned them on the line.

But there was such a humorous twinkle in his squinty answering gaze that once again her sense of the ridiculous was tickled. The sternness on her face softened into a smile. Oh well, one can be civil without being too friendly.

"How's Sara?" she asked.

"Fine. Gettin' ready for the weddin' t'morrow."

"And Joshua?" she put in too quickly.

"Contrary as ever."

"Willie's sweet on Amy. He'd scream at me if he ever found out I told you, but he's always making these little comments about her. 'Amy said this at school. Amy said that. Her hair was in ringlets. It was in braids.' And on and on."

"Amy takes after her mama, the same as Willie takes after you."

"Oh, do you think so? I always thought he had a bit of his father in him."

"He's your young-un. Ain't no doubt 'bout that. Been long since his daddy died?"

"More than three years."

"Musta been hard bein' left all alone with a young-un t'raise."

"My late husband captained a merchant ship," she said matter-of-factly. "He was gone most of the time, anyway."

Wondering if she'd meant that the way it sounded, he studied her, but her face remained impassive.

Jessica finished hanging the last of her clothes. As she walked around the clotheslines, she caught sight of the rusty wagon wheel rim careering out of control, straight toward her fresh-washed laundry. She leaped forward, intercepting the rim a split second before it would have hit a wet bed sheet broadside.

"Boys!" she scolded, angrily rolling it back. "Keep that dirty thing away from my wash!"

"Why don't you tell the little shavers t'take that ole rim outa the yard an' play somewheres else with it?" Coke suggested.

"I can't do that," she said, coming toward him. She set the basket down next to the porch and hesitated, considering what to do next. Finally she sat down on the end of the step a few feet away from him and, untying her scarf, drew off her hat and began fanning herself with it. "Willie's being punished, Mr. Sanders. He's confined to either this yard or the store for a week."

"What'd the little feller do?"

"Last Wednesday he and two of his friends climbed up to the hayloft in Ramiro's stable."

"What's wrong with that?"

"Nothing . . . if they'd stayed there. But they shimmied out through the hayloft window and up onto the roof. I stepped out of the store that afternoon, looked up, and there's my Willie and two other little boys way up there, weaving along the top of the stable roof like tightrope walkers. It must be thirty feet high up there, you know." She shuddered. "I didn't start breathing again until Ramiro fetched his ladder and got them down."

"You give him a good whuppin'?"

"No."

"Just clipped his wings a bit, eh? A whuppin' woulda been better. Settled the matter once an' for all. These long, drawn-out kinda punishments never work with little whippersnappers Willie's age, Jessie. They can always figger out a way round 'em, figger out a way round you."

It was the first time that he'd called her by her given name, and she wasn't sure that she liked the familiarity it implied. She stopped fanning herself and regarded him askant. "Have you ever been married . . . Mr. Sanders?"

"Nope."

"I assume, then, that you've never had children."

"Nope . . . leastways, not to my knowledge."

She let that pass. "Then tell me, from what experience do you draw in order to advise me on the proper rearing of my son?"

"I'm a former boy," he replied.

She resumed fanning herself. "Well, Mr. Sanders, it's easy to know what's best for a child when the child in question isn't your own. When you're the parent of that child, it's not so easy to be . . . detached. I can't be. Not with Willie. I can read myself in him as one can read oneself inside anything one has helped create." She paused, resting her hat on her knees, her eyes following her son as he played across the yard. "Children are so full of life, so cocksure of it, that oftentimes they just can't see the terrible fragility of it.'' She shrugged. ''Perhaps you're right, and I should have whipped him. But by the time I got him down off that roof and safe in my arms, I was too overjoyed to summon up any anger.''

He was a little surprised that she'd admit to any self-doubt with him. ''If you felt that you was right, Jessie,'' he said gently, ''then most likely you was.''

''If I had it in my power,'' she went on wistfully, still watching her son, ''I'd gather up a hundred full and happy years, place them on a golden platter, and hand them to my child . . . even if sixty of those years were my own.''

He was strangely touched. This wasn't the lady he'd met at the store last week. Her nearness to him was working a powerful physical effect upon him. Sitting there, less than a few feet away, with her hair undone, she seemed younger, softer. Her skin held a sensual sheen in the heat, and her loose-fitting work dress made the unshackled curves inside seem more nearly available to him.

''Now, don't you ever fret 'bout doin' right by that boy,'' he said softly. ''He's turnin' out real fine . . . even though you ain't had his pa round t'help out.''

Somewhere along the line the spell had been broken, for she was regarding him in a half-mocking way.

''An' I reckon,'' she drawled mimickingly, ''that you ain't likely t'slug the pore widowed mother of an innocent, fatherless child.'' There. That was the closest thing to an apology that he was ever going to get out of her.

''Nope.'' His eyes twinkled back. ''Though there been times when I sure been temp—''

''Omigod!'' Her hands flew to her face. ''Cindy's wedding!''

''What?'' he frowned, startled.

But she was already up and wedging the door open behind him. ''I just remembered, I left two pies for the wedding supper baking in the oven.'' The door dropped shut behind her and she was gone.

Coke sat there on the stoop. ''Gettin' this-un pinned down is akin t'trying' t'lasso a roadrunner,'' he muttered.

At least now, however, he had her corralled. He got up, opened the door, and followed her inside.

* * *

A smoky haze hung in the kitchen, thick with the sweet-acrid scent of burned apple syrup. Coke leaned back against the kitchen wall, watching Jessica as she feverishly yanked cabinet drawers open searching for her pot holders.

"They're over there." He nodded toward the counter.

She whirled around, and sure enough, there the pot holders were, out in plain sight on the countertop. She snatched them up, and with fluttery hands threw the oven door open. Smoke ballooned out. Searing heat slapped her face. She yanked one pie out and dropped it noisily on the stove top, then the other. Instead of two golden mounds, the pies were two sunken, chocolate-colored craters.

"Really!" She stood glaring at the petrified pies. "Serves Lucy Blankenship right. She came into the store two days ago and told Meg and me—mind you, she *told* us—that we could bring two pies to her daughter's wedding supper. And she hadn't even invited us to the wedding."

"Well, most everybody round here takes in the weddin's if they're feelin' up to 'em . . . whether they're invited proper or not. An' the ladies always provide the food for the suppers. That's just the way it's done. An' it's up to the mamas o' the brides t'keep the menus balanced. So afore you could offer, ole Lucy just went on ahead an' told you what she needed."

"Meg should have done the baking," Jessica reflected, quietening. "She's much better at it than I am. But today she kept insisting and insisting that I stay behind and get the baking done, since tomorrow is Saturday, the busiest day of the week at the store, and it's my turn to do some of the cooking around here, anyway."

"Why'd she think it was your turn t'do the cookin'?"

"Oh, because she's done all the cooking this week," she replied, then caught herself, her eyes growing guarded.

"Why's that? You lazy or somethin'?"

"Uh . . . yes." She nodded circumspectly. "I guess you could say that." He may have gotten her flustered, but he hadn't gotten her flustered nearly enough to admit that a week free from cooking had been her reward for winning that bet with Meg. She cleared her throat. "Anyway, I decided to try my hand at baking the pies. They seemed simple enough to make."

He glanced at the two blackened craters on the stove. "Seems you was wrong."

"Cooking, baking, they're not my strong points," she airily replied.

"Oh?"

"Such a waste of time. All those tiresome hours. Why, just look at it objectively, Mr. Sanders. A person's hungry. He eats and is no longer hungry. And whether the food he eats is simple or complicated, what counts is that the hunger itself is satisfied." She paused, a defiant little smile playing on her lips.

"The way I see it, Jessie," he replied in a low voice, his eyes perusing her, "the hunger for food is like all the other physical appetites o' man. Some ways is a sight more pleasurable in the satisfyin' than others."

The smile froze. "It's Jessica," she said.

"Beg pardon?"

"My name is Jessica. Not Jessie. You call tottering, swayback old buggy horses with blinders Ole Jessie."

"Nope. You call 'em Ole Bessie. That's my ma's name, too."

"*Old* Bessie?"

"Nope. Just Bessie." He glanced toward the stove. "I reckon you'll be tryin' your hand now at makin' two more pies."

"No. I'll probably just go ahead and take these to the wedding."

"That a fact."

"I take no pride in how I do things that don't interest me."

"It pleases folks when you try."

"Why should I go around trying to please everybody? The way I see it, if I go ahead and take those two"—she waved a careless hand toward the pies—"disasters to the wedding, then people will think twice before asking me to do it in the future. Which would suit me just fine. Besides, I made the bride's wedding dress. What else could the Blankenships expect out of me?"

"Didn't you get paid for it?"

"Not yet."

"All right, then, Jessie, I'd be right honored t'take you, Willie, an' your two special-prepared, burnt-out potholes t'Cindy's weddin'."

He got it out. Finally. And it caught Jessica quite off balance, for she thought perhaps she'd succeeded in deflecting the invitation. Apparently, the way out of this man's heart wasn't by way of his stomach. She turned away, soberly straightening the canisters on the counter.

"I'm sorry, but I can't accept."

"Why not?"

"Because if Willie and I go with you, then Meg'll have to go alone. She's such a dear friend. I'd hate to just abandon her."

"Meg won't be goin' alone," he said.

"How do you know that?"

"Because she'll be goin' with Cactus."

"She never mentioned that to me."

"That's probably because she takes it purty much for granted. She an' Cactus always take in the local doin's together . . . weddin's, baptisms, revivals, church socials. They'd take in the buryin's too, 'ceptin' that's Cactus's business. So you see, Jessie, you'll be the one who'd be goin' alone."

"Well, it's been a tiring week. I probably won't go at all."

"Wouldn't recommend that. Be bad for business. Folks'd think you liked 'em fine when they got buyin' t'do for you, but you don't like 'em enough t'take part in their important occasions."

She began rapidly fanning herself with her hand. Funny how an outdoor man kept on squinting even while he was indoors, and one could rarely be sure where he was looking without going up close. And yet, she could feel his eyes boring into her. A lot of confidence must lay behind that easygoing exterior. And stubbornness. Any other man would have been put off or scared off by now. This one was neither. She should have sold him something cheaper the other day.

"It's hot in here," she blurted. "I'm going outside." And she swept past him out the door.

The yard was deserted. Willie had disobeyed her, and he and his friends were nowhere in sight. There was no one around, no single thing, that she could use to move Coke from his course.

Without breaking stride, she marched straight between the wires on the clothesline and began going through the motions of feeling the laundry for dampness. As she reached for a petticoat, he materialized on the other side of it, looming over her.

"Tell you what," she said with insincere enthusiasm. "I'll go with my son to the wedding and meet you there, all right?"

"Wouldn't recommend it. A lotta unattached gents will be at that weddin' tomorrow, Jessie. You show up there all by yourself, they'll figger you're free for the pickin'. An' afore ten minutes has gone by, one or two of 'em will have attached hisself to your side closer'n a blood-hungry tick on a houn' dog's ear."

"And I suppose I'd be ever so much better off if you happened to be that blood-hungry tick."

"Couldn't help but be," he replied. "What with me havin' my Bible-thumpin' ma an' my nosy baby sister there t'eyeball me."

This brought a sudden smile, which she quickly suppressed. "You're very persistent," she said, moving down the clothesline.

"Yup. Persistence is one o' my strongest traits."

"That has got to be about the most depressing thing I've heard all week," she muttered to a pair of Willie's underdrawers.

He appeared above the underdrawers. "Well, that's how I got me 216,862 an' a quarter acres, Jessie . . . some of it prize bottomland. Pure dogged persistence."

She drew herself up and confronted him. "Well, you can just give up," she declared. "For I, sir, am not a piece of prize bottomla—" She caught herself.

"I never said you was, ma'am," he averred solemnly.

Her mouth twisting at a smile, her eyes darting here and there, everywhere but at him, she struggled to repress her laughter. But it surfaced anyway. "All right . . . all right . . . all right!" She threw her hands up. "I'll go with you . . . but only on one condition."

"What's that?"

"That you don't get any romantic notions about me because I agreed to go with you."

"Why, I'm surprised at you, Jessie," he replied. "Truly surprised. Seems like a purty little gal like you would be hankerin' t'be puttin' a little romance in her life."

"Romance?" Her nose crinkled. "Romance is nothing but a pipe dream. The great deception or self-deception of all time, and women should discard it with their little-girl pinafores. Romance never solves any problems, Mr. Sanders. What it does is inject disruption, tension, and doubt into otherwise serene, uncomplicated lives." She slumped, her shoulders sagging. "Romance just tends to muck everything up."

"You're the first young an' unattached gal I ever met, Jessie, what wasn't traipsin' round lookin' for some man t'carry her away."

"Carry me away? From what?" Arching a brow, she looked up and down the line of wash. "From this? Listen, if I ever allowed myself to become manacled to another man again, I'd still wind up having to do this same diddly poo—only more of it." As though to illustrate her point, she turned away to test the dampness of the collar on Meg's upside-down blouse.

"You know, Jessie," he said to the black velvet bow at the nape of her neck, "there's somethin' special 'bout this South Texas climate."

"You don't say," she replied without looking around.

"Yup. This South Texas climate, why, it never lets up. Take that ole sun up there. It just keeps on a-beatin' down an' a-beatin' down . . . down through your skull, down through your body, all the way down to the soles o' your feet. You put on a hat, carry a parasol. Won't make no difference. You'll still feel that ole sun up there burnin' straight on down through you.

"An' the wind . . . it never lets up, neither. It keeps on a-blowin' an' a-blowin'. You lock your doors, latch tight your window shutters, an' that still won't keep that ole wind out. You check out the furniture o' your house an' somehow that ole wind blew the dust in."

Sensing where this might be leading, she half turned and, her hand on a dish towel, regarded him obliquely. "So?"

"So there's one thing I ain't never seen this ole South Texas sun an' this ole' South Texas wind do."

"What?"

"Dry a clothesline full o' wash in less'n thirty minutes." He tipped his hat. "Be by for you an' Willie come six t'morrow."

Still clutching the dish towel, she stood there, watching him walk away. As he rounded the corner of the house, he thought he heard a low "Oh, damn!" behind him.

Untying Sin Cerebro's reins, he smiled.

He led his horse to Main Street and tied him to the hitching rail in front of the emporium. He found Meg rocking by the potbellied stove needlepointing daisies onto the edging of a pillowcase. Cactus rocked opposite her, puffing on his unlit pipe and, probably for the umpteenth time, thumbing through the week-old San Antonio newspaper that had arrived on the stage yesterday.

"Hiya, Coke," Meg said, her eyes burning questioningly at him.

"Hiya, Meg," he replied. "Was right glad t'hear that you an' Cactus is goin' t'Cindy's weddin' t'gether t'morrow."

"What?" Meg asked.

"We are?" Cactus frowned over his newspaper.

"Yup," Coke said. " 'Bout time you two took in some o' the doin's round here t'gether."

Brows furrowed, Meg studied him, then, shaking her head, slowly grinned. She'd gotten the message that somehow her attending the wedding with Cactus in tow was tied in to Coke's being able to take Jessica.

She leaned over and gave Cactus a swat on the knee. "You might as well take me, you ole buzzard, you. Wouldn't hurt you a bit . . . seein' as how you spend half o' your life in here with me, anyhow."

The mortician gave Meg a long, weary look. "If you say so."

"So you really truly got Jessica to agree t'go to the weddin' with you?" Meg marveled at Coke.

"Yup," he nodded. "Though I think I coulda tolerated just a tad more enthusiasm."

❧ Chapter 9

AFTER TEN DAYS of shoving deeper and deeper into the rock-hard ground, chucking out a mountainous welt of dirt and pouring out enough sweat to sink a Rio Grande sandbar, the well diggers had turned up nothing more for their trouble than an assortment of bones, stones, and arrowheads, a dozen lizards, two scorpions, a tarantula, and one very indignant rattler. Tomorrow morning they'd cover over one more deep dry hole, load up their gear, and lumber away to another piece of ground and start at the top all over again. Coke *knew* that there was untapped water still to be found running somewhere underneath his two hundred thousand parched, rolling, rather indistinguishable acres.

That morning another wagon train of hides had rolled away for the tanners. The money they'd bring wouldn't meet half the Sidewinder's monthly expenses. Coke was grateful that he owed no man nor banking institution, otherwise his land would be sliding out of his grasp right now, and not just his stockpiled cash. Bad enough as that was.

He went to his bedroom window and looked out. He'd spent the day paying the hands their wages. Some of the men hadn't yet been by to collect their pay. He knew they wouldn't be around for it, either, until the need arose or until Christmas, whichever came first.

The compound grounds were singularly quiet. Most of the vaqueros' families had climbed aboard ranch wagons and gone to town to spend some of their men's pay, and Coke had heard that another big wedding was being held that night at the Catholic church. He regretted that he'd had to keep some of their menfolk back this weekend; he was posting extra guards in his north section.

He squinted up glumly at the cotton ball clouds floating eastward. The wind out of the west seldom brought rain.

He stepped over to his washstand, dipped his comb in the washbowl and, frowning into the oval mirror on the wall, carefully parted his hair to the side and wetted it down. He spat on a thumb and flattened an errant curl poking out over his ear. He stood back to gauge the effect, then gave his head a shake and ran his fingers through his hair, ruffling it back to its normal unruliness. As soon as they dried, the short-cropped curls would go their own way, anyhow. And he wasn't about to glue them down with axle grease as some would do tonight. He refused to go around looking like a peeled onion.

He'd gone to enough trouble already, he decided. He'd shined his better boots, had a new bandanna around his neck, would wear his cleaner Stetson, and had put on his newest shirt, which Sarie had given him two birthdays back and he'd worn only twice. Wouldn't do to look too eager. He figured he was ready enough for Jessie West.

"H'lo, Coke," Willie said, holding the door open for him. "Ma ain't ready. She hasn't even got her dress on yet."

"That's all right," Coke replied, and stepped over Herman, who lay dozing across the stoop. "I'm a mite early."

"I know. When Ma heard your knock, she looked at the clock on the chiffonier and said oh hell."

"That so?"

"Yes. But don't you worry any. I don't think it was you she was mad at. It was her bun."

"Her bun?"

"Yep. Said it came out looking **lopsided. Made** the entire back of her head looked warped. I think it **was the** mirrors—she looks backwards through 'em." His eyes followed Coke's hand as he placed the brown paper package he'd been holding on the entry-way refectory table. "What's that?"

"A little present my sister, Amy's ma, fixed up."

"What's in it?"

"A doily."

"Oh," the child said, losing interest.

"An' some walnut fudge."

He perked up, but quickly covered his sudden interest with an air of nonchalance as he led Coke into the parlor.

"Sit down," he ordered, gesturing toward the sofa. He perched on the edge of the overstuffed chair opposite. "Ma told me to tell you to sit down, then to engage you in polite conversation."

"All right," Coke said, taking the seat Willie had indicated. "I'm sittin'. Now go 'head an' start engagin'."

The child rolled his eyes mischievously. He looked a shinier replica of himself, face scrubbed pink, hair parted down the middle and wetted to his scalp. Already little wisps were starting to rise up in back like damp pin feathers.

He sighed, squirmed a bit, face screwing up and straightening out, betraying the uncertain mixture of emotions at play behind it.

Finally, curiosity won out. He leaned toward Coke, looking him straight in the eye. "Do you really like my mother?" he asked, sounding more like an overprotective father than a son.

"Sure do."

He settled back, regarding Coke dubiously. "She can be one big tussle t'live with, you know."

"No doubt."

"Do you know what that . . . that mother in there"—he jabbed a finger toward the closed bedroom door—"tried to make me wear tonight?"

"No . . . what?"

"A sailor suit!" he said disgustedly. "The little-boy sailor suit I used to wear in San Francisco. Can you imagine? Me . . . having to go to the party tonight in that! Boy!" He shook his head. "Did we have one big go-round."

"Looks like you won out, though."

"Yes, I guess so. I don't much like this new stiff shirt and these wide black pants she dragged me back to the store and hustled me into. But they sure are a whole lot better'n that baby suit.'' He fell silent, fingers drumming on the chair arm, eyes roving to the package on the refectory table and back again. ''I suppose that fudge your sister sent is for my mother,'' he conjectured slyly.

''An' for you, too, I expect.''

''I suppose we're not supposed to eat it till later.''

''I don't believe my sister much minds when you decide t'eat it.''

Casting a cautious glance toward the bedroom door, Willie slid off the chair and stepped next to Coke. Placing an arm on his shoulder, he looked at him man to man. ''What say we give that fudge of your sister's a try.''

''I think I'll pass on it this time . . . but you go 'head, Will.''

''All right.'' He beamed. ''If you say so.''

He skipped to the refectory table and tore greedily into the package, sending paper scraps fluttering to the floor. The doily flopped to his feet. While cramming a full square of fudge into his mouth, he plucked up the disarrayed doily and deposited it on the table. Then he filled his fists with more fudge and strolled back to his chair. He plumped down, dropped back in the chair and, feet swinging, gave Coke a blissful ornery grin, the fudge filming over his new, half-grown-in permanent teeth.

Didn't take much to make a young-un feel right with the world, Coke mused.

''Meg's over at the schoolhouse collecting the food people fixed for the wedding,'' Willie volunteered. As he spoke, he brushed at the fudge crumbs sprinkling his chest, and in so doing marked the immaculate white shirt with thin brown streaks.

''Your mama takin' those pies she baked up yesterday?''

''Naw. She gave them to Ruby over at the saloon.''

''What you reckon Ruby's gonna do with 'em?''

''Feed 'em to her pig.'' He shrugged.

''Your mama fixin' on takin' somethin' else instead?''

''Baked potatoes. Meg already took them.''

''That's good. Ain't much injury your mama could do t'plain ole baked taters.''

''You don't know my mother,'' he breathed, then gave a little shrug. ''Course, she's better here.''

''How you mean?''

''She left her books in San Francisco, and there isn't any lending library here that she can borrow out of. Ain't nothing worse, Coke, than a ma with her nose jammed in a book while she's cooking. Everything gets boiled away and glued to the bottom of the pan thataway. 'Twasn't till we came here that I found out that peas aren't supposed to lose their skins and sloosh together.''

''Why your mama leave her books behind? Y'all leave San Fran-cisco kinda sudden-like?''

The child seemed to close up. Lowering his gaze, he wiped his sticky palms on his thighs. ''I'm not supposed to talk about San Francisco.''

''That's all right,'' Coke replied easily. ''Her cookin' aside, I'll bet your mama has her share o' good points, too.''

Willie considered a moment. ''Yup.'' He nodded thoughtfully. ''I guess she does. If you can put up with her long enough, prob-ably you could really get to like my mother.''

''I sure can believe that, too.''

As though the one thought naturally fed into the other, he tilted his head speculatively and said, ''Meg told me you had one of the biggest ranches in the entire county. That true?''

''Reckon so.''

''How big is it?''

''More'n two hundred thousand acres, all told.''

''Is that big?''

''I guess you could call it a tad above medium-sized.''

''I've never been on a real ranch before,'' the child said wist-fully.

''An' it's a daggone dirty shame, too, seein' as how you're sittin' smack-dab in the middle o' ranchin' country. Tell you what, Will, why don't you an' your mama come on out an' spend a coupla days at my place come next weekend.''

''You really mean it?'' Willie breathed.

''Yup.''

''Oh, boy!'' Willie leaped to his feet. ''Wait'll I tell Ma!''

''Uh, hold on there, Will,'' Coke stopped him. ''Let's chew this over a mite, all right? Could be that now may not be the best time t'be askin' her 'bout visitin' my place . . . her bein' so busy in there gettin' herself dolled up an' all.''

Willie looked at the bedroom door, then slowly sat back down in the chair. ''She could say no, you mean.''

''When you reckon would be the best time t'ask her so's she'd be more inclined t'say yes?''

He frowned. "I guess sometime when Meg's around. Meg can be a real help when Ma gets herself in a mood."

"Will," Coke said, "you are one savvy little fellow."

The bedroom door whipped open and Jessica strode into the room, a black dress hat in her hand.

"I'm sorry I kept you waiting, Mr. Sanders," she said in a formal tone. "I've never seen Dispenseme as crowded as it was today. I closed the store barely an hour ago. Then I had to get Willie ready." She gave her son a sidelong look, and her tone of voice dropped. "Or should I say, discuss with my son what he would or would not wear this evening. That in itself took up most of the hour, leaving me very little time for myself. I do hope that he kept you good company, though."

"Sure did. We had a right fine time discussin' the ranchin' business." He exchanged a knowing glance with Willie.

Jessica didn't notice. Her eyes were fixed upon the telltale brown stains at the corners of her son's mouth and the streaks down the new starched shirt. "Willie." She spoke his name ominously. "Have you been eating anything?"

"Yes," he answered smugly. "Fudge. Coke's sister sent it to us, and Coke told me to go right on ahead and eat some."

"Oh, he did . . . did he?" Her glance slid to Coke. Then, realizing that she might sound a little ungrateful, she forced a smile. "How thoughtful of Sara." She strolled to the wreckage of the package on the refectory table and picked up the doily. "How lovely!" she exclaimed with artificial delight. "Your mother's, Mr. Sanders?"

"Yup, that's Ma's."

"Your mother practically supports our handiwork department, you know." She glanced at her son. "Willie, please pick up these paper scraps."

Willie dutifully complied.

"Take them into the kitchen and throw them into the dustbin," she continued. "And please bring back a plate for this fudge."

"Yes, ma'am," Willie said.

Brows knitted, she watched her son disappear into the kitchen. Then, with a shrug, she set her hat on the refectory table and took the doily into the dining room. Picking up the painted clay vase that served as a centerpiece on the dinner table, she spread the doily before her, than set the vase upon it. "Fits perfectly here, don't you think, Mr. Sanders?'' she asked, forcing another tight smile.

''If you say so,'' he replied, not at all appreciating this I'm-going-to-be-nice-even-if-it-kills-me attitude that she'd adopted.

Willie came out of the kitchen with the plate. ''Now, go in the bedroom and wash your face,'' she said, taking the plate.

''Yes, ma'am,'' he replied, and headed off as directed.

Again, her puzzled eyes followed her son. ''Hmm. Strange,'' she said, arranging the fudge on the plate.

''What's strange?''

''Willie. He's so . . . so happy to be obedient. He's never this docile and civilized before a party.''

''Mebbe he's savin' up energy.''

''Oh, no, Mr. Sanders,'' she said, setting the plate of fudge on the dining room table and walking back to the refectory table. ''My son usually spends as much energy in anticipation of an event as he spends on the event itself. The only times he's ever this quiet and obliging are when he's done some mischief or is contemplating doing some mischief.''

She picked up her dress hat and, looking into the entryway mirror, held it above her head, tilting it this way and that in search of the most flattering angle.

But, like himself, he decided, she evidently didn't want to show too much anticipation of the evening ahead. She wore the same simple black skirt and high-buttoned blouse she'd had on the day he met her, the only difference being a little added fluff to her hair. And, at her throat, a small cameo brooch he'd seen Meg wearing from time to time. But the plainness of her attire only made him notice all the more how soft her beauty was. Each time he saw her, he was struck down by it anew.

Their eyes met in the mirror. She gave him another distant little smile, then shoved her hatpin in place.

She's holding herself in, he thought, playing the proper lady, sloshing propriety on thick so's to keep me at a distance.

Willie emerged from the bedroom. He'd washed the chocolate stains off his face, but he'd also mussed up his hair. Apparently the slicked-down look didn't appeal to him either, thought Coke.

Jessica slowly shook her head at the sight. Then, giving Willie's cause up for lost, she turned to her escort. ''Shall we be off, Mr. Sanders?''

''It's Coke,'' he said, opening the door.

She appeared not to hear. Her attention was on Herman, who still lay snoozing across the stoop. "Move," she said, nudging the hound with the side of her foot. And when the animal's only response was a groaning unfolding of his body from stomach to side, she lifted her skirt and stepped over him.

As they reached the front gate, the bell in the tower of the Catholic church struck its first deep, sonorous bong.

They walked on, side by side along the quiet road, without touching. Willie lagged a few feet behind, kicking a stone along and powdering his pant cuffs and newly polished shoes with dust. Between the long-echoing bongs of the bell, other sounds became magnified . . . the padded beat of their footsteps, the rustle of her skirt, the skittering and bouncing of the stone Willie was kicking. Somewhere, in someone's backyard, two women were carrying on an animated conversation in Spanish. Between the deep, plangent tolls of the bell, the words rang in the air, seeming to issue from some indefinable spot that was always just before the three of them as they made their way along the road.

Jessica sighed, and looked up at the sky. With the approach of evening, it had ripened to a deeper, richer blue, the descending sun turning candescent the billowy undersides of the clouds that now drifted above it. They glowed a milky pink that reminded Jessica of scalloped mother of pearl.

"What a lovely evening for a wedding," she remarked. Weather was such a nice, neutral subject, she thought. Except, perhaps, when it was *this* beautiful.

"A good soakin' rain's what would really make folks feel like celebratin'."

"Oh, come now, Mr. Sanders—"

"Coke."

"Coke. No one would want to go to a wedding and get himself and his dinner drenched in a rainstorm."

"The way things are here, Jessie, I don't think folks'd give a da—uh, a fiddler's whistle what got drenched, so long as their ranchlands got it, too."

"Even so. I've found that for such monotonous, arid country, you have the most stunningly colorful sunsets here."

"Comes from all the dust in the air."

"Whatever causes it . . . just look up there. What a magnificent cerulean sky."

"What kinda sky?"

"Pretty blue one."

He squinted up at it. "Yup, it's blue, all right, bluer'n a Eskimo seal hunter's bottom."

"How poetic!" she exclaimed. "Why, I do believe you're another Shelley, Coke."

He frowned. "Shelley who? Are you likenin' me to a lady, Jessie?"

"Oh, heaven's no!" The will-o'-the-wisp dimple flickered. "I'd never stoop so low as to resort to such a vile, snide insult. Shelley was a man. Percy Bysshe Shelley was his entire name. He was a great English poet who drowned in a boating accident many years ago."

"Well, that's one way o' signin' out that folks hereabouts sure don't hafta worry 'bout," he observed. "Percy . . . Bysshe . . . Shelley," he repeated slowly, then shook his head. "Whew! Pore honcho. Havin' t'go through life with a handle like that."

"I suppose it does sound effeminate . . . to you. Here, a man should have a tough, menacing name. Like Killer, Dead-Eye, Brute, Butch, Bear, Bull . . ." she said, her voice trailing off tiredly.

He lifted a brow at her. "You left out Stud."

"Oh, that's right," she replied, her footsteps slowing as, reaching back, she pulled Willie up between them. "And his twin brother, Deluded."

And that's my Jessie, he thought as they stepped onto the boardwalk of town.

✿ Chapter 10

BUGGIES, SURREYS, RANCH wagons, and saddle horses lined the approaches to Miss Muriel's Day School. Smoke rose from the mesquite fire in the backyard pit over which a steer was barbecuing. It lofted above the schoolhouse roof in lazy, tenuous whorls, brushing the quiet air with the mingling aromas of meat, smoke, and mesquite.

The menfolk loitered outside in the street, delaying to the last the moment that they'd be herded inside to witness another of their number being hog-tied and branded forevermore. Too, word had been passed by Cactus Caleb that Coke had snared the town's most elusive prize for the evening, the mysterious Jessica West. They wanted to be among the first on hand to mark if it was true. Standing around in loose clusters, slouch-shouldered, hands jammed in their front pants pockets, thumbs out, and elbows slack, they compared notes on the drought, speculated on the identity of the rustlers—the consensus was that they were Mexicans—and discussed the unexpected reversal of Hector Navarro's fortunes. Many put in that they wished that they had a rich cousin somewhere, too.

The day school had once been a family home, but years ago Miss Muriel had converted it to a school by having most of the inner walls in the forward part of the house taken out. That left a spacious area in front for her classroom, and narrow living quarters in the rear for Miss Muriel herself. As a young woman she had attended a small ladies' college in San Antonio for a year, a distinction that qualified her as the most educated Anglo in town. From it the forty-one-year-old spinster schoolmarm had derived the notion that she knew what was best for everyone. Her certitude fed on itself, and was further fattened by Miss Muriel's interpretation of an uncompromising fundamentalist faith. Unacknowledged kindred spirit to Bessie Sanders, she saw the world as a zebra's behind: enlightened, heaven-bound white set against decadent, hell-bound black . . . and stupid assholes (poor white trash and those of murkier hue) in the middle. Miss Muriel herself was, of course, the only surefire white in a virtual sea of the latter. And so it was only natural that in the absence of a real Protestant church, she should insist that her schoolhouse serve in its stead whenever the circuit preacher came to town. It was, after all, the only undefiled building around.

Soot was the first of the crowd to see Coke and Jessica turn the corner onto the street. He elbowed the fellow next to him, who turned, eyeballed the twosome, and let out a loud "Whooeee!" That brought the rest of the menfolk around.

"Hey, Jack," a young drover teased, making no effort to hide his glee that Handsome Jack couldn't win them all. "You must be losin' your touch. Looks like that hot campaign you had goin' came up short. Coke Sanders beat you out.''

Jack had been standing for some time a little away from the crowd, leaning back against the schoolhouse, hat low on his brow, and eyes leveled on that same corner that Coke and Jessica had turned onto. Now he broke into his easy smile, except that this time it seemed more tooth than smile. ''Must be some new kinda bribery I ain't heard of yet.''

And all the men who had young wives or sweethearts and couldn't help feeling uneasy whenever Handsome Jack showed up around their gals, and a few who'd found at different times that they had sound reason to be uneasy, gloated over this rare blow to Handsome Jack's lady-killer reputation. And their glee found release in the whistles, hoots, and catcalls they delivered to the couple coming up the street.

Jessica's steps slowed under the barrage. Every movement she made felt stiff and awkward to her. She resisted the impulse to run her fingers down the front of her blouse to check that all her buttons were secured, or to peek behind to see that her petticoat hadn't strayed below her skirt or that something else hadn't shaken loose onto the boardwalk behind her.

She felt Willie's hand grasp the back of her waistband. Stumbling on at her heels, he peered around her in bewilderment. She instinctively drew a little closer to Coke, and if she could have pulled it off with any aplomb, would have followed her son's example and hidden herself behind him.

When they reached the edge of the boisterous crowd, she hesitated, uncertain. Should she duck her head and plow straight through to the schoolhouse door? Or should she acknowledge this rabble in some fashion? How she might do that, she hadn't the foggiest notion.

''Howdy,'' Coke said with a stoicism that bordered on boredom.

Taking his lead, she gave a little nod and reaching back, unlatched her son's hand from her waistband.

At that moment Willie saw himself caught out, in all the world's eyes and his own, as a scaredy-cat baby clinging to his mother. He stared at her hand as though it were a rotted fish, then jerked free of it.

He bounded up the schoolhouse steps, leaving Jessica holding air and feeling even more absurd.

"Holy Hell, Coke!" bellowed a toothless old geezer in bib overalls from the back of the crowd. "How'd you bag this-un?"

"It was rough goin', let me tell you," Coke responded easily, directing Jessica up the steps. "But in the end, I gave in an' said, 'yup.'"

"Arm-wrestled you into it, eh?" The geezer grinned.

"It's this sweet, charmin' smile o' mine," Coke deadpanned, pulling the door open. "Get's 'em every time."

A jumbly chitchat of women's voices filled the schoolroom. As they entered, a lady in a straw bonnet at the end of the last row was the first to see them. She jabbed the lady next to her. Nudges and taps ran swiftly down the rows, and the chattering sputtered away as, one by one, each of the ladies turned around to inspect Dispenseme's latest romantic twosome, then turned again to nod knowingly to her neighbor.

"Oh, poopie-dog, Unca Coke! Not you, too!" a little boy squeaked off to the side. And Joshua, in a wild pantomime of shock, clutched his chest and threw himself backward off the plank seat into the lap of the lady behind him. Sarie, next to Joshua, was the only one in that entire goggling gaggle whose face was open and a bit triumphant as she gestured to her brother to take the empty plank seat in front of her and the rest of the family.

Jessica wasn't as intimidated by the members of her own sex as she had been moments before by the men. And when she read on the faces of a few of the unmarried ladies and their mothers begrudging envy, letdown, and barely concealed hostility, her confidence was completely restored. For the first time that evening she possessively took Coke's arm, and sauntered down the aisle beside him. She pointed Willie down the row in front of the Sanders family. And the child, maintaining a nose-up demeanor before all those observant eyes, led his mother and her suitor to their places.

"Thanks ever so much for that delicious fudge you sent, Sara," Jessica said to her while the room listened in. "And, Mrs. Sanders, that doily you made was simply lovely."

"What doily?" Ma exclaimed, then frowned at Sarie. "Which o' my doilies didyuh give 'er?"

"Ah, Ma," Sarie sighed. "It was the pink one outa that pile in the corner we've never used."

"Hummmph!"

"Hush, Ma," Sarie whispered.

As soon as Jessica faced forward, intense whispering erupted behind them like air escaping from a leaky flue. Patting her chignon as though she might deflect the heat from all those eyes burning into the back of her head, she looked with studied coolness about the room.

Miss Muriel's scuffed desk had been moved front and center. On it stood a large wooden cross, framed from behind by a vase of wild and domestic flowers. A well-thumbed Bible lay open on the desk before it. The children's desks and chairs had been stacked along the side walls, having been replaced by the lengths of backless wooden plank seating for the wedding congregation. An upright piano, its black varnish scratched, sat at the front of the room, catty-corner to the chalkboard.

Whenever Coke found himself stuck in one spot where he was obliged to do nothing but sit and listen, and especially when such an occasion was a church service, he would fold his arms, cross his legs at the boot, hunker down, and turn his thoughts inward, sinking into a kind of open-eyed dozing off. Not even when he took Ma to camp revival meetings could the fiery-mouthed evangelist penetrate the shell.

As a young soldier fighting under General Hood at the Battles of Franklin and Nashville, he'd come to terms with defeat and death, which were what these things were about, anyhow. And he doubted that a reader, a dreamer, or a Bible-pounding screamer could impart to him more.

Caught once again in that familiar setting, that old automatic response in Coke had already taken hold.

Jessica, on the other hand, was alive to every little whisper, shuffle, and nuance in her charged surroundings. She heard whisperings two rows back whose words she could make out. Without needing to look around, she identified the whiny heavily accented Southern drawl as belonging to Susan Shaftesbury, the sheriff's wife.

"Could be, Bessie," Susan was saying, "tha-ut yo-ah boy, Coke, may be gettin' the weddin' bug hisself."

"Not a chance," Ma Sanders blurted, loudly enough to be shushed again, this time by Susan. "I gave up on that-un ten year ago."

"Ah, come na-ow," Susan said. "Coke ain't tha-ut old."

"Old's not the point," Ma replied in her same loud voice. "He's just dad-burned muleheaded. Eight, nine year back, when

Sarie here got herself hitched and moved out, I was feelin' mighty lonesome. The place felt empty all the way down to the hollows o' my bones. So I goes to that boy o' mine an' I says t'him, I says, 'Sure'd make me happy if you brung yourself home a wife. You ain't got no idee, son, how I yearn an' burn before the good Lord calls me to my great re-ward, t'hear the pitter-patter o' little feet 'bout this ole house o' ours.'

"An' that critter, he says t'me, he says, 'Ma, as I live an' breathe, have I ever denied you?' " Ma paused and sniffed. "Next day, he brung me home a crate o' chickens."

Susan tittered. "One day he just ma-ut suhprise you, Bessie," she averred. "An' you'll find yo'self with a pittuh-pattuh that waa's an' burps instead o' one that pecks an' peeps."

"Can you get a jackass t'whistle?" Ma snorted.

Jessica peeked over her shoulder. Her eyes met Sarie's. A little smile touched their mouths, and simultaneously they both caved forward, convulsing with silent laughter. The quaking next to him shook Coke out of his stupor. Looking down, he saw Jessica doubled over, holding her shaking sides. Frowning, he ran his eyes around the room, finding not a single solitary humorous-looking thing.

Willie fidgeted, and pulled his mother's sleeve. "When's this thing gonna begin?" he demanded.

She straightened up, brushing the tears of laughter from her eyes. "Soon . . . soon." She patted him on the knee.

"Why aren't the people genuflecting to the cross when they come in? Where're the candles and the holy water? Where's the silver wine chalice and the curtained box for the hosts?"

"I don't believe that Protestants use those things, love."

"You a Catholic?" Coke asked.

"Yes."

The people seated in the row in front of them turned and fixed their eyes on Jessica as if she were an alien creature.

"Don't you folks believe it's a sin t'take part in Protestant services?" Coke asked, and the people in the row in front shifted their eyes from him to her.

"Yes," she replied to them all. "My coming here with you, Coke, will cost me a century in purgatory."

He thought that over. "You sure do have a way o' makin' a hombre feel important, Jessie."

"Oh, I wouldn't want to do that," she answered dryly. "Actually, I don't believe that this will cost me at all, because we're not in a genuine Protestant church. It's a schoolhouse. And as for the service, Willie and I just won't pay attention."

"Oh?" he teased. "So you *figger* your way around your sinnin', do you?"

"Of course." She smiled to the people in front of her. "Doesn't everybody?"

"I don't," Coke said. "Ain't rightly settled in my mind what's a sin an' what ain't."

"Well." She shrugged. "That's how *you* figure *your* way around your sinning."

A door opened at the side of the room leading to the schoolyard, and Meg and Cactus stepped inside. They brought with them a tide of air, now heavy with the stomach-tugging aroma of barbecuing meat. Untying her apron and folding it, Meg led Cactus to the plank seat across the aisle and two rows up from Coke and Jessica. The ladies at the back of the room craned their necks at this unexpected pairing, then frowned in consternation at one another. Everyone knew that the mortician and Meg spent a lot of time together at the store, but at social gatherings they behaved like any old married couple, all but ignoring each other.

Mopping her face with her folded apron, Meg whispered into Cactus's ear. He got stiff-jointed up, hobbled to the nearby window, and jerked it open. Reminded of their own discomfort, two ladies in other parts of the room did the same, bringing in the clatter of the men's voices from outside. Fanning themselves, the women fell silent in order to listen in on their menfolk, whose gossip tended to be so much timelier and juicier than their own.

Signaling that the important proceedings were about to begin, the door at the front of the room to Miss Muriel's quarters was flung open. Slamming it behind her, Miss Muriel strutted imperiously to the upright piano, clutching her sheet music to the side of her pendulous bosom and towing across the floor behind her an exaggerated, bustled tail end that she must have dug up especially for the occasion. Her dress was a stark navy in color, hitched so tightly at the throat that a layer of pinched-up chin lay folded over the top of her collar like a pink, dimpled ruffle. The schoolmarm's only concession to frivolity was in her hat. Almost as wide as a wagon wheel, it was festooned with garish cloth flowers and painted wooden grapes, all topped by a large crystal bird. The bird tilted forward and pecked at a wooden grape as Miss

Muriel bent over the round piano seat and, with jutting index finger, twirled it to the proper height. She delicately sat down, bustle overlapping the stool behind like the overbite of a camel. Snapping open the gold watch that was attached to a heavy gold pin that in turn was clipped to her bodice, she frowned disapprovingly at the time. She snapped shut the watch and spread her music out on the piano rest. Lifting her lorgnette, attached by a chain to the same gold bodice pin that supported her watch, she poked her head forward and frowned through the lenses at her music. The wind through the opened windows riffled the sheets. She slapped them back. Suddenly a gust swooped two of the sheets away, carrying them in a graceful arc behind the desk-altar. From there they veered back, skimming down under the plank seats of the congregation.

The lorgnette poised before her eyes shot off sparks of light. Miss Muriel rose to her feet, sending condemnatory glances in the direction of the offending sheets of music, than at the blameworthy open windows.

Bang!

Bang! Bang!

The three windows were slammed shut by three spooked ladies, former students of Miss Muriel's. Though long grown and years out of school, they hadn't forgotten the sting of her yardstick against knuckles and cranium, or the effortlessness with which she could lift even hefty, half-grown boys off their feet and send them sailing to the Fool's Stool. Miss Muriel had remained such an imposing figure in their mind's eye that they still failed to see that she was barely five feet tall.

Feet shuffled, people grumbled and knocked noggins as they bent this way and that to retrieve Miss Muriel's music. Finally it was passed back up to her. Without a word or a nod of gratitude, small courtesies being her due, she accepted it, clomped back to the piano and, with a billowy whump, swallowed the stool top once again in her bustled, petticoated hind end.

At last, rigidly upright, face severe, and sustaining pedal clamped to the floor, Miss Muriel slammed out her opening chords. Heeding the clamorous summons, the men started trickling in from the street and filing down the rows to their womenfolk.

The door to the schoolyard opened again, this time timidly. The preacher peeped in, then fairly tiptoed to his place before the altar. He was a young one. They always got young ones in Dispenseme. Just out of seminary and needing someone to practice upon, the newly ordained were given the scut-work of spreading the Word to the one-horse towns before being awarded with permanent churches of their own.

And this preacher wasn't displaying an overabundance of confidence. His Book of Services might have been a hot potato, bouncing around the way it did in his trembly hands. His eyes skipped about to avoid making contact with anyone in the room; his mouth twitched between a smile and a frown. It appeared that he was scared to death. And indeed, the Dispenseme churchgoers did have a reputation that reached all the way back to the seminary in Dallas for discomposing their wet-behind-the-ears young preachers.

With the preacher in place—though looking like he might make a break for it at any moment—the mother of the bride, Lucy Blankenship, made her entrance, twittering nervously down the aisle like a drunken butterfly and alighting so tentatively at the end of her front-row plank seat that if anyone had reached out and slapped the opposite end of the plank, she'd have gone fluttering up in the air again and have to be swatted back down.

The side door opened again, and the groom, Freddie Winsnap, stepped in, followed by his best man, another wrangler from the Blankenship ranch. Red-eyed and hung over from a night and a morning of passing the bottle to fuel Freddie's courage, they both looked in worse shape than the preacher.

Massaging the numbness out of his hands, the groom stood gazing over the heads of the congregation, eyes sliding in and out of focus, Adam's apple bobbing up and down his throat in a vain effort to pump spittle into his panic-parched mouth. The poor boy looked so goosey and unsteady on his feet that a sneeze could have knocked him into a backward somersault.

Miss Muriel stopped pounding the piano, the abrupt silence sending eardrums ringing into dizzying deafness and out again, and almost bringing the hung over bridegroom buckling to the floor. She spun around on her stool and scowled through her lorgnette at the back of the room. With a significant nod, she turned back, shuffled a piece of sheet music forward, and slammed into a stirring rendition of the old hymn "Almost Persuaded." It was her schoolhouse, her piano, and she'd play whatever she darn well pleased.

The flower girl, a three-year-old Blankenship cousin, was first down the aisle, shooting through the door at the back of the room as though she'd been jettisoned from behind. About a third of the way down, her knees locked and she stood rooted to the floor, tightly clutching the flower basket to her chest, the tears of fright welling in her eyes . . . until she was rammed from behind by the ring bearer, Cindy's brother. Mort was having the time of his life being the center of all this attention while dispensing the important duty of keeping his little cousin in motion. Catching sight of Willie, he crossed his eyes and made a face, mindlessly tilting the ring pillow. The ring slid to the edge, raising a gasp among the congregation. Willie giggled. And Miss Muriel, with unerring teacher's instinct, turned her face from her music and singled Willie out with a withering glare.

The bridesmaid, another Blankenship cousin, appeared next. A rawboned, stringy-haired gal who wouldn't have looked well put together in a two-hundred-dollar New York gown, she carried herself with such disdainful hauteur that she must have fancied herself a raving beauty.

The bride on her father's arm was a picture of loveliness. Flushed with the triumph of this day, she looked prettier than she ever had before or would ever look again, while her ruddy-faced pa looked merely put out at having to take part in another of these foolish rituals that women browbeat their menfolk into when he'd sooner be out on his ranch worrying about rustlers, counting drought-starved beef carcasses, and otherwise inflaming his peptic ulcer.

The ring bearer bunting the flower girl along, the wedding party progressed jerkily down the aisle, dutifully arranged themselves before the preacher, and waited.

It turned out to be a long wait, for Miss Muriel, caught up in the grandeur of her music, kept pounding away. Shifting their feet, the wedding party exchanged glances back and forth. Then the young preacher leaned toward Miss Muriel and, blushing, whistled low to catch her attention. But the schoolmarm pounded on, stiff-backed, her projected elbows bouncing militantly.

Muttering a curse, Cindy's pa cupped his hands around his mouth. "Shut it off, Muriel!" he boomed. "For God's sake, give somebody else a chance!"

Miss Muriel leaped a foot off her stool, coming down in a jarring plop that knocked her hat lopsided. Huddled over the keyboard, she peered suspiciously askant, then abruptly rose up and slammed out an ending chord, hitting half the keys wrong. The congregation winced. She tried again. And made it worse. She decided to go at it from a different angle. Starting low in the bass clef, she rolled her fingers up the keyboard and, with magnificent flourish, crossed her left hand over her right and delicately hit the wrong note, flat, high in the treble clef.

Uncertain if she was indeed finished, the young preacher stared slack-jawed at her. Slapping her hat straight, she whipped around on her stool and, bringing her lorgnette to her eyes, faced him.

"Dearly Beloved," he squeaked at her, then caught himself, cleared his throat, and turned to the wedding couple. He began again, about an octave lower: "Dearly Beloved . . ."

His voice cracking here and there, and stumbling over the easy words, the preacher sweated through the vows until he came to a key line. It came out, "Do you, Frederick, take this woman to be your lawfully bedded wife?"

He blanched. "Oops," he said in a wee voice, his small hand going to his mouth.

At the back of the room, someone snickered.

"Bedded?" Cactus remarked to Meg in a stage whisper. "Wedded an' bedded. That's outa Shakespeare, I do believe, *The Shamin' o' the Screw*."

"Pore fella," a cowpuncher mumbled to his companion. "Cain't tell his rear end from a hole in the ground."

His mind a blank, the preacher looked desperately about for someone or something to jog his memory.

"You was a-askin' Freddie here iffen he was a-wantin' me for his wife. . . ." Cindy prompted.

"Oh, yes," the young preacher breathed. And picking up the vows where he'd left off, he stampeded through the rest of the ceremony at double time, hoping to outdistance any other catastrophe that waited to befall him along the way. Until, at last, he declared the couple husband and wife.

Cindy's pa belched and said, "Thank God." Mort tossed the ring pillow in the air. And the newlyweds, despite hundreds of steamy hours spent over the past many months in groping each other and rolling around out on the prairie or in the Blankenship hayloft, brought their faces together in a shy little kiss like two innocent six-year-olds.

The sustaining pedal clunked at the piano. And to the deafening accompaniment of "Shall We Gather at the River," Cindy supported her ashen-faced groom down the aisle. The bridesmaid and best man followed, the scraggly-haired girl flirting shamelessly up at him, her body glued so tightly to his that there was no way that he could come unstuck and walk at the same time.

The wedding guests streamed into the aisle and, buffeted behind by Miss Muriel's sledgehammer musical delivery, spurted out the front door. Some of the men stayed behind to pass the plank seats out the side door and into the yard.

"That poor minister," Jessica remarked to Coke as they came down the steps.

"What's so pore 'bout him?" he asked.

"He looks so young, and that little slip of the tongue threw him off so."

"What slip o' the tongue?" Coke asked.

✤ Chapter 11

THE WEDDING GUESTS scattered themselves across the schoolyard. Like leaves caught in an eddy of wind, they swirled about the steer roasting over the pitted mesquite fire. Nodding importantly and bestowing opinions and judgments upon it, they gave the steer as much notice as they gave the newlyweds. They inhaled deeply of its aroma, assuring their grumbling bellies that help was on the way.

The Blankenship camp cook was in his glory. Circling and recircling the browning beef, dipping his brush into his bucket of secret sauce, he dabbed and stroked his masterpiece-in-progress.

From far away, in the vicinity of the Catholic church, vagabond wisps of mariachi music flitted across the schoolyard. Most of them were blotted out by blasts of laughter, the swell of voices, and the squeals of children pattering through the throng, their footsteps slowing only when their feet carried them by the serving table. There, with shiny bright eyes, the young ones surveyed the desserts being set out.

The crowd soon sorted itself out along its customary lines. The landowners, talking land, money, cattle, and the market, claimed the dominant position around the beer keg. The younger men, their sons and drovers, stood along the periphery of the yard. The conversation among them was meandering, since their attention was trained mainly on the unmarried young women milling before them. The married women, discussing recipes, children, pregnancy, and childbearing, bustled around preparing the serving tables. The older ladies, having already put in their time as the workers at such affairs as this, had appropriated the first plank seat that the men had toted out the door. Roosting in a row, they fanned the gnats out of their faces and avidly discoursed on their own illnesses, other people's illnesses, disease in general, and the dead and the dying.

Meg gestured Jessica over to the back steps of the school, which were overcrowded with picnic baskets.

"I forgot t'tell you when I took off this afternoon," she said. "I put our plates, cups, an' ironware in this here basket marked with the green yarn on the handle."

"Thanks, Meg," Jessica replied. "It never even occurred to me that we'd have to provide our own eating utensils."

"I reckoned as much. You know, Jessica"—Meg grinned—"I been watchin' you an' Coke. You two sure do make one handsome couple."

"So do you and Cactus."

"Naw. Cactus an' me are a coupla tough ole flints. Ain't much spark left in us no more."

"Then you should start flirting," Jessica teased. "Get Cactus's old heart beating."

"That'd be 'bout the meanest thing I could do to him."

"Why?"

"I suppose you've noticed I ain't got that many teeth left in my mouth." Meg made a face to show the gaps.

"So?"

"Have you ever seen Cactus yawn? He's got even fewer choppers than I do. Our guard rails is plumb rot out. Why, all I'd hafta do is t'rare up an' give him one o' my superduper smackeroos, an' he'd come a-slidin' straight on down my gullet. Suffocate t'death on my Adam's apple, he would."

Jessica smiled. "I wish I had your talent for superduper kisses."

Then she paused, growing serious. "There's a man I wouldn't mind suffocating to death any which way I could."

"Coke?"

"No. He doesn't qualify . . . yet."

"This other fellow . . . he the reason you get so down sometimes?"

"I'm not sad," Jessica said.

"Oh yes you are. Somethin's troublin' you down deep, honey. I know it. I seen it."

"Seen what?" Jessica said, bending over the basket and opening it to get out the plates and ironware.

"Well, for one, your happiness don't never seem t'hold. It keeps flickerin' off an' on like a gutted candle. Look, Jessica, tonight you should feel like the world's in your pocket. You're young, you're purty, you got a darlin' little son, an' one o' the most eligible men in this part o' the country has taken a interest in you. Yet I hear you pacin' the floor half the night. I can see how you dread the sight o' the stage pullin' in."

Jessica's eyes shot to Meg's face.

"I see the way you stand there at the store window watchin' that stage empty out," Meg went on, "all doubtful an' a little bit skittish. Like it's a gun that's probably loaded with blanks, but there's a off chance a real bullet's hidin' somewhere in there in the cylinder."

Seeing the wariness in Jessica's eyes, Meg put an arm around her. "I'm sorry t'be bringin' this up right now, but I want you to *enjoy* yourself tonight. I know you're slow in trustin' folks, an' from the little you've let me in on 'bout yourself, I can see why. I just want you t'know you an' Willie's like kin t'me. Time ever comes you need someone, I'll be just a holler away."

Jessica was touched. "You're a dear, dear person, Meg. You've been too good to us already."

"But you see, Jessica, I ain't the only one here you can trust. Look around, you'll see plenty others. Coke for one. You get t'know him better, you'll find that once you got him on your side, he won't walk away from it. He'll do t'ride the river with."

"At what cost to me?" Jessica put in.

Meg shook her head. "There you go again, countin' folks out without givin' 'em half a chance. Sure, most of us got faults big enough t'drive a steam-powered locomotive through. But we look

out for our own. An' you're startin' t'become one of us, Jessica.
So hold to your happiness. You're among friends tonight.''

"Is that man over there considered one of us?" Jessica asked.
She nodded toward a broad-shouldered, middle-aged man, clothed
in a brown business suit and carrying a cane, who'd entered the
schoolyard. A younger man followed him, then a third, tough-
looking man with hard, wary eyes.

Meg's face clouded. "T. C. Barrett. Yeah, I reckon he could
be considered a part of us. Like screwworms can be considered
a part of a cow.''

Jessica's eyes followed the man. She'd seen him in town a few
times, and it seemed that wherever he went, a layer of space
surrounded him. Now, too, people were clearing a path for him
as he walked toward the Blankenship family.

As awareness of Barrett's arrival spread through the crowd, the
cascades of easy laughter became suddenly self-conscious and
trickled away. The canopy of voices that had seemed to bubble
high in the air above the throng lost effervescence and settled in
closer to the speakers.

T. C. Barrett looked as stiff and stolid as his suit. Though
Jessica had sensed that his slow gaze had taken in her presence as
he passed by, she'd been unable to find any expression at all in
his hooded eyes. His thick brows seemed permanently fixed at
low tide. The younger man was his son, whom Jessica had heard
was called Beau. He was an angular, plain-looking young man of
about nineteen or twenty with thin dishwater hair. She read amused
superiority in his eyes and in his slow swagger. He seemed to be
trying to pose his way into manhood and power as he followed
his father through the crowd.

Lucas Blankenship, Cindy's father, and the newlyweds accepted T.C.'s congratulations with an uneasy reserve, while Cindy's mother, Lucy, tried to cover over the uneasiness by launching
a raft of cordialities. "So nice of you to drop by, Mr. Barrett.
Would you and your son like a beer? Would you join us at our
table for dinner?''

"Don't think he'd like our fixin's." A rancher by the name of
Graham McKetchin had spoken out from the crowd.

"Graham.'' His wife put a hand on his arm, but McKetchin
shook it off and stepped forward.

"All we got is a steer on the spit," McKetchin went on. "Ain't
likely t'satisfy a cannibal like you.''

Barrett's expression didn't change. "Well, look at that," he said to Beau. "He still kept his mouth. Mortgaged every other organ away."

"You—" Graham moved forward.

The thug with Barrett stepped in front of him, his hand on his gun.

"No!" Mary McKetchin cried.

"This is a weddin'," Lucas Blankenship said. "An' I would like my little girl an' our friends t'have a nice memory of it. Now, Graham, calm down. All this emotion is gonna effect your music playin'. An' we all was countin' on your fiddle t'put the spirit in the dancin' t'night."

Mary McKetchin took her husband's arm and tugged him back.

Coke stood at the corner of the schoolhouse near the road and watched T.C. approach, the cane scoring the ground by his steps. Their eyes met and held until Barrett moved on by to his carriage, waiting in the road. His armed guard got on his horse; his son Beau climbed up beside the driver.

As T. C. Barrett put his arm up on the carriage, he paused and turned back to Coke. "Interesting, Sanders," he said, "how that greaser Navarro came up with the cash the other day t'buy back his mortgage."

"Rich cousin, I heard," Coke replied impassively.

"I wonder. Wouldn't come as a surprise t'me that you'd be the sort that'd take sides against your own kind."

"Gotta take exception to that," Coke retorted. "The notion that you an' me could be two o' the same kind."

Barrett's eyes held steady. "Wasn't charity that built the Sidewinder."

"I bought folks out, Barrett. I didn't offer 'em a quick vaccine for what ails 'em . . . then draw all their blood out through the same needle."

Barrett set his hands on the top of his cane. "Maybe I learned one powerful lesson from your pa twenty-seven years ago."

"Maybe it was the wrong kinda lesson. Ain't that many widows left around here anymore, land-rich an' cash-poor."

Barrett climbed into his carriage. "Enjoy the money-lending business while you can, Sanders, you won't be in it long. I own the franchise for that game in these parts."

Coke glanced at Barrett's armed guard. "You'd be wise to avoid startin' any blood feud hereabouts. You might not be able t'pull back from it just any old time you wanted.''

Barrett considered. "Good advice. Too bad you didn't give it to your pa." He tapped his driver on the shoulder with his cane, and the carriage pulled away.

Coke watched the carriage move down the dark road, then went back to the schoolyard, stopping at a place apart from the crowd where the evening breeze could reach him unbroken and he had an unobstructed view of the crowd. He'd already learned a lot from observing how folks reacted to T. C. Barrett this evening. Some had watched him from a distance, nodding slowly when Barrett looked their way. A few had stood at the ready, looking eager for him to notice them. And there were others who'd looked upset and avoided glancing his way at all. It was the latter group that Coke surmised was—as Navarro had been—on the edge of losing it all to the drought and the Warner Savings and Loan.

But now Coke's gaze settled on Jack Siden, standing on the opposite side of the yard from him, slowly drawing on his thin cigar. The smoke curled around his head in the quiet air as he looked steadily in the direction of Jessica. Other rivals for her attention gave Coke no cause for concern. But Handsome Jack Siden was a man of a different stripe. And though he'd lost out tonight, Siden clearly hadn't given up the fight.

Coke looked at Jessica, over by the schoolhouse steps talking with Meg, and made his way toward her through a scattering ring of children. He was impatient for the dinner to be over and the dancing to begin. Then he'd have an easy excuse for taking her into his arms.

It was during dinner that Willie sprang on Jessica Coke's invitation to visit his ranch. With Coke there to make the invite official, Sarie to throw in her support, Meg to insist that she could manage the store just fine next weekend without her, and with about a half dozen other people looking on, Jessica had to give in.

Coke sent Willie a wink behind her back. It had been a smart idea to leave the timing to the boy. A young-un always has a natural talent for knowing when best to bushwhack his mother.

❧ Chapter 12

CONVERSATION SWELLED AS dinner plates were emptied one last time, having made their third or fourth go-around to the serving tables, and women here and there started the cleanup. Striking matches to after-dinner pipes and cigars, the menfolk hunkered down to serious talk, inhaling opinions with their smoke and exhaling better ones. Children slithered away from their families, ready to play and chatter by lamplight.

In the shadows alongside the schoolhouse, Graham McKetchin and another man drew fiddles out of battered cases and began waxing bows and plucking and tuning strings. Nearby, another man was strumming and tuning a guitar; the man next to him, a banjo. Warming up on his Skye Pilot's folding organ, a handsome young cowboy skipped from one snippet of song to another while casting a roguish eye toward each pretty gal who looked his way. The musicians collected into a huddle and came out throwing themselves into an ear-battering rendition of "Turkey in the Straw." Fragments of discernible tune surfaced fleetingly out of the melee of sounds.

"This early in the doin's, 'bout all they can agree on is the song," Coke explained to Jessica. "Takes 'em a spell t'put together the rhythm an' the key, but they'll get there."

He was proved right. And by the fifth go-around of "Green Corn, Green Corn, Bring on the Demijohn," wedding guests began to turn from their cleaning and conversation to shout out the words.

"Ever take in any hoedowns in San Fran-cisco?" Coke asked Jessica.

"No," she replied.

"You pore city folk just don't know what a good time is."

"I wouldn't be so sure about that. A person can go to many places in San Francisco and have a good time."

"But ain't them sorta places for a passel o' strangers?"

113

"So? What's wrong with that?"

"Seems t'me tryin' t'make fun amongst folks you ain't never seen before an' ain't likely t'see again would be leavin' somethin' important out . . . kinda like ham without raisin sauce. A smile without the eye twinkle."

The musicians flew into the bawdy tune "Black Bull Came Down the Mountain." More people were up and about, shuffling and jogging across the yard to the infectious rhythm of the music even as they finished their chores—women scraping plates out in the barrels that Sol Wingate, the local hog farmer, had provided, needing all the slops he could get for his nursing sows; men toting the tables and plank seats to the edge of the yard to clear space for the dancing.

"Folks around here sure do need a good shindig," Meg observed. "Ever once in a while a body needs remindin' that there are other things t'life than drought an' ruination an' T. C. Barrett."

"Yup," Sarie agreed. "It's good just bein' able t'feel the music runnin' through you an' seein' the worry frowns easin' back on your neighbors' faces."

Jessica smiled at the two women. She was beginning to feel a kinship with these people, a communion with their joys and sorrows that she hadn't felt before. She had about decided, too, that if she had to be stuck with a man tonight, Coke Sanders was probably the best of the lot. She liked the easy relationship he had with his sister and her children and Meg, as though he really enjoyed their company. And she appreciated that he wasn't crowding her tonight. His manner was as subtle as a whisper. Interesting, she thought, how his restraint in touching her had led to her wanting to reach over and touch him. Or, at least, get him to touch her.

The music stopped, and leaving a buoyant atmosphere in their wake, the musicians withdrew to catch their second wind and pass the bottle.

Jessica, Meg, and Sarie gathered up their plates. As they headed for the barrels to scrape them off, they deposited the lantern from their table at the back of the yard. Other ladies were doing the same, placing lanterns in a line down two long tables. Their light cast a concentrated glow over the space cleared for dancing.

With the dinner over, the first wave of leave-takers gathered up their things. They included the very elderly, those from far outlying ranches, and the strict fundamentalists, who held dancing to be sinful. Ma Sanders left with Lou Wilson's grandmother, who lived on the outskirts of town. Ma, Sarie, and the children would be staying the night with Granny Wilson, sparing themselves a long trip back for church in the morning. The shedding off of this first group of people lightened the mood for the rest. Now they could get down to the serious business of having themselves a blazing good time.

The musicians emerged from the shadows, leaned into a brief conference, then broke into "Lizard in the Sun," the spirits in their innards inspiriting their music. Two beribboned, ringleted little girls grabbed hands and, noses up, cheek pasted to cheek, arms outstretched, seesawed back and forth in front of them.

When the lively tune was judged ready, the banjo picker stepped forward. "Awright, ladies and gents, form your squares!"

Skipping ahead of her bashful groom, Cindy started the first square. Men reclaimed their women, and women searched out their men, and four-couple squares started forming around the yard.

"You lookin' forward to the dancin'?" Meg asked Jessica as they put their dishes back into the basket.

"Won't I be sitting it out?"

"Why d'you think that?"

"Well, doesn't a big tough king rancher like Coke Sanders think dancing is sissified?"

"Nope," Coke said, coming up behind her and taking her arm. "Let's go on out an' shake a leg."

"Shake a leg?" she repeated, the will-o'-the-wisp dimple at the corner of her mouth blinking. "Forgive me, Coke, but for the life of me I can't imagine you shaking a leg."

"Depends on what crawled up it," he replied, walking her into the fourth side of a square.

Looking around at the other couples, Jessica realized that this form of dancing was entirely new to her. "I've no idea how to do this," she announced, wide-eyed.

"That's awright," the girl at her side assured her. "All you gotta do is listen. The caller'll tell you what t'do."

"Nee-ow fellers, stake your pen!" the banjo picker yelled. And he paused, chin jutting in and out to the rhythm, to let a few beats pass.

"Lock horns t'all them heifers an' wrestle 'em like men. . . ."

"What?" Jessica squeaked, but Coke had already flipped her into his arms and was swinging her around.

"Salute yer lovely critters; ne-ow swing an' let 'em go. . . . Climb the grapevine round 'em. All hands do-si-do."

As casually as if he were unwinding a yo-yo, Coke rolled Jessica out of his arm, popping her off to the man to his right. That man grabbed her hand and thrust her on to the next, with whom she scrabbled, intent on giving him the wrong hand. They sorted themselves out. He swung her on to the next man, who chucked her away, bouncing her off Coke. Jessica frowned up at him, but he was gazing nonchalantly straight ahead, whistling to himself.

For the next thirty minutes Jessica was in an absolute state. New calls kept coming so fast and furiously—"Box the gnat," "Weave the ring," "Break and trail"—that the caller could have been yelping Cherokee for all the help it did her. Soon she couldn't tell her left hand from her right, and would go slamming off into an allemande left when she should have been allemande righting. Coke would coolly reach out, take hold of the back of her waistband, and shoot her off in the right direction.

Once she stopped in the middle of the square and, hands on her hips, demanded, "What in the devil *is* 'seesaw your purty little taw,' anyway?" But before she'd gotten all the words out, Coke had scooped her up. As he rolled her away in a half sashay, it was all she could do to blow a wisp of hair off her nose and manage a shaky smile in response to the wave Meg sent her as she bounced along in another square.

Feeling Coke's arm angling down across her breast as he held her waist in a forward swing, she peeked up at him and caught the tiniest glint in his eye under the slant of his hat. You sneaky devil, you, she thought. He even danced sneakily, with such a sparsity of movement that he scarcely seemed to be moving at all. Yet he got the moves accomplished nonetheless . . . while she kept slam-banging around like a half-wit mule with its foot stuck in a bucket.

But as time passed, Jessica calmed and grew patient with herself, pausing to follow the others' leads. Soon the moves started coming naturally to her. A lightheartedness came to her step, and she gave herself over to the sheer primal joy of moving to the music.

"Ain't this fun?" "You havin' a good time?" One by one, people asked her that, as though Jessica's having a good time really was important to them. Feet shuffled, boot heels thudded, skirts whirled, generating happy feelings around the yard.

The dancing lantern light captured smiles and swinging bodies in brief suspension, its flickering gold erasing the flaws from the plainest of faces, making them smooth and mysterious. As the wedding guests swirled away in a circle of light, night, black and forbidding, surrounded them all around; and the bleakness of another cloudless morn awaited them on the morrow. They clung fast, now, to this island of happiness.

In the farthermost sweep of the lantern light, the children played scare games, the boys slinking through the shadows and charging with whoops at the girls. Squealing and holding to one another, the girls scurried away, though not so far away that they couldn't be scared again.

The musicians took another break, and Lucas Blankenship, looking worried, came over to talk to Coke. Jessica wandered off to join a small group of women who were laughing as they swapped anecdotes about their children.

After a time the music started up again, a waltz, and Jessica awaited Coke's arrival. He came up behind her, his hand going tightly around her upper arm. A little annoyed at him for reverting from his unpressured manner and grabbing her in such a possessive way, she glanced down, and realized that the hand around her arm wasn't Coke's. She turned and looked up into the green eyes of Handsome Jack Siden.

"Shall we?" he said.

Not wishing to rebuff him in front of the other women, she nodded, and walked with him to the dancing ground.

"I thought you planned to come here alone tonight," he chided as they moved through the waltz.

"I did plan to, Mr. Siden," she responded, somewhat guiltily, for that was what she had told him many times during the past two weeks. "But Coke can be very persuasive."

Jack Siden flashed his even white teeth, focusing his green eyes deeply into hers, his hand making a slight massaging motion at the back of her waist. "I thought I could be, too."

Instead of coloring, she pulled back a bit and regarded him coolly. "Well, there's persuasion, Mr. Siden, and then there's persuasion. Some can be rather stressful."

"Call me Jack."

"Oh? I thought your name was Handsome Jack," she remarked. And drawing herself in from his hand that still caressed her, she added, "Or could I just call you 'Hand' for short?"

"I surrender," he laughed, holding the hand up before her in an attitude of capitulation. "Let me try some less stressful persuasion. There's a dance over in Warner next Saturday night. Would you like to go?"

"I'm sorry," she replied, "but I've already accepted an invitation to visit the Sanders family next weekend."

The heat in those penetrating green eyes seemed to alter subtly. Jack Siden *was* an intimidatingly handsome man, but too smugly confident in his ability to overpower through his eyes and his person. She was relieved when Coke cut in, and responded to him more warmly than she had all evening.

"I'm glad you arrived," she smiled.

"That so?"

"Yes. It can get to be such a strain trying not to vex a man by failing to melt before his sales speech."

Coke's dark eyes warmed and he pulled her closer. "Too bad you didn't have somethin' handy here from the store t'latch on to t'sell him."

At the approach of midnight the newlyweds were sent off with laughter, cheers, and ribald jokes to honeymoon in a back bedroom of the Blankenship house. Soon after, a second wave of guests headed for home. And for those who danced on, the earlier easy gaiety took on an edge of determination to hold fast to the magic. But it drained away nevertheless with each departing wedding guest until a core of only ten couples remained. Unwilling to give in to the night yet, they lingered on, singing old familiar songs, "Swing Low, Sweet Chariot," "Dixie," "Jeannie with the Light Brown Hair," "What a Friend We Have in Jesus."

Finally the music stopped, and the plump man who played the fiddle, Graham McKetchin, stepped forward. He pulled a handkerchief out of his hip pocket and wiped his brow. "As y'all know by now," he said, "Mary an' me are losin' our ranch to T. C. Barrett and the Warner Savin's an' Loan. We're pullin' up stakes an' movin' t'Galveston, where maybe I got me a job in my brother-in-law's buildin' business.

"After more'n twenty years o' workin' this land an' raisin' our young-uns here, there warn't nothin' Mary an' me wanted more'n stickin' it out all the way, right here with you. But you cain't blow the breath o' life into a drought-starved steer. Cain't bring on a drencher with a wave o' the hand, nor squeeze nine percent loan interest outa dust. A body just cain't keep on takin' everythin' in his stride when man an' nature keep on a-trippin' him up.

"Who knows? Maybe we'll be able t'build us up another grub-stake an' come on back here for another go-round. Leastways, the thought'll stay with me whilst I'll be sawin' an' planin' an' hammerin' away, way over yonder in Galveston. I'll say my fare-thee-wells to you with this last an' favorite song o' mine."

He lifted his fiddle, touched his bow to it, and began to play "Oh, Bury Me Not on the Lone Prairie," the melody carrying sweet and plaintive into the gentle night air. And when the tall, gaunt man on the bull fiddle joined in, harmonizing in thirds, the poignancy of the moment cut through every heart.

Jessica sat turned away from Coke, her hand over her brow. And when the final note faded away, she abruptly got up to go through the motions of searching for Willie, though she already knew where he was. The wedding guests quietly collected their baskets, dishes, and children, blew out the last of the lanterns and, as though they were leaving a sanctuary, bade each other hushed good-byes and filed out of the schoolyard and into the night.

Coke and Jessica walked down the street. They didn't speak, absorbing the silence. Words would have felt too jarring. Willie plodded behind, willing one leaden foot in front of the other.

The evening had veered too much between laughter and sorrow for Jessica. She felt that all her emotions had been used up, and didn't at all mind Coke's holding her as they walked along. His closeness was a comfort to her, in fact, and she wondered if the anxiety and tension that had been plaguing her these past few months had been, temporarily at least, emptied out of her system. Maybe tonight, for the first night in weeks, she'd be able to sink into a deep, dreamless sleep.

As they neared the front gate to Meg's house, Willie picked up speed, moving on ahead of them up the path and into the house.

"Thank you, Coke," she said at the steps. And he could see that she meant it, though a ghost of that ironic smile still touched her lips.

He took her chin in his hand. "You know what I cotton to most 'bout you, Jessie?" he said. "It's that twist you sometimes get there at the corner o' your mouth that seems t'say you've just pulled up t'play another hand in Life's poker game . . . an' durn well oughta know better.''

He kissed her lightly on the lips then. And finding that she didn't protest or pull away, he gathered her into his arms and kissed her more deeply. She didn't give in to it so much as simply let it happen. Then, surprising Coke, she put her arms around him and embraced him, her face against his shoulder, in an attitude of a weary giving and receiving of consolation.

''Ahh, yuck!'' they heard Willie breathe through the nearby open window.

She separated herself from him and, gently touching his face, turned in to the house. He thought he glimpsed in the thin light a strange sheen in her eyes as she closed the door. He touched the place on his shirt where her face had pressed. It was damp. He hesitated, wanting to follow her inside to seek out the source of her sadness, but he realized that she wouldn't feel like she knew him well enough to confide any secrets of her heart. She had a right to retreat into her solitude. He turned from the door.

''See you Friday, Will,'' he said as he passed the window.

The child's response was swallowed in a yawn.

The wagon rolled slowly down the road out of Dispenseme. With rounded back and sunken shoulders, Graham McKetchin sat on the seat holding the reins, the only sounds the clip-clop of the horses' hooves, the rhythmic squeak of an axle, the occasional rattle of stones under the wheels, and Mary's soft breathing in back as she slumbered on the blankets piled on the wagon floor.

Then, suddenly, Graham heard a horse galloping up from behind. Putting a hand on his Winchester, he turned, squinting into the darkness. Not until the rider was almost beside him did Graham see who he was.

''Coke, you get turned around? Your place is on t'other side o' town.''

''Ain't turned around,'' Coke replied, slowing Ole Belcher to an amble alongside him. ''I just wanted a talk with you.''

''There's a oversupply o' empty silence round here, for sure,'' Graham said, pulling the horses to a stop. ''So I reckon I won't object t'fillin' it up with words.''

Coke tied Ole Belcher to the rear of the wagon and climbed up beside McKetchin.

''How much the Savin's an' Loan into you for?'' he said.

"Too much for me. Over four thousand dollars."

"Would you still be inclined t'try an' stick it out here if you had the chance?"

"Don't have the chance. The foreclosure will be descendin' in less'n two weeks."

"You can have the chance if you wanta take it, Graham. I'll loan you the cash t'pay off T. C. Barrett. I'll give you ten years t'pay me back at two percent interest."

"Well, ain't that somethin',", McKetchin said slowly. "Been goin' around for close to a month now sayin' good-bye t'everythin' in my mind. Now I find that all them toodle-oos may o' been a tad premature. You'll hafta give me some time t'readjust my brain."

They rode on for a while, Graham shaking his head every so often and muttering "Ain't that somethin'?"

"Well," he finally concluded, pulling the wagon to a stop. "Never did like carpenter work that much. Never did like my brother-in-law much. I reckon I'll take you up on your offer."

"I'll bring the money an' the IOU papers out to you in a coupla days," Coke said, getting down off the wagon. "Let's just keep this deal strictly between us, all right?"

"That I'll do," Graham said. "By the way, why're you doin' this, Coke?"

"Got t'thinkin'," he replied, untying Ole Belcher. "I'd miss your fiddlin'."

Chapter 13

ONE NIGHT THAT week a shower fell in the east section of the Sidewinder, and tender grass shoots sprouted along the cracks in the earth. The starving cattle went after them, dragging their heavy jaws across the thin mud so that by late morning most of the new growth had been shaved off. The few scraps that remained were soon baked brittle in the sun.

Each day, men forced out of work on other ranches drifted in, seeking employment. Coke hired a couple men he knew to be too good to pass up, and a couple more who were kin to some of the families that had been working for him for years and who had families of their own to feed. A man couldn't expect others to put themselves out for him and his if he couldn't be relied upon to come through for them and theirs in hard times.

Still, the men he'd taken on were only a small part of the number in need of work, and it pained him to see so many good men going to waste. The number of hands out of work could only increase in the coming months, though, as the consequences of a spring and summer of searing drought piled up. Ranchers whose herds had been decimated in the dry dust and had slim prospects of selling the scrawny cattle that they had still standing, while meanwhile they ran through the last of their cash set aside for operating expenses.

At least the rustlers had been quiet, giving him and the other ranchers in the area a rest. Coke took little comfort from that, however; no doubt the thieves were just biding their time to strike again.

He devoted most of his time, rustlers or no rustlers, to holding the line on his land. Day in and day out, somewhere on the Sidewinder they continued burning cactus to feed the cattle. Men dropped like flies from heat and smoke inhalation. Wagon axles broke, harnesses snapped. A valuable bull broke his leg and had to be destroyed.

Worn down, the men bickered constantly. Their senses were deadened by hours of backbreaking labor under a blistery sun, and accidents multiplied. Men were thrown from horses. Badly aimed hammers and pickaxes smashed fingers and toes. The *curandera* was kept busy working her magic. The aged mother-in-law of one of Coke's outfit bosses, the *curandera* knew the curative powers of every leaf, stem, branch, and root that grew in the region. Her *llerba del soldado* speeded healing, her *palo de muela* quieted toothaches. And Coke always kept a supply of her *estafate* handy to brew as a tea to quell the cyclone that boiled up in his belly whenever Gustina or the camp cook got overly inspired with the chili peppers they used to season their sauces.

So it was with bone-aching fatigue that each night Coke had stretched out on his bedroll, only to flicker off to sleep to the howls of the coyote summoning their brethren to another feast on his fallen beef. Except for a few brief encounters with Amy and

Joshua, the only bright spot on his horizon was in knowing that come today, Friday, he'd be seeing Jessica West. She was always there, not far from his thoughts.

Many times over the passing days he'd been tempted to cut short the space of time that he'd have to wait to see her, and take off for town then and there. But each time he stopped himself. He'd sort of tricked her into accepting his invitation to visit his place, and since then she might have had second thoughts. If he showed his face anywhere in her vicinity, she might use the occasion to back out of her visit.

Even now, as he turned the wagon down the road to Meg's house, he was wondering if she'd go through with it. But when he saw Willie, swinging on the gate, let out a whoop and go charging into the house hollering at his mother to get a move on, he relaxed.

She met him at the door. She wore the same stark black skirt and high-necked blouse that he'd seen her in most of the times before. And the notion crossed his mind for the first time that this lovely woman with the face and figure made to be adorned probably had very few dresses to her name.

She'd packed Willie's and her own things into a single scuffed valise, and had prepared a basket for his family of fruits, nuts, preserves, candy sticks, a roll of red ribbon for Amy, and two skeins of the latest shades of yarn for Ma. The gift seemed no more than a polite gesture, for once again her attitude toward him was remote. It seemed she didn't want to acknowledge or re-awaken the flashes of closeness that they had shared less than a week ago.

As the wagon joggled through the countryside, she sat impassive beside him, her hands folded in her lap. Once, the wagon tipped down a dip in the road and she was thrown against him. She moved away with a touching shyness that made him want to put his arm around her and snuggle her close.

Willie was too excited about the adventure ahead to be touched by his mother's restraint. Standing in the rear of the wagon and leaning over the top of the seat back, he prattled out questions.

"Got lotsa rattlers out on your place, Coke?"

" 'Nuff t'start a full-scale rattler ranch."

"D'you have lotsa fights with wild Injuns?"

"We just fight hard t'leave one another alone."

"If a fellow follows a scorpion, will it lead him to gold?"

"More likely it'll just lead him to another scorpion."

"Is it true what else Chacho says, that if a buzzard ever puked on you, you'd turn green and die?"

"Depends on how much he pukes."

At that last, Coke caught a spark of amusement in Jessica's eyes and knew that the wall that she'd been trying to maintain between them had finally been breached. They talked comfortably to each other the rest of the way to the Sidewinder.

Dusk was already stealing color from the world outside the windows when the Sanderses and their guests gathered for dinner. The two oil lamps on the table had been lighted in anticipation of the night, and dapples of their watery light danced like weak mirror reflections among the climbing roses on the wallpaper.

Coke and Ma sat at the heads of the table. Sarie and her children occupied one side, Jessica and Willie the other.

Ma didn't know how to take this stranger in their midst. She knew all there was to know about the young gals who lived in the area, including the queer strains in their family bloodlines to be on the lookout for—but she knew nothing about this Jessica West. Ma had never taken to outsiders. They had a peculiar way of looking at things that aroused her suspicions. Worse than this West woman's being any old outsider, though, she hailed in particular from California, a no-good, low-down state that had sided with the Union during the Great War. But if being a Yankee outsider weren't bad enough, it was mild in comparison to the main point against her, namely that Coke seemed to be taken by her. So taken by her was he that he'd committed the dumbfounding act of inviting her to stay at his home, the one and only time he'd ever done *that*. Now, as his mother, Bessie Sanders naturally reserved the right to doubt Coke's judgment in all things. But as to his choice in women, her son was blinder than a hoot owl at high noon.

So before Jessica had so much as stepped foot into the Sanders home, everything was against her in Ma's eyes, her every word and gesture subject to the most distrustful scrutiny and jaundiced interpretation by Ma. Jessica had picked up on that attitude right from the start. She wondered if she and Mrs. Sanders would be spending the next two days circling each other like a pair of jackals about to scrap over the same piece of carcass. And she immediately determined not to do a single thing to curry favor from Coke's mean-tempered mother.

The children's hands had already shot into the basket of biscuits before them when the sharp clink-clink-clink of Ma rapping her water glass with her butter knife prompted the little hands to be swiftly withdrawn.

"Amy, you may give the blessin' for today," Ma said.

"What?" Amy asked, puzzled.

"The blessin'," Ma repeated, sparse brows lifting above the faded metal rims of her spectacles. "As proper Christians, we-all gotta thank the Lord for providin' us with these here vittles."

"Oh," Amy recovered herself. "That's right. We got company." Knotting her hands under her chin, she looked sternly about the table to insure that everyone was adopting the properly reverential pose. "Thanks, Lord, for providin' us with these here vittles. Sincerely Yours. Amen."

Little Joshua concluded the pious interlude by making the sound of a locomotive chugging into its home station with a squeal of breaks and a pop of steam, and was the first to snap up a biscuit. Jessica and her son had crossed themselves in the Catholic way, and Ma, setting her jaw, duly took note.

As they passed the food around the table, Coke looked from his sister to Jessica, noting how pretty the two women were, each in her own way. Sarie's most fetching quality, though, was her openness, the easy way her feelings played across her features. Sarie hid nothing. She had no reason to, had nothing to fear. She had known sorrow but never hurt, not the kind of hurt, anyway, that shook her faith in herself and in her own worth or that undermined the foundation she'd built her life on. Someone's love had always been there serving as a shield.

Jessica, on the other hand . . . nothing was obvious about her. With her delicate features, she looked almost too fragile to long endure, or to withstand even a single sharp blow. But the ironical twist at the corner of her mouth said otherwise. No, she couldn't be broken so easily. There was flint in those finespun lines. And never would she be found running out to greet the world with wide-flung arms. Holding back, she'd wait, a wary cast to the eye. She'd known hurt. Deep hurt. And that insight touched Coke like unshuttered light.

"I heard tell, Mrs. West, that you was a widder lady." Ma commenced her interrogation, slapping butter on her biscuit. "How long has it been since your late husband passed on t'reap his heavenly re-ward?"

"Three years," Jessica replied.

"What he die of?"

"His ship was wrecked in a typhoon in the Pacific."

"What was he doin' way out yonder in the ocean?"

"He was the owner and captain of a trading vessel."

"That what he done for a livin'?"

"Yes."

"Heard tell y'all hail from San Fran-cisco. That right?"

"That's right."

"You got kin there?"

"Not to my knowledge."

"Got kin in these parts?"

"Not to my knowledge."

"You got any kin a-tall?"

"I suppose so."

"What d'you mean, you s'pose so?" Ma asked pertly. "Don't you know iffen you got kin or iffen you don't?"

"Ma!" Coke and Sarie broke in together.

"Now, don't you go pickin' on our guest," Coke warned.

"Son," answered Ma. "Now, I know that California sided with them no-good, dog-lickin' Yanks durin' the Great War. But that state ain't entirely north o' the Mason-Dixon line. An' it ain't entirely south of it, neither. I was only tryin' t'get a handle as t'which side Mrs. West here was on."

"I'd had the impression that that conflict had been resolved twenty years ago," Jessica said.

" 'Tain't for us," said Ma.

" 'Tis for me," said Coke.

"Let's change the subject," Sarie said.

There was a silence; then Joshua wiped the milk mustache off his lip and declared, "My baby brother has the measles."

"Didn't know you had a baby brother." Willie frowned.

"Sure do," the four-year-old answered.

"What's his name?" Willie.

"Goober."

"Idiot." Amy punched her brother in the side. "We ain't got no baby brother."

"I know," Joshua answered archly. "He just *died* o' the measles."

Sarie sighed. "Most o' the action round here takes place inside o' Joshie's little ole head."

"He won't use the outside privy anymore," Amy put in, sending her brother a superior little smirk. "Says a long, bony man lives deep down inside it. An' evertime he plunks his backside over the privy hole, that long, bony man reaches up . . . slowly, slowly rolls out his long bony finger . . . an' gives him a tickle on the behind."

Willie chortled.

"He does, too! He does, too!" Joshua shrieked at his sister's betrayal of his most intimate secret. Rising up combatively, he thwacked her on the top of the head with his spoon. Sarie got her arms around him, and separated her two scrappy youngsters before they could tussle each other to the floor.

"That's all right, Joshie," Coke said calmly. "If you think a long, bony man lives inside the privy, we'll take your word for it."

His righteous indignation sabotaged by having someone agree with him, Joshua directed it elsewhere. "Ma," he started off again. "I ain't a-gonna eat none o' them stinky peas you put on m'plate."

"What you mean you ain't too sure 'bout the whereabouts o' your kin?" Ma harked back to her unanswered question.

"Would you like t'see the ranch, Jessica?" Sarie quickly interjected. "Maybe Coke could take you on a horseback ride around it tomorrow."

"Yes," Jessica responded immediately. "I'd like that."

"So would I," Willie chimed in.

"Course, hon," Sarie said to the child. "We was plannin' on it." She directed her attention back to Jessica. "You ever ridden a horse before?"

"No," Jessica responded. "And it's time I learned."

"You city-made gals sure don't get much practical upbringin'," Ma observed, swabbing up her pea juice with a piece of biscuit.

"I reckon Jessie knows all she needs for makin' it just fine in the city," Coke said.

"Why you wanta know how t'handle a horse?" Ma asked slyly. "You fixin' on stayin' on in these parts?"

"Not really," Jessica replied. "I just think that when one visits other places, it's fun to do what the natives do."

"We ain't half-nekkid *natives*," Ma retorted. "We're proper brought-up Baptists."

"By the word *native*, I was hardly implying that you were savages," Jessica explained pleasantly. "I simply meant that when one visits a particular locale, it's worthwhile to try those activities indigenous to the area."

"We ain't indigent, neither," Ma said.

"I didn't say indigent," Jessica replied. "I said indigenous . . . whatever is common to an area. If it were the custom here to ride unicycles through the brush, I'd probably want to try that, too."

"That ain't bein' indigenous," Ma said. "That's monkey see, monkey do."

"Now, Ma," Coke said evenly. "We didn't bring Jessie out here just so's you could go leapin' an' pouncin' all over her words like a Eyetalian grape stomper."

"You a good cook?" Ma plowed incorrigibly on. "Coke always did like a well-set table."

Jessica grinned. "I'm an abominable cook. Simply abominable."

"Boy, that's the truth," Willie piped in. "The other morning Ma fried sausage for breakfast. It came out so black and shriveled lookin', Meg asked her where'd she hide the half-constipated sheep that had just staggered over our plates."

Jessica nodded proudly. "I detest cooking. I can't think of anything I detest more . . . except perhaps darning. If we weren't at the dinner table, I'd ask Willie to take off his shoes so you could see all the holes in his socks."

"Ma!" Willie protested. "I don't have any holes—" But his words were cut short by a sharp squeeze on the arm from his mother.

"You made Cindy Blankenship's weddin' dress, didn't you?" Sarie asked.

"Yes," Jessica replied. "Creating a dress can be a challenge . . . whereas a hole is, well, merely a hole."

"Cindy's dress was a mite short-waisted to my taste," Ma put in.

"That was the way she wanted it," Jessica said.

"Reckon so," Ma mused, "considerin' her condition an' all." She shook her head. "How these well brought up young gals from good families can get theirselves into such fixes, I'll never know."

"An' we ain't about t'tell you, neither," Coke drawled, carving off another slice of roast.

"No matter what her condition was," Sarie said, "Cindy was right purty in that dress you made for her, Jessica."

"She's purty, all right . . . now." Ma sent out a look that, bouncing off of Jessica, came to land meaningfully upon her son. "But give her a few years. These slender, purty, well put together young gals you find are always temptin'-lookin' . . . when they're young. But give 'em a few years. Wait till they've seen the backside o' thirty, had a few babes, an' they all start t'goin' t'seed . . . spreadin' out like bloated jellyfishes."

"That's right, Coke," Jessica said silkily. "When you men marry, you should choose only fat, sloppy women to be your brides. That way, they won't have so far downhill to go."

"Did you bring any ridin' clothes?" Sarie intervened.

"I got a riding skirt from the store," Jessica replied. "But I didn't find any ladies' boots. For some reason, Meg had very few in stock."

"That's probably because they ain't much in demand," Sarie explained. "The gals round here tend t'throw a leg over a horse an' gallop off without givin' it much thought aforehand. I do have a ole pair o' boots round here, though. You're welcome t'use 'em."

"Thanks. I'd appreciate that."

"What you mean you ain't got kin you know of?" Ma thrust in for the third time.

"That ain't none of our business," Coke said.

"You got a one-track mind, Ma," Sarie uttered.

"Oh, that's all right," Jessica responded in an artificially light tone. "It's nothing I'm ashamed of. And since your mother is so . . . curious, I'll tell her." She fixed her eyes levelly on Ma. "The reason I'm uncertain as to the whereabouts of my relations, Mrs. Sanders, is that when I was five years old, my mother and newborn brother died in childbirth. My family were new arrivals in California at that time. We had no other family there. And my father, feeling that I was too much of a burden to him, handed me over to the sisters of Holy Mary, Mother of Perpetual Help Refuge for Foundling Girls in San Francisco."

"Somewhere in that long name it sounded like an orphanage," Coke said quietly.

"Well, I suppose it was. Some of the children there were orphans. But there were many others like me who probably did have relatives somewhere . . . only, these relatives apparently didn't think these particular children worthy of the inconvenience of looking after them.''

Coke noticed that although her voice was still casual in tone, a tremor had appeared in her hands. And catching him looking at them, she quickly dropped them to her lap.

"Did he ever come back for you, your pa?" Sarie asked, her dark eyes softening.

"No, he never did," she said in a tone of voice so weightless that it seemed to hang in the air.

"Did you hear from him?" Coke.

"There were a few letters early on. He sent me a doll from Nicaragua for my tenth birthday . . . but after that I never heard from him again." She grew distant, reflective. Then, with a flicker of the eye, she seemed to become conscious again of their presence. "He did the right thing, my father," she said almost defiantly. "Yes he did. He did the right thing. Perhaps Holy Mary's wasn't a real home, but my needs were well looked after, and the sisters, though very strict, did give me an excellent education."

"Catholic education," Ma amended.

"Well, yes, I'm a Catholic . . . naturally."

Ma stuffed a forkful of mashed potatoes into her mouth. "A adulatress," she posited muffledly through the potatoes.

Jessica stiffened. "How dare you!" she breathed. "How dare you say that because I'm a Catholic, I'd make an unfaithful wife."

Ma's jaw froze in midchew, the wad of mashed potatoes making a crepey pouch of one wrinkled cheek. She gazed, beetle-browed, over the rims of her spectacles at Jessica, then cautiously moved her eyes to Sarie, who looked on the verge of throttling her. Her gaze finally settled on Coke. By the look in his eye, she deduced that she may have gone just a mite too far this time. She chewed twice more on the potatoes, then, stretching her neck, swallowed them in one eye-watering lump. She took a gulp of water, then thoughtfully set the glass down. "That was a strange sorta answer, child," she said. " 'Twasn't the sorta answer I was expectin' a-tall."

"Mebbe you better explain what *you* said, Ma," Coke muttered, "afore you start expectin' Jessie to explain her answer to it."

"Well, you Catholics do pray to them statues, don't you?" Ma asked carefully.

"Occasionally," Jessica responded tightly. "As symbols of the ones to whom we really do pray."

"By them 'ones' you mean saints, right?"

"Yes, sometimes we pray to saints."

"Don't you know, dearie," Ma pushed on with growing conviction, "that prayin' t'saints or the statues of 'em instead o' prayin' direct to the One True Lord God Almighty an' His Son, Jesus Christ, is flat-out the worshipin' o' graven images?"

Jessica stared at Ma a moment, then comprehension swept over her. "Oh, I see," she exclaimed. "You called me an idolatress . . . not an adultress. That's better."

"It is?" Ma frowned.

"Ma," Coke said in a low, restrained voice. "Whichever way Jessie feels like prayin' is her own dad-blamed business. So you might as well quit now . . . whilst you ain't runnin' too far behind."

Ma eyed her son, and fell silent. And she kept her opinions muzzled throughout the remainder of the evening.

Chapter 14

A FAMILIAR RING of lighthearted laughter chimed through the open window. Jessica groped for her blankets and pulled them over her head. The lighthearted laugh jingled again. Resignedly flipping the blankets off her face, she lay blinking at the window curtains, undulating gently in the morning breeze. She rolled onto her back, and with a groan, arched into a stretch that rippled deliciously up her body from toe to fingertip. She sank back, arms circling her head, luxuriating in the feel of the cool morning air mingling with the cozy warmth of her bedclothes.

Again the familiar breathless giggle bubbled up outside. And with it, she heard the chaotic flappings and squawkings of panicky chickens and a strange scuffly clip-clopping sound. Vaguely puzzling as to how her son's feet or those of a chicken could make such a sound, Jessica got out of bed. Parting the curtains at the window, she looked down on the yard below. She saw nothing unusual, though she still heard the perplexing sounds a little off to the side. Leaning out the window, she caught sight of Willie's heels disappearing around the far corner of the chicken coop. Moments later three chickens came exploding out the other end as if fired from a blunderbuss, followed by a stampeding nanny goat, and finally her son, barreling pell-mell after them.

"Willie!" she rasped.

The child and the goat slid to a stop and gaped at her.

Frowning severely, she put her finger to her lips. "Shshsh!"

Willie and the goat both looked downward. They seemed to consider a moment; then the goat's tail gave a little wag and they both shot off in concert, clattering around the corner of the house.

She opened her mouth to let out a yell, then stopped herself. The sky still held a dingy residue of the night. It must be very early. Muttering, she hurried to the wardrobe and flung open the door. Kneeling down, she unearthed the alarm clock she'd buried under a pile of blankets and doilies the night before, when its clackety ticking had kept breaking into her dreams.

Six twenty-five. Drat it. Her son would awaken the entire household.

She flew into action, untying the ribbons of her nightgown and shrugging it to the floor. Before fifteen minutes had elapsed, she'd splashed water on her face, cleaned her teeth, dressed, made the bed, and vigorously brushed the tangles out of her hair and pinned it into a tight coil at the nape of her neck. Throwing the bedroom door open, she tore down the hallway and took the stairs two at a time. As she dashed through the dining room for the front door, she stopped dead.

Ma Sanders was rocking placidly in the parlor, Amy kneeling on the floor before her, yarn looped over her extended hands. Ma, in rhythm to her rocking, was flipping the yarn off and wrapping it into a ball. The two looked like they'd been there for hours.

"Law, girl!" Ma sniffed. "We was beginnin' t'think you'd died up there."

"We've already had our breakfast," Amy put in primly. "And Willie, Joshie, and me got back from our horseback ride near a half hour ago."

"Why, it isn't even seven o'clock yet," Jessica panted. "What time do you people get up around here?"

"With the roosters," Ma replied. "Four A.M."

"Four A.M.!" Jessica exclaimed. "Why, that's almost ungodly!"

"Snorin' away the coolest part o' the day is what's ungodly," Ma retorted.

The door to the kitchen opened and Sarie poked her head in. "Mornin', Jessica." She smiled. "I was just now dustin' off my ridin' boots for you. Come on in, have some breakfast, an' try 'em on."

With relief, Jessica ducked away from the prima donna of the parlor and escaped into the kitchen.

"Goodness," she breathed, taking the chair Sarie offered her at the table. "Is your mother always this crabby?"

"It's Ma's nature t'be cantankerous," Sarie explained, handing Jessica the boots. "Don't let it get to you. If it wasn't for that mean streak she's got, she'd o' probably spent these last twenty years six feet under pushin' daisies. Want me t'fry you up some eggs? We got steak, beans, an' grits here on the stove an' biscuits keepin' warm in the oven."

"Just coffee and biscuits, please," Jessica replied, bending over to unbutton her shoes. Lifting her face, she looked wryly up at Sarie over the table. "Must be getting near your lunch hour by now."

"No, we eat lunch at twelve," Sarie answered seriously.

"How do you survive such a long time between breakfast and lunch?"

"We eat like pregnant sows at breakfast, then like pregnant sows at lunch," Sarie said, setting an empty coffee mug and a plate of hot biscuits on the table before Jessica. "Breakfast and lunch are our two biggest meals o' the day."

Jessica slid the boots on. Her feet hit bottom without touching the sides.

"How they fit?" Sarie asked as, using her apron as a hot pad, she picked up the coffeepot from the stove.

Pulling her skirt up, Jessica stuck her legs out. They looked like two sticks poking out of a pair of butter churns. Sarie's boots were way too big, but women resented having to hear how much bigger they were than other women. And besides, only boots would look appropriate with the new riding skirt she'd gotten at the emporium. "Uh, they'll do just fine," she said, dropping her feet to the floor and letting her skirt fall over them.

Sarie poured coffee into Jessica's cup. Jessica glanced at the liquid; then her eyes locked on it, for she couldn't detect the slightest glint of light through the solid black stream. She stared down into her cup, then cautiously picked it up and took a sip.

"My taste buds just rolled over and died," she gasped. "Sara, you do brew your coffee mighty strong, don't you?"

Grinning, Sarie sat down in the chair across from her. "When a body crawls outa bed at four in the mornin', it needs a good, swift kick in the pants t'get it goin'."

Heaping butter on her biscuit to counteract the acrid aftereffect of the coffee, Jessica glanced out the window. "Where's Coke? Will he be the one who'll take me horseback riding or is he too busy?" She asked the question matter-of-factly, though she knew that if he didn't consider her important enough to drop his work for, that would be the end of him as far as she was concerned.

"Oh, no, Coke'll take you out. He was here waitin' for you. An' when Willie dashed in a little while ago an' said he'd seen you up at your window, he went on out t'get your horse ready."

Now that everything was set as she'd wanted it to be, Jessica felt a flutter of apprehension. Alone . . . out there . . . with Coke?

"Why don't you go with us, Sara?" she asked hopefully.

Sarie shook her head. "I best be stayin' on here an' gettin' to my chores." She seemed to sense Jessica's unease. "Don't you worry, now, hear? Windy, the horse you'll be ridin', is a great grandma, the oldest, gentlest horse on the place."

The kitchen door banged open and Willie burst into the room. "Ma!" he scolded. "Coke's got your horse all saddled and he's out there waiting for you. And here you sit yapping."

Holding her hand up for silence, Jessica quickly dumped three spoonfuls of sugar into her coffee, stirred in enough cream to raise its level to the brim of the cup, and gulped it all down.

"Tell Mr. Sanders, Willie, that I'm going to my room to get my hat and put on my riding skirt and I'll be out shortly."

She walked, clomping, into the parlor, Sarie's oversized boots hitting the floor ahead of her feet. She shifted her weight forward onto the balls of her feet to prevent that from happening. Swaying a bit, she smiled woodenly down at Ma as, shoes in hand, she shuffled by.

She'd almost reached the parlor door when she heard Ma's sugarcoated voice behind her. "Be careful, child. Don't let your horse step in no holes. That's how Coke's pa broke his back an' died.''

"Oh, Ma!" Sarie breathed. "Pa was gallopin' full speed down a hill in the dead o' night when his horse stepped into that hole."

"That's right," Ma went on sweetly. "So don't you go gallop-in' 'bout in the dead o' night, neither.''

"Only if I'm on foot," Jessica called back equally sweetly as she slogged up the stairs.

🌸 Chapter 15

COKE WAITED AT the corral by the two mounts. The door of the house opened. Jessica emerged, and descended the porch steps ponderously. Gathering up her skirt, she primly picked her way across the dung-studded yard, her downturned face hidden under the slant of her straw washday hat. There was an odd skating motion in her steps, Coke noticed, and he wondered if she had a crick in the back.

"They're so much bigger close up," she said, gingerly skirting around a huge, moist, fly-dotted glob of feces freshly deposited by one of the mounts.

"Beg pardon? What's bigger?"

She lifted her face and looked at him. "Horses."

"Oh. Never thought of it."

She solemnly contemplated first one mount and then the other, their twitchy, fly-flicking buttocks rounding up above her head. "Which do I ride?"

"Windy here." He gave the animal a pat. It flopped its head around and snorted.

She recoiled slightly. "Does it bite?"

"Only if you got your back turned."

Digesting that bit of information, she warily eyed the mare's long, muscles hind legs. "Does it kick?"

"Not ole Windy. Take too much gumption."

She eyed the horse a moment longer, then pulled herself erect.

"Well, shall we be off?" she asked brightly as with trembly fingers she pulled on the riding gloves Sarie had handed her as she'd gone out the door. Like the boots, the gloves were too big, their fingertips flaps of deflated leather.

Taking her elbow, Coke led her to Windy's left side, the clean scent of lavender filling his nostrils and pleasing him; she'd put it on for him.

Windy's head was still turned in profile. Its rolling black eye seemed to be sizing Jessica up. Absorbed in the look of that eye and not liking it a bit, she drifted a hand upward to the saddle horn, level with her hat, and absently lifted her right leg.

"T'other leg," Coke said.

She lowered the right foot and raised the left. Looking down, she saw that a huge gulf separated her upraised foot from the stirrup, which hung about even with her stomach. She lowered her left foot the the ground and looked soberly at Coke.

"Do you have a shorter horse?"

"Yup, but none of 'em is near as easygoin' as ole Windy here. Just take hold o' the saddle horn an' give a little bounce. I'll tote you the rest o' the way."

She did as he said, grasping the saddle horn firmly in both hands. Coke stood behind her, his hands on her waist.

Feeling foolish, she gave a halfhearted little jump. Her weight caught in Coke's grip and she felt herself rising. Pulling up on the saddle horn, she tried to aim her foot into the stirrup. But only her toe was pointing inside the roomy boot, and the boot stayed stuck at a clumsy right angle to the stirrup. Letting go with one hand, she tried to force the boot into the stirrup. Then she realized that she'd slid in Coke's grip so that he was now clasping her around the ribs, just beneath her breasts. Alarmed, she let go of the saddle horn and found herself floundering in midair, hands grappling out and making feeble crawling motions up the side of the horse. She felt as helpless as a capsized turtle, and about as graceful. Still Coke didn't put her down. With a bounce, he shifted her up against his shoulder, his arm going around her waist, his free hand groping down her calf. She flung her arms around his head. Grasping her boot at the heel, he blindly wrestled it into the stirrup, then peeled her arm off his face and directed it to the saddle horn. Giving her a push on the backside, he boosted her on up.

"Whew!" he breathed, bending down to pick up his hat off the ground. "That was harder'n steer wrestlin'." His eyes danced mischievously. "Though I gotta admit, a sight more pleasurable."

Feeling herself blush all the way to the roots of her hair, she glowered at him. The sneaky devil. She winced, and a thump sounded on the other side of the horse. Glancing under Windy, he looked at the boot lying on its side in the dust. Maintaining a poker face, he strolled around the horse and looked at her stockinged foot. The toes curled chastely inward.

She gazed glassily down at him from atop the horse, then with some effort, unrolled her foot and pointed it at him. "Do you mind?"

He retrieved the boot. "Mebbe you better change back to your regular shoes," he said, shaking the dust off of it.

"Aren't boots designed to keep one's feet from sliding out of the stirrups?"

"Partly. But what's t'keep your feet from slidin' outa the boots?"

She thought that over. "Well," she answered tartly. "I'll just keep my feet pressed on the floors of them, that's what."

He regarded her skeptically.

"There's no way that you're going to get me down off of this horse . . . after all the trouble it took crawling up it!" she declared. She paused. "Besides, if I changed to my walking shoes, I'd look ridiculous . . . uncoordinated."

"Uncoordinated?"

"Yes. High-button shoes and a riding skirt don't go together at all."

"Well," he said, sliding the boot on her foot and fitting it into the stirrup, "I sure wouldn't wanta get caught offendin' your sense o' style."

He untied Windy's reins, lifted them over the mare's head, tied them together again, and put them into Jessica's hands.

"Now, this is your right hand," he patiently explained, giving it a pat. "An' this is your left. When you wanta go right, pull back with this hand here"; he gave it a pat. "An' when you wanta go left, pull back with this-un here"; pat.

Her breathing growing audible, her eyes sizzled at him. "Now, when you wanta stop," he drawled comically on, "pull back with this hand here an' this hand here"; pat . . . pat. ". . . both at the

same time, though. An' whilst you're about it, call out 'Whoa!'
. . . kinda loud-like.''

"I know that!" she rasped.

His eyes twinkled at her. "Just double-checkin'."

He pulled his mount's reins off the fence rail and swung into
the saddle. Windy jerked around and flung her head over the neck
of Coke's horse.

"Family affection," he explained as they sat knee to knee, at
right angles to each other. "Sin Cerebro, my horse, is Windy's
young-un."

Turning Sin Cerebro, he headed for the gate. Windy pranced
merrily after.

"Coke!" Jessica squeaked, clinging to the saddle horn, her
backside flumping crudely all over the saddle. "Slow down . . .
stop . . . whoa . . . please."

He turned aside, feasting on the luscious bounce-jiggle of that
perfect little body. He'd managed to get ahold of it once so far.

"Relax, Jessie," he said when she reached him. "Go with the
movement of your horse. Press your feet down flat in the stirrups
like you said you would. An' I know, as a rule, you ain't normally
told this," he finished with mock solemnity, "but try an' pull
your knees together."

"I'll try," she said schoolgirlishly. "But, Coke, please go
slowly until I get used to this . . . this thing."

"All right," he said. "Slow an' steady it is."

He directed Sin Cerebro down the trail; Windy followed oblig-
ingly after. It was too early in the day for Sin Cerebro to be held
in. Head tossing, he fought the bit, breaking into cantering bursts
and sparking Windy into the same little spurts of speed; Jessica
thought her heart might stop. After a time Sin Cerebro calmed,
and soon the two horses were sashaying side by side down the
trail, hips swinging to and fro like a pair of Kansas City fancy
gals.

Jessica began to relax. Inhaling the morning, she allowed herself to take in the countryside. She glanced at Coke and found
him watching her. Her face smoothed into an easy smile.

"What was that you called your horse?" she asked pleasantly.

"Sin Cerebro."

"What a lovely-sounding name. Almost musical. What does it
mean?"

"Brainless."

"Brainless! Why would you call your own horse 'brainless'?"

" 'Cause that's what he is. Years ago when my remudero tried t'train him, he wouldn't take t'cuttin', wouldn't take t'ropin' or herdin' or brushpoppin' or anythin' else worthwhile, either. So one day, Tomás, he's my remudero, points him out t'me an says . . . only in Spanish o' course, 'That has gotta be the dumbest critter I've ever tried my hands on. All he's good for is comin' an' goin' an' naught much else.'

"That's all I need a horse for most o' the time, anyway. So I took him over."

"Do you always give your horses such descriptive names?"

"On occasion."

"Hmmm. You called my horse 'Windy.' Is that because she used to run like the wind in her younger days?"

"Uh . . . no," Coke replied, a trifle uneasily.

"Oh, then is it because she gets winded easily?"

Coke shifted uncomfortably. "Beg pardon?"

"She gets short of breath easily. Is that why you named her Windy?"

"Uh . . . no."

At that moment Jessica noticed a stiffening in Windy's gait. Her step growing lopsided, the mare shuffled to the side of the path and stopped. Jessica's eyes widened, for the mare's sides seemed to be ballooning between her legs. Windy lowered her head, an odd pumping motion starting up in her body that, accelerating, grew more pronounced until Jessica felt like she was rocking back and forth in a water trough in a rudderless boat. Then with a cockeyed lurch of the tail, Windy pumped out a huge, rolling fart. Tail askew, body still pumping faintly, Windy slouched forward a couple steps and let loose a second terse fart like the period at the end of a sentence, then offhandedly took a nibble at a nearby tuft of grass as though no one could possibly accuse an innocent little darling like her of such a gross social impropriety.

"Sorry 'bout that," Coke said. "She burps like that, too. Guess that's why Windy's so easygoin'. All her unruliness takes place inside."

"No need to explain," Jessica muttered, her cheeks reddening for the second time that day. "I walked into that one."

They ambled to the top of the nearby hill. The horizon seemed to back up a hundred miles, expanding out and out into the distance until it fuzzed into the sky. They rode on, the trail curving and disintegrating into the stunted chaparral, absorbing them into the rugged countryside. The crisp scuffling sound of the dry brush in the wind and the stutter of insects had a crystalline, sterile quality that seemed otherworldly. To Jessica's right, an armadillo issued from a thicket and meandered toward the sun, trawling its elongated shadow behind.

"All this," Coke said, "far as your eye can see, belongs to me."

"It's . . . so desolate," she uttered.

"I reckon I got me the biggest piece o' privately owned desolation a body can find most anywhere," he replied. "Special made, this ragtag corner o' the world is, Jessie, special made it is, for the Lord's most ragtag, cantankerous critters . . . scorpions, buzzards, rattlers, tarantulas, jabalinas, coyotes . . . an' crusty ole polecats like me. For every five pounds o' sweat a body pours into it, he gets nary a pound in return, but that's still makin' headway. Homely an' troublesome though this piece o' earth is, though, it's still mine. An' I never feel all the way right with the world till I'm on it."

A chill grazed Jessica's flesh as if a ghost had brushed against her. Her husband, William, had once spoken of the sea like that. A vague melancholy stirred inside her, and an antagonism, too, toward Coke and this land.

"When I lived in San Francisco," she mused, "I had a similar feeling toward the ocean."

"Seein' as how you liked the ocean so much, did you ever take t'swimmin'?"

"And have a shark sink its teeth in my backside? Heavens no." She paused, focusing her eyes on his. "I may get romantic and sentimental about certain nonhuman things, Coke . . . but only up to a point."

Feeling vaguely stung as though a rebuke had been hidden somewhere in those last words, he studied her. Sometimes she seemed to speak on more than one level at once, like a simple, single-finger melody on a piano, transforming into a ten-finger organ chord with deep and disparate resonances and colorations.

"Why'd you come to Dispenseme?" he asked abruptly.

"Meg."

"Meg?"

"I've never known anyone like her. Being near her is nourishment for my soul."

"How do you mean?"

"When I was a child living in the Home, each year at Christmas the ladies of society gave us children a party. There they sat in their finery along one wall, apart from us, as we cast-off girls squealed and exclaimed over their children's or grandchildren's cast-off toys and clothes.

"Then, their annual ritual played through, they'd gather up their furs and glide out the door like Spanish galleons, happily freed till next year of an obligation. One that helped them maintain their social standing and their belief in their own benevolence.

"Benevolence. They had no idea what that meant. Oh, they gave—and left their beneficiaries feeling even more bereft. Now, dear Meg may not have a single material thing to give you, but she always leaves you feeling better about yourself."

"Yup," Coke agreed. "Somewhere back there, Meg plumb forgot t'stop likin' people." Patting Sin Cerebro, he fixed his dark eyes on her. "But I got a strong hunch that Meg ain't the only reason you showed up in these parts."

"I wanted to see more of our country," she said impassively.

"I can see you stoppin' off in Colorado t'take a gander at Pike's Peak. I can see you stoppin' off in Arizona for a eyeful o' that mighty big canyon they got over there. I can see you pausin' in Wyomin' for a look-see at them overheated water holes." He paused. "But I sure cain't see you droppin' by South Texas for a look-see at Dispenseme."

"Are you implying that I'm a liar?"

"There be times, I think, when you ain't too partial to over-workin' the truth."

She leaned toward him, her voice dropping conspiratorially. "Do you want the real reason why I came here?"

"Yep."

"My intentions are entirely honorable, you know. You see, I came to Dispenseme to catch me a rich landowner for a husband, and have the unsurpassed joy of spending, spending, spending him to the poorhouse."

"Whooeee!" he exclaimed lightly. "You sure do know how t'hit a hombre where it hurts."

"Don't worry." She smiled. "Staying poor and unmarried is still preferable, to my mind, to blindly anchoring myself to some man, and thereafter, whatever he became, I must become, too."

"Hold on there. Gettin' hitched doesn't hafta be done blind."

"Love is blind."

"Love is seein' durn clear an' bein' willin' to accept an' understand what you see."

"That's what I'd expect you to say," she replied, "because that's how a man defines how a *woman's* love should be—the same definition doesn't necessarily apply to him. To truly love, to be tolerant and forgiving, to give in to love, to make sacrifices and concessions to it, in a man's mind, is to be weak, like a woman. Neglecting wife and children, pickling his brains with liquor, stepping out with the dance hall girl, gambling his home away . . . those are his proper pursuits. And a man, if he's to be a real man, must cleave to every last one of those God-given male prerogatives. And this being a man's natural way of loving, his woman, if she's worth her salt, accepts and understands. Such a love I can live without, thank you very much."

"I don't know who you're talkin' 'bout, Jessie," Coke said quietly. "But it sure as hell ain't me."

"Let's ride faster," she said suddenly. "I think I can hold on better now." And to herself, a fervent prayer. "Oh, Lord, keep me on this dratted horse."

Coke pulled Sin Cerebro around, and with a nudge, let him break into an easy canter. Windy loped after. The horses' ears lay back, their manes lifting and dropping to the rhythm of their hooves. With each upward bounce, the breath caught in Jessica's throat, out of fear that she might not hit the saddle on target coming down. Still, with the wind in her face, it was exhilarating.

Coke eased Sin Cerebro down. Windy wheezingly dropped back to her lazy-going stroll.

"Where are your cows?" Jessica asked. "All the animals I've seen so far have been lizards and an armadillo."

"They're in other parts o' the ranch that ain't been grazed so threadbare," Coke said, turning Sin Cerebro up the slow incline of a sheepback hill that, curving, arched to a cliff in the distance.

"How many cows do you have?"

"Nine thousand, give or take a few hundred."

The bookkeeper in Jessica was offended. "You mean you don't keep an exact count of your own livestock?"

"Cows ain't chamber pots stacked up in a store. They have a kinda peculiar habit o' producin' more o' theirselves or keelin' over an' dyin'." He paused, a melancholy note coming to his voice. "With this dry-up, a helluvalot more is a-droppin' than a-croppin' up."

"Do you expect to lose many?"

"If this drought holds out two, three more months an' we don't find new water, we stand t'lose another thousand, fifteen hundred, head easy."

"How desperate this battle for survival must be."

"Right now, it's a full-scale war."

"Could it ruin you?"

"Nope. Bank don't own me like it owns a lotta ranchers. I lose my beef, I still got my land. Ain't never gonna let loose o' that. Folks keep on pressin' up against the open spaces like they been doin', it's gonna be valuable someday." He squinted at her. "I figger t'get myself hitched one o' these days. Have me eight, ten young-uns. If they ain't too stupid, got a little gumption, it'll set 'em up for life."

She eyed him askant, the dimple starting to play at the corner of her mouth. "It's so refreshing to meet a man with honorable intentions," she purred. "Have you chosen your victim yet?"

"My what?"

"Your victim . . . the fine lady who'll be providing you with that litter of heirs. You know, the one who'll be spending a dozen years waddling around all puffed out like an inflated Scottish bagpipe."

Coke reached for his Winchester.

"Don't shoot!" she squeaked, ducking down.

But he aimed well in front of her at a scrawny, dirt-colored animal that, with tail between its legs, was skittering diagonally down the slope. He squeezed the trigger. The gun jumped. The animal yelped, dropped, scrambled back up and, running on three legs, scuttled behind a hummock, the sparse grass poking out along its rim looking like the three-day-old growth on an old man's chin.

"Damn," he muttered, lowering the Winchester. Dropping it back in its boot, he looked at Jessica, who was still hunched down in saucer-eyed mortification. "Don't worry, Jessie," he deadpanned. "You're safe. Hell, I ain't shot a lady outa the saddle for near on—" he paused, calculating to himself "—sixty-two days now."

"Well! Well!" she spluttered, coming up. "Why would you do a thing like that?"

"Takin' potshots at coyote comes as natural as breathin' t'me," he said, nudging Sin Cerebro on.

"Why would you want to murder those poor creatures?"

"Well, they have this kinda annoyin' habit," he replied. "They like their beef same as we folks do. Trouble is, they don't pay for theirs. So if it's a choice betwixt a few dozen dead coyote an' ten, twenty thousand dollars worth o' beef on the hoof, I'm a-feared it's the coyote that's gonna lose."

They continued plodding up the hill, the surrounding country-side sinking around them.

"So you think a gal hitched t'me would be a victim," he said.

"Ten children?" She shook her head. "Easier said than done."

"Even if the lady had help?"

The dimple blinked. "Help at what?"

"Cookin', cleanin', chasin'."

"I can just picture all those hundred sticky little fingers gum-ming up your mother's doilies."

"I can see your point," he reflected. "Ten young-uns could get t'be a mite disruptive. Five'd be better."

"Five . . . ten . . . fifteen . . . twenty." She shrugged. "Have as many as you want."

He regarded her good-naturedly. "You're purty durn independent, ain't you?"

"Challenging, is it?"

They reached the top of the bluff. The wind breaking over it surged through their clothing. The brittle grass sprinkling the cracked ground leaned stiffly over. It would break before it would bend. Coke climbed out of the saddle and came around to help her down.

"Let's rest the horses."

Her eyes had grown guarded. "They don't seem tired to me."

"It's a good place t'stop."

Moistening her lips, she squinted up at the sun-dazzled sky, then turned her eyes down on him, regarding him with about the same kind of wariness with which she'd first regarded Windy that morning.

"Better watch out," he drawled. "I might bite your ear."

A smile flickered up. "Maybe you're the one who'd better watch out."

It was pleasant where they stood, in front of a large boulder set a few feet back from the cliff face. The canyon, splotched with clumps of brush and marked by an occasional gully wrinkle and wimple, flowed gracefully out before them. Far in the distance, cattle were grazing, tiny warped ovals, inching like roly-poly bugs toward the cliffs to the east.

✿ Chapter 16

THE ALTITUDE LENT a feeling of pleasant estrangement from the world below. The wind veering up the cliff steadily cooled them while the boulder at their backs cast a shadow over them and served as a buffer against the crosscurrents lashing over the hill from behind.

Jessica sat back against the boulder. Though her attitude was relaxed, she was not. She was intently aware of Coke, the nearness of his body, his breathing, his subtlest gesture. She was as keenly aware of herself, the unevenness of the ground beneath her, the roughness of the boulder through the thin fabric at the back of her blouse, the touch of her clothing on her body; her skin was sensitive almost to the point of soreness. She wished this hypersensitivity would leave her, kindled as she knew it was by the magnetic tension simmering between them. And yet it felt too good and she was greedy. She feared his touch, though, and would have recoiled from it. She distrusted her own instincts as deeply as she distrusted him.

Watching him, she wondered if he was as much at ease as he looked sitting there less than a foot away, leaning loosely forward flipping pebbles over the edge of the cliff. He remained so for some time, as if, adrift on surface silence, he was sounding out the depths below for some deep undercurrent by which to set his course.

At last he settled back against the boulder and looked at her. She held his gaze and they both seemed to be searching out through the eyes of the other the key to a riddle.

"You musta had one hell of a miserable marriage," he said.

The sudden bluntness of his remark took her by surprise. "Why?" she stammered. "Why would you say that?"

"Though I ain't denyin' it's a part o' your charm, you seem a mite like a festerin' sore."

"That's not very complimentary."

"Didn't say you looked like one . . . only that there be times when you act like one. Seems t'me if you'd had a good marriage, you wouldn't be so spiky at the edges now. What happen? Your late husband let you down?"

"Coke, I'm not going to glorify my husband's memory, deifying him like a proper widow."

"Nope."

"I don't wear hypocrisy well. You said that I'm on the prickly side. Well, if it weren't for the trust in my little boy's eyes, I'd have no doubt turned out harder than this boulder here, inside and out."

"What'd your husband do t'you?"

"In a marriage it may not necessarily be what you do or what the other person does, but how the two of you come to work on one another, poison one another."

"Were you still livin' at that Home when you met him?"

"No. When I was seventeen Holy Mary's placed me in a small dressmaker's shop in the city to work as an apprentice. The proprietress of the shop, Miss Hanover, was a good Catholic, getting on in years and in need of an extra pair of hands.

"From the sisters' point of view it must have seemed the perfect place for me to be. There were only the two of us in the shop. Miss Hanover was straitlaced to the point of prudery, so she'd certainly have a proper influence on a young woman just out in the world. And in the business we dealt almost exclusively with women."

"Bet you still had a lotta fellas comin' round."

"A few. But I didn't like them."

"I'd a-thought you'd a-been rarin' t'go."

"Not really. During those first months out of the Home, everyone seemed strange to me. It seemed that everyone was playing some game I didn't know the rules to."

"Why'd you feel that way, Jessie?"

"I guess being brought up in a place like Holy Mary's, a refuge that protected, yet confined you, one emerges with a kind of distorted view of the world—and sensing it, too.

"So once I got out, I locked myself into a routine. Busy all day long even when I didn't have to be. I moved through the world with the stone walls of Holy Mary's still around me."

"Seems that woulda gotten old fast."

"Yes. Slowly I started finding a few people, mostly elderly ones, whom I could greet without feeling threatened. I discovered the lending library . . . novels. During the day I'd meet with the customers, take measurements, stitch beading, keep the account books straight for Miss Hanover, then at night I'd escape to my quarters in the loft overhead and pore over those novels.

"But after a while, books and dreams were no longer enough. Somewhere out there, people were laughing, having a good time, living. And I was too much of a coward to break out and join them."

Running pebbles back and forth in her hands, she looked at Coke. "It was at about that time that I met William. He walked into the shop one morning with a lady who'd come to fetch a gown I'd made. The woman had quite a reputation. She sang in one of the dance halls on the Barbary Coast. I'd always been a little in awe of her, secretly envied her. But the man who was with her that day made me really envy her."

Jessica smiled sadly. "Oh, my William looked so handsome that morning, dressed all in black, captain's hat atilt on his head, devil-may-care gleam in his eye. It was like he'd stepped out of the novels I'd read.

"As his lady and Miss Hanover talked about accessories, I was as conscious of their voices as the hum of street sounds outside. I was conscious only of William. And whenever he'd steal a look my way . . . and he did a lot that afternoon, I blushed all the way to the soles of my feet. Words stuck in my throat, and whenever I pried any loose, they tumbled out all wrong. If my legs had been set back about a foot behind my body, I do believe I'd have kicked myself blue that afternoon. And when William and his lady left, he paid for everything, the gown, the accessories . . . which filled me with all kinds of spicy speculation."

"I reckon you ran into him purty fast after that."

"Two days later. I came upon him standing in the street gazing in a nearby shop window. I knew, just knew, that he was waiting there for me.

"He greeted me by name. I was thrilled. He took my marketing basket and asked me to join him for a cup of coffee and a croissant at the corner stand across the street.

"I couldn't refuse. I knew that I'd hate myself if I did.

"He was waiting for me every morning after that. He flattered me, told me how lovely I was. . . ." She smiled ruefully. "And I believed every word he said. I blossomed in his presence. And soon my life revolved around our morning meetings. And each hour that I was away from him, I daydreamed over every gesture that had passed between us.

"William's father had abandoned the family, in New Orleans, when he was a small child. At fourteen, William himself ran away and went to sea. We were alike that way—had no sentimental ties to family. At the time, I thought that a positive sign."

Sighing, she gazed up at the sky. "Later I realized what a fool I'd been. William had been playing a game with me, a game that he was a master at, a game that he'd played many times before." She paused. "I don't think William liked women very much."

"Why, Jessie?"

"Well, somehow he'd come to believe that the female sex were emotional deceivers, schemers, and manipulators. And that attitude later marked our marriage."

"How do you mean?"

"William could never accept any of my expressions of love or concern as being sincere. To him they were the devices that women use to lay guilt, get a tight hold on a man, and manipulate him out of his freedom."

She paused, soberly tossing the stones one by one over the cliff. "It wasn't that I hadn't been warned about William. I had. When Miss Hanover found out that I was meeting William, she tried to warn me.

" 'Don't get mixed up with the likes of him,' Miss Hanover would tell me. 'He's much too worldly for a child like you. Has a reputation as a drinker, a gambler, a womanizer. Done some smuggling, too, I've heard.'

"And I'd think, what does this old prude know of life . . . sealed up here in this dark shop, hiding behind her bolts of muslin and linen? Her feelings probably moldered to dust twenty years ago along with her youth.

"Miss Hanover's disapproval made William seem even more intriguing. And I was flattered that an adventurer like him had found anything appealing in bookish, timid me.

"Then one morning William wasn't there at our place to meet me. I thought, I should have expected this. He can have all those experienced, sophisticated women. Why would he want me?

"But that night, after Miss Hanover had gone home, William came. I felt life come singing back to me. I was thrilled. Up until that time, I'd always shied away from his offer to take me around at night. But that night I did go. At first I went mainly because I didn't want to lose him, but soon I went because I was attracted to the kind of world that he took me into, a world that I'd always wondered about. And I thought William sophisticated when he drank his liquor, and daring when he risked large sums of money at the gaming tables. And I thought myself sophisticated and daring being with him.

"Then one night, William said he loved me. I'd never known such bliss. At the Home we'd spoken of love in an abstract way . . . the love of mankind, that sort of thing. Never before in my life had anyone expressed love to me in a personal way. And I was naive enough to believe it and accept it as eternal truth.

"It didn't take long for word to get back to Miss Hanover that I was going around with William at night. She took me back to Holy Mary's, and Mother Superior lectured me on the evils of the world and how they can imperil a young woman's soul.

"I enjoyed it all immensely. Just because they were frightened by all that was alive in the world, why should I be? Why should I care what God's opinion of me was? It was William who loved me, and William was all-wise and all-knowing. I had gone beyond their stale, recited arguments . . . or so I thought." She fell silent, reflecting. "But perhaps I hadn't gone far enough."

"What do you mean?"

"Well, three days later, shortly before he was to leave on another voyage, William asked me to marry him. And I leaped at the chance. It was too deeply ingrained in me that marriage was the only avenue by which indecent passion can be made decent. I'd known William less than two months when we married."

Gazing off into the distance, she absently fingered the wisps of hair floating over her temple. "Over the years I've often wondered why William decided to marry me. I suppose, being over the age of thirty, he just decided that the time had come to have a proper wife and a proper home."

"Coulda been, Jessie, that he didn't want them things till he met you."

She shrugged. "William could've gotten a wife a great deal more advantageous to him than I was. Perhaps what it came down to in the end was that I, the one who was so innocent and trusting, made him feel a little guilty."

"Why can't you believe that he loved you?"

"Well, whatever it was, it didn't last long. Though we started out well enough, I suppose. When William returned from his voyage, he won big at a casino and we put the money down on the freighter. He'd work for himself, not other men. It would be a legitimate operation, no gun running, no smuggling. And when we'd paid that freighter off, we'd put money down on another. Oh, we had big plans. . . ." Her voice dropped. "Or should I say, I had big plans."

"Not William?"

"Not William. They were my dreams . . . his responsibility . . . a responsibility that he didn't really want. And soon, I think, I became a responsibility that he didn't want."

"Why d'you think that?"

"A feeling that was often there. But then, I guess I expected too much. I expected an end to my loneliness.

"I soon learned, though, that in marrying this devil-may-care adventurer, I'd be spending most of my life alone. He was away on voyages for months. And when he was home? Well, he preferred the company of men, and he was usually with them. He was never there when I needed him, and I don't think that he wanted to be. He was off on a voyage when Willie was born."

She gave a humorless laugh. "I remember I could hardly wait till he got home. I had this lovely picture in my mind . . . proud, beaming father, a family complete. But he acted toward Willie as though he were one more chain upon his freedom. And whenever Willie got noisy, as tiny children often do, William would send me a look of such reproach. I'd brought this nuisance into his life. It was my fault."

"Maybe William didn't know how t'take t'children, Jessie."

"Well, all I know is that I always felt that I had to somehow justify to William our little boy's right to be. That bewildered me. And it hurt.

"William's drinking and gambling kept growing worse with each home stay. He believed that it was his right to do as he pleased, that I must twist my own needs to it. Yet he'd tolerate no attempt by me to influence him."

"A man is who he is, Jessie. He ain't a puppet on a string that a woman can make t'dance as she pleases."

"That's true. A man is not a puppet on a string. He's a child. Forever a child, putting himself first as children do. Oh, I learned. I was slow, but I learned. I learned that I had to stop dreaming and grow up. After the baby came, one of us had to."

"What about William? Wasn't he earnin' you a decent livin'?"

"He was earning it . . . but he wasn't holding on to it. And it was so easy for him, Coke, after throwing away every cent in casinos or all-night poker games, to go sailing off on a ten-week voyage, leaving me to juggle the books and sweet-talk our creditors."

She lifted a brow at Coke. "And he was skillful at making me feel responsible for what he did. Then, during one of those long, hurtful nights when William was out carousing, I grew up a bit more.

"That night I asked myself, Why should I feel this guilt? I didn't force him to marry me. I've tried to live up to my side of the bargain. A thousand times, I'd have been overjoyed to fulfill his needs if only he'd have let me know what those needs were. No, *I'm* not the one who gets drunk, who gambles away every cent that comes in. He is. He's responsible for his own behavior.

"That realization brought me comfort. But it was a cold comfort, since it marked the hardening of my heart against William. The beginning of indifference."

She paused, then continued in a faraway voice. "On those nights when William got home drunk . . . and he was drunk a lot that last year . . . he'd say such hurtful things to me. Then, next morning, he'd put his arms around me, kiss me, and say he hadn't meant those things at all. It had been the liquor talking."

Her voice grew bitter. "Oh, but he had meant them. I believe that the only time that William was ever truly honest was at two A.M. with a bottle in his hand. It was the morning after that he lied. And the words 'I'm sorry,' when they're only meant to smooth things over and are not backed by any real intention to change, have about as much substance to them as—" she gestured over her shoulder—"as a backshot out of Windy down there.

"So, our marriage had been a huge mistake. But what was I to do about it? Often, when I tried to block him from his drinking and gambling, William would growl, 'If you don't like it . . . get out.'

"Nice sentiment. But where would I go? If William was trapped, I was doubly so. How could I provide for my little boy and myself? So swallowing my pride, I held on, more out of cowardice and the need for financial support than out of love . . . or of hope."

Her last words trailing away, she looked unseeingly down at the canyon. "When I learned that William, his men, and our ship had been lost in that typhoon, I did grieve—but not for myself. How can you mourn the loss of something that it took you long, tormented years to learn that you never had in the first place? It was for William's loss that I grieved. He could have had something precious in his little boy and me, but he refused to see it."

She turned her aqua eyes toward Coke, unaware that sometime during the past half hour he'd taken her hand. "I guess it's unfair for me to speak to you of William this way, since he can't speak for himself. But you seemed to want the truth about how it was with me and my marriage. And today, I don't feel inclined to lie."

She turned away, taking her hand from him. "I do know that as I folded William's clothes for the last time and put them away in boxes, I had one regret."

"What was that, Jessie?" Coke asked softly.

"That I'd never gone on a voyage myself, never experienced the thrill of the open sea as William had, the sights and the sounds of faraway places." She sadly smiled. "I guess I wanted things both ways . . . adventure and security at the same time."

"It's the lack o' something' bein' a sure thing that makes it adventuresome," Coke said.

"And either way I'd choose to live my life, I think I'd come away feeling that I was missing out on something." She touched his arm. "Is that how it is with you, Coke?"

"I'm past that now. I've accepted that there's only one way that I'd be goin'." He nodded toward the canyon. "An' this is it."

"Destiny."

"Destiny? Hell, no. After all the years o' work an' sweat I've poured into gatherin' up this passel o' land, I might as well thank myself." He paused, musing. "It coulda just as easy a-been my destiny to have wound up planted by a well-shot cannonball at Nashville or Franklin . . . like a lotta better men than me was."

"You were in the war."

"Wouldna missed it for the world," he said dryly.

"On the side of the Confederacy . . ."

"In these parts, there warn't no other side."

"It must have been hard to take . . . the defeat, I mean."

He looked at her, the playfulness gone from his eyes. "War is one education I coulda done just fine without. To a wet-behind-the-ears young fella with dreams o' glory, war is sure one gut-wrenchin' letdown. When the shootin' was finally done, I was just relieved knowin' that I was one o' the lucky ones, able t'come back home upright."

"You weren't bitter?" She frowned.

"I was ragin' inside at the whole damn thing, Jessie. Biggest waste I've ever seen. Folks spend near on a hundred years buildin' somethin' purty durn good up, then commence t'rippin' it apart. Women use up their youth pourin' out love, raisin' their sons the best way they know how . . . only to get the news their boys have been buried on some Godforsaken battlefield near some strange-named town, their lives countin' for no more'n the bean tails you snap off an' toss to the chickens. Such a God-awful waste.

"I don't like talkin' 'bout it much. It makes me so bone-deep sad, rememberin' my part in it an' not bein' able t'reach down past all them noisy words o' hate an' put my finger on the exact why of it. Nothin' I can think of could be worth that awful cost."

An errant curl was poking out over his temple. She half lifted her hand to smooth it back, but thought the better of it.

"I've heard that it hasn't been exactly peaceful around here," she said. "Indian wars, things like that. So what's the difference between the two?"

"Here, it's my land we're talkin' 'bout, Jessie. My land. Somethin' my pa an' me worked hard for. Somethin' I can touch an' see. It's personal, like my family is. An' it ain't got nothin' to do with any highfalutin words spouted by some far-off politician.

"Dead in that war," he went on, "what I woulda wanted wouldna made no difference anyhow. Dead it still won't." He turned his eyes on her. "But whilst I'm still a-kickin', I know what I want an' I'm damn sure gonna go for it."

Her composure threatened by the intensity in his eyes, she looked away. "Is . . . is this the prize bottomland you told me about at Meg's house last week?"

His eyes got back their good-natured twinkle. "I reckon from way up here, that down there does look like bottomland. But no, that ain't it. That piece o' land is about six miles west o' here."

He squinted up at the sun and got to his feet. "We'd better start headin' back. I get you home too late, I'll be findin' Sarie an' Gustina eyeballin' me nasty out the window 'cause their special-prepared supper dried up in the waitin'."

Taking her hand, he pulled her to her feet. As she followed him down the slope toward the horses, it occurred to Jessica that with the exception of a few casual touches, Coke had kept his physical distance from her here. Yet she felt amazingly close to him.

Coke untied their horses, and she walked at his side as he led their mounts to more level ground. Windy, plodding behind Jessica, took notice of the motion that had started up in Jessica's backside. Stretching her long neck down, the mare let out a snort barely an inch from Jessica's hip.

With a yelp, Jessica leaped in the air. She came down hard, seated on the ground.

"Really, Coke!" she breathed, angrily yanking up the boots, which had slipped down. "What kind of dumb idiot horse did you stick me with? A person can't walk in front of her. And . . . obviously it would be risky to walk behind her too."

"I think you may've overreacted a tad, Jessie."

"Overreacted?" she exclaimed. "You told me this morning that that animal bites when your back's turned."

"Naw, 'twasn't that," he said, Virginia drawl broadening as, taking hold of her upper arms, he drew her to her feet. "Ole Windy just got a mite curious, that's all . . . as all animals tend t'get when their eyes latch on to a temptin' movement."

He kissed her. And though moments before she'd been praying for this, still it came as a surprise, a happy surprise, because it felt so right, and mingled in the kiss was the intoxicant of shared laughter. And she responded openheartedly, sliding her arms around his neck.

When the kiss ended, she put her hands to the side of his face and finally smoothed back that curl over his ear. "Hey," she admonished gently. "I didn't say you could do that."

"That's all right," he replied. "I have good ideas on my own from time to time."

And they kissed again. But this time the lightheartedness fled, the contact deepening, and she could feel the will of this man who knew what he wanted and would damn sure go for it. At first she melted into it, the greediness building in her to be held harder and touched more and more. Then the panic started and he felt a reassertion in her bones. She pulled her face away from his, drawing her arms in tight against her.

"You know, Jessie," he said, running his fingers through the silky hair under her chignon. "I could want a woman like you."

He felt her bones harden again. She pushed back. "And what, pray tell," she asked, brushing her hair back with a trembling hand, "would you be wanting a woman like me for?"

He saw the disturbance in her eyes and eased back. "What do you think I want you for?" he responded lightly. "I want you t'go have lunch with Ma."

She relaxed visibly. "You have no idea of the sacrifice that you're asking of me," she said drolly.

She moved away, walking in a wide path halfway around him. When she was a safe enough distance away, she stopped, and slowly lifting her hat off her shoulders and setting it back on her head, regarded him quizzically. Then she sighed and looked at Windy.

"You know," she mused, "it shouldn't be that hard getting aboard that dumb horse. It was my boots that held me up before."

She kicked them off, stood them side by side. Pulling the gloves out of her belt and slipping her hands into them, Jessica took a few steps back. She took a deep breath and, sending Coke a look of defiant glee, darted off, sprinting stocking-footed across the ground and vaulting into the saddle.

"See!" she cried jubilantly. "I bet you didn't think I could get on a horse that fast."

"Never doubted it at all," he replied, handing her boots up to her. "If you had the proper motivation."

Chapter 17

AS THEY DESCENDED the slope, Jessica's spirits seemed to sag as well. The light fading in her eyes, she gazed pensively off into the distance.

"You mad 'cause I kissed you back there?" He broke the silence.

"No. It's kind of sad, though, that some things just don't stand a chance." She gave him a sad smile. "You should be satisfied, I suppose."

"How do you mean?"

"Well, I behaved both up and down to your expectations. Isn't it what you men want in a woman . . . that she be as enticing as a lady of the evening yet as cold and remote as a marble statue high up on a ten-foot pedestal?"

"I can do without the statue part. You ain't big-boned enough for the statue type, anyhow. An' for your information, Jessie, ladies o' the evenin' ain't that enticin'. Dealin' with them is like stoppin' off at a water hole after a thousand head o' cattle have just been herded through. A body's gotta have one mighty powerful thirst t'wanta get down t'drink."

"This is an arid country, I've noticed."

"Not near as arid as you think. And I'd appreciate it if you'd stop rankin' me with everybody else. I ain't other men. I ain't got no expectations for you t'live up nor down to. I find you, just bein' you, purty durn charmin'."

"But you don't know me," she said. And seeing the dissent in his eyes, she went on, choosing her words carefully. "I may not be the kind of person that you think I am. Remember last week when you asked me to go to the wedding? I told you that it wasn't the time for me to get involved with anyone. That was true then. It's true now. I've made my plans. The die's been cast. And I can't make a truth go away no matter how much I may want it to.

"You have a lot to be proud of, Coke, your home, your family, all that you've built here. You know where you've come from and you know where you're going. I can't see myself fitting into that. There's no way I can be the woman that, as I read in you, you'd want me to be."

"Then you'd better get yourself a new set o' readin' glasses 'cause you're readin' me wrong. I take folks the way they come."

She thought that over. "Then thanks for giving me so much of your time today," she said with finality. "Thanks for lending an ear to my foolish fretting about things I should've set aside years ago. And oh yes, thanks for teaching me a little about horseback riding."

"So when the time comes, you can hightail it to Mexico?"

"What do you mean?" she asked quietly.

" 'Bout the only way t'get t'Mexico from Dispenseme is by horse."

"I don't want to go to Mexico."

"Didn't say you wanted to. Only there might come a time when you'd wanta clear outa the country pronto."

"You're wrong," she said, regarding him levelly.

"After your husband died, how did you earn your livin'?"

"I sewed. I got a job in a tailor's shop and I sewed."

"That all?"

"I sewed some more," she said, an edge in her voice. ". . . and I earned more money sewing."

"That all?"

"What do you want from me?" she flared. "You don't own me. Let it go, Coke. Just let it go." And prodding Windy, she pulled ahead of him.

They rode on in silence. He drew alongside, sending her an occasional squinty look, but she kept her face turned away.

"Shoulda known it," he drawled.

She said nothing, fixing her attention on a bramble bush she was riding by.

"Yup," he went on. "Sure shoulda known it. That's one lesson I shoulda learned a long time back."

"What!" she snapped in a tone that would have discouraged a reply from most other people.

"Oh, that horseback ridin' ain't the best way t'spark a gal."

That brought her eyes to him.

"Happened when I was sixteen," he went on, holding fast to that fragile line of curiosity. "It was just after I went up t'San Antone t'join the Rebel cause. After spendin' three borin' weeks bein' taught how t'march here, how t'march there, an' how t'turn 'bout without stompin' on the other fella's heel . . . as though dislocatin' a body's boot was 'bout the worse offense a body could commit in the army . . . they let me come back home here t'rest up a spell before shippin' me off to the war.

"Now, I sure did feel spiffy comin' back here in my new Johnny Reb uniform." He reflected a moment. "Truth be told, it was naught but half a uniform. They'd run outa the pants by the time I joined up. Never did get them uniform pants. Spent the war not lookin' . . . what was that word you used 'bout matchin' your boots with your skirt?"

"Coordinated."

"That's right. Fought close t'two years lookin' half-assed."
The dimple flitted.

"Well, here I was, a brand spankin' new soldier out t'win the
war for our side. Now, there was this gal, lived on t'other side o'
town. I remember that gal so clear . . . clear as I can picture the
inside o' Sin Cerebro's mouth. Liddy was her name. Purtiest little
thing. Dancin' black eyes, long, fluttery eyelashes, dimples in her
cheeks, an' these little bitty spit curls that came a-twirlin' on down
in front of her ears. She had this giggle . . . that now I think back
on it . . . listenin' to that cackle for twenty years runnin' would
likely drive an hombre loco. But back then, that giggle had a way
of attractin' the fellas like tarantulas take to the high ground durin'
a drencher."

He paused, patting Sin Cerebro. " 'Twas the day after I got
home from my trainin' that I headed into town t'get the broken
breech tail on Pa's gun brazed at Ramiro's forge. Mostly, though,
I was itchin' t'strut m'stuff in my new Johnny Reb coat. Droppin'
Pa's gun off at Ramiro's, I commenced t'workin' my way down
the street.

"Steppin' into the feed store, why, who should I bump into but
Liddy. I could tell by the shine in her eye that I was 'bout the most
excitin' thing t'come into her life since the night the Lipans raided
her daddy's ranch and burned off a corner o' their tool shed.
Wormin' in words betwixt the giggles, we made plans t'meet out
back of her daddy's barn the next day for a little horseback ride.

"Next mornin' I got up, polished my buttons, shined my boots,
and glued my hair to my scalp with axle grease. Now, bein' a
conquerin' hero 'bout t'go t'battle for the greatest cause the world
has ever known—whatever that was—I couldn't ride just any ole
horse t'see my gal. It had t'be El Rojo."

"El Rojo?" Jessica asked, now drawn into Coke's tale.

"Yup. Big Red. The prize stud Pa paid over a thousand dollars
for to improve our stock. Reglar snarlin', stompin' mountain o'
power. Havin' a horse like that under you can sure make a sixteen-
year-old kid feel like one tough hombre.

"Well, I chased Rojo down, wrestled the saddle on him, an'
wrestled him all the way t'Liddy's place. There she was . . .
waitin' out back of her daddy's barn like she said she'd be. Sightin'
me gallopin' up macho as you please in my new Johnny Reb coat

and on my pa's prize stud, she leaped onto this little speckled mare an' came a-gigglin' on out t'meet me.''

He sighed. ''I'll never forget how she looked that mornin' . . . them black eyes glitterin' like a pair o' new-polished agates, big smile makin' them dimples look deeper'n Rio Grande potholes.''

'' 'Where you wantin' t'go?' she asks, flutterin' them long eye-lashes.

'' 'Anywhere is fine with me,' I answer back, 'just lead the way.' '' His voice went flat. ''. . . a statement I shall regret to my dyin' day.''

''Why?''

''Well, unbeknownst t'Liddy an' me, that speckled mare o' hers had just started into heat.''

''Oh-oh.''

''We hadn't made it up the first rise when I noticed Rojo gettin' a mite squirrelly.

'' 'Liddy,' I says. 'Is that mare o' your-un . . .' But before I could finish up what I'd a-started t'say, I had t'holler, 'Jump!'

''For that speckled mare, tail hiked, had stopped dead in her tracks. An' Rojo, breathin' like a yardful o' het-up train loco-motives, was a-rarin' up.'' Coke fell silent, paying funereal hom-age to the memory. ''Cracked a tooth.''

''Who? You? Liddy?''

''Rojo. Happened when he smacked his jaw on the top o' pore Liddy's skull. Pore gal. Was laid out cold close t'eight hours.'' He dourly shook his head. ''Coulda shot that damn horse.''

''I can see why . . . considering what he'd done to your girl.''

''That, too. Here I'd set out expectin' to experience one o' the high points o' my entire life an' it's m'damn horse that goes sa-shayin' off with the prize.

''It was a mite strained there for a spell. Liddy's pa was fixin' t'brain me. Kept sayin', 'If she dies, what'll I tell the folks back east?' My pa was pissed off at me. Betwixt here an' there, no place was too comfortable. But then, when Liddy came round all right, her daddy settled down some. An' the next year, when that little speckled mare foaled twins, he became downright friendly. Made my pa meaner, though.''

''Why?''

''Well, his prize stud had succeeded in matin' a neighbor's mare an' he couldn't rightly collect the hundred-dollar stud fee.''

''Coke,'' Jessica laughed. ''Are you trying to shock me?''

"I got a strong suspicion, honey, that you don't shock that easy."

❧ Chapter 18

LOU WILSON ARRIVED that evening for his Saturday courtship of Sarie. He brought with him a thing prized almost as much as gold in that part of the country—a block of ice, which he'd wheedled out of Ruby that afternoon after noticing that the saloon was receiving a shipment of ice along with its regular supply of keg beer.

They made ice cream after dinner, marvelous, cold ice cream, the mere prospect of which sent the children frolicking across the shadowed yard. Afterward, they popped corn and the grownups gathered around the dining room table to play card games.

Jessica's zeal for card games was fully matched by Ma's. Ma had mellowed enough in her latter years to have scratched this one vice off her list of mortal sins, and she, like Jessica, was a crafty player. And she cheated. Jessica was sure that she'd seen Ma dealing off the bottom of the deck a few times. But she couldn't call her on it. As Ma was counting on, a person just couldn't snitch on a frail, white-haired, little old lady. Swallowing a smile, she took several hands out of sheer cheekiness.

Coke was an indifferent player. He went through the motions, betraying neither pleasure nor displeasure, win or lose. Card games were mere time spinning to him, too much akin to sittin' work. Eventually he grew restless and left the table to wander outside.

Lou was an apathetic player as well. He was feeling too romantic. Plump apple cheeks aglow, he stole long, yearning looks at Sarie and made the most exasperating mistakes at his game.

Sarie's response to romance didn't affect her game. She already knew how the unleashing of uninhibited romantic passion one day could easily result on a later day in the rattle-splish of an infant unleashing in his diaper just as she collapsed, pale with exhaustion, at the table for dinner.

Soon Lou tired of handling cards when it was really Sarie that he wished to handle. He left the game and followed Coke outside. Coke was leaning on the corral fence, lost in thought.

"Quiet evening," Lou said, strolling up to the fence, his hands in his pockets.

"Too quiet," Coke replied. "There's a tame kinda quiet an' a lurkin' kind." Reflecting, he squinted toward the brush fringing out from the margin of the pasture, spectral in the hazy moonlight. "It's the lurkin' kind that's too quiet." He gazed out at the night for a while longer, then turned around and leaned back against the fence rail. "Not interested in card games, neither, I see. Why don't you get Sarie away from the table?"

"Amy's still up."

"Amy?"

Lou nodded. "The little dickens has taken it upon herself t'learn the finer points of spoonin' by observin' her ma and me in action. She's turned into a regular shadow. I put an arm around Sarie . . . comes a giggle, and there she is peeking around the corner. I lean over to give Sarie a kiss, look up and find a big eye peeping out at us through a crack in the door. It's like being followed around by a bucket of cold water about t'be thrown." He sighed. "How's it working for you and Miss Jessica?"

"Took her five miles away from the house."

"Guess I'll hafta try that." Lou shrugged. " 'Ceptin' Amy'd follow us on her pony." He reached over and stroked the muzzle of a horse that had wandered up to the fence. "Jack ain't said anything, but I do believe he's not that pleased 'bout losin' out to you. This is about the first time I can recall that my partner's been so brought up short by an eligible gal."

"Where is Jack, anyway?"

"In Warner, I think. Had some hides to ship out."

"Must know the railroad folks over there pretty well."

"Sure gives 'em plenty of business."

"This tannin' sideline o' his must be bringin' in quite a bit o' money."

"Yep," Lou said. "I was kinda doubtful 'bout Jack comin' into the business with me, what's it been, five and a half years ago. I guess it may've been a good deal after all."

Coke thought he detected some reservation in Lou's tone. "You two've gotten t'know each other pretty well?"

Lou frowned. "Well, Jack's kinda like comin' to a river. The water looks all blue and pretty, waves on top rifflin' soft. Yet you can't tell for sure, if you was t'dive in, you might could knock yourself out 'cause the water's naught but half a foot deep. Or maybe you'd be pulled under in a whirlpool runnin' a hundred feet down. Yup, Jack's been with me in the business for close to six years, and outside of thinking he's agreeable enough, I only know that he hails from Missouri and has aggravated some o' my good customers by skirt-chasin' their wives and daughters." Disapproval soured Lou's tone, for he was a straitlaced sort of man in many ways. "Yup," he went on. "I got good profits coming in through him . . . though I still ain't too sure if they're worth it."

In the house, as Ma and Jessica competed across the table over cards, a begrudging kinship was beginning to evolve between them. Ma had always cottoned to the red-necked fighters of the world, and without a doubt this West woman had pluck. She held her ground, looked Ma straight in the eye, and seemed not to give a whit whether Ma took to her or not. And astoundingly to Ma, this was one young gal who really didn't seem bent on snaring her son. It appeared to be the other way around. Coke had finally come across a woman to contend with, which was exactly the sort of woman that he'd *want* to contend with.

Jessica, for her part, had to concede that though the lady opposite her, magnified eyes flashing in the spirit of competition, was old, she was far from giving up the ghost. She was definitely something solid to deal with. And Jessica was grateful to Ma, too, in that Ma's hostility toward her hadn't extended to Willie. Coke's mother treated Willie in the same way she treated her own grandchildren, playfully goading him and teasing him into speaking up to her. Willie was a sparkly-eyed back-talker in Ma Sanders's presence, which his instincts had picked up on from the start as being precisely what she wanted out of him.

As the night deepened, Sarie and Jessica took their charged-up offspring in hand and browbeat them into bed. When they descended the stairs, free women at last, Lou materialized in the parlor. Apple cheeks flushing deeper, making him look positively handsome, he at last took possession of Sarie, and the two strolled arm in arm out into the night.

Seeing Coke, Jessica felt a rush of panic. She was growing too susceptible to him. Too many feelings, long dormant, were starting to awaken. She didn't want to like him more. She didn't want to cause him pain or risk it to herself. She was searching for a way to maneuver out of following Sarie's lead and going out into the night with him, when her deliverance arrived by way of a vaquero at the door.

Coke's reaction puzzled Jessica. At the vaquero's knock he'd moved swiftly to the door, as though he'd been expecting something. Then he seemed relieved at the news—that a tack wagon had overturned in a gully coming into the compound. She saw him look at her, waver, as though weighing the idea of saying, ''T'hell with the wagon.'' Then his sense of obligation took hold and he left with the vaquero.

Jessica knew that he'd be back in the least amount of time that it would take to check the damage and make the return ride home. She looked over at Ma, still sitting at the dining room table, and determined to make the old lady stay put.

''Let me teach you a new game,'' she said brightly, slipping into the chair across from Ma.

''What's it called?'' Ma asked.

''Has a French name, vingt-et-un. We'll need something to play for . . . rocks, matchsticks, buttons.''

''Got a cigar box full o' cast-off buttons,'' Ma declared.

She fetched the cigar box from her bedroom; and as Jessica divided the buttons between them, Ma made her first friendly gesture toward her guest since her arrival yesterday. Hobbling into the kitchen, Ma set the teakettle on the stove and brewed them both a hot toddy.

''Drink up,'' she commanded, setting the steaming cup before Jessica. ''It's for medicinal purposes. Keeps a body's circle-lation a-hummin' right along.''

When Coke arrived an hour later, he found Ma just where he'd left her, at the dining room table, popcorn bowl now empty at her elbow. Her spectacles teetering heedlessly on the end of her nose, walnut-sized bun askew on the top of her head like a cropped horn, hair leaking out of it, she sat crouched over her hoard of buttons like a menaced cat, eyes blazing at the cards whisking her way, body wire-taut, as though at any moment she might spit and leap into the air. Whenever a hand was played out, she'd grab up her cup, take a swig of hot toddy, and clank it back into the saucer.

Frowning, Coke wondered how much of her favorite nighttime brew his mother had been guzzling, for every so often she'd slap at the air in front of her face and gripe that the place was "a-gettin' a mite stuffy."

But it was Jessica who really captured Coke's attention. She was dealing the cards with an elasticity of wrist and hand that looked quite professional. He recalled that she hadn't been that adept at handling the cards earlier that evening. He pulled out the chair next to Ma and sat fascinated, watching Jessica as, with a finger-blurring, card-blurring, flowing rhythm, she shuffled the cards, snapped them into alignment, set the deck out for Ma to cut, brought the two halves together with a crisp snap, turned the top card up for Ma, burned it and skimmed out a facedown card to Ma and to herself, another facedown card to Ma, and a faceup king to herself.

Glancing dourly at Jessica's king, Ma pinched her two cards up and took a peek. "Hit me!"

A face-up four immediately skimmed under her nose. Lips puckered, Ma took another peek at her cards and about ten seconds out for thought. "Hit me again!"

A queen sluiced her way.

"Busted!" Ma snorted, turning up the remainder of her cards and peevishly grabbing her cup. She took a gulp and smacked it back into the saucer.

Jessica swept Ma's stake of two tiny white buttons and her own three-button stake into her pile of winnings, whisked the played cards up, and with an undulation of her hands popped them into alignment, face-up, at the bottom of her dealing deck.

"Was the wagon badly damaged?" she asked Coke.

"It'll need some fixin'."

"Nobody was injured?"

"Nope. Driver jumped free."

Noticing a fidget from Ma, Jessica resumed dealing. "Would you like to join in? We'll stake you some buttons."

"No, thanks," he replied, the web of lines at the outer corners of his eyes deepening as he watched her. "Tell me, Jessie, have you dealt blackjack for anything other than buttons?"

"On occasion," she said.

Ma took a glance at her cards. She frowned as if disbelieving what she'd seen. Body huddled protectively over as if she suspected Jessica's eyeballs capable of sliding under the table and sneaking a peek at her hand, she furtively pinched the cards up and checked them again.

"Banty-oon!" she whooped, flipping over an ace and a jack, then swooped Jessica's three-button stake into her own pile of winnings.

"This is durn good fun," she exulted, jerking her hankie out of her sleeve and mopping her brow. "What was that you called this newfangled city game, son?"

"Blackjack."

"That another name for this banty-oon we're a-playin'?" she asked Jessica over the rims of her specs.

"Yes," Jessica replied, dealing out the cards.

"Hmmm." Ma frowned, peeking at her cards. "Blackjack. Name has a familiar ring to it. Hit me."

"Really?" Jessica asked, shooting Ma an eight and flicking herself a nine.

"Twenty," Ma said, showing her cards.

"Blackjack," Jessica replied.

Disgruntled, Ma took another gulp of her toddy. "Coke asked if you played this banty-oon for anythin' other'n buttons. What other things do you play it for?"

"Chips," Jessica said.

"Chips? What kinda chips? Wood chips? Cow chips?"

"Flat discs, like coins, often red, white, and blue in color."

"Seems I've seen them there chips before. How you come by 'em?"

"You buy them."

"You just pop into any ole store an' say, 'Lay me in a supply o' them Yankee-colored chips'?"

"In some stores I suppose you could do that," Jessica replied, leaning on the table, suspending her card dealing. "But it isn't normally done that way."

"How's it normally done?"

"You buy them in the establishments where vingt-et-un, or blackjack, is being played. Each color of chip has a different money value placed on it. Whites might cost you a dollar each, reds five dollars, and blues ten or twenty dollars. There are usually other colors of chips besides red, white, and blue with other money values placed on them. It depends on the establishment."

Ma's brows furrowed. "Why the different colors cost different? They different sizes?"

"They're the same size."

"Then why they cost different?"

"Because people may choose to wager different amounts of money on the different games," Jessica patiently replied. "As we've been doing here, when you play against the dealer, you risk two to win three . . . two dollars to win three dollars . . . and so on."

"Why, that's gamblin'!" Ma breathed.

"Some people call it that," Jessica guilelessly replied.

"You taught me a gamblin' game!" Ma squawked. "You tempted me into sinnin' agin my knowledge an' my will!"

"Ah, Ma," Coke drawled. " 'Tain't nobody can sin agin his knowledge an' his will."

"We're not betting money here, Mrs. Sanders," Jessica pointed out. "Just buttons. And when the game is over, I promise, I'll give you back every last one of your buttons."

But Ma would have none of that. As Coke knew too well, when his ma got fired into one of her ranting tangents, there was no way to turn it off. A body could only hope to duck out of the heat until it burned itself out.

Ma leaned combatively toward Jessica. "Chips, buttons, or cabbage seeds. Don't make no difference. Gamblin' is still gamblin', an' gamblin' is sinnin'. You know what you done, young lady? You placed my immortal soul in jeopardy. That's what you done. Where in the world do you city gals pick up such disgraceful behavior?"

"From the same source that most young women acquire their disgraceful behavior," Jessica answered placidly. "From my husband, of course."

Drawing in her breath, Ma fell back in her chair. "Now, you listen here, dearie. I don't know what kinda man you caught, but Coke's pa, my late husband, was a upright, God-fearin' prince of a man. Never, in all the years we was married, would he a-thought o' temptin' me into sinnin'."

"He just went out an' done it on his own," Coke said.

But Ma gave no sign that she'd heard him. And very likely, she had not, it being her habit to retract her ears whenever any unacceptable, but undeniable fact was hurled her way.

She picked up her hot toddy and rose to her feet. Swaying slightly, she grabbed the chairback and stiffened her body. "I'm goin' to my room," she announced in a wintry tone. "I'm a-gonna get down on my knees an' pray to the Lord. Gonna tell Him of the sinful thing you done t'me t'night. Gonna tell Him t'reach down deep inside your soul an' turn it around."

"You're gonna tell Him a lot," Jessica rejoined. "Tell me, do you ever stop telling Him things long enough for Him to answer you back?"

"I already know the Lord's will," Ma retorted haughtily. ". . . Like any decent, upright Christian oughta." And just as Jessica was about to respond, she cut her off. "An' how *I* pray, di-rect to the one true Lord God Almighty, is a sight better'n the way you Catholics do . . . askin' a string o' mopey saints t'step in an' whisper in His ear for you. Why, it'd be 'nuff to make the good Lord wanta hike His robes an' take off runnin' soon as He sights any o' them fellers a-headed His way."

Jessica opened her mouth to speak, and again, Ma broke in. "An' if you have any regard for your immortal soul, young lady . . . any regard a-tall, you'd turn away from all that God-denyin' papist poppycock."

With that, she hobbled to the parlor. At the doorway, she abruptly stopped, remembering something. Turning, Ma narrowly peered at Jessica's hoard of buttons and then at her own. "I win by three," she stated piously as though this proved her point, then disappeared into the darkened parlor.

"Oh, Coke," Jessica sighed, reaching out and brushing the buttons into a single pile before her. "If all of us had the same uncompromising Christian certitude that your mother has . . . we'd wind up bludgeoning each other to death."

Leaning to the side, head in hand, she scooped up a handful of buttons, watching them dribble out of the bottom of her fist into the cigar box. "Would you believe that I was almost . . . almost, mind you, beginning to like your mother."

" 'Tain't that easy right off," he replied. "Ma's like a pair o' loose-fittin' boots. Gets more comfortable t'put up with, the thicker your calluses get." He paused, watching her. "Sure is purty outside, the moonglow washin' over everything. Let's go on out an' catch us some."

She hesitated, glancing at him warily. "Isn't it already crowded with Sarie and Lou?"

"I expect they won't be stayin' out in it too long," he said dryly. "We could find a place t'sit. . . ."

She shifted gingerly. "Since that horseback ride this morning, I doubt that I'd be able to sit anywhere with any conviction."

He settled back in his chair, eyeing her thoughtfully. "Where'd you learn how t'deal blackjack like that, Jessie?"

"Oh, I just have a knack for picking up useless skills," she lightly replied, then shrugged. "Anything involving numbers comes easily to me."

"Yes, I know you're good at that. You sure put Meg's business in order." He paused. "Have you been in my office?"

She smiled. "Yes, it's a mess, especially your desk."

"Well, since it appears that countin' is your favorite pastime, why don't you come out here next weekend an' straighten me out, same as you done for Meg?"

"Actually, dropping off to sleep is my favorite pastime," she said guardedly.

"All right, then," he replied compliantly. "Seein' as how you seem t'cotton to gamblin', too, why don't I make you a bet." He reached for the deck of cards and fanned it out on the table in front of her. "Best of two out of three draws. A hundred dollars if you win . . . against your comin' out here an' straightenin' out my ledgers if I do."

Leaning forward on the table, she regarded him skeptically, not quite believing his offer. "If I win . . . you'll give me a hundred dollars?"

He nodded. "An' you come out here next weekend an' straighten out my ledgers if I win."

She smiled slowly. "You're on."

He gestured for her to make the first draw. She reached for a card that had a slight crease in the upper right-hand corner.

"Ace o' spades," he said, before she turned it over. "I was kinda wonderin' if you'd go for that-un. So I reckon I'll go for this card here." He slid it out.

"Ace of clubs," she said before he turned it over.

They eyed each other across the table, then settled back, grinning.

"You were expecting to cheat me, weren't you?" she chided.

"Well, I sure wasn't the only potential double dealer at this table," he teased back.

"Who marked these cards?" she laughed. "Your mother?"

"Amy. She's a sore loser."

"Well," she said. "Since we both can read the backs of the high cards in this deck, I guess our bet's off."

"No. We'll just hafta bet on somethin' else."

"Like what?"

"Let's just flip a coin then," he reached into his pocket.

"Well, all right," she said unenthusiastically. "Though I've never been lucky at coin tosses."

The face of the dragon was red and black with golden tones. Its brows twisted fiercely over bulging yellow eyes, nostrils flaring, mouth crooked in a ghoulish grin, it slowly dipped and swung to the right and left down the narrow street, brandishing its pointed golden teeth. Dark-haired people leaned from overhead balconies, waving their arms and crying out. Golden light burned out of windows and doors, illuminating golden skin and glancing off golden highlights on the dragon's undulating, elongated back. Down the corridor of buildings the dragon snaked, its long tail bonelessly cresting and falling in broad waves, firecrackers hailing down on the pavement around its dozen feet that shuffled along in black slippers and white stockings. Sizzling and smoking, the firecrackers kept bursting in jittery flashes.

The dragon moved on by and was gone. The buildings and street ballooned, brightened, then hazed away, leaving behind only the echoing sputter of firecrackers and shouting voices.

Jessica's eyes fluttered open. This wasn't Chinatown. This was Coke's house; the room was not golden, it was night-black. But still . . . firecrackers were popping in the distance. She sat up. Those weren't firecrackers. They were gunshots.

She became aware of movement and voices outside the house, and went to the window. Down the road, lights were blinking on in the vaqueros' houses, women and children silhouetted at the doors. A man hurried out of one, pulling on his shirt. Another was exiting from the bunkhouse. Gunbelt hanging around his shoulder, he bent over and stomped his boot on before rushing on.

In the pasture by the corral, the horses were neighing and bunching. They lurched back and forth, charcoal clouds of dust rolling about their feet as they sought to evade the cowpunchers moving in on them. Lariats at the ready, their shirttails still lapping out, the vaqueros singled out their mounts. Swinging the ropes over their heads, they hurled them forward, the loops drop-ping nimbly about the horses' necks and springing taut as the vaqueros dug in their heels to pull in their mounts. They brought them, shying and bucking, to the fence where other horses were tethered, their bridles being slipped on and buckled. With heads tossing and feet fidgeting, the animals waited; saddle blankets and saddles were lifted and slung onto their backs.

Jessica left the window, snatched up her knitted shawl, and went down the hallway to the top of the stairs. Down below, the door of Coke's office was open, its light cutting an angle down through the darkness of the dining room. She descended the stairs.

Coke was seated on the arm of an overstuffed chair next to the gun case deftly loading a rifle, his hat on and shirt open, the lamplight glinting softly on the gold and silver hair on his chest. Sarie was kneeling on the floor next to him shoving cartridges into a shotgun, her white hair a single plait tracing the bend of her back.

Jessica hung back from the door, hesitant to intrude and feeling an outsider.

"You think it's rustlers, son?" Ma had come up behind her, her tiny form insubstantial in the darkness.

"I reckon we'll find out soon enough," he said, getting up and buckling on his gun belt. Picking up two rifles, he slipped them under an arm, barrels angled down over his forearm, and headed toward the door, Sarie following with the shotgun. Jessica backed up, but didn't get out of the way in time and found herself con-fronting him, looking up at him, speechless.

The hardness in his eyes seemed to soften. Lifting his hand, he lightly touched her shoulder as he turned toward the entryway and went outside. Taking the shotgun from Sarie, he strode across the yard. A vaquero reined in, pulling Ole Belcher behind him. Coke tossed the man the shotgun, barrel up, which he caught solidly in one hand and dropped into the boot by his saddle. Then Coke tossed his extra rifle to another rider who'd pulled up. And shov-ing his Winchester into its boot, he climbed onto Ole Belcher. The men from the Sidewinder compound galloped down the road past the vaqueros' houses and faded into the darkness.

Gunfire still popped in the distance, but there was more space between the sounds and they seemed more distant. Amy and Wil-lie had come down the stairs and stood in the doorway, their white nightshirts pouchy around the bends in their bodies, their hair poking out at odd angles, and faces still dull with sleep.

"You want me to go out an' check what's going on?" Lou Wilson asked. He approached the porch from the bunkhouse, having been relegated there for the night by Jessica's taking the spare room.

"No, honey," Sarie replied. "You don't know the terrain. An' with everyone armed an' edgy, swarmin' about in all that night out there, Lou, I'd be scared that you'd be mistaken for a hostile body."

Jessica's eyes turned to Ma Sanders. She was standing out in the middle of the yard, immobile, her hair in a skimpy braid, her thick shawl bulky on her frail shoulders. Jessica and Sarie seemed to have the same impulse. They walked down the porch stairs and across the yard to her. Sarie put her arm around her.

"I'm sure Coke's horse won't step into any hole, Mrs. Sanders," Jessica said, gently touching Ma's arm.

"He'd better not lean into any stray bullet passin' by, neither," she answered sternly.

At that instant, there was a sharp stutter of gunfire that seemed to come from no more than a quarter of a mile beyond the compound gates.

They'd been waiting for them behind a rise a little over two hundred yards ahead and to the right; three men, it looked like, by the rifle flashes. Coke and the others had just ridden into a clearing—where a clump of prickly pear probably saved Coke's life, for Ole Belcher had abruptly swung left to get around it.

An instant before the bushwhackers let go their fire, the hair on the back of Coke's neck prickled with sharp premonition, charging his senses to vivid clarity. Then a bullet zinged past his face, another ripped through the back of his shirt, and the third fell short, bursting a stem on the prickly pear. The bullet that lashed behind Coke tore into the flank of the horse galloping to his left. The animal squealed and reared up, then started bucking and twisting, hooves thrashing out.

Spurring Ole Belcher, Coke broke away from the others, charging headlong toward a line of chaparral about two hundred feet ahead and to his left, his body angled low and to the side of his horse away from the rifle blasts. The shots followed him as he expected they would, zinging over and around him. One grazed his right shoulder. Galloping into the thicket, he jerked his Winchester out of its boot and dropped to the ground, rolling until he came up against the low, tangled outgrowths of a shrub. Ole Belcher careened on, drawing fire as he loped through the brush.

The vaquero was still on his pain-crazed mount. His foot caught in a stirrup, he flopped about on the back of the spinning, pitching horse like a rag doll. The other men, reining their horses in so hard that the animals were rocking down on their haunches, were scrambling for cover.

Rising to a half-kneeling position, Coke fired off four rounds in quick succession; then, brush being cover but thin protection, he threw himself to the left and rolled away, the answering fusillade pinging and splintering through the dry brush he'd just quitted, thwacking thin funnels of dirt off the ground beyond. Lying prone, he took careful aim at the rifle flashes, squeezed off two more shots, and scooted away.

The vaquero had at last twisted free of the stirrup. He dove clear. His horse lurched away, blood foaming out of its mouth.

The other men were firing back now, drawing some of the bushwhackers' shots away from Coke. Though the rifle flashes on the rise had dropped to two, the Sidewinder men were still pinned on the low ground, their attackers firing down from above. Coke heard one of his men breathe a soft "Aiyee!" in pain.

Far to the right another rifle opened up in the night, its fire directed at the bushwhackers. The rifle flashes on the rise dropped to one, then fell silent. The vaqueros kept blasting away until the night air above the rise grew powdered from the attackers' fleeing horses. Three of the men leaped up and ran for their mounts. Swinging into the saddles, they wheeled around and took off after the bushwhackers.

"*Güero*," a voice called softly across the open space; Coke recognized it as belonging to old Tomás. "*Está bien, Güero?*" Are you all right?

"*Sí*," Coke replied. "*Quién está herido allá?*" Who is wounded over there?

"Miguel," Tomás said. "*En el hombro.*" In his shoulder.

Coke walked across the clearing. The silence after the gun battle was profound. Miguel was sitting on the ground, stoically holding in his pain. The wound didn't appear to be life-threatening.

"Take him back to the compound," he told Tomás. "See that the wound's cleaned up, then take him on to the doc's in Warner." He paused. "Tell 'em back at the compound that we stumbled onto a loose batch o' rustlers. The rest of us here is all right, though.''

One of the men had ridden to the top of the rise.'' *"Matamos a uno,"* he called. We killed one.

Coke found Ole Belcher and, feeling heavy and old inside, ambled up to investigate. The bushwhacker had taken a shot in the neck and had bled to death, the large black stain still spreading in the dirt around him. They rolled him over. Coke didn't recognize the man, but a couple of the hands did.

"A drifter. He came through here *hace dos semanas*," one said. Two weeks ago.

"Era un hombre muy extraño," said another. He was a very strange man. The vaquero put his hand to his eyes. "He watched everywhere.''

They heard the crunch of gravel of a horse coming up the draw behind them and spun around. It was Cruz Cortez, one of Coke's outfit bosses and the twenty-seven-year-old son of the ranch's foreman, Alejandro. He was riding bareback, holding his rifle loosely under his arm. He had been the rifleman in the distance.

"Qué pasó?" Cruz asked. What happened?

"We got bushwhacked," Coke replied. "Do you know what's been goin' on north o' here?''

"Rustlers. They stampeded about four hundred head through the north section campground." Cruz spoke English fluently with but a trace of accent. Alejandro, who'd always felt the disadvantage of having had less than six months of formal schooling in his life, had seen to it that all five of his children had been educated through secondary school. All were sent to live with their cousins in San Antonio to complete their schooling.

"They were clever, those rustlers," Cruz went on. "Two men rode in ahead, firing and chasing off the remuda. Then the cattle were stampeded through. We ran for cover. By the time that they were gone, our horses were scattered. I was about a third of the way here when I caught up with this horse. Then I heard the shooting in this direction.'' He looked around. "I guess that the rustlers did not want any of you from the compound to come out and interfere.''

"It's possible, Cruz," Coke said soberly, "that they *did* want us from the compound t'come out here an' interfere.'' He appreciated that the men had refrained from pointing out what had been evident from the first shot . . . that he had been the one whom the bushwhackers had leveled their sights upon.

He turned to one of the men. "Bring a wagon out from the compound an' take this bastard's corpse straight to Seth Shaftesbury in town. I don't want anyone in the compound gettin' upset by the sight of it."

The north section campgrounds were deserted. The squeak and clank of the windmill echoed forlornly in the hushed half-light of approaching dawn. The outer fence of one of the pens was bowed inward, apparently having been broadsided. Pieces of gear were scattered toward the west. The cold remains of a campfire had been trampled across the ground, its charred ashes strewn out to one side like the umbra of a flame. The chuck wagon was on its side, the tarpaulin fallen in and skewed up on one canted pole, the wagon's skillets, pots, and heavy contents lumped around, the flour from a split sack washing a piece of the ground white.

A few of the vaqueros with Coke galloped on to the west in the direction of the stampede. Coke hesitated, his eyes falling on two dark forms lying motionless at the outer perimeter of the grounds. Dread tightening his stomach, he rode toward them. They were only tangled bedrolls swept along by the trampling hooves of the cattle and deposited to one side.

"Much confusion," Cruz said. "We grabbed our guns and boots and ran for cover, either inside the pens or among the trees."

Dark forms were starting to dot the rolling hills to the west. Cattle, about a hundred fifty, were being peacefully brought in by two vaqueros.

"The thieves let some get away," said Rogelio, one of the vaqueros, riding in. Rogelio was old Tomás's grandson, called *El Payaso*, the clown, by the other men for his quick humor and penchant for playing practical jokes. He didn't look amusing now, though, for his bandanna was twisted up under his hat, dried blood caking the side of his face.

"You wounded, Rogelio?" Coke asked.

"*Sí*, but not in a very honorable way, *Jefe*," he replied. "When the thieves struck, I grabbed *mi pistola* and ran back toward the trees firing. *Muy aprisa* I run back. *Muy rápido* I fire . . . boom . . . boom . . . boom, *lo mismo que, cómo se llama?*" The same as, what's his name? ". . . Jesse James. Then I met this tree."

He put his hand to his head. "Very stubborn, that tree. *Muy cabezudo*. It refused to step out of my way."

"And the other men?" Coke asked. "Where are they?"

"Still riding after *los ladrones, yo creo*." The thieves, I believe. "I don't think that they'll catch them, though, for it took so long to get to our horses."

Alejandro and a few of the men were just riding in from the south compound, over fifteen miles away. Like Coke, Alejandro was drawn first to the two dark forms at the edge of the grounds, for two of his sons, three of his nephews, a couple of cousins, and some of his wife's family worked on the Sidewinder. He turned back toward Coke.

"Es difícil comprender," he said. It's difficult to understand. "There's so much open land around, yet the rustlers ran the cattle through these grounds, where they were sure to meet resistance."

"I guess they wanted t'get our attention," Coke said.

"Por qué?" asked Alejandro. Why?

"Could be," Coke replied, "there's a land-grabbin', music-hatin' hombre about who didn't appreciate my recent support of a certain fiddle player."

ᘏ Chapter 19

COKE DROVE THE buckboard along the road into town. He was on his way to fetch Jessica and Willie for their second weekend visit to his home. His wish to see her, the attraction that he felt for her, had evolved into a need. The need to have her near, to touch her. He'd already succumbed to that need twice earlier in the week, going into town on two afternoons before this one.

Both times, he'd also dropped by the saloon to talk with Ruby. Ruby was a longtime friend of Francine Daley, the madam of Francine's, the bordello outside of the county seat at Warner. On occasion Ruby and Francine swapped some of their girls between the two bawdy houses. Oftentimes, Coke had found, information squeezed itself out of the heat generated in brothels and collected along the baseboards and walls like mold. And he was on the hunt for information anywhere he could scrape it up.

But mostly he'd been drawn to town because of Jessica. The knot of resistance in her hadn't gone away. He'd see the light spring to her eyes when she saw him, then she'd quickly look down or turn her attention elsewhere in the store, trying hard to put a polite distance between them. Then, in the course of the visit, some small thing would happen. They'd see the liver-spotted, arthritic hand of the eighty-seven-year-old Widow Henry shakily taking a coin out of her purse for a stick of striped candy, or glance out the window and find Willie out there, his tiny form bent over a mound, busily picking roly-poly bugs out of the dirt and stuffing them into his pocket. And their eyes would meet as from a great distance, and in a flash their souls would connect down deep.

Never had Coke's feelings for a woman been so powerful or run so deep. He wanted her to be moved by the tenderness that he felt for her, while at the same time he hungered to pull her hard against him, to have the license to explore every part of her, the delicate softness of her body and the mystery of her soul. She was stirring remembered emotion all up and down the years of his life.

Perhaps it was that brush with death in the dim hours of early Sunday morning that was inflaming him so. He'd had many close calls with the Reaper over the years—from rustlers, Yankees, Comanche gunfire, mean-tempered bulls. Once he nearly drowned in a flash flood on a trail ride. He hadn't dwelt on those near shaves, though. He'd survived. And it was the glory of survival that he'd felt, the thump of life and not the shudder of death's passage so close by him.

He glanced over his shoulder. The dust wells sent up by the two riders were maintaining a steady quarter-mile distance behind him. The men on the Sidewinder were like family to one another. Many *were* family.

Alejandro would have heard fairly quickly from the men who'd ridden out of the compound with him that dark morning that Coke had been the target. Still, none of Coke's men had mentioned that discovery to him, nor had he to them. But since that day he found that whenever he left the ranch, he had escorts riding at a discreet distance behind him. Coke smiled to himself. After thirty years, Alejandro was still looking out for him. Well, he'd let the men go on thinking that he didn't notice. Too much was left uncompleted in his life—for one, Jessica West—for him to be inclined to forfeit it too easily.

The two bushwhackers had escaped, their tracks swinging north and blending into this same well-beaten road into town. Marshal Shaftesbury had managed to find a name to put on the third, dead bushwhacker. It was rumored that at one time he'd worked on a ranch north of Warner now owned by the Silver Mountain Land Company, though the people from the company claimed they hadn't seen the fellow in months. For that matter, no one would step forward and swear for a certainty that the dead man had ever worked on that ranch. But the bushwhacker was pinned with a name now, right or wrong, and would go on being labeled with it until the wind and the dust wore the letters off the wooden marker over his grave.

The rustlers, too, had gotten away, but with only a little over a hundred of the cattle that they'd stampeded, their tracks disappearing on the rocky floor of Caballo Blanco Canyon. The men had spent most of Sunday going through the canyon and bringing out pockets of cattle that had broken away from the stampede. Since the rustlers appeared to be oddly indifferent to holding on to the cattle they'd chased off the ranch, Coke could only conclude that the stampede, and not the seizing of his livestock, had been the object of their actions. Nevertheless, he was continuing to have his best herds scattered to different grazing fields across his ranch.

To Coke's right stood the hacienda of El Rancho San Sebastian, a monumental presence on the land. His thoughts turned to Juan Fernando Castillo, now dead these six years, heir to San Sebastian and last powerful custodian of its legacy. Since the attack against him last Sunday, Coke's thoughts had turned quite a lot to Juan Fernando and the manner of his death.

As he neared the entrance to San Sebastian, he caught sight of the slight figure of Ray Barrett. T.C.'s older son had just arrived at the hacienda and was climbing down from the buggy at the front steps. A servant was carrying his bag inside while T.C. and Beau waited on the porch.

The younger son, Coke thought, was a crude copy of his father at that age. But his older brother, Ray, seemed different. Coke had caught a kind of intelligence in his eyes that he couldn't fix as to whether it showed calculatedness or reflectiveness. The Barretts noticed Coke, too, moving by on the road outside their gates. And the two parties, all three Barretts and Coke, eyed each other across the expanse, no gesture of acknowledgment passing between them.

"Look at that bastard," T.C. muttered. "Acts like he owns the road."

"Looks to me more like he's using it," Ray said. He went on into the hacienda. Paying homage to the Old Man's grudges wore him down sometimes. He'd leave that to Beau.

Ray followed the servant up the wide staircase, past its imported Italian balustrades of ornately carved tangled grapevines from which cherubic faces peeped out. He went directly to the room that he used whenever he visited here . . . and he visited here as infrequently as he could. It was at his father's insistence that he'd come this weekend. The Old Man had business that he wanted to talk over with him, and it was Beau's nineteenth birthday.

Tossing his suit coat on the four-poster bed, Ray moved restlessly around the room. How he hated being in this domineering hacienda with its stone saints whose bowed heads and prayerful hands emerged from every nook and where down below the statue of Don Quixote stood with his lance, impassively guarding the foyer.

Ray doubted that if he resided here fifty years, he'd be able to leave any real imprint of himself on the strong character of this place. His would be no more than a chicken scratch in a cornfield that the wind could erase in an hour.

Perhaps if he could be more at ease with the way his father may have gotten the San Sebastian its atmosphere would settle more comfortably around him. Maybe his father should tear it down and ship it back to Mexico where it belonged. That would be one undertaking, razing this building with its five-foot-thick stone walls. It would be like trying to remove a mountain.

Yes, the Old Man had probably pulled some shady ploy to get this mausoleum. The straight and narrow didn't appeal to him, not even when it was the fastest and surest way to the prize. He preferred the dark and crooked paths. Beau would know most of the twists and turns of how it came into their hands. He was the son in whom the father confided these last few years, the Old Man's most admiring disciple.

Ray knew his father and brother were of like mind, scheming and ruthless and growing to be more so. If you stomped on a fellow, it was that fellow's fault for allowing himself to trip in the way of your foot. If you jerked the rug out from under him, you laughed at his stupidity for having gotten caught standing on it in the first place. In his blind idolatry, Beau just couldn't see, nor was he old enough to remember, that their father's ruthlessness was not confined to the world outside his home.

Well, let the two of them keep their secrets, whatever they were, Ray thought. He'd sooner not know any details except when called upon in his capacity as lawyer to kick legal dust over them. As much as he could, he'd keep his attention trained on the legal work, the impersonal documents, and avert his eyes from whatever dirty movements were going on underneath. That, in itself, involved him enough to keep him uneasy.

Ray looked out at the sky beyond the window. It wouldn't take on a decent coloration of blue until late afternoon. He missed Colorado. The elegance of the mountains, the scent of pines on the crisp air, the white winters, and the deep greens of trees and meadowlands of spring.

Ray could place the exact moment when the decision was made to abandon the country of his childhood for this parched, drab land of tans and browns. It was over eight years ago. Ray had been seventeen at the time. He and his father had ridden down into the high plains to the east of Colorado Springs. The Old Man was restless. The silver vein had played out, and in the playing out had made him a wealthy man. And three years before, the partner he'd been feuding with for years had been killed when a dynamite charge, set to open a new shaft, had exploded prematurely. The man's death left T.C. even wealthier. But it also left him with no one else to draw offense from. Life was suddenly too peaceful and fine.

Each spring T.C. felt the urge to ride down through the eastern meadowlands. A large part of the land was leased to Texas ranchers, either for winter quarantining of their herds or for spring grazing to fatten the cattle up for market. Though he'd prospected and mined in Colorado for years, T.C. thought of himself as a Texas cattleman. He'd still have been one, too, he often told his sons, had his family's land not been seized in an ambush by a neighboring, thieving rancher who murdered his pa and left T.C. himself lame. Many times the Old Man had recounted *that* story to Ray and Beau, a baneful glint in his eye from the curds of rancor he kept inside and regurgitated every so often, like a ruminant, up to his mouth to chew over and savor bitterly.

As T.C. and Ray rode through the meadowlands, they came upon a broad field. Cattle, their coats sleek from the rich spring grazing, were scattered out for miles. A couple cows were cropping the long, sweet stems along the road.

T.C.'s eyes fell upon the brand on the hips of those two cows, a strange, winding brand, and his face changed.

"What is it, Pa?" Ray had asked.

"Unfinished business," the Old Man replied. "Business I've put off for too long. But now . . . now I have the know-how *and* the wherewithal to go back and settle the accounts."

And pulling his revolver out of his belt, he fired two swift shots through the heads of both cows.

Within six months the family had moved to Warner, Texas, and the Old Man set out to settle accounts. The politics and business practices of South Texas and the unforgiving landscape itself turned out to suit Ray's father perfectly.

He became fired with new energy. Over dinner, eyes flashing with amusement, he'd boast of his triumphs of the day of trickery and double-dealing. Ray got into the habit of listening to those accounts stoically. If he drew back and asked a troubled question, the Old Man would flare at him.

"Get out of the clouds," he'd deride. "This is the real world we're dealing with here, the dog-eat-dog world. I can't believe any son of mine could be such a spineless, thumb-sucking goddamn girl with nothing but air between his legs."

Yep, Ray thought grimly, the Old Man knew how to punch a fellow into "the real world." And the successful politicians around here were the dogs that knew how to bark, ass-lick, or snarl at their neighbors whenever a jugular-ripping, dog-eating dog like dear old Dad trotted into the barnyard.

And as for scruples? A man could range all up and down the halls of power around here for years, and in and out of every room attached, and never bump into a single fully-formed scruple. His father's oft-repeated line said it all: "If you're not with me, you're against me."

Being uncommitted made you the enemy, giving T. C. Barrett the license when the time was right to go after and destroy you. Most of the people here had limits short of that. There were certain boundaries of behavior that they would not cross over whatever the pressure. It gnawed at Ray sometimes to know that the Old Man differed from them in that regard. Well, he wouldn't look too closely.

And although he had to admit that the power game could be challenging and engrossing, most of the time Ray would prefer to be no more than a spectator to it. Hell, he'd prefer to be back in Colorado.

Colorado, where his mother was buried. Ray couldn't claim that he missed her, or that he appreciated her or even loved her. His mother hadn't been a whole person to love. Anyway, she hadn't seemed to be by the time he was old enough to tell.

She was older than his father by four years. T.C. had met her in the Dakota Territory. She was the oldest of twelve children of a widowed, stone-poor farmer. Ray surmised that his father had taken her away and married her because he was a lusty young man in his early twenties and available white women were few and far between. What he'd been doing in the Dakotas at that time remained something of a mystery. Ray had picked up indications that he'd been a soldier in the Union army. But since it was only 1862 then, and there was plenty war left to go, Ray conjectured that dear old Dad had probably been a deserter.

She wasn't pretty, but her eyes had been beautiful, large and dark and soft. She probably hadn't expected much out of life, and after marrying T. C. Barrett, she'd probably gotten less than she expected.

Her second-born child after Ray, a daughter, had died before reaching her second birthday. His mother never spoke of the infant; the emotion was too close. But Ray's father brought the child up plenty of times. In the heat of lacerating his wife for her faults and deficiencies, he'd cut her through with the blame for the death of their daughter—as though she could be held responsible for cholera.

If his mother had once had a personality, her marriage had shredded most of it away. It was a rough hand-to-mouth existence that they led early on. For a long time, nothing seemed to work out for the Old Man, and he was seething with frustration and acrimony. He poured it out on Ray's mother.

Over a frayed hem on her shirt, coffee that was too weak, he'd fly into a cold rage at her, then refuse to speak to her for days, letting her twist under a tyranny of his contemptuous silence. Ray recalled many times during dinner when his father swept his plate of food off the table with the back of his arm because he didn't like the way she'd prepared it. His mother would sit frozen across from him, those dark, gentle eyes wide and the tears held back because she didn't want to be reviled for them, too.

At young ages, Ray and Beau took their cues from their father, turning into petty, evil-tempered tyrants themselves. It was their father whom they held in awe. He was the strong one who held the family in his grip, he was the one they wanted to be like. And he had demonstrated repeatedly through his derision that their mother existed solely for the convenience of the three of them, and even in that she failed miserably.

Then the Old Man's luck turned and he struck silver. They moved to a fine house, his father buying tailor-made clothes and expensive cigars. It was more peaceful in their house, too, but only because the Old Man was away most evenings with other women. Walking home from school in the afternoon, Ray and Beau would sometimes come upon their father riding by on the main road with some flashily dressed, pretty-faced, hard-eyed woman or other. He'd wave at them, grinning. And their mother diminished even more in their eyes.

Then one day she sat down in the chair in her room, without speaking, without trying. For a month dinner went unprepared, beds unmade, clothes unwashed and unmended. Dust gathered on the furniture. Ray heard his father in that room yelling at her, heard the cracks of his blows. But she'd given everything in her with nothing ever put back, so there was nothing at all left to be reached anymore.

Then, one morning, she was gone. They found her drowned several miles downstream in the river that rushed behind the town. Her spirit long reduced to nothing, she'd quietly withdrawn her presence as well. T.C. even begrudged her her death; she'd had no right to that, either.

Ray occasionally wondered who his mother really was. She must have cared. She stuck it out so long. In recent years, especially these last four, she'd grown in his memory. Time and rough experience had caused him to recognize her pain and sympathize with it. The Old Man would've been astounded to realize that his own actions had resurrected his detested wife in Ray's memory, humanized her to his son, and generated this sympathy in him for her.

Four years ago, T.C. jerked Ray into "the real world." And

the one person whom Ray saw revealed there, for the first time in unidealized clarity, was dear old Dad himself.

It was during Christmas vacation, when Ray was home from college, that he met Cathy at a local dance. She was eighteen then, the daughter of a rancher who owned a spread north of Warner. She had honey-colored hair, warm brown eyes, a fresh complexion, little freckled nose, and a quick, lighthearted smile. There was something wonderfully wholesome, open, and clean about her. Her delight in life seemed to bubble up from a spring deep inside her.

Life became full of promise for Ray when he was near Cathy. His natural gloom melted away and he felt that he could accomplish anything, be anybody. And he aspired to be honorable and good and worthy of her affection. He spent every day of the rest of that winter vacation with her. And when spring break from school arrived, he was a daily fixture at her family's ranch and at their dinner table. By the time he returned home for the summer, he knew he wanted Cathy with him through life.

Early in June he took her to meet his father. Surprisingly, T.C. was the soul of hospitality, and he even offered Cathy a job in the Savings and Loan, where Ray would be working that summer. The gesture seemed intended to encourage his son's romance; as well, it seemed a bestowal of generosity, since Cathy's family would have use of the additional income.

Ray was still beaming with pleasure when he walked into his home that night after dropping Cathy off at her house. His father was waiting for him.

"The girl's a charmer, I'll give you that," he said to Ray. "But she's a tramp. Everybody knows it. The only reason she's going after you is because I hold the mortgage on her daddy's place."

Ray was struck dumb. He fumblingly tried to defend Cathy. The Old Man merely smiled.

The following week Cathy started work at the Savings and Loan. It seemed that during the days of that summer Ray could do nothing right in the business. The Old Man was constantly at him, castigating him publicly.

"At the rate you're picking up the routine around here," the Old Man shot at him one day, "it's hard to believe you're college-educated. Hell, a six-year-old could learn it faster."

And indeed, nobody had sat Ray down and explained the work to him in detail. He was given tasks that had only been half outlined, insuring that he'd err in some way. And even when he thought he'd done a good job and had carefully double-checked himself, his father would find fault.

Ray was too slow, he was too careless, his penmanship looked like the scrawl of a feeble old lady. He treated this person too rudely and that one too deferentially. He left a drawer open. "Do we have to clean up after you like you're a slobbery-mouthed baby? Next you'll be expecting us to wipe your ass for you."

Ray had expected a certain amount of verbal flagellation from the Old Man, for that was his way. But this was brutal, and it confused Ray that his father would so belittle him in front of his fellow workers . . . and especially Cathy.

She'd look on as Ray's father ripped into him, her dark eyes shining with sympathy. Then later, she'd gently touch him as she passed by. When they were together in the evenings and he was upset and resentful, she'd urge him to be patient.

"Sometimes my daddy is hard on me, too," she'd say. "Maybe your father is real pressured right now. He does have a lot of responsibility."

As time passed, Ray sensed a cloud of doubt growing in Cathy—doubt that, perhaps, whispered that the chagrin Ray's father showed toward him had foundation, for to her Mr. Barrett was the most patient and kindhearted of men.

Ray couldn't blame Cathy for wondering if he might be a dunderheaded weakling. The Old Man almost had him believing it himself. Ray and Cathy's love for each other was yet too unformed, its structure not having had the time to grow solid enough to withstand the systematic undermining of it by such a seasoned manipulator as his father.

As August deepened, Cathy seemed to retreat inwardly from him as if repelled. Ray felt desperate for he still loved her deeply.

Those last weeks she seldom laughed or smiled. The look in her eyes grew circumspect and dull. And when she was in the Savings and Loan, her gaze followed T.C. and not Ray, although by that time T.C.'s attitude toward her had grown brusque.

One afternoon just before Ray was to return to college, he

arrived home early from an errand. He'd gone to a ranch to have some affidavits signed, and the ranch wasn't as far away as his father had thought, nor did the reading and signing of the documents take as long as he'd predicted.

Since it was almost noon when Ray got back to town, he decided to go on home for lunch. Beau was sitting at the table buttering a slice of bread when he walked in.

"Dad here?" Ray asked.

Amusement glinted in Beau's eyes. "Up in his bedroom. Told me to send you on up soon as you got here."

Ray went up the stairs. The house was unnaturally quiet. His father's door was slightly ajar. As Ray reached to open it, he heard muffled sounds inside, and paused. Then, a strange feeling coming over him, he pushed the door open.

Cathy was lying on the bed, her clothing scattered on the floor like molten feathers, her white skin looking pitifully defenseless in its nakedness. His father was on top of her, thrusting and pumping. Cathy's head moved, and her eyes met Ray's. He'd never forget the look in those eyes. There was no passion in them, only a lifeless resignation.

Ray quietly closed the door and walked out of the house. His father found him ten days later, passed out drunk in a prostitute's crib in Reynosa.

When he came to, he was lying in the bed of some hotel room. His father was at the washstand squeezing water out of a towel.

"Looks like you'll be startin' your college classes a little late this fall, son," he said affably, coming over and laying the damp towel across Ray's forehead. He sat down in the chair next to the bed. "You sure did tie one on." He chuckled.

"Why'd you do it?" Ray asked.

The Old Man shrugged. "I warned you that gal was a tramp, that all she was after was t'save her daddy's ranch. But you was so damn hot-blooded over her, it affected your hearin'. That gal's been after me half the summer. And hell, why shouldn't I take a sweet little piece like that when it's offered up to me on a silver platter all wrapped in pink ribbons? I may be your dad, but I ain't taken any vow of priesthood."

Ray didn't answer.

"One of these days you'll be grateful to me, son, for showin' her up for what she was. I already fired her from the business. Didn't think you'd feel easy havin' her around."

"That's very generous of you, Dad," Ray said acidly.

"Well, she ain't worth our wastin' time an' trouble over," he went on, ignoring Ray's irony. "Won't be long till you forget about her an' see things my way."

Ray set eyes on Cathy only once after that, during the Christmas holidays. They saw each other on the street in Warner and veered apart like repellent poles on two magnets. His father had turned them into something unclean and shameful, to themselves and to each other. Less than a month later, the Savings and Loan foreclosed on her daddy, and the family moved away.

After that morning in Reynosa Ray didn't mention Cathy to his father until the following summer. That summer, Ray could do no wrong in his father's eyes . . . though Ray was drinking heavily and was often late, hung over and indifferent at work.

One evening his father walked into the parlor, where Ray had been drinking steadily by himself.

"You can't tolerate the idea of anyone having more influence over Beau and me than you . . . can you, Dad?" Ray asked.

"Depends on the kind of influence," the Old Man replied. "Remember your own mother. The wrong woman can weaken a man, hold him back."

"Tell me," Ray said. "Would you've gone to the lengths you went to last summer to prove Cathy's unworthiness if she'd been from a rich and important family?"

T.C. laughed. "Son, you are startin' to live in the real world now."

"Yep." Ray poured more whiskey into his glass. "I guess I am."

"You got a nice rich gal in mind?" the Old Man asked amiably. "Bring her on by. I'd be happy to meet her."

Even with the aid of his liquor, Ray was taken aback. But he managed to regard his father levelly. "No, Dad," he said. "I'm your son. Not your procurer."

They'd be ice-skating in hell before he'd give his dad another chance to prove himself more of a man by turning Ray into less of one.

The Old Man must be pretty complacent about the hold that he had over him to presume that the betrayal and anguish that he'd inflicted on Ray that summer would be readily accepted, discounted, and forgotten. Or perhaps he assumed that Ray's capacity for love was as niggardly as his own. Well, it was four years now, and Ray hadn't forgotten.

* * *

A servant tapped on the door. Dinner was ready in the dining room down below. Ray washed up, put on a fresh shirt, and went downstairs. His father and Beau were already at the dinner table.

"I've heard reports," the Old Man was saying to Beau, "that you've taken to spendin' time with Jack Siden. You'd be wise, son, to steer clear of that fellow."

"Why?" Ray asked, pulling out a chair at the table. "The man runs a successful business in town. Seems more responsible to me than a lot of others Beau knows."

"He'd be a bad influence on your brother," the Old Man snapped.

"How do you know that, Dad?" Ray asked.

T.C. ignored him. Since Ray had passed the state bar, he asked too many questions. His firstborn son was getting less and less pleasurable to have around.

After dinner, Ray sat in a wing chair in the library with a book he'd gotten down from the shelf. But the words on the page kept knotting up, refusing to cohere into sustained thoughts. Even here in the library, the alien quality of San Sebastian oppressed him. Ray looked up and set the book aside. At least the face staring down at him from the mantel was that of a blank-eyed bust of Plato, not some doleful-eyed saint.

Beau had left the house and was out roaming somewhere. Ray's brother was too restless to stay long in any one place. The teachers he'd had in school had complained that Beau Barrett had a wild streak in him. They'd about torn their hair out over the boy.

Ray wondered anew why the Old Man found Beau's keeping company with Jack Siden objectionable. Was it that old possessiveness, the need to counter any possibility of anyone's threatening his absolute dominion over his sons? Given the riffraff Beau usually kept company with, Siden seemed likely to have a calming effect. Come to think of it, Beau already seemed quieter. But perhaps that was because he was spending more of his time here than in Warner, where his rowdy behavior would be in sight and sound of Ray. Yes, it was almost a relief to have Beau tucked away out here. When he was in Warner he fell in with an unruly crowd, most of them employees of the Old Man's Silver Mountain Land Company. By the looks of them, very few of the company's men would win any contest on virtue. They all looked like thugs, thieves, cutthroats, and gunslingers.

Running with them, Beau was in constant trouble, whoring around, getting into drunken brawls, committing battery on some poor stranger who happened to get in his way on the street, shooting up property. Beau would've cooled his heels in jail more than a few times if the county sheriff hadn't been in the Old Man's pay.

The door opened, and his father strode into the library brandishing a rolled-up sheepskin document, yellowed with age. He lit the lamp on the desk and gestured Ray over.

"Remember the mortgage papers we had Celestina Castillo sign two years ago, when she put this place up as collateral for her loan?" he said as he unrolled the document on the desktop. "We made sure to put in the phrase 'any and all holdings falling to El Rancho San Sebastian datin' back to the original Castillo land grant of 1723.' " A jubilant twist came to T.C.'s face. "If you'll look careful, son, you'll see that almost two-thirds of the Sanders ranch, the Sidewinder, falls inside those original land grant holdings."

With a sigh, Ray leaned forward and looked at the map. He'd continue being with T. C. Barrett and not against him. He'd clear for him all the legal paths he wanted, smother any smoking details that might flare into real trouble, and turn a blind eye as much as he could to the skulduggery and dirty dealing that went on underneath. And sometime down the road, he'd inherit, with Beau, the proceeds of it when the Old Man cashed in his chips for good.

❧ Chapter 20

"NOW, MA SAYS she doesn't want the new curtains t'clash with her doilies." Sarie rolled her eyes.

Jessica took in the Sanderses' parlor, where every piece of furniture boasted a doilie. There were doilies of every shape, size, color, and design. "I guess only solid white would do then . . . or black," she said dryly, laying out on the sofa the fabric samples she'd brought from the emporium. Out of old seamstress's habit, she'd already draped her tape measure around her neck and had absently touched her left wrist a couple times, where she ordinarily wore her pincushion like a bracelet.

Coke had asked her to make new curtains for the family parlor last week. First the wager to straighten out his accounts, now the parlor curtains, she reflected. Coke would use any ploy to draw her into his family.

"This is hardly a dainty room even with all these doilies," she went on. "Ruffles and frills wouldn't fit with these rough walls and wood beams."

"Like puttin' a little pink bow on the top curl of a battle-scarred grizzly," Sarie commented.

The *calabacita con pollo*, squash with chicken, bubbling in its tomato sauce in the *cazuela* on the stove, was filling the house with its thick, savory aroma. They could hear Ma's metallic voice in the kitchen making pronouncements on the sorry state of the world, to Gustina's low, neutral grunts.

Dishes and flatware had started clinking in the dining room as Amy, Willie, and Joshua set the table, Ma having maneuvered them out from underfoot in the kitchen by giving them this task. Already Amy had assumed the superior role, ordering the two younger fellows around.

"You don't do it that way, Willie. You do it *this* way," she clucked like a mother hen. But to her little brother, her tone turned stinging. "All right, stupid, what would Uncle Coke do with three forks? You can't do anything right."

"Won't be long before Joshie'll be chasin' his sister around the table tryin' t'skewer her on one o' Coke's three forks," Sarie grumbled, walking toward the dining room. "Joshie, sweetheart," she called. "Why don't you go help Gustina heat the tortillas?"

"That should hold him . . . for about five minutes," she said, coming back into the parlor. "Then poor Gustina will be tryin' t'pry him outa her hair like heated tar."

"What do you think of this one?" Jessica held up by the window a swatch of fabric with dark brown stripes on a light beige background.

The light from the window behind her shone through her hair, burnishing the loosened strands to glittery frost. Sarie wondered why she hadn't noticed it before, but she could see now why Coke and half the men in town were so taken by Jessica, and it wasn't only that delicate prettiness. At times there was a certain flow in her movements, a deepening of expression in her eyes that showed an awareness of her body, an enjoyment of its sensuality. She doubted that Jessica herself knew she was reflecting that catlike quality in her. Inexperienced young men would be taken by it and not quite know why.

Sarie smiled. "I can't get over Coke suggestin' that we get new curtains in here. He's never paid any mind to the inside o' the house before." Her eyes danced. "You must be workin' a spell on that brother o' mine." Yep, Sarie thought. Coke had probably homed in on that scent of sensuality in Jessica West in about thirty seconds after he'd met her.

"It's 'bout time Coke started thinkin' o' settlin' down," she added.

Jessica laughed. "Isn't this a two-hundred-thousand-acre home he owns? Seems to me he's already settled in as deep as he can get."

Sarie's attention had shifted out the window, where Coke was conversing intently with his outfit bosses. Her expression darkened. "There're too damn many low-voiced conversations goin' on around here."

"Because of that attack by those rustlers last week?" Jessica asked.

"We've been rustled before. But there's somethin' else goin' on that Coke ain't let me in on."

"Perhaps it has something to do with that rustler who got killed," Jessica said.

"That's another thing that's been botherin' me. Why would rustlers be roamin' so close to the compound where that gun battle took place? Our closest herds are four miles out. Have you heard anything?"

"I heard someone say that the rustlers were probably up from Mexico."

"That won't wash. The rustler who got killed wasn't Mexican."

Glancing one last time at her brother, Sarie turned from the window. "Well, at least with you here, Coke'll be sleepin' in the house tonight . . . for the first time this week."

"He doesn't come back here every night?"

"The ranch is flat-out too big for him t'make it in every night." She sent Jessica a significant look. "Course, he ain't never had a good enough reason drawin' him home every night, neither."

Jessica sat down in the chair across from Sarie, her fingers absently following the design of the doily on the armrest. "Sarie," she ventured slowly. "I've noticed a lot of very pretty young women among the vaquero families out here. A few were quite stunning, in fact. . . ."

Sarie seemed to follow the line of Jessica's thought, and for the first time since Jessica had known her, her warm eyes went icy.

"Though I'd never admit it to his face," she said stoutly, "if there's one thing my brother is . . . it's smart. He needs the loyalty of his men. An' if, in his position, he started movin' in on their wives, sweethearts, or daughters, it'd set into motion all kindsa strains an complications that we'd all be better off livin' without. No, Jessica, that is one thing Coke would *never* do."

"I'm sorry," Jessica stammered, stung by the indignation in Sarie's response. "I didn't mean to be insulting."

Sarie calmed. "You kinda took me aback implyin' that. You see, Jessica, some o' these families have been with us more'n twenty-five years. A few go back to the time when Coke was no more'n a little sprout of ten. Goin' after their daughters would be akin t'Coke goin' after a member of his household livin' under his protection. My brother is an honorable man."

There was a tightening around Jessica's eyes. "Not all men are as honorable as your brother," she said, going to the sofa, gathering up the fabric swatches, and tossing them back into their box.

Feeling uneasy, Sarie walked over to her. "Please forgive me for comin' back at you as hard as I just did."

"Coke is indeed fortunate to have a sister who so staunchly defends his honor," Jessica said, whipping off the tape measure and dropping it into the box.

"It doesn't need defendin' by me," Sarie answered gently. "But a thing like that takes time t'find out. It ain't stamped on a fellow's forehead. There's no way you could know in so little time."

Jessica turned around. She liked Coke's sister too much to sustain a disagreement with her. Sarie's nature was not one of sharp edges at the ready to abrade and wound. She was a healer.

"You love your brother," she said.

"I do love that ole cowpoke." Sarie smiled. "An' it'd be kinda nice if you could, too."

"Yes," Jessica admitted wistfully. "I suppose it would be nice . . . wouldn't it?"

Chapter 21

THE STILL AIR lay upon them like a cool sheet in the predawn darkness; yet Jessica felt Coke's presence as he rode beside her as a tingling warmth received within, as if the side of her that he was on were warmer than the side that he was not. Soon, crimson arteries of dawn began reaching into the sky above the eastern foothills, and the shadows blurring the land condensed the darkness into themselves, gaining definition. Still, the delay before the sun itself emerged seemed so prolonged to Jessica that she almost expected to hear in the far distance a low creak and rumble as it pushed through its rocky confinement in the earth and erupted onto the horizon. But at the last it simply shed its leadenness, breaking free of the land and levitating into the sky.

Over two hours before, Jessica had awakened with the alarm clock. Having grown fed up the night before with the gibes Ma Sanders kept slinging at her about her lazy, misbegotten city ways, she was determined to beat Ma down to the kitchen that morning. Quickly dressing, she'd gone downstairs, stuffed the corncobs under the stove lid, lit them, and got the coffee going. She was seated at the breakfast table, arms folded placidly, when Ma walked into the kitchen. Ma jerked upright at the sight of her, and the dismay on the old woman's face was all the payoff that Jessica needed.

"Your rooster running late?" Jessica asked good-naturedly. "It's almost four-thirty."

It took Ma a moment to recover. "Didn't think you city-made gals could get your engines stoked before noon."

"Oh, I have a method," Jessica responded easily. "You see, each night I pray to one of my saints to lean over and blow in my ear at the appointed hour." She paused. "A city-made saint."

Ma went over to the stove and, lifting another lid, stuffed some more corncobs inside. "That happen t'be the patron saint o' gamblers?" she asked with lifted brow.

"The very same," Jessica replied blandly.

But if Jessica thought that she'd outtrumped Bessie Sanders that morning, it wasn't for long. Ma took out a skillet, clanked it onto the stove, then set a basket on the table in front of Jessica.

"Mind gatherin' the eggs?"

Jessica peered up at her.

"Eggs," Ma repeated. "They come outa the no-nonsense end of a hen." She gestured toward the door. "Their livin' quarters is thataway."

Jessica picked up the egg basket and went outside. It still looked like the middle of the night, though the night seemed to be winding down, with only the fading moon providing its thin illumination. She could smell the musty odor radiating from the innards of the henhouse long before her foot landed in some fresh chicken dribble and she skied roughly into the door. Muttering, she jerked her skirt up and tried to scrape the viscous syrup off her shoe on the edge of the door frame. Then she stepped carefully into the henhouse. The bottom half of the room was steeped in oily shadow, and, squinting, she made out the chickens, tucked inside their ranks of boxlike cubicles along the walls, as blue-white blobs in the darkness. Her intrusion into their lair raised a flux of uneasy cluckings and fidgets on every side, stirring the fine dust that hung in the air.

Now, Jessica had consumed thousands of eggs in her lifetime, but she'd had only limited direct dealings with the creatures that cranked them out, except when they were dead and plucked. She went over to the first cubicle to her right and peered in at its occupant, sitting squarely on its straw nest, head cocking jerkily at her.

"Excuse me," she said, reaching under her. The hen promptly stabbed her beak into Jessica's hand. Then, clucking, she indignantly rocked back and forth and, puffing out her feathers, settled deeper into her straw mattress, eyeing Jessica contentiously.

Jessica rubbed her hand. "Can't say I blame you," she said. "Someone tried to poke a hand under me like that, I'd probably try to take it off, too."

She tried again to get at the eggs, carefully sliding her hand around the side of the hen. But the little culprit was on the alert, and drilled her twice more with that sharp beak.

Giving up on that one, Jessica looked about for a more cooperative candidate. A few of the chickens had spilled out of their rows of cubicles like undisciplined schoolchildren and were moving around on the ground or were perched perkily and noisily on the ledges, their tail feathers rippling subtly as they let loose their greasy drippings onto the floor.

Jessica collected the eggs from their abandoned nests, each of her forays deeper through the space of the henhouse setting off small bursts of cluckings from the ladies in the cubicles. They were a chattery, easily aggravated crew, she thought.

She felt in her egg basket. Six eggs. Not enough. But all of the remaining nests were occupied, the hens planted stoutly on their precious deposits. She'd have to be more aggressive, she decided.

She reached under another hen and got pecked again. But she didn't retreat, slipping her hand in deeper until it came upon the smooth rounded shape between the hen's warm underfeathers and the scratchy straw. The hen gave way, rising up. Then suddenly, beating her wings and squawking, she flew down at Jessica, exciting a chicken on the opposite side to swoop down out of her cubicle. Reacting as she would had they been cans tumbling out of shelves at her, Jessica instinctively threw her hand over her head and ducked aside. Three eggs leaped out of her basket and splatted to the floor. The chorus in the henhouse rose to a higher pitch. Feathers eddied in the air.

"You ladies must've learned your manners from Bessie Sanders," she said angrily, going outside to escape the racket and inhale some fresh air.

She peered down into her basket. Only three eggs. This was humiliating. She couldn't take this pathetic yield inside. It would fuel Bessie Sanders for the next two days of needling. Well, she wasn't about to allow herself to be done in by Ma Sanders and her band of militant chickens. But how to get at those eggs without further assault to her person and dignity?

Her eyes roamed the darkness, stopping at an old broom leaning against the back porch across the yard. Putting her basket down beside the henhouse door, she walked over to the broom, grabbed it, and marched back into the henhouse.

Within seconds a squawking, straw-flying, feather-flying full-scale riot broke out in the henhouse as Jessica, brandishing her broom, prodded and spanked the belligerent critters out of their nests. In infectious panic, chickens swooshed down out of their cubicles in crisscrossing patterns in the air, then sprinted and flapped in hysterical zigzags across the floor before she swept them, screeching, leaping, and stampeding over one another, out the door.

At last the henhouse was quiet except for a couple of perturbed holdouts strutting rapidly about. Setting her broom outside, Jessica retrieved her basket and, calm and unmolested, collected every egg her hands could find among the straw—twenty-one eggs in all.

She walked back to the house, sat down on the porch steps, and pulled off her shoes. Taking out her hankie, she wiped the chicken dribble and smashed egg off them. Then, leaving the shoes on the step to dry, she hefted her egg basket up and went inside.

Coke was leaning back against the kitchen counter drinking coffee. Gustina was frying beans in a pan. And Sarie was standing in the middle of the kitchen holding a rifle.

"Why, all that ruckus out there woke me up," she exclaimed. "Thought a opossum was gettin' our chickens." Then she looked at the pinfeathers standing up in Jessica's hair, and put her hand over her mouth to hide her smile. Coke was already grinning.

Pulling herself upright, Jessica strode across the kitchen in her stocking feet, feathers fluttering down from her clothes in her wake. She triumphantly set the heaping basket on the table before Ma.

"All right, Mrs. Sanders," she declared. "I got you your eggs." Then, squaring her shoulders, she stalwartly hooked her thumbs in her belt. "Now, where's the herd of bulls you want me to slaughter for your steaks?"

Ma was the only one who didn't laugh, and even she was hard put to keep a straight face.

When the breakfast arrived, Jessica was amazed at her own hearty appetite. She'd supposed that at that unaccustomed hour her stomach would be inclined to just hang there, limp inside her, like a drained water bag. But she went at the meal ravenously.

Perhaps it was all that hard work she'd done. Or perhaps that dark, primordial hour evoked a feeling of happily conspiratorial isolation, as if they were the only people moving on earth, and had a jump on all the rest. There was an air of festive coziness to the occasion. And throughout the meal, Jessica felt the glow of Coke's eyes upon her, warming her inside.

After breakfast, she went back upstairs and got dressed to go horseback riding with Coke. He was by the barn saddling the two horses when she came out of the house.

"This time I came prepared," she cheerfully announced, walking up to him. "See? . . . I got boots that fit." She pointed down at them, though it was unlikely that he could make out in the darkness whether they fit or not.

Without speaking, he pulled her around the corner of the barn, backed her to the wall and, pressing hard against her, hungrily found her mouth and kissed her roughly, his chest and arms and hands feverish in their unrelenting force upon her.

She struggled up for air. But his mouth came down hard on hers again, his body crushing against her, his hand moving around to the soft swell of her breast. She put her hand over it to pry his fingers off, but only clasped them feebly instead.

Gradually, as though from great exertion of will, he eased back a little. And still close against her, moved his hand up to her face and looked down at her, his dark eyes devouring her. She brought her hands down to her sides, knotting them against the wall behind her to steady herself, for she was shaking violently.

"My God," she gasped weakly. "Was it the eggs?"

The intensity in his eyes receded and the lines at the outer corners crinkled. With still considerable effort, he moved back and smoothed her collar.

"I've been wantin' t'do that for some time," he said. Then, setting her hat back on her head, he picked her up and put her on Windy. She stared down at him, wide-eyed and trembling.

"Well, actually," he added thoughtfully, "more than that."

She hadn't looked at him since they'd left the compound, though she yearned to, every moment. She was frightened at what she'd see in his eyes and he in hers. The equilibrium between them felt too precarious, the turbulence of emotions too delicately contained.

The aftereffect of what had happened was just now setting in, renewing her trembling inside. Her flesh where he'd pressed against her felt inflamed. Her lips felt swollen and tender from the pressure of his mouth. She felt too open to the tenor of the moment, and was glad that he could not read her mind. But if she looked at him, he'd see . . . he'd see that if he stopped and pulled her down into the darkness, she'd plunge into it with him unrestrainedly.

The breeze picked up as though escaping from a vent in the

earth. The rims of the hills and the tips of the brush caught fire and the sun broke onto the horizon in an outburst of glorious light.

Jessica instinctively turned toward Coke, a smile on her face as if to say, "Wasn't that splendid of it to do that for us?"

And he reached over and gently took her arm in a gesture that communicated that he would not hurt her. And the tension between them flowed out.

This was a moment to savor, Jessica thought, a magical slice of time to preserve in her memory like a keepsake. Already with him she was saying to herself, "This is a moment I want to keep. And this . . . and this"; for she knew that she could not allow herself the luxury of thinking in extended time for them.

She suddenly noticed that she felt less shaky and unnatural on Windy than she'd been the week before. She wasn't yet ready for steep chasms, racing, and bucking. But some trotting would be quite all right, she thought.

They rounded a thicket and came upon some men working in a dried-out creek bed. Jessica was amazed that fellow human beings could materialize so miraculously in the middle of nowhere and at this hour. The day-to-day business of the ranch, it seemed, was already plying along. One of the men was on horseback riding back and forth on the arroyo floor down below, dragging brush tied to a rope behind him, scraping up dirt and attempting, it appeared, to deepen the creek bed. Another man was building a wall of dirt and stone across the dry channel.

"Hola, Jefe . . . señora." They nodded, eyes lingering inquisitively on Jessica, but not so long as to appear too bold, before they returned to their chores.

"What're they doing?" Jessica asked as she and Coke ambled on.

"Buildin' a dam."

"But there isn't any water," she said.

"If there ever is, Jessie, we're durn shore gonna catch an' hold it."

The sharp report of a rifle sounded a short distance away, followed by the bawling of a cow. Winding through the brush, they came into a clearing where a newborn calf lay on the ground, black blood bubbling out of the small, innocent-looking bullet hole in its head, its feet going through their final spasms. A cow stood over it, nudging it, and bawling plaintively. A few feet away a vaquero sat on his mount, his rifle still smoking. The sight was a brutal violation, irreconcilable to the peaceful, roseate dawn.

"Why'd he kill that calf?" Jessica asked quietly.

"T'save the ma," Coke replied. "That cow's gonna have a hard enough time survivin' as it is, without a calf pullin' the strength outa her."

The land had lost its benign charm for Jessica. And as they rode along, she looked upon it with keener eyes. Near an outcropping she saw the bones of some small animal sown on the ground like the pieces of a fragile toy that could be gathered up and reassembled. Though spiked brush, clusters of prickly pear, and brown, bristly grass clumps were all around, the earth itself was bare of the thinnest fringe of green grass. The sweet aroma of greenery did not season the air, only the dry, vinegary scent of the tall, darkish weeds that grew among the brush, that scent neutralized slightly by the pervasive dust; dust that swelled weightlessly around the horses' legs like ashes even though they were moving at a slow, measured pace.

Now, Jessica was more personally acquainted than she'd ever have cared to be with all forms of cruelty in city life, both of the overt and covert kind; the cruelties of coldhearted apathy and of evil-hearted deeds . . . all of which were of man-made origin. But here she was witnessing a cruelty of a different kind, not one born out of action but of withholding, the passive cruelty of nature's withholding.

"Conditions just keep getting worse around here, don't they?" she remarked.

"It's been so long since things got better in these parts," he replied, "I'm beginnin' t'believe that gettin' worse is its natural condition. An' the dust keeps gettin' drier. An' the cattle keep shrivelin' t'bone, an' the bones keep molderin' back t'dry dust. I'm almost scared of a hurricane blowin' in outa the Gulf. This whole part o' the state would wind up buryin' New Mexico, an' all that anyone would find o' South Texas would be a coupla boulders an' one mighty deep, dry pothole."

Coke was escorting her through a different part of the ranch, she noticed, from the one that he'd taken her through last week, a section that was less deserted. They rode by about twenty cattle feeding in small clusters around chunks of singed prickly pear scattered on the ground.

"I thought your brand was a winding one," she said.

"It is."

"But those cows have a different brand."

He glanced at them. "Those beeves belong to a family that works for me, the Dominguezes. The four main families on the Sidewinder run their own herds out here. Every once in a while I'll give 'em the loan of a coupla my blooded bulls to improve their stock. When times is good, they profit, too."

Farther along, Jessica heard the faraway clanking of a bell. Shading her eyes, she spotted smallish white forms scattered in the brush.

"Are those goats?" she asked.

"Yep. Some o' the folks out here prefer their goat milk an' barbecued *cabrito* t'anything my beeves put out."

He was deliberately keeping his tone matter-of-fact, she thought. Every so often the fiery sensations generated in the darkness of the barn an hour ago seemed to resurge, quivering in the air between them and evoking stray silences. Occasionally she caught a dark, searching glimmer rising in Coke's eyes, and she guessed that he was wondering if he'd gone too far that morning or hadn't gone far enough.

They heard the plod of hooves behind them, and a large, middle-aged vaquero emerged from the brush.

"Alejandro," Coke said.

"Güero."

Coke glanced at Jessica. "Have you met my foreman, Alejandro Cortez?"

Jessica nodded. "At the emporium. How's your daughter, Teresa, Mr. Cortez?"

"Bien, señora," he responded, touching his hat to her, then he turned to Coke, speaking in Spanish.

Jessica let Windy wander away as they talked. It hadn't occurred to her that Coke would understand Spanish, though on reflection, it seemed natural that he would.

She'd met Alejandro Cortez on her second day of work at Meg's Emporium. When he'd entered the store, she'd gone speechless with fright. To her city eyes he'd been a tough-looking, menacing sight. Large in stature, with those hardened, dark Indian features, squinting, alert eyes, and impassive, spare movements, he was clad in rough cowboy garb, his hat low on his brow, a gun strapped to one hip and a long sheathed knife to the other. As he moved toward the counter, she'd backed to the wall and had stood frozen, preparing to hand over all the money in the cash drawer.

"*Un espejo,*" he said in a deep guttural voice.

She looked at him dumbly.

"Mirror," he said. "*Chiquito* . . . for the hand."

"Mirror . . . hand," she repeated.

"*Es para mí señora,*" he went on, compelled to explain further by the flabbergasted look on her face. He paused, searching for words. "It is for my wife. It is her . . . *cumpleaños* . . . birthday. For the birthday of my wife . . . a mirror."

"Oh!" Jessica exclaimed in a burst of relief, and started breathing again. "You want a hand mirror for your wife's birthday."

"*Sí,*" he said expressionlessly.

Never had Jessica searched out merchandise so fast, even scampering into the back room and flinging things aside to get at a mirror newly arrived on the stage. Within minutes she had all the different hand mirrors in the store lined up on the counter before him.

He examined them one by one, slowly touching the decorations on their backs with his callused, brown hands. Then he paused for a long time, his hand on his chin, considering.

"*Un momento, señora,*" he said, and went to the door.

Some girlish voices outside on the street stopped their chattering, and a pretty girl of about seventeen with flashing, laughing eyes walked into the store.

"Hello," she said, in slightly accented English. "I'm Teresa Cortez, Alejandro's youngest daughter. My father is having a hard time making up his mind."

Talking in Spanish, Alejandro and Teresa deliberated over the mirrors, and though Alejandro maintained that deadpan, spare manner, Jessica could tell by the way his eyes connected with his youngest daughter that the girl clearly held her father in the palm of her hand.

They moved away from the counter, examining the bolts of fabric on the table, Alejandro's grave expression never changing. Once he made a comment in that gutteral voice and the girl laughed, "*Papá,*" and mock jabbed him in the ribs with her elbow. By the time they were finished, they'd chosen the prettiest hand mirror in the store, two lengths of fabric for dresses, and ribbons and rickrack. By the look of mischievous triumph in Teresa's eyes, Jessica had little doubt about whose dress that second length of fabric was intended for.

Alejandro paid for their purchases, a pained, reluctant expression on his face that Jessica could tell was feigned to tease his daughter. For the rest of that afternoon, Jessica had shaken her head at herself that she could have misjudged a person so completely, for when she'd first laid eyes on Alejandro Cortez, she'd thought she was a goner.

Coke and Alejandro ended their conference and parted company, Alejandro touching his hat to Jessica as he swung his horse around.

"He called you '*Güero*,' " Jessica said. "Does that mean 'boss'?"

"There ain't no direct English translation for *Güero*," Coke explained. "It's a nickname, kinda a cross between 'Curlie' an' 'Blondie.' "

"The men who work for you call you 'Curlie'?" Jessica said incredulously.

"Only the real old-timers who knew me as a little sprout that every so often they'd hafta pull outa trouble. When I met Alejandro I couldna been more than, let's see, nine years old, an' he was purty well grown. Back then, he an' the other vaqueros who worked for my pa used t'tease me on my blond, curly hair, an' the name stuck. The newer men an' the younger fellows call me *Jefe*, which means 'Boss.' "

She thought of Coke as a child on this rugged, merciless land. "Must've been pretty hard and not that pleasant growing up around here," she commented.

"I just did it," he said. "I didn't reflect on it."

"Alejandro brought some good news," he went on. "The well diggers struck water in the northern part o' my east section last night."

"That is wonderful, isn't it? Does that mean that your cattle will survive now?"

"Not exactly. Unfortunately, wells don't provide grazin' grass along with their water."

"Maybe you will get rain soon," Jessica said. "I hope with all my heart for all of you that it will rain soon."

"If wishes came true," he said slowly, "the whitetail deer tryin' to outrace a pack o' hungry coyotes would sprout wings on her legs, an' to the hungry coyotes, that whitetail deer would get lead in 'em.

"If wishes came true, mountains would step out o' your way an' ragin' rivers slide aside." He paused, regarding her.

"An' if wishes came true, Jessie, you'd come downstairs an' be in my bed tonight."

She looked down at her hands, folded on the saddle horn, then raised her eyes to his. "If wishes came true, Coke, we'd all be a lot more careful about what we wished for . . . for I've seldom had a wish of mine that came true that I didn't live to regret."

Chapter 22

"I GUESS I shoulda had a bookkeeper's visor an' sleeve garters on hand for you," Coke remarked when Jessica arrived at his office door after cleaning up from the horseback ride. She looked the image of unassailable, no-nonsense efficiency in her high-necked white blouse and black shirt. She'd redone her hair, wetting it and pinning it into a sleeked-back, tight chignon.

She entered his office in a halting manner, aware that she was trespassing into another creature's native habitat with the creature in residence. This room was definitely Coke's, from the massive oak desk to the longhorns mounted on the wall, the gun case, the buffalo skin rug, and the brightly woven Navajo coverlet on the daybed.

From the way she moved around his office, hands clasped behind her, he realized that she wouldn't intrude into any part of this room that he didn't invite her into, leaving it up to him to decide which compartments of his life to lay open to her. And any privacies divulged to her here were unlikely to meet with any return in kind from her side.

She stopped before a large cowhide stretched out on the wall. A map had been dyed into the hide, the boundary lines expanding out and out, each expansion marked with penned-in acreage numbers and a date.

"The Sidewinder?" she asked.

"Most of it," he replied.

"That section down there appears to be marked out."

"Sold those five thousand acres to my foreman, Alejandro Cortez. Eight years back he told me he wanted t'buy 'em. Said his grandparents an' parents had tried t'scrabble a livin' outa that land for near on fifty years. Then one day the branch o' the Castillo family that inherited it came in an' run 'em off."

"So you let Alejandro have it."

"Not then an' there. I was a tad perturbed at the time. Told him he oughta know that I don't part with my land. Once it's mine, it stays mine.

"He never brought the subject up again. But I thought about it a lot. Kept rememberin' how he knocked me into a ditch durin' a gun battle when I was thirteen when my own pa woulda left me out t'fend for myself. I was riled at Alejandro for months after that. Kept slingin' mean comments at him. He'd just shrug his shoulders an' laugh. It took the war an' some growin' up for me to appreciate why he'd done it.

"So, close to a year after Alejandro made that offer, I bought those thirty-two thousand acres there to the northeast. I thought, 'Oh, hell, if those five thousand acres in the south mean so much to Alejandro, I might as well let him have 'em. He has the right to wanta leave his young-uns somethin' more'n the tradition o' workin' for somebody else. So I sold 'em to him.

"Turned out t'be a purty good buy. Once he an' his sons could sink a hole that didn't run into another pocket o' that damn gas he's got running' under that land, they found a purty good supply o' water. When this drought turned ugly, I moved some o' my stock onto that piece o' land."

"Nice of him to let you use it," she said.

"I'm leasin' it from him, Jessie . . . at fair market value. Hell, I sold it to him at fair market value. One o' the reasons my men an' me have gotten along so good for as long as we have is we keep the business side of our dealin's strictly business. An' we're right careful 'bout drawin' too deep on friendship an' loyalty."

"Fair is fair," she said.

"Yup," he replied, his eyes straying over her, causing the color to rise in her cheeks. Since this morning, it didn't take much to bring the color to her cheeks.

"When you're so scrubbed an' proper-lookin' like this, Jessie," he said, playing with the thin circlet earring in her ear, ". . . with every little hair in place, you know what I'm tempted t'do?"

She quickly turned away to his desk. "Do you have the papers here in these separate piles for any particular reason?" she asked in a forced, businesslike tone.

He came over beside her. "That pile o' notes on the left is things I need t'get or things I've ordered an' ain't got yet. That pile on the right is the things I got but still hafta pay for. Now, most o' my record keeping for these past months is in these two drawers to the right." He pulled out the top drawer. The hash of papers that had been squashed inside ballooned up, a couple sheets fluttering to the floor.

"You don't keep ledgers?" she asked incredulously.

"Got the ledger books a few years back. Never got around t'puttin' anything into 'em, though."

She regarded him sternly.

"Hell, it don't take hours sittin' on my backside writin' teeny tiny in narrow lines for me t'figger out if I'm makin' more'n I'm spendin' or spendin' more'n I'm makin'. All I gotta do is go outside an' look at my beeves. If they're lookin' good, I'll probably come out ahead. If they ain't, I won't. Course, the market has t'be agreeable, too."

"You don't enumerate anything?"

"Only the payroll . . . an' that I pay in cash."

"Always?"

" 'Tain't much reward in a puny little bank draft, Jessie. It's a helluvalot more satisfyin' havin' the silver dollars right there t'jingle in your pocket after puttin' in damn hard work for 'em."

Reaching up behind her, he stroked the hair at the nape of her neck. "We ain't too straitlaced in the way we do things round here."

She moved her head back against his hand, her eyes softening, then caught herself and grabbed up one of the stacks of notes on the desk.

"You paid forty dollars last month to the San Sebastian School?" she asked, leafing through the papers.

"I pay 'em forty dollars every month," he said, still stroking her hair.

She scooted away and sat down, straight-backed on the edge of the daybed. "Why do you pay that much?"

"Used t'pay 'em a whole lot less," he replied, leaning back

against the desk and regarding her unsteady primness with a hint of amusement. "Up until a year ago, when they was robbed o' their land, the Castillo family was the main support o' that school. About a week after Doña Celestina an' her family were forced out, Father Dominic came by. Brought that brother from the school along with him. Durin' that entire visit, that brother said nary a word. He just sat there, his hands tucked into those floppy sleeves o' his, an' lookin' mean enough t'swallow a porcupine whole.

"First off, the padre pointed out that they had sixteen Sidewinder children on their rolls at their school. The school was runnin' short o' money, he said. How would all these Sidewinder children get their educations if the school was forced t'close? It was my responsibility t'see that the children out here got their educations.

"So if the San Sebastian closed its doors, he went on, I'd be obliged t'build a school right out here, then go to the expense o' layin' in a supply o' books, desks, slates, an' such. Then," Coke put in dourly, "he said I'd hafta pay someone like Miss Muriel or the brother there t'come out here on the Sidewinder an' live with me t'teach these children."

Coke shook his head. "These old-style Spanish priests come at you like they're bullfightin'. First comes the *pecadores* . . . the need . . . the obligation . . . an' the guilt. Then they lash out that sword o' theirs . . . the threat o' eternal damnation. An' before you know it . . . they're strollin' off totin' both your ears an' your tail."

He sighed. "An' now I find I'm the main support o' the local Catholic school. Ma ever found out, she'd squawk like she'd just sat down on a prickly pear."

Jessica laughed.

But Coke had grown thoughtful. "The Castillo family sure did leave one mighty big empty space when they pulled out. The balance in these parts has been cockeyed ever since."

Chapter 23

JESSICA LIKED NUMBERS. They were crisp and unambiguous. Either the columns balanced or they were in error. She also liked forging order out of chaos, arranging it in neat little rows and alphabetizing it.

Since Coke had introduced her to his office and left her alone in it, she'd had a fine old time digging through the muddle of his office, finding patterns, and setting them out in clear-cut form.

The disorganized way in which Coke had had this office laid out, merchants could've charged him twice for goods and services and he'd have had no record of any prior payments. Yet Jessica doubted that details like that would slip by Coke. And anyone who got caught trying to cheat him once would never be given the chance to try it again.

Lately, she found herself smiling quite a lot when she thought of Coke. The smile slipped. Things were moving too fast between them.

She got up from the desk, and putting her hands to the small of her back, arched against them. She'd been right to tell Coke last weekend about her disastrous marriage. Perhaps it would give him pause, make him realize that she wasn't the answer to any man's dream. A man's dream? More his nightmare.

She sighed. This neat and clean Jessica West, so demurely fending off his advances . . . how could he guess where and what she'd been . . . what she was . . . a woman with an arrest warrant on her head and a past that could at any time well up and poison everything around her.

She remembered so clearly the moment that she'd spotted that arrest warrant in New Mexico. It was at the train station in one of those scrawny, half-grown towns that seem to sprout along the railroad tracks as if from windblown seeds. She'd still been reeling from the horror of what she'd seen that night. She'd immediately taken Willie and fled San Francisco on the first train she could find, disembarking at one station and immediately buying tickets for the next train headed east. But as the miles had rolled by at that tranquilizing clickety-clack rhythm and the landscape beyond the windows changed, her terror subsided. She began to study stagecoach and train schedules, plotting ways to throw any pursuers off her trail. She changed her name several times, zig-zagged her course, feinting in one direction and quickly reversing in the other.

She'd decided on New Orleans as her destination. Perhaps William still had family there. But even if he didn't, New Orleans was a place big enough to disappear into.

That morning she was feeling the first rays of confidence that she and her son would make it. The rush of hope was making her almost euphoric. Hadn't she dreamed and schemed of this for months? From here on out, she'd bear straight on into New Orleans.

She left Willie sitting on a bench out on the station platform near their bags and went inside the depot to buy tickets for the train that would be arriving within the hour. She bought the tickets and, having time on her hands, strolled aimlessly around the waiting room. Something on the wall opposite her caught her eye. Tacked in rows on one side of the room were around twenty wanted posters. Among them, on fresh-looking, unyellowed paper, appeared to be a likeness of herself.

Frowning, she approached. The words "Wanted for Embezzlement" sprang out at her. Then she saw her name. It was as if she'd been slammed in the chest by a two-by-four. Putting her hand over her heart, she read rapidly, "5 feet 4 inches tall, 100 pounds, light brown to blond hair, blue eyes, age, early twenties. Accompanied by a boy of six or seven years called 'Willie.' Reward $200 for information leading to this woman's capture and arrest. Contact Superior Court 8, San Francisco."

She didn't know how long she stood there staring at that poster before she again became aware of her surroundings. She peeked over her shoulder. Seeing the ticket master turned from the window talking to the telegraph operator, she reached up in a shamed way, pulled the poster off the wall and, crumpling it into a ball, walked out the door.

Feeling dazed and cold inside, she sat down on the first bench outside the station door, the poster knotted in her fist. In a far-off way, she heard Willie prattling with some middle-aged woman who was seated on a bench farther down.

She should've known, the words kept roiling up inside her. She should've known that Henri would never let her just walk away. He'd reach out and drag her back somehow. How many towns had this poster? How many people were lying in wait out there for a chance at an easy two hundred dollars? What would happen to her little boy?

"This is one adorable little fella." The middle-aged woman had approached Jessica without her having noticed.

Jessica didn't answer. She just sat there blinking numbly. All those wretched months, all those days and nights of shame and fear, had reared up before her. And black despair washed over her; a despair that she could not push back.

She felt the woman's touch on her shoulder. "Are you sick, child?"

It was the voice that got to Jessica. Something in it warmed her through and through. It was the same kind of tone that a mother, kneeling down, would use in asking her child who'd run crying into the house, "Love, where does it hurt?" That this stranger would even get up to come over and ask moved Jessica. And the tears started pouring out.

The woman sat down beside her and put her arm around her. "There, there, child," she consoled. "It cain't be all that bad. Where are you an' your little boy headed for?"

"Mexico," Jessica answered bleakly. "I guess it's Mexico now."

"Well, ain't that somethin'? I'm headed thataway myself. Hail from a town less'n thirty miles from the Texas-Mexican border. Why don't you an' your little-un travel along with me? Oh, by the way, my name is Margaret Mary Emerson. Folks call me Meg."

And Jessica had followed that warm voice as if through a darkness. Meg played games with Willie and kept him occupied as they traveled along, her voice flowing comfortingly through Jessica's long silences. She coaxed Jessica to eat when she sat gazing without appetite at the food before her. She offered to buy the tickets for her and Willie at the train station so that soon Jessica automatically handed Meg the ticket money when they arrived at the depot. Once Jessica thought she heard Meg say to the ticket clerk, "Three tickets . . . for my daughter, my grandson, an' myself."

Jessica couldn't figure this woman. Why would she bother, why would she care? What was in it for her? Where Jessica came from, people tended to steer clear of such despair. Or else they took advantage of it. But that wasn't in Meg's character, Jessica would learn later. Meg couldn't look upon a lonely and hurting soul without regarding it as an aberration of nature that needed rectifying.

When they reached Dispenseme, the lack of food and sleep, the weeks of fear and strain, had caught up with Jessica and she was ill with fever and exhaustion. Meg settled her and Willie into her own home.

"Stay here with me," she urged. "This has been a lonesome ole house since my son moved out on his own an' my husband passed on. You're in no shape t'keep pushin' on, Jessica. You're safe here. This ain't Mexico . . . but it's close enough."

And Jessica had stayed, at first because she needed Meg's healing warmth, to let someone take over for a while, to brighten the days for Willie when she hadn't the resources to do it herself. Then she stayed because she saw a certain logic in it. Perhaps she had shaken off her pursuers. With Mexico just next door where she could easily slip out of reach of any United States arrest warrants, Dispenseme seemed a good place to bide her time and find out.

As the days melted into weeks, Jessica found that she could sometimes go for hours without thinking of San Francisco. But it was always out there just beyond the horizon, waiting. And in the dark hours it slipped inside her room and haunted her nights. At odd moments, too, some offhand little comment would bring it all crashing back to her.

Sarie's words yesterday. "My brother is an honorable man," had done that. They'd stung her, for she knew that she herself was not an honorable woman. She knew that Meg's healing warmth, a new town, could not turn her into a new person. It could not simply chop away the past that she had lived or the person she'd been. That would always be a part of her.

This morning in the darkness of the barn, she realized that she was nearing a point of no return with Coke. Those hands, those sun-toughened hands moving over her, exploring, setting her flesh on fire, those eyes burning into her. It had been such a long, long time since she'd hungered like this for any man. If she allowed what was happening between them to strengthen and deepen, soon it could gain such force that she wouldn't be able to wrench free without leaving a part of herself behind.

Her eyes strayed to the cowhide map on the wall. But he was rich. The Sidewinder was a massive operation. If she'd gained anything from her work this afternoon, it was that knowledge. It would be such a blessed relief to be freed from the pressure of how to make ends meet today, this year, and the next, to know that Willie's future was assured.

Yes, she thought again, a two-hundred-thousand-acre home in the midst of a searing drought, occupied by a mother-in-law with a taste for combat. And Coke could have any woman he wanted. If he knew everything about her, he would not want her.

That's the way, she told herself. See things as they are, Jessica, not as some silvery dreamscape. Too often people fall into the trap of believing that there's a magic circle somewhere and it's never where they're standing, when the truth of the matter is, no such magic circle exists . . . anywhere.

🌿 Chapter 24

JESSICA'S SILENCE DURING the evening meal was like a hollow place in the atmosphere.

Even Ma was moved to remark, "Law, girl, you look 'bout as woebegone as the coyote whose only share o' the carcass was the wrong end o' the tail."

Jessica hadn't answered back, which troubled the others at the table. And Ma was confused. She'd been getting pretty satisfying sport out of their thrusts and parries.

She did look wan, Coke thought. Maybe he shouldn't have put her to work in his office this afternoon. Once she tackled a project, he judged, she held on tight to it until she overcame it no matter how much it cost her. He became aware again of her fragile slenderness and wondered if she took good enough care of herself, so that even though she had plenty of fire, the strength that she needed to fuel it gave out on her from time to time. Yet there seemed to be something more than simple bone-tiredness pressing her spirit down.

Later, the children put to bed, he took her into his office so she could show him what she'd done there.

"Cain't be all that hopeless," he said, closing the door behind him.

Her eyes held on the closing door, shutting them off from the rest of the house, then she looked at him in confusion. "What's hopeless?"

"My office."

"Oh. No, I didn't find it hopeless." She went to the desk. "Here, I've laid everything out for you. These are the ledger sheets for your suppliers. I've labeled the sections according to orders, deliveries, and payments." He noticed an edginess in her speech and mannerisms.

"In these two drawers," she went on, pulling one out, "I've arranged a filing system for current invoices."

His arm brushed hers. She moved quietly away.

He seemed not to notice, his eyes on the ledgers. "What did you think I'd meant?"

"About what?"

"When I said it cain't be all that hopeless."

He heard a small intake of breath. "Us," she said softly. "That's hopeless."

"Why do you think that what's goin' on between us is hopeless?" he asked, still looking at the ledger sheets.

"I'm afraid . . ." she began, then checked herself. "It's all wrong."

He set the ledger down, turning his dark eyes on her. "Are you sure that's all you're afraid of, Jessie?"

She moved back, that trapped look swimming up in her eyes. "Look," she blurted breathlessly as if struggling up to the surface of a pool. "We've both lived enough to know that a lot of what we want can't ever be realized."

"Not on its own, it can't," he said.

She tried to meet his gaze, but couldn't sustain the connection. Her eyes veered away. "It's not that I don't care for you," she stammered to the space between them. "But I can't afford any . . . involvement."

"You cain't deny that part o' you that wants it, neither," he said, touching the side of her face.

"You mean I can't deny you."

"Yes."

She backed away again. "All you want is a tawdry little affair," she charged.

He looked amused. "If I'd a-wanted only that, do you think I'd o' brought you home t'meet Ma?"

A tiny smile quivered up and vanished.

"I ain't playin' no games with you, Jessie," he said. "You know by now that a cheap little affair, like you call it, ain't what I'm after."

"Yes," she admitted. "I suppose I do know that. But you see, that's all it *could* be between us, and I wouldn't want that."

He drew nearer. "What do you want?"

"Peace."

Without preamble, he gathered her in his arms. She stiffened, but since all that he was doing was holding her, she resigned herself to it, settling against him.

"Talk to me, Jessie," he said against her hair. "Tell me what's keepin' you from that peace."

"I'm so tired," she said heavily. "And I fear—" she stopped.

His arms tightened around her. "Fear what?"

"Emotion," she said after a time. "Too much emotion." She paused. "You."

"Why do you fear me?"

"I fear your love . . . and . . ."

"An' what?"

"I fear your hate."

"I'd never hate you, Jessie."

She seemed to gather her strength. Moving back, she looked into his face. "Words. I've heard plenty of those before."

"I'm a man o' my word."

"Well, if you are, you're rarer than a desert thunderstorm." She tried to free herself, but he wouldn't let her go. "Don't do this to me," she whispered. "You're making this too painful."

"I wouldn't cause you pain, Jessie. Know that."

"Then let go, Coke. Give up. Let it be over between us."

He didn't let her go. "I'm a patient man, Jessie," he said softly. "An' I never give up."

She gave him a skeptical look, then reached back and removed his hands from her waist. "I'd be more careful about what I wanted if I were you." And she walked to the door and quietly let herself out.

"I already am," he said to himself. "That's why I want you."

🌹 Chapter 25

A THIN CLOUD drifted across the moon like moss sliding across the surface of a pool. The fence rider on his horse ambled through the chaparral, slouch-backed and drawing on his rolled cigarette, an orange pinpoint glow blinking in the darkness. The cigarette smoke trailing silkily behind him, he glanced only now and then at the fence extending on ahead of him, its measured posts casting sentry-length shadows against the land.

A cottony drowsiness was settling in on the fence rider. He'd been up most of the night playing poker with the boys outside the bunkhouse on the Blankenship compound. Allowed no liquor on the ranch, the men played card games endlessly in their space time. Tonight the cards had fallen in the fence rider's favor. By the time the game had broken up, he was twenty dollars ahead but due to start out on his rounds in less than an hour and a half. He was in too good a humor to turn in, so he saddled his horse and set out on his rounds early. He'd catch some shut-eye off and on along the way, when the sleep finally did overtake him. His horse knew the route.

Pulling up to a fence post, the fence rider crushed his cigarette out on top of it, then rolled the tobacco between his fingers to make sure that it was cool before letting it go in the breeze. The land was like a tinderbox.

Pulling his hat over his brows, he moved on, slouching lower in the saddle. Dream images were starting into motion in his mind, when he felt a muscle-tightening, head-lifting alertness in his horse. The fence rider snapped upright, blinking hard to clear his head.

They'd just descended a small hill. The air was hazed with dust. To his right the clean line of fence was broken. It looked like someone had roped five of the posts and pulled them down. He heard a rumble, low whistles, and the crackle of twigs to his left, and suddenly cattle were swarming out of the brush at him, the riders urging them on, black silhouettes in the moonglow.

Reaching for his rifle, the fence rider was starting to spur his horse to get out of their path when he found himself facing a man who'd come around, approaching from the side. He recognized that friendly face, had seen it here on the ranch two days before. And only a few weeks ago he'd sat at a table in the saloon drinking beer with this man. The fence rider hesitated as he looked into the other man's eyes, for they still were friendly. He didn't see the gun, but he saw the blasts—and felt the explosions of pain inside him.

At daybreak, two Blankenship men tracing the stolen cattle came upon the fence rider's trampled body tangled in the downed barbed wire, two bullet holes in his chest.

Willie scampered into the emporium and threw his school-books on the counter. "I'm going horseback riding," he announced breathlessly.

"You are?" Jessica frowned. "With whom?"

Coke appeared in the doorway. She looked up at him, trying to bring under control the rush of feelings that always rose inside her each time she saw him.

"I promised Willie yesterday before I brought y'all home from the Sidewinder that I'd take him on a ride around town one day this week," he said.

Jessica eyed him doubtfully, then looked at her son, dancing around with excitement. "You didn't wait long," she replied.

"Coke," Meg called, coming up from the back of the store, her normally jovial face grave. "You hear about the killin' of that drover this mornin' on the Blankenship place?"

"Yep," he answered. "Met the poor fellow a coupla times. Seemed a decent sort. You hear how many cattle was rustled?"

"Cactus told me eight hundred," she said. "So that'd probably be around four hundred." Sharing Coke's habit, she automatically halved Cactus's customary exaggerations. "Heard it was Lucas's best stock. Wonder how the thieves knew where t'find 'em."

"Don't know. I'm fixin' t'pay Lucas a visit after Willie an' me finish our ride." He turned to the boy. "Ready, son?"

"Yes, sir!" he cried.

"I'll have him back in less'n a hour," Coke said to Jessica.

She followed them to the door, watching as Coke picked up her sparkly-eyed little boy and swung him onto Windy's back.

"You're not playing fair," she said.

"Not if I can help it," he replied, adjusting the stirrups to her son's short legs.

Pulling the reins of the two horses off the hitching rail, he handed Willie Windy's reins, then went around to mount Ole Belcher.

"Coke?" she asked in a high voice.

He stopped. "Yes, Jessie?"

"You are taking care, aren't you?"

"What?"

She stepped off the boardwalk and came toward him. "This . . . this killing on the Blankenship ranch," she stammered. "Well, it reminded me of the attack on your land only a little over a week ago. You . . . and the others out on your ranch are taking care, aren't you?"

His eyes warmed. "Yes, Jessie, we're takin' care." Then, putting his arm around her shoulders, he kissed her lightly on the cheek. "An' it's sweet o' you to ask."

She put her hand over the place where he'd kissed her as he climbed onto Ole Belcher. "You're not playing fair," she repeated.

Smiling down at her, he turned his horse around.

"I know," she murmured to herself. "Not if you can help it."

After returning Willie to his mother, Coke rode out to the Blankenship ranch. Lucy's usual fluttery motions and breathless, giddy chatter had died out, as though the air that normally swirled around the inside of her head had sunk into a doldrum. Her husband's face was tightened to stone. Lucas Blankenship looked past rage, past mourning, and past hope. Coke needed no more confirmation of his suspicions.

As soon as he decently could, Coke asked Lucas straight out, "How much the Warner Savin's an' Loan into you for?"

Coke didn't think that a face could get tauter than Lucas's, but it did. "As of a week ago, eighteen thousand, nine hundred fifty-two dollars an' eighty-seven cents," Lucas intoned, the numbers seared on his brain.

"It ain't my habit t'bail folks out, but t'buy 'em out," Coke said, "but this time I'll give you an option."

And as Hector Navarro and Graham McKetchin had done before him, Lucas chose to take the two-percent loan. The papers were signed the following day and Coke advanced Lucas the money. The rancher set out for Warner to buy back his mortgage, climbing onto the wagon next to a wife in whose head the breeze had started up again, her tongue fanning it out at a prodigious rate.

Coke was at the site on his ranch where the well diggers had struck water the week before. Already the men were walling in the well, and hammers clanked as the men assembled the derrick on the ground nearby. Graham McKetchin came ambling across the field through the powdery furrow of dust churned up by his horse.

"Goldurn, thought I'd never find you," he remarked, lifting his hat and wiping his glistening head with his handkerchief. "With all this space you got here, seems like your men would be spendin' most o' their time just stumblin' aroun' tryin' t'get a fix as t'where they are."

"Most of 'em grew up here," Coke replied. "So they already got a lifelong acquaintance with it. What brought you this way, Graham?"

The fiddle player grew sober. "Heard some news outa Warner. Thought it'd be worth your while t'get it straightaway."

"What is it?"

"Well, you know my second cousin is a court clerk in Warner. His wife paid us a visit this mornin'. Seems the Silver Mountain Land Company filed a claim on a good piece o' your land late yesterday."

Coke's expression remained fixed. "You happen t'know on what grounds they filed this claim?"

"Accordin' to my cousin's wife, it's based on their acquirin' o' the San Sebastian. Seems there was a clause in the mortgage papers Celestina Castillo signed a coupla years back when she borrowed money from the Savings an' Loan. Clause said somethin' about the mortgage including all the land attached to the San Sebastian Ranch accruin' to it from the original Castillo land grant."

"In what court was this claim filed?" Coke asked.

"The Thirty-second."

"Judge Albertson's court.'Tain't surprisin'. Heard he was solid in T. C. Barrett's pocket these days." Coke was silent for a time. "The deeds I got on this land would probably have a hard time standin' up in that honcho's court even if they was signed in stone by God."

"I'm doggone sorry t'be bringin' news like this out to you," Graham apologized.

"I appreciate that you did, Graham. Though I don't much cotton t'gettin' hit with a ugly situation like this, it didn't come as too big a surprise."

"That so?"

"I been gettin' in T. C. Barrett's way lately. Been expectin' him t'come back at me for some while." Coke's eyes hardened. "I may have one helluva fight on my hands, but not one foot, not one single inch o' my land, will I ever give up to T. C. Barrett. Or anybody else. One o' these days, Barrett's gonna regret ever decidin' t'try t'take me on, one on one."

❧ Chapter 26

THE REGULAR ASSORTMENT of old-timers had parked themselves in their usual spaces on the benches around the courthouse square at Warner. Settling into their daily rounds of reminiscing and deliberating over politics and local doings, they presided over their small corner of the world, both judges and witnesses. The watchers' gaze trailed after anyone who moved down the street with any purposefulness, as they vaguely wondered where he was going or coming from and why.

Five empty wagons with "Siden" painted on their sides approached in a row from the train depot, having just transferred their loads of hides to the freight cars waiting in the station. The unweighted frames of the wagons rattled loose-jointedly as they rolled by the square.

Handsome Jack Siden strolled toward town from the depot,

Beau Barrett at his side. A pretty young woman stepped into their path, greeting Jack. The two men stopped, Siden's face reflecting cool amusement as she chatted coquettishly up at him while Beau, leaning forward, listened in, his adolescent features assuming an artificial soberness. With a wave, the woman moved on. Siden made a side comment to Beau, which the younger man, eyes eager, bent forward to catch. Then, turning, he looked after the woman and let out a lewd guffaw.

"Dammit," T. C. Barrett growled from his office window. "I told Siden t'leave Beau alone."

"It's Beau who's the hanger-on," Ray replied from the desk. "What do you think Siden should do? Slap him off like a mosquito?"

They were in T.C.'s office at the Savings and Loan, sounds of the bustle of business trickling in from the main reception area on the other side of the door.

Ray shook his head. "I can't see why you're so set against that man."

"He's trouble." T.C. turned from the window.

"Trouble?" I doubt that you'll ever catch him getting drunk and involving Beau in shooting out store windows, or pistol-whipping some seventy-five-year-old Mexican on the street into a coma like that riffraff you have working for your land company did a few weeks ago."

"The boys were just lettin' off a little steam," T.C. said, sitting down at his desk.

"Yes, I'm sure," Ray said tiredly. "So what kind of trouble could Siden be?"

"He's too unpredictable," Barrett returned. "Can only be controlled up to a point. The man's ice inside."

"I thought you regarded that as high recommendation for a man," Ray said. Then, seeing the hard look his father shot him, he decided to back off. He reached for a document. "Let's get to this foreclosure you want done on the Twin Rock Ranch. If we hold off a few more weeks, I think Red Mitchell will be able to come up with the money to keep the place."

"That ain't what I want an' you know it," T.C. retorted.

"It's only a small ranch, Dad." Ray liked Red Mitchell, a widower with a half dozen rough-and-tumble sons. "We won't miss a couple thousand acres."

"Land empires ain't built by lettin' opportunities slide by."

Ray sighed. There was no arguing with the Old Man. He never fought fairly anyhow. "I'm glad I don't have to serve the papers," he muttered.

"You just make 'em out," Barrett responded, reminding his son that he shared in the culpability.

They became aware that the babble of activity in the next room had suddenly dropped to a dead silence. Then they heard Wilkin Edmonds, whose desk was parked just outside the door, yelping in protest. The door crashed open and Coke Sanders was in the room, the office clerk leaping around behind him, spluttering, "I'm sorry, Mr. Barrett. He just barreled on by an'—" until Coke calmly reached back and closed the door in Edmonds's face.

Barrett's hand was sliding into his desk drawer.

"Wouldn't do that if I was you," Coke said expressionlessly. "I got some men who'd make damn sure that you'd pay . . . personal . . . if it ever turned out that I was on the receivin' end of a homicide."

His eyes steady on his enemy, T.C. withdrew his hand.

Arms folded, Coke coolly surveyed the room. "So this is where you commit your crimes."

"Need a loan?" Barrett inquired impassively.

"Nothin' you got, I'd want." His eyes included Ray. He approached the desk. "Though it appears I got somethin' that you want."

"And while I'm at it, I'm gonna get back that land you stole from my family."

"That a fact," Coke said coldly. "Well, you know somethin'? That claim o' yours got me t'thinkin'. If you want my land so all-fired bad, why, hell, I might as well give you a piece of it."

His eyes holding Barrett's, he drew a small cloth bag out of his belt. He loosened the string and, tipping the bag, slowly poured the dirt out onto the papers in the middle of T.C.'s desk. He dropped the empty bag on top.

"Now, go ahead, Barrett," he said. "Take off them high-polished city shoes o' yours an' prance aroun' in it all you want." Leaning his fists on the desk, Coke brought his face to within a foot of Barrett's. " 'Cause this here is the only piece o' my land that you're ever gonna be able t'stand on an' claim as your own."

"You might be in for a surprise, Sanders," Barrett growled.

Coke's eyes remained level. "I'm hardly ever taken by surprise.'' His voice lowered. ''. . . though I can be damn good at givin' em.''

Straightening up, he walked unhurriedly to the door. Putting his hand on the doorknob, he made a half turn and surveyed the room again.

''You gotta do somethin' 'bout your decor, Barrett. Room looks too normal. It don't reflect your personality a-tall. A stuffed turkey buzzard on the table might look right, pair o' fangs on the wall . . . mebbe a few gutted ranchers on the floor . . .''

And opening the door, he walked out.

The amber lights from the vaqueros' houses warmed the darkness in the Sidewinder's south compound. Inside one of the houses an infant squawled, then abruptly broke off as he was put to his mother's breast.

Coke and Alejandro wandered outside after dinner at Alejandro's home. October was settling in, and although heat still weighted the daylight hours, it was easing off at night. An inviting breeze riffled across the flatlands, luring folks outside. They sat on their front stoops or in chairs that they'd pulled out their doors, enjoying the fresh air and the warmed-over gossip. Off to the side, a half dozen youngsters played mumblety-peg, slinging knives at a target scratched out as a circle on the ground.

Over the years, an easy tempo of words and silences had developed between Coke and Alejandro whenever they were together. There was no need to point out that there was trouble ahead; Alejandro knew. It was understood, for Coke yielded to nothing and to no one where his land was concerned.

Knowing how deeply Coke was attached to his land, as though it were an extension of himself, Alejandro remained touched that Coke had relented a few years ago in allowing him to buy those five thousand acres.

''Interestin' ''—Coke broke the silence—''how this claim has arisen from Barrett's gettin' the San Sebastian. While he was alive, Juan Fernando Castillo never challenged my pa an' me over the land we bought from his cousins. He probably had documents sketchin' out the original Spanish land grant to his ancestry and how it was divided up over the generations. I wonder if Doña Celestina still has those papers.''

''Es posible,'' Alejandro replied.

''You know, Alejandro,'' Coke went on, ''that ambush out here a coupla weeks back got me thinkin'. If the same thing happened t'me as happened t'John Castillo, I doubt that Sarie'd be able t'hold the Sidewinder together over the long haul any better'n the doña did. Sarie's too trustin'. There're too many slick varmints out there, an' folks ain't scared enough of a woman." He fell silent, reflecting. "Wonder how the doña an' her young-uns are gettin' on?"

"Ellos todavía viven con la madre de Doña Celestina en Ciudad Guerrero," he replied. They still live with Doña Celestina's mother in the city of Guerrero.

"Been six years since Juan Fernando's murder an' somethin' about it still gnaws at me. I been wantin' t'talk to the doña for some time now. With this land challenge Barrett's flung at me, I got good reason to. Trouble is, my Spanish can give out on me when the talk turns complicated, an' I don't know how good a handle the doña's got on English."

"Llevate a Cruz contigo," Alejandro suggested. Take Cruz with you.

"Think I will. It'd be worthwhile havin' him along just t'make sure that the doña an' me don't wind up perplexin' each other too much."

🌸 Chapter 27

DOÑA CELESTINA CASTILLO was the only child born to Don Federico Guevara Ybarez and his wife, Sofia. Don Federico was fifty years old at the time of his daughter's birth, and a respected merchant in Ciudad Guerrero. Like many men of his gentle breeding, he also owned a small ranch outside of town, which he'd relegated into the care of a few trusted employees and, dutifully pulling on his boots, visited once a month. He wasn't a rich man, but he was held in rich esteem, for he was a scholar. The highly honored position of town historian had been conferred upon him by the people of Ciudad Guerrero. Until his death at the age of seventy, he wrote about the people of his town and region. The books that resulted from his labor of love survived him, occupying a prominent place on the mantel of his daughter's home.

Don Federico had been exceptionally close to his Celestina. Her arrival was like a miracle from heaven, as though God's light had unexpectedly shone upon him. And he poured upon his beloved daughter every attention and advantage that was his to dispose.

He saw that Celestina received the finest education available to a young woman in northern Mexico, sending her at the age of twelve to the convent school in Monterrey. There for six years, as she grew into a young woman of rare beauty, she studied Latin, French, Catholic theology, history, literature, art, and music. Each September and January, with great emotional sacrifice, Don Federico delivered her into the care of the nuns in Monterrey.

Celestina was fifteen years old when she met Juan Fernando Castillo, and he was twenty-seven. In Ciudad Guerrero only two events could bring together large gatherings of family and friends from far-flung places . . . weddings and funerals. It was the latter that occasioned their first meeting, the deceased being an uncle by marriage of Juan Fernando as well as the husband of the first cousin of Celestina's father.

At the funeral mass, as she alternately stood and knelt and sat between her parents through the service, Celestina became aware of a handsome man glancing across the church aisle at her. The experience wasn't unusual, although not until recently had Celestina become aware of the power of her beauty. She was flattered by the attention that it brought her, while at the same time she felt frightened and confounded that in doing nothing at all she could arouse such emotion.

At the family gathering following the burial, a cousin introduced Juan Fernando Castillo to her. Celestina thought him very handsome but far too proud. She couldn't imagine that anyone so proud as he could ever really care what she thought or felt. But he did. When, two afternoons later, in the company of her cousin, he paid the family a visit for *merienda*, he listened to every word she spoke with a singular raptness. It was as though he had seen a well-made musical instrument and had to know if the quality of the tone that it expressed was equally fine.

Celestina didn't think that one so proud as Juan Fernando Castillo would inconvenience himself to travel many miles to visit her home, where her maiden aunt, Hortencia, sat in the corner looking sternly on as they conversed in the parlor, then followed a few steps behind them as they strolled through the garden. Or that he'd travel even as far as Monterrey to visit her for only one hour in the reception room of the convent school, their meeting presided over by two fierce-looking nuns. But he did inconvenience himself.

She never thought that one so proud as Juan Fernando Castillo would bestir himself to romantic gestures, sending love letters and poems, bringing her flowers, paying a singer to serenade her outside her window not once, but many times. But he did.

She never thought that one so proud as Juan Fernando Castillo could ever be ill-at-ease. But when he came one night to ask Don Federico for his daughter's hand in marriage, he was very nervous. And indeed, her father did look more severe than an Old Testament God when he ushered Juan Fernando into his library.

Celestina never thought that one so proud as Juan Fernando Castillo would be willing to defer the gratification of any desire once he'd moved himself to speak for it. But when her father told him that he must wait a full year until Celestina completed her education and became seventeen, he did wait.

And until she married Juan Fernando Castillo, Celestina never thought that one so proud could be capable of such great passion or such patient, understanding tenderness. But he was.

And until she married Juan Fernando Castillo, Celestina never thought herself capable of such soaring joy and such fiery and sweet, sweet love . . . but she was.

As the years passed, she saw other qualities in Juan Fernando that gave her reason to admire him, qualities that maturity and endurance through life would require. Foremost was his sense of duty—to his heritage, to his land, to his people, to his church, and most important, to his family. Juan Fernando Castillo was, to his fingertips and to his marrow, the *patrón* of San Sebastian.

In no way had Celestina been prepared to lose him at the time that she did. It had seemed an ordinary day, like any other, when he prepared to leave for a visit with his cousins just across the border in Mexico. He had arisen early, looked in on his children still slumbering in their beds, then gone downstairs for his usual light breakfast. Having not yet shaken the queasiness of the morning sickness of her fifth pregnancy, she'd been a little late in joining him at the breakfast table. While she nibbled on a dry flour tortilla and sipped weak tea to settle her stomach, they talked of everyday things.

She followed him into the library and looked on while he gathered his things for his trip. Then she stopped him at the door, to smooth the shoulders of the shirt that didn't need smoothing and straighten the tie that didn't need straightening. And, in the privacy of the library, to brush a kiss upon his cheek. She didn't stand and watch him mount his horse and ride away, but only waved lightly at him from the library window before turning away to begin her household chores.

That evening after dinner, she was upstairs in the nursery, rocking and soothing her then youngest child, Alfredo Federico, who was feverish and fretful from a summer cold, when she heard horses pounding up the drive outside. Holding her baby against her, she went to the window and saw two vaqueros rein in sharply, leap off their mounts, and charge up the steps of the hacienda. At that moment, glimpsing the confusion and distress upon their faces, she felt a change in the atmosphere.

Passing little Alfredo Federico into the arms of the servant girl, she walked down the hallway. Sounds of whispered commotion were rising up from the foyer below. At the top of the stairs, she stopped. Servants from the kitchen and other parts of the house had streamed out and were collecting around the two vaqueros.

"Qué pasa?" she asked. What's the matter?

They froze and looked up at her in alarm, as though she'd caught them in some dreadful indiscretion. Yet she felt a tensed watchfulness in them like the silence before an explosion.

"Qué pasa?" she repeated, coming down the stairs.

Their eyes flicked aside at one another as though communicating a warning or searching for a sign. She noticed a film of tears gathering in the eyes of Manuela, the oldest servant. Celestina stopped before her and waited for an answer.

Manuela averted her eyes. *"Está muerto,"* she whispered. He's dead. Then pulling up her apron, she sobbed into its hem.

"Quién está muerto?" Celestina demanded, moving toward the closest vaquero. Who is dead?

Ducking his head, he peeked up at her in a mortified way as though he deserved a blow.

"Quién?" she repeated.

Unable to avoid her eyes, he winced as though the blow had fallen. *"El patrón."*

She didn't collapse or become hysterical. She didn't weep or wail. She didn't believe so outrageous a falsehood. She didn't believe it.

She quietly walked into the library and, brushing a hand over the book that Juan Fernando had left off reading the night before, sat down at his desk. Picking up his ivory letter opener, she thoughtfully ran her fingers along the flow of the design carved into its handle. She knew that one day death would separate her from Juan Fernando, but that day was a thousand years away. Not here, not now, on such an ordinary day.

She didn't believe it when Father Dominic burst into the library. Panting, his robes disheveled, he struggled to contain the shock and anguish written on his face, for he had a reputation to maintain as a tough old bird. Then he joined the others gathered silently around her, waiting for her to signal them how to respond.

Sitting there, fingering Juan Fernando's letter opener, she still didn't believe it as word spread and people started converging upon the hacienda, running up the road from town, galloping their horses in from the fields of the ranch, their voices outside asking the same question in hushed bewilderment, getting the same response, and like Celestina herself, stubbornly refusing to accept it.

She only started to believe it a little when a silence spread through the crowd outside. Carefully setting the letter opener down exactly as Juan Fernando had left it, she took Father Dominic's arm and walked to the front door.

A wagon had turned through the gate of the compound and, in the waning pink-golden dusk, was slowly rolling down the drive. A small procession moved with it. Many hands clasped the back and sides of the wagon rim, as though through their fingers on the wood they might receive some final impression of the *patrón*'s fading essence.

The measured, tired clop of the horses' hooves, the grate of iron wheels on the pebbled drive, the shuffle of feet, echoed in the unnatural silence. As the wagon passed slowly through the throng, hands fluttered up in butterfly movements, making the sign of the cross. Faces that had been set hard as marble quivered into tears. On the road outside the compound, Anglos from town had gathered, looking on from beyond the gates as though timid to intrude on such a tragic occasion, the deep resonances of which could be known only to Juan Fernando's own.

The wagon slowed to a stop at the foot of the steps. It didn't jerk in its stopping, but simply ceased motion. With Father Dominic on one side and Manuela on the other, Celestina descended the steps and, as in a trance, approached the wagon and looked in. She saw a plain brown blanket of coarse weave molded over a form, a form impassive in its stillness. As though merely curious, she slowly moved around the wagon, her eyes on that form, the scattered sobs in the crowd flittering about on the edge of her consciousness like fireflies.

Her gaze fell upon a hat lying in the corner of the wagon, so intimately familiar, yet its import registering only faintly in her mind. Then she stopped, staring down. The vibrations of the wagon as it moved down the road had dislocated the blanket a little. The side of a hand was visible at the edge of the coarse material. She knew that hand, had felt its touch, had run light kisses playfully over it. Comprehension exploded through Celestina, and with a sigh, she sank to the ground.

For weeks Celestina moved through life as if she were playacting a role. People who came to the hacienda to pay their respects remarked on her dignified serenity, attributing it to the power of her faith. But her mother and the servants who dealt with her day by day saw a change in her, a disconnection from the world. In the middle of a discussion about the meals for the day or while she was doing some simple, commonplace task, they'd feel a sudden vacuum of stillness and, looking up, find her motionless, her expression vacant. Casting troubled looks her way, they'd wait out her silence until her thoughts resurfaced and she connected with her surroundings once more.

Each day before dawn, she went down to the cemetery and sat beside Juan Fernando's grave. While he was alive, this was the hour, before the ranch came awake, that she and Juan Fernando had set aside exclusively for themselves. It was a treasured time known only to them, of cozy intimacies and quiet conversations, its tone melting a glaze of secret contentment over the remainder of the day. It was still a requirement of her heart, in those first few weeks, to share this hour with him.

She took her meals upstairs in the nursery with the children, because she could not stand to look across the table in the dining room and see that empty place before her. She returned to her bed at night only when she was too numb with exhaustion to feel that empty place on the mattress beside her spreading its chill emptiness through her soul. She avoided his library, where many of his favorite possessions were sprinkled about the room like the leaves deposited by a tree passing into its autumn dormancy. Only, there was no dormancy here; the life that had left them there had been uprooted and transported far beyond the stars, with only the leaves remaining, scattered around a circle of emptiness.

Not until after a month had passed was she able to truly weep, and then she couldn't stop. Sometimes, when the weight of her grief threatened to crush her, a black rage would take root inside her and crawl through her like dark-leafed ivy.

Who? Why? the questions cried out at her. Who was this monster of unspeakable arrogance who, by his savage act, presumed to interpose his will over God's, destroying a life before its time and purpose had been fulfilled? For what reason? Money? Power? Pride? Well, they were nothing, meaningless, less than ashes compared to a priceless life being well lived, a life beloved and irreplaceable to many others.

But no answers came to her, and the questions had not lost their power to torment her even now, over six long years later.

Too soon after Juan Fernando's death, the world had began to intrude upon her. Without the *patrón*, the people turned to her for direction when she hadn't found firm footing herself.

"The *patrón* said that we should sell these cattle by October. Do you wish to sell them, doña?" "Doña, the barbed wire that your husband ordered was delivered three months ago and we have yet to receive our payment." "Doña, the pump in the northeast windmill is badly in need of repair. Should we order another?" And when her trusted foreman, Javier, approached and with great embarrassment said that the men had not received their pay in two full months, Celestina finally betook herself into the library to probe the mysteries of Juan Fernando's desk.

She knew almost nothing about cattle and running a ranch. She knew even less about managing money. At first any request for money that she received she dispensed with as quickly as possible by writing out a check. She couldn't be bothered. Her family was her higher duty, and the center of her life. And when she did try to turn from her children to deal with other matters, they exerted themselves to make certain that they would not be disregarded.

Her two oldest children, their world thrown off balance by the loss of their father and unable to comprehend it, became angry and rebellious, provoking each other constantly. They also started having trouble with their school lessons, requiring her help. Her third child came down with scarlet fever and then pneumonia, and for almost a week Celestina was up with her night and day. One morning before breakfast, her four-year-old decided that it would be great sport to slide down the banister, and met with a bad concussion when she went flying off the end. Her two-year-old, Alfredo Federico, was a little tornado, having more energy than the two servants that she paid to control him had together. One night he climbed up on the side of his crib, tumbled off, and broke his wrist. Then her baby was born, a daughter, Angela Sofia. The birth depleted Celestina's strength; yet she had to nurse her infant at least three times a night and as many times during the day.

So divided did Celestina start to feel between the requirements of her family and those of the ranch that doing justice to either seemed an almost insurmountable task. She pictured herself trying to scale a pair of mountains at the same time, while rocks from both sides above kept shaking loose and tumbling down upon her head.

Then two years after Juan Fernando's death, her trusted foreman, Javier, on whom she'd come to depend totally to manage the ranch, became gravely ill and asked to return to his ancestral home in Mexico to die. To replace him Celestina hired a man highly recommended by Juan Fernando's cousin. Soon she began to receive hints, accelerating into complaints, from other employees. She turned them away, refusing for almost a year to believe them, because the new manager seemed so competent and so anxious to help her. Finally she was forced to confront the disgusting fact that he and the San Sebastian attorney had taken advantage of her inexperience and were enriching themselves at the ranch's expense.

Many of the San Sebastian people closed ranks around her, trying to protect her. Yet there were always a few who, with gentle and humble words, only pretended to protect her, and gaining her trust, immediately started betraying it. It was the aggregate of the acts of those few, who thought that a little pilfering of the ranch's resources wouldn't really affect it that much, that in the end was the most crippling to it. And always when their transgressions were revealed to her, Celestina went through a time of disbelief before she could confront their dishonesty. It was beyond her understanding how anyone could look her in the eye and behave so kindly and acquiescently toward her and at the same time be doing her injury when out of her sight. Celestina had never before dealt with betrayal. She'd always assumed that people would be kind to her.

Celestina was the center of the San Sebastian, the one around whom everyone revolved, and in time it became apparent that the center wasn't holding. Out of affection and loyalty, many of her employees gamely tried to stay close and keep the motion going, but it was hard to sustain the momentum once the money ran out.

Why had Juan Fernando been carrying so much money with him on the day he died? she asked herself over and over. That money now would have made all the difference in the world to the San Sebastian.

When she had run out of the money that had been left her, only T. C. Barrett of the Warner Savings and Loan stood willing to make the immense sacrifice to his institution to loan her more. Celestina was only a month late in her payments when Barrett called in her entire loan. She frantically scrambled to get the money, but her family's property in Mexico couldn't be sold in time to raise the cash . . . and even then, such a panic sale couldn't have brought enough to satify the entire loan.

And on the day she and her children were dispossessed of their home the people of the San Sebastian were reluctant to let them go. They followed along behind, then stopped on the hill, the tears streaming down their faces as they watched the Castillo's small wagon train recede into the distance, and moved down the road with their wagonloads of belongings. It was Celestina who finally felt the biggest betrayer. She had betrayed her husband's faith in her, betrayed his legacy, betrayed the many good people who had been loyal to the Castillo family for generations, and most painful of all, she'd betrayed her own children, allowing their legacy to slip from her hands.

Oh, if she had it back, she'd do everything differently, for she was not so naive anymore. But she didn't have it back and would probably never get it back, and she was bitter.

Most of all was she bitter at that unknown beast who had brought her husband down; he had brought everything down in his vile act. It was as though the bullet that he'd fired on that fateful day had passed through Juan Fernando and gone through her as well.

Chapter 28

COKE AND CRUZ Cortez walked through the streets of Ciudad Guerrero in the late Saturday afternoon sunlight. They were on their way to see Doña Celestina at her childhood home where she and her children were now living. The Doña, in response to an overture from Coke, had invited them to *merienda* at four o'clock.

As they neared the house, which was three blocks past the church, La Iglesia de Nuestra Señora del Refugio, Coke could feel Cruz's growing nervousness. He was about to be received as a guest by the aristocratic lady of the San Sebastian.

It wasn't only Cruz's ability to rattle off both Spanish and English that had prompted Coke to bring him along on this visit. Through the years, Coke had spoken with the doña only a few times, in brief and proper circumstances, and he was concerned that she might feel ill at ease meeting alone with him, the Anglo rancher who had often been at odds with her husband. As the *patrón*'s wife she'd known most of the Mexican people who lived around the San Sebastian, and Cruz's face would probably be familiar to her. Then, too, Alejandro's older son always stood out in a crowd. He had his father's height and broad shoulders, and the fairer complexion and refined features of his mother, María Luisa. He had a mouthful of strong, even, white teeth and—though he showed little of it at the moment—the smooth, easy grace of movement of one accustomed to exercises of speed and strength and skill. Since the age of fourteen he'd been fighting off the señoritas . . . and probably had given up the struggle on more occasions than his father would have approved.

Never had Coke seen Cruz so well turned out as he was this afternoon. There was a fresh-scrubbed look about him. His thick hair was meticulously parted at the side, and he had on a crisp new shirt, its color unfaded and unsoiled from use. Even his hat looked brushed of dust and scrubbed of stain. The moment they arrived at the gate of the Guevara residence, he flipped that hat off his head and held it self-consciously in both hands.

As they waited for the bell to be answered, Coke heard a horse approaching at a slow gallop down the road. He glanced in the direction of the sound, and was momentarily thunderstruck. The rider was no more than a boy, fourteen or fifteen, but the features of his face, the proud way he held himself as he rode, the familiar slight tilt of his hat, hit Coke with such sharp recognition that for an instant he felt that time had turned back. Moving to the side, he watched the boy guide his horse down the drive to the stables at the back of the house. A regretful sadness stirred in Coke, for Juan Fernando would have been very proud to see his son growing into such a fine likeness of himself.

A woman in her sixties admitted them into the foyer. It was also a hall breezeway, with wrought-iron gates opening onto the street and, at the opposite side, onto a private courtyard. The servant took their hats, leaving Cruz flummoxed as to what to do with his hands. Then she led them into the *sala* of the house and offered them a seat. The doña would be slightly delayed, the woman told them, for she had gone outside to talk to her oldest son, Juanito. He had been a full two hours late in returning from his horseback ride and had missed his violin lesson. By the way the old servant's nose wrinkled up at the mention of the violin lesson, it appeared *she* didn't regret that the boy had missed it.

She left Coke and Cruz sitting in the shadowed coolness of the room. One side of the *sala*, with high, arched windows, looked out onto an enclosed courtyard. A water fountain stood at its center, and curving brick paths ran through the flowering garden. The house was built on the square around the courtyard, with doors from its many rooms opening onto it.

Two huge portraits of a man and a woman dominated the *sala*, staring proudly down side by side from the twelve-foot wall. Ornate molding ran around the top and bottom of the walls, framing floor and ceiling alike. The dark furniture was all hand-carved, more artistic than comfortable. A grand piano filled the corner of the room. Draped over the piano was a fringed scarf on which rested a violin and bow. A wooden music stand carved like the treble clef stood beside the piano, sheet music scattered lightly on it. Situated before two chairs, near the courtyard windows the better to catch their light, were two easels bearing needlepoint designs stretched across frames. The needles had been stuck through the background fabric, their tails of pastel thread curving gracefully back to the point where the designs had left off. And everywhere on shelves and tables were porcelain figurines, books, photographs in ornate silver frames.

In Coke's estimation, he and Cruz were as much out of place in this room as two big brown boulders dropped in the middle of a bed of petunias.

The servant appeared again, with a frosty lemonade pitcher and glasses on a silver tray. She set the tray on the table before them, and served them the refreshment along with linen napkins. Another servant followed with an assortment of *pan de dulce*. A young girl, she discreetly eyed Cruz as she set her tray on the table.

Coke reached for one of the sweet rolls, gesturing for Cruz to take one. But the young man silently shook his head.

"Wouldn't know how t'deal with the crumbs, eh?" he teased. But Cruz was too tense to respond.

They heard footsteps on the tile floor of the breezeway and Doña Celestina walked into the room, followed by a wizened-looking woman carrying a cloth knitting bag over her arm. The two men stood, Cruz dropping his napkin and abashedly grabbing it up.

The doña's entry was like a shadow passing before a candle, for she was dressed in the solid black of mourning. Even the tops of her hands were covered by her black lacy half gloves, leaving only her slender fingers exposed. For jewelry she wore only simple gold earrings, a small, unadorned gold cross at her neck, and her thin gold wedding band on her finger. Many Mexican widows dressed in mourning for the remainder of their lives, Coke reflected, even if that meant wearing black for fifty years. He often felt something akin to a shiver at the sight of these women wrapped in black. Their appearance struck him as a bald reminder of the Grim Reaper, and a kind of rebuke to life.

Recovering himself, he realized that even in her widow's weeds, the doña was still strikingly beautiful. Her hair was a soft black velvet against alabaster skin. Her dark eyes were huge, and so deep it seemed they might draw a person in and hold him there ... r. Five years without pregnancy had restored her figure to ... hful slenderness, which her erect posture and the starkness ... ess emphasized. Hearing a soft sigh at his side, Coke wondered it Cruz had lost hold of both of his languages along with his appetite.

"I'm most sorry for causing you to wait, Señor Sanders," she said with an overly precise pronunciation that was almost an accent. "But I had a family matter to attend to."

Coke noticed the tiny sparks still shooting out of those dark eyes, and felt a twinge of sympathy for the horseback-riding, violin lesson-avoiding Juanito.

"It was no bother, doña," he responded. "Your people took good care of us. Have you met my outfit boss, Cruz Cortez?"

"Oh, yes." She smiled. "I remember Cruz from many years of Sunday masses at the church of San Sebastian. *Cómo está usted, Cruz?*"

Cruz's color rose at the mention of the Sunday masses.

"Bien, doña," He finally found his voice, thumping it out a little loudly.

"This is my mother, Doña Sofia Guevara," she introduced the silver-haired lady. "Señor Sanders *y* Señor Cruz Cortez."

Her mother nodded. *"Con mucho gusto."*

Gesturing for them to be seated, the doña took a chair directly across from them while her mother sat off to the side. Apparently only there to lend her support, Doña Sofia pulled a half-finished sweater, her yarn, and needles out of her cloth bag and commenced her knitting.

The doña, reared to be polite and gracious to guests in her home, sensed Cruz's discomfort and made an effort to put the younger man at ease. She inquired about his family, then about others on the Sidewinder.

"Does Petra Dominguez still suffer greatly from the arthritis?" she asked.

"Sí, doña," Cruz replied, and spoke of Petra.

Gradually, as they talked on, his tension subsided. And in truth, the doña did seem hungry for news about the people she had known.

Coke studied the doña as she spoke with Cruz. He'd wondered about her often during this past year since she'd lost the San Sebastian. There was still a sadness about her, he saw; but there was also, in the lift of her chin and the tightness at the corners of her eyes, an edge of hardness, of reined-in anger. No longer did the softness of her character run all the way through.

Maybe she was more than a little like Jessica, he thought. Dressed just about as plain, too.

"It was most generous of you, Señor Sanders," she was saying to him, "to assume support of our school."

Coke was a little surprised. "I wasn't aware that you knew o' that, doña."

"Oh, yes. I correspond with Father Dominic regularly. I hope that you will forgive my presumption, but it was I who suggested that he seek your help with the school. I know you are not Catholic, but I have often felt that it is your way to live in accord with the world around you." A small smile appeared. "Even though you and my husband were often in opposition."

"It was only over gettin' more land, doña," Coke responded. "I want you t'know, though, that every time a choice piece o' land came up for sale, I never questioned his right t'be where he was or t'take me on from time t'time. I'd o' never wished on him what happened."

"At my husband's funeral I studied many of the faces in the crowd," the doña confessed. "Your face, if you'll forgive me for saying it, was one of them. I could find no satisfaction on it. Indeed, Señor Sanders, you looked quite ill."

"I did feel sick," Coke admitted, "seein' you an' your little-uns there. Few things have ever hit me as hard as John's murder. I guess I'd kinda taken it for granted that he'd always be around. We was close to the same age. We had the same feelin' about our land. An' I knew that from that day on, I wouldn't be able anymore to look at a new piece o' land goin' up for auction an' think, wonder if John'll be goin' after it t'buy it, or else be enterin' into the biddin' just t'force the price up on me. Wonder if this time I should throw myself into the biddin' t'force the price up on him. Kept me sharp an' wide awake, knowin' that John was out there goin' after the same things I was."

"John," the doña repeated, and smiled.

The outer corners of Coke's eyes crinkled. "Well, ma'am," he drawled. "I never did feel altogether comfortable callin' him 'Don Juan.' "

"Sometimes I did," she said softly, then glanced subtly aside at her mother, looking a little embarrassed at her indiscretion in divulging the fond joke between her and her husband.

But seeing Coke across from her awakened a lot of old memories. He and Juan Fernando had had such a long-established habit of vying with each other for more land that seldom did the people who lived around Dispenseme think of one of them without the other coming to mind. And there was a quality in Coke that brought Juan Fernando back vividly to her. It wasn't that the two men were at all alike in either appearance or manner. But there was a suggestion about them both of being quietly vigilant, alert to everything going on around them. And even more, they had the same effortless way of dominating every space that they occupied, so it seemed too snug a fit for them. Perhaps that was the reason the two men had been hungry for so much land . . . to acquire a space big enough to fit themselves comfortably into.

"My husband never thought of you as his enemy, Señor Sanders," the doña went on. "But more as a competitor, somewhat like an opponent in a chess tournament."

"With a thousand dollars ridin' on the outcome o' the game," Coke finished. He grew serious. "An' now I find that I'm in another game, doña, only this one is a whole lot meaner than the one that I had goin' with John. This other hombre don't go after your king by cool maneuverin' accordin' to the rules o' the game . . . but by tryin' t'slam down all o' the pieces in between."

Celestina's face clouded. "T. C. Barrett."

Coke nodded.

"But how could that . . . that . . . *man*," she breathed, "be any threat to you?"

"Has t'do with that mortgage you signed, doña, when you borrowed money from Barrett's Savin's an' Loan."

She looked bewildered. "How could that be used against you, Señor Sanders?"

"Well, there was a phrase in it that referred to the original Castillo land grant. It's what has provided the openin' for Barrett t'go after me." And with Cruz's help he explained the phrase in the document she'd signed that was now the source of Barrett's claim on the Sidewinder.

"I remember that phrase," she said. "But I thought it of no consequence. The borders of the San Sebastian were clearly drawn. The other sections of the original Castillo land grant had been divided among my husband's ancestors generations ago. Could such a claim as that . . . that man has, based on a single line in a mortgage agreement, prevail over yours in court?"

"Depends on the judge, doña."

"Oh, yes . . . politics," Celestina said with distaste. "An entirely different game. One of dominion not over property but over people."

"An' through the right people . . . the property," Coke added.

"I neglected to consider the mischief that political influence in the wrong hands can sow. I am very sorry, señor, that my carelessness has created this problem for you."

"If Barrett couldna come at me from this direction, he'd o' found another," Coke said.

"Is there any way that I can help you?"

"There could be. I have the deeds, but I might need more. You said that the original Castillo land grant had been divided up generations ago. Is it possible that Juan Fernando had some old documents showin' how that was done?"

"It is possible," the doña replied. "My husband had many old journals, maps, and documents that he treasured. I've never looked at them. I had them locked in the safe at the bank here in Ciudad Guerrero."

"I know that this is askin' a lot, doña, but would you be willin' t'go through those documents lookin' for anything that'll help me prove that the land that my pa an' me bought over the years was already separated from the San Sebastian a long time before?"

She hesitated. Then her face hardened. "That man, Barrett, should not be allowed to steal *your* land, too. Yes, I will do as you request, Señor Sanders. Now, if I should find anything of use to you, when would you need it?"

"As soon as possible. Within a month, if you can."

"I will go tomorrow to start searching through those papers. . . ." She grew pensive. "Though it will give me no pleasure."

"It must cause you great pain, doña, to have to look at anything that reminds you of the San Sebastian," Cruz was moved to remark.

"You are very perceptive, Cruz," the doña replied, and Coke could almost see the warmth rising in Cruz's face at the compliment. "It does sadden me, knowing we have lost our home." A look of infinite anguish passed over her face, and disappeared like a ripple of water on a brook. "But it gives me even greater pain, Cruz, to know that it was I who lost it."

"You cain't blame yourself for not bein' brought up t'be suspicious enough or mean enough, doña," Coke said gently.

"But our home, Juan Fernando's beautiful and cherished home. For over one hundred fifty years, señor, through wars and revolutions, the San Sebastian endured, united, one with my husband's family. Until it fell into my hands.''

"It was through the murder o' your husband that you lost it," Coke said.

His words seemed to strike a chord in her, for those dark eyes electrified. "And—whatever animal murdered my husband is probably still getting up each morning, smelling the flowers of spring and eating cakes and sweets. Still enjoying the years that he savagely denied my husband.''

"Do you have any idea who the killer could be?" Coke asked.

That stopped her; she perplexedly shook her head. "I was told by the county sheriff . . . others . . . that the killer was probably a robber who'd heard about the money that Juan Fernando was carrying with him into Mexico. The money that he'd withdrawn from the Warner Savings and Loan two days before.''

"If you don't mind my askin', how much money *did* Juan Fernando draw?''

"According to the withdrawal paper I was shown, over forty-two thousand dollars.''

Coke lifted a brow. "Heard Juan Fernando had a good deal o' cash on him that day. Had no idea it was that much." He leaned forward, his dark eyes intense. 'When he went to Warner that last time, did you know that he was fixin' t'get him all that money?''

"I knew he was dissatisfied with something about the Savings and Loan. But no, when he went to Warner I thought that he was only going to withdraw, as he often did, enough cash to meet the ranch's monthly expenses . . . and no more.''

"Then, o' course, you had no idea he was carryin' all that cash into Mexico.''

"No idea at all. I didn't learn of it until a few days after his death. That was when the sheriff from Warner told me, and added that my husband had said he planned to take that money into Mexico. I must confess, hearing of the loss of so much money meant little to me at the time. I was still so deep in shock at the loss of my Juan Fernando. Not until months later did it occur to me that perhaps he *hadn't* taken the money with him that day, and I started searching through the hacienda for it. Every day for two weeks I searched, from the attic to the wine cellar. I searched, but of course, I found nothing.''

"Do you have any idea, then, why he'd be taking that much money into Mexico?''

She was leaning a little toward Coke now, her eyes as intense as his. "Sometimes he bought cattle and horses in Mexico. Sometimes he had business dealings with his cousins. Occasionally he became involved in the politics in northern Mexico . . . and that always took money. But so *much*? In six years, Señor Sanders, not one person has come forward and told me where that money was meant to go. Nor has anyone ever told me that he, or they, had been expecting to receive it."

"An' Juan Fernando wouldna told you himself?"

She settled back. "The ranch, business, money, those were the concerns of my husband. I was busy with my home and children. I had no interest in such things." Her voice dropped. "To my very deep regret later."

A child of around five had appeared in the doorway, clutching a doll against her with one arm. The other was wrapped around the edge of the doorway, at the ready to pop her back out of sight should the atmosphere of the room prove unwelcoming. In dress she was her mother's opposite. She sparkled in white, from the pert satin bow that topped her raven curls, to her pinafore, stockings, and shoes. She had her mother's huge, long-lashed eyes, and her own turned-up nose and impish little mouth.

"Ven aquí, mi corazón," the doña said gently. Come here, my heart.

Slipping her arm off the door, the child shyly entered the room, picking up speed as she neared the refuge of her mother.

"Señor Sanders, Señor Cruz, *mi hija*, Angela Sofia," the doña introduced her daughter.

The child curtsied, then snuggled back inside the circle of her mother's arm, rolling her eyes coyly up at them. This one would be a heartbreaker in ten years, Coke was certain.

"Your youngest, doña?" he asked.

Celestina nodded, then her eyes misted. "You know, Señor Sanders, worse to me than the loss of our home is knowing that my youngest children will go through life with no memory of their own of their living father."

"I saw Juanito ride up when we got here this afternoon. Gave me quite a start, he looked so much like his father. Has the same straight way o' holdin' hisself." He half smiled. "An' clothes seem t'fit on him the same neat way, too."

"I think this is the time in his life when he misses his father the most. Juan Fernando would already have begun preparing him to become *patrón.*'' She smiled proudly. ''On his own, my Juanito goes out to my father's small ranch almost every day, to learn all he can about cattle and the land. He will be ready, he tells me . . . for the day he is going to get the San Sebastian back.'' She paused, growing thoughtful. ''I advise him that he must not allow his anger to take too great a hold of him. One can use time better and reason with a clearer mind without such emotions.''

''And you, doña?'' Coke asked. ''How do you feel?''

The room seemed to grow cold from the chill that came to her eyes. ''I try not to infect my children with my feelings.''

''You have a right to 'em,'' Coke replied. ''Well, we'd better be goin'. Thanks for allowin' us this visit with you.''

They rose. Cruz was a little delayed in getting up, so thoroughly had his attention been fixed on the doña.

''I will go through the San Sebastian documents, Señor Sanders,'' the doña said as she walked them into the breezeway foyer. ''You will be hearing from me within two or three weeks.''

''*Muchas gracias,*'' Coke replied, taking his hat from the servant. ''*Estoy muy agradecido.*'' Many thanks. I am very grateful.

At the door he stopped and turned around. ''One thing has been botherin' me, *doña,* for all o' these six years.''

''What is that, Señor Sanders?'' she asked.

''Well, I just can't figger why Juan Fernando would be travelin' into Mexico all alone, without escort, an' all that cash on him.''

The doña nodded slowly. ''I have often wondered the same thing . . . for only a very foolish man would travel alone with so much money. And as you know, Señor Sanders, my husband was not a foolish man.''

Chapter 29

COKE STOOD IN Matthew Hamlin's waiting room in Warner, staring at the stuffed turkey buzzard that the young attorney had on his cabinet.

"My mother gave me that," he said a little sheepishly. "Thought it'd make a fine decoration for my office."

"Well, that's interestin'," Coke replied. "Most mas tend t'have your baby shoes bronzed when you open a office an' give 'em to you as bookends."

"Your ma do that, too?" Matthew asked.

Coke shook his head. "Woulda took too much bronze. Didn't get my first decent pair o' shoes till I started my schoolin'."

Matthew Hamlin was a young man, only a few years out of law school. He was something fresh and untainted amid Warner's polluted establishment, for Matthew still believed in the impartiality and rectitude of the law. It was his firm conviction that right must prevail. More important to Coke, though, was that Matthew didn't just philosophize over that conviction, he rolled up his sleeves and went out and fought for it. Matthew Hamlin was a scrapper, and a tenacious one.

They talked for a time in his office about the Silver Mountain Land Company's claim on the Sidewinder. Matthew wasn't naive. He apprehended quickly how Barrett planned to orchestrate the seizure of a large part of Coke's land. And he was already getting fired up for the fight.

"Play it low-key for a while," Coke advised. "Don't let Barrett's crowd know what you're up to. Let 'em think you won't be much of a threat to 'em, otherwise they could give you a purty rough time.

"Hope you realize," he added, "that your representin' me could cause you plenty o' trouble in any other cases you bring into Judge Albertson's court. He ain't a-gonna take kindly to your bein' willin' t'stand up for me, so he'll make durn sure that it won't be easy for you t'win anything else you bring before him."

"I realize that," Matthew replied. "What we're facing here, though, is a setup for highway robbery. It'll have to take the priority." He drummed his fingers on the desk. "I might explore some ways to get around Albertson."

"You mean go to the Forty-second? Ed Bierbaum's court?"

"Yes."

"What's your feelin' 'bout where he stands, Matt?"

"I haven't seen any sign that he's been drawn into Barrett's camp. On the other hand, he seems to have gotten mighty cautious lately. I think he'd be leery about getting dragged into any dispute between you and T. C. Barrett."

"Then you'll just hafta keep after him," Coke replied. "Now, I'm afeared that you won't be able t'bring him to our side by any high-toned arguments 'bout the right or wrong in this. You'll hafta go more basic than that. Ed Bierbaum loves bein' a judge. It does his heart proud each mornin' t'climb into that black robe an' have folks leapin' to their feet when he marches to his bench.

"He'll be facin' an election in about a year. It wouldn't hurt if you dropped him a few hints 'bout how I could swing a helluva-lotta votes in the south part o' the county. Hell, ain't no secret that T. C. Barrett—or anyone seen as bein' too close to him—would have a hard time winnin' a popularity contest in most parts o' the county."

"That's why I can't figure what Albertson hopes to gain by coming out too openly on Barrett's side."

"To retire a wealthy man," Coke responded. "Be on the lookout yourself, Matt, on that score, too. When word gets out that you're representin' me, could be you'd find some purty choice business droppin' into your lap all of a sudden from Barrett's people. Litigatin' for the county, maybe, or the railroad company . . . anything that might sweeten you up to their side, make you beholden to 'em, an' shy 'bout doin' somethin' that'd risk that fine new paddin' in your wallet."

"I don't compromise my principles," Matt said stiffly.

"An' it's them uncompromisin' principles o' yours, Matt, that's gonna make a big name for you around here one o' these days . . . or else get you shot." He half smiled. "I doubt they'll ever make you rich."

The testimony had droned on for over three hours. The battling McPherson brothers were at it again. This time the court fight between them was over the ownership of two hundred cows. Never mind that since they'd filed their suits, seventy of the cows had succumbed to the drought, that another sixty had been rustled, that whoever of the two brothers won the remainder of the beeves would have to sell them to pay his attorney's fees; still the brothers were going at each other over those nonassets as though their very own survival depended upon them. Last year their litigation had been over water rights. And the year before that, they'd battled over the exact location of the property line that divided between them the land they'd inherited from their uncle.

Judge Edwin Theopholus Bierbaum peeked at the cheap pocket

watch he kept on the bench, and with a sigh wished that the two brothers would put themselves and everyone else out of their misery and just shoot each other. At least any trial resulting from that would have some real spark to it.

But despite the tedium that some of these cases could take on, Bierbaum loved his position. He could make or break his fellow man with the tap of a gavel. And he alone decided when the business of the day was done.

"This court will reconvene at nine-thirty tomorrow morning," Judge Edwin Bierbaum declared, and slammed his gavel down.

"All rise," the bailiff called out. The sprinkling of participants and spectators to the day's nonaction rose tiredly to their feet.

Bierbaum strode briskly toward the side door, his black robe billowing around his short, pudgy figure, the two-inch heels of his cowboy boots clomping on the wood floor. He wore those boots more for the added height than for the purpose of riding a horse. He hadn't been on a horse in over twenty years. It was murder on the hemorrhoids.

He whipped into his darkened chambers, unhooking his robe. He stopped, seeing the figure lounging lazily in the chair in front of his desk.

"Hiya, Ed," Coke drawled.

His Honor became guarded, his eyes darting uneasily around the room.

"Don't worry," Coke said. "Nobody saw me slip in here."

Buying time, Bierbaum slowly pulled off his robe, hung it up on the coat tree in the corner, and carefully straightened its folds before crossing to his desk and sitting down. He frowned at the document the clerk had left on his desk, his hands curling it up at the top.

"Heard you were in Warner," he said, avoiding Coke's eyes. Hanging in the air between them was the awareness that in former times Bierbaum's reception of Coke would have almost blown Coke over with its effusiveness.

"Town's changed," Coke said.

Bierbaum cleared his throat. "That so? Hadn't noticed."

"Then you must be hookin' that black robe o' yours a foot too high." He paused. "Not a wise thing t'do, Ed."

Arching his brow, Bierbaum looked at Coke. Since he'd become judge, he'd perfected the stern brow lift almost to an art form.

Coke was unimpressed. "Looks like you might hafta make a choice," he said.

The brow sank. "It's my duty to maintain complete impartiality in all disputes," the judge stated solemnly.

"Wouldn't object to that. *If* I could expect that same fine impartiality from that honorable colleague o' yours . . . Albertson," Coke answered blandly. "But I can't. So that leaves you with a mighty big choice on your hands."

Bierbaum dropped his gaze, running a finger up and down the edges of the document. "This isn't the time . . ." he hedged.

"You ain't a-gonna have the time, Ed, t'keep your options open. You ain't a-gonna have the time t'find out whether Barrett or me will be out on top before you make up your mind as t'who t'cast your lot with. You're just gonna hafta cast that lot an' take your chances."

Bierbaum's glance skittered around the room as though he were hoping to spot an opening to break out. He cleared his throat again. "Maybe my choice will be to, uh, not to make one."

"Then you should turn in that black robe o' yours, for you're no longer qualified t'be judge," Coke answered. "You wanted this position, you got it. You've been enjoyin' it for over a dozen years. An' along with this fine position o' yours is the requirement that on occasion you'll have t'make some damn hard choices."

Hiking his chin, Bierbaum nervously tugged at his collar. "And if I declined to make a choice should the occasion present itself . . . ?" he ventured again.

"Then to my mind that'd be the same as your throwin' in with Barrett, because for me the outcome would be the same."

"Doggone it, Coke." The loose flesh under the judge's jaw shook with feeling. "I don't want to get dragged into this feud between you and Barrett. I refuse to be hounded either way."

Regarding Bierbaum evenly, Coke got up. "Well, Ed," he said quietly. "You know, don't you, what happened to the fellow who spent too long a time tryin' t'keep his feet planted square on both sides o' the fence?"

The judge's wavery gaze finally found its way to Coke's. "What?"

"He wound up gettin' splinters up his ass." And without another word, Coke walked to the door and out of the room.

* * *

"Cómo le fue?" Alejandro asked Coke as he sat down on the edge of the empty loading platform at the train station next to him. How'd it go?

"Got Matt Hamlin, my attorney, all stoked up an' ready t'roll, an applied a little heat to a certain judge." Coke frowned. "Atmosphere around here has changed some since word leaked out 'bout this land battle brewin' between Barrett an' me."

"Cómo?"

"Stopped by a few stores on my way over here. I could tell by the look in folks' eyes that they was wantin' to be friendly, but their careful movements seemed t'say they weren't too sure how friendly they should be."

"Barrett se ha de estar haciendo muy poderoso por aquí." Barrett must be getting very strong around here.

Cruz and Rogelio were approaching along the tracks from the stockyards.

"We checked the cattle back there," Cruz said. "The brands do not appear to be burned over."

"I know," Coke replied. "Checked 'em myself after we all separated this mornin'."

"Casi todos tienen la marca de la compañía de Barrett el T-bar-B," Alejandro put in soberly. Most have Barrett's T-bar-B brand.

Coke suppressed a smile as he noted that the same suspicion had crossed all their minds that morning. "I guess even low-down cattle thieves ain't so stupid as to deposit their takin's smack in the middle o' the county seat." He glanced at the crowded pens. "Reckon those beeves over there are gonna be loaded on the train out tonight."

"On our way over here," Rogelio said, "I saw *El Guapo* . . . the man of the hides."

"Jack Siden," Coke said.

"*Sí.* That son of Barrett was with him. I saw them through the window of the saloon. The Barrett boy was smoking those little *cigarros* the same way as Siden, the same motion of his hands." Rogelio did an exaggerated imitation that caused Cruz to grin and the poker-faced Alejandro to tighten his jaw to hold in his own smile. "He must think that he can inhale some o' Jack's handsome through those same *cigarros.*"

"Siden's another one whose been gettin' pretty sparin' in his friendliness lately," Coke commented.

"Es por la señora West," Alejandro said. It's because of Mrs. West.

That Handsome Jack's campaign to win the beautiful new woman in town had fallen flat while Coke Sanders had glided on by to claim the prize had caused a good deal of behind-the-hands snickering among the people of Dispenseme.

"Some of the men from Barrett's Land Company are on the street," Cruz said. "It's easy to spot them, they have guns strapped to their hips. They have hard faces, and sly eyes looking for a fight. They don't look like cowhands who've come for a day in town."

"They look more like they'd gun down the poor cow an' eat it raw," Rogelio commented.

"Seems like they started showin' up on the streets after we got here," Coke said.

"An' that sheriff . . . *cómo se llama?*" Rogelio began. What's his name?

"Calhoun," Alejandro said dourly. "Watt Calhoun."

"*Sí*. Like a tomcat he is, prowlin' up an' down the streets."

"Guess they ain't too sure how many o' you I brought with me," Coke said. Lifting his hat, he ran his fingers through his hair. "Bring the horses here 'bout five," he said to Cruz. "We're ridin' out at about that time."

"Is that all?" Cruz was disappointed. "We're just going to leave?"

"We're gonna look like we are," Coke replied. "Your pa an' me got some business to attend to round here tonight an' it'd be good for folks t'think that we was long gone by then. Now, for the rest o' the afternoon until five," he continued to Cruz, "lose yourselves in the Mexican section o' town . . . hear?"

"Por qué?" Rogelio asked. Why?

"You two get pegged as bein' with me, you're likely t'wind up gettin' bloodied—or worse."

Rogelio pulled himself up. "I ain't afraid to fight."

"Everything is stacked against you here," Coke warned. "With that sheriff bein' Barrett's man, if somebody tried t'kill you, it'd be you who'd get tossed in jail for the attempted murder. An' I'd kinda like you two sharp-eyed an' in good health t'night."

"Está bien, Jefe," Cruz replied, and to his father, *"Adiós, Papá."*

Alejandro's eyes followed the two young men as they walked

away. *"Qué es el negocio que debemos atender esta noche, Güero?"* What is this business that we have to attend to tonight?"

"We're gonna pay a visit to Francine's."

Alejandro frowned at the notion of their going to the local whorehouse. *"No tengo necesidad para eso,"* he objected. I have no need for that. *"Mi hijo está aquí."* My son is here. He shook his head. *"Y María Luisa, parece ser un gatito mansito, pero cuando se enoja, aiyee, es un tigre. No quiero pasar mis noches durmiendo en la zanja afuera de mi casa."* And María Luisa, my wife, may seem as gentle as a kitten, but when she's angry, *aiyee*, she's a tiger. I don't want to spend my nights sleeping in the ditch outside of my house.

Coke smiled. "The business I have in mind will only require the exposin' o' some money, mebbe some of our intentions . . . but not our tools. Tell you what," he teased. "If this'll cause some trouble at home, I'll have the papers sworn out tomorrow declarin' that you an' me walked outa Francine's with the same amount o' virtue that we walked in with."

Alejandro's eyes danced mischievously. *"Sí,"* he said dourly. *"Las piedras en esa zanja son muy picudas."* The rocks in that ditch can be very sharp.

🌼 Chapter 30

"NOW, I'M ONLY allowin' you t'do this at Ruby's recommend," Francine declared with a toss of her shoulder-length earrings.

Coke and Alejandro were seated in her private quarters. They'd slipped into the brodello through the alleyway cellar door, where Francine's maid had been waiting to let them in.

Francine seemed not a woman for understatement. Her blond hair was swept loosely up to a cluster of feathery curls nesting in a swell of fluff at the top of her head. Around her neck, strings of pearls competed with ropes of colored beads, heavy gold chains set with chunks of colored glass, and the amethyst-eyed lion brooch on her bosom. On her arms, metal bracelets caught the light, and six of her fingers were cluttered with rings. Every movement she made was punctuated by a click or a clink somewhere.

She was in her midforties, and her medium height and impressive curves added up to a hundred seventy pounds or more. That ample flesh looked unconfined by restrictive undergarments; it bobbed around the inside of her loose moss-green gown, seemingly in search of its own level. There was a comfortable weightlessness about her, though, that made Coke think of a plumped pillow. If a fellow ever jumped on her, he guessed, he'd sink halfway through before he hit bone.

That comfortable rotundity extended to her room as well, from her high, rounded bed with its fat pillows and swollen feather comforter, to the overstuffed chairs, to the globular lamps, to the chubby yellow long-haired cat curled in her lap, its wide golden eyes gazing out at them as she rhythmically stroked its noggin. Francine seemed to have an aversion for edges, for everywhere—tables, bureaus, lampshades—all the edges were softened by fringes and lace. But Francine's fingernails and her narrowed, gray-green eyes were razor sharp.

"Ruby's always been rock-solid about her convictions an' who t'throw her weight behind," Francine went on. "An' more often than not, she turns out t'be right." She lifted her hand and examined one of her manicured claws in the lamplight. "Course, if I was too concerned 'bout what was right, I wouldna gotten into this profession. A hundred dollars—up front."

Making no mention that the price had doubled since he'd spoken with Ruby the day before, Coke pulled a leather pouch out of his belt, shook out five twenty-dollar gold pieces, and set them on the table. Francine gave the coins such a long, hard look that Coke half expected her to pick one up and bite into it. Then she opened the top of the round carved wooden box at her elbow, snatched up the coins, and casually tossed them inside.

"What time do you expect this clerk o' Barrett's t'show up here?" Coke asked.

"Ten o'clock sharp. Wilkin Edmonds is one o' those types you can set your clock by. Has a standin' appointment, every Wednesday. Don't know why a Wednesday particularly. Just must need a rise on the sinkhole day o' the week."

"An' his regular gal, she's agreeable t'our plan?"

"Grasshopper Gertie? Yep, already talked t'her. Now, a coupla my gals mighta shied away from a setup like this. But not Gertie. She has a more casual attitude."

"When can I talk with her?"

"She's with another o' her regulars right now. Should be in shortly." Reaching up, Francine clinkingly patted the back of her hair. "Don't know how shortly, though. This regular o'hers is pushin' eighty. Ain't got no trouble gettin' the ole pistol raised an' loaded. Just can't ever seem t'get aroun' t'squeezing off the shot." A smile appeared, dimpling her cheeks. "Sweet fella, ole Cyrus. In love with Gertie. Brings her flowers all the time, an' chocolates, too. Proposes to her almost every one o' the four or five nights he shows up here each week."

Coke exchanged a look with Alejandro.

"Muy caro," Alejandro said soberly.

"Yup,"Coke nodded. "That kinda romancin' must get purty costly."

Francine shrugged her shoulders. "Said he saved up for his retirement. Course, the pore ole fella's getting mighty forgetful these days. Every night he walks in the door, he shouts up the stairs, 'Time for m'Thursday romp!' Guess 'bout every single day seems like a Thursday to him."

A look of doubt coming into her eyes, Francine stroked the cat faster, stirring it to a low, rattling hum.

"I wouldn't be goin' along with this business at all if it weren't as a favor to Ruby," she repeated. "An' I don't want wind o' it to ever find its way back t'me . . . you hear?"

"It won't," Coke said.

"If word ever leaked out, that sheriff o' Barrett's would close me down in about a minute . . . despite the fine finanacial arrangement he's got goin' with me.

"An' the men from Barrett's Land Company bring in quite a lotta business. Course, a few of 'em don't have what you might call a gentle touch. 'Bout every other month I gotta get my receivin' room repaired. An', like as not, one or t'other o' my gals."

There was a knock on the door. A woman with a Dutch boy haircut strode into the room, and Coke and Alejandro climbed out of their deep, cushiony chairs. Even with their boots adding to their height, the two men found themselves staring up at the woman. Grasshopper Gertie was well over six feet tall. And where Francine seemed all flesh and no bone, this one appeared all bone and no flesh. She was long, lanky arms and long, lanky legs, and little torso in between to yoke them together. Coke had heard that she'd come by her nickname by the look those long legs took when, bent up at the knee, she sat astraddle a fellow or took the underlying position. Above or below, those gangly legs made her look like a grasshopper squatting on a leaf.

Francine glanced at the china clock on her mantel. "Ole Cyrus musta got inspired," she said to Gertie.

"No. I did," Gertie replied, her voice having the tough edge of a boastful adolescent boy. "After 'bout thirty minutes o' vigorous pumpin' an' still comin' up dry, I said, 'Hot damn, Cyrus, you gonna do it twice, I'm gonna hafta charge you double.' " She grinned broadly. "Backed off lookin' right pleased with himself."

Francine looked disapproving. "You just walked off leavin' that pore ole fella only three-quarters done?"

"I already done my part," Gertie asserted. "I got him started good. Hell, he ain't without know-how, he can work the rest out on his own."

She turned to Coke. "You must be Sanders," she declared. "Put it there, fella." She thrust out her hand.

Coke's hesitation before he took it was almost imperceptible. "Right pleased t'meet you, Gertie," he responded. "Ain't never met up with so much size with so little to it."

"Got what it takes, though," she replied, moving over to Alejandro and surveying him narrowly up and down. Bending her head slightly, she looked him in the eye. "Some might say you're a tad on the dark side, fella, but you sure are close on the right height."

Alejandro didn't blink. *"Y tienes un bigote que me recuerda de mí tío Panfilo,"* he said expressionlessly. And you have a mustache that reminds me of my Uncle Panfilo.

Gertie switched her eyes suspiciously to Coke. "What'd he say?"

"Uh, he only said that he was right pleased t'be receivin' such a fine compliment from a fetchin' gal like yourself," he replied.

"That so?" she grinned. She flung an arm around Alejandro's shoulders. "How much money you got on you, fella?"

Alejandro slid a look at Coke that was almost murderous.

"Gertie," Francine warned. "You ain't got the time t'make

arrangements t'pop another-un off before your ten o'clock arrives, *an'* talk with Mr. Sanders, too. So settle yourself down.''

Giving Alejandro a friendly swat on the rump, Grasshopper Gertie dropped down into the nearest chair, her wide-apart knees jabbing up two corners in her skirt. ''You want me t'work some information outa m'next client, I understand,'' she said to Coke.

''That's about it,'' he replied.

''Now, if I do manage t'jerk some o' that information loose from this fella, what's in it for me outside o' your gratitude?''

Coke digested her choice of words. ''A hundred dollars.''

She drew back, eyes bright. ''Well, now, that's what I call downright motivatin'.''

''This clerk o' Barrett's that you'll be seein' shortly, he's been a regular o' yours for quite some time, I take it.''

''Yep, since the days when he worked for the former owners o' the Warner Savin's an' Loan. Eight, nine years, all told.''

''He much of a talker?''

''Well, after all these years o' weekly familiarity, there are occasions when he engages in 'bout as much jawin' as doin'.''

''Won't bother you t'take advantage of him after knowin' him all this time?''

She shrugged her bony shoulders. '' 'Tain't sentiment that I get paid for.'' She made a face. '' 'Sides, the little bugger's changed some since T. C. Barrett took over.''

''How?''

''Well, before, he always seemed a lonesome sort . . . kinda like a little bird that got kicked outa its nest too soon that you'd wanta stroke. After Barrett moved in, though, Wilkin changed. Bein' round all that cutthroat power's kinda infected him. An' I think he enjoys seein' all these big landowners that used t'make him feel small an' no-account, tiptoein' with their hats in their hands up t'T.C.'s door. An' Wilkin's the one who sits at that door.''

''Does he seem t'know what goes on behind it?''

''Hard t'tell,'' Gertie answered. ''I got a feelin' while he's over there in the business, it's 'Whatever you say, sir, Mr. Barrett,' while around here it's 'Ole T.C. an' me.' '' Flinging a leg up, she propped its ankle on the opposite knee. ''Yup, you'd think him an' T. C. Barrett was wound up tighter'n a pair o' sex-starved rattlers.''

Satisfied by her response, Coke settled back. "You ever hear of a man by the name of Juan Fernando Castillo, Gertie?"

She frowned. "Wasn't he the fella who bought a bullet crossin' into Mexico sometime back?"

"Yup, 'bout six years ago. Can you recall Wilkin ever mentionin' Juan Fernando?"

"Somethin' that was said did stick in my mind," Gertie mused. "It was a day or two after word got back here o' Castillo's killin'." She gave her head a shake. "You gotta understand, Mr. Sanders, that was a long time back. Heard a lotta mouthin' off on a wide range o' topics since then. T'tell the truth, I cain't even place for sure if it was Wilkin who said it."

"What was it you heard?"

"Well, nothin' so big it'd knock you offa that chair. It was a brag kinda like, 'Well, ole T.C. finished off that highfalutin Mexican for good today.' " She scratched her head. "But that comment stuck in my mind, 'cause like I said, it was made a day or two after news reached here o' Castillo's death, an' I wondered, 'How can you finish off a fella who's already dead an' buried?' "

Coke thought a moment, then leaned forward. "This is where I'd like you t'take your conversation with Edmonds tonight, Gertie. That is, if you can steer it thataway."

"Sanders," she put in. "With the right kinda grip on a fella's tiller, I can usually steer him 'bout any which way."

"Now, it's my business policy t'provide a straightforward sorta service to our customers, an' voyagerism is not to my best o' taste," Francine said loftily as she strolled to a knickknack case about six feet high, three feet wide, and a foot deep that stood against the back wall of her room. "But," she went on, taking hold of a side of the cabinet, "the fella I took over this business from had some customers willin' t'lay out good cash more for the pleasure o' watchin' than for the effort o' doin'."

She swung the cabinet out to the side, revealing an opening in the wall, the motion producing an awe-inspiring roll through her unbound curves, fore and aft. Protecting the fragile curls of her topknot with her hand, she bent down and led Coke and Alejandro through the chest-high opening into a musty passageway. It was so narrow that Francine's flanks brushed the walls on either side, forcing her to angle her body slightly.

"Just between you an' me," she said, as she moved along, "I

suspect that the former owner o' this business was his own best customer. Heard that durin' the war some Yank sharpshooter didn't raise his sights high enough an' deprived the pore fella o' most o' his privileges.'' She glanced meaningfully over her shoulder at them.

"Well, here we are," she said a moment later, and stopped.

In the scanty light filtering down the eight-foot passageway from Francine's room, Coke made out four small plywood squares, each attached to the wall by a single nail at various eye levels. Reaching up, Francine rotated two of the squares upward, uncovering a pair of peepholes about an inch across.

Coke squinted through one of them into the bedroom beyond. The head of the bed was against the opposite wall. A lamp stood on the bedside table, its glass tinted dark red, secreting a dim rose glow that receded into violet shadow along the edges of the room.

"We call this our Rose Room," Francine said, her voice taking a husky tinge. "These peepholes here are carved outa the dark centers o' the flowers in the wallpaper on t'other side. They look like part o' the design."

"Uh, interestin' setup," Coke replied, feeling obliged to say something. Maybe it was his imagination taking over as the two of them stood so close together peeking into that bedroom, but a kind of energy seemed to be stirring in Francine. It made him think of a stroked cat. He had the odd sensation that the bordello madam's flesh was swelling in these dark, confined quarters, filling them up. Her musky aroma was growing overpowering in the stagnant air. He felt an impulse to retreat from it, but Alejandro was in the passageway behind him and he was hemmed in.

"With only that one faint light by the bed in there," Francine went on, rolling subtly up and down against him, "this side o' the room in there is purty much covered in shadow. An' you ain't likely t'draw a bead on our little . . . peepholes . . . lessen you press up close against 'em."

Coke now knew what was coming, but there was nowhere he could hightail it to.

"Hope Gertie pulls the goods out for you," she said, her teeth gleaming in the darkness. Then she closed in on him to pass back to her room. It would have been a snug fit getting by him anyhow, and Francine made the most of it, giving him full-bodied exposure to her pillowy curves. Her warm body rotated determinedly into him, the jagged knots of her brooch and beads grinding into his chest and stomach.

Jammed up against the wall, Coke felt surrounded, helpless. If he got into a wrestling match with her, that might overheat her more. But with all those swells and depressions moving against him, he didn't know where to put his hands, and there was an off chance that a part of her might find its way·into them that he didn't want to get caught holding. For several moments the two seemed locked in a strange dance of shifts and nudges. Finally, surfacing for air above her curls, he saw his opening. Scraping himself out from under all that billowy movement, he sidestepped down the passageway, leaving Francine wallowing in space. Noticing that she was now engaged in a solo act, she popped her eyes open. She glanced at Coke, and saw by the look in his eye that she'd have to catch him first. She straightened up, expelled a little sigh, and continued on toward her room.

Having witnessed what he might be in for, Alejandro stood on tiptoe, flattened against the wall. His hat tilted back off his head, pinned against the wall behind him, he eyed her with forbidding wariness. But she bestowed upon him only the springy impresses of her passing promonotories before she arrived at the opening to her room. She put a flirtatious hand to her curls and ducked out. The shaft of light shrank to a sliver and clunked to darkness.

"Had me on the run," Coke muttered, coming back up the passageway. Pulling out his handkerchief, he wiped his brow. "Think I lost that round. M'pants still up?"

"*Hijole!*" Alejandro breathed, bringing his heels down on the floor, his hat dropping back on his head. "*No es un lugar seguro para un hombre.*" This is no safe place for a man.

"Well," Coke responded philosophically. "If there was a decent, upstandin' way o' gettin' at T. C. Barrett, I'd probably try it. But then again, mebbe I wouldn't neither."

They fell silent; the cylindrical beams of light from the peepholes had suddenly brightened, then darkened to rose again, with the opening and closing of the door to the rose bedroom. Wilkin Edmonds stood next to Gertie peering around the glowing room, his hat tipped low on his forehead at a tough angle, his suit coat lapping open, and his thumbs hooked staunchly under his suspenders. That brawny stance might have succeeded were it not for his spectacles, which magnified his eyes almost to the size of the lenses, and his height. The peak of his hat barely cleared Gertie's shoulder.

"Why'd we come in here instead of your regular room?" he was asking.

"My room's bein' repaired," she responded, plucking his hat off his head and flipping it onto the bedpost.

"What's wrong with it?" he asked, smoothing his thin hair.

"Roof sprung a leak."

He frowned up at her through his thick lenses. "But it hasn't rained in close to a year."

Gertie's face went momentarily blank. "How the hell should I know?" she exclaimed. "Francine takes strange notions sometimes." Then a sly light came to her eyes. "It was the wind blowin' through that hole in the roof that she didn't like. Said it sounded like a herd o' elephants fartin'. Asked me how I could get through a decent five-dollar fuck on a windy night without feelin' obliged t'say 'scuse me fourteen times."

Pulling herself up, she directed a smug look toward the peepholes, as though expecting an ovation for her inventiveness. Coke pulled back, shaking his head.

But Wilkin was already turned away, sliding out of his suit coat. Holding it by the collar, he folded the sleeves in at the shoulders, just so, smoothed them down to prevent wrinkling, then laid the coat on the bureau as carefully as if it were an infant. He gave equal and due ceremony to the watch he drew out of his pants pocket, checking the time, and to the spectacles he lifted from his nose, arranging both articles on the bureau. Then, turning, he walked blindly across the room, jerked down a side of Gertie's loose blouse, and rising up, began loudly suckling her breast.

"Well, ain't we one hungry little critter!" she declared.

Inside the passageway, Alejandro snapped upright and backed to the wall, folding his arms as he did whenever he severely disapproved of something. Voyagerism, Coke recognized, was a tad too much for Alejandro's taste, too.

But Gertie had already popped Wilkin off her and gotten him flat on his back on the bed.

"This is your lucky night, honey," she announced, hitching up her blouse. "I'm gonna give you my special tonight. Gonna do it *all* t'you this time. So lie back, relax—but not too much—an' let Big Mama treat her fella to a whole new slambangin' experience."

He stared up at her. "Why?"

She dived onto the bed beside him, his diminutive body lifting and falling over the swell passing through the mattress. "Why, it's these new surroundin's, sweetheart. That lamp over there oozin' red light has kindled m'coals like you wouldn't believe." Propping herself up, she began undoing his tie. "An' I guess I'm feelin' sentimental, too."

"Sentimental?"

"We're nearin' our eighth anniversary, you know, sweetheart. An' that does earn you the right to a dandy bonus, over an' above your standard fifteen-minute in an' out."

"It does?"

"Damn right. Think 'bout it. This is a occasion t'celebrate . . . your bein' faithful t'me for eight years runnin'." She took hold of the end of his tie. "An', honey, I been faithful t'you . . ."

Rising up, he looked myopically at her.

She snapped the tie out of his collar and tossed it over her shoulder. ". . . as much as the traffic would allow." Shoving him down, she leaned over him. "You want me t'peel your clothes off real slow-like?"

Flicking his tongue over his lips, he nodded.

"Which end you want me t'start on?"

"What?"

"You want me t'start at the bottom an' work up?" She ran her long, spidery fingers up his body from his crotch to his neck. "Or do you want me t'start at the top an' work down?" She ran her fingers down. "Either way, honey," she said, pressing in closer, "you know I'm gonna wind up gettin' snagged in the middle." She rubbed her hand over the swell in his pants.

With a smile, he settled back expectantly on the pillow. "Start at the bottom," he said, folding his hands behind his head.

She moved to the bottom of the bed and, kneeling, lifted his foot onto her lap. "Anything interestin' happen in the business today?" she asked matter-of-factly, undoing his spats and untying his shoelaces.

"We started foreclosure proceedings on two more places," he answered self-importantly.

She yanked off the shoe and tossed it over her shoulder, then reached up his pant leg to unhook his sock garters. "Anybody I know?"

"Red Mitchell and Hal Sullivan. Two more big-acting ranchers

who won't be traipsing around so big anymore. Yep.'' He smiled.
''Ole T.C. sure knows how t'cut the high and the mighty down
to size.'' He winced. ''Don't snap the garter, Gertie. That smarts
a bit.''

''Well, some folks do like a little pain with their pleasurin','''
she replied. ''Thinks it adds a touch o' seasonin' to it.''

''Not on the shins, it don't.''

She fished the garter out of his pant leg, stretched it out, and
took aim at a corner. ''Your tiniest wish is my command, sir.''
She shot it off. Jerking his sock off by the toe, she balled it up.
''Heard Coke Sanders was in town today,'' she said coyly. ''Heard
there was bad blood between him an' Mr. Barrett. Was there a
fight?'' She tossed the sock away.

''Sanders . . . take T. C. Barrett on?'' Wilkin scoffed. ''That'd
be the day! He and those greasers he always has round him made
durn sure t'clear outa town before nightfall.'' He chuckled.
''Probably halfway home t'greaserland by now, still running low,
their tails between their legs.''

Coke felt Alejandro stiffen in the darkness.

Gertie had been reaching up Wilkin's pant leg for his sock
garter, but instead of stopping her long arm kept going, slithering
on up the inside of his trouser leg to his crotch.

''Well, look what I found!'' she declared, pressing around.
''Burrried treasure!''

''Ah, Gertie!'' he breathed.

''Why I do believe—'' her fingers probed ''—somethin's comin'
alive in there . . . just a-pokin' t'get out.''

He giggled, arching back.

''Cain't help m'self,'' she went on, her hand groping about
inside his pants until he was squirming. ''Every time you start
into talkin' like you do 'bout all that power you an' Barrett have,
somethin' in me just starts squirtin' outa control.''

Abruptly, she slid her hand back down his leg. ''But I do gotta
control m'self.''

Panting, he raised his head off the pillow and looked at her,
disappointed.

''Well, we don't wanta do you too fast, honey.'' She drew forth
the second garter and shot that one off at the washstand. Then she
took the toe of his sock and started tugging at it. ''The most
satisfyin' explosions, you know, is the kind that's pulled out—''

She tugged at the sock "—an' pulled out—" she tugged "—over a slooooow buildup." She yanked the sock off and tossed it away.

"Wanta know a secret?" she asked, running her hand caressingly over the tips of his toes.

"What?" he asked, his breathing still ragged from her explorations up his pants.

"I'm a big admirer o' you an' that boss o' yours . . . an' all you rough, tough hombres over at the Savin's an' Loan."

He bent a look down at her. "You are?"

"Damn right, sweetheart." She crawled up beside him. "You cain't help but admire folks who don't let nothin' stand in their way like y'all do." She unhooked his suspenders. "Why, I'd bet that nobody, but nobody, can ever put anythin' over on your T. C. Barrett."

"That's a fact."

"It must make you right proud t'be such a important part o' his operation. Right proud." She pulled his suspenders down. "Why, sounds to me like you're T. C. Barrett's right-hand man."

"I wouldn't go *that* far," he said, implying by his tone of voice that he was really just being modest.

She glanced coyly aside at him. "But then, I hear that Sanders is a purty sly ole fox hisself."

"Nah," Wilkin sneered. "Just you watch, Gertie. Ole T.C., and the rest of us, are gonna squash Sanders like a junebug."

"Well, I don't know," she sighed, drawing the front of his shirt out of his pants and slipping her hand under it. "Heard that Sanders is one right powerful hombre down in the south part o' the county." She began slowly massaging his abdomen. "Might be hard t'get to."

"Won't be that hard," he boasted, his breathing deepening.

"How can you be so doggone sure?"

"Well, it wasn't that hard getting at that other fellow from down thataway," he answered in a tough tone.

"Oh? Who was that?" she inquired, unbuttoning his fly, her hand working slowly downward, opening the buttons one by one.

"I doubt that you'd remember him," he responded, eyes turned down, following her hand intently. "He was just another greaser . . . only one of those big fancy kinds, all stiff-backed . . . name of Castillo."

"Oh, yeah," she breathed, smoothing back the sides of his fly. "I recollect Castillo. Owned a big passel o' land, didn't he?"

"Did . . . till he tangled with us."

"Didn't Castillo die o' lead poisonin' five, six years back?"

Wilkin tensed. "We had nothing t'do with that!"

"Why, settle down, sweetheart," she soothed, her fingers sliding inside his underdrawers, his flesh quivering under her touch. "A notion like that never even crossed m'mind. Wasn't Castillo killed for all that cash he was carryin' on him, anyhow?"

"So the story goes," Wilkin replied mysteriously.

She snuggled closer. "Know somethin'?"

"What?" he half hiccuped, his breath catching.

"I think I been neglectin' your jewels too long." She touched target.

"Ah!" he puffed. "Ah!"

"What you say I make 'em shine t'night, sweetheart?"

"Oh, yes, yes," he warbled. "Have at 'em."

Giving them a long, lingering caress that sent a tremor up through him, she slid her hand out, got up, and straddled him. Taking hold of his trousers at the sides of the waist, she started pulling them down, exposing his long woolen underwear, peaked in the upper sector, Wilkin eagerly lifting his hips to hurry her along.

"How much was it they said Castillo had on him that day he died?" she inquired offhandedly, backing and peeling his pants down. "Twenty thousand dollars?"

"Forty-two thousand three hundred dollars," Wilkin crowed.

"How'd you know the exact amount?"

"Remember, it was the Savin's an' Loan that he withdrew it from." He wagged his head. "Sorta."

Taking hold of the bottoms of his pants, Gertie shook his feet out of them as if she were emptying a potato sack. Rising up on her heels, she whirled the trousers around her head. When she let them go, they flew across the room like half a man shot out of a cannon. Then she sprang forward and nestled beside him.

"Just between you an' me," she said in a low voice, her hand slipping under the waist of his underdrawers again, her fingers slowly rippling down, "I cain't imagine a smart operator like T. C. Barrett ever allowin' over forty thousand dollars o' his business's money t'get away from him . . . even if it did belong to that Mexican."

"He wouldn't," Wilkin said.

They gazed into each other's eyes, a smile passing between them.

"Lemme get that big fella o' yours," she whispered, jerking down his drawers. She ran her hand up the inside of his thighs and took hold of the shaft. "Rise 'n shine, big fella," she coaxed, her long fingers undulating and kneading at it.

"Whoop-de-do . . . howdy-do . . ." Wilkin groaned. "Goo-ood mornin'."

"Well, how'd y'all do it?" Her motion picked up.

"What?" he quavered.

"How'd you sharp hombres keep ahold o' that Mexican's forty thousand dollars?"

He didn't respond, his eyes flickering and rolling.

"I guess there could be only one way," she mused, her motion slowing. "A friend o' T.C.'s musta shot that Mexican an' got that money back for him."

Again Wilkin tensed and lifted his head. "We had nothing to do with any killing," he protested. Then, eyes glazing, he sank back onto the pillow, for Gertie's tempo had picked up.

"Course not, baby," she soothed, her skillful fingers squeezing and yanking at him now, sending rhythmic spasms up him. "But how could you savvy folks get that forty thousand dollars back that Castillo withdrew from the Savin's an' Loan if y'all didn't steal it back?"

"Didn't hafta," he panted. "Castillo didn't have it on him t'steal back the day he died," he answered weakly, head rolling.

"Well, if he didn't have that money on him," she urged, her body starting to slither and slide against him in tempo with her hand, "where'd he have it?"

"In the Savings and Loan," he gasped.

She worked faster. "How'd that forty thousand dollars wind up here in the Savin's an' Loan if Castillo drew it out a coupla days before he died?"

He didn't answer, the sweat pouring out of him, his arms and legs twitching.

She intensified her efforts, roughly wrenching at him. "How could that money o' been back here in the Savin's an' Loan," she demanded, "if Castillo took it with him before he died?"

But he was too far gone, panting, heaving to the rhythm of her hand. Abruptly she let go and pulled away from him.

"Don't stop," he gasped, fully primed and nowhere to put it. "Don't stop." He groped for her hand and put it back on him.

But she delicately lifted her hand away.

"Cain't a lady take time out to admire her handiwork?" she purred. "Just look at that. Why, if I was a virgin, I'd find a sight like that staggerin'. I do believe we're reachin' new heights t'night, honey."

Licking his parched lips, his pumping chest jerking out hollows under his diaphragm, he grabbed her hand and forced it down on him again. And again her fingers slid away.

"Mebbe you should start levelin' off, sweetheart," she cooed against his ear. "You know, Francine might not like it if she walked in here an' found another hole poked through her roof."

"No, get going!" he begged, jogging his hips.

"But, honey, when somethin's a-teasin' at m'mind like this, I cain't put my concentration where it oughta be. There's these two things—"

"What two things?" he shouted. "Gertie, *what*?"

"Well," she said demurely, skimming her finger up the back of the shaft, reaching its peak, and sliding it down, then up again. "It's like I got this deep, deep itch I cain't scratch. You know. I'm dyin', just dyin' t'understand how you slick hombres milked that forty thousand dollars outa Castillo . . . but I just keep hearin' these two things at the same time."

"I'm the one who's dying!" he rasped. "What two things?"

"Well," she considered, her finger flickering feather-light back and forth across the crown. "First I hear that Castillo took out over forty thousand dollars and carried it off with him two days before he died. Then I hear that that money was back here in the Savin's an' Loan the day he died. Seems it just keeps bein' in two places at once, while at the same time"—she tweaked the top, the sharp spasm arching him back—"*not* bein' in them same two places."

"That money was here! Here!" he rasped.

"Then, how'd it get here?"

"Dammit! It never *left* here!" he cried, his wet hair matted to his scalp, his body jerking and twisting about on the bed.

"He didn't withdraw it?"

"No, you bitch! No! Now, get at it, dammit!"

"No reason t'get feisty, honey," she said in a hurt tone. "You know Mama loves you. . . . But . . ."

"Gertie!" he yelped.

"Well, somethin's still teasin' at m'mind."

"What? What?"

"Well, didn't you folks at the Savin's an' Loan say that Castillo withdrew all that money?"

"We said it, but he didn't do it!" he rattled out.

"Huh?"

"Finish me up!" he yelled. "Hurry up and finish me up and I'll tell you all about it!"

"Cross your heart?" she held out.

"Yes! Yes!" he cried frantically.

"All right, sweetheart." She grinned, her long leg sliding over his thighs. "I'll take your word . . . an' somethin' else besides."

She rose up astraddle him, lifted her skirts up at the sides like the spread wings of a hawk, and hitching her hips in, took aim and came down on him.

"Giddyap . . . ride 'em, cowboy."

"My head's still spinnin'," Gertie collapsed onto the pillow beside him. "Felt that blast so strong, it like t'knocked m'brain lopsided." She affectionately rubbed his chest. "An' you cain't deny Big Mama gave her boy one lalapalooza t'night."

He smiled serenely, his breathing steadying.

"So . . ."

"So?" He blinked sleepily.

"How did all you savvy hombres at the Savin's an' Loan work it?" She caressed his neck. "You promised t'tell, you know."

His face became stern. "This better not leave this room."

"You think I'm a fool, honey? I ain't 'bout t'set m'self up t'get shot by that sheriff o' y'all's. Who'd put any stock in the word of a five-dollar whore, anyhow?" Lifting a corner of her skirt, she dabbed at the sweat on his face. "So . . . ?"

He was thoughtful for a time. "Well, you know that last time Castillo came in," he began a little defensively, "he was rude. Downright rude. Told T.C. that if he didn't start changing the way he did business, he, Castillo, was going to withdraw every cent that he had in the Savings and Loan."

"The pure crust o' the man."

"Well, you know T.C. don't take nothing from no one," he went on haughtily. "And especially not from any fancy-tailed greaser."

"Course not." She played with the hair above his temple. "So T.C. didn't let Castillo have the money?"

"No," Wilkin said slowly. "Castillo didn't demand his money that last time he was there. He only threatened to." He shrugged. "Good thing, too. We wouldna been able to hand the cash over to him then, anyhow."

"I thought the Savin's an' Loan was rich."

"Has its ups and downs. T.C. is set on building his land empire, see. He makes the loans more for the purpose of foreclosing than for the cash. Foreclosing fast like he does means plenty of land pouring in . . . but not that much cash. The high interest rates we charge keep up operating expenses, but the cash reserves can dip pretty low now and again."

"So that last time he was in the Savin's an' Loan, Castillo didn't take out any money at all," Gertie prompted.

"He did withdraw some money," Wilkin responded. "But it was only the usual amount that he took out from time to time t'meet the expenses on his ranch . . . twenty-three hundred dollars."

"So how did that twenty-three hundred dollars turn out t'be more'n forty thousand?"

Wilkin chuckled. "I gotta hand it to ole T.C. He's slick. A few days after Castillo paid that last visit to the Savings and Loan, we heard of his killing. That night, T.C. called us into his office an'—"

"Us?" she interrupted.

"Martin Filbert, the main accountant, an' me. We were the two who'd dealt with Castillo that last time. I was the one who paid out the twenty-three hundred dollars, Martin was the one who got the cash outa the vault and marked it down in his ledgers.

"Anyway, that same night that we heard of Castillo's death, ole T.C. called us into his office. Said, 'You boys wanta make an easy five hundred dollars each?'

" 'Sure,' we said, 'wouldn't fight it.'

"Then T.C. reached in his desk and took out the withdrawal paper for twenty-three hundred dollars that Castillo'd made out. T.C. told Martin to hunt up some old papers of Castillo's and he told me to look at those papers and study out just how Castillo wrote a 'four,' the digit kind, and a 'forty,' the written-out-word kind." Wilkin glanced proudly aside at Gertie. "Ole T.C. knows I'm a right good copier."

"Just another o' your talents, honey." Gertie snuggled closer.

"It was easy, Gertie," he went on. "So doggone simple. All I did was just slip a Castillo-looking number four in front of the number 'twenty-three hundred,' then a written 'forty' with a dash in front of Castillo's written-out 'two thousand three hundred dollars,' and quick as a wink that twenty-three-hundred-dollar withdrawal of Castillo's became forty-two thousand three hundred. Martin made the changes in his records, and next day T.C. made the announcement about Castillo's big withdrawal from the Savings and Loan." He peeked aside at her. "Smart, eh?"

"I ain't *never* heard o' anythin' so slick," she said admiringly. "Fleecin' a fella outa forty thousand dollars, an' no one, not even him, bein' the wiser. I gotta hand it to y'all."

"That night, after we'd made the changes," Wilkin boasted, "Ole T.C. got out a bottle of Kentucky bourbon. An' Filbert and me sat around in T.C.'s office till past two, the three of us just a-chucklin' over the smart trick we played on that greaser . . . and raising our glasses to his memory."

In the passageway, Coke put a hand on Alejandro's arm to stay him.

"You sly foxes, you," Gertie was saying, pinching Wilkin's cheek.

"Wanta hear something even funnier?" he asked.

"You bet," she answered eagerly.

"Well, five years later, when ole T.C. foreclosed on the Castillo spread," he giggled, "it was on a loan of less than thirty-five thousand dollars."

Gertie opened the cellar door. Coke had been waiting outside in the darkness, leaning back against the wall, his hands in his pockets.

"Heard you was out here," she said. "Why didn't you wait for me in Francine's room?"

"Francine was in it. . . . Wanted t'save m'strength."

"You may not know what you're missin' out on. Heard that nobody does it half like Francine does it."

"Think she already half did it," he replied.

"Well? Did I pry out the information you wanted?"

"Yup," he said, taking out his leather pouch. "You did right good . . . good enough to deserve a twenty-dollar bonus." He shook out six twenty-dollar gold coins.

Grinning, she took the coins, weighing them in her hands. "Come by any time, Sanders. It'll be on the house."

"Thanks for the offer, Gertie. I appreciate it."

She saw by the expression on his face that he was only being kind. Hurt flickered up in her eyes, then her toughness returned. "Already got a gal, huh?"

"Almost," he mused.

"Where's the fella who was with you?"

"Down the road a piece tryin' not t'smash anything valuable."

"That was a purty raw trick Wilkin an' those others pulled on Castillo's family, warn't it?"

"Yup."

"Well, I hope that friend o' yours didn't take the way Wilkin an' me talked too hurtful. Bein' in my line o' work, I ain't partial t'name callin' m'self. Hope he understands that you cain't get folks t'open up by shootin' down their attitudes."

"I think he understands, Gertie. You did real good."

"I do know my business," she said proudly.

"No question 'bout that, an' I'm obliged t'you." He half smiled. "Kinda nice t'know, too, that you ain't the biased sort."

"Hell," she replied. "If I was too overparticular 'bout folks, I wouldn't keep meetin' 'em from the angle that I do."

"Put it there, Gertie." He held out his hand to her. "I do believe I like you."

"An' I'd settle for that 'most any day, Sanders."

✿ Chapter 31

KEEPING TO THE shadows, Coke and Alejandro made their way through town toward the place on the outskirts where they'd arranged to meet Cruz and Rogelio. To their far right, a diaphanous arch of light shivered against the night sky above the train station. The distant sounds of cattle being forced up the chutes and onto the train that was to leave at midnight filtered through the wavery breeze, the hollow clatter of hooves hitting the upraised floorboards of the cattle cars, the spurts of bawling in tenor and bass resounding in the boxed spaces.

As they walked in silence along the back streets, Coke felt Alejandro's coiled rage, a rage so thinly contained that it might spring out in any direction. It wasn't until they'd passed by the last house in town that he spoke.

"We'll even things up, Alejandro."

They spotted Rogelio waiting with the mounts under an ancient huisache tree, its branches casting thick, embroidered shadows over the man and horses. Even from the distance Coke could see by Rogelio's springy movements that the young man was on edge.

"Where's Cruz?" Coke asked when they reached Rogelio.

"Waiting . . . seven, eight miles north of here."

"You found somethin'?"

"*Sí*, a pen with a chute next to the railroad tracks. It's holding a hundred seventy-five, two hundred cows."

"Anyone guardin' 'em?"

"Two men. They were sitting on the ground a little away from the pen, smoking *cigarros*. I watched those two hombres through the chaparral while Cruz got into the pens to check the brands. The men guarding those cows were no vaqueros," he added scornfully. "They did not even feel the change in the cattle when Cruz passed among them."

"An' the brands on those beeves?" Coke asked, taking Ole Belcher's reins.

"They belong to the Blankenship ranch."

"Must be some o' those rustled from Lucas a coupla weeks back. Probably fixin' t'put 'em on that train leavin' t'night."

"*Y escuchen,*" Rogelio said, an urgent note in his voice. And listen. "The cows at the station are being loaded now."

"I know," Coke replied, swinging into Ole Belcher. "Let's get goin'."

Circling back around town, the three men galloped north through the dark land along the railroad tracks. Almost six miles out of Warner, they rounded a bend and saw about a mile in the distance a quivery spot of light.

"That wasn't there when I was here before," Rogelio commented.

"Must be a signal they set out for the train," Coke responded.

They rode toward the light, then veered off from the tracks and into the brush. Winding through the maze of chaparral, they passed parallel to the signal light, a large lantern set out on the cleared ground about a dozen feet from the tracks. Rogelio leading, they angled more deeply into the brush country until they came upon Cruz's horse, tied to a mesquite bush. They dismounted, tethered their own horses nearby, and pulling their rifles out of their scabbards, crept diagonally back toward the tracks, bearing in on the rustle of the bunched cattle in the pen and the drone of a couple of men talking in the vicinity of the pen. Edging closer, they came upon Cruz lying prone behind a bush, peering through the undergrowth. Wordlessly they crouched around him. Coke noticed the signal light to his left, estimating that it was about three hundred yards back up the tracks.

Directly in front of him, a little over fifty feet away, two men were leaning on the fence with their backs to him, placidly talking. Around the side of the fence he saw four horses tied in a row. Nudging Coke, Cruz pointed to the right. A man was sitting on a horse a little way off to the side, idly spinning the end of a rope. Cruz gestured again in another direction. It took a moment before Coke was able to make out on the opposite side of the pen, next to the cattle chute, the sliding orange dot of light of a cigarette being lowered in the hand of a large form.

Signaling to the others, Coke backed away. Keeping low, they retreated into the brush.

"Three more men arrived after Rogelio left," Cruz said in a low voice.

"Where's the fifth man?" Coke asked.

"The last time I saw him, he was walking along the tracks in the direction of the signal light."

"The murderin' bastards are probably fixin' t' mix these here stolen beeves in with those that were bein' loaded on the train t'night," Coke muttered.

"The train had not started out from Warner, then?" Cruz.

"Hadn't when we left," Coke replied.

"What should we do?" Rogelio.

"Well, we sure as hell cain't go for the sheriff." He shook his head. "I ain't in a peaceable mood right now."

"*Robarlos otravez,*" Alejandro growled. Steal them back.

Coke glanced at Cruz. "Your pa's in less o' one. All right, let's take them beeves back t'Lucas."

"*Sí,*" Rogelio put in, all eagerness.

"Cover your faces," Coke ordered, pulling his bandanna up

over his nose. "An' keep your hats down low. Cruz an' me will do all the talkin'."

"Por qué?" Rogelio.

"Your Spanish tumbles out too much," he replied. "It's dark an' we might as well let 'em think they're dealin' with a bunch o' thievin' Anglos." He paused. "Though they're the ones who are genu-ine. Cruz, you stay here 'til we get things in order round the beeves, then you go after that fella down the tracks."

Coke, Alejandro and Rogelio headed back toward the pen.

Slumped with one leg up and bent back around the saddle horn, the man on the horse lazily tossed the rope and pulled it back in. He felt something small like a pebble glance off his shoulder. He turned, and found himself staring down the muzzle of a rifle.

"Keep your hands up," Coke said softly, his voice pitched a note or two lower than usual. "An' drop outa that saddle right careful."

Easing his hands upward, the man lifted his knee the rest of the way over the saddle horn and slid off. The moment he hit ground, Coke spun him around and pushed him face-first against the horse. Shoving the rifle muzzle against the back of his head, Coke pulled the six-shooter out of the man's holster and flung it away.

At the same moment, one of the two men by the fence sensed something solid filling the empty space behind him that hadn't been there before, and automatically glanced back. Breaking off his comment in midthought, he slowly lifted his hands and lowered his foot from the rail. His companion looked sharply aside at him, and became very careful himself. The first started turning around, but with a rough jab of the rifle, Alejandro forced him back, facing the pen. Then, stepping in close, he slipped the two men's guns out of their holsters.

The huge man next to the cattle chute had rolled and lit another cigarette, and was leaning back on the fence when something small and solid stuck him in the small of the back. Thinking that it was the horn of a cow that had gotten crowded against the fence, he irritably reached back to shove it off. It quickly withdrew, and poked him between the shoulder blades. No cow was that tall. He peeked around and jumped, seeing the small man with the rifle, his face hidden under a bandanna and low-slanted hat. Keeping the barrel pressed into him, Rogelio quickly relieved him of his gun and tossed it over the fence. Then, jabbing the man with his rifle for attention, he gestured for him to move around the pen.

As he turned around, the big fellow saw his companions standing in a row at the fence, facing him across the pen. Behind them were the shadowy shapes of two more armed men.

"Come an' join the party," one of them drawled.

Holding his rifle under his arm and against his side so that it was hidden by the shadow of his body, Cruz walked casually out of the brush and started up the tracks. He approached the large form pacing restlessly halfway between the pens and the signal light. Noticing Cruz, the man stopped. Head lowered, he peered at him.

"Who're you?" he demanded.

"Cross," Cruz said, striding steadily on.

"Cross? Cross who? I don't know no Cross." He hesitated, trying to make Cruz out in the insubstantial light. Then a wariness came over him and he made a motion for his gun.

Cruz snapped the rifle up. "Better not."

The hands wavered, then slowly lifted. Keeping his rifle leveled on him, Cruz circled behind, drew the man's gun out of its holster, and slung it away.

"Move," he ordered, prodding his captive with his rifle while at the same time swallowing his astonishment, for as he'd circled around the man, Cruz had glimpsed the badge on his chest. He'd just disarmed Watt Calhoun, the county sheriff.

Rogelio roguishly rolled his eyes when he recognized who the fifth man was that Cruz had brought in to join the others lined up and facing the pen. This night would provide him the gist for many a campfire yarn for years to come.

"Get some rope," Coke was saying to Cruz. "An' let's get these bastards trussed up."

Calhoun moved his head slightly aside to try to catch a look at Coke. "You sound familiar."

"Should," Coke lied easily. "I was on that sonuvabitch Barrett's payroll once."

Coke felt the other men lined up at the fence searching their minds trying to place him. That lie would set them off track for some time, he reckoned. Quite a few men on Barrett's payroll had probably come and gone these past half dozen years. The men whom T.C. hired for the kind of work he wanted done weren't the sort who were known for their staying power.

Coke glanced at Rogelio. "Take one o' those horses over there an' start movin' these cattle out."

"You know who I am?" Calhoun demanded.

"Yep," Coke said.

"You know what we do t'cattle thieves in these parts?"

"Oh?" Coke responded. "These here your cattle?"

The thin wail of a train whistle lifted out of the night. The ears of the cattle rotated. A horse nickered. The midnight train was on its way.

Suddenly the sheriff swung around and lunged at Alejandro. The big bruiser, who'd stood next to Calhoun, also broke away, charging after Rogelio, bringing the smaller man pounding to the ground. And a third took off running for the brush.

Coke stopped the outlaw in front of him in his tracks, bringing his rifle butt down hard on the back of his head. And for good measure, he took out the man beside him as he spun around, undercutting the rifle butt up into his jaw. And almost simultaneously the two men buckled, one dropping leadenly across the other.

The ropes he'd collected looped around his shoulder, Cruz watched the fleeing man sprinting by. As one of the Sidewinder's most skilled vaqueros, he did the natural thing. Letting all the ropes fall but one, he walked after the man, deftly looping the rope and slipping the knot. Then he swung the lariat over his head and sent it flying. It dropped cleanly around the fleeing man. And with a yank, Cruz jerked him, cussing and kicking, onto his backside.

Watt Calhoun, the sheriff, was renowned for his brutality, especially against Mexicans. But he hadn't bargained on an Alejandro Cortez who'd been spoiling for a fight. The instant that Calhoun turned on him and struck, Alejandro, casting his rifle aside, tore explosively into the sheriff, unleashing the black rage that had been building in him for over two hours. He gave Calhoun no quarter, his fists slamming home again and again.

So taken aback was Cruz by the sight of his father walloping the tar out of the mean and muscular county sheriff that he let the culprit he'd lassoed slip the rope and bolt for the brush. Muttering, he flipped the lasso in and ran for a horse.

Rogelio, though half the weight of the big brute who'd brought him down, was a wiry fellow. Jabbing the man in the eye with his elbow, he squirmed loose and scrabbled to his feet, looking for the rifle that had sprung out of his hands when he'd smashed to the ground. The big bruiser clambered up. Rogelio kicked him in the knee. With a squawk, the man flung his thick arm out, clobbering Rogelio over the fence and into the pen. He was rising up to climb over the rail after Rogelio when Coke strolled up behind him, calmly lifted the big man's hat, and whopped him on the head with his rifle butt. Eyes turning up, the huge lug pitched forward, folding over the rail, his body hooked over it at the hip.

"Dammit!" Rogelio burst out scrappily. "I had him."

"What' were you fixin' t'do, bite him on the leg?"

"I woulda had him."

Coke found Rogelio's rifle. "We ain't got the time t'work out all the niceties of a decent fight," he said, tossing it to him. The train whistle wailed. "Listen, that train's only 'bout three, four miles out. Get them cattle outa here."

Rogelio ran for the horses, and jerking the reins loose of one, leapfroged over the fence and scrambled into the saddle. Coke swung the gate open and Rogelio galloped into the pen.

Lasso in hand, Cruz spurred into the brush. Up ahead, he saw the sides of the brush rippling as his quarry fled through them. He loped after. The man burst across a small clearing. The lariat shot out low, snaring him around the ankle. But Cruz had forgotten that his mount wasn't a cow pony trained to stop on a coin the split second that the rope connected. This horse galloped awkwardly on, almost running the culprit over and knocking him on his face, the rope snapping taut on the opposite side of him, whipping him around and dragging him, twisting and bouncing, across the gnarled ground, hiccuping out profanities.

The cattle were on the move, pouring through the gate in a choppy line into the chaparral. Glancing south, Coke detected the faint cone of light from the headlight of the oncoming train, reaching out over the bend in the tracks a mile distant.

Stooping by the pair of men he'd brought down first, he rolled the top one over, pulled him up to a fisting position, and hoisted him onto his shoulder. Cruz was bringing in the outlaw he'd captured, walking him in front of his horse, the man so trussed up that only his legs were free to move.

Breathing hard, Alejandro had dropped down next to the inert form of the sheriff.

"Feel better?" Coke asked as he trudged by, toting his burden.

"Mucho mejor!" Alejandro rasped, shaking his battered fist. Much better! Then, sensing the sheriff stirring next to him, he walloped him again.

Coke dumped his own unconscious victim into the brush and came back out for the other one. The train had rounded the bend, its beacon a levitating orb of light advancing in the darkness, the smoke from its stack a blue-white, funnel-shaped smudge against the glittery night sky.

Coke glanced at the pen. About fifty cows remained.

"Leave that no-good you got there with us," he said to Cruz, "an' help Rogelio get them beeves the hell away from here."

Cruz swung into the pen and, loping around to the rear, started clearing them out. Rogelio galloped through the gate and into the brush to take control of the forward cattle.

Coke hoisted the second man up, and dumped him next to the first. Passing Alejandro, who was heaving the sheriff onto his shoulder, Coke hurried over to the place where Cruz had dropped the ropes. He collected them, and on the way back grabbed the outlaw Cruz had brought in. He walked him into the brush and set him down roughly next to the heaps of his unconscious companions.

"Hog-tie these lowlives good an' tight," he said, tossing Alejandro the ropes. "We don't want 'em workin' free before mornin'."

"You low-down sonuvabitchin' bastards," the bound man spat out.

"Such language," Coke gently scolded him. And lifting the culprit's hat, he thumped him on the head with his rifle butt, knocking him out, too.

"This could get t'be habit-formin'," he said, pulling his bandanna off his face.

They could hear the rumble of hooves, the crackle of twigs, and the low whistles of Cruz and Rogelio hustling the cattle away. Coke peered through the brush. The train was almost to the signal lantern, but was slowing, the outer range of the beam from its headlight sweeping forward and cutting a swath of thin gray light above the tracks alongside the pen.

"Damn," Coke muttered. "Gotta collect that no-good I left out there decoratin' the fence. Stay here."

Pushing through the brush, he hurried toward the fence where the big bruiser who'd gone after Rogelio was still draped over it. Mindful of steadily brightening light above the tracks as the train approached, Coke took hold of the fellow's collar and belt. Bracing a foot against the fence rail, he grappled him back and sent him thudding cumbrously to the ground, almost three hundred pounds of deadweight. Kneeling down behind him, Coke sat him up, grasped him under the arms and around the chest, then, getting to his feet, started dragging him backward, the unwieldy lug's splayed boot heels cutting tracks in the dust.

The train beacon was gliding slowly above the chaparral, the brakes creaking and spurting out sibilant exhalations, the boxcars rattling far back into the shadows. In only a matter of seconds, he'd be in view of the men in the engine cab, and he was still only halfway to the brush.

"Güero," Alejandro called softly, and the loop of a lasso came skittering out on the ground next to Coke. Letting his inert load drop, Coke stooped down, pulled the loop over, hooked it around the fellow's shoulders, found the man's hat, set it neatly on his stomach, and gave a shove. The rope sprang into a straight line into the brush as Alejandro started hauling back on it.

The engine was creeping across the clearing now. Coke got up and turned around. A form at the window of the cab waved. Coke waved back, while in the corner of his eye the huge boots of the unconscious lug slipped backward with a little lurch.

The engine and coal cars passed by, then the freight cars, well over a dozen. This was one mighty long train, Coke thought. Eventually the cattle cars rolled into the clearing, rocking gently with the movements of the cattle inside and echoing with their sporadic lowing.

The din of the train straining to a stop heightened, brakes belching out steam, iron wheels shooting off sparks and squealing and grinding on the rails. Finally, in a long, rattling spasm that rolled down its length, the train shuddered to a stop.

Already the brakeman had leaped off with his lantern and was striding up the tracks toward him, another man following behind.

"Where the hell are them cattle we're supposed t'load up t'night?" the brakeman barked cantankerously.

"Damned if I know," Coke drawled, leaning casually on the fence on the opposite side of the pen from him. "Boss told me t'get out here an' light that signal lantern for y'all. I been waitin' here close t'two hours for them beeves an' I ain't seen hide nor hair of 'em yet." He shrugged. "Reckon they were just too far out t'make it in here on time."

"Dammit t'blue hell," the brakeman grumped.

Scratching his jaw, Coke looked slowly up and down the long line of cars. "Guess y'all are welcome t'stop by here on Friday."

✿ Chapter 32

AUTUMN WAS IN the air. The withering heat of summer had at last given way to a fresh October balminess. Jessica perched on a long-legged stool in the emporium polishing pill and snuff-boxes, watch fobs, mirrors, and sundry knickknacks and placing them in the new wrought-iron and glass display case that Ramiro had made.

Suddenly the late afternoon slant of autumn-tinctured sunlight suffused the heart of the store, and the effect upon Jessica was almost visceral. This was the rich-textured sort of day that filled her with unformed yearnings. As with Christmas, it heightened her sense of time moving by, childhood dreams left behind. If she could, she would have liked to wallow in this mood, to linger over a verse of poetry, to lie in a hammock, gently swaying, while the breeze whispered through the trees. But there was bookkeeping to do, clothing to be mended and ironed, dinner to be prepared—all those prosaic chores of adulthood that tended to blight the pristine enchantment with life that a golden day like this awakened. Oh well, she consoled herself, buffing a small china trinket box, if she were to try to stretch a hammock between two trees in this bald town, the thing would have to be a mainsail a thousand feet long just to reach from tree to tree.

She heard Meg coming up the boardwalk, guffawing over a remark tossed out a door she passed by, yelling "Howdy!" at somebody rumbling down the road on a wagon, humming the same fragment of tune over and over. The tympanic beat of her heels on the wood planks grew louder and she popped into the store like a risen bubble on the champagne afternoon.

"Lordy, lordy," she jubilated. "The first cool day o' fall feels better'n the first good burp after a beer an' hot tamale dinner. How's it goin'?"

Jessica's lifted brow signaled her comment on the deserted store. "It isn't."

"Well, on a purty day like this, folks can think of a sight better things t'be doin' than buyin'," Meg replied. She scratched her nose. "Or sellin'. What you say we close up, take a walk in the country, an' have our dinner at Mañana Luis's tonight?"

"Meg, you're a mind reader."

" 'Twas my own mind I was a-readin'," Meg said. "Where's Cactus?"

"A drifter was found dead a few miles out of town," Jessica replied, putting the remaining knickknacks inside the cabinet below the counter. "So the Sage of Dispenseme left his usual post to ply his trade."

"Sure hope he goes light on the cheek an' lip rouge," Meg mused, locking the money drawer. "Last corpse he laid out looked livelier than any o' Ruby's hardworkin' gals across the street."

Jessica got her hat and shawl out of the back room, stuck the "Closed" sign in the window, and followed Meg out the door. They started down the road. The uncommon briskness in the air made Jessica feel so high-spirited that she could have skipped, danced, and twirled down the street like a child. Even the livestock, the chickens, cats, and dogs looked more chipper.

Jack Siden was standing outside the door of his ranch supply store joking with a pair of tough-looking men who'd recently appeared in town to work as cowhands for T. C. Barrett on the San Sebastian. Seeing Jessica, Siden's face clouded slightly. Leaving his companions, he came down the boardwalk, leaned on the hitching rail, and watched her as she approached with Meg, his green eyes following her, steady and unblinking. Jessica's lightheartedness faded.

"Mighty fine day, Meg . . . Jessica." He nodded; his tone was casual and not at all suggestive, though the keenness of his eyes on her was.

"Yes . . . Mr. Siden," she replied, coolly passing by.

She heard his step on the boardwalk behind her as he rejoined the two Barrett men, heard the silence that followed.

"That Jack Siden still has his cap set on you," Meg observed. "I do believe that fella's tormented no end by you."

"Oh, Meg, don't make me feel guilty, as Jack Siden's trying to do, for something I haven't done. I'm not about to encourage that man and lead him on."

"That's what's tormentin' him," Meg said mildly. "An' you cain't feel guilty for havin' better judgment than a lotta the gals round here."

"Nothing special in coming by that kind of sense," Jessica responded. "All it takes is being dealt some blows and bleeding a few times."

Meg waved at a trio of old geezers seated in a row on the boardwalk step, whittling and jawboning. "Where's Willie?" she asked. "School's been out well over an hour."

Jessica's spirits faded even more. "Coke took him fishing."

"Imagine that—that Coke could find a water hole round here big enough t'sustain a fish."

"He mentioned a little dam on a creek three miles north of here."

"Must be the dam on Pollo Creek on Jehu Wight's place. Ole Jehu ain't got but a coupla beeves to his name, but he hoards that little bowl o' water o' hisn closer'n a overaged daddy guards his only daughter's virtue. Reckon ole Jehu won't mind Coke an' Willie scarin' out a fish or two, so long as they don't violate the water much."

They strolled on in silence, Jessica's mood darkening. "I wish Coke wouldn't do that," she said.

"Do what?"

"Plan these outings without mentioning them to me beforehand so that I find myself faced with a little boy already jumping up and down about what they're planning to do. I have no choice but to give in."

"Why would you wanta refuse, anyhow? It's right good-hearted o' Coke t'take the time out for our little darlin'."

"Oh, Meg," Jessica breathed. "I don't want my son to be used to get to me."

Meg shook her head. "Why must you read ornery, self-servin' motives into folks' simple, kind acts?"

"I don't read self-serving motives into your kind acts," Jessica pointed out.

"Well, what makes Coke's kind acts any different than mine?"

"He's a man."

"Oh-ho! So that's Coke's crime. I just don't think you know who you're dealin' with here, Jessica. Don't lump Coke with other men you've known. He don't hafta trap you nor nobody else. Folks seek him out . . . not t'other way round. He ain't some shuffle-footed, love-starved boy out t'prove his manhood, or a Jack Siden out t'boost his pride by leapin' onto any agreeable gal's behind he can find. Coke don't hafta prove nothin' t'no one. Single-handed, he's built one o' the biggest ranchin' empires in the whole dad-blamed state.''

"I've known rich and powerful men before," Jessica said coldly.

"In spite o' some real hard times," Meg went on, disregarding Jessica's remark, "he took a seventy-thousand-acre spread an' more'n tripled it in size."

Jessica was quiet for a time. They were passing the Catholic church and school. Up ahead to the left stood the majestic hacienda of the San Sebastian, reminding Jessica of its owner.

"That man T. C. Barrett makes me think of someone else I've known," Jessica reflected. "What do you think is going to happen with this claim he has on Coke's land?"

"Coke ain't likely t'let T. C. Barrett or anybody else steal his land out from under him."

"What does that mean, Meg?" she asked softly.

Meg soberly shook her head. "It could mean anything, I'm afraid."

"I hope Coke takes care," she sighed.

"He's smart, Jessica," Meg responded. "He's one o' the smartest men I've ever known."

Jessica, seizing at the remnant of her anger over Coke's maneuvering, looked askant at her friend. "I bet he hasn't read a single book in his life," she challenged.

"Sure, lotsa men got book learnin'. All them big, long, heavy words come a-tumblin' outa their mouths smoother'n dirt clods kicked outa a hillside prairie dog hole. But do you wanta know somethin'? Most o' those kinda men wouldn't survive in these parts. There ain't no fat o' the land for 'em t'live off of. It's all bone an' gristle. A person fine an' refined as Dainty Daisy Talcum Powder would up an' blow away with the first o' the kinda troubles we get down here. Here, a body's gotta be grainier than a South Padre Island beach, full o' down-home common sense an' wood-bucket smarts."

"I knew you'd always take his side," Jessica returned.

"I ain't takin' nobody's side!" Meg exclaimed. She frowned at the younger woman. "What's gotten into you, gal? Don't you like Coke a-tall?"

"Yes, I do," Jessica admitted irritably. "I like him too dog-gone much. And that's the problem."

"Well, he's sure taken a shine to you. So where's the problem?"

Jessica sighed. "Meg, a man's affection has always come easily to me. There isn't anything in my life that comes as easily to me, that I don't have to work for, as a man's affection. It's only after I accept it that I find that I must pay and pay . . . dearly. If a woman truly hungers for enduring companionship, loyalty, and affection, she should just get herself a big, furry dog."

Meg thought that over. "Now, Jessica," she said at last. "I've had me a man an' I've had me a dawg. An' ain't no dawg can outclass my late husband, Clarence.

"Though I love that big-jointed ole houn' o' mine dear, Herman still ain't nothin' but a dawg. When I come home with a right funny joke, he cain't even work up a decent giggle. He just sits there, thumpin' the tail he ain't got. When I'm feelin' down an' lonesome, he cain't put his hairy ole arms round me an' tell me everything'll be all right. No. All he can do is lick me on the foot. Why, Herman cain't even give me any decent back talk when I'm feelin' cranky. He just slinks off to the barn an' hides with the cow."

Meg's broad face crinkled into a grin. "An' let me tell you, strokin' my Clarence's ole furry belly could sure bring on a sight more pleasurin' than strokin' Herman's."

"Well, there are always exceptions." Jessica smiled.

"There are 'nuff exceptions t'make 'em not t'be exceptions a-tall. An' you gotta know, Jessica, that there've been men who, for more'n half a century o' their lives, have kept on bein' good t'women with natures that'd freeze a turnip an' tongues that'd stun a pit viper.

"Men can make mighty fine friends, Jessica. The dearest friend in all my life was Clarence. What was important t'me, Clarence went to the trouble o' makin' important to him. An' t'other way around with me. We built each other up . . . never tore each other down. Clarence made our little boy feel real loved. An' there was times we had the most fun together, you just cain't imagine.

"Oh, I admit, there was some hard times, too, but we held t'gether, toughed 'em out, an' after a spell, crossed on out to the other side of 'em like rollin' off a rocky stretch in the road.

"Yup." Meg nodded. "All in all, it was the sweetest pleasure o' my life lovin' Clarence. He was my own dearest darlin'."

"And your Clarence wasn't a liar?"

"Not much o' one. Why?"

"Coke is."

"Naw!"

"Oh, yes, he is. Now, I can see where there may be times when a person may want to shade over certain facts that he doesn't feel are anyone else's business. But why would Coke lie to me about something that makes little difference to me one way or the other?"

"Like what?"

"Like how many cows he has. I don't care how many cows he has. A thousand, ten thousand, the numbers are meaningless to me. So if he can lie about something as unimportant as that, then he can lie to me about important things as well."

"When'd Coke tell you how many beeves he had?"

"A few weeks ago, during my first trip to his ranch. I asked him out of idle curiosity, and he said around nine thousand."

"An' when'd you hear different?"

"This past Friday. A man came into the store. He seemed to be very knowledgeable about this area. We started talking about how hard it was on the ranchers these days with the drought. He told me that he'd just gotten back from the Sidewinder and had had a long talk with Coke Sanders.

" 'Just think,' the man said. 'All that land, a big operation like that, and the drought leaving him nothing but a couple thousand head of cattle to his name.' So you see, Meg, Coke lied to me."

"This fella that came into the store, you happen to recollect his name?"

"I'm not sure." Jessica frowned. "Davis . . . Davidson, something like that."

"Did this fella have a gap between his two front teeth an' a long, red, greased handlebar mustache, curlicues on the ends?"

"Why, yes, that's the man."

"An' that's Lester Davenport . . . the county tax assessor. Hell, girl, everybody lies to him. Soon as folks see that red handlebar mustache a-bobbin' into sight, they start into gettin' so destitute an' hangdog that ole Lester's gotta think that nobody cracks a smile around here . . . ever."

"People always lie to the tax assessor?"

" 'Tain't his business, the county's business, the state's business, nor nobody else's business what a body's got, don't got, what he's done with it, nor what he's fixin' t'do with it. Next t'how you take your lovin', if there's anythin' that should be a person's own private business, that's it. Unless you're just a-hankerin' to pay a heap more taxes than you'd hafta."

Jessica stopped in her tracks. "Oh-oh."

"Oh-oh *what*?"

"When Mr. Davenport mentioned that Coke had only a couple thousand head of cattle, I said, 'Why, that's strange. Just a few weeks ago, he told me he had nine thousand.' "

"Oh-oh *right*," Meg agreed. Cocking her head, she eyed Jessica uneasily. "Tell me, durin' the time you was a-jawin' with ole Lester, did the subject o' the store's inventory happen to come up?"

"No. We didn't discuss it."

"Whew! There for a second, I was a-scared that you'd gone an' made a liar outa me, too."

❧ Chapter 33

"I GOT A bite! I got a bite!" Willie squealed, his tiny body bouncing with excitement.

He tugged in the line tied to the end of the fishing pole Coke had fashioned for him out of a twig. Throwing himself forward onto his stomach, he lifted his catch out of the water. His face fell at the sight of the wee fish wriggling at the end of the line.

Frowning, he lifted his catch higher and peered at it. "Hey, Coke!" he cried. "This one has the same spot on the side of its belly as that fish you caught a little while back and let go."

Coke leaned down next to the boy and squinted at the tiny form. "Yup, an' in fact, it bears a strikin' resemblance all over to that other fish you brought in before I did . . . an' we let go."

"You suppose we been catching the exact same fish every time?"

"Wouldn't be surprised," Coke said, taking the line from Willie. Wetting his hand in the pond, he reached out and grasped the fish. Holding it below the surface of the water, he worked the hook out of its mouth and let it slither away into the smoky green murk.

"Why d'you think it keeps letting us catch it over and over again?"

"Well," Coke drawled, settling down on an elbow, leg bent up at the knee. "If it is the only fish in this here pond, could be it's a tad suicidal."

Sticking his hand into the rusty lard can set at the foot of a tree, Willie ran his fingers through the mud inside, drew out a worm, and without ceremony, impaled it on his hook. With a flip of his twig pole, he cleanly sliced the water with his line. Mirroring Coke, he settled down on an elbow and soberly watched his cork as it rocked placidly at the middle of the pond.

Coke was enjoying this time with Willie. Since he'd gotten the news of Barrett's claim on his land, he'd been on the move almost constantly, traveling to Ciudad Guerrero, then to Warner. And only yesterday he'd returned from a trip to Realitos, where he'd met with Hunt Tyler, the Texas Ranger in charge of the Ranger station there, who'd been a friend of Coke's pa's since before the Civil War. And until this afternoon, Coke hadn't had the chance to pull back and get in tune with the simpler life.

This sandy-haired boy with his mother's face was easy to take to, Coke reflected, because Jessica had made him that way. He was sure of her love, and that made him open and confident. He could recognize sincere affection in others, accept it, and return it in an easy way. Willie was proof of his mother's capacity for loving.

"Your mama ever take you fishin' out in the ocean whilst y'all was a-livin' in San Fran-cisco?" Coke asked.

"No. But Auntie Rosie did once. She took me fishing off a jetty out in the bay."

"Auntie Rosie?"

"She wasn't my really, truly aunt, o' course . . . just an old neighbor lady that Ma paid to look after me while she was away at work."

"You go t'stay with your Auntie Rosie much?"

"Didn't go to stay with her. She came to stay with me."

"Most every day?"

"Most every night.'

"That when your mama set off for work?"

"Hmm-hmmm. She'd leave right after supper."

"Came home next mornin', I suppose."

"Don't know when she'd get home. She'd just always be there when I woke up, sitting in her robe at the kitchen table, all starey-eyed, an' sippin' coffee while the bacon burned."

Coke broke off a grass stem and chewed on the juicy end of it. "I suppose, when your mama set out for work each evenin', she'd have on that same ole black skirt an' white blouse that she wears all the time round here at the emporium."

"No, she'd have on dancin' dresses."

"Dancin' dresses? T'go t'work?"

"Hmm-hmmm."

"Sure they wasn't just dress-up dresses?"

The arm that Willie had been leaning on had gone to sleep. He sat up, rubbing it to get out the prickle. "Well, they sure looked like dancin' dresses to me. One was this kinda dark green velvet with gold rickrack running all around, and t'other was a dark red silk with shiny beads and doodads sprinkled all over and a bunch of little fluffy feathers sprouting outa one shoulder. Ma'd curl her hair up high with the curling iron, then stick this comb all covered with diamonds smack in the middle of it . . . only they weren't really truly diamonds."

"Why you think your mama'd get so gussied up just t'go t'work?"

Willie shrugged. "Guess that's what the people at Ivory Ives wanted her to do."

"Ivory Ives. That the place she worked at?"

"Hmm-hmmm."

"Was it a dancin' place, then?"

"Don't know. Ma never talked 'bout it much."

They lapsed into a comfortable silence, enjoying the cool shade surrounding the pond. The overhanging tree limbs cast kaleido-scopic shadows across the surface of the water, while beyond the bower, the encompassing open prairie was still aflame in golden sunlight.

Coke sat up and played his line. "Reckon you miss your home in San Fran-cisco."

"Once in a while," Willie admitted. "I miss some of the things I left behind. Had this big box of wooden soldiers that I kept under my bed. Used to play war with them. Clean forgot to bring them with me when we left. I miss my big bouncy bed back there. Sometimes I roll right off that little trundle bed I sleep on at Meg's. Miss Auntie Rosie, too. If she was looking after me in the afternoon and I'd want a piece of cake, she'd let me have it right off, Coke, not say it'd ruin my appetite for dinner, rot my teeth, all sortsa bad things. Like that ma o' mine would.''

"That's plain ole mama love," Coke explained. "Mas are always more interested in makin' their young-uns turn out right than in givin' 'em everything they want any ole time just t'please 'em quiet. A good lovin' mama is always willin' t'put up a fight.''

Willie thought that over, and decided he wasn't likely to get much sympathy from Coke on that particular point. "I miss my pals at school," he went on, then made a face. "But I sure don't miss those awful starched white shirts.''

"You had t'wear starched shirts?''

Willie nodded. "They were a part of the uniform we had to wear at Rutledge's. That was the school Ma sent me to, Rutledge Academy. Auntie Rosie used to tell me all the time that I should be right grateful that Ma could afford to send me to such a fine school. But I tell you, Coke, I sure wasn't grateful for that awful uniform.''

"Bet you still learned a lot at that Rutledge place.''

"I suppose so. It was memorize, memorize, all day long . . . number tables, Bible verses, dumb poems 'bout virtue and discipline. When I'd get home in the afternoons, Ma would help me with my memory work while the dinner she was fixing would boil away on the stove.''

"Reckon your mama would be a big help with your schoolin'. She's right good at a lotta things." He squinted at Willie. "Even dealin' out cards, when y'all was visitin' out at our place a few weeks back.''

Willie nodded. "She is good at that. When she first started working at Ivory Ives, that was all she did all day long—sit at the kitchen table dealing out cards, pulling them in, and dealing them out again. And she had these flat, round colored things that she'd set out in stacks. While she was practicing her dealing, she'd move those things here and move them there, from one stack to the other. Why, she got so good at her card dealing, Coke, that she could remember which cards she'd put out on the table and which ones were still in the deck she was holding in her hand.'' His voice dropped secretively. "And do you know what?" he said. "She had this extra special deck of cards that she could call out the numbers to without even having to look on the front sides of them."

"How's that?"

"I don't know how she did it, but she'd hold that there special deck facedown in her hand, say, 'three of clubs,' flip the top card over, and sure enough, there it'd be. She could go through the whole deck thataway, real fast, and be right every time . . . just like magic. I'd look on the back sides of those cards trying to figure out how she did it. But I never could make out any words or numbers on them, just squiggly designs."

"You reckon she brought her trick deck o' cards with her from San Fran-cisco?" Coke asked idly.

"Left them there, I guess," Willie said wistfully. "Along with my wooden soldiers."

"Why didn't you bring those soldiers with you, seein' as how you liked 'em so much?"

"We just didn't have the time to remember every single thing."

"You didn't make plans t'leave before ya'll took off?"

Willie shook his head. "No. We left real suddenlike. That night, I remember, Ma left for work same as she always did. Then next I knew, there she was, shaking me awake and it was still dark outside. Boy, was she all a-twitter—like I didn't ever see her before—scurrying here and scurrying there, throwing things into suitcases. And Auntie Rosie was standing there in the doorway, just a-bawling and wringing her hands.

"We were on the train leaving San Francisco just as the sun was starting to rise, and Ma was jabbering away ninety to nine 'bout this an' 'bout that . . . 'bout everything under the sun—" his voice slowed and his gaze slipped away from Coke "—'ceptin' why we were leaving and where we were going."

The boy seemed to pull back then, his mood darkening. A frown marring the purity of his child's face, he picked at the bark at the bottom of his twig fishing pole.

"Anything the matter, Will?" Coke asked.

There was a long silence. "Something bad is bothering my mother," he mumbled, his eyes turned down.

"Why do you think that, son?"

Willie slowly peeled a strip of bark up the twig. "She gets

worried sometimes . . . 'specially when the stagecoach pulls into town.''

''How d'you know that?''

The strip broke off halfway up. He let it drop. ''When she hears it coming, she goes to the window and watches till everybody's out of the coach.''

Coke recalled her doing the same thing the day he'd met her. ''You think she's expecting someone?'' he asked.

''Don't know.'' Willie shrugged his small shoulders. ''I think she's a little scared, Coke.''

''Why?''

''When we first got here, Ma would have these bad dreams at night, and get up and walk the floor. I'd go back to sleep. And when I'd wake up later, I'd still hear the floorboards in the parlor creaking.'' He peeked up at Coke, then looked down again. ''Do you think she's going to leave here?''

''Not without you,'' Coke replied gently.

The child picked another piece of bark loose at the base of his twig. ''Sometimes I wake up at night and there Mommy is, sitting in the chair by my bed . . . just looking and looking at me. Sometimes I pretend I'm still asleep. Other times I open my eyes. She lets out this big sigh, then gets down on the bed and holds me real tight till I go back to sleep again.''

''You recollect anything happening back in San Francisco?'' Coke asked softly.

''No,'' Willie said, slapping a mosquito that had alighted on his wrist. ''But when we were leaving San Francisco, Ma told me that from then on out I was to call myself Willie West.''

''What were you called before?''

''Willie Daniels. On proper times, William Joseph Daniels, Jr. . . . the same as my father. 'Ceptin' he was Captain William Joseph Daniels, Sr.''

''Why you think you had t'change your name?''

Willie pursed his lips. ''I wasn't supposed to tell anybody that.''

Coke regarded him for a time, then decided to move to ground less troubling for the child. ''You remember your daddy much?''

''Not too much. He was gone most of the time. But Ma told me once that my daddy loved us more than anything in the whole wide world. That was the reason he had to be gone so much, 'cause taking things far across the ocean was how he earned the money to pay for our nice home and clothes and food.'' The child turned on Coke those clear greenish eyes so like his mother's. "And that was true, too. 'Cause as soon as my daddy died in that typhoon, some mean men came and took all of our furniture away and made us leave our home."

"Where'd you go?" Coke asked quietly.

"Different places. Finally Ma found us a place." Willie's face screwed up. "It was these two itty-bitty dirty rooms at the top of this skinny, rickety building near the wharves. You had to walk up lotsa dark, creaky stairs to get to 'em." His freckled nose crinkled. "And just down the street was this fish market. Made the place stink like dead fish all the time."

"I thought your mama was sending you to a fancy boys' school."

"Oh, that was later, after we moved outa that creepy place."

"When you moved . . . that 'bout the time your mama started in workin' at that place called Ivory Ives?"

"Think so," Willie reflected as he turned his face toward the pond. "Anyway, it wasn't till after we were in our better home that Ma started working at nights and Auntie Rosie started coming in to look after me."

Suddenly, Willie lurched to attention.

"Hey, Coke! Look, you got a bite."

Coke pulled the line in. There was no resistance, just dead weight. He lifted his catch out of the water.

"Ugh!" Willie made a face. "A frog! Hook musta stabbed him clean through the brain."

"I guess this just ain't our day for catchin' fish, Will," Coke said, working the hook out and tossing the dead frog into the under-growth. He unlooped his line from the end of his twig fishing pole and began wrapping it around his hand. "Sun's startin' t'lean purty heavy toward the west. Guess we'd better head on home."

When they untied the horses and led them out of the thicket, Coke noted the relaxed manner with which the child handled Windy.

"You seem right at home with horses, Will."

"Rode horses in San Francisco," Willie answered.

"Oh? Your mama took you ridin'?"

The child's face darkened and he looked down. "No," he said ill-temperedly. "It was Mr. LaMarque's groom that took me."

"Who's Mr. LaMarque?"

"Mr. Henri LaMarque was his whole name," Willie responded. "He owned Ivory Ives, the place where Ma worked. Anyway, that's what Auntie Rosie told me once. He was rich."

"Why you think so?"

"Had this big fancy carriage. Had a big house in the country."

"Oh? You visited his place?"

"Only on Sundays. Sunday was the day that Auntie Rosie was always away visiting her daughter. So whenever Mr. LaMarque sent his carriage for Ma on Sundays, I had to go along, too, 'cause Auntie Rosie wasn't around for Ma to leave me with."

"So then you went with your mama to this Mr. LaMarque's house way out in the country. . . ." Coke prompted.

He could see a confused anger stirring in the child. "Mr. LaMarque never liked me taggin' along. Always got snotty when he saw me."

Coke held Windy's reins as Willie got up into his saddle. "Why you think he didn't like you comin' along?"

"Don't know. But every time he'd see me there in the carriage he'd say real nasty to Ma, 'Why'd you bring the kid?' "

"And your mama . . . what would she say?"

"Nothing. She'd just look down and say nothing." His eyes brightened. "Except for the very last time we went out there. That time she talked real mean right back. Said he should just find himself some other woman to amuse him."

Coke eyed the child. "What'd the inside o' Mr. LaMarque's big house look like?" he asked, trying to sound casual. "Fancy, I'd bet."

"Don't know what it looked like, never went inside. Mr. LaMarque would always call Herbert out of the stables—Herbert was his groom, see—and tell him to take me riding. Then Ma'd tell Herbert, like she did all the time with Auntie Rosie, to mind, keep a close watch, now. Then Herbert would set me on this spotted pony and lead me all around the pasture. But after a while he'd get bored and go off and lie down in the shade. And I'd ride the pony all by myself."

"And your mama . . . where would she be?"

"In the house with Mr. LaMarque. Seemed like a long time. But soon as she'd come out, we'd get right back into Mr. La-Marque's fancy carriage and head on back home."

"Your mama and Mr. LaMarque were purty good friends, I take it," Coke said, climbing onto Ole Belcher.

"No!" Willie shot out. "She'd never like that man!"

Coke glanced aside at him. "Why don't you think so?"

"Ma always acted different when she was around Mr. La-Marque. Kinda careful. And she'd be real quiet and tense-like while we were going out to his place. She'd just sit there. And even when we'd get back home, she wouldn't start acting like my mother again till a long time later. No." He shook his head emphatically. "She didn't like that Mr. LaMarque at all. I don't see how anybody could."

"Why?"

"He was mean and he didn't have any eyebrows," Willie said. "And he was fat. Squishy fat . . . squishier than that frog you caught. And he had these light gray eyes, that when he looked at you, you couldn't see inside." He paused, his eyes flashing angrily. "And I don't like the way he looked at my mother."

"How was that?"

"Hard . . . like he could hurt her."

"Then why you suppose she kept on visiting him?"

The child fell silent, considering. "I asked Ma that once, when Mr. LaMarque's carriage was waiting out by the gate. And she said to me, kinda sad, that sometimes when you want to keep the bacon on the table, you have to feed the swine. I didn't understand that. Didn't understand that at all. Do you understand that, Coke?"

❧ Chapter 34

THE DYING SUN was soaking up the last of the light from the sky. Tomato-red and swollen, it was sinking into the horizon, and there was a chill in the air.

Willie shivered as they turned down the road toward home. Several times that afternoon he'd dangled his hands and feet in the pond water, and his damp sleeve and pant cuffs felt like bands of ice.

Jessica had apparently been watching for them, for as soon as they rounded the corner, she drifted out of the house and stood waiting behind the picket fence. Her hair was plaited in a thick braid that lay over her head like a wreath. The hairstyle defined her high cheekbones and emphasized the haunting solemnity of her appearance as she stood watching them, clutching close to her bosom the knitted shawl around her shoulders, the thin, misty light absorbing her eyes in shadow yet catching onto the wispy filaments of hair floating out of the crown of braid and turning them to silver.

As he and Willie rode slowly down the road toward her, Coke could not take his eyes off her. Another man had invaded that fragile loveliness, known the softness of her unprotected breasts, the grace of her legs, the smoothness of her thighs. A man named Henri LaMarque had pleasured himself with her, trespassing into her most tender and secret of places while probably scorning the Jessica inside.

Coke felt no scorn toward Jessica, but only a tender sorrow for her. And at that moment he knew that he did truly love her.

"You're late. I was getting worried," she said as they drew up. "Did you catch anything?"

"Only one dumb little fish, Ma," Willie responded, jumping off Windy. He tied the mare's reins to the fence and skipped through the gate. "Three times we caught that one dumb little fish. Then we caught a big dumb dead frog."

Jessie put a hand to her son's icy cheek, then wrapped her arms around him, snuggling him against her inside the shawl. "If you don't get into some dry clothes soon, my little man, I'm afraid that you're going to be catching something else as well." She let him go, giving him a playful pat on the rump. "Now, scoot on into the house." But before he could scamper off, she touched his shoulder, staying him. "Didn't you forget something, love? What do you say to Mr. Sanders?"

Willie rolled his eyes. This was some of that pesky social stuff that menfolk had to do for the ladies. "Thanks a lot, Coke. Sure had a good time."

"My pleasure, son," he replied.

Catching a peculiar, somber shading in Coke's voice, Jessica looked at him questioningly.

"Go on in the house, my love," she repeated absently, still eyeing Coke. "I'll be in soon."

"Meg!" Willie hollered, bounding up the step. They heard the muffled start of Meg's response before it was cut short by the bang of the door.

Inhaling, she set her shoulders. "Coke . . ."

"Yes, Jessie."

Again, she was stopped by that solemn note in his voice, the thoughtful sadness in his eyes.

"Is anything the matter?" she asked uneasily. "About the claim on your land, I mean?"

"Nothin' I can't handle, Jessie," he said.

She regarded him a moment longer, trying to fathom what was amiss, then apparently deciding to disregard it, plunged on. "There's a matter I'd like to discuss with you."

"Well, there's somethin' I'd like to discuss with you, too," he replied. "Let's find a place to sit down and talk it out."

Head tilted slightly, she studied him. Then, a mistrustfulness coming into her eyes, she glanced at the house, then back at him. "No," she said warily. "What I have to say can be said here and now."

"All right," he responded. "I'm listenin'."

"I don't appreciate this habit that you have of making plans with Willie before consulting with me first. It's unfair of you to do this to me, and I want it to stop."

"All I did was take a little boy fishin'. What're you really afraid of, Jessie?" he asked quietly.

"I'm not afraid," she said.

"I don't think you're bein' entirely truthful 'bout that."

"Well, that's my business, isn't it?" she answered stiffly.

He gave her a long, contemplative look, seeing that the resistance was building in her. "All right, Jessie," he said gently. "From here on out, when I wanta plan somethin' with Willie, I'll talk it over with you first. You have my word."

Her eyes widened. She hadn't expected him to capitulate that easily.

"Now that that's settled," he went on, "there're still some matters that I wanta talk over with you, so let's go sit down on the step over there an' talk 'em out."

"No," she answered cautiously after a pause. "Whatever you have to say, say it now."

"Willie's worried about you."

She frowned, confused. "He is? My little boy?"

"He can feel that somethin's not right with you an' it's got him scared. What kinda trouble are you in?"

"I'm in no kind of trouble," she answered quickly.

"Then why'd you hightail it outa San Francisco sudden-like in the dead o' night?"

"I didn't," she retorted.

"Then, if you ain't in no trouble, why'd you change your name from Daniels t'West?"

She didn't answer, her eyes hardening.

"After your husband died," he went on, "you didn't earn your livin' sewin' in no tailor's shop, did you? You dealt blackjack at a place called Ivory Ives."

She was clutching her shawl so tightly now that her knuckles were whitening. "I knew it," she uttered in a low voice. "I just knew that that was what you were up to, trying to pry information out of my son about me."

"It wasn't like that, Jessie. I do care for that little fellow."

"Ha!" she laughed mirthlessly. "I'm sure. All right, sir, what else did you trick my little boy into saying about me?"

He hesitated. He might as well lay it all out. "Who's this dude called Ornery LaMarque?"

There was a subtle lowering of her shoulders as if a weight had dropped inside her. Her eyes were two dark, glossy circles in a stark white mask. "You know all the answers," she said unevenly. "What did you get Willie to tell you?"

"Nothin' much . . . 'ceptin' Willie's scared o' LaMarque an' hates him 'cause he thinks he'd hurt you."

But she could tell by the look in his eyes that he knew more than that. He knew. And the mortification started rising up in her, choking her breath away.

"What kinda trouble are you in, Jessie?" he repeated.

"That isn't your business," she replied barely above a whisper.

"I think it is," he said, almost as softly. "An' maybe I can help."

For a fraction of a second he thought he saw her waver. He felt a glimmer of hope that she'd give up the fight, speak a soft word to him, or even weep and walk into his arms as he ached for her to do.

But the moment passed, for one of the lessons that life had battered into her was to betray no weaknesses—especially to a man—for they can be used against you.

"Well, I certainly don't need any assistance from the kind of man who'd use a child's innocence and trust to manipulate him into betraying confidences about his mother," she breathed contemptuously. "I don't want your help. I don't want you in my life. Are you too arrogant to accept that? Are you too blind to see it?"

"There's nothin' wrong with my sight, Jessie. It's yours, clouded so you cain't tell weeds from wheat, hawks from bluebirds, briar patches from vegetable gardens. So you discount 'em all. But, Jessie, if you got problems, I wanta help you."

"How generous," she replied acidly. "Since you really want to help me, Coke Sanders, just get out of my life and stay out of it."

He searched her face, then untied the reins of the two horses. "If that's what you want," he said, "I'll let you be."

He climbed into the saddle, pulled the mounts around, and when he'd ridden down the road a bit, finished his thought. "Till your mood improves."

She remained in place, watching him recede into the dusk, pulling Windy alongside, until he turned the corner and was gone. The old ache of shame swelled through her, and with it a pang of guilt and regret for what she'd done. The world was a glossy blur before she realized that she was weeping. The tension that had been building in her these past few minutes spilled out into her extremities, and her hands and knees shook. She pulled her shawl tighter around her, shuddering into it, and like a palsied old woman, walked into the house.

Meg was sitting on the parlor sofa, darning underwear. "Where's Coke?" she asked. "Ain't he goin' out t'eat with us?" Then she stopped, frowning bewilderedly at Jessica's downcast form as she passed by to the kitchen. Meg got up and followed her.

"Anything the matter, honey?" she asked Jessica's back from the kitchen doorway.

"Nothing." She shrugged, keeping turned away. Snuffling, she wiped her nose with the back of her hand. "It . . . it's getting cold outside." She opened the back door and picked up the pail on the porch. "I'll milk Cuspidora tonight," she said hoarsely, and went on outside.

She trudged into the stable yard and numbly gave Cuspidora a swat on the rump. The tame old cow ambled into the stable, and stood waiting in her customary place for Jessica to come milk her. Jessica closed the stable doors against the dying day. "Well, you did it,'' she whispered. "You really did it this time, Jessica Daniels, you low-down bitch, you.''

The stable was absorbed in shadow except for a single shaft of gray light slanting down through the hayloft window. It provided barely enough illumination for her to make out shapes in the darkness. But she didn't want any light. The enclosed darkness suited her. It was warm and soothing and covered over her shame.

She set the bucket under the cow's swollen udder, then placed the milking stool next to Cuspidora and sat down on it. Jessica had found milking to be the one country chore that she'd taken to. Somehow, being near this warm, placid cow had a calming effect on her. For a time, she sat slumped with her hands hanging limply from her knees, waiting for some of that calm to start settling through her. But it wouldn't come.

"Oh, Jessica, Jessica," she breathed jaggedly. "When will you ever stop feeling so dirty and no-good?" And leaning her head against Cuspidora's soft flank, she let the dam inside her burst.

❧ Chapter 35

SUNDAYS ALEJANDRO RESERVED for his own land. Before dawn his solitary figure moved across it. As the sun's glow spread into the sky, silhouetting the far horizon, he paused, as he always did, at the ruins of the adobe hut where he was born, listening for the echoes of distant voices and memories. Then he rode on. Less than a mile away, he was building his home.

Its walls stood only a few feet high, uneven, and spiked with markers and supports. He was building his home of stone. Alejandro tied his horse to the wheel of an old wagon crusted with dust, and pulled his rifle out of his saddle. He propped it against one jagged wall, then moved on to the pile of stone he'd quarried from a creek bed twenty miles away.

It was bone-aching, muscle-draining work, building this house, stone by stone. And though he knew that the Sidewinder's carpenters would've built him a fine one for the asking, this he chose to build on his own. It was *his* home on *his* land. María Luisa understood and forgave him his absences from mass. She knew that it was here, on the certitude of this land that was his, that he took his communion, paid his devotions, made his peace.

As he labored, mixing mortar, smoothing it out, planting stone upon stone, he saw not the bare primitiveness of the place as it was, but his dream of what it would be one day. María Luisa's garden would be there, and over there the barn, and there the fruit trees. And all around would sparkle the spirit of his grandchildren. Not a one of his five stubborn children had cooperated so far, but he expected twenty grandchildren at least.

So absorbed was he that he failed to notice the man riding across the plain toward him. And when he finally did see him, the figure was only a thin shadow against the sun. Leaning heavily against the wheelbarrow he was loading with stones, Alejandro wiped the sweat and sun-dazzle from his eyes with the back of his sleeve.

Recognition stirred through him. He tensed, glancing aside at his rifle twenty feet away. He felt men approaching from behind and looked over his shoulder. There were three of them, riding slowly in his direction, their rifles leveled on him.

The lone rider passed through the glare of light. The bruises on Watt Calhoun's face from the pounding Alejandro had given it had faded to a greenish yellow. The keen pleasure of blood vengeance about to be gratified burned from his eyes. He lifted something from his saddle and swung it slowly. It was a rope, a lynching rope.

No! every fiber in Alejandro cried. His home would not be so violated. These *víboras* might choose the time of his death, but they would never choose its manner.

Roaring, he yanked the knife out of his belt and charged Calhoun. He heard the blasts of the rifles, felt the bullets slashing into his back, the sudden, burning leadenness within him. He threw himself onward. Calhoun's gun was popping, the rifles blasting, bullets ripping into him from all sides, Alejandro hearing the reports distantly. The fiery leadenness deepened and spread, then flickered to numbness. Light drained from the day, the ground beneath his feet wavered and slid out from under him like a loose carpet.

At least I made it home. The thought drifted through his mind like a whisper and was gone.

"Damn," Calhoun muttered to his companions. "I had to empty my carbine into that bastard before he'd go down."

The people of the Sidewinder were scattered over the hill beyond the stone roots of Alejandro's home, Father Dominic had finished his absolutions, the box had been lowered into the ground, and still they hung on. They were all family here, if not by blood, by soul.

The spades clinked into the earth as the men shoveled the dirt onto the box. They shook it out timidly at first, as though tiptoeing, for a heavy clatter on the box would've resounded through them all as hard, cold, and final as granite. María Luisa stood between her two oldest children, dressed in the stark black of the doña; the light-absorbing black of death. Her normally animated, youthful face looked old, the skin drawn across it thin as onionskin, strong but translucent, showing a hint of quiveriness underneath.

Coke wanted to speak to her, to offer comfort. But no words came, and if he'd found any, they'd have felt like wisps of straw cast over a chasm. His bleak silence spoke more than words.

Ma was the first to move. She silently squeezed María Luisa's hand, gave each of Alejandro's children a nod as she passed by, and casting a suspicious look at the padre, hobbled down toward the wagon.

"We loved him," Sarie said, and brushed a kiss on María Luisa's cheek, then looked closely into her face. "I know," she whispered, one widow to the other. "It's so hard to let go."

She paid her condolences to the rest of Alejandro's family, then came to Coke. He avoided Sarie's compassionate eyes, for the pain was too close.

"I don't suppose you'll be comin' home with us," she said.

He shook his head. "I think I'll be spendin' a coupla days alone."

By twos and threes, the crowd drifted softly away, and still he remained.

"He spoke Spanish." Coke heard Cruz's quiet voice beside him. "At the railroad tracks when we stole back the Blankenship cattle, *mi papá* spoke Spanish."

"Shouldna asked him if he was feelin' better for all his beatin' on the sheriff that night," Coke said grimly.

Chapter 36

WILKIN EDMONDS PULLED the weighted chain out of his pocket, found the two keys he needed, and secured the rear door of the Warner Savings and Loan. It was past seven on a Friday night, Wilkin having stayed on to finish up some correspondence for Mr. Barrett to a cattle dealer in Trail City, Colorado. A steady income poured into Mr. Barrett's Silver Mountain Land Company, Wilkin knew, from cattle sales through that agent—more than enough to support the small army of men who worked for the Land Company, most of them paid double the wages of regular cowhands. Wilkin knew this because Land Company business passed through the Savings and Loan. And though Martin Filbert, the head accountant, was the only one allowed access to the Land Company's records, Wilkin had found occasions to peek over Martin's shoulder while he was at work on them.

Wilkin wouldn't have had to stay the extra hour to complete that correspondence for Mr. Barrett; he wouldn't sign it until next Tuesday, when he got back from a long weekend at the San Sebastian. But anything was better than rushing back to that cheerless room on the third floor of Jenner's boardinghouse, where nothing had changed in the twelve years since Wilkin had moved in there. It just kept looking more washed-out from year to year, and Wilkin almost expected to open the door one day and find nothing on the other side because the entire room had faded away.

He stepped out of the alley and onto the street, strolling toward the courthouse square. The last threads of daylight had about trailed out of the sky, and the gleaming spheres atop the lampposts on the square were gaining vibrance in the deepening darkness. The flavor of Friday night was upon the town, the lift of liveliness prolonged, the retreat into repose postponed. Several stores remained open. Strollers were out taking their constitutionals. The shouts of children still playing outside rang out of the encircling neighborhoods. Loose clusters of older children, not yet out of adolescence, roamed about, eyeing each other.

Wilkin strolled into Hank's Restaurant, on the corner. At the boardinghouse tonight they'd be serving beef pie; and twelve uninterrupted years of Friday night beef pie at the boardinghouse had left Wilkin with a hatred toward that dish.

Of course, the offerings here at Hank's weren't much of an improvement, he reflected, taking his usual seat at the back of the restaurant. Their Friday special was always chili and cornbread.

"I'll have the fried chicken and cornbread," he said to Molly, Hank's wife.

Molly stomped off to the kitchen, and Wilkin could hear someone back there slamming around for a fry pan. That would throw them off, Wilkin thought, feeling ornery.

Pulling off his spectacles, Wilkin wiped the lenses on a corner of a tablecloth, sporting enough red scars from the day's chili suppers to look like it had been worn by the victim of a scatter-gun attack.

It was on these Friday evenings that Wilkin most resented Martin Filbert's defection. Had Martin not taken up with that dour widow six months ago, he'd be sitting across from Wilkin now. As bachelors pushing forty with no close relatives around, or no relatives around whom they'd want to be close to, as colleagues in business, Wilkin and Martin had gravitated toward each other. For almost ten years they'd taken many of their meals together, drawn courage from each other when they went to dances at Cattleman's Hall, afterward reviewing the gals they'd met there and their various defects. Friday nights would find Wilkin and Martin here at the café, and later at Martin's tiny three-room cottage playing checkers or gin rummy, maybe drinking a shot of whiskey and talking tough and feeling racy. But all that ended when Martin took up with that sourpuss widow. Wilkin felt his friend's abandonment as a betrayal, and by his waspish comments let Martin know it, too.

Hope he gets married, Wilkin thought maliciously, knowing Mr. Barrett preferred his employees to be unmarried. As soon as any of them tied the knot, the boss grew suspicious, closed off certain portions of the business to them, and sooner or later, let them go. Mr. Barrett seemed of the opinion that a wife and children divided a man's loyalty. And he was right about that, too, Wilkin concurred.

The food arrived, indifferently prepared, and indifferently did Wilkin eat it. Buttering his cornbread, he wondered what the devil had happened to Martin today. He'd left for lunch late this afternoon and never come back. When he hadn't returned by four o'clock, young Tim passed the joke around that maybe Martin had gone to the widow's and was indulging in more than her homemade apple pie. Wilkin hadn't found that the least bit amusing. Just because Mr. Barrett had left town, he huffed at Tim, that didn't mean his employees could take advantage.

Wilkin couldn't figure what Martin saw in the widow anyway, outside of her home cooking and her money. She was stiff-lipped, stiff-backed, and almost as bony as Grasshopper Gertie.

The thought of Gertie brought a tiny smile to Wilkin's face. She'd always been his special secret. Wilkin's Wednesdays made him feel superior to Martin, who as far as Wilkin knew had always lived like a monk.

Maybe he'd pay Gertie a visit tonight, he mused, wiping the crumb-speckled grease off his plate with a piece of cornbread.

No, it was Friday night. Francine's receiving room would be crowded, and so would Gertie's datebook. Since that deliriously arousing night nine days ago, Wilkin had broken with his ironclad routine of eight years, and with high expectations had paid Gertie two extra visits. But she'd left him unsatisfied. Wilkin drained the last of his coffee and, with a sigh, wondered if he'd have to wait another eight years before Gertie would be inspired to give him a repeat performance.

He paid his check and, taking a toothpick out of the bowl, strolled outside. Digging the dregs of the dinner out of his teeth, working them onto the tip of his tongue, and lightly spitting them out, he started down the street.

Up ahead, someone was playing the piano in Dusty's Saloon, the clamor of voices and laughter spilling out into the gloom. The boys were starting up early tonight, Wilkin thought proprietarily. For a moment, he was drawn to the saloon. He reached into the inside pocket of his suit coat, touching the two dime novels he'd bought that afternoon after lunch. Well, he'd pass by the saloon; he'd already made his plans for the evening.

Wilkin walked another two blocks, then turned left. Jenner's boardinghouse stood at the opposite end of the long, dark street. Wilkin saw the large house in the distance as a checkerboard of lights glimmering out of the windows along its side. Only about a dozen other houses sat on either side of the street on the blocks in between. The houses were widely spaced, separated by empty lots that were either overgrown with weeds and briars or cultivated into neat rows of browning tomato plants, stalks of corn, and other vegetables.

Wilkin strolled on down the shadow-smeared, silent road. Life had withdrawn indoors.

Two thirds of the way down the road, Wilkin's steps slowed. A wagon and a team of horses were parked off to the side next to an empty lot. Two men were leaning back against the wagon. As he walked on, Wilkin realized that both of the men were Mexican, small in stature, yet rough-looking. His brows knitted. What were Mexicans doing in his part of town at this hour? The effrontery of them, to presume that they could just park themselves anywhere. He was going to complain to somebody about this tomorrow.

Keeping his manner casual, Wilkin walked on by without looking at them. Up ahead, another house stood on the opposite side of the street, then a pair of empty lots and finally the boarding-house.

Behind him Wilkin heard the soft snap of the reins, the heavy clop of hooves, and the grate of the wagon wheels turning on the gravelly road. He walked on, ears bent to the sounds behind. Before he'd gone another ten steps, the suspicion started prickling through him that the wagon was creeping along behind him.

Suddenly he heard footsteps close on his heels. An arm sprang out of the darkness, locked around Wilkin's neck, and jerked him back. He felt the man's warm breath against his neck, smelled the sweat and dust in his clothes. Then, with a pang of horror, Wilkin felt the point of a knife press under his chin.

"Pendejo," the Mexican rasped. "Let's go for a leetle ride, *pendejo.*"

Every bone, every square inch of flesh, in Wilkin Edmonds's body ached from the rattling bumps and vibrations grinding up through the wagon bed into him. His skin burned from the coarse hemp of the burlap sack that he was tied inside. It was already late afternoon and though the air was cooling, the declining sun angled down upon him and he was soaked in sweat, not only from the heat but from tight-jawed apprehension. He could smell his own spiked fear intimately inside the sack, its tang even more pungent than the fumes of dead animals that rose from the floor-boards of the wagon.

He heard the two men talking. Twisting around, he could make them out through the broad weave of the sack, sitting on the wagon seat up above him. They were speaking Spanish—probably talking about how they were going to kill him, Wilkin thought, the terror rising acidly in his throat.

When the two Mexicans had seized him last night, and bound him, gagged him, stuffed him into the sack, he'd been so stunned that he'd been unable to find the voice to protest or the strength to resist before they were on their way. His mind still reeled in disbelief. This must be some terrible mistake. What've I done to them?

Wilkin didn't know how many hours they'd been on the move when they stopped the wagon that first time, except that it was still dark outside when he heard the back flap of the wagon come unhooked and drop down. The sack was untied beneath his feet, then the rope around his ankles was loosened and slipped off. He was pulled out by the feet and stood on the ground, teetering, until his legs found the strength to hold him. He'd lost his spectacles in the sack and could make out his captors as only blurred shadows in the darkness. But something about the one nearer him, who'd pulled him out of the wagon, suggested that he was young. He located the other Mexican by a soft, rhythmic slapping sound. The man was leaning forward with his arms over the side of the wagon, lightly hitting the flat side of something long against the palm of his hand. The moonlight glinted off it. It was the blade of a knife.

Wilkin's heart contracted. This is it, his mind cried. The Mexican nearer him was untying his hands. He slipped off Wilkin's gag and turned him toward a blur to his right.

"Piss," he said.

Wilkin blinked uncomprehendingly at the blur. The younger man stepped over to the wagon and shook the burlap sack. Something light plinked onto the wagon bed. The younger man reached for it and came back to Wilkin. Wilkin's spectacles dropped onto his nose and the bleary world sprang into focus.

"Piss," the younger man repeated, gesturing toward the brush.

Wilkin's attention was drawn again to the Mexican by the wagon. He was cleaning his nails now with the point of that long knife. The man glanced up at Wilkin, one eye squinty, the other open, giving his features a shifty, treacherous cast. The man looked a weather-beaten fifty years old, his few-days-old growth of grizzled whiskers a whitish haze on his cheeks and chin. He gave Wilkin only the one glance before resuming the cleaning of his nails, but something in his attitude as he handled that vicious-looking knife suggested to Wilkin that he was very aware of him.

"Piss," the younger man repeated again.

Wilkin stumbled over to the brush, stepped modestly around it, and unbuttoned his fly. He did have to go . . . painfully. But the stream refused to come out. It would inch down and when it was just at the point of letting go, it'd balk, back up, then creep forward and shrink back again, needling forward and backward, backward and forward, until the sweat was pouring out of Wilkin.

After a time, the younger Mexican's face appeared on the opposite side of the bush. This was the first good look that Wilkin had gotten of it. It was a devilish face, Wilkin thought, with wicked eyes, a thin mustache, and a small black goatee that smoothed to a point at his chin.

"It won't come," Wilkin said helplessly.

The Mexican's face grew even more devilish. "I've heard o' bein' scared shitless," he remarked in a long, drawled accent, the last word sounding like "cheetless," then he shrugged. *"Pero cómo se llama este?"* Turning, he strolled a short distance away.

Now, in the past when Wilkin had a strong need to go and his equipment refused to cooperate, stopping up either because he felt pressed for time or because he felt someone's presence close by, he found that he could usually summon the stream forth by whistling low between his teeth. So he stood there whistling and whistling until the timorous stream finally worked down to the end and, with a stutter, shot out.

After buttoning his pants, he glanced around, wondering if he really dared to feel, as he was beginning to, twice relieved. If his captors had allowed him the courtesy of emptying his bladder, would it make sense that they would then kill him? That they'd care one way or the other whether he relieved himself first?

Wilkin emerged from behind the bush and walked toward the wagon. "You've made a mistake," he ventured. "You have the wrong man. I'm only a clerk in an office."

The grizzled Mexican with the knife seemed only mildly interested. "What's your name?" he rasped.

"Edmonds," Wilkin responded as if he weren't too sure of it himself, for the younger Mexican had already started tying his hands behind him. "Wilkin Edmonds."

The older Mexican eyed him in that lopsided way, then spat on the ground. "No mistake," he growled. "You the one we want."

Before Wilkin could form the question that was rising in his mind, the younger Mexican flapped the bandanna across his mouth and tied it. The burlap sack dropped over his head and he was hauled into the wagon again.

For the next several hours as they rattled across the land, the questions swarmed though Wilkin's mind. What did they want with him? What were they planning to do to him? He wasn't a violent man, hadn't harmed anybody. He was only a clerk, a simple clerk. . . . Finally exhaustion overcame him and he lapsed into a disturbed sleep.

When he opened his eyes, the night had lifted to the sallow beige of dawn. The needlelike fear slithered through him again and the flurry of questions rose up.

It was the full light of midmorning when they stopped again. They left him in the wagon. He could hear their footsteps beyond the wagon walls. After a spell, he smelled smoke, then coffee boiling and beans sizzling in a fry pan. They must not plan to kill him here, Wilkin thought hopefully, for surely they wouldn't sit down to eat first. After a time, he was pulled out of the wagon once more.

The grizzled Mexican was sitting by the campfire, expertly slicing dried beef with that long knife, satisfaction touching his features each time he chunked the blade down through the meat. The younger Mexican untied Wilkin and gestured for him to go to the campfire. Neither man said a word to him.

Trying to down that bitter paste of beans he was given, Wilkin squinted around. He had no conception of how far they had traveled in the past dozen hours or so, or in what direction. They were in the middle of wild brush country. No thin ribbon of chimney smoke could he see twining against the sky. No roads, trails, or rutted wagon wheel tracks marked the land. Not even a cow could he see grazing in the distance. Escape was out of the question, he thought, for, if by some miracle he did manage to get away from these men, he'd surely die trying to find his way.

Finally Wilkin could no longer stand the weight of his captors' silence. He cleared his throat. "Where are we?" he asked in a high voice that sounded foreign to his ears.

Slowly wiping the blade of that long knife back and forth across his thigh, the older Mexican turned his half-squinty look upon him. "Steel *Tejas*," he said after a pause.

"Where . . . where are you taking me?"

"*Méjico.*"

"Why Mexico?"

The Mexican ran his thumb and forefinger fondly up the sides of the blade. "It weel be very easy to keel you there . . . *pendejo.*"

Wilkin gulped. Hands trembling, he set his plate, rattling, on the pebbly ground.

"Of course," the grizzled Mexican added, "it would be very easy to keel you here, too."

Wilkin turned his widened eyes toward the younger Mexican, the man shrugged. "Piss?" he asked.

Wilkin had to whistle long and hard before he could summon forth the weakest trickle. So long did he stand behind the bush whistling that the younger Mexican stopped kicking dust on the campfire and, hands on his hips, looked around.

"Now, where is this leetle dog you are always calling?"

"I . . . I don't understand," Wilkin stammered as the young Mexican started tying him up again. "What have I done to you?"

The grizzled Mexican squinted at him, deliberating. He always seemed to speak with great reluctance.

"We are the ones who do not understand," he finally said.

"Wh—what?"

"What did the widow of Juan Fernando Castillo and his five leetle children . . . one not yet born, steel growing inside her mother's belly . . . do to you?"

"I don't know them," Wilkin said.

"But you stole from them."

"I—I didn't!"

"You robbed them of a very great sum, *pendejo* . . . forty thousand dollars."

Wilkin stared at him, stupefied. "How . . . how did you know—" He stopped himself. "I didn't take forty thousand dollars from them."

The grizzled Mexican spat derisively. "You, how you say,

changed the accounts. You, clerk of that stealing place. It is the same thing." He shrugged. "So we weel have to keel you." He eyed the evil-looking knife hungrily. "But I think we weel wait teel we get to *Méjico*."

And that black thought kept Wilkin close company in his burlap sack as, once more, the wagon rattled onward.

It was late afternoon when they creaked to a stop again. When Wilkin heard above him in the wagon the familiar slap . . . slap . . . slap of the flat of that long knife blade, he felt a biting terror. If he could have dug his teeth into a floorboard of that wagon to keep from being pulled out, he would have.

This time, after the younger Mexican pulled him out of the sack and the wagon, Wilkin just sat down on the ground. The grizzled Mexican was leaning with his arms over the side of the wagon in the same pose he'd held the night before.

"Is this Mexico?" Wilkin cringed.

The grizzled Mexican eyed him for a time. "Steel *Tejas*."

Putting his hand up on the wagon, Wilkin pulled himself to his feet and leaned weakly against it. His younger captor handed him a canteen, but Wilkin was so shaken that more water spilled down his chin than into his mouth.

"It was Gertie," he said when he could find his voice. "It was Grasshopper Gertie, wasn't it?"·

His two captors exchanged looks and then shrugged.

"*Qué es este* . . . grasshopper?" asked the younger one.

"*Es un chapulín,*" the grizzled one explained to him, then looked at Wilkin. "Who is this grasshopper you call Gertie?"

"A whore . . . the tall whore at Francine's," Wilkin replied. "It was Grasshopper Gertie who talked, wasn't it?"

"We know of no whore by name of a grasshopper." The grizzled one regarded Wilkin craftily. "It was a man name of Marteen."

"Martin?" Wilkin gasped. "Martin Filbert?"

"*Sí*. He was talking to his woman, that widow. He does not see servants, I think, not think they have ears, too."

"Martin? Martin told that widow?" Wilkin asked, an edge of anger in his voice.

"*Sí*. He said you changed numbers on accounts, you stole from the family of Juan Fernando Castillo."

"He was a part of it, too!" Wilkin burst out.

"It is of no matter. The money, it has been taken. The family of Juan Fernando Castillo, it has suffered for your crime.'' The grizzled man paused, and gingerly touched the edge of the blade. He lifted his finger, showing Wilkin the thin line of blood. ''I am a man with a very special skeel,'' he said slyly. ''Do you know what that skeel is, *pendejo*?''

''K—killing?'' Wilkin said thinly.

''No. Skeening. I am very good at taking the skin of animals. Whether they are dead or alive.'' A gleam rose in his eyes, a smile played across his craggy features, chilling Wilkin to the bone.

''The next time we stop,'' he rasped, ''it will be *Méjico*.''

''Piss?'' the younger one asked.

But Wilkin had neither the spittle to whistle nor the wits to piss.

The sun was now hovering just above the back of the wagon. In less than a couple hours it would be gone from the sky. And though he was shivering and his hands and feet felt icy, Wilkin was perspiring. He could feel himself being borne steadily toward Mexico and to his unspeakable fate.

And why? Merely because he'd added a number and a word to a withdrawal paper six years ago, only wanting to prove to Mr. Barrett that he could be one of the boys . . . and because that low-down traitor, Martin Filbert, could not keep his mouth shut.

The specter of his impending execution, of all the ways they might go about it, inhabited his every thought. He lost all track of time.

The wagon stopped. *''Es Méjico,''* the voice hissed above him.

Then the back flap of the wagon creaked down, and, still inside the sack, Wilkin was carried into some shadowy place and plunked on the ground.

And then he was unbound for what was to be the last time. Wilkin looked desperately about him. They were inside some kind of abandoned adobe hut, cottony with the dust of disuse, its walls flaking away. The grizzled Mexican was leaning back against the side of the doorway, the red sun sinking peacefully into the horizon beyond. He was swinging that evil-looking knife back and forth, back and forth, like an inverted pendulum.

''Please,'' Wilkin pleaded. ''Maybe''—he grasped at any straw—''I could talk to somebody, find a way to get Castillo's money back.''

"I don't trust you. It is too late, anyway. So I will keel you now."

"Don't!" Wilkin gasped. "You have to believe me . . . I didn't think that what I did would make a big difference to Castillo's family."

The grizzled Mexican eyed him coldly. "If you do not know your victim, it *never* makes a difference." Moving from the doorway, he stooped down in front of Wilkin. "An' I do not know *you*, either." He held the point of the knife at Wilkin's chin. "Call me greaser . . . gringo."

Wilkin shrank back. "I . . . I'd never do that," he quavered.

The Mexican smiled, his leathery face so close that Wilkin could see every seam in it, every thorny hair of his unshaved whiskers. "I do not think that I will stick this knife into you right away," his voice scraped out. Wilkin let out his breath. "No, I think that I weel skeen you first. Your skeen, it looks very, very thin. It should be very easy to peel off. Oh, it will make a very fine noise of popping as I jerk it away from your flesh."

Wilkin's eyes were goggling almost beyond the sizes of the magnified lenses. The Mexican's eyes broke contact with Wilkin's. Something seemed to catch in his throat and he turned away coughing.

"*Ay, este polvo!*" he croaked, getting up, then limped bowleggedly out of the hut where Wilkin heard him wheezing and gasping on the other side of the wall.

Wilkin's goggled eyes turned to the younger Mexican, who was leaning placidly against the wall.

"It is the dust," he shrugged. "He has a *cómo se llama un alergia*? Allergy. *Sí*, he has a very bad allergy to dust."

A drumming of hooves sounded in the distance. The grizzled Mexican leaned suddenly in the door, his squinty eyes flashing. "*Vamonos a la chingada de aquí!*" he shouted, then took off. Let's get the motherfuck out of here.

The younger Mexican charged to the door and seeing the dust of the oncoming riders, took to his heels after his companion.

Confused and quailing, Wilkin scrabbled into a corner of the hut. The horses pounded up outside and Wilkin heard heavy footsteps rushing toward the hut. A large figure appeared in the door, followed by two others. The man in the lead was middle-aged, heavily wrinkled around the eyes. He squinted around, finding Wilkin cowering on his knees in the corner.

"Edmonds?" he asked with a Texas twang. "You Wilkin Edmonds?"

Wilkin could only nod weakly.

"My partners an' me been trackin' that wagon outside since before dawn this mornin.' We was lookin' for you last night when we heard that a fellow who lives down the road from your boarding house had reported seein' you gettin' kidnapped an' tossed in that wagon. Where're your abductors?"

Wilkin gulped. The thought of them heightened his trembling. "Gone . . . I think."

"You know who they are?"

"T . . . two Mexicans . . ."

"By the way, the name's Hunt Tyler. I'm captain o' the Ranger station at Realitos, and I think I got me a pretty good idea why those Mexicans mighta wanted t'get you. We got a statement yesterday afternoon signed by Martin Filbert. Said he seen you doctor some papers at the Warner Savings an' Loan. Said you moved a big passel o' money outa the account o' some fellow by the name o' Castillo without Castillo's say-so."

Wilkin scrambled to his feet. "Martin did it, too," he babbled. "He was part of it. Martin was the one who changed the records in the account books. . . ."

The laughter bubbled up again, and when Hunt Tyler rode out and found them, the two Mexicans were slapping each other on the back and chortling as they sat amid the scattered brush.

"He talkin'?" the wicked-looking younger one asked.

"He's singin' . . . so high an' fast, you'd think he was tryin' out for the Paris Opera."

"An' that Marteen," the grizzled one inquired. "Marteen Filbert, did he talk?"

"Your compadres did a good job on that-un, too. All I did was mention that his ole pal, Wilkin Edmonds, had been squealin' on him, an' damn if Filbert didn't start singin'. The two of 'em together could 'bout make a barbershop quartet, seems like . . . though I ain't likely t'be puttin' 'em together till they've polished off their solo performances."

"He thinks that he is in *Méjico*, you know," the younger one said. "He did not notice that we move east instead of south."

The laughter started rising again. "He shake so hard inside that sack, he did not even notice that we cross no river to get to *Méjico*. He must no have heard of Rio Grande."

Cruz Cortez sat alone by the side of the road, his horse tied in the brush nearby. A cool breeze was sweeping out of the plains, the starlight fading under the milky moonglow. He watched the dust of the approaching wagon, then got slowly to his feet as the two men pulled up.

"*Cómo le fue?*" he asked. How'd it go?

"*Muy bien.*" Homero grinned.

"*Sí,*" Rogelio added. "*Me gustó mas que emborracharme en sábado en la noche.*" I liked that more than getting drunk on Saturday night.

🌺 Chapter 37

THE RANCH CARPENTER moved down the ladder on the new windmill derrick, making his final adjustments on the vertical shaft inside. The sky was a clean-swept blue, but the wind kept whipping up dust swells that stained the air and stung the eyes. Here and there dust devils rose up in the distance, glided over the land like shadowy phantoms, then faded away.

Coke rode through the haze, tied his horse to a cenizo bush, and walked over to Cruz, who was standing apart from the other men gathered there.

"Got a message from Hunt Tyler this mornin'," he said. "Said that soon as Wilkin an' Filbert sign their statements, he'll be headin' out to a state judge t'get a subpoena t'go through the records o' the Warner Savin's an' Loan. Could be, Cruz, that the Castillos weren't the only ones hurt by some number jigglin' at that place."

He glanced aside at the young man. "You an' the others musta done one hell of a thorough job softenin' up those two office fellas for ole Hunt."

Cruz shrugged. Though he appreciated that Coke had turned him loose in setting up that piece of business, he'd gotten little satisfaction from it. It fell far short of what he was feeling; it was like tossing a pebble at your enemy when your rage demanded cannons.

The ranch carpenter had finished his adjustments and stepped back. Lifting his hat, Coke held it forward to shade his face as he squinted up the windmill tower. The wind had caught the slices of blades at the top and smeared them into a spherical cloud, sending a vibration down through the shaft.

With a gurgle deep inside, the pump disgorged a single dust-glazed water droplet. It crept out its mouth, clung timorously to its lower lip, and stretching out, let go, dropping to the water trough below. Another droplet inched out, hesitated, and let go, then another; and picking up tempo, the droplets began chasing one another out, beating a staccato rhythm on the trough below.

Through the soles of their feet, the men felt a pressure building in the entrails of the earth. The pressure found voice in a guttural rumble. The rumble swelled to a roar and the water blasted out of the pump, hurtled down the trough, and plunged, foaming, into the tank.

A vaquero waved his hat at a rider on a far-off ridge. The men watched the water rising in the tank. The realization that hundreds of formerly condemned cattle would be reclaimed by the Side-winder by this well didn't bring them the lift of whooping jubilation that they'd have shown at other times. These days everything had a flatness to it.

"Won't be a day that'll go by when I won't miss your pa," Coke said to Cruz. "He's too much in all o' this . . . like the earth . . . like the cenizo." He paused. "Funny thing, your pa could always see in me, an' too damn much o' the time, through me . . . though I could never quite say the same 'bout him."

"*Mucho hombre, mi papá,*" Cruz said, a flinch of pain passing over his face. Then Coke saw the rage rising in his eyes.

"I been thinkin'," he said matter-of-factly. "Doña Celestina should be told what's been happenin' here. An' I need t'know if she's found any papers that'd be o' use to me in a court battle. Why don't you go to Guerrero, pay her a visit for me."

"I want to stay here," Cruz replied.

"Don't you think the doña has a right t'know how all that money o' the *patrón*'s was stolen?"

"I suppose," Cruz admitted tightly. "But I want to stay here."

"Gettin' away would do you good," Coke said. "It'd ease your mama's mind. She's been worried 'bout you. An' the doña knows you, you'd be the best one t'go. Will you take care o' this for me?"

Cruz sighed, and was silent for a time. "All right," he said reluctantly. "I'll go."

A herd was starting to move in, its approach made known at first by an echoey, disembodied bawling, too faint and far-off to be pinpointed on the vast encircling land. To the east, a portion of the horizen blurred to a thin haze. Watery-looking specks emerged inside the haze, swimming together and stringing apart. They advanced, seemingly suspended above the earth in sight as well as sound, until they broke past some invisible line on the prairie floor. The rumble of their hooves struck the men's ears all at once, as though the herd had dropped, en masse, to the ground. The rumble grew to thunder, the individual forms became distinct as the cattle pitched forward.

Tongues swollen out, tails twisted up over their haunches, the herd hit the water head on, the steers at the rear slamming in from behind, upended and pawing the backs of the cattle in front of them, fighting their way to the water.

As the water reached more of the scorched bovine throats, the frenzy of the herd gradually died down and a droopy-eyed, boggy calm settled over them.

Coke absently watched the cattle wandering away from the tank. "When you talk to the doña," he said to Cruz, "tell her it'd be wise for her t'stay put for the time bein'. Things are still too unsettled here for her t'come stormin' back into the middle of 'em. We may o' got some movement goin' against the Savin's an' Loan, but Barrett an' those cutthroats aroun' him can still be meaner an' more slippery than rattlers trapped in a can o' lard." He looked at Cruz. "Keep that in mind yourself. Don't try gun-nin' for those bastards on your own. Your father wouldn't want more sorrow t'come to your ma. She already has more'n her heart can hold."

He could see that the stubbornness in Cruz still hadn't been put down.

"Remember," he went on gently. "You ain't alone in what

you're feelin'. But we don't wanta just kill 'em, Cruz, we wanta destroy 'em . . . bring that entire rotten structure that they've built up crashin' down, wipe every trace of it from this part o' the country.''

Coke rode back to the compound. He unsaddled Sin Cerebro, set him free in the pasture, and walked into his house, heading straight through his office to his bedroom. He sank down in the chair by his window and propped his feet up on the edge of his bed. Outside, Sarie was vigorously wiping out the vat and tubs from the day's washing. Gustina was seated on the windmill platform nearby, holding her brown fists up before Joshua and playing guess-in-which-hand-the-stone-is-hidden. Whenever her four-year-old got into one of his badgering, impossible-to-satisfy moods and Sarie had taken all the torment that she could bear, she passed him over to Gustina and eagerly took over the household chores herself.

Sarie'd been to town yesterday and seen Jessica. She said that in a roundabout way, Jessica had kept turning the conversation back to him, pumping Sarie for news on how he'd taken Alejandro's murder . . . but she'd sent no message to him herself.

Jessie. Coke's eyes moved from the window to his bed. A picture formed in his mind of how she'd look lying there, her fine, shining hair fanned over the pillow like golden gossamer, one arm gently folded on the sheet, her sweet flesh warm and full and well satisfied, those greenish blue eyes dewy with quiet contentment. Yes, that was one thing that he'd like to see on her face one day, make happen, if he could . . . quiet contentment.

Suddenly Coke felt as closed off as if he were at the bottom of a pool. He'd gone his own way for so many years that the prospect of carrying on to the end that way didn't impose any great dread upon him. Yet he felt lonesome.

Yesterday he'd wanted to forge, acre by acre, an empire out of the South Texas dust. And the dream of it, the struggle to persevere in fulfilling that dream and the fight to keep it from ever being stolen from him, had been enough to fill his life. That drive would never leave him. But now it didn't seem enough. Not nearly enough.

His eyes settled on his worn work boots, propped up on the bed before him. He eyed them a moment, then got up. No matter that

Jessie didn't want to see him. A man had a right to shop for a new pair of boots.

"Yup," Maribelle Bolan declared to her cousin, Lucille. "This petticoat is purty, all right . . . on the outside." She turned the garment inside out. "But look at them there seams. Be comin' apart on you afore the year's out, mark my words."

Lucille adjusted her bifocals, then gathered the material into her two knobby fists and proceeded to jerk at it, down both sides of an inner seam of the petticoat.

Meg stood noncommitally nearby. Even if that seam did withstand Lucille's assault, the two cousins wouldn't buy it anyhow, it being such a deep-seated notion in them that pretty meant flimsy. In the end, Meg knew, they'd walk out with the plainest petticoat she had to offer.

A footstep sounded at the doorway. Meg looked up. Her plump face dimpled into a slow grin. The petticoat suspended between them, Maribelle and Lucille exchanged a meaningful look, then their heads rotated in unison toward Jessica. She stood at the side of the room with her back to them, taking inventory of children's ready-to-wear.

Jessica immediately felt the change in the atmosphere. Coke. Her heart gave a thump. Her back stiffened as if she were expecting a blow from behind. Her fingers tightening on the clipboard in her hands, she tried to focus hard on the words and numbers written there, but her mind recorded only gibberish.

"Jessica." Meg's voice punctured the loaded silence. "You mind helpin' Coke?"

The shoulders slowly lowered. A slender hand appeared, fluttering briefly over the back of her chignon. Then she pulled herself up and turned around.

The color had drained from her face, giving her eyes the dark luster of polished stones. She looked at him questioningly. A softening appeared in her eyes, then was gone.

"Good afternoon, Mr. Sanders," she said, strolling toward him, hugging the clipboard to her chest. "More yarn for your mother, I presume."

She was going to affect the cool and proper lady, he noted, throw up that smoke screen.

"Not today," he said. "Today I wanta buy a new pair o' boots."

"Boots?" Her tapered brows lifted with the pitch of her voice.

"Yup. You know, them leathery things that protect a honcho's steppers from splinters, rocks, burrs, manure, an' such."

"Oh." She frowned, then added quickly, "Sorry, but I can't help you."

"You ain't got no boots t'sell?"

"Yes," she admitted circumspectly. "But you wouldn't like them. They aren't of good quality."

"Why, Jessie," he chided. "I ain't never heard o' you turnin' back a sale before."

"Well, why waste your money on cheap ready-to-wear?" she responded. "A man of your prominent position in local society should have his leather goods custom-made."

" 'Tain't much so-ciety round here for me t'worry 'bout bein' positioned in," he countered. Then, with a lift of a brow, he sent a look at Maribelle and Lucille, who were still standing in rapt silence, the petticoat suspended between them as though they were trying to flag down a passing ship. The women jumped. And the petticoat caving in between them, they burst into chatter over its merits and demerits.

"Look at it this way," he went on to Jessica. "I need somethin' cheap t'go with that belt you sold me a while back. 'Tain't proper for an hombre t'go traipsin' about with his belt an' boots lookin' . . . uh . . . what's that word again, the one you used that first time you were out at my place when you didn't wanta change outa Sarie's boots to your walkin' shoes?"

"Uncoordinated," she said in a flat tone.

"Yup. Why, it'd be a doggone dirty shame for a man like me t'be caught walkin' round here uncoordinated."

She studied him, head tilted slightly as if listening for something. Then he saw the spirit rise in her. "All right," she said curtly. "I'll get you some boots to try on." She glanced at his feet. "Size small?"

"Look again. These ain't the daintiest little steppers that ever stepped into this store," he said, taking heart from her spark of sarcasm. He had needed this. Already the numbness that he'd been feeling was crumbling away inside him.

"Sit down." She gestured toward the rockers by the potbelly stove. "I'll take the boots over to you."

"Whatever you say, ma'am." He doffed his hat.

Tossing her clipboard on the counter, she walked to the shelves at the front of the store, and stood there staring walleyed at the boot boxes stacked before her. She stole a peek over her shoulder. Maribelle, Lucille, and Meg were all grinning at her. Giving them a thin smile in response to the significant nods and winks they sent to root her on, she reached for a box. Trapped, she thought, jerking it out. She was going to have to play this charade through.

Running her fingers down a stack, she yanked out two more boxes, carried them over to Coke, and dumped them at his feet.

"If you decide on anything, I'll be at the counter."

She was poised to stalk off when she heard a quiet voice behind her. "Jessie."

She hesitated and slowly turned around. His eyes were serious, direct, no game in them. And though she saw only kindness in them, it touched off a storm deep inside her and she knew she couldn't sustain the charade. Distress, turmoil, fear registering on her face, she backed away until she came up against the fabric table, then she spun around and bolted out the door.

🌸 Chapter 38

JESSICA'S HEART WAS hammering as she fled down the road, conflicting emotions whirling inside her. She wanted to hug Coke so hard that it hurt and to push him away, to be intimate with him and miles away, to bare her soul to him and hide it away. She wanted desperately to escape, to find steady ground . . . somewhere . . . because she knew that the next time that she felt Coke Sanders near, the lid would spring off those feelings again and once more they'd start ricocheting and caroming all over, like popcorn let loose from a hot skillet.

"Hello, Jessica." She heard the drawled greeting behind her and lurched to a stop, suddenly realizing she'd been fairly scurrying down the street, trying to leave her demons behind her in the dust. What a sight she must be making.

Jack Siden was leaning in the shade against the saloon, smoking one of his thin cigars. Standing in the glare of the sunlight on the road, Jessica saw his form as hardly more than a shadow, out of which faintly glimmered the two luminous slits of his eyes.

"Hello, Mr. Siden," she replied detachedly, her mind still in turmoil.

He flipped the cigar onto the boardwalk, crushing it out with a slithery movement of a leg.

"What's the big hurry?" he asked, moving out of the shadows and leaning against a pillar.

"I . . . uh . . . I remembered I had something to do at home."

His eyes moved toward the emporium. Coke was coming out the door. Siden looked back at her. Her face had colored. An astute smile turned the corners of his mouth.

"Well, Miss Jessica," he said, stepping off the boardwalk. "Would you like me to walk you home?" All courtliness, he offered her his arm.

As though held in suspension, she was still watching Coke. He was turning toward her.

"Yes," she blurted with a start, drawing closer to Jack. "I'd appreciate that." She slipped her hand through his arm and they turned back down the road.

Handsome Jack talked amiably as they walked along; Jessica nodded and said "yes" whenever it seemed that a response was required, though his words didn't penetrate her thoughts. They were turned away to the sound of the horse moving slowly down the street in the opposite direction.

As they crossed to the road toward home, she looked back. Coke was almost to the end of Main Street now and soon would be gone. Suddenly she felt desolate. She wanted him so much. No affected coolness could distance her anymore. Nor could she cling to and hide behind declarations of honor and decency, for he knew that she'd already given those things away. She was tainted. And knowing that he knew brought it stingingly back to her every time he looked at her. Maybe tomorrow she'd take Willie and leave this country, she thought wildly. But she knew that she couldn't uproot her son so soon after he'd just settled into his new school and had made friends. And she didn't want to uproot herself from Meg yet, either.

She saw the house up ahead, and longed to be inside it. Perhaps if she had another good cry, she'd feel better, she reflected, still nodding to Handsome Jack and smiling faintly.

They arrived at the door. She tried it. It was locked. If Meg had dropped back home since Jessica had last been here, it wouldn't have been. Meg's attitude was that if anyone wanted anything she had badly enough to steal it, he was welcome to it. Reaching into the pocket of her skirt, Jessica brought out the key.

"Let me do that," Jack said, his hand folding warmly around hers as he took the key. Then, standing behind her, close enough so that she could feel his heat, he reached around her, unlocked the door, and pushed it open.

She glanced up at him, becoming keenly conscious of Jack Siden for the first time. She caught the glint of greedy expectancy in his eyes, the look of the child who has spotted the chocolate cake waiting in the kitchen for dessert. Oh, no, she thought tiredly, she wasn't up to this.

Turning around, she faced him, placing herself between him and the open door.

"Thank you for the company, Mr. Siden," she said coolly. "I appreciate it. Could I have my key?"

She saw a stubborn determination stirring behind those green eyes. A teasing smile playing on his lips, he casually stretched out an arm, set his hand on the doorframe, and leaned over her so that he almost surrounded her.

"Aren't you going to offer me a cool drink?" he wheedled. "That was a dry walk."

"And if you hurry back to the place that you started from, you'll be in the saloon in about five minutes."

His gaze seemed to darken, though his manner remained smooth. "You're not being very friendly, you know, to someone who's been nice to you."

"I don't think our short walk together constitutes a great sacrifice on your part, Mr. Siden,'' she countered. ''Besides, as I told you, I have some things to do. My key, please.''

He didn't move, looking down at her with those bold, green eyes. ''What's so important that you have to do?''

''I have to finish draperies,'' she said evenly. ''For the Sanders family.''

''They can wait.''

''No they can't. The key, Mr. Siden.''

He held it up, swinging it provocatively between his thumb and forefinger. ''Try to catch it.''

She sighed. ''I'm going back to the emporium. You can bring the key to me there when you decide to stop playing these little-boy games.''

She made a move to go, but his other hand instantly came down against the other side of the doorframe, blocking her on both sides.

''You can't put me off any longer,'' he said in a low voice.

Her face hardened. ''Back away!''

His eyes narrowed, then suddenly he grabbed the front of her blouse and shoved her into the house. Her head hit the door as it swung back. He stepped inside, closed the door behind him and leaned against it, the corners of his mouth twisting in sly triumph.

She backed a few steps, her eyes flickering subtly about for something to get hold of to use as a weapon. She could feel the roused animal power rising in him.

She stood her ground, stiffening. ''Get out of my house. I didn't invite you in here.''

''Ah, Miss Jessica,'' he chided silkily. ''Why must you be so sparin' with your invitations?''

He slowly walked toward her and put his hand to the side of her hair. There was no reaction at all from her.

''Since you first came here, I've been watching you,'' he whispered, sliding his fingers slowly through her hair, playing with the ends of the strands that slipped loose. ''You've been teasing me, you know . . . moving round here, teasing me.''

''So that's the excuse you're going to use,'' she said icily.

His fingers tightened on her hair. Gripping it, he yanked her around, slamming her back against the wall. A framed, needle-pointed picture banged to the floor, the sound a faraway echo to her ears.

He bore in upon her, his lips moving hotly over her face, his hand pressing and exploring her. But she remained coldly motionless, her body rigid, her mouth pressed shut.

He slowed. He had expected fire, wanted fire. He became aware of his tight grip on her hair.

His fingers relaxed and he lifted his hand, looking at her as though she should be grateful for that thoughtful gesture.

"I been wantin' you since I first laid eyes on you," he said roughly. But she didn't respond, her eyes leveled straight ahead.

He came at her again with greater force, tearing at her blouse. "C'mon, baby," he urged. "You know you want it."

But she was as still as a piece of furniture, so that it came as almost a shock to him when she spoke. "If none of Ruby's girls will do, Mr. Siden, the countryside is swarming with cows for you to stick 'it' in . . . though I wouldn't wish this on any cow."

He pulled back, looking hard into her face. She lifted her eyes and met his. Though her face was youthful, its features as softly feminine as any he'd seen, her eyes looked old to him now, hard-boiled, worldly-wise. This was no fragile little innocent that he could frighten or break.

"Of course," she went on expressionlessly, "there's also that knothole in the tree out back of the Bolan house."

"You're one tough little cookie, aren't you," he muttered. "I bet Sanders has already had his share."

She looked at him evenly. "At least he's a real man, Mr. Siden. But you wouldn't know what that is, would you?"

"Just because Sanders has all that land—"

"Without an acre to his name, without a dollar, he'd still be ten times the man that you are."

The back of his hand flew up and struck her face, knocking her to the side. She drew back up, her hand over the place that he'd hit, the eye tearing from the stinging pain.

"I take that back," she said. "He's a hundred times the man that you are."

He saw now that she'd passed by this way before and knew how to close off a part of herself. He could rip her clothes off, do any profane thing to her, and that part of her would still be out of his reach. And it was that part that he wanted to get to and destroy.

His eyes changed. She saw that change and recognized it—for it was the look of a killer.

"People have seen us together," she said quietly. "Anything happens to me, they'll know who did it."

Outside on the street came the jingle-jangle of children's voices. School had let out. A foot lightly dropped on the stoop outside. The doorknob turned and Willie stood at the threshold, holding his books by the strap. Three other children waited at the gate.

"The key, Mr. Siden," she said.

His eyes full of hatred, he pulled the key out of his pocket and flung it on the floor, then turned and strode out, pushing past Willie. Willie looked after Siden, then stepped uncertainly into the house.

"What's the matter, Ma? How'd you get that red place on your cheek? Why's your shirtwaist torn?"

She put her hand on the refectory table to steady herself, then stumbled to the nearest chair and sat down.

"I'm all right, love," she whispered, rocking and hugging herself. "I'm all right. I'm all right. I'm all right."

Coke felt uneasy. For the third time since he'd left Dispenseme, he stopped Sin Cerebro and turned halfway around. As he toyed once again with the idea of going back, Beau Barrett galloped up behind him. The boy was mounted on an expensive-looking, blooded bay mare. He reined in sharply, wrenching the bay's head around, then circled Coke and stopped in front of him.

"You forget somethin', Sanders?" he gibed. "The land you swiped? A decent mount?"

Coke only looked at him. And when it settled in on the boy that his father's enemy didn't regard him as worth a rejoinder and would be content to sit there forever without going to the effort of making one, Beau flushed, and yanked the bay around. He jabbed his fancy spurs into the mare's flanks, unloosing a trickle of blood, and galloped down the road toward the San Sebastian.

Barrett's younger son was about ten years overdue for a good strapping, Coke thought, turning back toward home. As the slow miles passed, though, he couldn't shake the feeling that something was wrong. It had nettled him some seeing Jessica walk off with Jack Siden, but he guessed that she'd taken his arm only to hold Coke off until she got home. If Cactus had been there, he'd have served as well, or Soot Fisher, or probably even another woman.

No, jealousy wasn't the cause of Coke's unrest. He knew that there was real feeling in Jessica for him; that tug was there between them all the time now, no matter how hard she pretended otherwise. And if she was keeping him at arm's length, he doubted that she'd open those arms to a Jack Siden. She'd always reacted to him like a hen sensing a coyote in the barnyard.

She shouldn't encourage Siden at all, though, Coke thought uneasily. The man had made no secret of the nature of his intentions toward her and under that bland surface there was something that seemed off-key, a malcontentment, a covetousness of and resentment for anything not his. Open the door a crack, and Siden might assume he'd been given leave to steal the entire house away.

Still, it was a bright midafternoon when the two had walked away, and Meg's home was less than two blocks off Main Street. No, Coke thought, reining Sin Cerebro back toward the Sidewinder. Jessie would have turned Siden away at her door.

He was almost a mile from his ranch when he heard someone riding up from behind. Settling his hand around his rifle handle, he turned aside. It was Obie Given hurrying to catch up. Coke waited resignedly. He was in no humor to have his ears bombarded by the kid's prattle.

The boy had spent a little money at the emporium. He had a pair of five-pound flour sacks tied on either side at the front of his saddle, for his ma, no doubt. Atop one of the sacks, flapping and twisting in the wind, was a small cowboy hat, probably a gift for one of Obie's four younger brothers.

Coke noted that the boy still rode like a farm boy, more accustomed to trudging behind a horse pushing a plow than sitting astride one. And the ranch horses were a vinegary lot that could sense right off if the fellow on them was green or not.

"I thought that was y—" Obie began, awkwardly pulling up, then misplaced his words as his horse quickly sidestepped away,

let loose a few abbreviated back kicks, slapping up puffs of flour
from the bouncing sacks into the boy's face, then came to a head-
tossing stop. It must not have been a very relaxing ride for the
boy.

"That's a lotta horse for you, son," Coke commented.

"Well, I'm learnin', sir," he replied when he started breathing
again, his chest and jaw dusted with flour.

Coke turned toward home. Maybe tussling with that ranch horse
would divert some of the boy's energy away from his mouth.
Eventually Obie managed to pull almost even with Coke.

"You come directly from town, Obie?" Coke asked. He
glanced at the boy's skittery horse. "Or as directly as you
could?"

"Yessir."

Coke rode in silence for a time. "You happen t'see Jack Siden
before you headed out?"

"Saw him comin' up the road 'bout the time I was fixin' t'leave.
Was movin' right along like he had a train t'catch."

Coke felt a little easier. Jessie was safely home. Up ahead
stood the entrance to his ranch, a long plank of wood with
"Sidewinder" burned into it nailed atop two tall posts over the
gate.

The contrary streak in Obie's mount broke loose again. Bouncing testily up on its hind legs, it abruptly sidestepped, carrying
Obie diagonally behind Coke.

The burst of rifle fire was like dry twigs snapping. Coke wheeled
around, jerking his Winchester out of its boot, and looked into
the dismayed eyes of Obie Given. His mouth working silently, the
boy swayed as though a breeze had caught him, then gently folded
forward onto the neck of his horse, a dark oozing spot glistening
on the back of his shirt.

Beyond him, at an outcropping, Coke saw a sharp discharge of
smoke. The bullet thwacked by his neck, setting the skin prickling. Shouldering his rifle, Coke rapidly squeezed off three shots.
Then, swinging Sin Cerebro around against the side of Obie's
agitated mount, he grabbed the boy's collar and pulled him down
with him between the horses.

The two horses careered off in opposite directions, Coke's
horse loping slowly, ears rotating questioningly, Obie's bucking and kicking down the line of fence, flour spurting down its
side.

Coke got up firing, and keeping up a steady fire, walked forward and dropped behind the only cover, a low boulder. Reaching back, he snapped the bullets out of his belt and shoved them into the rifle, then propped the barrel on the boulder.

But the outcropping had fallen silent. The silence puzzled Coke, for the bushwhacker still had the advantage. He waited, squinting around for any movement, then a funnel of dust lifted in the distance as the fleeing rider burst into the open beyond a line of brush, his form a small, dark blur in its base.

Coke glanced over his shoulder. Already men were galloping down the road from the compound. The scattered dust clouds of three other riders were converging toward the gate.

Coke hurried back to Obie and stooped over him. The boy was lying on his face, the wet red splotch on his shirt still expanding from the hole in his back about four inches above his belt to the right of his spine. Coke put his hand on the boy's shoulder and felt the reassuring stir of life underneath. With a squeaking sound like a rusty hinge, Obie tried to raise up.

"Lie steady, son," Coke said, knowing that the boy was still stunned, that the pain hadn't started searing through him yet.

"I'm sorry, sir," Obie whispered.

"No, son," Coke gently replied. The boy was so used to tripping up at every turn on the ranch that he even assumed that getting shot was his fault. "I'm the one who's sorry." Taking out his pocket knife, he cut and ripped Obie's shirt away from the wound. "This bullet you took had my name on it."

He'd pulled off his bandanna and was pressing it over the bullet hole to stanch the blood when the first vaqueros pulled up. Their rifles were out of their scabbards, at the ready.

"We was ambushed from that outcropping over there," Coke said. "The bastard took off already. We gotta get this boy to the doc. Get a wagon from the compound, plenty o' blankets, an' tell my sister t'bring her medicine kit." As a vaquero pulled his horse around to gallop back to the ranch, Coke stopped him. "An' tell the *curandera* t'send out somethin' for the pain."

More of the men were trickling out from the ranch. Homero dismounted, silently stooped down beside Coke, and took over the compress on Obie's wound. His eyes squeezing shut, the boy was starting to squirm. The pain was getting to him.

"Lie still, son," Coke said kindly. "Try not t'move."

"Do you think I'm gonna die, sir?" Obie gasped.

"Not if we can help it," Coke replied.

"My mom an' dad . . . it'd be hard on 'em."

"Hell, you ain't gonna die," Homero rasped. "I myself will see that you get to the doc's in plenty o' time."

Obie's eyes popped open. Turning his head, he peered glassily back at the grizzled hide skinner. "When'd you learn t'speak English?" he asked weakly.

Homero scratched his stubbly chin. "Thees mornin'," he finally growled. "Before breakfast."

Coke's attention had been drawn to the outcropping. Something was going on over there. A few of the vaqueros had ridden over to it and were gathering in a circle, looking down. Two dismounted.

Coke stood up. One of the vaqueros, Homero's son, Alfredo, was loping back.

"You got one, *Jefe*," he said.

So there'd been two out there, Coke thought. It had happened at such a confused pace that he hadn't been able to tell.

"The bushwhacker dead?" he asked.

"He is badly wounded . . . in the chest." A troubled look came to Alfredo's eyes. "The man who is lying over there, *Jefe* . . . he is the son of Señor Barrett . . . the younger one that they call Beau."

Coke was silent for a time. "Bring another wagon from the compound."

He turned to Homero. "We got us two boys with bullets inside 'em," he said, "an' but the one doc sixty miles away."

Homero rose up and spat on the ground. "*Sí, Jefe*, we'll see to it that it is our boy who gets there first."

~ Chapter 39

THE LANTERN SAT on the stable floor, its light a concentrated glow amid the gloom. Jessica was milking Cuspidora at a feverish pace, the streams snapping into the bucket below.

The news of the gunfight outside the gates of the Sidewinder had whipped through town a few hours ago. Jessica had been one of the townspeople lining the street who'd watched first one wagon carrying a wounded boy tear through town in a flurry of whirling dust and trampling hooves, then about fifteen minutes later, the second wagon. Men knelt within to tend to the boys; riders galloped alongside and behind, pulling reserve strings of wagon horses.

Jessica looked for Coke but hadn't seen him. He had not been hurt, she'd heard, but the Given boy, who'd been riding with him, and the second son of T. C. Barrett had been shot. She didn't tarry on to talk with the others about what had happened and what it might mean. She'd had too many things to do.

Since late that afternoon, after burning to ashes the blouse that Jack had torn, she'd been a cleaning, scrubbing, polishing demon. Few things in the house escaped her attention. And when the last wagon had faded down the road, she'd hurried back to the house and thrown herself into her work with redoubled ferocity.

She'd left fixing dinner to Meg. Cooking would've required her to stand in one place for too long. After gulping only a few bites, she'd leaped up to clear the table while Meg's and Willie's plates were still half-full. And when they objected, she rebounded into the parlor and washed a couple windows.

She couldn't account for this compulsion she felt to make the house immaculate. It hadn't been that untidy to begin with. From time to time, Meg followed her around, scratching her head. Jessica hadn't spoken a complete sentence to her since Meg had gotten home. Finally, after lifting her feet off the floor as Jessica, on hands and knees, went scrubbing by in a trail of suds, Meg could stand it no longer.

"Now, if you wanta go after some real dirt," she remarked, "we gotta whole yard outside that could do with a moppin'."

The milk splatting into the pail was losing strength. Cuspidora's udder was emptying. She'd get out the churn next, Jessica decided, and make butter. She'd churn and churn a lot of butter. And after that she'd do the wash. The laundry was piling up. Not a bad idea, washing the clothes at night. It'd be cooler.

Meg entered the stable and came to Jessica's side. She put a hand on her shoulder. Jessica's tempo didn't let up, though the bucket was full; the threads of milk were thinning and Cuspidora was growing restless.

"Did he hurt you?" Meg said quietly.

"What?" Jessica asked.

"Jack Siden. Willie told me Jack was in the house with you when he got home from school today. Said you seemed upset after he left. Did Jack put that welt on your face?"

Jessica dropped her hands to her lap. Her chest heaved once up and down in half a sigh. Then, looking down, she nodded.

Meg lifted the milk bucket out from under Cuspidora and set it aside. The cow plodded away to the hayrack, the straw sticking out, a large, shadowy bristle on the opposite wall.

Meg stooped down beside Jessica and looked up into her face. "Did he hurt you, child?" she repeated.

Jessica studied her hands. "No . . . not that way."

"Did he try?"

She nodded.

Meg tenderly smoothed Jessica's hair. "You shoulda sent for me."

"I'm not used to having anyone to send for."

"You have someone now. We should set Marshal Seth on Jack. He cain't be allowed t'get away with this."

"No," Jessica said softly. "I don't want to draw attention to this. And I'd have to talk about it."

"Jessica . . ."

"No, Meg. I wasn't hurt. I'm all right." Again her chest lifted and dropped once. "And I don't want to have to think about it anymore." Her brows knitted. "Meg?"

"Yes, child."

"I wonder if it's my fault."

"What's your fault?" Meg frowned. "You done nothin' t'cause Jack Siden t'turn mean on you."

"But could I have caused him to turn on Coke? And that poor Given boy was hurt for it."

"Law, girl," Meg scoffed. "The notions you take. You had nothin' t'do with that ambush outside the Sidewinder. It was the Barrett boy who was a part of it, an' it was 'cause o' the bad blood his pa has against Coke. Jack Siden got nothin' t'do with that."

Lifting her face, Jessica met Meg's gaze. "He's a killer, Meg. I saw it in his eyes."

The clock on the mantel in Doc Elam's waiting room was set in a wooden shell carved in a facsimile of the Parthenon with miniature Doric columns on either side. It ticked restlessly on, tinging at the half hour and bonging out the hour. Someone had overwound it, Ray Barrett thought, for it was an hour and twenty minutes fast. But time held everyone in the room in its thrall; they could feel its passage as it crawled and wound through their entrails, their eyes catching on that clock time and again even though the dimension that it measured out read falsely.

Ray's eyes moved to Mrs. Given, seated on the divan across from him. There was something familiar about her, a quality redolent of treeless, windblown prairies. She'd probably been pretty once, he reflected, her flesh full and springy, her eyes alive with laughter and hope. But probably too many torturous births in lonely, dirt-walled huts, too many years of toil under the deadweight of bone-aching fatigue, had crushed the juices from that flesh, leaving it a withered gauntness as the erosion of hope had dulled and hollowed out her eyes. Her husband, seated next to her, had the equally rawboned, haggard look of a man whose every effort had come out just a hair short of making it. Ray's eyes lingered on Mrs. Given's red thick-knuckled hands folded awkwardly in her lap, wondering why the sight of them moved him so.

He was seeing everything too keenly, he decided. Liquor sometimes did that to him, put an edge on things. And he'd been well into a solitary drunk when he and the Old Man had been summoned here with the news that his little brother, Beau, had been shot.

Ray knew that the couple opposite him were named Given, for that was the name that the doc's wife had called them when they'd been brought here a while ago. He knew, too, that it was their son, Obie, on whom the doc was operating . . . while Beau Barrett, the son of the most powerful man in Warner, was left lying on a hard table outside the surgery door like the starving beggar who'd arrived too late for the feast.

Glancing at his father, standing against the wall next to Watt Calhoun, his hands propped on the head of his cane, Ray could tell that it rankled the Old Man that his son would place second in the doc's attention after the spawn of these dirt-poor folk and that he resented being stuck in the same room with them.

Beau hadn't looked that bad, Ray had thought, when he and the Old Man had been led into that austere room in which his brother was lying. Except for the small, smooth-edged puncture in his chest and a rattle in his breathing, he was as still and unblemished as white marble.

"We gave him medication to ease his stress," Mrs. Elam volunteered, standing on the opposite side of the table that held Beau.

Seeing that old familiar cowlick that had sprung up on the side of Beau's head like a burr, Ray's heart moved with affection. He had always felt that it was Beau who'd been the more deeply marked of the two of them by the disintegration of their mother under the tyranny of their father that had mangled every joy of their youth, so that Beau never seemed able to find a solid place on which to set his feet but kept hopping around, attaching himself to first one person and then the other in search of one.

Splintered images of their shared childhood glimmered up in his mind. His eyes stinging with tears, he impulsively reached over and touched his father's arm, though he should've known by the hard line of the Old Man's jaw that that was an imprudent thing to do. The arm instantly turned to stone and jerked upright so that Ray had to snap his head back to avoid taking a jab in the face from his elbow. The Old Man turned on Ray, his eyes hooded with the contempt he always displayed whenever he descried weakness in his son, as when he smelled liquor on him, as he did now and with growing frequency lately.

"Get outa here," he snarled.

"No," Ray said.

Realizing that shoving his half-drunk son out of the room would create a scene he didn't want, he turned on Mrs. Elam.

"Get Doc out here," he demanded. "My son needs his attention."

"The boy that the doctor is working on now is bad shot, too," Mrs. Elam retorted, her eyes sharp as blades. "And that boy got first claim. If you can't accept that, take your boy to the doc in Beeville."

They glared at each other across the table, but the gray-haired Mrs. Elam stood firm, for she and her husband operated from the fundamental power of life and death while the power of a T. C. Barrett was merely the ornamentation of money and position.

For an instant Ray feared that his father might do something rash like crash into the surgery and drag Doc Elam out himself. Ray kept silent, though. He'd already decided to keep his distance from the Old Man. He could do without his abuse.

"If you want to work out who gets priority here," Mrs. Elam went on, "talk to Coke Sanders outside."

Hatred flared in T.C.'s eyes. He hesitated, an odd thing for him, then slowly gave way. He couldn't afford to antagonize the tough Doc Elam . . . not now.

"Doc ain't had the last o' this," he muttered, then turned and, hooking the door open with the handle of his cane, stalked out.

Ray sat down in the chair next to Beau. Taking his brother's hand, he spoke softly to him, but Beau was too far removed to be reached by a brother's love. After a time, Ray got up, tried once to smooth down that cowlick, and went back to the waiting room.

The clock kept fidgeting out the seconds, T. C. Barrett standing against the wall, his will thwarted, while across from him as though in counterbalance, arms folded, eyes steady on the Old Man and Calhoun, had appeared the solid will of Coke Sanders, insuring that the son of these common prairie folk got his full due. A parallel of this loaded atmosphere was developing outside. The Sidewinder vaqueros were clustered with their wagons and horses along one side of the yard while a dozen of the toughs employed by the Silver Mountain Land Company had gathered across from them. The Land Company men, their Colts strapped to their hips, and the vaqueros, their rifles prickling out from their silhouettes in the darkness, silently eyed each other through the thin white-wash of moonglow.

It was still sketchy to Ray how the gunfight had taken place. He only knew that it had happened at the Sidewinder. Some time ago, the sheriff had made a show of interrogating the vaqueros who'd brought the boys in, but had met with only insolent shrugs.

None of the vaqueros could speak English, it seemed, or were willing to.

Neither Calhoun nor the Old Man made a move to ask Sanders, here in the same room with them, what had happened near his place, for that would've required them to speak to him. And standing there stolid, his eyes steely on them, Sanders seemed content to wait them out. A part of Ray shrank from hearing the particulars, too.

There'd been too many nagging questions these past couple of days, Ray thought. Yesterday he'd learned that the secretary and head accountant at the Savings and Loan had vanished. At first Ray suspected that the two old-maidenish office workers had made off with the cash from the Savings and Loan vault. Plenty of money was still there, though. Ray and the assistant accountant had counted it, and everything tallied. But the sheriff had had no success in tracking the two men down. They hadn't taken the train, nor had they rented horses and buggies from the livery stables in town. Relatives and acquaintances hadn't seen them, either. Indeed, neither man had been seen since Friday.

When the Old Man got back from the San Sebastian that morning, he seemed at first perplexed by the two men's disappearance. But as the day moved along, he began muttering how he should've gotten rid of that pair of eunuchs years ago.

Again Ray looked at the Givens. They seemed ill at ease sitting there, seemingly too aware of their humble origins. His mother had been like that. Unequal to the task of fitting into unfamiliar surroundings, she'd duck her head and try to fade out of sight, while the Old Man didn't fit in so much as occupied the space around him as an invader might. Yes, Ray realized, it was his mother whom Mrs. Given reminded him of.

Doc Elam walked into the waiting room, drying his hands on a towel, his surgical apron spattered with blood. He was in his sixties, slight in build, with thinning silver hair and a fresh pink complexion. His bifocals were set low on his nose, his stethoscope slung lopsidedly at his neck as though he jerked it around a lot like a necktie tied too tight.

"We're moving your boy out of surgery now," he said to the Givens, then glanced at Barrett. "And settin' up for yours."

"Will . . . will our boy make it?" Mr. Given stammered.

"If we can keep the infection down, he will; if we can't, he won't." The doc was known for his economy with words, and when he used them, they had a tendency to pop folks between the eyes.

"Boy's likely t'have more poundin' pain in his head when he comes to tomorrow than in his innards," he added briskly. "Got so waterlogged with tequila on the way in, he hardly needed the ether."

This seemed to stir Mrs. Given out of her tired grayness. "We're Methodist, Doc," she said, rising. "My son would never allow alcoholic spirits t'pass his lips."

Too pressed for time to argue a point with a Methodist, the doc only arched a brow, then turned back, a whiskey flask molding his hip pocket.

"Hope your boy's made his peace with his Maker," he tossed off to Barrett as he strode out the door.

Mrs. Elam motioned the Givens into the next room to sit with their son. But Sanders stayed on. Ray found this curious. What was his stake in this? The cattleman's eyes were still leveled at the Old Man, then at Calhoun. With what in them? Hate? Condemnation? Calhoun avoided the man's gaze, eyeing instead a claw foot of the divan. Barrett looked at Sanders once, his eyes sharp and slightly analytical. Then, clearing his throat, he sat down on the sofa the Givens had vacated. Finding the Old Man invasive to his thoughts, occupying as he did the space directly in Ray's sight, Ray got up and moved to another chair.

And two armed camps eyed each other across the yard outside. And the Grecian clock badgered on, whittling away the night, tinging the half hour, bonging out the hour, an hour and twenty minutes too fast, until Ray wanted to bash it to splinters.

It was bound to happen sooner or later. Someone from the Land Company began trying to draw the vaqueros out. Ray heard a low, derisive remark outside the window aimed at the vaqueros, raising a chuckle among the Land Company men. A hectoring voice answered back in Spanish, setting off hoots among the vaqueros.

Jaw tight, Barrett rose to his feet and stalked out the door. Watt Calhoun followed behind. The cane jabbing the ground, Barrett marched straight toward the vaqueros. The Land Company men, growing coolly alert, started forming a line, the vaqueros sliding off the wagons and getting up from the ground, gathering across from them.

"One o' you garlic-eatin' son o' whores musta shot my boy," Barrett charged, looking them hard down the line. "You better turn the bastard over to me now, or my men an' me will be teachin' you a lesson you ain't likely t'forget.''

"My men need no lesson from yours," Coke said at the door. "At least they collect their wages for doin' a helluvalot more worthwhile than thievin', destructin', an' killin'.'' He walked across the yard, stopped in front of T.C., and looked him squarely in the eye. "I shot your boy."

"You—"

"I warned you once you better not start a blood feud with me 'cause you might not be able to pull away from it when you wanted. Well, it started." His eyes moved to Calhoun. "More'n a week ago."

"An' you went after my boy," Barrett growled.

"Had no interest in your boy," Coke retorted. "But when some low-down bushwhacker is takin' potshots at my back, I ain't about t'stroll over an' check out who it is before I let loose myself."

"We only got your word on that, Sanders," Calhoun put in.

Coke sent him only a disdainful look before fixing his eyes back on Barrett. "The young hand who was ridin' with me is lyin' in there with a hole in his back that your son, or the other snake in the grass ridin' with him, put there. I've filed charges against your son with the marshal in Dispenseme. If the Given boy dies an' your son survives, I'll see to it, personal, that your boy swings for it." He glanced at Calhoun. "The rest o' the bushwhackers in your pay had better be on guard, too. An' you can gather up every hungry judge in South Texas an' stuff 'em in your pocket an' it won't make a damn bit o' difference."

"You ain't gonna get away with this, Sanders," Barrett growled. "You're gonna pay for what you done to my son."

"Wasn't me who made a murderin' bushwhacker outa him," Coke shot back. "You oughta be grateful, Barrett, that we even bothered t'bring him in here t'Doc's. We coulda just as easy left him lyin' out on the ground t'die as the lowlife who was with him done."

He shook his head. "I thought you was too smart t'want me dead now. Seems it'd deprive you o' the joy o' tryin' t'steal my land if I ain't around t'see it."

"And you'll see it," Barrett vowed. "Then you'll die."

"You'll see hell first," Coke said contemptuously, then turned and walked away.

"Nobody turns his back on me," Barrett uttered.

The tension in the air had electrified. The sound of the hammers of guns snapping back was like a snake rattle through the lines. Calhoun glanced around. He, Barrett, and Sanders were between the two lines, close enough to the vaqueros for him to see the bloodthirst glittering in their dark eyes above their rifle sights.

Doc Elam appeared at the door, framed in the light. He was still drying his hands on a towel, his stethoscope twisted askew at another angle, the fresh blood of Beau Barrett spattered over the dried darker splotches of that of Obie Given on his apron. He stepped off the porch.

"I just dug a bullet outa the back o' one young fellow in there," he said in a low voice, prowling slowly up and down the lines. "And performed a similar excavation into the chest of another. Now, digging out bullets is one occupation that I've always had a profound abhorrence to. Fact is, it puts me in a damn sour mood. That's why the wife limits me t'diggin' out no more'n two bullets a day."

He came to a stop at the head of the yard and, setting his hands on his hips, lowered his head, peering over the rims of his spectacles at the two lines of men. "Well, I've done my quota. So any more o' you sons o' bitches happens t'get plugged out here, you can damn well keep your bullets an' take 'em t'hell with you. I'm through for the night. Now, move your asses offa my yard."

Calhoun had felt the subtle nudge of a rifle sliding out of the darkness into his side. "Doc's right," he muttered to Barrett. "This ain't the place. Move out, boys!" he called. Barrett's men started reluctantly to back off.

"We'll meet again, Sanders," Barrett vowed. "Sure as damnation, we'll meet again."

"Lookin' forward to it," Coke replied. He stepped in front of Calhoun. "Odds were too even out here, weren't they?" he muttered. "Mowin' down a man workin' alone is more your style, ain't it?"

"I don't know what you're talkin' 'bout," Calhoun responded. "You got no proof of anything."

"Stay clear o' my part o' the country," Coke warned. "Suspicion will kill down there sometimes."

Chapter 40

THE STAGE WAS being loaded up. Soon it would be pulling out. Jessica turned away from the window of the emporium. She'd missed watching its arrival today, only the second time that she'd missed it since she'd come to live in Dispenseme. But Flora Henry, the eighty-year-old widow who lived alone on the edge of town, hadn't shown up for her daily visit to the store.

Jessica and Meg could usually set their clocks by Flora. Each morning at eleven o'clock, she'd hobble through the door, buy a stick of penny candy, break off a piece, and suck it up into her toothless mouth. As she enjoyed her treat, she'd wander through the store, lingering over new goods that had been set out.

Flora would signal her desire for some item in the store by examining it long and pointedly. Next day she'd arrive with a pound cake for Meg to put out for sale to enable her to raise the money toward the purchase price. The cake was usually a pitiful thing, scorched on top. And it was always lopsided, baked at a tilt—a defect she tried to plaster over with extra-thick layers of butter frosting across the decline. More often than not, Meg wound up buying the cake herself, then located the item that Flora fancied and marked it down to the same amount.

"That's not a fourth of what that picture frame's worth," Jessica had once objected as Meg cut its price down in readiness for Flora's arrival.

"Well, I don't want t'hafta buy another three cakes," Meg had remarked.

But this morning, Flora hadn't made her usual appearance at the store. By eleven-thirty, after going outside a few times to look down the street, Meg and Jessica had grown concerned, and Jessica set out for Flora's house.

She found the old woman lying, shaken, on her back steps. She'd twisted her ankle going down them to feed her chickens, and had taken a hard fall. Jessica brushed off the food scraps sprinkled over her; and when Flora seemed willing to make the try, Jessica helped her up, supporting her through her house, easing her down in her rocker in her crowded parlor. The old woman felt featherlight to Jessica, all thin little bird bones and empty skin.

Jessica took Flora's shoe off, helped her out of her stockings, and pressed gently around her swollen ankle. It seemed unbroken, but badly sprained. She went into the kitchen and found a large pot. She pumped water into it, found some salts and shook them into the water, then carried the pot into the parlor and lifted Flora's injured foot into it. By slow degrees, Flora seemed to be coming out of her shock. But Jessica thought she still looked alarmingly weak and pale.

"Do you hurt anywhere else?" she inquired.

"Only a spatterin' o' bruises up this side, I think," she responded. "But my back steps is a mess."

Jessica smiled. The housekeeper in the poor woman couldn't be set aside. "I'll sweep the food scraps off your steps for you."

When she returned, Flora was lying back in the rocker, her eyes closed. Jessica wandered about the shabby, cluttered parlor, her eyes falling on the flowered vase that Flora's slanted cakes had bought. On a cabinet she saw the picture frame Meg had practically given away. It held a photograph of two young boys. Jessica picked it up, and a corner of the frame glanced off the candy dish alongside it.

"My sons," Flora said. Her wrinkled eyelids were still closed. "The blond one, Todd, was killed at the Battle o' Chickamauga, Tennessee. And the younger boy, Andy, he died o' typhoid fever in a Yankee prison camp . . . Point Lookout, Maryland."

Meg knew when to soften up, Jessica reflected. Yes, let this poor woman have all the picture frames her heart desired to hold the images of her lost sons.

Flora stirred and opened her eyes, her crooked, withered fingers lifting to her straggly hair. "Lordy, I do hate bein' so untidy this late in the day."

Almost reverently, Jessica set down the photograph of the two boys. "I'll fix your hair if you'd like me to, Flora."

Surprise flickered up in her old eyes. "That'd be so kindly of you, dear."

So Jessica went into Flora's closet-sized bedroom, fetched her hairbrush, and taking her hairpins out, began brushing Flora's crackly dry salt-and-pepper hair that reached in slivers to her waist.

"That feels so soothin'," Flora sighed.

And in companionable silence, Jessica brushed on, the feeling radiating up through her arms with each slow stroke, how long had gone unanswered this lonely old woman's longing for a loving human touch.

Jessica had just finished dressing Flora's hair when two women who lived down the road arrived at the door, worried because they hadn't seen their old neighbor up and around. Shortly thereafter, another woman showed up, sent by Meg to find out what was afoot.

"Yep, that sure musta been one humdinger of a thump you took outside," one of the women declared. " 'Cause it knocked your hair into a whole different style."

Flora was brightening up now, and despite her throbbing ankle and general soreness, she was starting to enjoy herself. Her neighbors went back to their homes, returning with beef stock soup, fruits, and lemonade for lunch. Another neighbor dropped in, and soon the afternoon took on the tenor of a tea party among intimate friends. Flora presided over it from her rocker, one weedy leg sprouting out of her pot of salts, her wizened face beaming.

Never had Jessica known such a feeling of belonging. Under its warm glow, time glided by. Then, she heard in the distance, like an admonition, the rumble and rattle of the stagecoach rolling through town, setting off a cacophony of aggravated dogs. A shadow passed over her at this reminder of the fragile texture of the life that she had created here and the thread of deceitfulness running through it.

It wasn't easy pulling free of that congenial gathering. She had to do it gently, so as not to break the fond spell for Flora. By the time she reached Main Street, the stage had already emptied.

Hearing behind her the snap of the reins and the sound of the stagecoach pulling away from the Wilson-Siden Ranch Supply Store and Post Office, Jessica walked back to the counter and started opening the box of merchandise that had just been delivered. Missing the stage's arrival left her more with the feeling of something's being undone than of anxiety. After over ten weeks of almost constant vigilance of it, nothing had materialized yet.

"Ain't you supposed t'meet Sarie sometime this afternoon?" Meg asked.

"Oh, yes," Jessica exclaimed. "I forgot that she was coming today, and I left the draperies that I made for her back at the house." She went into the back room and got her hat. "When Sarie comes in, ask her to go over to the house. I'll have some coffee on."

"An' your ears primed t'hear the news o' Coke?" Meg teased.

Jessica only smiled as she walked out the door. It would be useless to protest; and she did want to know how it was going with Coke. At last report from Warner, both of the wounded boys were still hanging on. That should be a comfort to him. Maybe both sides in that land dispute would decide to back off now.

Jack Siden had dropped out of sight for a few days after that Monday afternoon, when he tried to force himself on her. Perhaps he feared that she'd bring charges against him. She'd almost begun to hope that he was gone for good when, yesterday, she saw him on the street again. He avoided looking her way, slinking back into his store. It was loathsome and discomposing to her to feel him still around, but at least he wanted to steer clear of her now.

She frowned. Across the street up ahead, Siden had come out of the saloon. His thin cigar in his hand, its thread of smoke twining slowly up, he was looking at her steadily, insolently. Jessica hesitated; then, giving him a censuring look, she continued down the boardwalk, passing Cactus's dentistry, barber shop, and mortuary. She stepped off the boardwalk into the gap between that three-in-one building and Cactus's bathhouse.

She gasped. A hand had shot out and grabbed her arm, yanking her back between the buildings. Dismayed, she looked down at the smooth hand gripping her wrist, the shirt ruffle jutting out from the bottom of the sleeve of an expensive city-style suit coat. When he stopped, her eyes fell on the brocade vest. And with spiraling terror, she looked up into the face that had reeled up out of the inferno of her nightmares into reality.

"You . . ." she whispered.

He smiled. Though his attire was that of the overdressed city slicker, his face had the look of a sly, greedy alley rat that had crawled out of some dark hole to usurp the only spot of sunlight.

"Yes, 'tis me, your old pal, Mike O'Banion," he replied in that oily brogue that he'd often affected with the ladies in San Francisco or with gullible males whom he was out to fleece. "Now, c'mon, lassie," he chided. "Did you really think you could get away from me?"

"You can't . . . you can't . . ." she breathed. "You have no place to hide here if you—" She swallowed. "I have friends here."

"Seems you can't count every one of the hayseeds in this burg as your friend. I found one who was only too pleased t'point you out t'me." He glanced aside.

Out of the corner of her eye she saw Jack Siden flip his cigar onto the road, then slide his hands into his pockets and stroll away.

"Now, c'mon, m'love." O'Banion's fingers tightened on her arm. "You an' me are goin' on a little trip."

Her arm stiffened against her. "I'm not going anywhere. You can't force me."

His hand eased up on her wrist. "Oh, but I can, m'love. I can. One way or the other, I surely can." He tapped under the lapel of his suit coat. "Do you know what I have here in my inside pocket?"

She flinched.

"Oh, no," he chuckled. "That's not where I keep my knife. What I have here are two documents . . . all official, signed and notarized. One is a warrant for your arrest charging you with the embezzlement of eight hundred fifty dollars from the business establishment of Ivory Ives. And the other . . ." He grinned. "I think only you can appreciate this, m'love. It identifies me, your dear ole buddy, Michael Jay O'Banion, as a deputy of the court in San Francisco, empowering me to apprehend you and return you there to stand trial."

Disbelief rose in her eyes. "Henri . . . chose you?"

"That he did," he replied through that feral grin. "Our dear and sainted patron, Henri LaMarque, it was, who arranged my deputizin' by the court."

"He . . . wouldn't."

"He wants his strumpet back," he said simply. "But in a rather different condition than the plucky one that she walked out on him with. That's why he chose me to do the job." A lewd twist came to his mouth. "He knows my tastes. Yes," he went on, a heavily sardonic note in his voice, "Mr. LaMarque knows how to reward a valuable minion for his faithful service. I'm sure you, of all people, can appreciate the sweet irony in that, can't you, love?"

Jessica stared at him in horror. A look of unspoken knowledge passed between them, and she knew that she'd never reach San Francisco alive.

She twisted her arm free and dashed for the street. He caught her around the waist and started dragging her back. She threw her hands out, grasping the window ledge of the mortuary and desperately trying to pull away. Reaching up, he tore one of her arms away from the window ledge and then the other.

"You better behave," he threatened, holding her from behind, pinioning her arms against her. "You want me t'use these papers? You want all these good Bible-thumpin' friends of yours around here t'know that you're a thief and a rich man's whore?"

But she knew that if he got her away from here, she'd be dead. And she struggled harder, lashing a heel back into his shin. He held fast to an arm, though, and she lost her balance, falling forward, her hat tipping over her face.

"You're startin' to annoy me, love," he said in a calm, deadly tone, reaching under his coat for his knife.

He felt a jab in his back.

"Reach for the firmament, you despicable outpourin' of a sheep's anus." It was Cactus Caleb, holding a rusty antique muzzle-loading rifle that was almost as long as he was. Lou Wilson was standing behind him. "Get away from that lady," Cactus commanded. "And stick your proboscis against the wall. An' if you ain't got a educated ear, that means your nose."

"You all right, Miss Jessica?" Lou asked, helping her up.

She nodded, not looking at him.

Lou automatically straightened her hat so that he could see her face. "I'd just brought Cactus some things that'd arrived on the stage," he jabbered on. "I don't like anything that he's ordered t'lie around in my business for too long. Then we heard this ruckus. . . . You sure you're all right?"

Again, she only nodded.

"I got documents here," O'Banion snapped. "They give me the right—"

"I don't give the piss of a syphilitic hyena," Cactus interrupted, "if you got the entire Constitution o' the United States, the Bill o' Rights, an' every last one o' the fifteen amendments engraved in gold letterin' up the inside o' your intergluteus fold, you don't got the right t'drop into our town an' proceed t'manhandle our womenfolk. Now, move. I'm takin' you to our local constabulary."

"Seth ain't there," Lou said. "Told me this mornin' he was headin' out t'track some cattle thieves."

"Then we'll just lock this cayhoot up till he gets back," Cactus replied. "Now, start locomotin', feller."

O'Banion sneered at the rusty flintlock in Cactus's hands. "I bet that piece of scrap metal can't even shoot."

Cactus didn't blink. "At this range, it's bound t'do somethin' . . . an' I'm as curious as you are."

"You're gonna feel like a fool, old man," O'Banion warned.

Cactus rammed him in the stomach with that ancient rifle. "Seems you keep locomotin' the wrong portion o' your anatomy. It's your feet that I wanta see movin', not your jaw."

Lou put his hand on Jessica's shoulder. She recoiled, and he took it away. "Would you like me t'walk you back to the emporium?"

"No, I'm all right, Lou," she said woodenly. "Just fine, thank you. You go on. Please go on."

Leaning against the wall, she listened to them walk away.

"Lou, you hear o' any bovines bein' swiped in recent days?" Cactus was asking in a perplexed voice.

"Not in close to two weeks."

"Then send that young feller you got helpin' out at your store to that fishin' hole over on Jehu Wight's place. Most likely Seth'll be stretched out on the bank over there tryin' t'apprehend a fish or two instead o' any long gone outlaws."

Their voices drifted away. Jessica stood there, her heart laboring hard inside her chest though it seemed to be working backward, pumping the warm blood out of her arms and legs instead of into them. The fragile crystal of hope that she'd been nurturing these last few weeks had burst apart. The moment that she had dreaded for so long was upon her.

On benumbed legs, she started toward home, struggling to get her stunned mind to function in some logical sequence. How much time did she have before the marshal got back to town and came to arrest her? An hour? Two? She was trotting now.

And how soon after that before Seth turned her over to O'Banion? Tonight, probably. The scene that had been haunting her for over a dozen weeks rose in her mind: the shadowed, narrow staircase, the thin, rust-colored light trailing out of the room at the foot of it, the dank odor of the cellar, water dripping somewhere, the faraway voices of the crowd in the casino up above, a heavy footstep reverberating overhead, and a clear, strange gurgling sound that didn't seem to come from a drain but didn't seem human, either. He was on his knees, his eyes wide, so wide, gaping up at her in terror and a kind of bafflement. Shrinking back in the shadows, she noticed the line, a thin crease like a wrinkle that seemed to extend under his chin from ear to ear. He made a gasping motion with his mouth but gurgled instead. His head wobbled. The crease seemed to swell, the blood oozing and trickling down out of it, then he toppled forward onto the floor. And beyond him, deeper inside the room among the wine racks, Mike O'Banion stood calmly cleaning his knife blade with his handkerchief.

They'd turn her over to him: they had no choice. Jessica broke into a run. O'Banion had the papers to legally take her away. Henri had fixed that.

She fumbled in her pocket for the key, got the door open, and slammed it shut behind her as she tore for the bedroom. She attacked the hooks and eyes on her new skirt, ripping them apart, shoving the skirt down her hips. She yanked her old black skirt out of the wardrobe and, jerking her hat off, pulled the skirt over her cold, sweating body. She hooked it unevenly with blunted fingertips, then wrenched off her shoes and pulled on a pair she hadn't worn since her arrival here. Grabbing up her straw washday hat from the corner of a chairback, she slapped it on her head, stuffed her hair up inside it, and tied the scarf under her chin in a lopsided knot. She snatched up the longest hatpin poking out of the pincushion on the bureau and nearly jabbed it into her skull sticking it into the hat. She yanked the pin out, fumbled it, dropped it, plucked it up, and shoved it back into her head. She had to get out of here.

She sprinted out the back door and, leaping over the snoozing Herman, dashed into the stable. Grabbing a dusty old canteen off a hook on a beam where it hung next to a horse collar, she charged back out of the stable, leaping over the still-prostrate hound, and raced into the kitchen. Holding the canteen under the pump spout, she frantically jerked up and down on the handle. The machine coughed and wheezed, but not a drop of water did it give up. Gagging on the air she was breathing, wiping the sweat off her brow with the back of her trembling hand, she spotted the cup of primer water that she herself had filled and set here this morning.

She dumped the water into the pump and began swinging the handle again.

"Jessica, Jessica," she chanted to herself. "Get hold of yourself, get hold of yourself. If you get so hysterical that you overlook simple things, you're lost, really lost."

Gulping deep breaths of air, she rinsed out the canteen, filled it with water, and hooked the top. Hurrying into her bedroom, she grabbed up her purse, then her suit coat. Pulling it on, she bolted out the back door and nearly slammed into Sarie, who was coming around the back corner of the house.

"You didn't hear my knock?" she said. Then she saw Jessica's panic-stricken face. "What's wrong?"

"I've gotta get away," Jessica gasped. "There's a man here. He's going to kill me."

Putting a hand on Jessica's arm, Sarie looked fearfully around. "Where?" she whispered. "Where is he?"

"In town. He's going to take me away and kill me. I've gotta get away from here." She pulled free of Sarie, and started backing, a pained expression coming to her face. "Check on Willie from time to time for me, will you?"

Her eyes stark with bewilderment, Sarie nodded faintly. She started to speak, but Jessica was gone.

Jessica opened the door at the rear of the emporium and stumbled inside to the storage and fitting room. She leaned against the wall, eyes closed, her breathing thrashing in her ears. When she opened her eyes again, her gaze lit on the mirror across from her and she jumped at the haunted, hunted visage that she found there. She dragged herself away from the wall and crept to the doorway that opened into the store. Nudging the curtain, she peeked inside, the siesta-time normalcy of the store feeling alien to her.

Meg sat in the rocker by the potbelly stove. The angle of her head and the subtle movement of her shoulders told Jessica that she was knitting.

"Meg!" Jessica called.

Meg lifted her head and frowned around.

"Over here!" Jessica beckoned.

"Why're you back here?" Meg asked, coming into the room.

"I'm leaving, Meg."

"What?" Meg spluttered. "Why?"

"There's a man in town. His name is Mike O'Banion. He's come to take me away."

" 'Tain't nobody can make anybody go anywhere that they don't wanta go to," Meg said indignantly.

"This man can. He has a warrant for my arrest. But if he gets hold of me, he'll kill me. I have to get away."

"Where to?" Meg asked, still confounded.

"Mexico. I'm going to try to cross at San Pedro de Roma sometime this afternoon or tonight, then—" She caught her breath, panic freezing in her eyes; someone had just walked into the store.

Her troubled eyes holding Jessica's, Meg backed to the curtained doorway. She peeked out. "Be out shortly," she called. "Helpin' someone with a fittin' right now."

She let the curtain drop. "It's only Graham an' Mary McKetchin."

Jessica let her breath out. "Meg, getting away—now—is the only chance I have. Will you loan me two dollars?"

"Why . . . o'course," Meg fumbled.

"Please hurry."

Meg walked gravely back through the store, responding to a remark from Mary McKetchin in a flat, preoccupied tone. She opened the money drawer and scooped out all the cash it contained. Clasping it to her bosom, she returned to the fitting room and tried to hand it all over to Jessica.

"Someday you're going to bankrupt yourself, dear heart," Jessica said with wistful affection, picking out only the two dollars.

"Really, child, two dollars cain't be near enough. Let me go over to the safe at Lou's, get some real money."

"No," Jessica responded. "I have money. I do. In my shoes." She paused, trying to summon her strength. "There's something more . . . a giant favor." A tortured look came to her eyes. "Willie," she whispered, and stopped, unable to go on.

"You want me t'look after him," Meg said. "Don't worry, I do love that little darlin'. I'll take good care o' him until you . . . until you . . ." She paused and cleared her throat, realizing by the look in Jessica's eyes that what she was about to say might not come to pass. "Until you come back," she finished feebly.

Jessica's eyes filled. "Oh, Meg," she breathed. "You're so good . . . too good for the likes of me."

"There . . . there," Meg soothed. "Livin' side by side with a person like I have with you, a body just knows in his soul if that person is good or not. An' I sure know that 'bout you. If you ever done any wrong, Jessica, it's because you just couldn't see any other road t'choose.''

Jessica straightened up, wiping the tears off her cheeks. ''Good or bad, sooner or later, it all catches up with you. If I can't— If worse comes to worst . . .'' She swallowed hard. ''I've made arrangements to provide for Willie. When winter comes, you'll know . . .''

''Jessica,'' Meg pleaded. ''This whole thing, it don't set right with me. There must be some other way.''

''There isn't that I can see. I should've kept going right past Dispenseme, but I hoped . . . I prayed . . .'' She shook herself. ''Well, none of that's important now. I don't regret these last three months here. But oh, Meg, I'm so terribly sorry for bringing this worry on you.''

''Child . . .''

Tears welling in her eyes again, Jessica embraced Meg. ''You're the best, the very best there is. I wish I'd known you all my life. I wish I'd had you for my mother. I love you, Meg.''

Letting her arms slide away, she turned and stepped to the back door. Taking a deep breath, she opened it a crack and looked outside.

''Jessica . . .'' Meg began, but Jessica was already on her way.

''Oh, Jessica,'' Meg said helplessly to the empty room. ''How the sam hill are you even gonna get yourself to the border . . . you bein' such a dad-blamed tenderfoot an' all?''

❧ Chapter 41

RAMIRO TOILED AT his forge, shaping an iron shoe for the horse he had tethered nearby, his iron hammer clanking down with hard, measured strokes against the red-glowing bar.

''Ramiro?'' But the voice, high and breathless, could not compete with the ringing clangor of iron striking iron.

Feeling a tap on his shoulder, Ramiro started. Glancing around, he found Meg's pretty helper looking anxiously up at him.

"Un momento, señora." He turned back to the horseshoe and, his arm swings growing more abbreviated, worked the ends into their final shape. Then he lifted the hot horseshoe off the anvil with iron tongs and set it, hissing, into the vat of water. He turned to her, wiping his hands on his leather apron. "I can help you?"

"I want to rent a horse, right away."

He hesitated, eyeing her uncertainly. There was a strange, wild look in her eyes as she stood there fingering the straps of the canteen and purse she held. Her hat was clamped on so tightly that it hugged her brows, and the little jut of nose underneath was redder than her cheeks.

"You drunk, señora?"

"Me? Of course not! I want to rent a horse. That's all. You do have them to rent, don't you?"

"Sí."

"Then please get one for me right away. I'm in a hurry."

With a shrug, Ramiro trudged out the side door of the barn into the corral, and singled out an ancient bay gelding. It was the best choice, he decided, a safe ride for a tipsy tenderfoot like Willie's mama. There was one thing that could set it off its lazy-going pace, though—getting pricked by a burr. So Ramiro took extra care to check over the saddle blanket, shaking it out and running his hands over the rough material before throwing it on the gelding's back.

Heaving the saddle off the fence, Ramiro took another look at Jessica, and decided she didn't seem to be drunk so much as spooked. She was in constant motion as she waited for him to get her horse ready. Wringing her hands, she'd go scampering to the front door of the stable, peer down Main Street, wheel around, scurry back to the corral door, send him a pleading look to get a move on, then rush to the front door again to peer down Main Street.

Ramiro finished saddling the gelding and led him into the barn.

"You have ridden horses before, señora?" he asked doubtfully.

"Yes," she curtly replied, slapping the two dollars into his hand and grabbing the reins. She pulled on them, but the animal seemed disinclined to stir. She turned around and, with the reins over her shoulder, leaned forward. Digging her toes into the ground like she was climbing a hill, she dragged the heavy-footed horse outside and made a sharp turn to the right.

Ramiro wandered to the doorway and watched her as she wrested the gelding off Main Street. She proceeded to make her way through town, creeping stealthily from behind one building to the next . . . or as stealthily as possible considering that she had a nine-hundred-pound horse in tow. He watched her tiptoe behind a woodshed. Her head poked out warily on the opposite side, while unbeknownst to her, the end of the gelding was sticking out past the end of the shed behind her. Its lazily swinging tail might as well have been a flag. Shaking his head, Ramiro turned back to his forge.

Miss Muriel sat at her desk checking the students' work slates. They waited in hushed, watchful rows before her. The schoolmarm was in a deadly mood. A few of the boys had discovered that dropping insects down the backs of the girls' pinafores could be devilishly amusing. After lunch, their pockets loaded with ammunition, they'd gone at it with a gusto, sending little girls leaping out of their chairs and twitching and jiggling and squealing across the room. Miss Muriel had managed to collar one of the culprits, and the little bugger was still serving out his time perched sullenly on the Fool's Stool in the corner.

Miss Muriel heard a sharp tap-tapping. Lifting her face, she sent an eagle-eyed glower across the room. The tap-tapping sounded again, more insistently. She ducked down and peered under her desk. Nothing. She sat up, moving her eyes ominously around the room, and nearly jumped out of her drawers when her gaze met up with the huge face of a horse, framed in the nearby window.

At first she thought that one of the children's horses had come untethered. Lifting her lorgnette, she eyeballed the animal closely. It definitely didn't belong to any of her pupils.

Rising from her chair, she spotted the roof of a straw hat just a fraction of an inch below the windowsill. She leaned over and yanked the window up.

"I must speak to my son," Jessica West whispered urgently up at her.

Miss Muriel always made it a policy to never argue with any crazy-eyed mother, especially if that mother happened to be one of those strange, unpredictable out-of-staters who now and then drifted into Dispenseme like loose sediment to the bottom of a river pool. Willie was promptly shunted out the back door.

Seeing her son's small, vulnerable form, Jessica's heart swelled inside her.

"What're you doing here, Ma?" he asked in his sweet, innocent voice. He looked at the horse. "Are we going somewhere?"

"Sit down, my love," she said, struggling to control her voice. "I want to talk to you and I haven't much time."

Willie obeyed, eyeing her uneasily. Jessica tied the horse's reins to the low-hanging branch of a nearby tree. The saddle horn caught her eye, and she realized for the first time that she could hang her canteen and purse on it. She did so.

She walked over to her son and sat down on the step beside him. "Willie, my love," she said gently, putting her arms around him and resting her chin on his head. "Do you remember I told you once when we first got here that a time might come—"

"No!" he protested, pushing away. Now he knew where this was leading. "You have to stay right here with me."

"Oh, Willie, there's nothing in this world I'd want more than that. Nothing. It's possible, dear," she said, putting her hand to his cheek, "that I'll only be gone a short time."

He regarded her mistrustfully. "Where are you going?"

She took him in her arms again and kissed his feathery hair, touched with the beloved boy-scent of earth and wind and dry, tumbled leaves. "It's a special secret between you and Meg and me. So don't tell anyone, not even Chacho or Mort—but I'll be in Mexico."

Lifting his head, he looked into her face. "Why do you have to go at all, Mommy?"

The last word twisted her heart. "If I stay, dearest, chances are that I'll be taken away . . . for a long, long time."

"It's that ugly Mr. LaMarque's fault, isn't it?" he said angrily.

"Partly," she answered softly.

He saw the tremor in her eyes. "Why does he want to hurt you, Mommy?"

The need to comprehend shone so brightly on his face that it burned her. Her breathing shallowing and catching in her throat, she took his hand, using that as an excuse to turn her eyes away from his. "I've made mistakes, Willie. Bad choices," she said in a tight voice. "I can't explain it all to you now. It would take too long and you're too little to understand."

He regarded her reproachfully, that she would resort at a time like this to those same old flimsy words that grownups used all the time when they didn't want to tell the truth but couldn't quite bring themselves to lie.

"I may not be gone so very long," she repeated lamely.

But he saw through that.

"Take me with you," he cried. "Please, Mommy, please. I won't be a bother. Really, I won't."

Her throat ached. Her eyes stung. "Oh, my dearest darling, you're never a bother. Never. It's just that you'll be safer here, that's all. Meg adores you so. She'll take good care of you while I'm . . . I'm away. You have your friends here. You have Amy's family—her mother, her granny, her Uncle Coke. Count on them, Willie. What you have right here in Dispenseme is far, far better than what you'd have in me right now—a mother who may know where she's going but not what it'll be like once she gets there." She hugged him, then, with a fierce, desperate yearning; oh, to press him so tightly to her that he would fuse into her flesh and she could carry him away under her heart. "Try to be good, little love. Mind Meg. Promise?"

She felt the little nod of his head against her breast.

"Remember, I love you, William Joseph Daniels, Jr. I love you more than anyone or anything in this whole entire world."

With all the strength that she could muster, she let go of him and, giving him one last caress, got to her feet. She was relieved that he didn't cling to her. He seemed resigned, aware that further protest would only make it harder for both of them. He just remained where he was, a child, her child, sitting, forlorn and defenseless, on a step.

Turning away to untie the horse, she let the tears stream out. She felt like such a traitor. Despite his flashes of contrariness, his occasional assertions of independence from her, she was still the font from which he drew his strength and security, the looking glass through which he viewed the world and grew to understand it. Guilt overwhelmed her for the unhappiness that she was bringing upon him because of her own failings, because of her own blind stupidity in believing that she could come in contact with a ruthless, fundamental force in the world like an Henri LaMarque and walk away from it still whole. She had failed her son. Despite the lengths that she had gone to, even at the cost of her own honor and worthiness, she had still failed to shield her child from pain.

She stood for a time with her back to him, struggling to regain control over the grief surging through her. Taking the gelding's reins, she heaved a long, shuddery sigh and looked up at the rolling hills beyond town. A sad, secret smile formed on her lips. "Willie . . ."

He bounded to his feet. "Yes, Mommy."

"For all my thinking about taking this trip, there's one thing I completely forgot. Maybe you can help me."

His face fell when he saw that she hadn't changed her mind about taking him along. "What's that?" he asked dejectedly.

"Well, I know that *that* direction is west—" she pointed "—because the sun's headed that way. And I know that it's east over there, because it isn't— But, honey, when I'm out in the country, all that empty land looks the same to me and I'm afraid that I'll get turned around. How can I know for certain that I'm going south?"

"Oh, Ma!" he breathed. "You don't even know that? When you wanta go south and the sun's going down, you keep it on your right."

"All right." She smiled. "Thanks, my little man. How on earth could I ever get by without you?"

She turned away, pulling the horse behind her. Willie followed to the edge of the schoolyard. He felt better, a little more confident. He was part of her plans, he was necessary to her. When she'd gone some distance away, he cupped his hands around his mouth. "Ma!"

She turned.

"Don't forget. When it's morningtime, keep it on your left."

Smiling tenderly, she waved.

His eyes followed her as she threaded her way in and out around the buildings and brush, growing smaller. At the outskirts of town, she lifted up a bucket that was hanging off a fence post and turned it upside down on the ground. Stepping onto it, she put her foot into the stirrup and climbed up into the saddle. Willie watched the tiny figure of his mother ascending the hill, elbows flailing as she slapped the reins, body bouncing, her feet thrashing to urge her mount onward while the animal kept plodding along at the same plow-horse pace.

❧ Chapter 42

THE SAFFRON SUN hovered low over the western foothills, and Jessica felt herself enveloped in a dreamlike, dusty rose haze. She estimated the time to be around six-thirty. Seemed she should've reached Mexico by now. But then, maybe not; she wasn't such a good judge of time. Neither was she a good judge of distance. Especially not now, with her mind and emotions keyed to such a fevered pitch. And how could she adequately gauge time and distance when the worthless animal that she was on took forever to slog to any point on the horizon for which she set her course? Over the miles she'd often wondered if she might not have made better time on foot.

Now that the day was ebbing, another worry was starting to manifest itself. She hadn't counted on being out at night. She'd read about the planets, the galaxies, and the constellations, but hadn't achieved any practical knowledge. Whenever she'd looked up at the night sky, all that she'd been able to make out had been a spray of twinkling lights, with no more discernible pattern in them than had they been dress spangles tossed on black cloth. How, then, could she get her bearings when night closed in? Mysterious, menacing night . . . when the creatures came out.

She'd make it, she assured herself, quieting this new fear. She was in control. She'd get away. And another emotion had taken root inside her—anger. She was outraged at Henri LaMarque for what he'd done. She was incensed at all the injustices in her life that had brought her to this point. She'd pull them out and relive them in every ugly, poisonous detail, to fire that anger, for rage was her most dependable ally. It would keep her mean and tough. Just let a wolf attack; she'd break its scrawny neck.

Suddenly she had the vague sensation that something had altered in her surroundings. She stopped the horse and looked around. The setting sun was on her right, as it should be. And then it struck her: It was the wind. Instead of the gentle, ruffling

348

breeze out of the east, the wind was now sweeping in from the southwest, cooler, and strong enough to sway the brush. An expectant hush had settled over the land. Not an insect crackled around her. Not a bird did she see swimming across the sky.

Far to the southwest, a trembly glow caught her eye. Then she saw it. A black pall had coagulated over the southwestern horizon.

Yep, she thought, nudging the gelding back into its sunken-headed shuffle. It'd be her luck, wouldn't it, to be the personal recipient of South Texas's first drencher in almost two years. Well, so what? If rain-soaked, clammy clothes repelled her, she'd just have to think of how her skin would crawl if Mike O'Banion touched her. And touch her he most certainly would do if he ever caught up with her, the contempt never fading from those greedy, predatory eyes of his. And then he'd kill her.

A rainstorm might work to her advantage, her thoughts hurried on. It would wash away her tracks. And even better, the prospect of getting wet might deter Mike O'Banion. For a back-alley killer, he was uncommonly fastidious about his person. Yes, a rainstorm mightn't be that bad after all, she decided, considering that it would keep the night beasts at bay.

Out of the corner of her eye, Jessica picked up a movement that seemed at odds with the windswept land. She squinted at it. At first the movement, perhaps less than a mile away, was but a blur skimming the ground, a shadow crossing through shadows. But as she kept looking back, it dawned on her that the skimming shadow was a rider galloping hard after her. She wasn't about to wait around to find out who he was.

She sprang into action, slapping the reins and pounding her heels. "Giddap! Move!"

The gelding altered its gait. It certainly wasn't galloping, wasn't even trotting. It was twisting its rear end a little faster from side to side as it moped along.

She glanced back. The rider was gaining.

"Move, Lead Butt, move!" She slapped the horse's neck with the reins, kicked him hard in the sides.

Letting loose a little snort commensurate to a human shoulder shrug, the gelding arched its tail and lifted its hooves a bit higher.

The rider was closing. Leaning forward and holding the reins up before her in a tight fist, she started bouncing rhythmically in the saddle, as if she were galloping full tilt into the wind. But the gelding didn't pick up the hint. Twisting around in the saddle, she pounded his rump with her fists. As she did so, she unwittingly jerked back on the reins. The gelding stopped dead in its tracks.

Wheeling around, she frantically whipped the reins and beat her heels. But the horse remained as fixed as a fence post.

She slumped, her heart throbbing in her ears, her mind racing. Her eyes narrowed. Reaching up, she drew the long hatpin out of her hat. Holding the reins slack in one hand, she turned and, raising the pin high in her fist like a dagger, drove it down hard into the horse's rump.

Squealing, the gelding bucked once and shot away. In slow motion, Jessica saw the world turn upside down. The ground flew up and slammed into her.

Still clutching her hatpin, she lay sprawled in the dirt, the wind clouted out of her. Her equilibrium returning, she spat the dust out of her mouth and lifted her face, peering with one eye through the tunnel her hat made as it leaned on her nose. The gelding was finally responding as she'd intended; it was now a wavy blob bowling rapidly up a hill a quarter of a mile away.

The hoofbeats of the oncoming rider pulsated through the ground into her stomach.

She dropped her head, dust drifting over her as the rider reined in. She heard the creak of a saddle, then his feet thudding to the ground. She stiffened. Her grip on the hatpin tightening, she prayed she'd know when and how to strike, listened to the crunch of gravel as he stepped over to her. His heavy breathing suddenly became frighteningly close and intimate as he stooped down beside her. With a shock, she felt her hat being pulled off.

"Goldurn it, Jessie," came that familiar Virginia drawl. "When in the hell are you gonna stop this dad-blamed overreactin'? I hope you ain't hurt yourself this time."

Coke. Relief swept over her, but she wasn't about to let him see it.

"I should've known it was you!" she exploded, squirming away. Snatching up her hat, she smashed it on her head backward. "Every time you're within a mile of a horse and me, I wind up planted on the ground!"

The worry eased from his face. "Not every time," he answered mildly. "You shoulda seen yourself turnin' that backward somersault. All them petticoats a-flyin', you looked like a blossomin' white rose." He became concerned again. "Sure you're all right?

Better check yourself over, make sure you didn't loosen up any o' your joints.''

"I'm fine," she asserted. "Just fine . . . except, as you may have noticed, my horse decided to finish the trip without me."

He looked at the stiletto-sized hatpin in her fist. "Can't say I blame him. Don't worry, though. He'll find his way back home."

"That wasn't what I was concerned about," she replied with exaggerated dignity. "I'd like to have him back, you know. You have your horse. Kindly go get mine."

"Where'd he go?" he asked with exasperating innocence.

"Thataway." She poked a thumb toward the hill. "You saw him take off."

He got up and, hands on his hips, blinked placidly at the darkening hills. "Sure don't see him now."

"Well, then"—her voice rose—"go find him!"

"Naw," he said easily. "Be a waste o' energy. Take up all the light we got left."

She sighed. She might as well give up on that. He could be as muleheaded as she was. More so. In his own easygoing way, he could never be prevailed upon to do a single thing that he hadn't already set his mind to do. She was still getting over her amazement that he was here at all.

"Tell you what," he said. "I'll take you to wherever you were whuppin' off to. Mexico, ain't it?"

"Who told you? Sara?"

"Sorta. She an' Meg went chargin' into the back room o' the saloon—you know, that room full o' cots that Ruby provides for her customers too bleary-eyed t'find their way back home. They flung a bucket o' water into the face o' one o' m'drovers stretched out in there an' shook him till his teeth rattled t'get him awake. Then Ruby grabbed him by the hair an' poured a pot o' scaldin' coffee down his gullet so's he'd be sober enough t'run the message out t'me pronto that you was hightailin' it thisaway."

He paused and shook his head. "Pore Rogelio. Scared the hell out of him. Said a little tap on the shoulder woulda got him goin' just as good, seein' as how he hadn't tied one on but was only a mite tuckered out."

Jessica couldn't help smiling. But then her eyes clouded. She was still pretty much in the same fix she'd been in before, the same shameful, God-awful fix. He'd expect to be told about it, too, and there could be no more evasions. Yes, she thought, he'd pursue her down every corridor, allowing her no dark corner to duck demurely into. He had her now, stuck out here in the middle of nowhere . . . and he was the one with the horse.

He was looking up at the sky. The thunderhead had swollen across more of the horizon. "Well, sweet potato." He offered her his hand. "If you're a-wantin' t'get t'Meheeco, we'd better get a move on."

Pursing her lips, she eyed him circumspectly.

"You wanta spend the night proppin' up the side o' this here hill?" he asked.

For better or worse . . . she thought, and took his hand.

"That wasn't too savvy o' you, Jessie, settin' off all alone like that," he shouted over his shoulder as they rode through the churning wind. "You ain't familiar with this neck o' the woods. Don't know the dangers. For all you'd o' knowed, I coulda been a rustler. Or a comanchero, a hardhearted drifter, or a bad-mannered Injun."

"And I coulda been a water buffalo, an Arabian camel, or Attila the Hun's polka-dotted elephant," she yelled back. "But I'm not and you're not, so stop trying to put fear in me." Her voice lost its spirit. "I have enough of that already."

"Cain't blame me for the way things are," he replied, then added, "Though I reckon you will, seein' as how I'm the only hombre in sight t'slap it on." He reined in Ole Belcher and half turned in the saddle. "I understand that a fellow showed up in town today that you think is fixin' t'kill you."

"Yes," she admitted softly.

"Then why didn't you stay close t'folks who'd look out for you?"

She didn't answer.

"The fellow has an arrest warrant against you, doesn't he?"

She still didn't respond.

He peered back at her. "Doesn't he, Jessie?"

She looked away. "Yes."

Like a huge iron galleon, the thunderhead was bearing down upon them now, its towering, arched contours illuminated by flare-ups from within. And they could hear its deep, grumbling groans from the exertion.

Coke looked up into the sky. "Sure don't like the looks o' that thing."

"Why?" she asked. "It means rain. You know . . . rain. Water. Green grass. Little birdies twitting through the mudholes. I'd think you'd be delighted.''

'' 'Tain't my land that it's over.'' He prodded Ole Belcher on. "Looks like we'll hafta find some shelter an' sit this out.''

"Oh no we don't!'' she exclaimed, her voice wavering in the wind. "I want to get to Mexico—tonight!''

"Jessie, you ain't got no idee what it's like when a cloud like that starts lettin' loose in these parts, 'specially after a dry-up. Lightnin' hittin' from outa nowhere, crumblin' terrain, flash floods. With the night comin' on, when the lightnin' ain't strikin', it'll be so thick an' black all aroun', we won't be able t'make out our noses smack-dab in the middle of our kissers lookin' cross-eyed. Don't fret. A few hours delay won't make no difference.''

"That's easy for you to say,'' she retorted. "You're not the one in danger. I'd wager that your ole drinkin' buddy, the town marshal, is already halfway here.''

"Seth'll give you the time t'make it.''

"How do you know that?''

"Know Seth. He looks out for his own. He'll put off this fella what's come for you.''

"I'm not one of his own. He doesn't know *me* that well,'' she replied, ducking behind him as a huge tumbleweed came bounding down on them from out of nowhere. It whopped against a boulder and veered away.

"Seth knows you better'n that outsider what's come for you,'' Coke explained. "He tends t'get a tad on the lazy side from time t'time. An' I got a strong hunch that this'll sure 'nuff be one o' those times. Won't be till tomorrow, when this outsider starts gettin' itchy an' shootin' off his mouth, that Seth'll make a stab at goin' after you . . . just so's he won't hafta be aroun' t'listen.''

"I don't see why he'd do that for me,'' she puzzled. "He hardly knows me.''

"He knows that Meg, Cactus, an' me are on your side. Though you wouldn't know it t'look at him, Seth's a right good politician. Knows when t'give ole blindfolded Justice a little tickle on the fanny so's the scales'll tip in the right di-rection. That's why he's so popular round here. Gets elected every time.''

Jessica digested that in silence. It was starting to take too much effort to talk anyway. The wind helped carry his words back to her, but she could yell at the top of her lungs and her words had become chaff that the stiffening wind whipped away and scattered across the prairie behind them. The only way that she could make herself easily heard now would be by snuggling up against him and speaking directly into his ear—the prospect of which she found most disconcerting. So conscious was she of the strength of his shoulders and arms before her and the physical pull that had always been there between them, that each little touch seemed to carry suggestive undertones. She was keeping herself as far back on the saddle as she possibly could, the touch of her hands on his waist as light as possible. That contact with him served both to steady her on the horse and to help her hold her distance from him.

Night had erased the daylight away. Behind them, to the northeast, the stars glimmered serenely out of a limpid, untroubled sky; before them the world was in turmoil, convulsive flashes of lightning eerily exposing the landscape. Gusts of wind kept spattering them with dust and debris. Ole Belcher sidling against the blasts, they kept their heads turned away in order to breathe.

Suddenly they dipped downward. Squinting over Coke's shoulder, Jessica saw that they were descending into a deep arroyo. As they approached the bottom, the wind that had been bawling in their ears abruptly disengaged and lifted, wailing fitfully on above them. Looking to her left and right at the ghostly fissured walls illuminated in the jabs of gray light, Jessica imagined a flash flood thundering down upon them. Perhaps Coke was right. Perhaps they should find some shelter and sit this out.

Without preamble, Ole Belcher lurched up the opposite bank, catching Jessica totally by surprise. Thrown backward, she lost her hold on Coke's waist. Flinging a hand out, she caught his shirt. For a moment it held her. There was a loud rip and she found herself clutching only a loose scrap of cloth, and teetering on the top of his bedroll on the verge of tumbling back into the arroyo. Grabbing her wrist, he hauled her up, holding her until they reached level ground on top.

"Doggone it, Jessie, it ain't a-gonna hurt you t'put your arms about me," he muttered, pulling her arms around him and fixing her hands on top of each other over his stomach as though he were hooking his belt. "Hell, I ain't so squirrelly as t'get romantic astraddle a horse goin' up a gorge in a lightnin' storm."

Her face burning, Jessica debated whether a better placement for her hands might not be a couple of feet higher . . . like around his neck.

They pressed on, their faces down, and hats low against the stinging upsurges from the ground. In a dazzling zigzag of lightning, Jessica glimpsed a copse of trees far ahead, fronted by what appeared to be some strange, jagged boulders. As they drew closer, she realized that the boulders were three buildings—an adobe hut, an open-faced stable, and some kind of storage shed—surrounded by a fence that sagged in some places and was completely caved in in others.

Ole Belcher delicately picked his way across a section of the collapsed fence and they entered the debris-strewn yard. The thunderstorm seemed to be fermenting directly overhead. Vertical stabs of lightning lacerated the night. Tympanic thunder vibrated through the air. In the copse of trees the tree limbs thrashed frenetically about in the screaming wind as if trying to grab something just out of reach. And the door of the adobe hut, hooked to its frame by a single hinge near the top, kept slapping lopsidedly back and forth with a spasmodic squeak-bang! squeak-bang!

"Well, it's better'n nothin'," Coke said. Taking her arm, he helped her slide off Ole Belcher, then he dismounted beside her. "Go on into the hut. I'll get Ole Belcher bedded down."

He led the horse away. Holding her twisting hat, she started toward the hut, her legs feeling weak and wobbly from her hours astride a horse. Her eyes became fixed on that crazily lurching door, in turns baring the blackness behind, then clapping over it. It reminded her of a macabre, babbling mouth. Alone . . . with Coke? In there?

She fought the door back and stumbled inside. Dust swirled off the floor, its dry, musty odor filling her nostrils and making them prickle. Having no inclination to venture deeper into the darkness, she turned and knelt down a few feet from the door. A soft residue coated the floor, and she couldn't tell if she was kneeling on wood, slated stone, or packed earth.

The prickle in her nose sharpened and she sneezed again and again. Wiping her nose, she became aware of how chafed and stiff her fingers were, and for the first time realized that she'd forgotten her gloves. Left them behind in the right front corner, second drawer down, in the bureau in her bedroom an afternoon ago, a century ago. Poor Willie. Left behind like her gloves. He should be asleep by now, one tiny white foot curled over the blanket, arm dangling down, his body, pillowy warm and cuddly, giving off the sweet-sour scent of unripened fruit. A deep sadness stirred inside her, a poignant longing. She missed him already. Oh, how grievously she missed him. Poor sweet blessed child. Had her father felt this way when he'd left her behind at the Home twenty years ago? Odd; this was the first time in over ten years that she'd broken past her unbending bitterness toward the man to ascribe any feelings at all to him. Would her own child be so unsparing toward her? She shuddered. She wasn't cold, but she shuddered.

Where was Coke, anyway? Seemed like he'd been gone a long time.

Perhaps he'd been attacked by a pack of wolves. Or an Indian, or an escaped murderer. She peered out into the wild night. She couldn't possibly tell what was going on out there, what with the banging of this accursed cockeyed door, the strident wail of the wind outside, and this incessant breathy whistle shimmying through a chink in the fireplace like a teakettle building steam.

She felt a stab of fear, and peered again outside. Maybe Mike O'Banion was out there and had killed Coke . . . or was killing him now. Or Jack Siden. Logic told her that this was unlikely, quite unlikely; still she was growing panicky. If either of those beasts hurt Coke, it would be her fault.

She was just on the point of leaping up and charging out to find him when, in a flash of light, she spotted him beyond the careening door. His saddlebags flung over a shoulder, bedroll tucked under an arm, rifle in hand, he was stooped down in front of the copse of trees examining the ground. He rose up and walked, slowly looking down, nudging stones or chaff out of the way with his foot. Lifting his head, he gazed off toward the east for a moment, then turned toward the hut.

He approached, the only steadily moving silhouette among writhing ones. His form filled the doorway. Shrugging off his saddlebags, he tossed them, along with his bedroll, inside.

Then, holding the door back, he lifted his rifle and brought the butt of it down against the rusty hinge. She knelt in his shadow, staring up at him as he brought the rifle butt down again and again against that hinge, the jittery light beyond magnifying his shoulders and arms and turning the determined set of his jaw to chiseled granite. He ceased pounding, stood the rifle against the wall, and muscles hardening, gripped the door in his hands and wrenched it off. And at that instant she felt all her disparate feelings boiling up inside her as ungovernable as that storm raging outside. And it was all that she could do to keep from springing to her feet and fleeing into the night.

⚜ Chapter 43

THE HUT MOANED and shuddered in the wind. Jessica listened for the drum of raindrops that would relieve the storm of its fury, drain it of its bluster; but all she heard was the fusillade of debris spewed against the roof and walls.

Coke had started a fire in the fireplace and had put coffee on to boil. The chimney was partly clogged, and whenever the gales shifted overhead, smoke belched out of the fireplace, swelled into the air, lingered a moment, then was snuffed out the door.

The smoke stung Jessica's eyes, but she needed that fire. There was solace in its homey flames, distraction in its dancing light. Without it, the savage night outside would have seemed too oppressive to bear.

She sat against the opposite wall, her legs curled under her. As soon as Coke had entered the hut, she'd taken her place there, an uneasy wariness in her attitude that she couldn't disguise. Watching him unroll the blanket of his bedroll near the fire, she wondered if the space between them teased at him as much as it teased at her. Yet the more keenly she felt the magnetism between them, the stronger was her instinct to shrink from it; for the growing susceptibility she felt toward him was reviving something else in her, too—the deep-seated distrust that she felt toward all men. The inner conflict, the threat, the shame . . .

Their eyes met. A smile trembled across her face and was gone.

"What were you looking at out there by the trees?" she asked.

"Cattle tracks," he said, smoothing out the blanket. "Seems like a good number o' cattle have been moved through here in recent months."

"Why does that interest you?"

"The tracks seem t'come from the direction of a canyon not

too far from here. A lotta the cattle that was swiped from around here these past few months disappeared into that canyon.''

"Do you think the thieves were moving them into Mexico?''

"It's possible," he replied slowly, settling down on the blanket. "But the rustlers coulda turned 'em back north an' moved 'em toward the train lines outa Warner. More money t'be made in that direction.''

"Seems as though someone would've seen those cattle being moved.''

"Not if the thieves had a safe place t'hold 'em till things cooled down, then moved 'em with herds from some ranch that's known in these parts." He grew thoughtful. "The San Sebastian Ranch is directly north o' here—T. C. Barrett's land now. Fact is, the former owner o' the San Sebastian, Juan Fernando Castillo, was gunned down less'n a coupla miles from here.''

His eyes fell on one of the small, dark, insect-sized things scattered by the fire that he'd noticed earlier. He picked it up and held it to the light. It was the butt of a thin cigar.

"Makes sense," he mused. "With that hide-gatherin' operation o' his, Jack Siden would know all the ranches in this area an' the hands that work on 'em, too. Wouldn't be hard for him t'find out where the prime herds on the spreads was located.''

Jessica's face had changed when she'd recognized what Coke was holding. "Throw that dirty thing in the fire!" she blurted.

"Why?" he asked, perplexed by the sharpness of her tone.

"I don't want to be reminded of that man.''

"You ain't too partial to Siden these days, I take it.''

"I think he was the one who shot at you last Monday, and it's my fault.''

He gazed at her for a time, then looked amused. "Ah, Jessie, seems like all you family women have a talent for gatherin' up most o' the guilt in a area and claimin' it as your own. 'Ceptin' Ma, that is. She doesn't gather it up, she spreads it around." He saw that she was serious. "Now, why do you think it was Siden who tried t'ambush me?''

"Because . . . because earlier that same afternoon he got a little . . . forward and . . .''

He frowned. "How forward, Jessie?''

She nervously tucked her skirt about her knees.

"How forward?''

"It's no matter," she replied, unable to meet the intensity in his eyes. "Willie walked in from school and it came to nothing. But I said some things that could've angered Jack Siden against you."

"Like what?"

"Well, I implied that there was more between you and me than there really was. And . . . I told him that . . . that you were a hundred times the man that he could ever be." She drew up defensively. "Well, I wanted to . . . to—" she searched for the words "—take the wind out of his sails." She became pensive. "This . . . look came into his eyes, Coke. Then Willie came through the door, and he left. Later, when I heard of that attack against you, I thought—Jack Siden. Jack Siden did it. But Meg said no, that the cause of that ambush was T. C. Barrett's grudge against you. It still nags at me, though . . . that look in Siden's eyes. It chilled my soul."

He was quiet, gazing at her. "Were you hurt by this, Jessie?"

"Me? No. I'm tough."

He tossed the cigar butt aside. "Come over here, Jessie." He patted the blanket. "Closer to the fire."

She regarded him suspiciously. "It's liable to get too . . . hot over there." Her eyes shifted to the fireplace. "Your coffee's boiling."

Reaching in his saddlebags, he took out the tin cup and held it up for her. "Here," he teased. "If you keep both hands on the cup an' I hold the pot, think that'll keep things cool enough for you?"

With a wry smile, she got up and sat down closer to him, though still a few feet away, and took the cup. He poured the coffee into it. The hot tin stung her blistered fingers and sent a sharp tingle down her spine. The aromatic steam rising into her nostrils made her suddenly ravenous.

He was opening his food wallet. "Hungry?"

"A little," she admitted, the blandness of her reply belied by the eager gleam in her eye.

She immediately seized the biscuit that he offered her and bit off a chunk. It was so dry that it sponged up all the moisture in her mouth and had to be forced down in a single scurfy knot. She sipped the coffee to lubricate its descent down her throat. The parched sourness of the biscuit made the bitter coffee taste sweet by comparison. Nevertheless, she devoured the whole thing. Then, folding her hands around the coffee cup, she watched expectantly as he sawed a strip off a long, dark brown slab of something with his pocketknife.

He handed it to her. Frowning, she examined it in the firelight. It was grainy in texture and gave off a pungent meaty scent. "What animal did this come from?"

"A beef."

"How long has it been dead?"

"Don't rightly know. Don't worry, though. It's safe."

She looked at him doubtfully. "Then how did it get this way?"

"From dryin' out in the sun."

She thought a moment. "Do you, by any chance, dry this meat by hanging it out along the eaves of your barn roof?"

"On occasion we do."

"So *that's* what those things were."

"What?"

"The things that you had hanging out along the side of your barn that last weekend that Willie and I visited you. As I recall, they were completely covered with flies. They were so infested that from a distance, I thought that they were each black shining living creatures . . . greased bats or something. It wasn't until I'd gone up close that I discovered that they were things with flies swarming all over them. I thought they were your fly diverters."

"My whats?"

"Your fly diverters. Something that you ranchers put out to draw the flies away from your livestock."

His eyes crinkled. "Nope. They was the jerky."

She delicately held the jerky up before her by her fingertips. "Oh, well," she sighed. "I guess it serves its purpose. May not satisfy the hunger, but kills the appetite nonetheless." And she resolutely bit into it.

"That how you got yourself hooked up with Ornery La-Marque?" he asked quietly.

She'd just managed to tear off a hunk of the meat. She stared at him, chewing. She continued to stare at him, her eyes bulging more and more as she chewed and chewed and chewed. Finally, abandoning all hope of ever grinding that jerky down to swallow-able size and thinking it indelicate to take the mangled mess out of her mouth, she put two fingers to her throat and gulped. The chunk of meat stuck and she started gagging.

Pulling her over, Coke began massaging her back in slow, circular motions. Taking sips from the canteen that he held before her, she finally scraped the jerky down her throat.

"Oh, Coke," she gasped, wiping her watery eyes. "Have you ever considered trying the roundabout approach once in a while?"

"There's a time for circlin' an' a time for homin' on in," he replied. "Me, I always prefer startin' at the bottom line an' workin' back from there."

He set the canteen down and, putting his hand on her shoulder, kept on gently massaging her back, feeling a responsiveness growing in her. "You know I care for you an' Willie, don't you?" he said softly.

With a sigh, she moved away and faced him. "I don't want you to lose that feeling," she said sadly. "I'd like you to think of me as an honorable, decent lady . . . someone who has never been touched by evil. I'd like you to think of me as a perfect, untarnished gilded angel."

"Perfect angel?" he considered. "Hell, Jessie, I knew you wasn't that the day I met you. If you had a-been, I wouldna gotten this taken by you."

"Hell Jessie," she repeated ruefully. "The name's appropriate. . . . I've fallen so low that I'm stuck on the devil's pitchfork. The devil is Henri LaMarque, and his pitchfork is Mike O'Banion . . . that man who arrived in Dispenseme this afternoon with that warrant against me."

The color drained from her face. Her eyes grew bright in fearful challenge. "To answer your question—yes, when I was hungry enough, I was willing to try almost anything . . . trade away my self-respect, my name, and my honor . . . to earn a living for my son and me. To lay it on the bottom line as you would have me lay it on the bottom line, I let a man I cared nothing for, a man I found physically revolting, even, have his way with me. I let that man have his way with me not just once, but many, many times. For money."

Her confession seemed to make no impact on him. He calmly took the cup and poured more coffee into it. "I got the impression from Willie that you an' he was real hard up when your husband died."

She shot him an astonished look. Then, pulling farther back, she studied him. "That's generous of you . . . providing excuses for me so that I don't have to provide them myself. Anyone can give countless justifications for an immoral act, you know. Lord knows, I've tried. But as the sisters at Holy Mary's drummed into us girls often enough, a million shouted excuses cannot drown out an unconscionable act. The unconscionable act has a voice of its own and speaks for itself.''

"I see 'em as reasons, Jessie. Not excuses. I reckon I don't see sin the same way you do.''

"Of course you don't. You're a man. And men don't waste time fretting over the morality of an act . . . only whether it's expedient.''

" 'Cause the world ain't that clearly marked,'' he replied. ''Ain't a single one of us can claim t'hold the corner on virtue. You was left purty hard up when your husband died, wasn't you?''

It flustered her a little that he was so accepting. His disapproval would've given her something to fight against, at least. ''Yes!'' she said angrily. ''Yes! When that ship went down, we lost everything. Everything. Willie and I were destitute. Beggared.''

"You had no money a-tall put back?''

"Look, as I told you, my husband was a gambler, a compulsive gambler. Almost every cent he earned was bled away to feed that obsession of his . . . and then some. Naturally, I always tried to hide away what money I could.

"Only three days before he left on that last voyage, he came to me and begged for the money that he knew I'd kept from him. He desperately needed it, he said, to pay off a few old sporting debts.

"Sporting debts! What a delicate term. He told me, Coke, that if these people didn't get the money that he owed them right away, they might burn down our house or do harm to him or Willie or me. So I handed over the money, or almost all of it. What else could I do? When William sailed away that last time, I'd kept back enough cash, barely enough, to cover the month's rent on the house and buy food for Willie and me.''

Her eyes burned bitterly. ''When I learned that William, the crew, and the ship were lost, I didn't even have time to come to terms with my tragedy. Soon as word got out, our creditors swooped down on me. Waving promissory notes William had signed, those carrion birds carried away even the pictures on the walls. And since, by that time, the rent on our house was past due, Willie and I were out on the street within the month.''

Coke shook his head. ''Almost a crime for a man t'leave his love-uns in such a fix.''

"William was William," she said heavily. "I'm still angry at him, but I don't hate him anymore. Somewhere, buried down deep under all those months of pain and disillusion, there had been a beautiful time." She smiled perversely. "Could it be that I actually did love the man once? Says a lot for my judgment, doesn't it?"

"The only one who's supposed t'have perfect judgment is God," he replied. "But then, I ain't too sure 'bout that. He invented us folks, didn't he? Pore Fella. Must be kickin' Hisself raw over that-un." He paused, growing serious. "Tell me, Jessie, was it when you an' Willie found yourselves out on the street that you took up with this Ornery LaMarque?"

"Oh, no. It never entered my mind to do anything like that . . . then. I had hope. I still had a jade necklace and some other pieces of jewelry that William had brought me from some of his voyages early in our marriage. I'd sewn them into my skirt months before—to keep them out of William's hands. The jewelry wasn't worth much, really, but I thought that the money I'd get from their sale would tide us over until I found work.

"And I did look for work, Coke. I knew I wasn't stupid. I'd handled the ledgers for William's ship for years, and for us to have held on to it as long as we did took real genius, believe me. But jobs that would pay me a decent living, or at least offer the prospect of it sometime in the future, just weren't out there. Oh, I did get a few good offers from foremen, businessmen . . . but my eagerness to learn a job and do it well weren't the attractions they were after. Not from me, anyway.

"I soon learned, too, that even when it came to the most menial of jobs, deboning fish or cleaning houses, nobody wanted a woman with a four-year-old child in tow. Yet those jobs paid so little that they hardly covered the cost of food and shelter, with nothing at all left over for me to pay someone reliable to look after Willie while I was out working.

"I was almost at the end of my rope when I did find work as a seamstress for an old tailor. It paid only fifteen dollars a month, but the tailor allowed me to keep Willie with me in the shop so long as I kept him quiet and out from underfoot."

"Fifteen dollars a month sure ain't much t'go on."

"We barely scraped by. Barely. We moved into a dingy two-room walk-up."

"I think Willie told me 'bout that place."

"It was in the sleaziest part of town near the wharves. Still," she went on, a note of irony in her voice, "I earned my living honorably. The old tailor and I worked well together . . . though I knew that my days with him were numbered."

"How come?"

"He was married and he was henpecked and his wife had taken an instant dislike to me."

"Why?"

"She feared that I was out to seduce her old man, steal him from her. Her attitude baffled me, I recall, not so much because she thought so little of me but because she thought so little of her husband. As men go, he was a rather decent fellow. Unfortunately, though, his wife was making his life a battlefield. And I sensed that if he was to ever get out from under that misery and regain any peace, he'd have to divest himself of the principal cause of the strife—me."

"How long did you stay with him?"

"Almost seven months. It seemed that in those last days, fate conspired to give me some rough shakes to snap me out of my passivity, to force me to act to get Willie and me out of the dreadful circumstances we'd fallen into."

"What happened?"

"Well. To start with, there lurked on the street where we lived this . . . this creature. He was addled. From what, I don't know, maybe brain disease, or some narcotic. For some reason he'd attached himself to Willie and me. I should have taken pity on him, I suppose, but whenever I sensed him lumbering along the walkway behind us, I went cold inside.

"That last Friday, I stopped off at the market on the way home from work to buy food. It was already dusk when Willie and I turned the last corner toward home. As oftentimes in the past, that creature was there waiting. But instead of watching us pass with those disturbed, infected eyes of his, then lurching out behind us as he'd always done before, he reached out and grabbed Willie's arm. He tried to say something to Willie, but his slobbery mouthings made no sense at all.

"Willie was terrified. He cried out and struggled to get away. I tried not to panic. I asked that animal as calmly as I could to please let go of my little boy. But the more Willie screamed and fought against him, the more insistent he became.

"There were several people out on the street, I recall, but not a one of them lifted a finger to help us. They merely paused from whatever they were doing and looked on with empty eyes.

"I ordered that beast to let go of Willie. But it had no effect. I tried to pry and scratch his fingers away from Willie's arm, but they were dug in too deeply.

"Then suddenly, seeing my little boy squirming like that in that animal's clutches, like a trapped rabbit, reaching out to me, something inside me burst. I swung my marketing basket and hit him in the face with it. He yowled, and I kept hitting him in the face until he threw his hands up to protect himself. I grabbed up Willie then, and ran down the street. He loped after us, bellowing. Clasping Willie against me, I barely beat him up the steps to our rooms. I shot the bolt on the door a moment before he flung himself against it.

"He kept throwing himself against it. Willie was hysterical, sobbing, and I was shoving every piece of furniture I could move against that door to brace it. He kept raging on like that, off and on, for I don't know how long.

"Mercifully, as that awful night wore on, Willie's hysteria exhausted itself and he fell into a fitful sleep. I carried him to my bed in the next room. And while he tossed and whimpered there and that monster raged outside our door or slumped against it, I sat in a kitchen chair facing that door, a butcher knife across my lap. I was icy calm, I remember, for I knew without the slightest doubt that if that beast ever broke through and so much as took a step inside that room, I'd shove that blade into his belly.

"Fortunately for that pitiful beast and me, the door was the only sturdy thing in that entire decayed building, and it held. When, in the wee hours, he'd been silent for a long stretch of time, I pushed the furniture aside and peeked through the keyhole. He'd fallen asleep on the stair landing. Curled up there, he looked about as menacing as Meg's hound dog.

"He was still snoring there when it was time for Willie and me to leave for work. Positioned as he was across the landing, we'd have had to climb over him to get down the stairs. So we stayed put behind our door.

"A couple hours later, I heard the door to the walk-up across from ours open. I peeked through the keyhole and saw a sailor, no doubt one of my neighbor lady's customers, standing on the landing prodding that awful man with his foot. I saw that brute that had held my child and me terrorized for hours heave to his feet, look bewilderedly about, and shamble on down the stairs, scratching his head as though something had just slipped his mind.

"Willie and I were three hours late for work. When we arrived at the shop, the tailor's wife was there. I could tell by her look of malignant satisfaction that my tardiness would be the excuse they would use to get rid of me. I didn't plead, I didn't argue. I was too beaten down already. It would have only delayed the inevitable, anyway. To the tailor's credit, and his wife's disgust, he gave me an extra fifteen dollars in severance pay. But he couldn't look me in the eye.

"I took Willie's hand and we started the long walk back to that rattrap we called home. I moved in a kind of mechanical stupor, I recall. Despair, Coke, is when all emotion has dried up to a heavy stone inside you and has sunken to a point just below your knees.

"I guess if I'd been as conscious of my surroundings as I usually was, I'd have avoided what happened next. We were still blocks from home when this child—anyway, I think he was a child, children in that part of town looked like dwarfs with forty-year-old faces—anyway, this little ruffian came bolting out of an alley. He knocked Willie into the gutter and made off with my purse.

"That purse contained my severance pay, and now the only money I had left in the world was the two dollars I always kept hidden in my shoes. The rent on our apartment was due the following week. And there was almost no food in our cupboards, since the food I'd bought the night before, I'd lost in getting Willie away from that beast.

"The next morning, Sunday, I was dressing for mass when Willie called me from the bedroom, 'Mommy, do people sleep with their eyes open?' I hurried into the room and went to the window where he was standing.

"It's chilling, Coke, to realize that while I'd slept, just on the other side of the wall, twenty feet down, some poor man had been viciously murdered. I'd probably even heard his dying moans blending among all the other night noises.

"I sent Willie out of the room, yet I couldn't pull myself away from that window. I kept staring down into those lifeless eyes as though I were looking into a mirror. I realized how much of this squalor we'd numbed ourselves to, had become blind to.

"I walked into the other room and looked at my Willie through changed eyes. I saw that no longer was he the rosy-cheeked little busybody who'd once kept our home bubbling with life. Now he barely cast a shadow in a room. At four years old, he couldn't help but to absorb my silent defeat and make it his own.

"We didn't go to mass that morning. Instead we went for a walk, and we kept walking until we'd left that forsaken part of town behind, and found ourselves on lovely broad boulevards.

"It was as though we'd crossed into another land. There was space to breathe, without that feeling of heavy defeat pressing in from all sides. The air was fresh, and sweet with flowers. The birds truly sang there, the people we passed had a certitude, a self-possession about them. And it cut through me all the more deeply how Willie and I had changed.

"And yet, perhaps it wasn't too late. I'd noticed that in merely crossing into this other world, Willie had shed much of his list-lessness. He was perking up, chattering and pointing things out to me almost in his old way, a little skip in his step.

"We came to a park, and I sat down on the ground in the shade of a tree. I didn't take a park bench, I was afraid that would look too presumptuous. I'd caught the sidelong glances people had sent us along the way, and knew that our faded and worn clothes had identified us as trespassers into their sunlight life.

"Oh, how I hated those fashionable people! How I despised them! They seemed far too vital, too carefree, too self-satisfied. I wanted to leap on them and strip away all that pious certitude, those trappings, and see what kind of animals they'd become then.

"Never again did I want my son and me to be allotted among that city's refuse. We didn't deserve it, neither Willie nor me. I wanted to break away from such an unfair place where such disparity among people could be allowed to exist. But all the money I had to my name was a dollar and fifty cents.

"I looked at my little boy scampering there. He had a right to a childhood free from fear and deprivation, the kind of childhood that would fill him with hope for the future and belief in himself. I was not doing right by him.

"The sisters at Holy Mary's had often said that the meek shall inherit the earth. Well, I'd been meek, all right, and I was grove-ling in life's dirt. To hell with inheriting the earth.

"Up until that day, I'd taken the blows that life had dealt me and I'd reacted to them with honor and decency. Oh, yes, I'd been decent. I'd held fast to my principles and my honor . . . while the

368   Ann Gabriel

bright promise that burned in my son was steadily being extin-
guished. What are principles, pride, and honor, anyway, but
vanities that only the well-fixed can afford.

"I'd tried to find honest employment by offering my intelligence and my willingness to learn and to do hard work. Those
qualities in me had counted for nothing. There was only one thing
that I could see that I did have going for me in this world. I was
pretty."

She swept up a handful of kindling and hurled it into the fire.
It immediately became popping sparks that were snuffled up the
chimney.

"Now, the number of ways that a woman in my circumstances
might use her prettiness was very limited. Half measures would
not suffice. With less than two dollars to my name, I couldn't
sally forth to cultivate some man's affection and support while
decorously fending off his advances. Such demure and coy flir-
tation from a penniless widow with a child would seem pitifully
self-deceptive. Laughable. Any man would see through it, and
realize that he needn't play any of the conventional games.

"Yet the thought of becoming a lady of the evening or working
in a fancy house—that sort of life turned my stomach. It wouldn't
do Willie any good to have a mother like that, anyway. So I decided, if I must sell myself, I should try to do it in such a way as
to give the *appearance* of respectability.

"I went over in my mind, then, those men I'd encountered
during my search for work who'd hinted that they'd hire me and
pay me well . . . provided I was 'cooperative.' After considering
them, I decided that they were not, a single one of them, in po-
sitions strong enough to compensate me sufficiently for what I
deemed my 'cooperation' to be worth. If I was to prostitute myself, I decided, I should try to get as much out of it as I could. It
was at about that time that I saw a carriage that looked like Henri's
turn a corner down the street, and I thought of him."

"You already knew him?"

"Yes, I'd gotten to know him a few years before, in my role
as William's bookkeeper. Among other things, Henri owns an
import-export firm. William occasionally carried freight for his
company. And, I later learned, he did some smuggling and gunrunning for Henri, too.

"I met Henri one summer while William was away on a voyage. William's gambling was getting out of control at that time

and we were strapped for money. So I went through my ledgers and made a list of those people and firms that were delinquent in paying the fees they owed us. Then I set out to collect them.

"The very rich are often the most negligent in paying their debts, you know. They assume, I suppose, that the privilege of serving them should be payment enough. Or else they find some debts just too petty for them to concern themselves with, though the people that they owe are in no position to consider them petty.

"In any case, Henri's company was among those that were past due in paying us. When I stopped at his office, I didn't expect to meet the great Henri LaMarque himself. But he was there and he took an immediate interest in me.

"Ordering a clerk to make out a bank draft for me, he led me into his huge office and offered me a chair and some brandy. I didn't object. I'd walked miles that day. I was thirsty and my feet hurt.

"On the surface Henri's manner was gentlemanly. But every so often he'd send me a conjecturing look or slip in some doubled-edged comment or question. Ordinarily it would've put me on my guard. But I felt in no danger from him; couldn't take him that seriously. I thought the situation amusing.

"You see, Coke, Henri was so fat, he was a clutter of circles. Overhanging circles, semicircles, half circles . . . loose circles forming and dissolving with his movements. Everywhere your eyes fell, there were those wiggly, jiggly circles. And I couldn't spot a single hair on him, either. His head was shinier than an ostrich egg. I found it rather comical that he'd believe I might fall victim to his charms.

"Eventually the conversation turned down that same old, well-trod path . . . how lonely it must be for me with my husband gone so much of the time. I said it didn't bother me at all, I just kept repainting the kitchen. When he hinted about how much business he'd channel William's way given the proper inducements, I decided it was time to go.

"I ran into Henri quite often after that. He'd be passing in his carriage on those mornings when I'd be out walking to the market. He'd direct his driver to stop and offer to take me wherever I wanted to go.

"I accepted . . . always left him laughing and preening himself." She shrugged. "Same old game. It was good for William's business, and I saw no reason to hurt Henri by turning him down outright.

"After William's death, I thought of Henri only once, during those first weeks when I'd been searching for work. The notion crossed my mind to ask him to help me get a job. And that notion brought me the first amusement I'd known in months. There was little doubt in my mind about the price of his help, and picturing myself in a compromising position with that hairless blob made me burst out laughing.

"But that was when I still had hope. Sitting in that park on that bitter Sunday morning, I no longer had such illusions. And picturing myself in a compromising position with Henri LaMarque didn't seem the least bit funny. It seemed frighteningly, revoltingly real. I knew I *would* carry it out, to get Willie and me out of that sewer we'd sunken into.

"That afternoon I threw most of my money away on a good meal for Willie, and pony rides. I didn't want to leave myself a single out from the course I'd set for myself.

"Next day, I went in search of Henri. I didn't find him. I sold my wedding band for food and kept trying. A couple days later I caught up with him at his office.

"He was surprised to see me. And very pleased, I could tell. He said that he'd tried to find me when the news of William's death reached him but that I'd already dropped out of sight. He asked me where I'd gone. When I told him where Willie and I lived, he deduced our plight immediately, and for the first time seemed to notice the condition of our shoes and clothes. His eyes took on that cynical look that the rich tend to get when they suspect you might be one of the multitude out to relieve them of a bit of their bankroll. That look didn't last long, though. It turned into a sly gleam. With a side wink to one of his clerks, he handed Willie over to his secretary and invited me to go for a ride in his carriage."

She paused, her face working. "When we got back from that carriage ride, I had my job—blackjack dealer at a place Henri owned called Ivory Ives. It paid a hundred twenty dollars a month."

Eyes narrowing, she looked away, a rough edge coming to her voice. "As soon as I'd gotten Willie away from Henri's office and was back on the street, I went to a shop and stared at my reflection in the window. I don't know what I expected to find . . . some change in my features, I guess. Mostly, though, I puzzled at my own absence of emotion. It was as though during the time in Henri's carriage, the real me had slipped away somewhere, and was pulling the strings of my actions from afar . . . like a puppeteer who didn't care to associate himself with the performance he was giving.

"I became aware then of the coins that Henri had pressed into my hand when we'd left his carriage. I looked down at them—four twenty-dollar gold pieces. I should've been ashamed at that moment, I guess, but all I could feel was relief, enormous relief. That money meant food and shelter for my son and me.

"Over the next several days I tried to keep occupied with learning my new job and looking for a new home for Willie and me. I tried not to think of that other thing, that bargain I'd made to secure that home and that job." A look of desolation rose in her eyes. "I tried not to think of the way Henri's flesh had jiggled with the rocking of the carriage, the way the tiny gold rings on his hands pinched into his fat fingers, the dissipation around his eyes, the puffy looseness about his mouth. And whenever the reality of it threatened to cut me through with self-revulsion, I'd tell myself that this was the way of the world, these were the terms I must bend to. But there were times when no matter how hard I tried to reason it away, I felt vile, contaminated. The entire Pacific Ocean wouldn't have been enough water to wash me clean.

"At those times I'd try to console myself. I'd reason that once Henri had satisfied himself with me a couple more times, he'd begin to lose interest. After all, he could put that same money into other palms, have the pleasure and variety of new conquests. And by that time I'd have proven myself such a top-notch dealer at Ivory Ives that I'd be allowed to continue working there."

She stopped, and frowning, tilted her head. With the exception of the lazy drone of a cricket and an occasional feeble sputter from the dying fire, the hut was quiet. The storm had moved on.

Coke became aware of the silence, too, and looked away. It came as almost a relief to her when he did, for during the time she'd been talking, his eyes had never left hers; those attentive, reassuring eyes, steadily drawing out her most painful memories and emotions.

She marveled at her own candor. Yesterday she'd have tried any evasion, any subterfuge. But now it was all over. She had nothing to lose. She'd be gone from here tomorrow.

🌸 Chapter 44

COKE GOT UP and walked to the doorway. Arm up, he leaned to the side in it and looked outside. The night was still, breathless. Not a twig or a blade of grass stirred. Leaves and debris lay nestled around the house and at the feet of brush and trees like discarded nightclothes. The last of the line of fence that had been standing an hour ago had been wrested from the ground and lay slung across the yard. Not a glint of moisture could he see on stone, wood, or wall. Or earth.

Hooking his thumbs in his belt, he gazed up at the sky. One by one the stars were sprinkling through the gently unraveling blue-gray fleece of clouds.

"God-damn constipated sky," he muttered. "All it ever does is rumble an' blow hot air."

"I'm sorry," she said.

He turned back into the room. "That's all right. Though I'd like t'put the blame on someone, I reckon it won't be you."

He stooped down, tossed a large hack of wood onto the sleepy embers of the fire, prodded them awake with a stick, then meditatively watched the hungry flames go gobbling down the wood in a line.

"Did you have this Ornery pegged right?" he asked, lifting his dark eyes to hers.

"No," she said disgustedly. "He bought a toupee. He gave me trinkets, which I sold. And treated me as his ornament—which he'd bought. He enjoyed flaunting me, though only in back rooms. I was his and always, he held the threat of imminent poverty over my head. Whenever I tried to evade his 'summons' to his country home, he had it relayed to me by way of the pit boss at the casino. The implication in that was clear.

"And let me tell you, my holding down that job was in no way Henri's charity. I was a darn good dealer. I took in three, four times as much money each and every night that I was there than that measly hundred twenty a month that they paid me.''

"I cain't see why you had t'work for your keep a-tall.''

"You mean, why couldn't he have just kept me?''

"Yup, seein' as how he was so well heeled an' all.''

"Well, in the beginning, I don't think that it was something that would occur to him.''

"How come?''

"For one, I'd made it clear that it was the job I wanted from him. And for another, he wouldn't want his wife to find out.''

"He had a wife?''

"Yes, from a very prominent San Francisco family. The sort of family with the old, aristocratic name that opens all the right doors. Trouble was, though, that in the branch of family Henri's wife came from, the kind of money needed to maintain that high-falutin style of living had about run out. So, as a marriageable young woman, she'd been respectability on the hunt for new money. And Henri, of course, had been new money on the hunt for respectability. The perfect match . . . only not quite. I got the impression that Henri's blue-blood in-laws never quite deigned to bestow upon him the acceptance he wanted. But they got what they wanted out of him—money. I found a perverted sort of justice in that. What Henri was doing to me, they were doing to him.''

"Reglar slab-sided, brushpopped steer tryin' t'pose as a registered Hereford bull.''

"Weren't they all,'' she answered scornfully. She winced, and looking down, shook her head. "As for me, I'd made a loathsome trade-off. Loathsome. Yes, I did get my little boy into a nice neighborhood. He had a yard to play in, fresh food to eat. I could afford to pay a good woman to look after him while I was at my job. And I did like my work, especially the hours. They allowed me to be at home during the day while Willie was awake and needed me the most. And later I could afford to enroll Willie in a fine private school. . . .''

She fell silent, brooding. "Yet all those things I stood to lose if I refused Henri anything.'' She looked away.

"He didn't lose interest, as I'd hoped. And the longer I was involved with him, the more I came to realize what he was capable of and the more fear I felt. It's like thinking you're becoming entangled with only a foul, squishy worm and discovering that it's really a serpent.''

"How d'you mean, Jessie?"

"I doubt Henri's in-laws had the least idea that he was leading a double life. Working in the casino, though, I heard a lot and I saw a lot.

"Gradually it began to sink in on me that Henri probably had his hand in half the sordid things that went on in the city, from bribery of judges, public officials, and the police, to murder. Most of his riches came from gunrunning and smuggling . . . smuggling not only of banned goods but of desperate human cargoes from China . . . and opium.

"In the darker world that I saw him in, he was always surrounded by dubious types. They were cigar-chomping braggarts in cheap, showy clothes, quick with the wink and the vulgar remark and slick at slipping the money into their pockets. Or they were the kind that could slither in and out of a room virtually unnoticed, leaving only a chill in the air.

"During the day I might read in the newspaper that Mr. and Mrs. Henri LaMarque had held a glittering reception in their mansion on Nob Hill, honoring some European soprano in town for a performance. And that night I'd notice him whispering to Mike O'Banion, then I'd watch Mike go slinking out the door, a little smile on his face as though he'd been sent on a mission he expected to enjoy carrying out.

"I'd begun to see what an ugly trap I'd gotten myself into; how powerful and dangerous Henri was. I feared the consequences if I ever tried to get free of him. He wouldn't have tolerated that. I knew then that my only hope would be to take Willie and just disappear one day, vanish without a trace. I didn't have the means, though, or any idea how to carry that off. So, biding my time, I began putting money aside and planning toward that day. . . ."

Her eyes took on a lifeless, forsaken cast. "And believe me, Coke, it's hard to bide your time when you're repeatedly called upon to subject yourself to the most unbearable and demeaning of torments and to pretend that you like it. And I did pretend . . . a lot." Her voice faded to a whisper. "It was less rough that way."

Then she gathered her strength and pulled herself up. "Henri's will was strong, but so is mine . . . only, I move it underground from time to time.

"I set a week in July as the time for Willie and me to make our escape. Every July Henri and his wife and the circle they moved in vacationed at some fancy resort down the coast. Having him out of town, I figured, would give me several days' head start.

"But in May, trouble started brewing in Henri's organization. One morning I read in the newspaper that a ship had been found adrift south of San Francisco. All hands on board had been massacred and the cargo stolen. From evidence found in the hold, it was determined that the ship had been smuggling opium. The pirates had probably lain in wait in some inlet, then intercepted the ship before it moved in to make its delivery.

"That night the atmosphere in the casino was loaded with tension, whispered meetings everywhere, hurried comings and goings. Jonah, the pit boss, came over. He told me that the pirated ship was Henri's, that somebody in on the operation had obviously turned renegade. Only an insider could've known the course, and just when and where that ship was supposed to arrive. Jonah, knowing my relationship with Henri, probably thought I cared.

"Three weeks later another of Henri's opium ships was intercepted, with the same result. Jonah told me then that he was going to get to the bottom of it. If the opium turned up on the streets, he'd use his connections to trace it back to the turncoat in Henri's organization. I thought Jonah was only strutting and puffing. As far as I could tell, he was only a minor functionary distributing bribes to policemen and lower-lever politicians. He was ambitious to move up with Henri, though, and he did come from a rough neighborhood where a lot of shady activity was going on."

She paused, a tortured look rising in her eyes. "The night two days later will always be with me." Blinking rapidly, she grimaced and looked away.

Coke took her hand. "What happened, honey?" he coaxed.

She hesitated, then sighed heavily. "I was working at my table at the casino. Business was brisk that night. The place was a beehive, and the commotion, the confusion of voices, the cigar smoke thick in the air, were suffocating me. I felt sick inside, and so downhearted." She looked down, forcing her words out with great difficulty. "Henri had sent for me that afternoon and it had been an ordeal, so . . . so horrid. He was still incensed, burning with vengeance at the treachery inside his organization. And . . . and . . . ." She put a trembling hand to her forehead. "And he took it out on me. He sensed a change in me, I think. It was only a month to the time that I'd set to escape and I wasn't pretending so much anymore. I was growing distant—which he could never,

never abide.'' Her face changed as some agonizing memory rose up and caught her by the throat.

She peeked up at Coke, and flinched. ''Don't look at me like that,'' she whispered.

''Jessie . . .''

She turned away, covering the side of her face with hand. ''It hurts when you look at me.''

He moved then, around behind her. Putting an arm around her waist and another around her shoulders, he gently leaned her back against him. ''All right, honey,'' he said. ''I ain't lookin'. You can go on.''

She seemed to recoil from him a little, but then, slowly, she gave way.

''It's all right,'' he repeated softly, thinking how fragile and tender she felt in his arms. ''You can go on.''

A kind of heaviness seemed to settle through her. ''I was still trembling inside when I came down the stairs of Henri's country home,'' she went on tonelessly. ''I heard Jonah. He was in the library boasting to Henri that he was within a breath of pinpointing the Judas in Henri's organization. Henri was skeptical about that.

''That night at the casino I didn't see Jonah out on the floor, but I thought I glimpsed him once moving out of a back room. The feeling that I was drowning in that heavy atmosphere grew overpowering, and I closed my table and went out to the alley at the back of the casino to catch my breath and be alone. It had just rained, and everything looked varnished.

''I knew I had to hang on for another month. I hoped I could stomach it that long. Henri would summon me back the next afternoon, I knew, give me perfume or some bauble to atone for being a bad boy. But''—her voice grew hollow—''the outcome would still be the same. One month . . . an eternity.

''I went back into the casino. I'd just stepped inside, when I heard a kind of mewling down below in the cellar, then a soft thump. Thinking that a cat had gotten trapped down there, I started down the stairs. I was only a few steps from the bottom when something put me on my guard, a shadow sliding through the dim light from the door . . . an odd gurgling sound.'' He could feel her body tensing in his arms. ''I crossed over to the shadows and crept the rest of the way down. . . .'' She seemed to run out of breath then; it was coming in small, hiccuping spasms as if it were being squeezed out of her. "I saw Jonah," she said in a tortured voice, and swallowed hard, unable to go on.

Snuggling her closer, Coke put his hand over her forehead and pressed her head back against his shoulder. "Look at the fire, Jessie. What did you see?"

She gazed into the flicking flames. "He was on his knees . . . Jonah . . . trying to breathe. But he couldn't."

"Why couldn't he, honey?"

"His throat . . . it had been"—her voice rose to a squeak —"sliced. The blood . . . it started trickling out. Then Jonah gurgled, and slowly crumbled forward to the door. And far behind him . . . back in the cellar, looking down . . . cleaning his knife . . ."

His arms tightened around her. "Who?"

"Mike O'Banion." A shudder ran through her and she turned her head, pressing her forehead against his neck.

Resting his face in her hair, he soothingly stroked her temple. "What did you do then?" he whispered.

She was quiet for a time, then turned her head back to face the hypnotic movement of the fire. "I started backing up the steps. I had one hand out against the limestone wall, bracing me. A small, pebbly chunk of it crumbled loose under my hand about halfway up, and it rattled down the steps. I sensed a swift movement down below . . . like a displacement of air. I spun around and ran the rest of the way up. As I whipped around the corner at the top of the stairs, my skirt snagged on a nail sticking out. I ripped it loose and fled into the casino. I moved over to the wall and started edging to the front entrance. The bright lights, the laughter, felt obscene.

"I saw Mike appear in the doorway I'd just come through, and peer around at the crowds. I slipped behind some men gathered around a roulette table. I was afraid for Mike to see my face. I knew it would give me away. When I peeked at the doorway again, he was gone. I didn't know if he'd turned back or had come out into the casino and was moving through the crowds. I made it to the front entrance, slipped outside, and started running.

"I must've run almost five blocks before I started becoming aware of where I was. I collapsed to my hands and knees in a recessed doorway. I don't know how long I crouched there, staring into a glassy pool of water. Finally I stood up and started listening . . . listening . . . for the sound of footsteps moving up the street behind me. Then it occurred to me that Mike O'Banion wasn't the kind whose footsteps would sound if he didn't want them to.

"It took me a long, long time before I gathered the courage to come out of that doorway and start making my way, hugging the shadows, toward the cable car stop. It was a relief to see up ahead a small group of people waiting there under the streetlight. I wondered why they stared at me as I approached. Then I realized I had no wrap, and they were looking at a woman wearing a gaudy evening gown, all splattered and streaked with mud, and a rhinestone hair comb. It was supposed to be anchoring my curls at the top of my head, but now I felt it dangling behind an ear. And I remembered that I'd left my purse back in the cloakroom of the casino. The bench at the stop was full. Three old women sat there, looking at me with pert disapproval. I silently blessed them for being there, anyway, even though it didn't improve their opinion of me when I sat down on the curb, pulled off my shoe, and shook out the money for my fare.

"While I was riding in the cable car, I noticed the tear in the side of my skirt and discovered that a piece had ripped off. I realized that it was probably still hooked on that nail at the top of the cellar stairs at the casino—if Mike O'Banion hadn't found it yet. Even if he never found it, he'd soon notice who was conspicuously missing. He'd know I'd seen what he'd done in the cellar, that I could finger him as the traitor in Henri's organization. Willie and I were on the train heading west before dawn."

Jessica stopped, and became aware of his cheek nestling in her hair. She tilted her head a little toward it, gently moving it from side to side in a kind of caressing motion.

"Was it just today that you found out 'bout that warrant against you?" he asked softly, inhaling the windblown aroma of her, the clean, faint scent of soap and lavender.

"I already knew about it," she said tiredly. "I saw a wanted poster against me while I was on the run. It was tacked up on the wall of a train station in New Mexico."

"You know the charge against you, then."

"Embezzlement. The embezzlement of eight hundred fifty dollars," she repeated slowly. "Henri must've pulled that number out of the air." A lonesome sadness seemed to settle over her. "You know, I'd thought he might resort to the law to get me back. But seeing that poster there that morning . . . it came as a hard blow. I was just beginning to feel safe. Hopeful. Seeing that poster brought me to my knees.'' She paused, then added softly, ''But it was there at that same railroad station that I met a beautiful . . . beautiful lady called Meg, and she pulled me up again.''

Her melancholy seemed to deepen. ''Coke . . .'' she began, pensively fingering a button on his shirt cuff.

''Yes.''

''I want you to know that if, after you think about all this, you find that you despise me . . . it's all right. You have no obligation toward me. I can go on. I'll—''

''Jessie.'' Taking her shoulders, he turned her around to face him. ''Look at me, Jessie. C'mon, now.'' He lifted her chin. ''Look at me. I don't despise you.''

''You haven't thought about it.''

''I've thought 'bout it.''

''No.'' She shook her head. ''Not really.''

''Dispenseme may seem like the end o' the world, honey, but it ain't dropped off it yet. Seth showed me that wanted poster over a month ago.''

It took her a while to grasp what he'd said. ''Why didn't you tell me?'' she breathed.

''Didn't know how you'd take the news. An' I was gettin' kinda partial t'havin' you around.'' He drew her forward into his arms again. ''As close around as I could manage.''

''Meg?'' she said after a time. ''Does Meg know?''

''She told Seth a long while back t'be on the lookout for that poster an' t'burn it.''

Jessica remembered a dusty train depot somewhere in West Texas, Meg at the ticket window. ''Three . . . for m'daughter, m'grandson, an' me.'' Dear Meg had known all along, and had still believed in her.

She became aware of his hand slowly stroking her back, and grew very still. ''You haven't thought about Henri,'' she whispered.

''It's you I've thought 'bout . . . not that Ornery. Wanta know somethin'? I think you're pretty decent.''

She lifted her face and frowned at him. ''Me? Decent?''

''Yep, 'cause there're some things you just cain't seem able to accept about yourself, whether you had good reason for doin' 'em or not. An' outa all the gorgeous women I've ever seen, you don't use it half as much as you could. You don't use it t'play on men's emotions, play 'em against one another, t'work 'em t'get what you want outa 'em like I've seen a lotta purty women do if only t'feed their vanity. You may be a mite on the ornery side, an' that's all right 'cause there's somethin' honest about it. But I don't think that you have it in you t'hurt reglar folks too deep. *I'd* say you're probably too damn honest for your own damn good.''

She seemed to find that a bit discomfiting. ''Yes . . . sure,'' she answered dryly. ''I make a better harlot than a hypocrite.''

''Ah, Jessie,'' he said, his arms tightening around her. ''Did I say that? You're the one who's hardest on yourself. Not me. Try t'rest easy, honey. Nobody you care 'bout round here is heatin' up t'hate you.'' He brushed a kiss on her temple. ''It's more in t'other di-rection.''

She softened against him. It felt so good. Until this moment she hadn't realized how much she'd needed this . . . someone, someplace to rest her head. The comfort and acceptance that she found in him was like warmth to a chilled and unprotected soul, sweet water to a thirsting throat, and she drank it in and savored it.

Then stealthily, the tenor of those feelings started changing. She felt the solidity of his body burning through her, and hungered to press herself, harder and harder, into it. She felt his lips moving insistently along her face and neck, his hands traveling through the back of her hair and over her shoulders and waist, gaining momentum and intensity.

She thought of that dark dawn outside the barn and remembered that it was this other thing that he was after from her, too . . . like those others. And though she tried to keep them closed off, the raw memories, the noxious images and sensations, broke loose and clawed through her, twisting the passion that was stirring in her to self-disgust and shame.

''No!'' She struggled away, distraught, on the edge of panic. She scrambled back, and clambered to her feet.

''I've got to get out of here,'' she gasped, keeping her face turned away from him. ''I've got to get out of here and be alone.''

And wheeling around, she plunged outside into the darkness.

Chapter 45

THE VAPOR OF light drifted down from the door, condensing on the ground in a patch, pale gold and rippling like new-poured beer. He found her standing in the shadows at the edge of it, gazing down, the most solitary-looking figure he'd ever seen.

"I'm still going to Mexico," she said, not looking up. "A moment ago I even thought of stealing your horse and doing it now."

"But you didn't."

"Didn't think you deserved it. Only those who deserve it should be robbed. Besides, I hate horses. The last one I had wouldn't move, and yours would probably stampede me straight back to Dispenseme." She lifted her eyes, a grave uneasiness moving behind them. "Do you think Mike O'Banion's on his way, Coke?"

"Nope. Seth'll hold him in town till you get clear."

"Oh, but Mike's very, very devious," she replied. "He can assume almost any guise, be disarmingly smooth, even charming. He knows the law, and he's been deputized by a San Francisco court."

"How come he knows law?"

"Before Henri took him under his wing, he'd had so many close scrapes with it that he couldn't help but learn the system, pick up its jargon. When he wants to, he can sound like a Supreme Court justice. He can be so persuasive, Coke."

"An' he can talk his big-city britches off," Coke replied. "But it's Meg that Seth'll listen to."

"He could kill Seth. He could kill Meg," she said in a hushed tone.

"An' that'd be borrowin' a helluvalotta trouble that he don't need. C'mon, Jessie, I thought you said that the bastard was cunning. He's a city fella. His hind cheeks have probably never been smacked by the topside of a saddle. How's he gonna track you down? Ain't no city streets in these parts for him t'go prowlin' aroun'. He needs Seth t'find you, an' he needs Seth if he's gonna

381

use that warrant t'get you away. An' Seth'll make durn sure t'hold him in place t'night.''

His assurance still hadn't erased the fear from her eyes.

"Come here," he said, putting an arm around her shoulders. He guided her over to the corner of the hut. "Look." He nodded toward the northeast, where on the distant horizon the dense, leaden clouds kept quivering and reddening. "The storm's bearin' down on Dispenseme now. Nobody'll be settin' out from there t'night. You're safe here. Now, let's go into the hut."

She looked back at the door and quickly stepped away from him.

"What?"

Avoiding his eyes, she fidgeted at the hair on her temple. "You might expect . . . and I don't know if I can . . ."

He realized at that moment the other cause of her fear. "Ah, Jessie," he admonished gently. "Just 'cause the first few hombres you met up with in your life was dirty skunks . . . that don't necessarily make the rest of us stinkers."

Surprise rose in her eyes, then the tension subsided a little and a wistful smile touched her lips. "Well . . . I don't know, Coke. . . . As I recall that first day I met you . . ."

"You'd spent sittin' in the store, addin' up ledgers, dabbin' lavender behind your ears, an' leg-pullin' love-starved cow-boys," he finished for her. "Whilst I'd been out in the boilin' sun soppin' up smoke, dust, an' cattle fumes."

The smile almost lifted to her eyes. "Oh, Coke." She shyly touched his arm. "Hard as I try, I can't help liking you. When I'm gone from here, thinking of you will make me happy."

"I ain't dead yet," he said. "Let's go back in the hut."

"I still aim to go to Mexico," she warned. "I've made my plans."

The fire seemed to have a settling effect on her, so he dropped another dry log on it. "How's your Spanish?" he asked, keeping his tone matter-of-fact.

"What?" she asked, kneeling down on his bedroll.

"You're set on goin' t'Mexico, so how's your Spanish?"

"Well, I've picked up a few words here and there since I arrived in Dispenseme," she replied, primly smoothing her skirt around her.

"Like what?"

"Like *buenos días, por favor, sí, muchas gracias, adiós.*"

"Hell," he muttered, sitting down before her. "Them words is more likely t'get you into trouble than ever get you out. Seems like you left out a damn important part o' your plannin'."

The spirit flared in her eyes. "I've only been in Dispenseme three months," she retorted indignantly. "To my knowledge there isn't a single Spanish grammar book in the entire town. What should I have done to learn the language, huh? Toss a gunnysack over some poor Mexican passing by, drag him home, and order him to start talkin'?"

He suppressed a smile. He enjoyed seeing her snapping back. "How do you expect t'get by down there," he answered mildly, "them not understandin' what you're a-sayin' an' you not understandin' what they're a-sayin'?"

"There must be some people in Mexico who speak English."

"Wouldn't bank on it." He paused, growing circumspect. "Course, it's possible you could find somebody t'help . . . if the persuasion's right. How much money you got on you?"

She mumbled something.

"How much?"

"Four twenty-dollar gold pieces . . . in my shoes."

"That all? Eighty dollars?"

"Mexico is an inexpensive country, I've heard," she said lamely.

"Depends on how savvy you are. An' far as I can tell, Jessie, you ain't bein' savvy 'bout this a-tall."

"You don't need to be insulting."

"Well, ye gods, woman. Here you are, fixin' t'go tearin' off into a foreign country. You don't know the lingo. You don't know no one livin' there. You don't know how t'live offa the land. An' you ain't got but a piddlin' eighty dollars to your name." He shook his head. That has got t'be 'bout the most boggy-brained thing that I have ever heard."

"Don't underestimate me, Coke," she retorted. "My life hasn't been easy, but I've learned from it. So much that I can be even as dirty and underhanded as a tough-talkin', gun-totin' Texas cowboy. I can be smarter and more resourceful than you give me credit for."

"But O'Banion did catch up with you here," he pointed out.

She seemed to waver a bit, then straightened up. "I've learned from that, too. I'll be more clever next time."

"What do you plan t'do better, if you don't mind my askin'?"

"O'Banion won't be looking for a woman with a little boy anymore. By myself in Mexico I can change my appearance, move a lot faster. Then when I see an opening, I'll slip back into the States and head for some large city along the Atlantic, maybe New York or Boston. It was a mistake to hope that I could disappear in South Texas, where I'll always stick out as the new woman around. In a big city, though, almost everyone you see is a stranger. I'll get a job, and when I feel that the coast is clear, I'll send for Willie."

He regarded her quietly. "I think you should go back to Dispenseme."

"No!" she almost shouted.

"You're not alone here."

"I don't want to have to deal with those monsters from San Francisco. I don't want to have to look at them, to think of them. I don't want them anywhere near me," she shouted out. "Can't you understand?"

"You won't solve nothin' by runnin'."

"What do you think I should do, eh? That warrant is still out there. Henri has all the big guns and the ammunition. I don't even have a slingshot. My only recourse is to have the fastest feet in the West."

"An' what'll that get you? You could just be puttin' it off till the next time, runnin' the risk o' havin' t'face 'em down in a lot lonesomer place to you than this is."

His words had struck a nerve, and it showed on her face. "Maybe that won't happen," she said unconvincingly.

He only looked at her.

"Well, it's a risk I'll just have to take," she went on. "I know my enemy, Coke, and believe me, the unknown in Mexico, or wherever else, is far, far better. There is no way that you can convince me to go back. No way."

"Jessie," he said reasonably. "You'll still stick out in a city. Wherever you go you'll draw attention to yourself 'cause your too damn purty. An' as you've learned by now, purty can work for you an' it can work against you. An' even if we can throw O'Banion off your tracks for good for you down here, that warrant can still catch up with you down the line."

"Well . . . so . . ." she cried exasperatedly. "So luck is against me and I am taken back to San Francisco in chains. Henri may think that he has me where he wants me—prison over my head instead of poverty. But let me tell you, it won't work. Not this time. Never again. He can just throw me in jail. I don't care. I wouldn't mind. That's the way I grew up—confined.''

"An' Willie . . . what about him?''

The defiance went out of her. "Willie," she repeated, her shoulders sagging. "He'd probably be better off without me.''

"No, he wouldn't.''

"Ever since I left the Home, every choice I've made has been the wrong one. I can't hold anyone to blame for that but myself.''

"But you love the little fellow.''

"Children need more than love. Meg could provide him a better, more stable home than I could.''

"But Meg ain't you.''

"Yes," she conceded bleakly. "Meg isn't me. Blind, headstrong fool though I am, nobody, not even dear Meg, can love that little boy the way I do. We're so close sometimes, my Willie and me, that we almost breathe together.'' Catching her breath at the thought, she cupped her hands over her eyes as though the room had suddenly grown too bright. "If I were to . . . to leave him, it would wound him. More deeply than anything else ever could. And it would be the kind of wound that would never heal properly. How . . . how could I do that to my little boy?'' Tears were streaming down her cheeks, and with shaking fingers she tried to wipe them away.

"You know that if you're ever taken back t'San Fran-cisco,'' he pressed on, "it ain't likely t'be no jail that you'll wind up in.''

She looked up at him through her tears, the anguish deepening on her face. "Why're you doing this to me, Coke?'' she asked brokenly. "You know I can't go back to Dispenseme. I thought you were my friend.''

He pulled his handkerchief out of his pocket and put it into her hand. "I am, Jessie. I am.''

He watched her for a time, then heaved a sigh. "Tell you what,'' he began, eyeing her closely. "There's a fella I know, lives 'bout twenty miles south o' the border. Married. Has a big spread, big hacienda. He might could put you up while we buy a little time.''

She stopped dabbing her eyes and looked up at him. "He's a friend of yours?'' she asked hopefully.

"Well, not exactly,'' he replied. "Ever since we Sanderses settled in these parts, whenever this fella's herds started gettin' a little low, he'd slip across the Rio Grande and borry a few from us. An' now an' again, we've taken it upon ourselves t'borry a few back. Every once in a long while this fella an' me meet up with each other, an' like a pair o' wide-eyed innocents, we start into wonderin' why all this shameful pilferin's been goin' on. We talk it out, shake hands, an' go our separate ways. After a spell, though, thing's start gettin' prickly again.

"But here's the point; every time I meet up with this honcho, he says real po-lite t'come an' visit him sometime. Says, *'Mi casa es su casa.'* My house is your house.'' he shrugged. ''Fella cain't blame me if I take him up on it.''

"I'd be imposing," she said glumly.

"Well, so what? They'd still treat you good. Go agin their in-bred, upper-crust Mexicano graciousness not to. An' you'd be safe, have a good place t'hide out in till we figger your next move.''

"But Mike O'Banion . . . he's so evil. My going there could put these people in danger without their knowing it.''

"Don't worry 'bout O'Banion.''

"Don't *worry* about him!'' she exclaimed.

"We'll take care of him on this side.''

"But you don't know him, Coke. You don't know what he can be like.''

"You gave me a pretty good idea. But, Jessie, he don't know me. And there are some folks in these parts who owe me a few favors. We'll send that Bunion polecat off on such a wild-goose chase that it'll take him a good six months just t'find his way back to here.''

She drew closer to him. "You'd really do that for me . . . wouldn't you?''

"O' course," he said, finding it increasingly difficult to keep sounding so calm and reasonable when he yearned to reach out and draw her to him. "Don't you worry. We're gonna pull you an' Willie outa this.''

She leaned closer, her eyes searching his. "You really do care for me, don't you . . .'' she marveled, "despite . . . despite . . .''

His gaze warming, he touched her face. "Yes, I do care for you . . . despite.''

She gathered his hand into both of hers and clasped it tightly. "When . . . when I ran out of here before . . . I want you to know . . . it wasn't because I didn't . . . I didn't want you to . . . or I didn't want to . . . You've been so understanding and generous-hearted toward me. If anyone, I'd want . . . it would be you. It's just that since . . . since Henri, I've changed inside, Coke. I always felt so dirty when he . . . when he . . ." Closing her eyes, she shook her head. "And my feelings get tangled up. When you touch me like you did before . . . those same feelings come back, that . . . that I had with Henri. I don't want to feel that way . . . especially not with you. I only want to . . . to feel good with you." She smiled, embarrassed. "Talk about damaged goods."

"You ain't damaged goods," he said gently. "You're Jessie hurtin' inside."

"I'm so sorry."

He reached out and smoothed her hair, as soft to the touch as feather down. "I'll just hold you if you want me to, Jessie. Would you like me to just hold you?"

"Yes," she whispered. "I'd like that . . . very much."

He held his arms open to her, and smiling timidly, she moved inside. He held her lightly, knowing that she was only testing, not only him but her own emotions. He became conscious again of how slight she was, the feeling that his arm could go around her waist twice.

"You should eat more," he commented.

She seemed to find that amusing. "That . . . from you," she chided, relaxing more against him, "who gave me only one hard biscuit, then choked me on a piece of that dreadful jerky."

"Sorry," he replied, his hold on her strengthening. "If I'd o' known you was expectin' a feast out here, I'd o' flung a side o' beef an' a sack o' potatoes over my saddle before chasing out after you."

With that, she kissed him lightly on the cheek and snuggled closer, nuzzling his neck. As though it was a natural progression, he lowered her onto the blanket. He could feel a spasm of tension running through her.

"Still scared?" he asked.

"I'm scared of all you men," she admitted shyly. "Sometimes I think that you're another species of animal, one I can't predict, and that I'd be wise to live out my life steering clear of every last one of you."

"Sounds like your attitude toward horses," he drawled, settling down beside her, propping his head in his hands. "I'm ashamed to admit it, Jessie," he went on, playing with her fingers, "but there are some horses even this tough Texas cowboy ain't been able t'tolerate. But iffen I'd decided thirty years ago after I'd been tossed a coupla times that they was all no-goods an' I wasn't gonna have nothin' t'do with any of 'em anymore, I sure wouldna been able t'build me no 216,862-an'-a-quarter-acre spread.''

Moving his hand up, he lightly touched the thin gold loop in her ear. ''Why, I could just picture me an' my drovers sashayin' about on foot jawbonin' at a herd o' cows. It'd be near on impossible just gettin' the critters t'stand up . . . much less persuadin' 'em offa the spread an' hoofin' it all the way t'Kansas.''

''Cows don't pay attention to anyone on foot?''

His eyes crinkled. ''Not whilst they're rollin' on their sides an' laughin' themselves t'death.''

She giggled and, turning toward him, wound her arms around him. He responded, enfolding her against him. The fire crackled cozily on, lapping light and shadow over them, but he was aware only of her. Slowly he felt a change in her, like a subtle give in those delicate bones, bringing her body more fully into his.

Lifting her hands and riffling her fingers through his hair, she began kissing him softly down the side of the face. He turned his face and captured the last kiss with his mouth, pressing her back onto the blanket. The kiss deepened and he could feel her breathing coursing through him, her warmth melting into him, the secret pulsing of her heart.

He pulled back, looking down at her. ''I ain't made o' stone, Jessie,'' he said, feeling his throat tighten. ''I've wanted you for a damn long time.''

Her eyes were luminous in the quavering light. ''Touch me more,'' she whispered, caressing his face with the back of her fingers. ''I want you to touch me more.''

His eyes steadily holding hers, his hand moved down, slowly undoing the buttons on her blouse. Then, sliding his fingertips lightly under the dainty ridges of her collarbone, he spread the blouse open. He glanced down. Her breasts were deep and full in the firelight, swelling up to shadowed silhouettes inside her loose chemisette, its thin, puffy cotton an almost transparent cloud against the light. A rush of feeling overtook him, but he held it in control. He knew that she was still testing, and about all this, she was as fragile as spun glass.

Leaning down again, kissing the silky hair around her temple, he untied the ribbons of her chemisette, then slid his hand inside to that defenseless, surpassingly sensitive softness. Her breathing caught and deepened and she turned her face to the side of his, so close that he could feel the quiver of her eyelashes on his skin. Slowly he passed his hand from one side to the other under the warm cloth, his fingers tracing out her fullness, moving softly and lingeringly around and over the tips, feeling the response beneath his touch. Then he parted the chemisette, letting it fall back to the sides, and looked down, wanting to know all of her with all of him. Though her breasts weren't large or heavy, the areolas were full and ripe, implying a deep, rich sensuality to be found and to be unsealed.

His arousal became more consuming, and he'd have grown insistent were it not that he glimpsed, with that delectable fullness, the delicate definitions of her ribs, reminding him that this was Jessie and that she was vulnerable. Unable to keep away from that tender lushness just above, he gently handled and stroked her there, and shifting his body more over her, began sliding kisses along her neck, moving down to the front of her shoulders, down to the declivity between her breasts and moving slowly to the side. She started arching back when suddenly he felt a tightening in her and a burst of shaking. He looked up. Her face was turned away, her eyes pressed shut, her hands knotting into fists.

He moved up and wrapped his arms protectively around her. She clung to him, trembling.

"Do you want me to stop?" he asked.

He could feel the surprise go through her. "Won't it . . . leave you?"

"Ain't nothin' I'm likely t'die from," he said.

She drew back and looked at him with disbelief.

He took her face between his hands. "This cain't be for me alone, honey," he said gently. "I want to pleasure you . . . not take from you."

Her eyes, and everything else in her, seemed to soften. She took his hand and kissed it, then slid it down against her breast. "Don't stop."

Though the fire burned in his eyes, they hadn't lost the ability to take on a twinkle. "God," he breathed. "I was hopin' you'd say that."

And that night, Coke discovered a tenderness in him beyond any that he'd ever dreamed himself capable of. For though he wanted her, he wanted even more to give her back her preciousness. He knew that one key to unlocking her passion was trust; and whenever he sensed a resistance building in her against her own desire, he retreated a little, his touch growing lighter and gentler until he felt that give in her, then a quickening that demanded more again.

When he'd freed her of all her clothes, the fine-boned loveliness of her, the silky feel of her, drove the heat of his desire to such a pitch that it demanded every ounce of his control to think only of her and to hold back and move her along gently. But every advance became a discovery and a rediscovery for them both to savor. And with infinite compassion and steadfast persistence he carried her beyond fear and self-hateful memory, gasping and clinging to him . . . until this Jessica, who'd been at first only a beautiful facade that he'd hankered for as all men hanker after beauty; and this Jessica, who, in taking that shallow hankering and turning it against him, had forced him to look deeper; and then this Jessica, who, in turns, by her wit, her defiance, and her undeniable originality, had kept him intrigued and challenged since that very first afternoon, then had touched and endeared him by the eloquence of her love for her son, and had always held him captive by her irrepressible spirit; this Jessica was at last able to let go and let him love her. And the moment was exquisitely poignant for both of them. And afterward, she wept.

When, later, she started reaching for her clothes to cover up her nakedness, he stopped her.

"I been thinkin' o' havin' you like this almost every hour o' every day since I met you," he said. "An' I don't want t'let go of this moment yet."

She settled back against him, letting him run his hands slowly over her. After a time, she sat up and gazed at him with shining eyes. Then, that sweet little dimple dancing at the corner of her mouth, she leaned over, her hair cascading over a shoulder, and started kissing him across the chest. And with hundreds of soft kisses and tender caresses, she taught him all the sweet delights of a truly affectionate woman. And this second time, paid him back.

🌺 Chapter 46

LIGHTNING LASHED, BLEACHING the darkness with its sterile light. They seemed almost alive standing down there, Ray thought, those granite crosses and gravestones marking the Castillo burial ground. Through the spasms of light, the mangling wind, the tides of scourging dust, they stood there; through the cataclysms of atmosphere, earth, and mortal men, they stood there, erect, waiting. Even when he kept the shutters closed, these heavy drapes drawn, Ray often felt the weight of their presence out there beyond this bedroom window. Bleeding shadows, implacable . . . waiting.

He reached for his bottle. The lip of it rattling against his glass, he poured out more whiskey. It was faithfully well kept, the Castillo burial ground, he'd noticed, the rosebushes and hedges watered, the stone vases always holding fresh wildflowers, the grass manicured—and not a weed allowed to invade that hallowed ground. Whoever tended it must come at night, Ray thought as he downed the whiskey. Whoever he is, he, too, must be waiting.

He saw two shadows moving down the road toward the hacienda. More Land Company men riding in, no doubt. They wore slickers, put on to protect them from a rain that the storm hadn't delivered.

He saw another figure, riding down the road behind the other two. That would make nine who had arrived just since he'd been sitting up here at his bedroom window, seventeen for the day. By late tomorrow, the rest of his father's private army should have drifted in.

Ray heard a low musical bong! the clapper in the church bell stirring in the wind. He looked toward the knoll, and saw that he wasn't the only one witnessing the influx. Father Dominic and that dour brother who ran the school were standing in front of the church doors.

Ray pushed unsteadily out of the chair and, the whiskey bottle

391

swinging from one hand and the glass from the other, wandered out of his room and down the broad hallway. At the end of it, he stopped, poured himself a drink, and raised a toast to the sorry-eyed stone saint that dwelt in the niche there. Then he descended the stairs, flat-footed, step by careful step. Reaching the bottom, he turned to the marble Don Quixote. Gazing up at the grim face, he raised another toast. Before the night was done, he intended to toast every stone-cold face in the place. Including the Old Man's.

He ambled into the library. T.C. was seated at the desk going through some papers, the heavy drapes drawn behind him. Ray kept close to the walls, skirting the sweep of the lamplight. It burned his eyes, as did his father's visage behind it.

He opened the liquor cabinet and broke open the seal on a fresh bottle. Turning to the bust of Plato, he poured himself another short one, then decided against making the toast. This fellow would probably understand. He shuffled over to the chair that sat at an angle from the Old Man, and dropped into it. He hooked a knee over its arm, composed a dignified face.

"I think you're moving too fast on this, Dad," he said.

"Oh?" T.C.'s tone was caustic. "Still able t'think, are you?"

"My legs are numb, fingers numb, lips and tongue a little numb. But my brain . . ." He gave his head a tap "It isn't nearly numb enough. You should give yourself a few more days before you decide on this action," he ventured on. "There's no need to push it. Let the system work it out for you."

"Why waste the time," T.C. retorted, "when I can buy it, bend it aroun' t'suit me, an' use it as I choose?"

"Judge Albertson sure didn't hide that he had some serious reservations about this move."

"But he's goin' along with it, anyway," T.C. pointed out. "It's too late in the day for him t'start puttin' on the airs of a tight-kneed little virgin, when he's already spread his legs an' gave out at a good price years ago."

"Those Rangers coming into the Savings and Loan with that subpoena the other day got him real spooked," Ray commented.

"Well, we managed t'get the ledger books moved out in time," Barrett replied. "It ain't likely to occur t'no Ranger t'subpoena the San Sebastian wine cellar. So what do they got against me now? Only the signed statements of a pair o' disgruntled employees tryin' t'get back at me for firin' 'em."

Ray ran his index finger slowly around the rim of his glass.

"Sanders isn't likely to just back off and let you take that land," he mused.

"Nope."

He licked the whiskey off his finger and poured out some more. "This'll bring on a standoff. There's likely to be a battle."

"Yep."

Ray squinted up at his father. There was an edge of tensing expectancy about him. "It's the battle, you really want, isn't it, Dad? Not the land. Far as I can tell, you have no taste for ranching." He gulped down the whiskey. It didn't burn his throat anymore. That was numb, too. "It's not having the prize at the end of the road that you get your pleasure from, it's the mowing down of anyone who happens to be in your way."

T.C. irritably shoved the papers aside. "Yup." He glowered. "That's the reasonin' I'd expect outa the lily-livered sorta man who tries t'draw his balls outa the bottom of a whiskey bottle."

"I can think of worse ways to try to get them."

T.C.'s eyes flared ominously. "You're pushin' me, boy. You better not push me."

"Or . . . what?" Ray shrugged indifferently.

Barrett's fury seemed about to break out when a knock sounded at the door and his face changed, a mask of calm sliding over it. One of the Land Company men opened the door, and Handsome Jack Siden strolled unhurriedly into the library, hands in his pockets, lazily surveying his surroundings. "First time I've been in this room," he commented. "Fancy. Mighty fancy." His green eyes fell on Ray, and sharpened. "Ray's in on our business here?"

"All the way," Barrett said, sitting back, playing with a silver chain he'd taken out of his pocket. He nodded toward the chair across the desk from him. "Have a seat."

Handsome Jack complied, sitting down opposite Barrett. His eyes flickered appreciatively around the room again. "If I'd've known what you'd be gettin' out of it," he said smoothly, "I'd've charged you more for that little piece of business I performed for you six years back."

"You got enough," Barrett replied.

"But you got a helluvalot more," Siden answered affably. He eased more comfortably into the chair, propping his ankle up on the opposite knee. "Why'd you call me in here?" he asked. "And all these other men of yours. I've been watchin' 'em ride by all evenin'."

"Day after tomorrow Watt Calhoun'll be servin' a court order issued by Albertson. I'm preparin' t'back him up."

"Court order?" Siden inquired. "Orderin' what?"

"Orderin' Coke Sanders to vacate the land t'me that I'm challengin' him on in court."

Handsome Jack whistled silently. "Sounds like somethin' I wouldn't want t'miss out on. Mind if I join your party when you serve that court order?"

"You ready t'come out in the open round here?" Barrett asked. "Ain't you afraid that it'll cost you your popularity?"

"That's not important anymore." Siden replied. "I've decided t'shake the dust of this place off my boots and move on."

"Don't you have a business here . . . ranch supply or somethin'?" Barrett asked, fingering the gray chain.

"Oh, that. It's finished. This mornin' Lou Wilson informed me that he was buyin' me out an' endin' our partnership for good." A smile broke across his face. "You an' Sanders," he went on in an amused tone, "loadin' your carbines, pushin' an' maneuverin' for the power in these parts . . . while the real power's in the hands of a fifty-five-year-old woman with half her teeth missin'."

For the first time Barrett moved his attention from the chain in his hand. "Who's that?"

"Meg Emerson. She owns the two-bit general store in town."

"What she got?"

"Influence."

"Money?"

"Nope, just influence."

Barrett frowned uncomprehendingly.

"You figger it," Handsome Jack said. "But the folks round here tend t'follow her judgments an' attitudes like they was delivered direct from God. She sets her bonnet against you . . . well, folks start t'treat you 'bout as cordial as dogs treat the only tree in town." Siden reached inside his vest and drew a cigar out of his shirt pocket. "An' a few days ago, I made the serious mistake o' gettin' on Meg Emerson's bad side."

"What happened?" Barrett asked, idly lifting the end of that silver chain up and letting it curl back down into the hand cupped below.

"Wasn't much," Siden said, striking a match off the sole of his boot and lighting his cigar. "Meg just decided I'd behaved impolite to that little bitch she's got stayin' with her. One word from

her an' that fool partner o' mine is cuttin' himself out of a prof-
itable piece of his own business, the local marshal is eyein' me
fishy, an' even Ruby over at the saloon isn't makin' me too welcome in her place anymore.'' He slowly drew on his cigar. ''Guess
I shoulda directed more of my energy toward workin' on Meg
. . . though she ain't my type at all.''

''Guess so,'' Barrett said, having lost interest as, looking down,
he slowly ran the smooth, even bumps of the chain between his
thumb and index finger.

Ray felt uneasy. Something was off; he couldn't put his finger
on it. Though the Old Man was talking easily with Siden, he
wasn't looking at him. That wasn't his way. His way was to freeze
a person with his eyes, or bore holes through him.

''This place was gettin old to me anyhow,'' Siden was saying.
''It's time I pulled up stakes.'' He drew on his cigar. ''Wanta buy
a hide-shippin' operation cheap?''

''You lettin' it go?''

''It's about petered out. Got all the use I could get outa it,
spottin' the best herds hereabouts. Most o' the good cattle have
already been swiped by your boys an' sent on their way . . .'ceptin' those on the Sidewinder, o' course. But day after tomorrow,
once you got that land, you can hunt those up on your own.''

''I expect we will,'' Barrett said absently.

Siden studied the end of his cigar. ''So how 'bout buyin' me
out of that hide operation? You an' me got accounts to settle
anyhow.''

''That we do,'' Barrett said slowly. ''That we surely do.'' He
seemed to rouse himself. ''How much you askin' for it?''

''Thirty-five hundred dollars.''

''It ain't worth that.''

''Well, that price includes those last two rustlin' operations I
directed for you. You still owe me on those.''

''That's true,'' T.C. nodded musingly.

''Now, ridin' with you when you deliver that court order, I
won't charge you for my services there. There's a score I wouldn't
mind settlin' with Sanders.''

''I got that impression,'' Barrett said, lifting his eyes. ''You
already tried t' gun him down twice, didn't you?''

Siden immediately became guarded. He said nothing, his green
eyes narrowed, probing.

"Beau told me," Barrett volunteered offhandedly. "Why'd you go after Sanders?"

"Why not? You were plenty grateful to have that other fellow round here taken out."

"But this killin' I didn't order."

"This was personal. Sanders was gettin' in my way," Siden said evenly. "I thought you'd appreciate it, anyhow."

"I guess I would've at that," Barrett admitted, wrapping the chain around his hand. "Well, you'll have your chance at him day after tomorrow."

Siden relaxed visibly. "That is one fight I am lookin' forward to. Guess Beau's gonna regret missin' out on the action."

"It's considerate of you to think of Beau," T.C. commented. "Right considerate." He put his hand on the desk drawer. "Now, what did you say it'd take t'settle our accounts?" he asked, sliding the drawer open.

"Thirty-five hundred dollars." Handsome Jack pulled contemplatively on his cigar. "Thought I'd go over to Doc's sometime soon an' pay Beau a visit. How's he gettin' on, anyhow?"

"He died this mornin', you bastard," Barrett said in a cold, deadly voice, lifting the gun out of the drawer and leveling it on Siden. "We buried him at noon today."

Handsome Jack froze. A mist of smoke drifting out of his mouth, his green eyes widened at the sight of the gun. He made a reflex motion toward his belt. Barrett squeezed the trigger. The blast of the gun and the crash of Ray's whiskey bottle splintering on the floor were almost simultaneous. With unblinking eyes, Barrett fired again. Jack Siden jerked backward, then, coughing feebly, started squirming in the chair. The holes in his stomach oozed blood through his shirt.

His gun still smoking, T.C. calmly got up, strolled around the desk, and stopped directly in front of Handsome Jack.

"I told you t'stay away from Beau," he said, raising the gun and pointing it at Jack's forehead. "But you took him with you that day anyhow, didn't you? Then, you yellowbelly, you just rode off, leavin' my poor boy lyin' wounded in the dust."

Ray had crawled up in his chair. "Dad!" he croaked.

The gun exploded. Handsome Jack's head snapped back, glancing sickeningly off the wooden chairback.

As though from a great distance, Ray heard the footsteps of men running from the rear of the hacienda and across the porch.

Bending down, T.C. was picking Siden's smoking cigar off the rug. "Stinking habit," he muttered as the room started to fill with Land Company men.

The explosion of that last shot still resounding through him as if he'd become a hollow drum inside, Ray was held mesmerized, horrified, by the awkwardly slung form of Jack Siden. Only a moment ago, this man had been amiably talking, making plans.

He heard the faraway sound of his father's voice. "The bastard drew on me. Get rid o' him."

Two of the men pulled Siden's body out of the chair. Ray's eyes stayed locked on it as it moved past him out the door.

"Get rid of the chair, too," he heard the Old Man say casually, as though in afterthought. "Got blood on it."

Another shadow lifted the chair. Ray's eyes followed it, too, as it passed by to the door.

The Old Man sat back down behind his desk and turned his eyes on Ray, his countenance glacial in that shrill light.

"Clear out," he said to the shadows still tarrying, his eyes steady on Ray.

They blended together and streamed away until only Ray and his father were left in that room.

" 'Or what?' you were askin'?" T.C. said, unwinding the chain from his hand. Ray saw the silver nugget at the end of it. It was the chain the Old Man had given Beau almost a dozen years ago, when he made that silver strike. "Did you pee your pants, son, or is that a good bottle o' whiskey that you just wasted on the floor?"

"Dad," Ray choked out. "You didn't have to—"

"He was half the cause of your brother's death," Barrett replied. "An' two days from now, I'll take care o' the other half."

Ray shook his head, his mind a maelstrom. "It's not Sanders's fault," he said softly.

"What!" Barrett's tone was heavy with accusation as he put the chain back in his pocket. "You ain't even gonna stand up for your own dead brother?"

"They were trying to kill Sanders," Ray said. "He was only defending himself. Beau shouldn't have been there."

"Get you some backbone, Ray. It ain't the how that's important. It's the outcome. An' Sanders killed your brother."

Ray's head was pounding. He turned his eyes away; looking at his father stung them. Squinting up, he noticed for the first time in the play of light on the yellowed wall above the library door, the whitened imprint of a crucifix that had once hung there. It tripped the remembrance of something that had been working on him before.

"When . . . when he came in here," he began, finding it hard to say the name, for the man was still alive in his mind, his voice still hanging in the air like the scent of the smoke from his cigar.

"What?"

"S—Siden," Ray got out. "He said that he took care of some business for you six years ago."

"Yep, he did," Barrett said, picking up his gun and breaking it open.

Ray forced himself onward, picking his way toward that revolting thing that every fiber in him recoiled from confronting. "Did Siden kill Castillo . . . for you?"

Reaching inside a box in his desk drawer, Barrett picked out some bullets. "Both Castillo an' Sanders were dug in so solid in this part o' the country," he said, shoving the bullets into the cylinder, "that I had t'pry one of 'em out just to be able t'get at the other." He snapped the gun shut.

Again Ray had the feeling that he was a hollow drum with tiny echoes rattling faintly about inside.

"I knew . . . I always knew . . . that the limits of normal men didn't apply with you. But I guess I'd always hoped that there were some lines that you'd never cross. . . ." He realized that a pleading note had crept into his voice, but he couldn't erase it. "How, Dad, could you have had a man killed that you hardly knew?"

"Look what I got outa it," Barrett replied.

Ray couldn't look. Everything in this room, especially that indelible imprint of a crucifix above the door, had become like a rebuke.

"Dad." Ray tried to control his voice, for he knew that he was sounding weak and that the Old Man enjoyed that. "You've done this before?"

"When the situation required it."

Ray only stared, nausea rising in him.

Barrett let out a humorless laugh. "Do you think that that dynamite charge that killed my partner back in Colorado really went off premature?"

"This is all wrong," Ray said.

"That's your weak, dirt-dumb ma talkin'," Barrett said derisively. "I win out, nobody else is gonna pay right or wrong any mind."

"It's still wrong," Ray said softly. "Wrong." He shook his head. "I think I'm gonna be sick."

"Must be from how fast your head came snappin' down outa the clouds tonight an' landed in the real world. You like bein' rich, havin' power. You just don't wanta get down an' get your hands dirty t'get it or know for a fact that someone else is in the ditches gettin' their hands dirty for you."

"But do you have to get them bloody, too?" Ray asked.

"You'll never understand," Barrett retorted. "You've wound up with the spine of a worm an' the whine of a cat in heat. Now, Beau—he understood. *He* was turnin' into a real man. Had what it takes, Beau did—real spine."

"And he's dead," Ray said tiredly. "Because Beau, with that steely spine of his, still bent to you. Sanders was right. Wasn't him that made a bushwhackin' killer out of Beau." He raised his eyes to his father.

Barrett came out of his chair. "Don't you quote your brother's killer t'me!" he exploded. "You, sittin' there with your head in the clouds—analyzin', analyzin', the blood in your veins runnin' neither hot nor cold. You've never wanted anything bad enough."

He stopped talking, seeing that his words were not touching Ray. A viciousness rose in Barrett's eyes.

"You couldn't even keep ahold o' that gal, Carol, a few years back," he sneered, and noted with satisfaction that he now had Ray's attention. "You, Mr. Lukewarm, Mr. Namby-pamby." He twisted the knife deeper. "Always pussyfootin' round right or wrong. Why, you wasn't even man enough, I bet, t'get aroun' t'puttin' it in her." Setting his hands on his desk, he leaned toward Ray, his voice dropping to a coarse whisper. "But your Old Man was."

"Do you see people when you look at them?" Ray said, rising out of his chair. "When you look at them, what do you see?"

"Tell you what I see when I look at you, boy. I—"

"Her name was Cathy," Ray said quietly. His voice rose to a shout. "Her name was Cathy!" And spinning around, he rushed headlong out of the room and out of the hacienda, stumbling blindly through the storm until, arriving on land that was not the Castillos', he felt it was all right to fall to his knees and be sick.

🌿 Chapter 47

THE LAST SURVIVING embers in the fireplace had yielded up their souls in coils of smoke. Jessica didn't care that the fire had gone out, for with Coke there, the darkness felt benign.

Moving her head back, she peered at him, a sleepy smile in her eyes. Gradually the smile came to life, twinkling across her face. Ruffling his hair and giving him a kiss on the nose, she sat up and, bending to and fro, began plucking up her clothes scattered on the floor about her, gathering them into a bundle against her breasts.

"Just doesn't seem right," she said, her voice still husky with sated desire.

"What don't seem right?" he asked lazily.

"Oh, that in the past hour or so, I was shucked out of one chemisette, a pair of drawers, a petticoat . . .'' she recited, pulling the garments one by one out of the bundle and holding them up to the thin rectangle of light falling through the doorway, ". . . a shirtwaist, a stocking . . . another stocking, a skirt, and somewhere, I don't know where, a pair of shoes . . . while all you had to do was button your shirt and pull up your pants."

"Wayull," he drawled philosophically. "I reckon that's 'cause there are some things in this world that're just flat-out harder t'get to than others."

"Ah, Coke," she sighed, disappearing into the balloon of her petticoat and pulling it down to her hips. "How I love the sweet nothin's you whisper in my ear."

He raised up on an elbow. "Is it sweet nothin's that you want, Jessie? Well, then . . ." Reaching out, he traced the curve of her waist from rib to hip with his finger. "Take that line there. 'Tain't nothin' can compare. No sculptor, sketcher, or painter, creatin' hard as he can for a hundred years, could ever come up with a more fetchin' line." He sat up beside her. "An' your eyes . . . they're clearer an' deeper an' bluer than a Rocky Mountain sky

400

on a January mornin'. An' they change. With each shift an' turn o' your mood, they change so you cain't ever hide altogether what it is that you're a-feelin'.'' With the back of his fingers, he caressed her shoulder. ''An' your skin. 'Tain't nothin' on this earth tenderer an' sweeter to the touch. Why, every time I'm near you, I'm reminded all over again that the good Lord sure knew what He was about when He created a woman like you, for He put in you all that there is or ever could be to pleasure a man.''

''Whew!'' she breathed, hastily slipping into her chemisette. ''I'd better get back into my clothes fast.''

He didn't want her to diminish what had happened between them by making too much light of it. ''I love you, Jessie.''

The vein of melancholy that had been there all along surfaced. ''Don't say that,'' she said quietly. ''Please don't say that.''

It was as he'd feared. After taking her first steps across that forbidden line with him, she'd become beset by doubt, and felt she needed to pull back from him again. He was determined to keep that from happening.

''You don't believe that I love you?''

''Yes,'' she said softly. ''I believe you.'' She sighed. ''You know, words like that when they come easily aren't really meant. And when they come hard, they mean too much. And it all becomes too imposing, too perilous. Too frightening.''

''Why would you think that? You an' Willie could have a right good life with me on the Sidewinder.''

''Maybe. I don't know. And see, you're already thinking in terms of the future.''

''Well, I sure don't see any peril in it.''

''You wouldn't . . . because if I came to live with you, you'd still go on doing the same things you've been doing all along. But I'd have to change everything to fit into your life. I'd have to give up my own dreams. This, tonight, is one thing, and by itself it's beautiful, so beautiful. But surrendering everything that is in me to you? For the rest of my life?'' She gave him a wry, wan smile. ''Hell, Coke, I ain't that easy.''

''Jessie, I don't think that you're seein' it the way it could be.''

''You're not seeing it the way that it could be, either,'' she replied. ''A while ago you implied that I was impractical. Well, I'm being practical now. Romance that leads into marriage, too often can lead to disillusion and hostility as well, one problem and heartache after the other crowding in on you.''

"That's like sayin' you can tell it's a honeysuckle vine by the hummin'bird turds," he responded. "Sure, the beginnin' of anything always seems more thrillin' just 'cause it's so brand-spankin' new an' you cain't help but t'put your own imaginin's into it t'fill in the gaps o' what you cain't make out too clear yet. So when the real parts start into showin' through, sometimes they just gotta seem less."

"That's because they are less," she said, buttoning her blouse. "If I decided to stay with you, ten years from now you wouldn't say all those lovely things to me about my form, my eyes, my skin. Those words, those sentiments, wouldn't even occur to you then. By that time, you might even look at me and see, well, kind of a well-used wagon with an ill-fitting axle or something."

"Honey, I doubt that I'd ever come t'think of you that way. You're too damn smart. You'd always give me a run for my money."

"But marriage changes people. Sooner or later, you'd probably turn away from me, not let me close. Coke, I couldn't stand to watch something that was once perfect and lovely erode away into callousness, bitterness."

"Jessie, remember, I'm me. I ain't anybody else. What we see in each other, what the other causes us t'see in ourselves, is somethin' special. It cain't be copied with anyone else an' it sure cain't be compared with 'em, neither.

"You gotta know by now that I ain't some green kid puttin' a starry view on the world. Ain't a one of us ever come into this life with the guarantee that it'd be easy. Chances are, there'll be plenty o' times when it won't be. An' times when any two people, no matter how close they are, they won't be able t'see eye t'eye. An' when the drought sets in, they'll wanta retreat to their own private wells t'draw their strength. But them times just gotta be expected. They gotta be taken for granted an' not be made too much of, so the union that the two people are forgin' together won't get loosened.

"What I'm sayin', Jessie, is that it's that day t'day o' goin' through life, the rough an' the easy of it, knowin' that that special someone is there, carin' an' keepin' the faith with you that'll make the years a whole lot richer an' sweeter. Sure, I admit, bailin' out, you'll be escapin' some bad times, but you'll be losin' out on the good times, too."

"I have other problems, Coke," she said quietly. "Don't forget."

"Come back with me tomorrow an' we'll work 'em out. I'll figger you a way outa this."

"You don't know Henri. You don't know the ways in San Fran-cisco."

"We ain't in San Fran-cisco. We're in my neck o' the woods, remember?"

"Oh, Coke," she sighed. "I thought we'd already decided our course. I'd go stay with that rancher friend of yours in Mexico while you find a way to send Mike O'Banion off on a wild-goose chase."

"But that still ain't solvin' nothin'."

"It allows me time to work out a good escape for Willie and me. This other . . . this going back . . . it's too risky."

"An' you don't wanta take a chance on anything . . . or anyone, right?"

"I think I've used up my chances," she said roughly. But looking at him in the shadows, she softened. Reaching up, she caressed his face. "I'm sorry. Please don't be too disappointed in me and hate me. I think I love you, too. Tonight, what happened between us tonight, has shaken me more than you could possibly know. I felt with you something that I'd thought I'd never be able to feel with any man again.

"Circumstances being different, I probably would've been willing to take the chance and stay with you. And years from now I'll look back on this moment and wonder what I may have forfeited, and probably I'll think that I've been a fool. But if I took the chance and went back with you and I lost, then I'd be forfeiting everything—including you. That'd make me an even greater fool. So please, I have to be strong now. I'm going to Mexico tomorrow."

She turned away and got to her feet. "Pass me my skirt and the canteen, please. I want to go outside and freshen up."

He picked up her skirt, weighing it in his hands. "These wool things can sure be heavy. Why didn't you put on that ridin' skirt you got at Meg's?"

"I had no intention to keep on riding a horse once I got to Mexico. I planned to take some other conveyance, a stagecoach, a train, anything other than having to rely on a damn, dumb horse." She ran a hand over her tousled hair. "Sure wish I had a comb and a mirror. I don't much like the idea of hitting Mexico, hair a-flying in the air like I'd just been chased down by a dozen cheetahs and a boa constrictor.'' She paused, the fugitive dimple at the corner of her mouth flickering. "Come to think of it, I have."

She went to the door, stopped, and turning around, gazed down at him with wistful tenderness. "It's nice to know that I was right about at least one thing this week."

"What's that, Jessie?"

Her eyes filled. "You *are* a hundred times the man of any man I've ever known, Coke Sanders."

She stepped out the door and into the night. He watched her go. The hardship and heartbreak that had plagued her life had too powerful a hold on her still to be wiped away in a single night. She'd already known a man's fine words and acts of love, and she'd learned a long time ago that a man's love too often meant not something gained, but something given up. Still, if there was one thing that Coke was not . . . it was a quitter.

❧ Chapter 48

THE SUN HAD been edging up in the sky for almost two hours, its heat and brilliance intensifying with each degree it ascended. They were in for a scorcher. Already the air felt close and muggy, as though the rains that had not been let loose the night before had saturated it.

Coke stooped down by the campfire he had going in the yard and poured himself a cup of coffee. He'd just gotten back from circling to the west, north, and east of the hut and had confirmed his suspicions. The cattle tracks that ran past here came from the direction of Caballo Blanco Canyon, to the west; and they didn't veer south into Mexico to the east of the hut, but swung northward toward the San Sebastian. That holding pen next to the railroad tracks north of Warner had been kept pretty busy, he figured.

Stolen South Texas beeves were probably now swelling herds from Montana to the Dakotas.

He detected a stirring inside the hut, then heard a low groan, a snuffle, a firecracker sneeze. Jessica limped to the doorway. Recoiling from the blast of sunlight, she shaded her eyes with her hand and peered down at him. Her skin looked drawn and pasty. And though she'd tried to coil her hair and pin it back up last night, a long streamer had come loose and poked out at the side of her head, looping over and down like a drooping Indian feather.

"Why'd you make the fire out here?" She frowned.

"Didn't wanta disturb you."

Still shielding her eyes, she groggily lifted her face to look at the sun and was almost knocked off balance by the movement.

"What time is it?" she asked, grabbing the doorframe to steady herself.

"Eight, eight-thirty . . . thereabouts."

"That late?" she exclaimed. "Why did you let me sleep so long?"

"Thought you needed it. What's the matter? You ain't feelin' good?"

She pulled a doleful face. "I feel awful. Really awful. I'm not used to pounding in a saddle all day. I'm not used to sleeping on the hard, hard ground all night. My legs won't unbend, my arms won't unbend. Even my fingers won't unbend. And my backside"— she gingerly put a hand on her hip—"feels like it's been scourged by a red-hot iron." She heaved a long, woebegone sigh. "All in all, I feel about as cheery right now as three-day-old horse ptooey. Any more questions?"

"I think you've 'bout covered 'em all. Hungry? Want a piece of jerky?"

"My teeth would break off."

He added more coffee to the cup, got up, and took it to her. "Here," he said, patting her consolingly on the back. "Drink up. It'll make you feel better."

She gazed morosely down into the cup. "Now . . . if I could only soak my tail in it . . ."

"Jessie," he began seriously, "you recollect what we talked about last night?"

She peeked up at him. "Oh, I recollect a lot of things about last night."

"Remember we talked 'bout goin' back to Dispenseme and tacklin' this problem o' yours head on."

"Oh, that," she answered in a flat tone. "You talked about that, I didn't. It's too chancy. O'Banion's too evil. I can't go back. Why can't you accept that?"

"Don't wanta let go," he said, gently smoothing the hair back from her forehead. "I want you t'be willin' t'take a chance on me. I wanta be given the chance t'take care o' you an' Willie. Willie's a fine little fella, Jessie. He needs a pa. An' there ain't no finer place for a young-un t'grow up on than a ranch. All that open space to run an' play. He'd learn what work means . . . and responsibility. An' patience. He'd learn what's important in life an' what ain't. It'd be good for you, too, havin' a strong, solid home."

She looked at him, deeply moved, her hand lifting to touch his face. Then she stopped herself, the caress that she'd started turning into a playful pat on the cheek. "Haven't you learned by now that just 'cause you've been in Meg's Emporium a couple of times, it doesn't follow that you have to buy the entire store . . . lock, stock, and barrel?"

He fixed his dark eyes on her. "Last night was no piddlin' little shoppin' spree, an' you know that."

"Yes," she whispered, looking away. "I know that. You just won't let me off easy, will you? It's just that everything's happening so fast. Maybe I'll be able to think things through if I can just get away to a safe place." She paused. "Speaking of which, how long will it take us to get to Mexico?"

"Less'n an hour, I reckon."

She handed him the cup. "I'll get my things."

By the time she limped out of the hut, he'd washed and packed his coffeepot and cup and was kicking dirt on the fire. He took the bedroll that she'd rolled up haphazardly, shook it out, rerolled it, and tied it to the back of the saddle.

She was a far cry from the tidy, perfectly groomed Jessica he was accustomed to. She looked spent, and needed a good day to rest up, he thought, then felt a little guilty because she wasn't going to get it today.

He swung onto ole Belcher, then wrestled a wooden-limbed, grouching Jessica up behind him. They bounced off, with a griped "Must you?" from the passenger seated to the rear.

Skirting the copse of trees, they ascended the nearby hill. As they rode up it, Jessica turned back to look one last time at the old homestead. She wanted to remember it, carve this one image out of her kaleidoscope of memories and preserve it.

She felt the rush of air as they attained the crest of the hill and turned back around. Her eyes widened . . . for there below, basking in the sun like a glossy, whiskey-colored snake, lay the Rio Grande. And not a quarter of a mile to their right reposed the sleepy border hamlet of Roma de Saens, with its Mexican counterpart, San Pedro de Roma, across the river from it. They'd spent the entire night less than five minutes from the border.

"You dirty skunk!" she sputtered.

"Now, Jessie," he said, nudging Ole Belcher down the hill. "I told you it'd take less'n an hour t'get here . . . an' it did."

"You misled me last night," she steamed, grabbing his shoulders and trying to shake him. "You low-down snake in the grass, you waylaid me at that hut last night just so you could have your way with me."

"All right," he conceded. "For the sake o' peace I'll give you that one. My thoughts 'bout you ain't never been o' the kind that'd sail me into heaven . . . but there sure cain't be no denyin' which one of us had the honorable intentions."

She knocked his hat over his face. "Now you're implying that I'm dishonorable. Well, you can just take your holier-than-thou superiority and you can . . . you can—"

"Jessie!"

"I can't stand being on the same horse with you," she muttered. Leaning back, she pulled her leg over and jumped off, the hard ground hitting her feet, sending pangs up through her aching thighs.

He rode stoically on.

"I'm not through with you yet!" she cried, limping after him, holding her hip. "Unscrupulous . . . untrustworthy . . . low-down . . ."

And thus they made their entrance into Roma de Saens. The town was a small trading center. Most of the houses in Roma were squatty and flat-roofed, and of sunbaked shades of brown that looked like tumorous growths on the skin of the earth. Only a few buildings that abutted the town plaza had attained a height of two stories, these second stories girdled by balconies, fringed with curlicue wrought-iron railings.

After months of drought, the trading vessels had long ago ceased trying to push up the river past the sandbars bared by the receding

water level. And the business activity in Roma had drained away
with the river that fed it, the town sinking into a somnolent suspension, the long, low warehouses lining the riverbank standing
hollow.

Coke drew up at the general store, climbed down from Ole
Belcher, and waited patiently for her. She was lagging a hundred
feet behind. The heat and the humidity and the strain of dragging
her stiff body down the road had taken most of the ginger out of
her. She straggled up, threw herself against the pillar supporting
the porch of the store, then plumped down bruisingly onto the
step.

He stood looking down at her for a time. "I still love you."

She gave him a long, haggard look.

"Jessie," he went on, "would you o' told me 'bout that fix you
was in if we'd come straight on here?"

"Yes," she said, then met his eyes. "No." She threw her hands
up. "Oh, I don't know."

"How could I be able t'help you, honey, if I hadn't had the
chance t'find out what your trouble was? Look." He pointed. "If
you'll just look a tad to your right, you'll see it. The Rio Grande.
Mexico. You've made it. You're home free. Nothin' was lost by
our stoppin' at that homestead last night. I sure don't regret it."
His dark eyes penetrated into hers. "Do you?"

She flushed. "No," she said softly, then looked dartingly
around to see whether anyone was around to overhear. She finally
brought her eyes back up, meeting with the glint in his, and
couldn't hold back their laughter. Doggone it, why couldn't she
ever keep her anger fired up when she was around him?

"No!" she burst out. "I don't regret it. But you did deceive
me."

"Yup," he admitted. "An' for that I'm sorry." His gaze wandered over her. "But not too sorry. You still want me t'help you,
don't you?"

The question was rhetorical, she knew. He'd help her. No matter what she said or did, whether she wanted him to or not, come
hell or high water, he'd stick by her. She saw that it was fundamental, ingrained in his nature, that once a bond was formed, it
became a constancy in his life. And she'd allowed that bond to
form, walked right into it, sealed it with him last night.

Last night. The sensations, the images, came alive and tingled
through her. She devoutly wished that Mike O'Banion and the

marshal were weeks away instead of only hours; they could go back to the hut and keep on doing what they'd begun last night. Perhaps, somewhere on the way to the hacienda of this acquaintance of his . . .

She squinted up at him. The sexual charge fairly sizzled between them. "Yes, I want you to help me," she said, unable to hide a wicked little smile, "but you're still a dirty skunk."

The river had shrunk so far down its banks that only the outermost legs of the ferryboat pier still stood in water. Its rearward legs were left stranded, stiltlike in the mud, giving the structure the look of a praying mantis. The flat-bottomed ferryboat was chained and padlocked to a leg at the end of the pier, rocking far below in a few inches of muddy water. The ferryboat was linked to a long cable that, curving down from elevated pulleys standing on opposite sides of the river, ran through an iron ring soldered to the boat's flank.

Coke pulled the rope, ringing a bell suspended from brackets at the top of the post at the end of the pier. He got no response, and jangled the bell again.

A chunk of brush up on the riverbank shivered and swelled, then birthed out a man, tail end first. On all fours, he backed out of the undergrowth, then reached back in and fished out his sombrero. He got to his feet and loped, yawning, down the pier toward them. Wordlessly accepting the two-bit toll fee from Coke, he swung down the ladder. Reaching to his waist, he took hold of the large key tied to the rope that doubled as his belt, and unlocked the padlock that held the ferryboat chained to the leg of the pier.

As Coke and Jessica climbed down into the boat, he hauled in the chain. Picking up a long pole, he leaned over the railing and used it to push the boat away from the bank. Then, standing the pole in a corner, he took hold of the cable, and with steady, pulley-creaking yanks, began propelling the boat along the cable toward Mexico.

"First off, " Coke said, "we'll get your entry paper."

"Entry paper?" She frowned. "What's that?"

"It's the law that any foreigner fixin' t'travel more'n ten miles into the interior o' Mexico has t'have that paper. It's for the purpose o' keepin' out undesirables."

"This applies even to United States citizens?"

"That's where most o' their undesirables come from."

"Why should I need to get this paper? There must be hundreds of people who cross back and forth along the border all the time who don't have it."

"That's true, but most o' them are likely t'travel through the open country. If the time ever came that you'd wanta head out from Ramon's spread, I'd expect that you'd wanta stick to the main roads, where it's safer, travel from town to town, stay in ho-tels. Travelin' thataway, you're more likely t'meet up with lawmen, government officials, who'd wanta see your entry paper. And them dudes could give you a mighty hard time if it turned out that you didn't have it on you."

She studied him. This was the first acknowledgment he'd ever made to her that he recognized she had freedom of will, and a reminder that any decisions she might make in the future could very well be hers alone.

"How do I get this document?" she asked. "I have no identification on me. And with that warrant against me, I'm not exactly what the Mexicans would regard as a desirable, either."

"Won't be too hard t'get . . . for the proper *mordida*."

"Mordida?"

"Bite . . . bribe. I know a fella in San Pedro. For the right price, he'll fix it for us."

She shook her head. "I'm glad you know your way around here. I'd never realized that absconding to Mexico could be so complicated."

❧ Chapter 49

HOLDING HER ELBOW, Coke guided her through the streets of San Pedro de Roma. With its stumpy rock and stucco buildings, narrow in front and long down the sides, it was almost a twin of its American counterpart across the river. Yet there was a different flavor to the place. It was Mexico—more life, more sound, more motion, more people out and about, passing on the streets, gathering at the small produce and fruit stands on the plaza; and everywhere, the cries and commotions of children in rippling, musical Spanish.

They kept walking, Coke guiding her through the narrow dirt streets, on the lookout for someone or something. Not until they'd reached the outskirts of town did he seem to latch on to what he was searching for. Taking her hand, he led her down a winding path that terminated in a ramshackle farmhouse a short distance away. As they followed along the path, they passed a small corral holding about a dozen emaciated cows, some littering the ground in the scant shade of a dried-out tree, others standing stuporously about on weak, spindly legs, their rib cages little more than stretching racks for their hides.

Jessica's nose turned up at the stench. "I should've known you'd make a beeline for familiar smellings," she groused.

"They're awful bunched up in there," he said.

"And now I know why you Texans hanker for the wide open spaces."

In the front yard, an old Mexican woman knelt at a short-legged workbench making flour tortillas. She was rhythmically plucking the balls of dough out of a bowl, flattening them out with a clack of a small rolling pin, then browning them on a griddle over coals. Coke asked her something in Spanish. Answering, she pointed toward a shed at the back of the house.

"Wait here." He started toward the shed. "I'll be back shortly."

Jessica wandered to the porch, found a place near the edge that wasn't bedaubed with any fresh chicken droppings, and gingerly sat down.

She heard Coke's voice raised in greeting behind the house. It was answered by a guttural male voice. Listening in on their Spanish conversation, she smiled, for even while speaking a foreign tongue, that drawl he'd told her was Virginian still flavored Coke's intonation.

Eventually the men's voices fell silent and she heard their footsteps coming up the side of the house. But instead of turning toward her when they came into view, they kept on going, passing between her and the old woman and heading on up the pathway. As Jessica watched in bewilderment, the two men crawled through the corral and began moving through the cattle, their voices rising and dropping as though they were dickering over something.

Straining her ears, Jessica tried to pick up some English-sounding word or phrase that might give her a clue to what they were haggling about; but she couldn't make out any.

The bickering ceased. They climbed back through the fence and came trudging down the path toward her.

"You mind givin' me one o' them twenty-dollar gold pieces you got tucked in your shoe?" Coke asked.

"What for?" she asked.

"The bribe. Ain't got but a coupla bits on me."

"How much will I get back?" she said, reluctantly bending down to unbutton her shoe.

"Not much, I'm afraid. We got more'n the one honcho t'pay off."

Tsk-tsking at mankind's greed, she pulled her shoe off, reached inside it, took out the gold piece, and handed it to Coke. Her sole contribution to the proceedings dispensed with, the two men went into the house, leaving her sitting on the porch. As she pulled on her shoe, she heard a jingling of coins in the house behind her, then something from Coke in Spanish. The Mexican replied in a baffled tone, and once again the two men's voices seemed raised in dispute, Coke sounding insistent, and the Mexican, disconcerted and reluctant.

By and by they came out of the house, the Mexican trailing behind and looking bemused. Scratching his head, he said something to the old woman.

"*Qué?*" she asked, the wrinkles in her face deepening in astonishment.

The farmer repeated what he'd said. Shaking her head, the old woman looked Coke and Jessica up and down in unabashed mystification. Coke took Jessica's hand; and accompanied by the farmer, they headed back toward town.

"What was the matter?" Jessica asked.

"Oh, they was a tad surprised that we didn't have more money on us," he replied easily. "Thought we was a mite cheeky in expectin' t'get your entry paper for such a piddlin' price."

"They will get it for me, won't they?" she asked, growing concerned.

"Yup. Took some persuadin', but finally ole Pepe here agreed t'take a cut in his usual fee."

They were now walking by the corral. "Why did you two go in there?" she asked.

"Pepe wanted a little advice. Thought his beeves was comin' down with somethin'."

She stared at the skeletal creatures behind the fence. "My goodness, didn't you tell him that the disease is called starvation?"

"They got somethin' else, too," he said vaguely, implying that only a fellow cattleman could understand the intricacies of such matters.

As they walked along, Jessica began to notice that the Mexican was eyeing them in a peculiar way. She kept feeling his eyes on her, scrutinizing her quizzically, then shifting to Coke, then stealing back to her. She moved closer to Coke.

"Why is he looking at us like that?" she asked under her breath.

He put his arm around her and kissed her. "These Mexicanos are hot-blooded, romantic devils, Jessie," he murmured in her ear. "Fact is, they got a powerful sixth sense when it comes t'lovin', an' I reckon the suspicion's just crossed ole Pepe's mind that you an' me sure musta had us one helluva tumble in the bushes not long ago."

"What?" she squeaked, coming to a stop. "No!" Then uncertainly, "Really?"

" 'Fraid so," he replied, straightening her collar. "You gotta admit, honey, you an' me sure do have that ole familiar used-up look."

Glancing in horror at the farmer, she batted Coke's hand off her collar. "Oh, my goodness!" she exclaimed, tucking at her blouse and pulling at her skirt. "Why didn't you say something?"

Jerking her hat off, she started down the path, furiously trying to smooth her tousled hair. Her fingers lit on a string of dried grass woven into the back. Peeking at the farmer, her face burning, she snatched it out.

"Got another," Coke said, reaching over and plucking another piece of chaff out of her hair, then another. "Whoooeee! You got close to a dozen trapped in there."

Cramming her hat back on her head with both hands, she hurried on ahead of them. Leaning forward and holding on to her hat, she moved at a faster and faster clip into town, her eyes leveled straight ahead, mortified that if she met anyone's gaze, she'd see on their faces the same dreadful detection of her recent wantonness with Coke that the farmer had picked up on. She'd already double-timed it past a low adobe building similar to all the others except that it had a faded flag hanging limply from a pole over the door, when she heard Coke whistle behind her.

"Whoa, Jessie! In here!"

Without breaking stride, she circled back and scuttled through the door he was holding open for her. As the interior of the dark-shuttered room evolved out of the shadows, Jessica found that they were in some kind of government office. It was a cluttered place evincing the kind of slipshod negligence of the low-level bureaucrat who has secured his post because he knows someone who knows someone. San Pedro de Roma was the sort of out-of-the-way place, Jessica surmised, that was perfect for filing away inept cousins who would be mooching wasters if left to their own devices.

A large, important-looking desk dominated the center of the room, every square inch of its surface strewn with papers, clouded with dust. Above the filing cabinets against the wall hung a copper-tinted daguerrotype of El Presidente Díaz in a stiff-backed, eye-popping pose that looked like he'd just had his neck starched. An empty tequila bottle lay on its side atop one of the filing cabinets with two sticky-looking shot glasses alongside. Indeed, the whole room reeked of alcohol, kept potent, Jessica guessed, by the man snoring out of sight in the next room.

Hands twisting at the rim of his sombrero, the Mexican farmer tiptoed timidly into the room where the snores were issuing from.

Suddenly the snores broke off with a snort and a thick-tongued, cantankerous mutter. They heard sibilant whisperings from the farmer, the official responding in a string of befogged grunts—sounds the farmer nervously tried to shush. Bedsprings creaked, then came a long female groan, which both men nervously tried to shush.

There was a heavy creak of protesting bedsprings, a pause, a muttered curse, and general sounds of stirring. Then came the pop-pop of a pair of suspenders. One boot clomped on, then another, and finally the official appeared, wandering stonily through the doorway, dragging over his holey undershirt a crimson coat that had long ago become dwarfed by its owner's ballooning tequila paunch.

"Ah, Señor Sanders," he blurted.

He shuffled to the desk, pulled out the chair and, with a sigh, folded his body into it. He ran his fingers through his gnarled hair, making it stand even further on end, and vainly tried to twirl together one side of the stiff-greased handlebar mustache that had come splayed on both ends. His grooming completed, he leaned back in his chair, folded his hands on the swell of his paunch, and with a regal arch of the brow, signaled that the business at hand could now proceed.

Fingers still fretting along the rim of his sombrero, the farmer started off, the flow of his words becoming more faltering and apologetic as he went along until finally they drizzled away to a doleful shrug. Coke pitched in, taking up the slack. As he drawled away in his hominy-grits-and-hog-jowls Spanish, the bureaucrat's eyes drifted to Jessica, lazily roaming up and down her in heavy-lidded, lip-curling, erotic appraisal. She blanched, then stiffened and sent the bureaucrat a tight-lipped, withering glare that chased his eyes back to Coke.

Shortly after, Coke said something that caused the official to lean forward, his bloated face pleated as though he wasn't sure he'd heard Coke right.

"*Uno? Por solo diez dólares?*" he exclaimed.

"*Sí,*" Coke replied.

"*Diez dólares . . . norteamericano,*" the farmer amended with another apologetic shrug.

"*Es necesario, éste?*" the bureaucrat inquired bewilderedly.

"*Es necesario,*" Coke replied.

The farmer merely shrugged dolefully again.

With a roll of the eyes and a sad shake of the head, the bureaucrat resignedly started searching through the papers on his desk. Failing to unearth what he was hunting for there, he turned to digging through his desk drawers, hauling out piles of forms, riffling through them, and abandoning them on top of the desk. Not turning up what he was looking for there either, he dropped his hands to his knees and, with a grunt, heaved out of his chair and lumbered over to the filing cabinets. He gazed, walleyed, at them a moment, then pulled out a drawer. He let out another grunt, this one of surprise and delight, and thrusting his hand inside the drawer, exultantly drew out a full, unopened tequila bottle. Dusting it off with his hand, he checked its label, then reverently set it on top of the cabinet before turning his attention back to the open drawer. Elbows poking out, he shoveled through it and, with another grunt, this of simple gratification, lifted out a yellowed, dog-eared form.

He waddled back to his desk with it and sat down. Plunging

his hand into a hillock of papers, he solemnly drew out the symbol of his power, his notary seal.

He picked up the dog-eared form and, holding it up at arm's length, commenced reading it aloud. Every once in a while, he'd pause and look up; Coke or the farmer would supply a word, whereupon he'd set the form down and, prissily dabbing his quill pen in the inkwell, scribble the word into the appropriate blank.

At last the form was completed. With trembling, uncertain hand, the farmer signed it. Coke signed it. Jessica was pulled over to sign it, and finally the bureaucrat grandiosely affixed his seal and signed it. He rolled the form up and opened the center drawer of his desk. He reached in and drew out a pink ribbon, which he wrapped around the document and painstakingly tied into a neat little bow.

"Veinticuatro pesos," he grunted, slapping the document into Coke's palm.

Coke handed him the coins. They ceremoniously shook hands all around, then Coke, Jessica, and the farmer stepped back out into the blinding sunlight.

"Muchas gracias," Coke drawled to the farmer.

"De nada," he replied, giving them one last odd look before he turned around and wandered away, shaking his head and muttering.

"Well, we got it," Coke said, stuffing the document into his belt. He took her arm and they strolled back toward the Rio Grande.

"Why did everyone have to sign it?" she asked.

"Well, ole Pepe signed it as a law-abidin' Mexicano citizen attestin' to your good character. I signed it as a law-abidin' *norteamericano* citizen attestin' to your good character. You signed it as the good character that we all was attestin' to. An' the official signed it 'cause it was his doc-you-ment, notary seal, little pink ribbon an' all."

"There was a point back there when that official seemed confused about something that you'd said. What was that about?"

"Oh, the *mordida* again," he answered offhandedly. "We got your entry paper at a real good bargain, Jessie. Dirt-cheap, in fact."

"I wouldn't call twenty dollars dirt-cheap."

"Didn't take all the twenty dollars. We got enough money left over t'buy us one humdinger of a breakfast. Hungry?"

"Famished."

"There's a real good restaurant in Roma, back on the other side o' the river."

She shook her head. "I wouldn't feel safe over there. Let's just get something at one of these stands on the plaza."

"Wouldn't recommend it. They got things in their cookin' that sometimes don't agree with a *norteamericano*'s belly. An' you might could wind up gallopin' to Ramon's hacienda—only without the horse, an' leavin' the wrong kinda trail—"

"I got the idea," she broke in. "I guess I'll just have to wait until we reach your friend's house before getting anything to eat."

"That's a mighty long time t'have t'go without food," he cautioned.

"Well, I can't go back to the United States side. What if Mike O'Banion and the marshal arrive while we're there? What if they're there already?"

"They ain't, Jessie," he said patiently. "Seth ain't a early riser. He'll be doin' good just t'reach the border by two this afternoon at the earliest. That is, iffen he takes it in his mind t'head thisaway a-tall."

They were now strolling across the busy plaza. A man hurrying by bumped into Jessica, then twisted around to stare after her. Two peasant women arranging vegetables on a stand slowed their motions to follow her with their eyes. She shrank down inside her clothes, her tangled, uncombed hair prickling her neck. "Oh, for a bowl of water, a hairbrush, and a mirror," she sighed.

"If we cross over to the other side for breakfast, you could stop off at the general store there and use their fittin' room t'fix yourself up."

"Well, I guess I'll just have to go on looking this way."

They had reached the bank of the Rio Grande and were standing at the foot of the ferryboat dock.

"It's a dog-gone dirty shame," he lamented, gazing across the river at the town opposite. "I was really lookin' forward t'havin' a big, stomach-fillin' breakfast over there once we was done with our business here. That there restaurant in Roma serves up the best vittles in all South Texas . . . thick, juicy steaks, eggs fresh outa the hen, sunny side up, hash browns, frijoles. An' biscuits, pipin' hot, the sweet-churned butter fairly drippin' outa them."

Her stomach growled and she guiltily put her hand over it. "I don't think I'd enjoy my food if I had to worry about Mike O'Banion and the marshal showing up.''

"If we go right now, you'd be safe," he assured her. "We'd have lotsa time t'eat before there's any chance a-tall of Seth hittin' these parts.''

She said nothing, thinking.

"Jessie," he said reasonably. "Would I o' gone to all this trouble t'get this entry paper for you if I didn't expect you t'use it? Look.'' He put his arm around her and pointed across the river. "The ferryboat's tied up on the American side. Always is. If there's any sign o' trouble . . . which I don't expect there t'be, but iffen there is, it'd be easy t'hop right aboard an' get back here, pronto.''

She started to speak, but he interrupted her, having anticipated her objection. "See that buildin'—" he raised his finger "—the one two doors up from the general store? That's the restaurant we'd be goin' to. See, it's facin' onto the main road into town. Sittin' at the window, we'd spot anybody comin' from away far off. We'd have plenty o' time t'get back to the boat.''

She pondered the idea, and her stomach gurgled again. The bit of coffee she'd swallowed that morning had set the machinery of her innards working without giving them anything to work upon. Sweet-churned butter, hot biscuits . . . She idly twisted a tangled chunk of hair poking down under her hat.

"If it'll make you feel better," he went on, "I'll keep watch outside the general store while you're in there sprucin' up.'' He looked her over closely. "An' if you don't mind my sayin' so, you sure could use a sprucin' up. An', Jessie, there ain't no good reason t'miss out on our single chance at solid food all day. It's a long, rough, wearisome way t'Ramon's spread.''

"What time is it?" she asked.

He squinted up at the sun. "Ten, ten-thirty. If we're gonna cross, we'd better get a move on while we still got plenty o' time. I gotta go back an' fetch Ole Belcher anyhow.''

That's right, she thought. Coke's horse was still over there. She probably wasn't being fair in letting her nerves and her stubbornness deprive him of the meal he'd been looking forward to so. Hadn't *he* gone out of his way for *her*, time and time again?

"All right," she caved in. "Ring the bell.''

🥀 Chapter 50

THE INSTANT SHE set foot on the United States side of the river, Jessica felt a rush of misgivings, her confidence sliding out from under her as if she were standing in sand in an undercurrent.

Coke's easygoing composure told her that her skittishness was irrational. Still, even his hand holding hers and the steady confidence of his manner didn't ease the constriction of anxiety she felt each time they moved past a building; that in the emerging space beyond she'd find herself confronting Mike O'Banion and the marshal. Still, she walked on, allowing her footsteps to carry her, one by one, away from the Rio Grande.

They arrived at the general store. Leaving Coke sitting on the stoop outside to keep watch, she forced herself through the moil of her uneasiness to go inside.

The neighborly storekeeper cheerfully assented to her request for the use of his fitting room. Once inside it, she was able to see herself in a mirror for the first time that day. She was a little astonished at what she saw, not because she looked so dreadful but because she didn't look quite as bad as she'd imagined. Leaning closer to the mirror, she peered at herself, trying to figure out exactly what had given her away, signaling to all those Mexicans across the river of her recent indiscretions with Coke, rather than that she'd come by this windblown, worn-out look merely by being out in the open air too long and not getting enough sleep. Yes, Mexicans must have some kind of sixth sense about such matters, she mused, pulling off her hat and flicking out her hairpins.

She unbuttoned her blouse to the waist, letting it fall around her hips, then bent over the washbowl and splashed water on her face. She hesitated, and turning, frowned in the mirror again. Yet why was it, she asked herself, that Coke had kept hinting that she looked such a fright when she, the severest critic of herself, didn't especially think so? The thought sent a needle of apprehension running through her.

Dipping a corner of the towel in the washbowl, she scrubbed her face, neck, and arms with a hurried briskness that made her skin tingle, then rapidly brushed her hair, sending the chaff flying, and rolled it up and pinned it in place. With mounting alarm, she scrabbled back into her blouse, buttoned it, straightened up the fitting room, and, grabbing her hat, rushed through the store, almost shouting her thanks to the storekeeper as she bolted outside.

Coke was where she'd left him, amid the lazy sunlight, the sleepy streets. He sat there on the stoop, idly tossing stones, making her jitteriness seem once again like featherheaded folly.

"I'm ready," she blurted, then added in a high, supplicating voice, "Let's go back to Mexico now."

"Why?" he asked, getting to his feet. "Town's peaceable enough. Ain't nobody came down that road since I've been sittin' out here."

"Still . . . still," she fumbled. "I feel uncomfortable being here."

"That's 'cause you're hungry," he answered confidently. "Flatout starved t'death. C'mon," he went on cheerily, taking her arm. "We'll get some hot grub into that little ole belly o' your-un an' you'll be ready t'face down the entire world, I guar-an-tee."

His solid certitude reassured her a little. Perhaps he was right. Perhaps the disquietude that she was feeling inside was due to hunger, and food would calm her, enable her to see things in a clearer, more rational perspective.

They were about to step into the restaurant when the far-off, familiar creak of the ferryboat pulleys starting up, stopped her. She spun around.

"Look!" she squealed. "The ferryboat's pulling away! Stop it!"

"Aw, Jessie," he drawled. "It's just goin' over t'pick someone up."

She wandered back down the road, scanning the opposite bank of the river. "I don't see anyone waiting over there."

"Ferryboat operator prob'ly just spotted one o' his regular customers headin' thisaway. C'mon," he coaxed, putting an arm around her and turning her back. "That boat'll be back here afore you know it."

Made helpless by confusion and indecision, she allowed herself to be walked into the restaurant. She and Coke turned out to be the only customers there. Jessica couldn't blame people for wanting to steer clear of the place. The sickening-sweet stench of food going bad hit you smack in the face the moment you stepped through the door. But she sat down in the chair he pulled out for her, while switching the burden of her breathing from her nose to her mouth to minimize the assault on her nostrils.

They were seated at a table by the front window. Coke leaned over and jerked it up. But since it was a breathless day, little air winnowed in. Jessica noticed that although the window did look directly onto the main road into town, as Coke had pointed out when they'd been on the Mexican side, one of the few trees in town that had managed to grow to a respectable size stood alongside a slight hook in the road a hundred feet away, its dense branches obstructing their view of the land beyond. Anyone riding down that road into town would have to be almost upon them before they'd realize he was there.

Coke and the cook, a mischievous-eyed Mexican, seemed to know each other pretty well. The skillets clanked onto the stove, the food started sizzling, and Jessica sat stewing as the two men bantered back and forth in Spanish. Her perturbation kept rising. She was sick to death of being bombarded by all this gabble that nobody bothered to translate for her.

"What in the devil's taking him so long?" she fretted. "Is he waiting for the hen to drop her egg? Is he searching his garbage for the meat?"

Scraping her chair back, she got up and tramped out the door. Standing in front of the restaurant, she searched the river for the ferryboat. It was still on the Mexican side, chained to the dock and looking abandoned. She ran her eyes along the far riverbank for the ferryboat operator, but couldn't spot him anywhere. Wringing her hands, she turned back into the restaurant. By the time the food arrived, anxiety was a razor-toothed rat, gnawing at her stomach where her hunger might have been.

After setting out their plates, the cook tarried on to continue his conversation with Coke. Jabbering away, he hovered over them, watching them eat, his blood- and grease-smeared apron barely a foot from Jessica's face.

She mechanically sawed at the thin, burned husk of meat. The fried eggs were gray, rubbery, and slick with grease. The beans had that metallic reheated-a-few-times-too-many taste. There were no hash browns. The biscuits were cold, hard, and dry, and the butter, rancid.

Feeling hemmed in, claustrophobic, she lowered her knife and fork and stared glassily down at the pale rainbows floating in the grease slick on her plate. Her mouth started watering sickeningly; her stomach heaved.

Gagging, she lunged to her feet and, shoving the cook aside, ran out the door. She kept on running, her hand clamped over her mouth, leaping over obstacles and chuckholes until at last she stumbled down the pier and collapsed to her knees against the bell post.

She clung to it, gasping. Gradually the nausea started easing off. The tightness in her throat subsided. She inhaled deeply. The bubbly spots swimming before her eyes faded away.

Turning around, she slumped against the bell post, her panting fragmented by hiccups. After a time, she rolled her head to the side and gazed haggardly at the ferryboat chained to the pier directly across the river from her. Flapping a hand over her head, she found the bell rope and gave it three sharp yanks. She paused, watching the opposite bank for the ferryboat operator.

"You all right?" She heard Coke clomping down the pier behind her.

She turned her exhausted eyes up at him.

"Pore ole Diego," he said, patting her affectionately on the top of the head. "You sure didn't pay him much of a compliment on his cookin'."

"It'd make a goat throw up!" she retorted, flinging her arm up and knocking his hand away. "Hot, fluffy biscuits! Hash browns! Indeed!"

"Wasn't one o' his better days," he drawled.

Giving him a reproachful look, she grasped the bell post and pulled to her feet. She jangled the bell and, shading her eyes, searched the opposite bank. She jangled it again, longer and louder. Still the ferryboat operator didn't appear.

"Where is he?" she cried exasperatedly. "Why doesn't he come?"

"Folks don't snap to in these parts like they do up north," he explained matter-of-factly. "It's contrary to their nature. They move at their own pace."

"Thanks! Thanks a lot!" she shot back. "I appreciate that, I really do! It's a great comfort!" She set her jaw. "I'm gonna get on his nerves so badly that he'll have to come."

With that, she jangled the bell, long and loudly, tapping her toe and chanting in a rising voice, "Come . . . come . . . come . . . you nincompoop!"

Icy wires of panic were starting to vibrate at the back of her skull. She pushed past Coke, and bustled up to the pier and into town. Turning to the right, she stopped behind a stable, where she could get an unobstructed view of the road into town. No one was coming down it. Only a handful of people were meandering, here and there, across it. She raised her eyes, fixing them on the crest of the hill over which the road disappeared. Imagining Mike O'Banion and the marshal ascending that hill on the opposite side this very minute, she whirled around and scampered back to the pier.

Coke had vanished. Looking desperately about, she found him up on the riverbank sitting placidly on the ground in the shade of a warehouse.

"Do something!" she yelled, charging at him. "For God's sake, get that boat back here!"

"Ah, Jessie," he groaned. "What you want me t'do? Traipse across the river for it? Now, just calm down. That ol' ferryboat'll come scootin' back here before you know it."

"Sure! You told me that almost an hour ago, when you talked me into that pigsty for breakfast."

Giving him a contemptuous look, she turned on her heel, and stomped back down the pier. Angrily grabbing the rope, she jangled the bell so long and emphatically that folks on both sides of the river leaned around to see what was the matter. But the ferryboat operator wasn't among them.

A Mexican peasant, neck wreathed with ropes of garlic, came strolling down the riverbank. Noting that the ferryboat was on the other side and that some deranged *mujer* was jangling the bell for him, he sat down next to Coke and, pulling his sombrero over his face, settled back for a little siesta.

It galled Jessica, this passive tolerance of everyone to the ferryboat operator's rude disregard of his duty. She wanted to shake them all until their teeth fell out. Instead, she tore back up the riverbank, sliding to a stop at her lookout post behind the stable. She searched the road sloping into town. It remained deserted.

She fixed her eyes on the ridge. No other riders appeared there. Giving it one last hard look, warning it to stay that way, she fretted back down to the pier, had no better luck with the bell than she'd had before.

Defeated, she plodded up the riverbank to Coke. Pushing his hat back, he squinted up at her. "Now, simmer down, honey. 'Tain't healthy t'go flyin' offa the handle in this heat, you could get sunstroke. Just sit down an' relax, all right?"

"It just isn't fair," she replied, sinking down beside him, "his stranding people this way."

But the peasant with the wreathes of garlic wasn't suffering from an excess of impatience. Sprawled on his back, arms outflung, he was snoring softly, a rope of garlic hooked over his upper lip just underneath his nostrils.

Looking across the river, Jessica found herself meeting the blank stares of the string of people who were sitting on the opposite bank, waiting mutely for the ferryboat operator to bring them to the U.S. side. Mexico, safety, seemed so close yet so out of reach.

Where was Ole Belcher? The question sprang out at her. Why hadn't Coke brought him here so that he could lead him straightaway onto the ferry as soon as it arrived? Hadn't he told her over in Mexico that he had to get Ole Belcher? Why, then, had he left him still tied to the hitching rail back in town?

She leaned back, her mind working. Coke had misled her a few times these last twelve hours. And three times, she distinctly recalled, three times, he'd urged her to go back to Dispenseme with him—and Coke Sanders was the type of man who usually got his way. By hook or crook. But no; he wouldn't have gotten the entry paper for her if he didn't intend her to use it. Would he?

Suddenly she couldn't stand being near him any longer. She scrambled to her feet and began pacing the riverbank. After a time, she wandered down the pier, gave the bell a halfhearted little clank and sat down. She tilted her face up and squinted at the sun. It had to be noon . . . or later. She peeked over her shoulder. His arms folded, hat over his face, Coke was slouched half-recumbent against the wall, apparently having just dozed off.

A sly gleam came to her eye. Slowly, methodically, she began unbuttoning a shoe. She'd just jerked it off when Coke's shadow fell over her.

"What're you doin'?" he asked pleasantly.

"Preparing to wade the river."

"Why?"

"Ferryboat's not coming back."

"It'll be back."

"Not in my lifetime." She jerked off her other shoe.

"Wouldn't try t'wade that river if I was you."

"You're not me."

"Got potholes."

She peeked up at him. "What?"

"The river. May look smooth an' shallow from here, but it's chock-full o' potholes. Big-un's."

"Yes, I'm sure there are potholes around here," she said tiredly. "But they're not in that river. They're in my head, for ever allowing you to talk me into coming back here."

Upending each shoe, she shook out her gold pieces and, unbuttoning the top of her blouse, dropped them into her cleavage. "Now, don't you fret, dear," she went on as, with a twist of the shoulder and a pat of the hand, she worked the gold pieces into place. "If I happen t'step into one o' those ole potholes you got out there, why, I'll just let my little ole backside go a-floatin' on up an' paddle across it."

"Wouldn't be too sure you could do that. That winter skirt you got on is durn heavy. Full o' water, it could drag you under. Maybe you should take it off before you try your hand at swimmin' this here river."

"Oh, certainly, certainly," she retorted caustically, getting up to face him. "And when I reach Mexico and start sloppin' down their streets in my underwear, your dear, scandalized compadres will have something to say about that!"

Bending over, she took hold of the hem at the back of her skirt, pulled it up between her legs, and tucked it into the front of her waistband so that her skirt fit her like a pair of loose pantaloons.

"Got snappin' turtles out there," he said.

"Oh, slibber-saucer," she responded, picking up her shoes. Flattening them out, she squeezed them into her waistband on either side, heels sticking out so that she looked like she was sporting a pair of six-shooters. "Now, don't concern your little ole self 'bout them ole snappin' turtles out there, hon," she went on. "I'll keep a sharp lookout for them, I surely will—" her voice dropped "—as well as for the octopuses, sharks, whales, an' rabid beavers you got out there."

"'Tain't no octopuses, sharks, whales, nor rabid beavers out there," he replied unflappably. "Just snappin' turtles. Big-uns."

"BULLSHIT!"

"Why, Jessie," he breathed.

"Yes, BULLSHIT!" she blasted him again. "There are snapping turtles out there, fella—like that ferryboat is always tied to this side of the river. There are snapping turtles out there—like . . . like that shack we stayed in last night was the only shelter for miles around." She caught her breath. "Really, Coke, just how noodle-brained do you think I am?"

"Now, Jessie . . ." he said reasonably.

"JessICA!" she cut him off. "The name's JessICA!"

"Now, listen—" he tried again.

"No! You listen—you—you." She shook her finger at him. "I don't trust you. I was out of my mind to have ever trusted you. A complete jackass! Well, I won't be making that mistake again. I'm through with you. Got that? Through. I don't want your help. I don't need your help. Go back to that precious ranch of yours and keep your cows company. I'm leaving. So wish me luck, and thanks heaps for getting me—" Her eyes brightened. "That's right! Give me that entry paper I paid for."

He didn't move, eyeing her. Then, shaking his head, he heaved a long-suffering sigh. "All right, Jessie, if you're so set on swimmin' that damn river, I'll take you across on Ole Belcher. Least, thataway only your bottom half'll come out soppin' wet."

She regarded him skeptically.

He grasped her shoulders, locking her in place. "Now, don't move. Don't go divin' in yet. I'll get Ole Belcher an' be back in a jiffy."

Without waiting for a reply, he turned and strode up the bank into town.

"Lordy, lordy," she muttered, sinking down on the end of the pier, "the lengths a woman has to go to, to get a man to move." It wasn't long before she started feeling uneasy again. It seemed like it was taking Coke a mighty long time just to get his horse. Maybe she should start across the river anyway. She peered down into the water. *Were* there snapping turtles out there? Big-uns? Was it really deeper in places than it looked? In spite of what she'd told Coke, she'd once discovered the hard way, years ago, that she was about as buoyant in water as a two-ton boulder.

No, she banished those doubts. That double-dealer, Coke, was still stringing her along. She'd better start wading that river—now.

She'd edged around the pier and had one stockinged foot on the ladder, ready to swing down, when she heard footsteps and the clip-clop of a horse coming down the riverbank. She looked around, relieved. The blood froze in her veins, for she was looking into the sadistic, triumphant eyes of Mike O'Banion. And a few feet behind him, sitting astride his horse, was Marshal Shaftesbury, staring down at her in openmouthed amazement.

"Hot damn, Jethica!" he exclaimed. "What in holy hell are you thtill doin' on *thith* thide o' the river?"

"We was waitin' for you," Coke drawled, strolling up behind them. "We was just sittin' round a-waitin' for you."

✿ Chapter 51

MIKE O'BANION SLAPPED the reins, and the rented surrey carrying him and Jessica speeded up. The marshal and Coke, on horseback, were pushing their mounts at a rigorous pace. Mike didn't appreciate having to keep up. It only aggravated the teeth-chattering clatter of the iron wheels on the rocky ground. He wondered, why the haste? They had the woman now.

He glanced aside at Jessica, sitting as far away from him on the seat as she could get, as if he harbored some revolting disease. He smirked. Now he had her, the chippy whose charms had kept LaMarque itchy for two years. He'd often watched her in the casino. She had a smooth, contained style that attracted the pigeons. And when a customer raised her ire, she turned on that icy charm, dealt out the cards, and made him pay. Now she would pay.

With his long black hair slick-varnished to his head, and his faded complexion stained blue-gray, like an old bruise, around the jaw from a thick growth of inerasable whiskers, Mike didn't look Irish. Indeed, he was but a fraction of the stock, a dilution of a miscellany of nameless, faceless travelers in the night, Mike's own father included. Dear old dad was but a random seed that had happened to find its way into the fertile womb of a fourteen-year-old barmaid by the name of Sally O'Banion, the first of seven such random seeds that had taken root and ripened into seven bastard babies, no two alike.

That he was a man of crude and virulent nature did not keep Mike O'Banion from being highly sensitive about his ignoble origins. He sought to compensate for the defect, not by improving himself and becoming a gentleman of honor, but by assiduously adopting the trappings of a gentleman of honor, taking especial care in the cut, style, and fabric of his clothing. The effect was that of a vampire bat in peacock feathers.

"You weren't the one waitin' for us at the river, now were you, love?" he gibed in the Irish brogue he affected with the ladies. "It was the cowboy who was waitin'. Not you. Tricked you, he did. Musta heard o' the reward." He snickered. "Who'd have thought it—you, a city-wise gal, gettin' suckered by a back-country hayseed."

She ignored him, her eyes smoldering into the cowboy. Mike shot a contemptuous look of his own at Seth.

"A fool and a numbskull, that marshal," he muttered. "I knew you was off t'Mexico, I did. But that bumpkin wouldn't hear of it. Led me on a house-to-house search, he did. All afternoon long from house t'barn t'stable we went. Then he spent half the night standin' outside the jail watchin' cowpokes driftin' by to some place on the other side o' town. This mornin', though, was a different story. He was itchin' to go after you like a fire had been lit under him."

O'Banion tensed. "What's this?"

Jessica pulled her eyes from Coke. Four riders were galloping at breakneck speed toward them. One she recognized as the older son of Coke's murdered foreman.

The four men swung around behind them, the dust from their horses swirling over the surrey. Jessica noticed with sly satisfaction O'Banion's confusion as to how to take this forceful arrival of four rough, foreign-looking men.

Cruz said something in quick Spanish to Coke.

"Seth told me," Coke responded grimly.

The rest of their conversation was lost in the racket of the surrey going down a gravelly decline. When they moved out of it, she heard Coke say to Cruz.

". . . t'Warner pronto. Get fresh horses at the Navarro spread.

Tell that attorney o' mine now's the time t'bust outa the gate like a bull spurtin' steam.''

Cruz, followed by a young, smaller vaquero, split away from the group, shooting off at full gallop toward the north. The other two vaqueros veered away to the east.

"What in the—" O'Banion began, then lost his words as a front wheel of the surrey dropped into a hole, skidding the rear wheels to the side.

Their arrival in Dispenseme came too soon for Jessica. If they'd dragged the trip out a week, their arrival would've come too soon for her, for now she knew she must face the townspeople's certain knowledge of the conterfeit life that she'd led among them.

As they moved through the town's sun-scorched streets, she felt on display, like a naughty little girl being brought back by more sensible adults to take her medicine. And she was ashamed at the thought of anyone she cared for seeing her this way. So as the surrey rolled along, her gaze traveled over the street with a distant, unfocusing dread as if she were skimming a newspaper for that one fateful headline.

They slowed to a stop in front of the jail. Jessica sat upright, blinking rapidly about as though coming out of a bad dream. She became aware of two heavily armed strangers riding toward them, their forms elongated and wavery in the glaring, hazy light. Then she noticed a half dozen vaqueros leaning in the shadows against a store across the street. They, too, were armed and strangely quiet. She recognized one and realized that they were from the Sidewinder.

Coke came around to help her down. A convulsion sweeping through her, she jerked her arm away, bounded off the surrey, and strode frostily by him into Seth's office.

"I'll take the prisoner into custody now," O'Banion said when they'd gathered inside.

Seth lay back in his chair, propped his feet up on his desk, and laced his fingers behind his head. "Can't do that," he said.

"And why not?" O'Banion asked.

" 'Tain't legal," Coke replied.

"Oh, that it is," O'Banion responded, sliding his hand into the inside pocket of his day coat and drawing out a long, bulging envelope. "I have here a warrant for this woman's arrest, issued on the ninth day of June in the year of our Lord 1886, by the Right

Honorable Willis B. Wayne, Judge of Superior Court Eight, in and for the City of San Francisco, County of San Francisco, State of California. Furthermore, I have here with me a notarized document designating me as a duly sworn deputy of the aforementioned court, empowering me to take into custody one Jessica Wade Daniels, whensoever and wheresoever I may encounter her."

"That's quite a mouthful," Coke said blandly. "An' I do believe that ole Judge Willis'd be right proud o' you. 'Ceptin' you overlooked one tiny detail."

"And what might that be?"

"This ain't San Francisco an' it ain't California. This is Dispenseme, in the county of Falcon, state o' Texas. We got our own laws here. An' I do believe that one or two of 'em got somethin' t'do with hustlin' folks outa this state without their say-so . . . legal-like."

O'Banion's eyes narrowed as he studied this cowboy who seemed to be calling the shots. There was an air of authority about him that contradicted the worn plainness of his cattlepuncher's garb.

"And where might I find a judge to whom I could present these documents," he asked affably, "and thereby petition authorization to remove this felon from this jurisdiction?" He sent Coke a barbed look. "Legal-like."

"Ed Bierbaum, the circuit judge, will be in town holdin' court day after tomorrow," Seth replied.

"Tell Ed t'set us up a hearin'," Coke said to Seth.

The prompt endorsement by the cowboy, not to mention his ready use of the judge's first name and his apparent ability to set the man's schedule, stopped O'Banion. He'd better maneuver himself out of this likely trap, he decided. He'd focus on the marshal, and try to supersede the cowboy's influence over him.

He smiled benignly at Seth. "I can see no practicable merit in a court proceeding. As a veteran of innumerable court appearances yourself, Marshal, I'm sure you appreciate how tedious, how time-consuming, the aforementioned proceedings can become. In this matter they'd be a sheer and utter waste of your time, my time, the court's time, as well as of taxpayer monies inasmuch as these documents I hold in my possession are in good order, properly executed and incontrovertible. They'd stand up under any and the most rigorous scrutiny, leaving this court, or any other court, for that matter, no alternative but to direct you to remand this felon into my custody.''

''Whatever our Texas courts decide, Bunion,'' Coke said, ''they will have the chance t'go ahead an' decide it.''

Ignoring Coke, O'Banion leaned forward on Seth's desk. ''Prolonged and unnecessary delay could jeopardize your entitlement to the two-hundred-dollar reward being offered for the expeditious return of this felon to California. We must be mindful, Marshal, of how justice would best be served here. Remember, this woman is not dissimilar from any other perpetrator of felonious crime that has infected your township and its citizenry thereof. True, she may not look like a felon, nor may have she conducted herself like a felon during her tenure in your jurisdiction. But I must remind you that she's been accused of a most perfidious crime against the law-abiding citizenry of San Francisco. Justice has been too long delayed there already. Therefore, I adjure you to dispense with the proposed de trop court proceeding and remand this woman into my custody forthwith.''

Seth gazed blankly at O'Banion for a time, then looked at Coke. ''Damn! Thith ith like lithenin' to a dicthionary fartin'.''

''You've battered our ears long enough, Bunion,'' Coke said. ''We'll see you in court in two days' time.'' He looked pointedly at Seth.

With a sigh, Seth sat up and got to his feet. ''Mind comin' thith way, Mith Jethica?'' he said, reaching for the key ring hanging on a hook on the wall.

Jessica looked at him uncomprehendingly.

''I . . . uh . . . hafta lock you up.''

Jessica walked over to Seth and stared at him in disbelief. ''You're putting me in jail?'' she asked in a high voice.

Seth didn't meet her eyes. ''It'th the law.''

''But, how *can* you?'' She turned on Coke. He was looking away, whistling soundlessly to himself.

Seth swung the cell door open.

''You . . .'' she began, then turned on her heel and marched into the cell, wincing at the clatter of the iron door slamming shut behind her. Grasping two of the bars on either side of her face, she peered out between them like a caged animal at the men departing, seeing with spiteful satisfaction the twinge of guilt on Coke's face as he went out the door. He put her here—the louse. But why?

Seth locked the jailhouse door, then turned to O'Banion. "You roughed up thith lady in here yethterday," he warned. "I better not catch you within a hundred feet o' thith jail. Got that?"

"She was resisting arrest," O'Banion replied. "I'm not the kind of man who'd intentionally hurt a lady." And, turning, he walked coolly away.

"That'th like a wolf claimin' it don't eat meat," Seth muttered. He glanced over Coke's shoulder. "Oh, thit!"

Coke turned, and saw Meg coming up the street. "Well, I gotta get to my ranch," he said quickly, pulling Ole Belcher's reins off the hitching rail.

"I'm gettin' away quicker!" Seth strode off.

"Where's Jessica?" Meg asked.

Coke glanced back. The chicken-hearted sheriff had already beaten a path halfway to the saloon.

Coke nodded toward the jail. "In there."

"What's she doing in there?" Meg asked suspiciously.

Coke climbed into the saddle. The vaqueros were already mounted and waiting. "She's locked up."

"What!" Meg exploded. "Why'd you put her in jail?"

"I got this other thing t'deal with, Meg."

"That don't give you no call t'lock that girl in jail!"

"It's the safest place for her right now," he answered. "Locked in there, I know she ain't gonna try t'hightail it off again, an' that city cutthroat cain't get at her."

Meg settled down some. "This is sure one sorry way t'court a gal." She shook her head. "She ain't likely to overlook this, you know."

"I know," he answered dourly.

Meg's eyes had gentled. "My prayers are with you, Coke . . . with all o' you." A spark of mischief rose in her eyes. "You better take care, Coke. Remember, you got a gal waitin' for you here." She glanced at the jail. "You made damn sure o' that."

Chapter 52

MEG HADN'T SEEN Jessica look this despairing since that morning at the train depot in New Mexico three months ago. She cast a worried look at Lou, whom Seth had left to watch over the jail. He hadn't noticed; he wouldn't. But Meg knew. Jessica had pulled back into an unnatural stillness, and those dark borders had appeared around her eyes, making them seem both faraway and magnified. So little of her was there, it seemed, that she wouldn't stir the air about her. Even her voice lacked weight. It sounded as far removed as an echo on its third reflection.

At least seeing Willie seemed to revive her a bit. He sat on her lap showing her the paper flower that he'd made for her with "I love you Mommy" scrawled at the center.

"It's beautiful," Jessica said. "I love it."

Willie wrinkled his nose, seeing his flower now through someone else's eyes, its petals of uneven length, pasted clumsily, with smudges. "It's not that good."

"Oh, but it's beautiful to me," she said, kissing his hair, "because it has you in it." The feeling of diminishment in her lifted a little.

Willie looked up at her, their eyes touching like a caress. He settled back, swinging his feet. "All right, when are you coming home?"

"I don't know."

"Why're you in here at all?"

Jessica hesitated. "Because I trusted someone I shouldn't have."

Meg cleared her throat. "Could be your trustin' there wasn't a bad choice."

"It put me here."

Willie picked up on that. "Who made you be here?"

There was another long pause. "Mr. LaMarque and a mean man named Mike O'Banion."

433

Meg sighed inwardly. Riled as Jessica was at Coke, she wouldn't destroy her son's affection for him.

Concern filled Jessica's eyes. "Are your friends, the other children, teasing you because I'm here? Are they saying that I'm bad?"

"They act more like you're sick than like you're bad."

Jessica looked over Willie's head at Meg for confirmation.

"Don't measure folks here by others that you've known," she said.

"I don't have to be protected, Meg. The people here must think that I've deceived them about myself."

"Most folks just take it for granted that anyone who shows up here all of a sudden like you did, and is as close-mouthed 'bout herself like you was, must've left somethin' purty ugly behind."

A shy knock sounded at the door, and Willie slid off Jessica's lap. He was young enough to want to be held, but old enough to want not to get caught at it.

Meg opened the door. Chacho was standing there holding a plate with a checkered napkin spread over it.

"My mother made *buñuelos* this mornin', Meg," he said. "She thought that Willie's mama might like some for her *merienda*."

Jessica looked confused. "They're for me?"

"Looks like it." Meg smiled.

"Tell your mama 'Thank you,' " Jessica said softly to Chacho. "And that she's very kind."

The two little boys' eyes connected. Leaning to the side, Willie spotted another child waiting in the street. Restlessness stirred through him. His mother was here. She was all right. Now he could play. He looked questioningly at her.

"Go on," she said, setting his hat on his head. Leaning down, she hugged and kissed him one last time before sending him on his way.

She watched the tops of the boys' hats whisk by the window outside. "Coke shouldn't have done this, Meg. He shouldn't have betrayed me."

"He didn't betray you."

"Then why did he have me locked in here? Why did he arrange for that court hearing tomorrow? What's the purpose of it? Those papers Mike O'Banion has will send me straight back to San Francisco. Is that what Coke wants?"

"I'm sure it ain't. I'm sure he'd never allow that. I don't know what he's got up his sleeve, but you can count on it, he's got somethin'."

"Too bad he didn't let *me* in on his fine scheme . . . instead of having me clamped in jail, then riding off. I had my own plans, Meg. Coke knew them. Yet he disregarded them like they were unimportant. I made the mistake of accepting his help once . . . and boom! like the typical thick-skulled male . . . he just moved right in and took over."

"Whatever Coke has in mind, I'm sure he feels it'd be better for you his way."

"Well, that's mighty big of him."

"Jessica, when you love someone, you wanta protect 'em . . . especially when you think they're headed for what could turn out to be a big mistake. Coke *did* have a hand in puttin' you here. An' the reason probably was selfishness on his part."

Jessica frowned. "What could he gain?"

"Havin' you close an' havin' you safe," Meg answered gently. "Because if harm came to you, it'd hurt him, too. That's the selfishness."

That forlorn look returned to her eyes. She got up and went to the window. Meg could see by the drop of her shoulders that she was still deeply troubled. Meg puzzled how being locked in jail could leave Jessica this distraught now that she knew Coke's motive.

"The marshal told me that T. C. Barrett has a court order to take over a large part of Coke's land," she said in that echoey voice. "Coke won't accept that."

"No, he won't."

"The marshal told me that Barrett has an army of paid gunfighters."

"I heard that."

"Do you think Coke will get hurt?"

Now Meg saw the source of Jessica's lingering distress. "You know Coke," she said. "Soon as a body thinks he's got Coke Sanders movin' along a particular line, Coke'll loop it aroun' an' tangle him in it."

"I know," Jessica said.

"I guess you would," Meg responded softly.

"It's because Barrett's son, the one Coke shot defending himself, died, isn't it? That's the reason Barrett's out to get Coke."

"Barrett was already gettin' set t'do it."

Jessica turned. "I shouldn't have allowed Jack Siden to walk me home that day."

"You still believe that Jack was a part o' that ambush?"

Jessica nodded.

"Child, a real killer sets his own self off. He can always find an excuse. If it's not you, then it's someone else; if it's not today, it's tomorrow. Score settlin' is his way o' life. You ain't responsible for that." Meg put her arm around Jessica. "Now, bear up. This day will pass."

Jessica took her arm. "You let me know how it goes with Coke." She blinked. "Not that I care."

"I will."

Jessica still held on. "The very minute you hear, you let me know . . . not that I care."

Meg smiled faintly. "The very minute I hear, I'll let you know. Even though you don't care."

Mike O'Banion watched the three boys scamper by him down the road, his eyes on the boy who'd come out of the jail. Must belong to the Daniels baggage, had the same features, he thought, his eyes following the boy until the three whipped around a corner and were gone.

He turned and walked back toward the center of town, his footsteps drumming hollowly on the boardwalk. It was a dingy, overcast morning. The town seemed almost deserted. A peculiar hush had settled over it, a silence almost heavy enough to be felt pressing against the skin. This was one sour place, he thought as he regarded the pinched, turned-away faces of the few people he encountered.

And he didn't even have a place to stay tonight. When he'd come out of his room this morning, his landlady had been waiting at his door.

"Sorry," she blurted, her hand nervously springing over the loose gray curls in her hair, "but you'll hafta find some other place t'bunk t'night. That room ain't available anymore."

"Why?" O'Banion demanded.

"My brother's payin' me a visit."

"So?" Mike folded his arms.

"He's a regulator," she said with a widening of an eye. "Wolf-Face Pete Buchanon is what they call him. These past eighteen months he's been mighty busy gunnin' down or stringin' up close to two dozen cattle thieves an' desperadoes all the way from Montana to New Mexico. Thought he needed a rest." She sighed, her hand still springing over her curls. "He's a high-strung feller, Pete. Got a hair-trigger temper. An' he wouldn't look kindly on crawlin' into that bed in there t'night an' findin' a whiskery Irishman in it." She gave him a fleeting smile. "So, clear out." And turning, she disappeared into the kitchen.

Mike had followed her, only to be stopped by the sight of four other middle-aged women sitting staunchly at the kitchen table like army generals conferring over battle plans.

Now he was starting to wonder if there wasn't some sort of conspiracy against him around here.

Mike looked at the saloon across the road from him. Here was respite, he thought, starting toward it.

He pushed through the swinging doors into the dark, cavernous room. The bartender was standing at the end of the bar, chin propped in his hand, reading a newspaper spread out on the bar top before him. O'Banion's attention was drawn by an odd, rhythmic *schlip . . . schlip . . . schlip* sound, like someone was lightly slapping a drippy cloth against a chairback. His eyes followed the sound to a huge man sitting at a table jawing a plug of chewing tobacco, the top half of his face buried under a tall, greasy hat and the shadow that fell from it. A woman in a tight-fitting gown sat across from the huge man, her girlish red, ringletted hair clashing with a tough face that was almost a dead ringer for Andrew Jackson's during the second term of his presidency. Between the fat man and the woman was a third man, who set his beer down, got up, and headed toward the door. He brushed past O'Banion on his way out.

"Didn't know you served Mexicans here," Mike said congenially to the bartender with just a touch of the brogue.

The man said nothing, slowly turning a page of his newspaper.

"It's either that or go bankrupt," the woman spoke up in a sharp tone. She got up and, a fresh-rolled cigarette in one hand and a match in the other, strolled toward O'Banion. She stopped in front of him and, looking him hard in the eyes, fired her match with a flip of the thumb and sucked the flame into her cigarette. Shaking the match out, she looked O'Banion up and down, her eyes fixing on his brocade vest and the ruffles of his shirt. Smoke trailing out of her mouth, she moved off, slowly circling around him.

O'Banion tensed. "What're you doin'?"

She came to a stop in front of him again. "Just checkin' t'see if your ass was ruffled, too."

She drew on her cigarette, letting the smoke out in his face. "Ain't never seen such fancy duds on a man before. Next to you, my whores'd look pale."

"Next to a stucco wall, your whores'd look pale," the fat man twanged, lolling his swinging jaw.

"Cain't take too deep offense, Soot," she answered, her flinty eyes still on O'Banion, "from a cattleman who's such a sorry judge o' cow flesh, even, that he's the only rancher in a hunnert miles who ain't been rustled."

She leaned toward O'Banion, squinting into his face. "How you keep 'em from slidin' off you?"

"What?" he asked suspiciously.

"Your duds. Must be hard keepin' clothes up on city slime."

O'Banion reddened. He felt a subtle movement to the side. A six-shooter had materialized on top of the newspaper the bartender was reading.

"Soot," the woman called over to the big man at the table. "You should come over here an' stand next to this dude. You two could start a travelin' show. Call yourselves Grime an' Slime."

"You could join us," the fat man twanged. "Call yourself 'Anythin' for a dime.' " He spat pingingly into the spittoon. "At that, the price'd be inflated."

"That's all right," the woman said. "I understand. A man can turn bitter when he starts outweighin' his horse an' outsmellin' his cows. But you're welcome here anyway, Soot."

She turned on O'Banion. "But you . . . you city slime . . . you ain't welcome. Now, get out."

O'Banion hesitated, shot through with rage.

"What's the matter?" the woman snarled. "The slime pluggin' up your ears? This place is closed t'your kind. So take your ass back t'where it came from. Foul up the streets o' your own town."

O'Banion's eyes moved toward the bartender again. He was still gazing placidly at the newspaper, but his hand had settled over the six-shooter.

"Hellcat!" O'Banion spat out. "Bitch! Whore!" And whipping around, he slammed out through the barroom doors.

The woman's voice followed him outside. "You catch him slitherin' back in under the door, Smitty . . . stomp on him."

"Damn, I'm feelin' fretful," Ruby muttered, sitting down across from Soot. "Wonder when Reymondo's gonna get back with the news o' what's going on at the San Sebastian." She drew on her cigarette. "Sure wish you'd kept your mouth shut while that city dude was here," she said, blowing out the smoke with her words. "You was interferin' with my concentration."

"I know, Ruby," Soot replied. "It can get t'be a strain jugglin' the insultin' o' two hombres at the same time."

"Dude wasn't much of a challenge anyway. All he could do was turn red and name-call." She shot a look at Smitty. "Well, dammit," she snapped. "Say somethin'."

"Scared to," he said, quietly turning a page in his newspaper.

O'Banion hurtled down the road, rage tearing him inside. They think they've won. But they'll find out. Wasn't for nothing that he was known in San Francisco as the Shark of the Shadows.

Chapter 53

CHUNKS OF CLOUDS crowded low in the sky, blocking off the sun. The air lay still and cool against the earth. The dust drubbed up by the pounding hooves of the riders swarming over the hill curled quickly earthward, lacking a breeze to puff it upward or heat to make it buoyant. The army of men scattered into a line of chaparral, and trickled out the other side in groups of twos and threes along the Sidewinder's eastern fence.

T. C. Barrett scanned the area before him. The land inside the fence looked no different from the land outside. But to Barrett's eye it was different, in the way that all money looked alike yet took on the nature of the hand that held it. He looked at the fence threading out on either side, the posts stitching along the contours of the land, their spacing contracting in the distance until they fused to a point and pricked through the horizon. That fence stood there like a challenge from Sanders: "This is where I draw the line."

"Pull it down!" Barrett called.

Lassos were flung out and the fence posts began bending and crackling down.

"I was expectin' a reception committee," Watt Calhoun said.

Barrett shrugged, though he'd been thinking the same thing himself. "Let Sanders meet us where he wants. We got him outgunned two to one."

"Why ain't Ray here?" Calhoun asked. "Seems it'd make this court order I got more official havin' a lawyer along t'spell it out fancy."

Barrett's brows lowered. "Took off a coupla nights ago."

"Takin' Beau's death hard, I guess."

"Boy ain't learned that gettin' back like this is the best way t'handle a blow." Barrett's scowl deepened. "I'll probably have t'follow the trail o' empty whiskey bottles through half the whorehouses along the border before I track him down."

He checked his rifle, then nudged his horse over the downed fence. "Keep a close lookout!"

Guns at the ready, eyes darting about, Barrett's army passed into the Sidewinder. They rode on, pressing deeper into the land. Stringing back in a loose line, Barrett's army wended down dry creek beds and up the other sides, over bare, scorched hills, past the bleached skulls of cows and over the bones of a deer, crunching under their horses' hooves like dry twigs. Still the silence wore on, the plump of hooves, the crackle of brush, the only sounds.

Where was Sanders? they asked themselves. Would he just let them wander about here forever, guns jerking up at a roadrunner bursting out of a thicket, heads turning at the sudden stutter of an insect, eyes catching on the odd flutter of a twig? They couldn't seize this vast expanse of land without anyone on hand to take it from. They'd be left with only the immensity itself, drifting loose around inside it like a dash of salt in a two-gallon jug.

They were losing their edge and growing apathetic when, about noon, they came upon a windmill towering over a grove of trees. Winding around the thicket, Barrett's column came to a line of corrals that ran along one side of it. There, sitting on their horses at the other end of the corrals and facing Barrett, were five men—Coke Sanders; the local marshal, Seth Shaftesbury; and three other ranchers, Hector Navarro, Graham McKetchin, and Lucas Blankenship. A tall, straight-backed young vaquero sat apart from the others on his horse in front of the trees and facing the corrals.

Coke, and the men with him, didn't move, but waited there silently at the opposite end of the corrals. Barrett hesitated; then, feeling the power of his paid army, he rode toward Sanders, drawing the line of gunslingers behind him, filing between the corrals on the one side and the vaquero in front of the trees on the other.

Feeling an odd prickling along the flesh in his back, Calhoun looked around at the Mexican by the trees. The man was watching him steadily. Something in his eyes . . .

"Thought you'd turn up here," Coke said to Barrett. "This place has changed some in the last twenty-seven years, hasn't it?"

"Not that much," Barrett replied. He nodded toward the trees. "Over there my pa an' me got shot an' I had my first hard lesson."

"Lessons," Coke repeated. "Seems you're a man o' hard lessons, either gettin' 'em or givin' 'em out. Yet I doubt that you've learned a damn thing from any of 'em."

"I have," Barrett responded. "Sheriff, hand over that court order. You're trespassin' on my land, Sanders. I got the law backin' me up now."

Coke took the paper. "Looks legal, all right," he said, glancing indifferently at it. His eyes turned flinty. "Interestin' how hombres like you always try t'serve up for other folks t'swallow, the same meat that you've been shittin' on all your lives."

"We're curious," Graham McKetchin said. "We wanta know, Barrett, what happened to those cattle that was trailed outa Caballo Blanco Canyon these past few months . . . and herded into the San Sebastian. A good number o' them cows we figger was ours."

"Hunches," Barrett scoffed. "We all got 'em. Not much proof in 'em, though."

Feeling the sting of the vaquero's eyes on him, Calhoun kept glancing back at the man. Giving Calhoun one last long, hooded look, the vaquero turned his horse, seemingly bored, and ambled unhurriedly along the edge of the trees. He'd rounded them and was gone before Calhoun could sound the alarm.

"Those clerks o' yours from the Savin's an' Loan had more t'talk about than bank fraud, Barrett," Coke was saying.

"So a pair o' disgruntled employees is tellin' lies t'get back at me," Barrett responded.

"They're tellin' more. They're tellin' names. Like the name of a cattle broker in Trail City who's been sellin' quite of number o' Texas beeves with questionable ownership. Like the names o' some railroad employees who've been collectin' bonuses that the

railroad company ain't been payin' 'em. While you been collectin' your gunslingers here t'steal my land, a roundin' up of a
different sort has started up—back in Warner and Colorado."

Barrett's eyes had turned sulfurous. "Only words. Empty
words. When the time comes t'bring those words out in court, if
it ever comes to that, you can be damn sure you won't have even
those anymore. Now, that court order has been served. Sheriff,
clear 'em offa my land now."

"I got somethin' t'give you first," Coke said. "Seth?"

The marshal ambled forward and handed a paper to Barrett.

Barrett looked at it, his face hardening.

"In case you're wonderin', Calhoun," Coke said, "that's a
court order signed by Judge Edwin T. Bierbaum. It vacates the
one you just handed me."

"The wind can blow paper," Barrett scoffed. "It only carries
weight when there's muscle t'back it up. An' I got the muscle."
He stopped, for vaqueros were riding in a line out from the copse,
and were forming an arc in front of him almost two hundred yards
distant. Scattered among them were men from the Navarro and
Blankenship ranches.

"Ranch hands are no match for gunmen," Barrett said. "We
got 'em way outgunned. Are they willin' t'die for you?"

"It ain't me exactly that those men out there are willin' t'fight
for. The question is, are these paid cutthroats o' yours willin' t'die
for your money?"

Barrett looked almost amused. "Doesn't look like it'll be much
of a fight."

"Guess we're back t'talkin' lessons again, Barrett . . .'cause
there's one lesson from South Texas that you ain't never picked
up."

"What's that?"

"Never piss a Spanish priest."

Barrett's brows knitted.

"I doubt that the padre in these parts gives a rosary bead 'bout
the Sidewinder. But you got him damn pissed by what you done
to the Castillo family. Now, since the padre ain't allowed t'follow
his natural inclinations no more an' barbecue sinners at the stake,
he done the next best thing . . . passed the word. Look behind
you, Barrett."

Barrett turned. Another line of vaqueros had formed behind
them.

"I doubt you'd recognize 'em," Coke continued. "But a good

number o' those are Castillo's men . . . the former vaqueros of the San Sebastian.''

Barrett swung back forward to face Coke, his face tight with fury.

"Damn!" Coke said. "I wish you'd signed up as a Yank general durin' the war. Lee woulda whipped your ass an' taken Washington in an afternoon. In case you ain't noticed it yet, Barrett . . . though I see that Calhoun an' some o' your men are startin' t'get the picture . . . you, an' your high-powered troops, are bottled up here. Enemy's in front of 'em, enemy's starin' down their rear. As to their flanks—won't be easy crashin' through these corrals here on their right. That leaves the stand o' trees over there. Wouldn't recommend headin' thataway, neither. Some o' my best shots are sprinkled among those trees itchin' for an excuse t'do a little target practice.''

Barrett's face burned. Laying back, Coke had let him pass through miles of the Sidewinder to come to him. Then, sitting calmly at the opposite end of these corrals, he'd waited again, letting Barrett come to him again . . . drawing him into his trap. Sanders had made a fool of him. And nobody ever made of fool of T. C. Barrett.

He snapped his rifle up. Spurring his horse, Coke rammed it into Barrett's. The gun discharged into the air overhead. Coke grabbed at the weapon.

"Start shootin'!" Barrett shouted to his men.

But they were already wheeling around in disarray. Shoot at what? Coke and the men with him weren't clear of Barrett's own men at the head of the column. The vaqueros were too far off and too widely spaced to present easy targets, while they were bunched up in these close quarters, sitting ducks.

Calhoun had swung around. Slamming into Coke on the outside, he brought his gun up. A rifle rang out. Calhoun clutched his throat. Twisting to the side, his last sight was of the vaquero who'd been watching him.

Cruz Cortez stood at the edge of the trees, his rifle smoking as Calhoun teetered and toppled to the ground.

The killing of the sheriff threw Barrett's men into a panic. Two tried to gallop for the cover of the thicket, but were brought up short by a hail of bullets from inside. Letting go of the rifle Coke was grappling for, Barrett wheeled around and was plowing back through his men. "Fire, you bastards! Fire!"

But his men were already in full rout, spurring their horses and trying to make a break for it in the direction from which they'd come. The vaqueros' lines broke and they took off after them. The stutter of gunfire echoed farther and farther away.

It was past five when Coke returned to the north windmill campsite. Most of Barrett's men had been captured and were being collected there. A few were shot, some had broken arms and collarbones from being lassoed and dragged off their horses. Most, though, had pulled to a stop and surrendered when they saw Coke's men pounding up hard on their heels.

"Barrett?" Coke asked Cruz, who'd just galloped in from another direction.

"He's still out there somewhere," Cruz said irritably.

"Thought he'd give up when he saw the box we had him in." Coke looked at the wounded by the corrals and shook his head. "Shoulda known I could only credit the bastard with viciousness an' not any sense."

The roar vibrated through the jail. A dank, cavelike chill suffused the air. Jessica rolled onto her back and looked at the ceiling. It almost seemed to tremble under the percussion overhead. Silvery light rippled in the marshal's office and spurted through the barred cell window, flinging stripes of blurred shadow across the room.

Through the surges of rain thrashing over the roof, she heard gunshots and shouting voices. Wrapping the blanket from the cot around her, she went to the window. The rain was driving down in thick, glossy curtains. She reached through the bars to catch some. The force of it pounded her hand down.

A gun popped close by. She drew back. In a blaze of lightning, she saw one of Meg's neighbors, dressed only in his long johns and stovepipe boots, galumphing through the mud puddles, firing his pistol in the air and yipping like a dog. She smiled. Celebration had taken over the town. It was a drencher, a gully washer. The rains had come at last. Her heart lifted with joy. And Coke was all right. He'd survived this day. . . .

A breath of air swelled in, spraying her with icy water. Her eyes fixed on the bars of the window. . . . The dirty skunk.

Chapter 54

THE ROAD OUTSIDE the jail was a quagmire that morning, the slimy mud sucking at horses' hooves and wagon wheels passing through. The deeply recessed window in Seth's office narrowed the sweep of Jessica's view outside to only a couple hundred feet in either direction. But colors looked singularly vivid to her. The grain in the wood on the building across from her, the cracks scribbling down its stucco, held a needlelike clarity in the pure sunlight. This was the first time, she realized, that she wasn't seeing Main Street, Dispenseme, through a fine gauze of dust.

She'd been ready for her appearance in court by eight that morning, dressed in the new black skirt and clean, starched blouse that Meg had brought her. The hearing had been set for nine o'clock. Nine passed, then it was ten. At eleven, Lou dropped in to tell her that the stage bringing the judge was stuck in the mud ten miles outside of town.

So Jessica paced, locked up alone in this box of a jail to watch the mud thicken outside, with only her thoughts to keep her company. She had no idea what to expect from this court hearing. Neither Coke nor the marshal had shown up. She had a few choice things to say to Coke; and as the waiting wore on, she kept adding more.

Meg brought her lunch. "You gotta understand," she said as Jessica paced and groused. "Coke's got over eighty Land Company men on his hands still dryin' out from the drencher. If they ain't got shot, they got head colds. Doc passed through here only a coupla hours ago on his way out there t'patch 'em up." She nibbled on a biscuit Jessica had ignored. "They been scourin' the country all night for T. C. Barrett. If the polecat has the sense of a turnip, he's a hundred miles away from here by now."

It was past two when Seth arrived, a day's growth of whiskers bristling his chin, his boots and pants caked in mud up to the knee, trailing crumbs of it across the floor. "We'll be takin' you to your hearin' now," he declared.

Jessica went to her cell and got her hat. Coming out, she stopped, for Coke was standing at the door—surviving and whole, despite her fears of yesterday. A smile sprang to her lips; she bit it back and crossed to the window. Seth diplomatically slipped back out the door.

Seeing her looking so starched and perfect there, he smiled, remembering how two nights ago, that hair had been mussed and tumbling down, and her eyes, fevered with desire, had gleamed brighter than the firelight.

She must have read his thoughts, for she flushed. "I'm glad you were able to keep your land," she said, and added with a touch of irony, "I know how much it means to you."

He walked over to her. "Not yieldin' up what I've earned to a murderin' thief means just as much, Jessie."

"The name's Jessica."

He gazed down at her, then in a sudden movement, swept her into his arms, crushing her against him. "Lord," he whispered against her hair. "You don't know how I've hungered for you."

She let him hold her, her body limp and unresponsive. "Do you feel better now?" she asked acerbically after a time.

He let her go. She imperiously patted her hair back in place. "You can leave now. That should hold you for another few days, I expect."

"You're still mad at me, ain't you?"

"You double-crossed me. You put me in jail. Do you think for a minute I'd take that lying down?"

His eyes twinkled. "Well, I was kinda hopin' you would."

Giving him a tired look, she slapped her hat on her head and walked out the door.

"My handcuffs, please," she said, holding her wrists up to Seth.

"Ah, now, Mith Jethica." He looked chagrined.

"I insist," she said. "I'm a dangerous desperado, you know, a threat to the community."

"You ain't gonna be handcuffed an' you know it," Coke said, taking her arm.

She yanked it away. "I'm perfectly capable of walking on my own. Where's this dad-blamed hearing, anyhow?"

"The saloon," Coke said.

She walked along the edge of the road. The mud had stiffened there, but toward the middle it was still stirred up and gooey. The saloon was on the opposite side. Someone had laid a narrow wood plank over the mud for people to pass from side to side. It was sagging in the middle from the trampling it had taken all day. Lifting her skirt, she started down it. About halfway along it started vibrating under her. Reaching out to steady her, Coke grabbed one arm, and Seth the other. She took a few more steps, and, at the spot where the plank sagged into the mud, abruptly stopped, yanking an arm free to gather up her skirt in back and sending Seth skidding in a slick spot. Coke held her up while Seth clung to her arm to steady himself. Then she tried to shake her arm free again.

"This is a new skirt," she insisted stubbornly, not about to make it easy on either of them. "And I'm not going to get its hem muddy."

"Hell, Jessie," Coke muttered. Scooping her up, he carried her to the boardwalk and deposited her there, whereupon she prissily smoothed her clothes as if to wipe off the imprint of his touch.

Jessica frowned down the road. An unusual number of horses and buggies seemed to be strung out along the hitching rail for a Monday afternoon.

"Is something going on in town?" she asked.

Coke pushed a flap of the barroom door open for her. She hesitated, sensing the weight of people massed inside, then warily stepped through the door. She froze. Half the population of Dispenseme, Texas, and its immediate environs seemed to be crowded in there, including the shopkeepers, and every neighbor lady along their street. Cowhands lined the bar. And off to the side, Flora Henry and her brigade of widow ladies sat around a bar table looking like they should have mugs of beer sitting in front of them.

"What're these people doing here?" she asked Coke rigidly.

"Lendin' their support."

"I don't need their support. I don't want anyone to know about this." She glared at him. "I'm getting out of here."

He grasped her elbow. "You're seein' this through."

His steely grip on her arm, she moved woodenly down the aisle, eyes shifting from side to side, stiff little smiles blinking on and off at the people who grinned and waved their fingers at her.

Coke walked her to the front row of chairs, sat down, and pulled her down in the chair next to him.

"Try to cooperate, Jessie," he said. "Go along with everything I say an' don't act surprised."

"Why should I want to cooperate with you?" she whispered hotly. "Because of you, every sordid detail of my life will probably be paraded out here for the entire town to goggle over."

"These people are here because they like you."

"They can like me all they want," she shot back. "They just don't have to know about me. And my good name? What about that, huh?"

"Didn't think other folks' opinions meant that much to you."

"This month they do."

"Jessie, gettin' outa havin' t'go t'San Francisco is what's important now. An' for that, you need me."

"Need you?" she rasped. "I need you like a snake needs garters."

"I'm all you got t'get you outa this," he warned.

"Oh, that's reassuring. It makes me feel about as secure as a long-tailed pheasant surrounded by a tribe of hatless Indians."

Resting the heel of his hand on the back of her chair, he riffled her hair. "Try t'trust me, honey."

She seemed to soften a bit, but quickly rallied and turned on him. "Trust you!" she squeaked. She glanced back, her voice dropping to a whisper. "Have you given me any reason to trust you? Why, all you've done these past three days is betray and deceive me. You men!" Her voice rose to a squeak again. "You're all alike. Putting love in you—putting trust in you—is such a waste of a woman's emotion. It's like trying to create an ocean out of pouring water down an ant hole."

"Why, Jessie," he teased. "You're startin' t'speak our lingo.'"

Muttering, she folded her arms and turned away. Then, like a solar eclipse, Mike O'Banion entered the saloon. Shifting her line of vision, she followed him out of the corner of her eye as he glided to the opposite end of her row of chairs and sat down. She inwardly drew a little closer to Coke, who was turned aside talking to Cactus, seated in the row behind.

With a commanding shove of the barroom doors, Judge Bierbaum stepped into the room. His meek-looking clerk, who'd been seated at a corner table, leaped to his feet and announced in a startlingly deep voice, "All rise. Hear ye . . . hear ye . . . hear ye . . . Superior Court Forty-two, in and for the county of Falcon, is now in seh-shun. The Right Honorable Edwin Theopholus Bierbaum pree-ziding.''

Like a pope on parade, the judge marched down the aisle, his high-heeled cowboy boots clomping on the wooden floor. He sat down, sternly running his eyes around the room, the politician in him stirring at the sight of so many voters.

''Is the petitioner for extradition here present?'' he asked.

''I am, Your Honor.'' O'Banion rose to his feet. ''May I approach the bench?''

''You may.''

Taking the thick envelope out of his coat, O'Banion delivered it to the judge.

''And how are you called?'' Bierbaum inquired, removing the documents from the envelope.

''Michael Jay O'Banion, Your Honor.''

Bierbaum gave O'Banion a long, flat look. ''That's Irish, is it not?''

''That it is . . . on me dear father's side.''

''My wife's cousin had a dozen of his finest horses rustled by an Irishman.''

''Uh, most regrettable, sir.''

''Was for the Irishman, Mr. O'Banion,'' Bierbaum said expressionlessly, flipping through the documents. ''Hal sicced his entire pack of bloodthirsty ketch dogs on him. When they were done, all that was left of the waster was a scrap of hide with a tuft of hair sticking out.'' He paused, then added matter-of-factly, ''Buried him in a snuff box out on Hangman's Hill.''

''Well, I'm but an eighth Irish,'' O'Banion said.

''Takes but a pinch of arsenic t'poison the stew,'' Bierbaum muttered. ''The complaint here listed is the business establishment of Ivory Ives. It's in the person of whom?''

''One Henri LaMarque,'' O'Banion answered.

''That's French, is it not?''

''Could be,'' Mike hedged.

Bierbaum considered a moment, then decided to let that one pass. He glanced down at the document again. ''Is the subject of this warrant here ascribed, one Jessica Wade Daniels, present?''

''Here,'' Jessica responded, barely above a whisper.

''Are you represented?'' Bierbaum inquired, switching to the condescending, protecting tone which he adopted with the ladies, especially young and pretty ones and most especially one who was allied with the man who could swing the vote in this part of the county.

"I'll be representin' her," Coke said.

"By what authority does this man claim to represent this felon?" O'Banion demanded. "He's no attorney at law . . . just a cowboy."

"Cattleman," Coke said. "Got me more'n the one cow an' I'm over twenty-one." He got up, pulling the entry paper out of his belt that he and Jessica had gotten in San Pedro de Roma two days before. He handed it to the judge. "This gives me the license t'represent her," he said. "An', I reckon', take on the obligation for her problems."

Bierbaum peered at the paper, then looked up helplessly at Coke. "I can't read this. It's in Spanish."

"That's all right," Coke replied. "I'll tell you what it says."

"I object!" O'Banion leaped to his feet.

"You object?" Bierbaum frowned.

"Most strenuously. I can't accept Mr. Sanders's translation of a document that he himself has proffered before this court."

"I can," Bierbaum said.

"May I remind you, sir," O'Banion answered angrily, "that I come before you in good faith, charged with the duty to apprehend one Jessica Wade Daniels and to return her to the jurisdiction of Superior Court Eight, San Francisco, to stand trial for the felony embezzlement of eight hundred fifty dollars. Superior Court Eight, San Francisco, is a legally constituted court of law of equivalent authority to this of Falcon. And it is a court of law which I must point out cannot speak for itself at this time. As the agent of said court, I adjure you, therefore, to assiduously exercise discretion in this matter, that you weigh each piece of evidence here presented with the utmost gravity and impartiality."

"Are you implying, Irishman, that I won't?" Bierbaum asked poisonously.

"Uh . . . no," O'Banion sputtered angrily, but quickly recovered himself. "But in the interest of justice, I ask, nay, I insist that an impartial witness be called to render translation of this document."

Shaking his head, the judge peered around the crowd, searching out Seth. "Marshal, do you know anyone around here who's impartial?"

"Haven't come upon one yet," he responded.

"Do you know anyone who's conversant in both Spanish and English?"

"A few. Ramiro over there is." He gestured with his thumb.

"Please approach the bench," Bierbaum said to Ramiro. Ramiro did.

"Are you associated with or related to Mr. Sanders in any way?" O'Banion asked.

"We're not cousins," Ramiro replied.

"State your full name, please," Bierbaum said.

"Ignacio Xavier Ramiro."

"Will you render translation of this document Mr. Sanders has here presented?"

Ramiro shrugged. *"Sí."*

Bierbaum handed him the document. Ramiro's eyes swept over it; then, brows knitting, he looked at Coke. "My . . . uh, congratulations to you an' the señora," he said carefully.

"Thank you kindly," Coke replied. "Sure do appreciate it."

"What does that mean?" O'Banion snapped. "It's out of order . . . completely out of order."

"It ain't only in order," Coke drawled, "but proper an' fittin', that Jessie Daniels an' me be congratulated on the occasion of our marriage two days ago in Mexico."

Jessica stiffened and choked. A stir ran through the crowd.

"Mr. Ramiro didn't attest to that," O'Banion said suspiciously.

"Mr. Ramiro," Bierbaum put in. "Is it your determination that the document you now hold is a marriage contract between Mr. Sanders and Mrs. Daniels?"

"Ah, *sí*," he replied, eyes dancing. "This official paper clearly says what it is, and it was signed by Heriberto Alvarado, an official of the *Gobierno Federal de Méjico*. He is a man I know well, for his grandfather was a second cousin of my wife's uncle by marriage." Grinning, he shook Coke's hand. "May the milk o' life flow sweetly to you an' your señora."

"So you and Mrs. Daniels are married," Bierbaum mused.

"We decided that it'd be wise t'do it pronto," Coke replied.

"The fact that Sanders married the felon still doesn't absolve her of the theft of eight hundred fifty dollars that she committed against the law-abiding citizenry of San Francisco," O'Banion pointed out contemptuously.

"The place that Jessie is accused o' stealin' from, Ivory Ives, ain't no decent, law-abidin' business like sellin' pots an' pans, Ed," Coke responded. "It's a gamblin' place, the sorta place that every night no doubt relieves the decent, law-abidin' citizens o' San Francisco o' three, four times the piddlin' amount that Jessie, here, is accused o' takin'. Hell, I'll just pay 'em that eight hundred fifty dollars. In exchange, of course, for their droppin' the charges against her. It'd give 'em a good profit, considerin' that the charges are trumped up anyhow."

"They are?" Bierbaum inquired.

"The man who made 'em is usin' it t'force Jessie back t'San Francisco 'cause she knows things that'd be a threat to him."

"Do you have proof of this?" Bierbaum asked.

"Refutin' empty charges ain't that easy. We all know how in these corrupt big cities, the law can be used by the wrong kinda elements with the right amount o' money."

Bierbaum cleared his throat and straightened up.

"Fact is," Coke went on, "makin' Jessie go back t'San Francisco would be puttin' her in serious danger." He shook his head. "Ain't no way that any God-fearin', upright Texas man would allow his"—he glanced down at Jessica—"adorin' little woman t'be put in such a situation."

"No man would," Bierbaum allowed.

Coke slid a look at O'Banion. "We got good reason to believe, too, that the trip itself would be a serious endangerment to her health." He paused. "An' to the health o' the child that we're expectin'."

Going livid, Jessica slid down in her chair.

"Now, that puts a whole different light on the situation," Bierbaum considered. "Mrs. Sanders's delicate condition does provide clear and compelling reason for her to remain in the state." He picked up his gavel. "Petition for extradition to California is hereby denied." He slammed it down. "This court will contact Superior Court Eight in San Francisco with its findings," he went on to Coke, "and convey your offer of restitution in exchange for abrogation of all charges against your lovely wife."

Cactus got up and walked over to Coke. "That's the second time old Bierbaum's come through for you," he whispered.

"Got the courage t'climb offa the fence when he felt the ground crumblin' under his foot on t'other side."

His eyes malignant on Jessica, O'Banion rose to his feet.

Coke moved in front of him. "Be outa here before sundown," he warned.

He watched O'Banion walk away, then went back to Jessica. She was still hunched over, her hands over her forehead, too mortified to look at anyone. "What've you done?" she breathed. "These people think that we—"

"It buys us the time t'get you outa those charges in San Francisco," he said.

"I'm not going to respond to that," she said through her teeth, "for it'd be an endangerment to you . . . and to the child that I am carrying."

꧁ Chapter 55

COKE WALKED DOWN the road from Meg's house on his way to Ramiro's to rent a wagon to take his new family home. Jessica stood at the door watching him.

"You sure do look outa sorts for a brand-spankin' new bride," Meg commented.

"Coke may've tricked me into that Mexican wedding," Jessica said angrily. "But I'm not pregnant. He made that up. It was only a few days ago that we first—"

As Jessica stopped short, Meg swallowed a smile. "Well, we best be keepin' that under our hats till you get clear o' this trouble in San Francisco."

The four Winston children, who lived two houses down, were trooping by, swinging their books.

"Willie should be home from school soon," Jessica mused. "I should talk to him before Coke gets back, I suppose."

A pair of pigtailed girls went chattering by. A boy scampered up behind them, leaped into a puddle, and splattered muddy water on their legs, then dodged away as the chase was on. A couple more children trickled by. But no Willie.

"He's probably dawdling somewhere," Jessica said to Meg. "Probably found some worms in a puddle to mull over."

She waited awhile longer, then went outside and stood on the stoop. Willie was nowhere in sight.

"I'd better go for him," she called to Meg, and started off.

She reached Main Street. A few clusters of children were scattered along it, but Willie's quick little figure wasn't among them. Perhaps he had to stay after school. She walked toward it.

"Have you seen Willie?" she asked a freckle-faced chum of his on the street.

He pulled the apple he was chomping out of his mouth and pointed it between the buildings. "Said he was gonna catch some hoptoads."

She headed off between the buildings, cut across the yards of a few homes, her eyes searching, until she reached the fields on the outskirts of town. Still no Willie. She walked along the borders of the yards that merged into the fields. The fields were alive with leaping toads, plopping among the grass and weeds like heavy raindrops. Perhaps Willie had caught his toad and was already on his way home.

Her steps slowed, for cast among the weeds in the field to her right were some books bound with a familiar strap. She walked over to them. Willie's primer and ciphering book were slick from the wetness of the plants. She looked irritably around. Willie was probably crawling through all this wetness. She wandered farther out into the field, and stopped. Willie's hat was lying on its side in the tall grass ten feet away. She went to it and looked around again. No children were out here, only weeds, brush, and toads—and the tracks of a single buggy curving away.

She slowly picked up the hat, alarm taking root inside her. Willie would never let go of his hat without raising a ruckus to get it back. It was one of his favorite things. The dire possibilities started bubbling up inside her, and one, mainly one, kept roiling out at her.

She began running back toward home. "Oh, please," she prayed as she reached the road, "let him be there."

"Señora!" a child called behind her.

She spun around. It was Chacho Ramiro.

"Have you seen Willie?" she cried.

"No," he answered breathlessly, running up to her. "But while I was walking home from the school of the San Sebastian, a man came up to me. He told me to give this to you." He held a scrap of paper up in his fist. "And only you."

"Who was this man?" Jessica asked roughly, snatching the paper.

"That stranger who dresses funny."

Jessica ran her eyes over the words. "Got the kid. If you want him alive, come *alone*, 2/3 m. East, right fork in the road, the abandoned shed."

Her heart twisted. She grabbed Chacho's hand, pressing the paper into it. "Take it to Coke!" she cried, then took off running.

In front of the feed store she found a horse tied to the hitching rail. She yanked the reins off, scrambled into the saddle, and thrashed her heels. An angry voice shouted, "Hey!" behind her as she tore out of town.

She kept pounding her heels, for though the horse's legs were reaching out at full stride, sending mud clots pattering onto the road behind, it didn't seem to be going fast enough. One image burned in front of her eyes—the pit boss, Jonah, on his knees, the helpless terror in his eyes, his mouth moving wordlessly, and the line, the thin line, slicing down from his ears.

No! her heart cried out. Not my baby! Whatever wrongs I've done in my life, I'll atone . . . I'll atone.

She saw the fork in the road and veered off to the right. She slowed; she didn't want to miss that shack.

She was on a narrow wagon trail that wove along the edge of the San Sebastian. The roofs of the compound and the church steeple loomed in the distance. Twigs and flakes of leaves torn loose in last night's storm were scattered over the trail, cleaving to the damp earth and imprinting it with their forms. The fresh grooves of the wheels of a small buggy cut along through them.

Rounding a crook in the trail, she saw a decayed wooden shed half-buried in the tall, yellowish weeds, a line of scrub trees curving behind it. The buggy tracks turned toward it.

She beat her heels, galloping toward the shack, then slowed as she passed beyond it. The buggy stood in the shadows of the thicket. A shadow separated from the others and moved into the light.

"Took you long enough," O'Banion said.

"Where's my son?"

"Get off the horse and I'll show you."

She didn't move. "Tell me where my little boy is."

He looked amused. "Back there." He gestured over his shoulder at the thicket.

Keeping her distance, she rode at an angle toward the trees and looked inside. The thicket was split by a deep ravine, chocolate-colored water streaming along its bed. With a stab, she glimpsed what looked like little feet jutting out from behind a tree near the bank of the ravine, about fifteen feet behind O'Banion.

"Willie!" she screamed.

The feet moved. He was alive!

"Now, get off that horse," O'Banion said.

She held back. Once O'Banion had her, he'd have no need for Willie. He'd kill him.

"Let my son go first," she said.

He eyed her. "Seems we've reached an impasse, lassie," he said lightly. A thin smile formed on his dark features. She remembered that look—that night of Jonah—as he stood there calmly wiping the blade of his knife with his handkerchief while Jonah's life drained out on the cellar floor. Now O'Banion made a motion with his arm as though straightening his belt, and the knife was in his hand.

"Get off the horse."

She didn't move. The thin smile still on his face, he turned back into the thicket toward Willie.

"No!" she screamed, jabbing her heels into the horse's flanks. They crashed into the thicket, hitting it at an angle, the tangled twigs and branches clawing and thwacking at her.

O'Banion spun around, astonishment on his face. He'd been fixing to hold the knife to the kid's throat to force the woman off the horse. He hadn't expected her to come plunging straight at him through the thicket on the beast. He tried to leap out of the way and lost his footing on the slippery mud of the embankment. The knife flying out of his hands, he toppled backward into the ravine.

Jessica scrambled free of the horse, throwing herself onto her stomach as the animal skidded over the edge of the ravine. She heard the loud, confused splashing, then smaller splashes as it loped away. She saw the knife propped against a rock on the embankment. She scrabbled over to it, grabbed it, and rushed to Willie. Dropping to her knees, she cut the rope from his wrists and ankles, then yanked the gag from his mouth. He flung his arms around her. She held him with all her strength as he sobbed against her neck.

She looked up. O'Banion had crawled over the embankment

less than ten feet away. She rose to her feet, pulling Willie up with one hand and maneuvering him behind her.

"Go," she said quietly to him. "Get away from here as fast as you can."

Willie backed away a little, the tears streaming down his face.

"Did you hear me!" she shouted angrily. "Run!" Willie turned and started uncertainly off. "Faster!" she yelled. "Get help!"

O'Banion's eyes were on the running child.

She lifted the knife in both her hands. "Don't think of it."

He looked amused. "So LaMarque's choice piece is now a tigress protectin' her cub." He moved toward her. "Ah, c'mon, lassie," he murmured in an almost seductive tone, starting to circle slowly around her. "You're not a killer."

"I'm not a fool," she said, turning and following him with the knife. "But you're a fool to have tried this."

"I didn't come all this way just t'turn back leavin' the job undone. Loose ends bother me."

He made a quick movement toward her. She lashed out, hitting only air.

Laughter rose in his eyes. "Oh, this'll be a fine game," he taunted, slowly circling. He made another feint and she lashed out, missing again. The third time, she was ready and struck.

The air going out of him, he jerked his arm back, looked at the line of blood oozing through his sleeve, then up at her; his eyes turned to ice. He lunged at her. She lashed out. He grabbed her wrist. She instantly dropped the knife, kicking it back with her heel. It skittered to the edge of the ravine. They both went after it, grappling on the embankment. She knocked it over the side. He grabbed at her and they lost their balance, tumbling down the mud-slick bank into the stream. She tried to scrabble away. He got her around the waist and flung her onto her back. Throwing his weight on top of her, he grasped her throat, squeezing down hard. Gagging, she grabbed a fistful of mud and smashed it into his eyes. The tension on her windpipe eased. She clawed at his face and, wresting a knee up, pried him up enough to twist out from under. He tore at her hair and the back of her blouse, but she was slippery with mud and squirmed free, crawling through the brown water. She struggled to her feet and tried to wade away, her movements hampered by her soaked skirt, twisted heavily around her legs.

"Lassie." The tone was seductive again.

She looked back. The knife was in his fist. She knew she couldn't outrun him, so she turned and faced him, backing. Moving the dagger teasingly back and forth before her, he slowly came on. At least Willie had Coke now, she thought.

The shots sounded like snapping twigs. O'Banion arched up and dropped at an angle onto the bank. Gasping, she stared at his body, then waded a little way downstream and sat down on the opposite bank.

She felt Coke's hand on her shoulder, then the gentle sliding of his arm around her as he sat beside her. The shaking had started up, and she hugged herself to hold it in.

"Do you hurt anywhere?" he asked, tenderly wiping the muddy threads of hair back from her face. "Did he cut you?"

"Willie . . ." she said.

"He's safe. He was climbin' into the back of Mary McKetchin's wagon while I was gallopin' out here." His arm tightened around her. "Can you stand?"

She nodded.

He helped her up. She looked at O'Banion, his legs lazily swinging in the muddy water, then suddenly wrapped her arms around Coke's waist, pressing her face against his chest. He held her tightly.

"He would've killed Willie," she said.

"I know," he replied, realizing that she regarded O'Banion's intent to kill her as to be so expected that it wasn't worth mentioning. He stroked her back. "Don't think about it."

He half carried her up the embankment; her trembling had made her too unsteady to make it on her own. They walked through the thicket and he lifted her onto O'Banion's buggy. As he untied the horse, he saw her staring down at him in bewilderment.

"Why, you're all covered with mud!" she exclaimed.

"Got it off you, Jessie."

She looked down at herself. She was indeed plastered in mud from head to foot.

He climbed up beside her and placed a hand on her shoulder. "Sure you're all right, honey?"

"Me?" she asked, focusing on a spot of mud on his cheek. "Course I'm all right. I'm tough." And reaching into her muddy pocket, she pulled out her muddy hankie and dabbed more mud on his cheek.

Chapter 56

COKE LET THE buggy horse amble along at its own slow tempo. Jessica's trembling had subsided to sporadic bursts of shuddering, as she expelled from her system the last chills of her life-and-death struggle with O'Banion. She saw a hawk gliding low through the sky, then noticed the golden vividness of the sun on the fields below, these sights seeming new to her. By the time they reached the road to town, enough of her numbness had worn off for her to feel the mud pasted in her hair, under her nails, and in her shoes. It was drawing on her skin as it dried, making it feel like sandpaper.

"I'm not ready to see people yet," she said.

"What would you like t'do?" he asked.

"Stop someplace where there's a water pump. I'd like to clean up a bit. I don't want people seeing me this way."

"I think they'd understand, Jessie."

"I have some pride left." She smiled wanly. "My name has been dragged through the mud." She looked down at herself. "And now the rest of me."

He squeezed her hand. "Whatever you want, honey."

He turned the buggy off the road into the broad field, and they cut a path through the tall grass toward the San Sebastian. The buildings of the compound waited in empty silence. The hacienda stood apart, no life stirring behind its sightless windows.

Coke turned onto the firm earth that ran behind the barn. As they passed behind it, a flurry of dust and straw spilled down on them from a hayloft window overhead. Jessica glanced upward, brushing off her shoulders.

Coke stopped at the water pump that stood just outside the yard of the hacienda. The bushes that bordered the yard, usually a smoky green color, had transformed overnight to a delicate light purple.

"How pretty," Jessica said. "What are they?"

"Cenizo," he replied. "They only blossom after a rain."

He helped her down, then paused to lift her chin and kiss her lips.

"Oh, Coke, I'm a terrible sight."

"But a livin' one, thank God."

Hand in hand, they walked to the pump. Coke swung the handle. The pump burped out a trickle, then the flow glistened forth. Jessica knelt beside the trough, catching the water in her hands and scrubbing her face. The crust of mud cleaved to her skin, breaking away in flakes and dissolving to clouds in the water below. She pulled out her hairpins, shook out her hair and, bending down, turned her face up to the water, letting it pour back into her hair.

The sharp crack of rifle fire was dimmed by the water rushing over her face. Sweeping the water back from her face with her hands, she sat back on her heels and glanced up at Coke. He'd stiffened, grasping the top of the pump hard, pain tightening his face. She clambered up, catching him in her arms as his weight fell against her.

"Coke!" She felt him trying to move, but unable to gather the strength. She sank with him to her knees, his head on her lap. She took her hand from his back and saw the blood on her fingers. He was trying to raise up, his eyes fixing on something near the barn.

T. C. Barrett stood there, the rifle in his hands, triumph gleaming in his hard eyes. "Looks like you ain't gonna win after all, Sanders."

Jessica cradled Coke closer against her.

Barrett ejected the spent shell and walked forward. "Get outa the way, woman. I want him t'see it comin' the same way that bastard Siden saw it comin'."

"Move, Jessie," Coke said, his hand nudging her. The weakness of his touch registered deep inside her.

"You can't tell me what to do!" she answered desperately, hugging him tighter.

Barrett was only a few feet away. He raised the rifle, "I got no qualms about shootin' a woman. This is your last chance. Move."

Eyes holding on the rifle, Jessica silently lowered Coke to the ground, then got to her feet in front of him.

"Step aside." Barrett gestured with the rifle.

Jessica flung herself at it. She grabbed it, trying to wrest the barrel away. Her strength was no match for Barrett's. He twisted the rifle roughly around, jerking it out of her grip. She went after it again. He knocked her away, sending her sprawling on the ground.

She was scrabbling back up when the gun exploded a second time, the percussion so powerful that it ran through her. The echo seemed to go on forever, rattling something deep in the hollows of the hacienda.

"No!" she cried, dropping back down and clawing the earth.

Something clattered to the ground a few feet in front of her. She peeked up through her tears. It was Barrett's rifle. She stared dazedly at the long shadow next to it, for it was undulating oddly. She raised her eyes to Barrett.

Knees buckling, he'd pivoted around, the entire side of him soaked in blood and looking like small chunks had been chopped out of it. His gaze was fixed on something above and behind her.

"You!" he rasped, then dropped to his knees. Eyes fading, T. C. Barrett pitched forward onto his face.

Jessica heard steps dragging heavily up behind her. She didn't recognize the man. He could've been young, but suffering had lined and hollowed out his face and put a leaden weight on his shoulders. He shuffled by her and stopped in front of Coke, letting the shotgun drop.

"Ray," Coke said weakly. "I thought you was like your pa."

Ray was silent a moment, then something seemed to stir inside him. "Only in the grudge part, I guess." But Coke had already slipped into unconsciousness.

Coke heard small metal objects clinking. He stirred, wishing someone would pull that damn hot branding iron out of him. He opened his eyes and found himself staring at the whiskey flask in Doc Elam's back pocket. The doc was turned away, bent over a pot, steam swelling out of it, fishing his surgical instruments out with tongs and setting them on a folded towel. Coke was lying on his stomach on a table in the hacienda's kitchen. He groaned, the sound seeming to rise out of him on its own.

"Oh, so you're with us," Elam said. He picked up the towel and set his instruments on the table next to Coke. "Never thought I'd be slicing and picking through you today."

"Doc . . ." Coke began, then stopped, catching his breath.

"You wanta know if you're gonna make it?" Doc asked, adjusting his spectacles downward on his nose.

"No . . . wanta know if you draw much from that whiskey flask in your pocket."

Elam considered. "Not so much that anybody'd notice. Do think it gives my patients religion, though. When they come out of their ether and find that they've survived . . . they start singin' praises to the Lord." And the ether mask went over Coke's face.

Coke felt like he was trying to grope his way through a curtain. At times it was thick, allowing no light through. Sometimes it thinned enough for him to feel the shadows moving beyond it. He recognized Ma's edgy, birdlike touch, the warmth of his sister, and the quiet tenderness of Jessie. The surgery seemed to have deepened the pain and made it more raw, intensifying as the curtain thinned, receding when it thickened.

A soft, damp cloth was moving gently over his forehead. He passed through the curtain. His eyes cracked open and he saw Jessica, the low lamplight deepening her eyes and turning her skin golden. He looked at the unfamiliar room.

"You're in the hacienda," she said. "How's the pain?"

"In better shape than me."

She was quiet for a time, slowly caressing his temple with the back of her fingers. "I'm so sorry, Coke. If it hadn't been for my stupid vanity, this wouldn't have happened to you." Tears welled in her eyes. "I don't know why you ever bothered with me."

He grasped her wrist hard. " 'Cause we're alike, Jessie. We'd both walk through hell, if we had to, for somethin' we believed in."

It was a familiar creak-creak that brought him around the next time. He looked at Ma, rocking and crocheting by his bed.

"You brought your rocker out here to the San Sebastian?" he whispered.

She gave him a long, blank look. "Cain't crochet without it."

"Operatin' with your usual sense," he mumbled, drifting off again.

It wasn't until the third day that Coke connected fully with his surroundings. Jessica was changing the dressing on his back. He liked her doing it the best. Sarie was smooth and fast while Ma, always impatient and operating on the principle that pain was an inevitability of life, would say, "Grit your teeth, son," and then ripped. Jessica, on the other hand, timid about causing him pain, took a long time, the feathery touch of her fingers a pleasant tickle on his skin that seemed to lighten the soreness.

She helped him sit up, wrapped the strips of gauze around him, and tied them together on his chest. Then, leaning forward, she pressed her face next to his. "You have a mole on your hind cheek," she whispered, and scooted away.

"You saw me that night at the hut," he began.

"Not that side of you," she said, bending over and efficiently brushing the wrinkles out of the blankets. "Anything you'd like?"

"You could trade that throat-huggin' blouse o' yours in for somethin' looser an' lower in front so that while you're doin' all this leanin' over me—"

"You're in no condition."

"Give me somethin' t'think about, though."

"An' here I thought it was my soup that was supposed t'pump the life back into this man," Sarie said from the door, dinner tray in her hands.

"Seems t'me," Ma declared to Coke the following afternoon while she and Jessica were straightening up the room, "that that snap Mexican weddin' o' yours leaves somethin' t'be desired. Hard t'see how a quick civil ceremony afore a Mexicano bureaucrat could have much holdin' power." She plumped a pillow, thinking. "Kinda like tryin' t'strap a pair o' big stubborn mules to a wagon yoke with a length o' sewin' thread. To my way o' thinkin', son, if you're gonna do it, you should do it up right— say your vows before the Lord, proper-like. Maybe the next time the circuit preacher hits town."

"How about Father Dominic?" Jessica couldn't resist saying.

"Don't see how Latino mouthin's from a priest could be any better'n Mexicano mouthin's from a bureaucrat," Ma retorted. "Either way, it'd be hard t'tell iffen you was or iffen you warn't married." Ma paused, reflecting, "I suppose there might could be some holiness in a papist weddin'; though, for the life o' me, I cain't see where." She shrugged her bony shoulders. "But I reckon half a tad o' God is better'n no God a-tall."

"You're losing your bigotry!" Jessica breathed with mock incredulity.

"I know it's big o' me," Ma responded, gathering up the laundry and going to the door. "But as the Good Book says, 'When the earthquakes o' life start t'hit . . . a body's gotta . . . shift a bit.' Ezekiel eight, verse eighteen." And she was gone.

Arms folded, Jessica leaned against the wall next to the door. "Though it grieves me deeply to admit it," she said thoughtfully, "you're mother does have a point. Snap Mexican weddings do leave something to be desired. The concurrence of the bride, for example." Then she, too, turned and was gone.

"Well," Coke said to Cruz, who'd just arrived at the door. "Looks like I'm gonna survive. Ma's already startin' t'nag . . . an' Jessie t'needle."

It was while they were going over ranch matters that the church bell thundered out its first bong, setting the pitcher and basin on the marble-topped washstand nearby vibrating.

"What the hell!" Coke said. "Who died?"

"It's in celebration," Cruz replied. "Father Dominic received the message today that the Castillos are returning to the San Sebastian."

"That's good. It'll make things feel right around here." The bell crashed again. Coke waited for the jiggling in the room to die down. "The dōna fixin' t'take the Land Company to court?"

"She won't have to. Ray Barrett signed the San Sebastian back to her two days ago, then climbed on the train out of Warner. People up there say he's left South Texas for good."

The bell crashed again. Coke winced. "Now I know what coulda drove Barrett homicidal," he muttered. "Tell Father Dominic that if he decides t'trade that bell I got him in for somethin' smaller, I won't take offense."

"I'm afraid he likes it." Cruz grinned. "You know the padre. He sees no subtlety in God."

Chapter 57

COKE WENT HOME to the Sidewinder the next day. The trip wore him out. His arms and legs still felt like they were made of stone, and he slept like one as soon as he got home.

It felt good waking up in his own bed. He lay listening to the compound awakening, the doors clapping shut down the road, the arthritic creak of the corral gate, the murmur of the men outside, the snap of reins and the clatter of horses and wagons moving out for the day's work. He heard the sizzle of bacon hitting the fry pan in the kitchen, the children's feet pattering down the stairs, and their high voices as they ate their breakfast. All these sounds he marked and gathered close that morning.

The only flaw was that Jessica wasn't there. That first night she'd taken the room upstairs, the one she'd stayed in during her visits; and it was there that she remained. Though she was still gentle and affectionate with him and seldom far away, the return home seemed to have triggered a reserve in her. It wasn't anything that he could pinpoint, but he often caught her watching him obliquely, weighing something in her mind. He knew she stole into his room at night. He'd feel her presence in the shadows, but by the time he fully awakened, she'd be gone. Something unresolved hung in the air between them.

He'd been home less than a week when at dawn he went upstairs and walked into her room. She was in her nightgown making her bed.

"Get dressed," he said. "We're goin' for a horseback ride."

"Are you crazy?" she replied. "You're not strong enough to ride yet."

"I'll be crazy if I stay cooped up in here any longer. Get dressed. We got some things t'clear up, you an' me."

That oblique look returned to her eyes, then she slowly nodded. "I'll go . . . but only if we take a wagon. I'll fix a picnic basket."

He paused at the door. "Dress purty."

465

* * *

They'd spread a blanket in the shade of a quiet grove on the bank of a stream. Jessica lay back on her elbows watching the water, the cool autumn breeze riffling her hair. She wore a soft-green blouse that made her eyes a decided green, and she'd left her hair down, tying it back at the neck with a full green bow. She looked fresh and airy enough to be carried on the breeze, were it not for the anchor of her staid black skirt.

"You look purty," he said, caressing her shoulder. "Don't know why you're so attached to that heavy black skirt, though. Seems I cain't ever get you outa that damn sober thing."

She peeked wryly aside at him. "Well, it hasn't been for want of trying."

"Speakin' of which," he said slowly, "let's get married."

She let her gaze drift back to the stream. "We already are."

"No, we ain't," he said.

"That document you got in Mexico says we are."

"Uh, no, Jessie, it doesn't say that . . . exactly."

She rolled over and looked at him. "Well, what does it say exactly, Coke?"

He reached inside his vest, pulled out the document, and handed it to her. "That Mexican bureaucrat was a right sloppy writer, but if you'll check out that scribble three blanks down, you might be able t'make out a word."

"*Vaca.*"

"Do you know what *vaca* means?"

"Yes, I've been here long enough to know that it means 'cow.' " She peered down at the word, then up at him, eyes narrowing.

"No, Jessie," he drawled. "They don't call brides 'cows' in Mexico. Now, if you'll check out that blank below it, you'll see the words *'Diez dólares, E.E.U.U.'* "

"Yes."

"That means 'ten dollars, *norteamericano*.' Now, can you think o' any reason why 'cow' an' 'ten dollars, *norteamericano*,' would be teamed up on the same official document?"

"That Mexican official was faking something."

"Nope, that document is gen-you-wine."

"It isn't an entry paper."

"Nope. It's a bill o' sale."

"Bill of sale?"

"Yep. That there paper says that you an' me is the proud owners of a slab-sided, half-dead, Mexican-bred ten-dollar cow." Leaning over, he kissed her lightly on the top of the head. "Welcome to the cattle business, honey."

She started laughing, then sat up. "Are you telling me the truth? The judge accepted this as a marriage license?"

"Ed Bierbaum didn't know what it said."

"But Ramiro testified—"

"He didn't exactly say that that there paper was a marriage license. He just kinda went along with what I said. Fact is, the court hearin' was the easy part. It was the buyin' o' that cow in San Pedro that mornin' that got a tad on the ticklish side."

"You mean, that Mexican farmer didn't want to sell you his cow?"

"No. He was right pleased to be gettin' a little money for that animal. It was just that the whole situation had him damn confused."

"Confused?"

" 'Tain't every day that a gringo cowpoke an' his tousle-haired gal come a-sashayin' up to his place wantin' t'buy one of his half-dead beeves. As a rule, gringos don't buy cattle that close to the border. They tend t'just drop on over an' chase 'em back across the river without any howdy-do to the owner at all.

"But there I was hagglin' with him over the price of a single cow that him an' me both knew wouldn't last out the month. An' when we finally settled on the price, why, hell, I didn't even wanta take the critter with me. Instead, I demanded that we all traipse into town an' take us out a official, notarized bill o' sale on that one dyin' cow."

Jessica was starting to laugh again.

"Now, that really got him goin'," Coke went on. "Said there was no need for us t'go to all the botheration. Hell, he'd let me have that cow any time I wanted, dead or alive. But I wouldn't back down, an' if he wanted t'keep that ten dollars, he had t'go along with me." Coke paused. "Thought you an' me was plumb loco, though."

Jessica thought back to that morning in Mexico, sitting there on the farmer's chicken-doodled front porch, waiting for Coke to settle with the farmer on what Coke had told her was the amount of bribe she'd have to pay to get her entry paper into Mexico. She recalled Coke and the farmer moving through the cattle pen, dickering; that was their picking out the cow and wrangling over the price. And that second flurry of squabbling that had broken out when they went into the house; that was the farmer balking at having to go into town to take out a bill of sale.

She remembered how the farmer had been shaking his head when he and Coke came out of the house. . . .

Her eyes widened. Those fishy looks the farmer kept sending them as they walked into town hadn't been because he was such a romantic devil and had detected in her bedraggled appearance signs of a recent roll in the bushes with Coke—as Coke had told her! Oh, no! The poor man was simply stumped as to why these two crazy gringos had insisted on going all the way into town to take out a bill of sale on a single half-dead ten-dollar cow!

The image of herself rushing down that road, plucking the chaff out of her hair, flashed through her mind and she burst out laughing. "You dirty skunk!" When her laughter ended, she leaned toward him, looking up into his face. "I gave you twenty dollars that morning. That cow cost ten. What did you do with the rest of my money?"

"Paid for that document."

"Only change. I saw you hand that bureaucrat only a few coins."

"I bought us lunch."

"Don't remind me. I've done some thinking myself, you know. C'mon, Coke," she prodded. "While I was inside the general store that morning fixing myself up, what did you do with that money of mine you still had on you?"

"You recollect the fella who was operatin' the ferryboat?"

"I recollect him."

"Well, he needed a little persuadin' t'tie his boat up on the Mexican side o' the river an' take hisself a nice, long siesta over there."

"That's what I thought." She fell back on the blanket, grinning. "Got me with my own money. I gotta hand it to you, Coke. When you decide to pull a fast one, you can really pull it off in style."

He curled a tress of her hair around a finger. "Well, now you know, honey, you still gotta marry me. I ain't made an honest woman of you yet."

She sat up, regarding him askance. "Not that easy to do."

"How's that?"

She looked down, picking at the threads in the blanket. "You know those charges that I stole eight hundred fifty dollars from Henri's place were trumped up. You do believe that, don't you?"

"Yup. An' I believed you when you told me before."

"Henri would never have believed that I'd have the gall to steal from him." She peeked up at Coke. "Otherwise he wouldn't have settled on such a piddlin' amount to have accused me of taking."

"What do you mean?"

"Once I worked out my method, Coke, I never left my table at the casino empty-handed. Never. Remember that night at the hut, you asked me how much money I had on me?"

"Yup. You said you had four twenty-dollar gold pieces tucked in your shoes—which you had."

"Yes," she mused, "I was truthful. About my shoes."

She moved in front of him and lifted her skirt. "I had this on that night. Rip it."

"What?"

"I know you've been wanting to do this for a long time. So go ahead—rip it."

Squinting at her curiously, he picked up the hem and tore a bit of the side seam apart. A twenty-dollar gold piece tumbled onto the blanket. He ripped harder and about twenty more cascaded out.

"Fun, isn't it?" She grinned, ripping another part of her skirt. And they kept ripping away, the gold coins raining out, puddling in her lap and sprinkling across the blanket.

When at last her skirt was emptied, hanging tattered around her, she blissfully ran her fingers through the coins.

"My treasure trove . . . my grubstake . . . my freedom. A store of my own like Meg's, a first-class education for Willie. Those beasts in San Francisco could've railroaded me to hell and back, but no way would they've been able to pry a single one of these darlings away from me."

"How many," he asked.

"Here? Two hundred and three."

"Here?" he repeated.

"I'd never have taken off from Dispenseme leaving my little boy unprovided for. I stashed another two hundred between the walls in the backroom of the emporium. I left a note for Meg hidden in a drawer among her winter blankets, telling her where to find them. If it turned out that I was still gone by winter, she'd find those coins when the nights got cold.''

Coke whistled low. ''Why, that's over eight thousand dollars, all told, Jessie. You robbed that bastard in San Francisco bare-assed.''

''He deserved it.'' Her eyes searched his. ''So I am what they said I was, Coke. I am a thief. I am a felon. Do you still want me now?''

''Yep.''

''But how could any man in his right mind want a woman like me?''

He touched her face. '' 'Cause for all you've been through in your life, you still got more spirit an' spunk in your little finger than any dozen o' virtuous, silver-spooned princesses rolled into one.''

She picked up a handful of coins, letting them pour out of the bottom of her hand. ''Well at least I can give you that eight hundred fifty dollars to get me off.''

''No, keep it. Just let it be your sneaky prize.''

''Could be it's you who's won the sneaky prize.'' Smiling, she slid her arms around his neck. ''I love you, Coke. You're stuck with me.'' She pressed her face next to his. ''Besides, a dirty skunk like you deserves a woman like me.''

''I was kinda hopin' you'd finally see it my way,'' he whispered, pressing her back onto the blanket.

''Coke,'' she breathed, ''what're you doing?''

''Ain't mined all the gold in this here skirt yet.''

''But Coke,'' she said, her breath catching. ''Your wound. Do you think you should? Do you think you can?''

''Hell, Jessie,'' he murmured against her neck. ''It was only my *back* that I got shot in.''

ABOUT THE AUTHOR

Ann Gabriel was born in Kansas. She lived there as well as in the states of Iowa and South Dakota during her growing-up years. For the past twenty-four years she's resided in South Texas. A schoolteacher and the mother of two teenage sons, she is married to a Laredo, Texas, physician. Her husband is a native South Texan whose family at one time owned ranches on both sides of the Texas-Mexican border and still holds land in South Texas today. Ms. Gabriel is currently at work on a new novel.

EDWARD MATHIS

A DAN ROMAN TE★AS MYSTERY